SPECIAL

THE COMPLETE NOVELS

SPECIALS
THE COMPLETE NOVELS

Created, written and produced by

BRIAN DEGAS
&
HARRY ROBERTSON

COLLINS
CRIME
CLUB

COLLINS CRIME CLUB
An imprint of HarperCollins*Publishers*
1 London Bridge Street
London SE1 9GF
www.harpercollins.co.uk

This omnibus edition 2017

Specials: Have a Nice Parade and *Specials: Ask 'Em, Tell 'Em, Lift 'Em*
first published in Great Britain by Fontana 1991
Specials: Over and Out first published in this volume 2017

A catalogue record for this book is available from the British Library

ISBN 978-0-00-826059-0

Typeset in Sabon LT Std by Palimpsest Book Production Ltd,
Falkirk, Stirlingshire
Printed and bound by CPI Group (UK) Ltd, Croydon CR0 4YY

MIX
Paper from
responsible sources
FSC™ C007454
www.fsc.org

FSC™ is a non-profit international organisation established to promote
the responsible management of the world's forests. Products carrying the
FSC label are independently certified to assure consumers that they come
from forests that are managed to meet the social, economic and
ecological needs of present and future generations,
and other controlled sources.

Find out more about HarperCollins and the environment at
www.harpercollins.co.uk/green

CONTENTS

I

•••••

Have a Nice Parade

1

He barely noticed the car on his tail, holding just behind and to the right, where it shouldn't be. Yet somehow he could sense the danger lurking over his shoulder.

Unfortunately, as he made his way along the freeway into Birmingham, Special Constable Freddy Calder's conscious mind was elsewhere. In fact, he was on the car-phone.

'Hi, John. Look here, I'll be with you in . . .'

Raising his wrist with a snap, almost a salute, Freddy checked his Rolex – actually, an imitation Rolex, but at a quick glance no one was ever the wiser.

'. . . twenty minutes. And, old chum, what I have to show you is *sensational.*'

His gaze momentarily shifted to the sample case lying on the passenger seat, open just enough to offer a tantalizing glimpse of lingerie, a pair of sheer lace panties to be exact. Freddy's talent was to imagine just how they would look on virtually anyone he knew, or thought he knew, or even conceived in his waking dreams of knowing. Of course, lying on the back seat was his model, 'Salvador Dolly', a curvaceous cut-out figure of an ideal woman wearing only her underwear every hour of the day.

'Listen, this latest stuff's so light you better hold on tight to your secretary when she wears them.'

They shared a low, lascivious laugh reserved for men talking about women. Whenever he sensed a customer had the same thoughts in mind, Freddy would start counting his money.

Accidentally and simultaneously, his car veered into the right

3

lane, although he made a swift correction in steering with a slight move of his finger. It was then that he noticed the car on his tail: a maroon Audi, a 'mean machine'. Suddenly he was alert, but gave no outward or visible sign of alarm.

'Well, 'course in that case she's travelling as light as she can get. Yeah. Fantasy Island . . . Don't we all! See you.'

Before he could put away the car-phone and look back to his wing mirror, he heard a Luftwaffe motor roaring behind him. Getting louder, the Audi pulled in parallel with him, then swerved toward him and back, as if testing his mettle, before finally surging ahead full throttle.

Freddy cursed. The fool in the mean machine didn't realize whom he was fooling with. Never cross Freddy Calder.

The chase was on. Guarding his intent – Freddy didn't want the fool to know it yet – he tucked his blue Sierra neatly in behind the Audi and started a little tailing of his own. His Sierra provided the ultimate camouflage: not new, perhaps, but trim, tidy, respectable, bright as a button, polished by a lingerie salesman's loving hands and totally inconspicuous in ordinary traffic.

Freddy reached for the car-phone and punched the number for Divisional Headquarters 'S' while keeping his aim fixed on the Audi ahead. Moment by moment, the solitary suspect appeared to be accelerating, forcing the pace, maybe trying to shake his tail.

Nevertheless Freddy Calder was on the case. His mood had changed with his identity: now he was a secret agent of the law – a Special – trailing someone in a hurry.

'Put me through to Sheila Baxter in Control, would you, Bill? Yeah, it's Freddy Calder here.'

There was no reason to assume that the response would be immediate, efficient or professionally respectful. Nor was it.

'Fred-dy Cal-der . . . Sure I'll hold, but this is important.'

Damn the bureaucratic mind. It was this kind of red tape, he reflected, that had delayed Napoleon's conquest of Russia, which would have been better for everyone concerned, as history had demonstrated . . .

Meanwhile, the Sirens were beckoning Odysseus, not only from his sample case stuffed with intimate and racy unmentionables but also from his anticipation of official sirens heralding the imminent arrival of the everyday police. And what would they think of Dolly?

Should he cover them in some way? Hide them? Absolutely not, for that was the secret of his disguise: a 'Special' in ladies' underwear. Who would think to look at *him*? The fool in the Audi wouldn't know what had hit him until it was too late. Freddy might appear to the casual eye to be pudgy and unimpressive, but underneath was a lion ready to pounce. When fists were flying, Freddy Calder would be the gent you'd want in there as a back-up. Many a fool had learned that lesson the hard way.

Meanwhile, at Division 'S' headquarters, WPC Sheila Baxter was manning the control room – and that wasn't the only contradiction in terms. In truth, the awesome-sounding 'control room' constituted four walls, no windows and no room whatsoever to manoeuvre. The sole generous proportion in this room was a desk too large, and the only semblance of control, computer terminals and the usual communication gear.

But it wasn't home, and that's what Sheila liked best about the place. She wanted to stay and keep this job, so she had to exercise a Job-like patience with some of the Specials.

'Freddy Calder, how many times do I have to tell you? Don't call on this line.'

In an attempt to win her sympathy, he told her that he 'couldn't get through by the proper channels,' and he had a hot item that couldn't wait.

'What? What car? Listen, Freddy, unless it's dropping gold bricks I'm not interested . . . Well, for one thing, you're not on duty. For another, I'm not supposed to give that kind of information to a Special. You know that.'

Perhaps he did, yet what difference should that make now, when pursuit was in progress through traffic becoming thicker as the city grew closer?

'Sheila, believe me. I got a tingle in my nose about this one. The number is . . . Ready?'

WPC Baxter grabbed her notebook. 'Just a second, give me that again.'

While entering the numbers into the computer terminal, she failed to observe the entering of Darth Vader – Police Sergeant Andy McAllister – behind her, looming above like a misery-seeking missile. Just as she realized his sinister presence, she also discovered something of an obstacle on the computer screen.

'Freddy! Blow your nose. You're tailing an unmarked police car, you wally!'

With that little piece of information, Freddy squeezed down on the brake and slowed considerably, while the idiot woman driver behind him pulled out and around with a screaming blast of the horn, although he and his brave Cortina did manage to escape intact.

Suddenly there was another vicious burst of noise from the car-phone Freddy was just putting to his ear.

'Calder! This is Sergeant McAllister.'

Trying to keep his grip, McAllister held the phone – which he had abruptly acquired from WPC Baxter at the instant he resumed command – like a club.

'Calder, you may think you're a bloody Miami Vice, but I've news for you. You're a *Special*, and that puts you lower than the lowest PC still in his nappies. And right now you're a damned nuisance. In future, leave highway duty to those who know what they're doing.'

The line went dead, and Freddy blinked hard. That's the thanks you get for risking your life, he thought to himself, still unable to calm his trembling fingers . . . and as a *volunteer* yet! Bunch of bloody desk jockeys.

'Damned Hobby Bobby!' McAllister muttered at no one in particular, although scared rabbit Baxter was at least ostensibly paying attention to his every word.

'Pretend police, who don't take their function at all seriously . . . who sell brassieres! This is no place for a clown.'

As far as McAllister was concerned it was enough to bring the entire Specials programme into question.

'Who's his senior Special?'

'His SDO is Barker . . .' replied Baxter.

An easy name for her to remember, McAllister mused.

'. . . but he's not been putting in much of an appearance lately, and things are being handled by the section officer, Bob Loach.'

I must have a quiet chat with Loach then, thought McAllister with a smile.

6

2

Cougar Coaches was busy in the late afternoon, hosting the methodical movement of vehicles being driven in and out of the garage. Prominently parked in the yard area reserved for the staff were the infamous Loach-mobiles, Bob's white Jag next to Noreen's Renault 25: hardly a matched pair.

Inside the garage were several buses of varying size and capacity, a few still waiting for repair or some adjustment: the mechanics were clocking off for the day. Unable to stop fussing over a particularly stubborn exhaust-system problem grounding one of the coaches for the last couple of days, works foreman John Barraclough was finishing the job himself. He had advised the frustrated young mechanic he could push off home after informing at least one of the Loaches as to the current status of and prognosis for the obstinate exhaust system.

In one corner of the garage, in the office constructed of white-painted breeze blocks, Noreen Loach was feeling trapped while trying to get somewhere: trying to leave a bit early so she could get to her appointment at the beauty parlour. There was always too much 'getting' to do.

She had tidied her desk until it was a model of efficient organization, and made her final tour of the kitchen, wash-up and lavatory in the annexe. Now all that remained to obstruct her was her husband, as usual.

'I'm off, then. I'll tidy up the Edinburgh entries tomorrow. It looks as though we did well on that one.' – While she practised her nonchalant tone of voice at every opportunity, in her own mind she realized full well that it convinced nobody, again with the possible exception of her husband, the one hope she clung to in the present circumstances.

'Oh aye.'

Another response typical of his ever-so-revealing remarks, she reminded herself.

'Yes. Anyway, I'm late for my appointment.' Before he could interrupt, she kept right on going, moving to the door one step at a time. 'Can I trust you to call them up and say I'm on my way?'

'Call who?'

Whatever her wishful thinking about making a quick exit, two words from him could dash such notions in an instant.

'Judy's Beauty Salon. And no cracks, Loach. I don't have time for cracks.'

'I was only going to ask, Noreen, how long you'd be there.'

Immediately she was defensive. 'What for? I don't have time to bother about your tea, if that's what you're asking.'

Obviously that was not what he was asking. What was she keeping to herself this time, he wondered.

'I can grab a sandwich. It won't be the first time.'

Apparently his gesture of self-sufficiency had tipped her over the edge.

'I'm off,' she shrugged, swinging her leather bag over her shoulder in a huff and throwing him a warning glance. 'I can't stand it when you use that little-boy-lost voice.'

After waiting another few moments to assure himself she was definitely gone, he lifted himself from the chair, straightened his shoulders and assumed an altogether different frame of mind on his way to the back room.

When he emerged with his freshly cleaned and pressed uniform, he was a new man. Carefully he stripped away the long plastic dry-cleaner bag, and there it was: the armour of a peaceful people, a dignified suit of mere cloth, yet signifying to every citizen of the realm that this man, Robert Loach, was a Special, section-officer grade.

Inhaling a deep breath to expand his chest, he held the smart uniform up against himself as a mannequin, looked in the tiny wall mirror Noreen used to patch up her powder and picked imaginary specks of foreign matter and even a few filaments of nearly invisible dust already beginning to float on to the stiff collar.

That was when the door behind him opened, the moment Noreen had chosen for her curtain call.

'Forgot my keys.'

With as much diplomacy, aplomb and deception as he could muster at this moment, he backed away from the mirror as inconspicuously as possible while swiftly shifting his scrutiny to the illusory minutiae on the collar of his uniform.

Noreen went straight to her desk to fetch the keys, without taking much notice of her husband caught preening himself in her mirror.

'Did you make the call?'

'I will. Give me a chance.'

'I did that once and ended up marrying you.'

8

'Very funny,' he said.

On her way out again, she almost bumped into John Barraclough on his way in, holding up his oily black hands in front of her face, thus barring her path with a crude display of the vulgar side of his occupation. As she always remembered at such inopportune incidents, it was also her husband's calling.

'I'm sorry, Mrs Loach. Didn't like knocking on the door. Not with these.'

To impress his blunt point upon her even further, Barraclough extended his hands closer to her eyes so that she might focus on the grease slicking down the hair on his knuckles.

'That's all right. See you tomorrow, Mr Barraclough.'

He nodded politely, still with his dripping hands held up to his face. She managed what she hoped would pass for a tolerant smile and closed the door behind her.

Barraclough walked over to Bob Loach, keeping his hands away from the uniform and away from anything else wherever possible. With an eyebrow instead of words, Loach asked him what he wanted.

'Sorry 'bout this, Mr Loach, but could you have a look at the Daf?'

'Can't it wait, John? I'm . . .'

He tried to indicate what he meant to say by showing his uniform, almost like a grandparent cradling a new baby.

'. . . all set, you see.'

John's response was also wordless, but Loach could easily discern the meaning from his anxious face.

'All right, let's see it.'

Gently putting his uniform aside, Loach retrieved and pulled on a pair of overalls. There was no loss of pride and self-respect when he switched uniforms, at least that's what he kept telling himself.

While lying on his back on a pallet under the Daf coach in the garage, Loach could hear the BMW of his partner, Dicky Padgett, howl into the yard and squeak to a halt just in time to avoid crashing into the garage itself. Sure enough, nary half a minute passed before Dicky's polished Italian shoe was tapping the sole of Loach's boot, which, unfortunately, was sticking out from under the coach.

In addition, there was another set of legs next to Dicky's – shapely, stockinged calves.

'Mr P-Padgett.'

'John. This is Michelle.'

Loach instantly determined that he had better get up and take a look for himself. It was well worth the trip: a flaming redhead, all leg and bosom (and more than abundant in that department).

Loach tried to concentrate his attention on Barraclough.

'I think somebody's botched the welding. That exhaust system'll need another go.'

When Loach turned to the happy couple, Dicky suddenly adopted an aspect of mock horror.

'No wonder our profit margin is small, Bob, if we do the same job twice.'

His next wisecrack Dicky addressed to the graciously smiling redhead.

'And he tells me he wants to be the first millionaire Special,' Dicky muttered into Michelle's ear, an irony palpably lost on her, as she struggled to make some sense of what he was saying.

Dicky must have sensed her questioning mind.

'A Special? You know, part-time bluebottle. He plays policeman in his time off.'

Sadly, Dicky's remarks did not seem to be making their way past Michelle's heavy dangling earrings. So she decided to play with them, perhaps in some attempt to realign her vibrations.

''Ullo, Dicky,' Loach offered.

Dicky acknowledged Loach's presence without further ado.

'You got my call about the Stratford job?'

Loach answered with a nod. An unsettling irritability stirred his middle as he strode across to the office.

'Americans and Japs. Good money. And in the bin up front, Bobby boy.'

That was evidently going to be another exhibition of the genius for business that supposedly convinced Loach, long ago, to enter into partnership with Dicky Padgett.

'This is Michelle, by the way.' Again he turned to confide in her. 'Bob Loach. My partner. The one who gets his hands dirty.'

He emitted a dry laugh, then winked at Loach.

'Lucky I met up with her.'

'Oh, aye?'

'Damn right,' Dicky asserted. 'The Stratford run will leave us short-handed. Unless we ask the joyous Noreen to step in and do the courier job. And I remember how nasty that was the last time . . .' Dicky's voice trailed away.

Loach was dumbfounded, although he tried to conceal it. 'You can't be serious? Her as a courier?'

'Watch it, Bob,' Dicky smirked. 'Equal opportunities. Sexist remarks. Ooh . . .'

Getting no glint of a smile from Loach, Dicky sucked in his breath, then proceeded in a somewhat more serious vein. 'All right. Humour me. I think she can do it. Tourists like a bit of glamour.'

By jove, he *was* serious. Loach had to take him aside.

'Dicky, it's Noreen's job to fix the couriers. She'll take one look at this one's knockers, and –'

'Bob, let's not forget who put this deal together in the first place, okay?'

End of discussion. Loach could sense that time was running out on this issue.

'Right now I don't have the time to discuss it. I'm late as it is for duty.'

With deliberate speed, he gathered his uniform in one motion as he walked out of the office. Even so he couldn't fail to hear Dicky calling after him.

'Since when did playing policeman come before Company business?'

What he did *not* hear was the next remark Dicky Padgett made. By then Loach was long gone and well beyond earshot.

'If you're not going to be around, Bobby boy, then some of us will have to start making the executive decisions.'

3

Special Constable Anjali Shah waited at the bus stop thinking there was nothing in particular about her appearance to suggest to other bystanders that they should be wary of a part-time member of a police organization in their midst.

Although she was always proud to identify herself as first-generation English, in many ways she still found herself uncomfortably in the middle of contrary and changing cultural influences, often self-conscious of the position she was taking in any group situation.

11

She also considered herself a feminist, so she really couldn't rationalize standing meekly at the rear of a group of strangers waiting for a bus. Paradoxically, she also had to wage a continuing internal struggle against ancient traditions urging her not to stand near the front of the group, and, especially as a woman, and most certainly as a woman alone and unaccompanied by a gentleman, not to be 'much too conspicuous', as Uncle Ram would say.

Standing in front of her were two women of her age who were indeed conspicuous and none too timid about asserting their presence, a couple of Sharons, their hair teased into clouds and their names surely immortalized on the sun visors of cars driven by their Kevins. While in some sense Anjali could envy the bold, even brave disguise they adopted to face a world crowded with anxieties, nevertheless she could never assume that disguise for herself.

Suddenly she recognized someone familiar – her section officer, Bob Loach – sailing by the bus stop in his fancy Jag. Impulsively she waved at him, a gesture perhaps uncharacteristic of the woman she imagined other people saw her to be.

Against all odds, Bob Loach saw her wave, and although he had overshot the mark, the Jag quickly slowed to a stop. Then he turned and waved back to Anjali, motioning for her to join him for the ride to Division 'S' headquarters.

The Sharons standing in front of her simultaneously got the same message, misinterpreting Loach's wave and come-on as intended for them. The short one even had the nerve to return Loach's wave. The two exchanged glances, half-seriously asking 'What d'you think?'

Before they could decide among themselves, Anjali had run and jumped into the Jaguar. She wasn't out of hearing range when the short one remarked loudly, 'What a tart!'

Anjali had to laugh but she couldn't quite convince herself to explain what she was laughing about to her section officer. He might see her as a bit silly but neither he nor anyone else would have any grounds to think of her as a tart. Yet she wasn't positive that someone else, indeed a man who had waved at her from afar and picked her up in his handsome carriage, would laugh at the misunderstanding. So she smiled and kept the story to herself.

In turn, Bob Loach didn't seem very forthcoming either: he appeared to mirror her distant attitude. He was friendly, and made some attempt to offer polite conversation, but still he was reserved. Perhaps that was proper for a man in his position – as well as for an unmarried woman in hers.

Maybe that was one of the reasons Anjali looked up to Robert Loach. He was sympathetic to the concerns of the individuals under his command and was certainly thought to be 'one of us'. Nonetheless, he clearly took his responsibilities seriously. Anjali decided he was more in tune with his role than she was with hers, at least in terms of what she could discern from his outward behaviour. His strength of character made him attractive to any woman, and Anjali was not unaware of her own desires and secret fantasies stimulated by a mature, older man who personified qualities she admired.

Later in the parade room for Specials at the Division 'S' station, Anjali and Section Officer Loach were looking smart in their neat, crisp uniforms, and she felt more comfortable with their defined roles. Yes, he was a section officer, but Anjali Shah could hold her head just as high: she too was a Special in her own right.

Of about a dozen Specials in the parade room, their ages varying from early twenties to mid-forties, one in four were women. Anjali felt honoured to be one of them.

The section officer cleared his throat, and she knew the meeting was about to come to order.

After reviewing the roster of duties on his clipboard and the faces of the Specials present, Section Officer Loach barked 'All right, settle down, troops.' It was time to move along, take parade and get the show on the road.

'I know you've heard it all before, but I want you to remember three things when you're out on the street . . .'

He paused for effect.

'. . . Respect . . . respect . . . and respect.'

Loach once again noticed eyeballs rolling skyward and wished that perhaps the Lord High Executioner would authorize him to order their heads to roll instead.

'Yeah, I know it's boring. But watch out when you turn the next corner. All hell could break loose, and you'd better be ready for it.'

He prayed, as he did every single time, that each of them would take his words to heart and return home safe and sound. However, before he could deliver the climax of his address, the door opened and Police Sergeant Andrew McAllister popped his head into the breach. Raising a quizzical eyebrow in Loach's direction, McAllister curled his finger, beckoning the section officer to him.

Loach held up his hand to signal a pause in the parade ceremony, then joined Sergeant McAllister at the door.

'Before you get started . . . a wee word in your lug, Section Officer Loach.'

Knowing how rarely McAllister assumed that tone of voice, Loach did not relish the anticipation of the nails being driven into his coffin.

'While we both know in what high esteem the Specials are held by the regular force, it would seem that some Specials hold themselves in even higher esteem.'

What was McAllister trying to say?

'I am, of course, referring to Special Constable Freddy Calder. He seems to see himself as Captain Marvel of the Flying Squad.'

Oh-oh, what was it this time?

'While we appreciate enthusiasm, Loach, Mister Calder is exactly *that* when off-duty: *Mister* Calder.'

Freddy had probably arrested Princess Di for showing disrespect for the royal family.

'I trust you'll see that my words are inserted in the correct earhole. Over and out. And have a nice parade.'

And with that the sergeant left Cheshire-cat like, the vision of his teeth still hanging in the air.

Loach made a conscious effort to lift his eyes for action, as he returned to his place in front of the Specials. At the same time, he tried not to look into the eyes of the woman he had picked up at the bus stop and given a ride to only moments ago.

'Okay. Where were we? Ah, right. Special Constable Anjali Shah?'

When he did look at her he was pleased to see that she was alert and responsive. In that instant he was reminded that Special Constable Shah generally demonstrated 'the right stuff' for the job, even though she was by no means a powerhouse in the physical sense.

'Anjali, you're on car patrol in the panda with PC Toby Armstrong. Okay?'

She nodded, no questions; but one of the wits in the room couldn't leave well enough alone.

'Cushy number.'

There was general laughter. Loach tried to ignore the mini-rabble.

'Special Constable Viv Smith?'

When he looked up Viv Smith was applying some blush to her cheeks, but she indicated that at least she was listening. The next one wouldn't be so easy, and he made sure his voice carried the menace of impending doom.

'. . . And Special Constable Freddy Calder.'

Again the resident wit struck a blow for cynicism.

'Batman and Robin!'

Yet he wasn't quick-witted enough to escape Viv Smith clouting him with a graceful swinging arc of her shoulder bag.

Loach immediately forget about that nonsense when he realized Freddy Calder was nowhere in sight.

'Flippin' 'eck, where's Freddy?'

Another wit took his turn. 'Trying to get away from his mother.'

Loach could barely contain his irritation. 'That'll do. That's out of order.'

At that inopportune moment, Loach heard the door open behind him, and when he turned to confront the interruption, a little furry fox hand-puppet poked his nose in and spoke to the assembled Specials in a squeaky little voice with a distinct though amateurish American accent.

'Foxy's real sorry for being late, but there was this babe in a miniskirt.'

Freddy Calder had at last arrived. Loach was sorely tempted to strangle Foxy and break Freddy's fingers.

'Hey! Feel my whiskers. Are they burning, or are they burning?'

The hand-puppet entered the parade room, followed by a similarly red-faced Freddy Calder. His embarrassment didn't excuse his crime. It was time for a firmly administered example of keel-hauling.

'Sorry, sorry, sorry.' Sprinkling his apologies here and there, Freddy must have noticed that Loach was not amused. 'Really sorry, Bob.'

Freddy hurriedly joined Viv Smith, tossing her a Benny Hill grin. Loach's glare wiped the smile off Freddy's face.

'Be serious, Freddy, for once. D'you know that Sergeant McAllister has just been melting the wax in my ears? You been chasing stolen cars again?'

That random probe apparently struck a nerve, as Special Constable Calder could no longer hide the guilt on his face.

Loach tried to go easy on him, out of a basic respect for someone

15

like Freddy who had, after all, volunteered his services to become a Special, just as he and the others had.

'I know you don't miss much, but it doesn't help to antagonize the police.'

Loach shook his head. It was no use. For all of Freddy Calder's talents, as well as quirks, advice to him on diplomacy would always fall on deaf ears.

4

Constable Toby Armstrong was walking his partner, Anjali Shah, to the black-and-white panda they shared while out lurking through the jungles of Birmingham and local environs looking for trouble. Tonight they might find it simply by sitting in the panda and going nowhere. While talking about his wife, Toby was, for the time being anyway, happy to be happily married, or else he might be vulnerable to the temptations of this dark angel.

'She's pregnant.'

Anjali's eyes widened. 'Shirley?'

'Who else?'

Anjali instinctively took Toby's hand and squeezed it in hers.

'Congratulations, Toby.'

As an afterthought, she did some mental arithmetic before coming to the logical conclusion about the nearly newlyweds and their first offspring now in gestation.

'It's a honeymoon baby!'

That must have been the correct answer, as it provoked a robust laugh from Toby that he didn't explain until they were settled in the panda with their safety belts fastened.

'Don't mention the word "honeymoon,"' he sighed, shaking his head in bittersweet reverie. 'We stayed in this hotel down in the West Country . . .'

Her blank expression suggested to him that she might not have the faintest notion of the particular nuances and idiosyncrasies found in that region of the realm, so he took a step backward before proceeding.

'You know? The ones that say they've a lot of character. Where some King Johnny spent the night.' It was too late in the story to stop again and explain. 'I reckon we had the same bed *he* did,' implying its age. 'It was gross. Like that –'

Through the air he made a deep scooping arc with his hand, illustrating the shape of the sacrificial honeymoon altar upon which he had probably developed permanent curvature of the spine.

'– with squeaky bed springs.'

He had to chuckle in spite of himself.

'If you're right, and it is a honeymoon baby, I reckon we ought to call him Shakin' Stevens!'

Momentarily a question flashed across his mind as to whether Anjali might consider his remark 'not in the best of taste', as she would carefully say. He hoped so. At least she might provide an occasion for some innocent flirtation. After all, his safety belt was in place: he was a happily married old man.

Because Freddy Calder was the last one in and, as per usual, the last one out, Viv Smith virtually had to lead him by the hand through the front entrance of Division 'S' in order to have any chance of getting some work done before it was time to go home again. Putting it mildly, this little-big lad could be absolutely maddening.

Nonetheless, Viv was flattered to be assigned the responsibility of babysitting the problem child of the bunch. That alone proved Loach had confidence in her: a single, smashing, hip young bird in charge of Freddy – Super Sleuth.

She decided she might as well take advantage of her plight this evening, and perhaps exploit the genuine gullibility of her intended victim, by rehearsing her latest sales scheme on poor Freddy, as she used to rehearse the lead in her school play.

'You know something, Freddy? I've come to the conclusion that money is a very interesting thing.'

'I'll say.'

Brilliant repartee.

'No, give over. I mean it.' The time had arrived to establish credibility by making oblique reference to her regular position as a Teller in Accountancy.

'Since working at the Building Society, I've learned a few things. You know, like stocks and shares?'

It was a bizarre possibility, but maybe he *didn't* know.

'Surely you've thought about that, Freddy? At your age?'

'No,' he scowled. 'And less of the "at my age."'

Such a sensitive dinosaur, though.

'But you should. You won't get very far pushing your fingers up a puppet . . .'

Maybe there was a better phrase she might have turned there, and she quickly checked his eyes for any sign of awareness or intelligence for that matter, none of which could be detected in the subdued light.

'. . . But if you do it right, you can make a quick killing on the market.'

'By going out and cutting my throat, you mean,' answered Freddy.

Viv wondered if that might be a better plan than hers.

Through her side of the windscreen in the panda, Anjali Shah watched Special Constable Viv Smith and Freddy Calder passing by. Apparently concentrating on his driving, Toby wasn't talkative at the moment, so Anjali had a moment's respite. She was lost in her own thoughts of being close to and yet far from her family, from the frictions as well as the comforts of home . . .

'Not feeling broody, are you?' Toby interrupted her wanderings.

'I need a husband first.' Now why did she let that slip, even as a joke?

'Well, then?' Toby asked slyly, sneaking a quick look to gauge her reaction.

Now that the subject was out in the open, so to speak, better to approach it lightly.

'Don't you start. It's like a broken record back home.' She almost broke out laughing, remembering her mother's constant scolding. 'My Ma thinks I've missed the boat, and Uncle Ram keeps telling me no one will marry an old bat like me.'

Actually, although she challenged and generally opposed everything Uncle Ram said, on principle, she was often secretly inclined to agree with him on this unsettling topic. Not that she would admit that to Uncle Ram, or to Toby.

But again Toby interrupted her train of thought in a lower tone of voice.

'From where I'm sitting, I see a pretty attractive bird.'

Anjali instinctively lowered her eyes, then immediately wished she hadn't.

'Thank you, kind sir.'

18

'A bit tanned, maybe, but . . .'

She winced slightly, trying to let his remark slide by, to erase it from her memory. She knew his gesture was merely intended to defuse the age-old timebomb between their cultures rather than spark it off with a casual insult, so again she kept her thoughts to herself, allowing Toby to continue.

'. . . not bad, not bad at all.'

Indeed, he *was* trying to give her a compliment, and she could see that it was sincere, although she wasn't quite sure what to think about the new direction their conversation was taking. Just as quickly she banished her doubts, reasoning that there was nothing wrong in modestly accepting reassurance from a friend.

'You're good for my morale, Toby.'

She wished that that was the end of it, but Toby didn't give her a second to change the subject.

'Listen, you may not believe this,' he began in his slow, smooth, baritone voice, 'but I can remember the first time we met.'

The alarm went off somewhere in the back of her brain. Simply turning and raising her eyebrows was enough to question his intentions.

'I'm serious. I remember the day and the time, and what you were wearing.' He tossed a Prince Charming smile her way before resuming his scrutiny of the car ahead.

For the first time in their conversation, Anjali was embarrassed. She couldn't believe what she was hearing. In her way, she did love Toby, but she could not possibly love him in his way, and she would rather her ears be made of stone before listening to him continue any further along this path . . .

And yet she could barely wait for his next words.

'You were wearing . . .' Must he delay the suspense interminably? '. . . a white shirt, black skirt, a check tie and jacket with silver buttons,' he intoned lovingly.

She punched him in the arm. It had taken her that long to catch on that Toby was describing her uniform.

After investing her time and expertise in 'building a foundation' for the financial advisory role with Freddy Calder, Viv was unwilling to give up her chance of gaining his confidence, and eventually the management of his savings. As they scouted the pedestrian shopping area she tried to offer him a strong dose of fiscal common sense.

'People like you always think money is a complicated matter. It isn't. It's all a question of market forces, and getting your money to work for *you*.'

There. Maybe she could knock some of that common sense into his head after all.

'Oh, bless you, Obewan Kenobi!'

So much for the notion he was buying any of her carefully prepared argument.

The clown's voice soured. 'This sucker's always had to work for his.'

Viv was determined to be undaunted.

'Very funny. Listen. You buy shares in a company being took-over. Then when it gets took-over, the company doing the take-over has to pay you more for the shares. Because the shares are worth more now it's being took-over.'

Even the simplest, most basic human sounds apparently sometimes failed to penetrate Freddy's thick skull.

'It's all very simple, you know, Freddy.'

'Simple, my big toe.'

This monkey was exasperating. 'What don't you understand?'

Freddy had to think for a few moments before he could figure out his answer.

'Where I get the money to buy the shares in the first place.'

Viv Smith sighed, and paused to contemplate the company she was keeping of late.

'Freddy, talking to you is the quickest way of getting a headache I know.'

5

In the corridor of Division 'S' outside his office, the sign on his door said CHIEF SUPERINTENDENT FRANK ELLSMORE, and when he walked out of his office through that door into the open territory beyond he wanted people to see that he had a clear-cut destination in view, plus the ever-resolute determination to get there. That was the mark of leadership, and he reasoned, rationally enough, that here was indeed what the troops needed to see in his demeanour:

his attempt to embody the authority of the uniform, as well as to fill it. He wanted them to see a man of action.

Unfortunately, sometimes ordinary reality presented unexpected obstacles in his path: in this instance in the person of WPC Morrow, the new one. Just as Ellsmore was hitting full stride, he almost collided with WPC Morrow carrying a pile of folders, but just in the nick of time she managed to spin and evade him, yet still balance the folders in her arms so that only a few actually spilled to the floor.

'Sorry, sir.'

One of Ellsmore's oldest failings, and one of the rusty skills needing some polishing, was his conduct when caught in embarrassing situations, even of the most trivial nature.

'My fault . . . er . . .'

'Morrow, sir. WPC Morrow.'

Of course, Morrow. Neat. Agile. Attentive. What other mental resources might she be capable of contributing?

'You've only just started here, right?'

'Right, sir.'

Well, he had offered her the opportunity to introduce herself and make an impression, but she hadn't taken the step forward. Talent should always be ready to rise to the top in an instant, he wanted to remind her. Instead he reminded himself that she had performed a nimble feat.

'Well, if you're as quick as you are on your feet, Constable, we won't have much to worry about, eh?'

'No, sir.'

WPC Morrow didn't say anything more, and Ellsmore had nothing more to say. Standing here waiting for her laconic answers was getting him nowhere and only prolonging the agony of his embarrassment. So he did his best to nod a farewell, and left her for the lift.

WPC Morrow sighed and watched Chief Superintendent Ellsmore steam away with his sights firmly set on course. She was becoming accustomed to observing the Super sailing through life like a galleon in a high wind.

In the Specials' parade room, Section Officer Bob Loach was vainly trying to make some semblance of order in his paperwork. His audible groans and grunts of brute persuasion seemed of no use in consolidating scraps of assorted documents.

Abruptly there was a sharp rap on the door, which opened

21

immediately. To Loach's surprise, standing there like a royal oak was Chief Superintendent Ellsmore.

'Chief Superintendent?'

As Ellsmore entered, Loach hurriedly straightened and shuffled the paperwork to the side of his desk.

'Should've known you'd be here . . .' The Chief Superintendent didn't sound overjoyed at this discovery. 'Wanted a quick word, Loach.'

Loach was powerless to prohibit the Chief Superintendent from poking through the paperwork at random, like casually rummaging through someone else's toolbox, looking for nothing. It was an ominous diversion.

'Good God, it seems damn stupid you Specials giving up your free time to fight crime, just to end up processing bumff,' Ellsmore lectured, rippling a few pages of paper with evident contempt. 'Fruits of bureaucracy, that's what it is, Loach.'

Why was he stalling? All that this delay accomplished was to make him more nervous. Maybe that was the idea.

'We try and cope, Chief Superintendent.'

'Yes.' Ellsmore did not pursue that dead end. 'I haven't seen much of your SDO lately, but I hear he's been having some trouble at home.'

Telling himself there was no reason to panic, Loach was patiently taking in the information the Chief Superintendent was feeding him, but he still didn't quite understand what Ellsmore wanted him to swallow.

'Anyway, I . . . wanted to have a word with you about one of your lads, Loach.'

'Trouble, sir?' Here it comes, he thought.

'Oh, no, no, no.' Three times: he doth protest too much. 'Just a storm in an egg cup.'

Brace yourself, this is it.

'But you know, I hate there to be any friction between Specials and Police. There are enough jokes as it is.'

What is it, what happened? Who? Why?

'It's Freddy Calder.'

Loach's blood rose as his spirits descended to the satanic depths of the underworld. Freddy Calder was an Achilles' heel if ever there was one.

'How long's he been selling lingerie?' Ellsmore was, sad to say, dreadfully serious.

22

'About a year, sir.'

'Right. And before that, he flogged . . .'

This was getting more painful by the moment. 'Kitchen ware.'

Ellsmore clucked his tongue in mock regret. 'A pity he didn't stick to it. You know, he tried to sell a pair of peach cammy knickers to a visiting Woman Police Inspector.'

Loach was sure his cheeks were already as red as he was going to lash Freddy Calder's backside. But his own torture wasn't finished yet.

'And worse . . . cracked some blue jokes with that damned puppet of his.'

That was too much. Loach's will was sapped, any hope of suitable revenge dwarfed by Freddy's towering imbecility.

'Have a word with him, Loach. Nothing strong. Just tell him to stop selling his ladies' undies on the premises in the future.'

6

Investigating the eerie surrounds of the Ellman Superstore at night gave Special Constable Viv Smith a weird case of the 'creeps', and having Special Constable Freddy Calder at her side was worse than *Rosemary's Baby*: what loony Americans would call 'a horror show'. Angular slabs of concrete cast deep shadows and what few sources of light were within reach merely served to spread the shadows out longer.

Slower and slower they walked, until Viv stopped. Freddy looked at her with questioning eyes, although not a sound emerged from his throat. She prayed there wouldn't be another peep out of him, as she took a cigarette out of her shoulder bag.

'Don't say another word,' Viv warned him in a low, cemetery whisper. 'I said I'd give them up.'

The cigarette was in her mouth, and she was just about to light up, when a squeaky noise pierced the night air. She froze like a deer, although she might just as well have shrieked and jumped over the moon. Freddy also appeared to have been instantaneously transformed into a pillar of salt.

Slowly she turned, her antennae searching the horizon for the direction of the squeaking noise, which seemed to become louder every second, as if coming toward them from the shadows.

Suddenly one of the shadows was moving! And while it was moving closer, it was growing larger and the squeaking noise louder and louder.

The moving shadow expanded to fill an entire wall, appearing to be a giant creature of some sort inexorably screeching toward them. The cigarette fell out of Viv's mouth, yet she wasn't at all sure she could manage a scream.

Something appeared at the bottom of the wall, beneath and much smaller than the shadow: something that was causing the shadow.

It was a supermarket trolley with a young child inside, being pushed by another child.

Quickly the Specials headed for the trolley, trying not to frighten the children the same way that they had been spooked.

The children immediately saw them and waited where they were. Freddy got to them first.

'Whoa there, stranger,' he soothed with a friendly smile, almost in one of his character voice impersonations.

Pushing the trolley was a young boy, not more than six years old. In the trolley was a little girl even younger. The two looked up with fear, uncertainty and suspicion mixed into their expressions of bewilderment. Viv's heart went out to them.

'Hullo,' she said gently. 'What are you two doing here?'

The children said nothing.

'Been shopping then?' Freddy inquired.

The boy laughed, unable to repress his reaction. 'Silly. It's closed,' he scoffed.

Another laugh from the boy even made the little girl smile. God bless Freddy, he really did have a talent after all.

'How did you get here?' said Viv, trying to pry some basic information out of them.

The children still said nothing. Perhaps she was intimidating them with her direct inquiries.

'You haven't done much shopping,' Freddy remarked.

'No. Auntie's shopping,' the boy responded.

'Your auntie?' Viv asked him.

Again he didn't answer her. 'Charming,' she muttered to Freddy. 'They must think I'm the Witch of the West.'

The little boy looked at Freddy with imploring eyes. 'We're waiting for her. We're waiting for Auntie.'

24

The looks on their faces made Viv thank heaven she had taken the trouble to come to the Ellman Superstore on this dark and lonely night.

There was important, urgent work to be done, as fast and efficiently – and delicately – as they could.

7

Suddenly an alarm was screaming in the night, and would keep on screaming until answered.

Someone who didn't belong there had tripped an alarm at Byron-Newman, a prominent engineering works that presented formidable barriers to any would-be intruder, although the alarm obviously indicated that this someone had trespassed beyond the point of no return.

Driving the panda, Toby Armstrong responded instinctively to the alarm with a hard jerk on the wheel, several seconds before they were told the direction over the radio.

'We're on our way,' Anjali replied before the voice at the other end could finish a sentence.

The sound of the alarm grew steadily louder as they approached Byron-Newman Ltd. The panda screeched to a halt. Toby half-expected to see a drawbridge and moat guarding the fortress, but, alas, no such luck. This was the real world; nobility was ancient history. Menace was immediate, somewhere ahead in the dark, where that someone was hiding.

Constables Toby Armstrong and Special Constable Anjali Shah hit the ground running.

Police Sergeant McAllister was replacing the telephone as Viv Smith, along with her section officer, Bob Loach, waited for the report on the immediate disposition of the two lost children.

McAllister's frown didn't change. 'Social Services will send someone as soon as possible.'

His gaze focused on Viv like a zoom lens in a movie camera.

'Until they do, Bonnie and Clyde here'll need looking after.'

The sergeant was plainly referring to the wandering waifs, yet

Viv also gathered that McAllister was expecting *her* to do something about it. She bristled.

'Why look at me?' As if she didn't know.

McAllister expressed exasperation by moving a centimetre closer, raising his left eyebrow a millimetre and lowering his voice.

'Because you're a woman, for pity's sake.'

Enlightened Man, circa the Stone Age.

'It might come as a surprise to you, Sergeant, but not all women come with a built-in maternal expertise of how to deal with children.'

The laughter down the corridor distracted her, and unexpectedly served as a reminder that she was getting much too serious. Her rising blood pressure surely needed to be cooled.

Viv glanced at the distraction, then looked again. The laughter was coming from the high-pitched voices of three children: the little girl on one side, the older little boy on the other and Special Constable Freddy Calder in the middle.

Actually there was a fourth party at the party: Freddy's glove-puppet, Foxy, who was playing with a couple of coins. The two children were talking to Foxy as if he were more alive than Freddy – a frightening thought. Indeed it was Foxy who was showing them the coin tricks: Freddy was merely his quick-fingered assistant.

Each child was enthralled with Freddy's antics. Viv looked over at Loach and Sergeant McAllister. She caught them smiling, and they caught her looking, and for a brief moment, they shared a quiet, knowing laugh among themselves.

Their amusement was interrupted by a PC rushing in with an urgent message written all over his face, yet his uniform suggesting he'd been in the middle of a poll tax demo.

'We've got Big Jess in the hoolivan outside!'

The PC's announcement brought Sergeant McAllister to attention. Viv was impressed. Who was this Big Jess all of a sudden?

'Drunk?' McAllister asked routinely.

'As a cock-eyed owl, Sarge,' the PC responded in the same old routine.

McAllister turned to Viv and Loach with a blunt request.

'Give 'em a hand, will you?' he asked with an edge of weariness in his voice. 'They've got the Queen of the Night – Mrs Godzilla – out there.'

Apparently Loach was just as unaware of this notorious character as Viv was.

'Who's Big Jess?'

'You don't know?' McAllister's expression turned from incredulity to a nasty, knowing smile. 'Then you've a nice surprise coming, laddie.'

A moment before Toby got there, Anjali had reached the elderly security guard outside the Byron-Newman building and quickly elicited the information they needed.

'The noise came from round the back,' Anjali briefed Toby.

'Wait here,' Toby told the old guard. 'We should have some back-up pretty soon. Okay?'

Toby didn't wait for the guard's answer before signalling Anjali that they proceed with their own investigation, and they set off in hot pursuit around the corner of the building.

It wasn't long until the pair raced into an area crowded with an obstacle course of tall waste-bins. On the other side of the congested area they spotted two figures who suddenly bolted from the deep shadows and made a run for the perimeter fence.

In the semi-darkness, the suspects appeared to be two boys or young men.

Caught on the wrong side of the obstacle course, Toby and Anjali tried to hurry through the clutter of bins that were slowing them down and facilitating the escape of the fugitives.

Being afraid didn't paralyze Anjali; fear made her run faster. She had never been able to overcome her inner panic in the face of danger, and she had no idea what would happen if she caught up with these bandits, or quite what she would do if they suddenly turned to attack her. Rather, she was driven by a sense of urgency, a blind compulsion to force her legs to keep churning. She made herself do what she instinctively knew had to be done, suppressing any thought of the possible consequences.

As Toby and Anjali got closer, the young men were legging it to the high fence. One was clearly older than the other, and both appeared to be of Asian extraction. An inopportune thought flashed through Toby's mind, wondering what Anjali's reaction to them might be.

The fugitives started to claw their way up the perimeter fence. The older one was lugging a heavy metal box and trying to heave it over the top. Yet, despite being weighed down by the box, the older lad was making better progress, and had nearly reached his goal.

Unable to gain secure toeholds, the younger boy was panicking. Desperate, he grabbed ahold of the older one's jeans, trying to keep his grip, his only chance to escape again to freedom. The older fugitive was almost over the fence, and the outcome seemed to be in doubt: whether the older one would shake loose and boost himself over the top or the younger one would drag them both down.

Sensing his dilemma, the older one kicked out at the younger boy below, who lost his balance and fell to the ground, landing awkwardly with an anguished cry just as Anjali reached him.

She looked through the mesh of the fence as the older one slithered down the other side, tightened his grip on the metal box and vanished into the darkness beyond.

A moment later Toby caught up with Anjali. They heard a motorbike revving hard on the other side of the perimeter fence, ready for the getaway.

'He's gone,' Toby stated, accepting the obvious and resigning himself to capturing only one of the pair.

They turned to the younger boy trapped at their feet. Their prisoner was obviously in considerable pain.

'I think his leg's busted,' Toby surmised from the queer angle of the boy's lower left limb. The kid couldn't be more than 14 or 15 years old, he thought, shaking his head.

He unclipped his radio, as Anjali tended to the boy. Looking up at her, the kid was squeezing his eyes, wincing in pain.

'Hold on, lad. The ambulance is on its way,' Toby said.

There was a hint of recognition in Anjali's gaze at the lad.

'D'you know him?'

'He's Raj Patel. I know his family.'

Unsure of quite what to do with this bit of information, Toby asked the next logical question.

'What about the other one?'

'I don't know him,' Anjali acknowledged, looking out through the fence. Her eyes narrowed, without looking back at Toby, yet still peering into the black hole into which the other fugitive had disappeared.

'But I'll recognize him the next time.'

8

It took a superhuman effort for Andy McAllister, Bob Loach, Viv Smith, two PC's and the arresting officer to force the struggling mass of a miserable prostitute by the name of Big Jess into a nearby cell.

While the weird wrestling continued, suddenly Loach let out a yell of intense pain. Big Jess had Loach's thumb between her teeth as if she were chomping on a sausage.

Loach made a fist with his other hand and threw it into the exposed face of Big Jess.

The impact moved her entire head away from Loach's thumb, and she slumped to the floor. The others managed to get a firm grasp on the mass of flesh, raise her off the hard floor and dump her on the bunk-bed in the cell with a great sigh of relief. Big Jess just snored and snuffled, no longer conscious of a world awake and outside her pleasant dreams.

In the meantime, Loach was examining his wounded extremity.

McAllister made a sympathetic cluck with his tongue. 'I suppose I'd better make a report that the offender suffered an injury during the struggle.'

Loach displayed the bloody stump of his thumb. 'She was going to bite it off!'

Sergeant McAllister restrained himself from snickering. 'Don't worry, laddie. That goes in the report as well. G.B.H.T.T.'

There was an inquisitive look from Loach.

'Grievous Bodily Harm To a Thumb.' He allowed his diagnosis time to register in Loach's brain. 'And get it checked.'

Then McAllister turned to the arresting officer. 'Get the surgeon to check her.' Truth be known, he was more concerned with Loach's health than hers. Big Jess was the Frank Tyson of the prostitute world.

At the Byron-Newman engineering works, there was now an ambulance as well as three other patrol cars, and another vehicle belonging to the manager of the works. All of a sudden the scene had become as busy as it might be in the middle of the day.

Anjali Shah was looking down compassionately at young Raj Patel lying on the stretcher, waiting to be taken to the hospital to get some attention for his leg. He was visibly trying to contain his fear.

'Who was the one who did this to you, Raj? What's his name?' She was making every effort to relate to him, not as a uniformed officer of the law but rather as a concerned human being from a similar background.

Nonetheless, he gritted his teeth and shook his head defiantly.

There was nothing left to be said for now. Anjali and Toby watched the young man being placed carefully into the ambulance, as they were joined by the manager of the engineering works.

'Another hero,' Toby muttered.

The manager piped up in reply. 'If there was any justice, he should've broken his neck.'

Toby noticed Anjali's reaction.

'Bit over the top, don't you think, sir?' Toby gently chided him. 'I mean – they missed the money box. And what they stole was a bit of machinery, wasn't it?' Of course the manager was upset, but it was time to bring his anxieties back to earth.

'A very expensive drilling bit, officer,' the manager explained in a patronizing tone. 'Only about thirty-five thousand quid. Not that it makes much difference. Fat chance we'll ever hear of it again . . .'

The next remark the manager aimed toward Anjali. '. . . especially since ethnics are involved.'

After staring her down, the manager was about to turn away when Anjali spoke.

'Excuse me, sir. Will you let us try to get your property back before you press charges?'

The manager was immediately suspicious.

'Why? You know something I don't?'

Anjali's response was neither timid nor equivocal. 'I know one of the offenders. After all, I'm an ethnic myself.' She wasn't mincing her words, Toby noted. 'At least let me make enquiries.'

The last comment startled Toby. The manager gave her a lingering look, which gradually dwindled into a knowing smile.

'Why not? The head accountant won't be back for a couple o' days.' His smile turned up at one corner, the equivalent of a wink at Anjali, and he moved away.

Toby waited for the manager to get out of earshot before lashing into Special Constable Shah.

'What the hell are you doing?' he berated her. 'You can't make deals!' The request should have come from Toby, if anyone.

Anjali made no attempt to contradict him. 'I'm sorry. I had no right to do that.' Yet this time she did equivocate. 'But surely it's just as important to contain crime.'

Her statement implied a question, although Toby was sure she knew the answer as well as he did. 'That's not what worries me.'

He had to confront her with the larger question, the underlying issue, although he was almost sure to be misunderstood. He tried to show his concern, rather than his own attitude toward those of Asian extraction.

'Aren't you identifying too closely with your own kind?'

The look in her eyes was the same as she had given the manager of the engineering works.

9

The view of Birmingham from the expansive windows of the 'Pub on 4th' – the purpose-built social club on the top floor of the Division 'S' headquarters – is transcendent and serene, far from the madding crowd below: one of the few material benefits of volunteering for public service as a Special. Restricted to Police, Specials and their guests, it allowed them to relax from the pressures and travails of their work and meet socially in a secure, private environment with all the comforts of home, including a bar, TV area and snooker room. Yet besides its exclusive, even privileged company the Pub on 4th was the same as any other perhaps, preferable only in its panoramic views and family atmosphere.

Tonight the pub was quite full and alive with shop talk and laughter. Not in the mood, Toby was sitting at a table with Anjali, the centre of attention, surrounded by young bucks, Specials and PC's alike. Somewhat dispirited, he was just finishing his orange juice and getting up to leave.

'Ah! Young love,' one of the Specials remarked, obviously referring to Toby. 'Bed calls.'

It wasn't worth a sassy rejoinder, so instead Toby flicked his fingers at the guy's head, though he missed by a long shot. He mouthed 'goodnight' and 'see you' to the faces around the table. Finally his gaze stopped, and stayed, on Anjali. He looked at her for what seemed like an eternity without turning away; yet she returned his stare, challenging him with her eyes, unflinching. Beginning to wonder if the others were watching them, Toby eventually decided it was time to leave.

On his way out, Toby watched Viv Smith and Sandra Gibson at another table engaged in serious discussion. Sandra was the Mother of all Midland Specials, the administrative secretary who knew, filed, remembered and took care of all the Specials in the Birmingham area. Toby would have liked to have stopped and say hello, but Viv was immersed in the conversation in a manner that suggested any interruption would not be welcome, so he decided to amble on by, acknowledging Sandra with a quick wave and smile.

Viv took the occasion of Sandra's momentary distraction to knock back the rest of her vodka and orange. It wasn't her first. When Sandra returned to their conversation, Viv was ready to continue her diatribe. 'What really gets up my nose is what kind of a human being could leave kids wandering around a supermarket?'

Sandra nodded and pulled a quizzical face in agreement. Before Viv could continue her litany of complaints about the parentage of the lost children, Bob Loach wandered over to their table showing off the red-and-white badge of courage: his bandaged thumb.

Immediately Loach began to entertain the other PCs sitting at the table with Viv and Sandra. Although they had ceased following or even listening to Viv, they interrupted any semblance of civilized conversation by raising their glasses, voices and laughter in toasts to the valiant Loach. 'Why didn't you get Big Jess to kiss it better?' asked one wag.

'Been sucking your thumb, Bob?' simultaneously suggested one of the others.

Loach smiled sourly and silently pleaded with Sandra for some sympathy. But Viv was having none of his interruptions.

'Now don't go giving Sandra a hard time with your problems, Bob Loach. She's off-duty. Having a quiet drink,' And busy with my problems at present, Viv wanted to add. 'She's not interested in discussing compensation tonight.'

The disappointment on his face was that of a disheartened little boy which, as ever, Sandra didn't have the constitution to resist.

'What happened?' she asked innocently, at the same time automatically removing a secretarial pad and pencil from her shoulder bag.

Viv decided that the only way to cut this short was to speak up first. 'A lady of the night called Big Jess bit it. I'd say Loach got off lightly.'

Loach ignored Viv and concentrated on Sandra. 'I suppose it'll mean a court appearance,' he sighed. 'As if I didn't have enough on my plate.'

Just feeling sorry for himself, Viv reflected. 'He's a lot on his mind, has our Section Officer,' she cracked.

Unfortunately Loach took the opportunity to venture off on one of his pet peeves. 'Damned right. I've been Acting SDO for about three months. And doing all skiver SDO Barker's paper work . . .'

Viv tried to head him off at the pass. 'Loach . . .'

But it was already too late. 'Don't get me wrong. I don't mind doing the job. But how long am I supposed to act as an Acting?' Now that he was off and running, there would be virtually no stopping him. 'I wouldn't care, if I got a word of thank-you from our invisible SDO for the time I'm putting in.'

Loach's tirade against SDO Barker was having an unintended effect on Sandra, although he took no notice of the time-bomb he could be about to ignite.

'Change the channel, will you?' Viv implored, though her voice probably revealed her sense of futility.

As expected, Loach barely paused to catch his breath before running on again. 'Why can't the sod phone and say: "Thank you, Bob." It's not much.'

Loach seemed completely oblivious to the devastating effect the lambasting of his immediate superior, Sub-Divisional Officer Rob Barker, was having on Administrative Secretary Sandra Gibson. Obviously he didn't realize the connection.

'If you want my opinion,' Loach offered, although no one had solicited his views, 'he's got his leg over some bird, or maybe broken it getting off.'

That did it. Without a word, her face set in a bleak expression, Sandra got up and walked out.

Loach was dumbfounded, the puzzled look on his face asking Viv: What's that all about?

'You really are a daft egg,' Viv remonstrated.

'What are you on about?'

'Rob Barker this, Rob Barker that. You're as sensitive as a Harpic.'

'I'm only telling it the way I see it,' Loach tried to rationalize self-defensively.

Viv wasn't letting him off the hook. 'Well, I'll be glad to tell Rob Barker the next time I see him.'

'Fine. Do that,' Loach concluded. To hell with the gent. But then he started to replay her comment and reconsider what it meant.

'What d'you mean "next time?"' he inquired suspiciously. 'When did you see him?'

Abruptly Viv corrected her course, becoming a bit more evasive in her tone. 'I've seen him a couple o' times in the last week.'

Loach was surprised by her answer. 'Where?'

'Where I work,' Viv replied: 'The Bromsgrove.'

A frown settled on Loach's brow. 'The Building Society? What for? A mortgage?'

The conversation was leading in the wrong direction, but there wasn't much Viv could do about it.

'No. He's got a mortgage already. I'm not sure, but I think he was talking to the manager about selling . . . selling his house, that is.'

Luckily at that moment Viv spotted Freddy Calder standing in the doorway. Smiling, she turned to Bob Loach to cut off his line of inquiry.

'Oh, oh! There's Freddy. Gotta go.'

Loach remained in some confusion as to what was going on while Freddy motioned Viv to join him, bringing Loach back to the present. 'That reminds me . . .'

As Viv got up, Loach joined her, and together they crossed the room to meet Freddy.

'The woman from social's here,' Freddy informed her. 'A Miss Brownlow. I thought you might want to meet her.' Apparently, Freddy was happily impressed with Miss Brownlow. 'She's a smashing girl. And the kids like her . . .'

Freddy turned to leave with Viv to meet Miss Brownlow. Loach made a weak waggle with his hand in an attempt to stop him, then waved both of them away. No use trying to drag Viv back for further questioning at present.

Surveying the crowded Pub on 4th last time, Loach noticed

34

someone else he wanted to see . Weaving his way through the maze of people and chairs, he arrived at Anjali Shah's table as she, too, was trying to extricate herself and say her goodbyes. But the other Specials and PC's at her table were teasing her unmercifully and refusing to let her go.

'You want a lift home, Anjali?' suggested one with a sly smirk.

'I go past your way,' another mock-chivalrous Special chimed in.

'Forget it, he's only got a motorbike,' scoffed the latter's partner.

Still another pseudo-knight stepped into the fray: 'If Anjali's going with anyone, it's with me.'

His challenge was met by a chorus of birdsong from the fellow rivals for Anjali's company.

'You can all sit down,' she ordered them, a trace of a smile on her lips. 'The man who's taking me home is . . .'

She kept them panting, awaiting the maiden's fair choice.

'. . . the nice man who drives the 44 bus.'

A series of muted boos greeted her announcement. Anjali left the table laughing, passing Bob Loach on her way out.

'If you want to change your mind . . . ?' Loach offered politely, not teasing her any more.

Anjali simply smiled shyly and walked by with her head lowered to avoid his eyes.

Shaking his own head, Loach watched her departure, then joined her former suitors at the table.

'Well, George?' queried the first one: 'You blew out there.'

'You want me to really try?' responded the PC named George. 'Show me the colour of your money.'

One of them turned to Loach. 'What d'you think, Bob?'

'What do I think what?' he countered.

'Has she got a heavy boyfriend, or what?

'Nah!' his partner scoffed again. 'Maybe she's cheesed off giving massage all day.'

The others laughed at the lewd suggestion, but Loach turned on them sourly.

'Only dipsticks like you would make an NHS physio sound like a nymphomaniac,' he lectured them.

But his sobriety only spurred the others to lower depths.

'Hey!' one pseudo-knight interrupted as an idea popped into his head: 'Did someone mention my hobby?'

10

Still in uniform, Anjali Shah walked up to the door of the modest terraced house where she lived. Retrieving the key from her shoulder bag, she unlocked the door and went in.

In the sitting room, her brother Sanjay was playing carom – a form of table billiards – with several of his 'friends'. One strong main light was beaming down on the playing surface, so that several of the players' faces were in deep shadow.

When Anjali removed her coat in the doorway, her Specials uniform was revealed. From the corner of her eye she noticed that the sudden sight of her uniform made some of Sanjay's nervous 'friends' scatter their winnings across the board, in effect ruining the state of play.

Sanjay was livid. 'Look what you have done, Jelly Baby! Go to bed.'

A trifle amused at his attitude, Anjali stopped a moment to look around the table. One face moved out of the shadow into the light. It was the young man, the young thief, she had earlier seen on the other side of the perimeter fence at the engineering works.

Sanjay turned to his 'friends' to apologize for his sister's presence. 'I have a snoop for a sister, you know.'

Her face hardened, as a sneering smile played around the lips of the young thief. Without another word she left them and went into the kitchen.

While she was making herself a cup of coffee, the young thief opened the door, came in then closed the door behind him. From the sitting room, she had heard one of the others call him 'Dev'.

This Dev moved alongside Anjali. He picked up a sharp piece of cutlery and played with it, perhaps trying to appear more menacing.

'So the little police lady is Sanjay's sister,' he began slowly. 'Don't you think that's funny? I think it's funny.'

'I'm sure Raj finds it very funny in hospital. He broke his leg,' she replied calmly.

Dev seemed unperturbed, and still fingered the cutlery. 'He's a good kid. He'll keep his mouth shut.' A sneer curled his lip. 'Just as you will, Jelly Baby. Is that what Sanjay calls you?'

She tried to remain unruffled, continuing the task of making her coffee while contradicting his assumption that all was well. 'I wouldn't bank on it,' she warned.

Dev moved closer to her. 'Listen, police lady. All I need do is ask your brother to say I've been here all night.'

Deliberately the young thief began to stroke Anjali's hair. Although she was immediately alarmed, there wasn't a thing she could do about it, which Dev obviously realized, so he continued. For the time being, she told herself, she would have to suffer and endure the indignity.

'What do you do then?' Dev asked. 'Have the police bring your own brother in for questioning? You're not that stupid, are you?'

11

At five minutes past nine, Viv Smith rushed in through the front door of the small suburban branch of the Bromsgrove Building Society, late for work again. As she quickly hung up her coat, out of the corner of her eye she noticed Maynard, the manager, holding his office door ajar, watching her. He checked his watch with a jaundiced look.

She was just settling into her position at the counter and unlocking her till when she felt someone touch her shoulder. It was only Madge, the young trainee.

'There's a call for you, Miss Smith,' she said politely, yet with a bit of a frown. 'A Miss Brownlow. From Social Services?'

'That's right. Thanks, Madge.'

Viv stood up and walked back to the telephone with the young trainee. Meanwhile Madge's face was assuming a pained expression.

'Mr Maynard told me to tell you about personal calls during office hours.'

Her duty done, Madge melted away. Viv reached for the waiting phone.

'Miss Brownlow. It's good of you to call . . .'

The voice on the other end of the line was businesslike, yet personal and friendly as well.

'You've traced the mother of the two children? That's great.'

Lost and found. Viv sighed with some sense of relief, despite still wondering what kind of mother would set her children adrift in a supermarket trolley.

'Where? She was in *Wales*?'

This new development was unexpected, but Viv had to confess to herself that she was becoming ever more cautious.

'Of course I'm surprised,' she admitted to Miss Brownlow. 'Yes . . . of course I'll meet her.'

At that moment, Maynard was crossing the office and passing behind Viv. 'Staff on phone means a customer gone,' he admonished her in an adolescent singsong voice.

She made an obscene gesture behind his back.

'Today?' Not today, she wanted to protest. 'Lunch-time?' Not lunchtime, not today. 'I guess I could.' She didn't know how in hell she could. 'Okay, I'll wait for you here . . .'

Maynard was still keeping a wary eye on Viv. Yet immediately after ending her conversation with Miss Brownlow and replacing the receiver, she picked it up again and dialled another number. When the connection was completed, she tried to speak softly in a low voice to the love of her life (or, at least, of the moment).

'Ginger? It's Viv. About lunch . . .'

It was obvious he guessed what she was going to say, so she didn't have to suffer through it.

'I'm sorry. You're a love.' She blew him a wet kiss. She doubted whether its sensual texture, let alone moisture, would survive the transmission to reach his ear, but gave it all she had anyway. 'Mwah! Sweetie.' She would have to demonstrate first-hand what she meant sometime later when they were alone together.

In a hurry she replaced the receiver and turned around – only to find Maynard standing behind her, open-mouthed, in a state of shock.

Mrs Shah hovered around the stove figuring how to look busy with nothing much left to do, while her children, Anjali and Sanjay, finished their late breakfast. Though at times concerned about her son, she was always worrying about her daughter.

'It is ten o'clock, Anjali,' she cautioned, making a conscious effort not to sound too abrasive.

Anjali questioned her mother's memory with a gentle reminder. 'Ma? Tuesday I have a late start at the hospital.'

Observing her brother nonchalantly half-eating his breakfast and half-reading his newspaper, Anjali decided the time was appropriate to approach him lightly.

'I see you've got a new friend.'

Sanjay put down his newspaper and looked up slyly at his older sister.

'You mean Dev? I thought I saw the two of you in the kitchen together.' He winked at her. 'Fancy him, do you? He's a good-looking fellow. But you're much too old for him, Jelly Baby.'

He took another couple of sips of coffee before continuing. 'Anyway, he's up here visiting his uncle for a week or two, then he goes back to London.'

Speaking casually, Anjali tried to disguise the extent and purpose of her interest. 'How did you meet him?'

'He came along with Bati,' Sanjay replied, then looked to his mother. 'Ma? I need more coffee.' Mrs Shah complied without hesitation. He switched his glaring eyes to Anjali. 'You know, you're sounding more like a policeman every day,' he said sarcastically.

Their Uncle Ram, brother of their mother and adopted 'father' of the family of three, wandered into the kitchen. Apparently feeling stiff and sore at the old age of 60, Ram tried a tentative stretch of his tired limbs. As usual, his mood was cranky first thing in the morning.

'Don't all get up, it's only your Uncle Ram,' he mocked.

Sanjay needled Anjali at the earliest opportunity. 'You're just in time, Uncle. Anjali is giving me the third degree.' He glanced at his sister to see if his jabs were getting to her. 'About a friend of mine. I think she's lusting after him.' That should do it.

'What a nonsense!' Anjali muttered.

But Uncle Ram was suddenly interested, mildly rebuking her. 'I will decide if it's a nonsense.' He turned to young Sanjay.

'What boy are you speaking about? Do I know him? What is his family?'

An unfeminine and unbecoming grunting noise indicated Anjali's irritation, but Sanjay was only too happy to respond.

'He's visiting from London. His name is Dev Patel. You know his uncle – Prem Ghai, the one who sells spice.'

Uncle Ram flattened his lips, clearly impressed. 'Prem Ghai is a very major businessman.' His calculating look at Anjali suggested he might have underestimated her.

'You are a slyboots,' he told her, 'and no mistake.'

Anjali was unimpressed. 'Uncle, look at me, and watch what my lips say. I have no interest in this boy. I do not wish to be interested in this boy. This boy is of no account.'

Just then the doorbell rang. Mrs Shah was relieved and thankful for the chance to answer the door and escape another family squabble.

His mother now beyond hearing him, Sanjay's eyes narrowed. 'Then why ask these questions? Are you prying into my affairs again? Is that it? You see I have a new friend? So you snoop. Now you're in the police you think everyone is a criminal.' Angry and disgusted, he stormed out of the kitchen.

Uncle Ram flapped his hands helplessly. 'He is right.'

'He's nothing of the kind,' Anjali answered sharply.

'There you go! I say something, and you contradict. You have no respect. I am the head of the family now that your father is no longer with us. You would do well to heed my advice.'

In the brief silence that followed, Mrs Shah returned to the kitchen from answering the doorbell.

'It's Mrs Patel,' she announced. 'She's in the other room.'

Uncle Ram checked his watch. 'I am late already, but tell her I can spare a few minutes.'

Mrs Shah shook her head. 'No, no. It is Anjali she wishes to see.'

12

In the office of Cougar Coaches sitting opposite Bob Loach was a young man of 16 by the name of Kevin, about to be taken on as the new grease monkey. Loach looked at him and smiled, then turned his gaze to Noreen, who was checking Kevin's references.

'Fantastic!' Noreen proclaimed. 'He got a C in Woodwork.'

Loach winked at Kevin. 'I'm not taking him on to give a lecture in French, you know, Noreen. He's just an apprentice.'

Noreen intercepted the male club wink, abruptly deciding to examine callow Kevin a bit more closely. It was hardly a pleasant errand given his unwashed hair, unshaven face and the sweatmarks under his armpits.

'True,' she reluctantly concurred with her husband. 'But I think Kevin has a lot to learn about personal hygiene. Haven't you, Kevin?' She paused for a brief moment, to see if he understood what she meant. 'Beginning with what it means.'

Loach glowered at Noreen. 'All right, lad, go see John Barraclough.

Tell him you're hired.' He offered a last word of advice. 'Remember, Kevin. We all have to pull our weight here.'

Noreen returned the references to the boy. 'In other words, luv, the only passengers we carry pay to get on the bus.'

Kevin nodded, getting to his feet while mumbling his thanks, then stopped at the door. 'Hope your thumb gets better, Mr Loach.'

Noreen jumped in before Loach could reply. 'I'm sure Jack Horner will watch where he sticks his thumb next time.'

His expression unsure, Kevin made a quick exit.

When he was gone, Loach turned on Noreen.

'Look, Noreen . . .' he grumbled.

But she was already back at work and didn't bother to look up.

The mother of Raj Patel was not crying; she was weeping. For her there was little comfort in surroundings of the Shah home decorated to resemble an idealized memory of Bombay. For her there was nowhere to hide from being treated as an alien untouchable in a pervasive and powerful class society. For her son she felt powerless, helpless, terrified.

All this convulsive anguish Anjali could feel as well, holding Mrs Patel's hands and trying to calm her.

'My boy is a good boy,' she sobbed. 'You work with the policemen. You tell them that. My Raj could never do what they say he did. You tell them they have made a mistake.'

Anjali wasn't sure whether it was a good sign or a bad one that his mother could believe no evil of her son, but she knew it was natural, and she shared Mrs Patel's heartache. What was more difficult for Anjali was to be professional, and dispassionate.

'Mrs Patel, I know Raj is a good boy . . .' That was as much reassurance as she should offer, in her official capacity. 'I'll do what I can with the police,' she promised, although she was honour-bound to state the pertinent facts as well.

'. . . but he was there, so they may not listen.'

In the yard at Cougar Coaches, John Barraclough was launching Kevin's shakedown cruise, showing him how to check for problems hidden under the bonnet of one of the coaches.

'These oil levels are very important, Kevin. Any questions, lad?'

Kevin's brow furrowed, ostensibly he was thinking hard, trying to make a good show with an intelligent response.

'That Noreen. She doesn't half give the Boss a bit of stick.' He made a visible effort to figure it all out. 'You'd think they were married.'

'They are.' Barraclough informed him, then followed with an advisory observation. 'There's marriages what are made in Heaven, lad; and there's Noreen and Loach's what are made out of barbed wire.'

Before he could elaborate, there was a roar behind them, and as they turned to look a dazzling new Porsche screeched to a stop. By now they were intrigued, and sallied forth to see which wild and decadent aristocratic personage had taken a wrong turn and nearly crashed into the garage.

As the passenger door opened, a pair of polished women's shoes and well-turned ankles were exposed, immediately succeeded by shapely calves swinging out, smooth stockinged legs that seemed to go on forever, with no outer garment yet in sight.

They were a glory to behold, and Barraclough had beheld them once before. As much could not be said for poor Kevin, whose jaw dropped.

Out of the Porsche climbed the long, lovely, endless legs – Michelle's, Dicky Padgett's latest ecstasy. Finally, to top it all off, Kevin dropped his toolbox with a clatter. The lad was unhinged.

When Michelle made her appearance at the door of the office, she gave Mr Loach and the book-keeper what Dicky referred to as her 'devastating smile'.

Loach was devastated. Noreen favoured him with a calculating stare.

'Uh . . . this is Michelle,' he quickly improvised. 'Michelle . . . this is Noreen. She's the one you've to talk to.' There – it was out.

'Talk to me about what?' Noreen snapped. She faced the intruder with a harder smile. 'I'm his wife.'

'Michelle completely slipped my mind . . .'

Her smile softened for her husband, and she knew he would understand. 'Michelle slipped your mind?' She was careful not to allow any hint of glee in her eyes. 'Come on, Loach . . .'

Loach was flustered and flushed, and resented her outmanoeuvring him before he could begin to explain. 'Listen to me. Dicky wanted to sign up Michelle for the Stratford tour. You know – the one we've got booked in for the end of the week.' He didn't dare tell her yet that Michelle was also here to ask for an advance.

Unpredictable, Noreen had a glint of danger in her eyes as she turned her own devastating smile on Michelle. 'Let's try and establish something, shall we, Michelle?'

'Sure,' Michelle aped her smile with cheerful enthusiasm.

Noreen spoke to her slowly and carefully, as if to a child. 'Have you ever been to Stratford?'

'No,' Michelle answered blithely, guilelessly, completely unaware of the freight train now headed straight down the track where she was standing.

'Well . . .' Noreen began, closing in for the kill, 'when you do a courier job, Michelle, it's vital that you can answer any question that a tourist on the coach may ask.'

'Sure. I know that,' chirped Michelle, glad to be tossed an easy one.

'For instance . . .' Noreen suggested – plainly divulging to anyone with even the slightest sensitivity that she was setting a trap, 'what do you know about Shakespeare?'

At last there was a spark of recognition behind Michelle's empty eyes, and she nodded vigorously.

'You mean the wine bar up on the Marlow Road.'

Even Noreen was taken aback. 'What?'

Michelle was unfazed, finally finding herself in familiar territory.

'The *William Shakespeare*,' she expounded. 'You don't want to go there. He's got hands like an octopus, the owner. They're everywhere!' she pouted. 'I only worked there for two weeks and my bum was black and blue!'

Hopeless, Loach concluded. What a crying shame.

13

Miss Brownlow parked the car, avoiding stray glass and rubble as best she could, then she and Viv headed into the block, assessing the older residences of the housing estate as they walked. With growing admiration for Miss Brownlow's diplomacy, her tact, her firm yet gentle manner, Viv was unable to manifest her holy tolerance and emotional self-restraint.

'I just hope I can bottle my temper,' Viv confessed. Her memory of two innocent children abandoned at an Ellman Superstore blocked any sympathy she might have felt for a mother bringing up a family in this area. 'Mothers who dump their kids are slags, in my book.' As her anticipation of the approaching confrontation tightened in her stomach, she realized that she expected the worst: a tart with a fag in her mouth. 'And,' she added in a lower voice, 'they usually all look the same – sluts.'

When eventually they reached the door, Viv was shocked, but not at all in the way she had expected. Miss Brownlow formally introduced her to the lost children's mother, although Viv neither heard nor remembered her name. All she noticed was how decent she looked, in a neat, clean dress; the lips of her smile slightly trembling, her teary eyes both welcoming and imploring.

The young mother ushered them into the main room of her home, which sparkled like a new pin. Viv knew at a glance that such a state of affairs couldn't have been accomplished overnight. This degree of scrubbing one couldn't buy servant's labour to perform, let alone afford what it would cost these days. Over in the corner, the two children were off playing quietly by themselves, content to wave at Viv without interrupting their repeated attempts to construct a house of cards. They, too, were dressed in crisp, clean clothes.

When Viv glanced over at Miss Brownlow to share what she was seeing, the proper Miss Brownlow for once couldn't resist a smile at Viv's expense. Viv felt suitably contrite. Yet still she was unprepared to face the children's mother, whose eyes begged her attention, her voice trembling on the edge of tears.

She spoke directly to Viv's heart. 'I could've . . . lost them . . .' She shook her head to banish the thought. 'I'm just so thankful you were there . . . and found them . . .' She was trying to hold herself together long enough to find the right words.

'When I think of . . . what might've happened . . .'

She couldn't continue. The tears welled in her eyes, her body began to shake and she started to fall apart in front of them.

In spite of herself, with an awkward lurch Viv moved to embrace her. To hold her, support her, hug her, and share the agony of how precious were the fragile lives of her children.

Anjali Shah entered the warehouse of Prem Ghai's Asian wholesale spice business and asked the first worker she met where she could find him.

'Excuse me. I'm looking for Mr Ghai.'

Before the worker could speak, someone else stepped in front of Anjali: the fugitive on the other side of the fence, the bully who tried to intimidate her in her own home – Dev himself.

'That's all right, Veejay. I will attend to the lady.'

Dev led Anjali to a quiet corner of the warehouse, but he couldn't control the volume of his anger. 'How dare you come here. To my uncle's place of business!'

The loud echo of his voice made him realize that letting his temper get out of control might precipitate his losing face among the employees of his uncle, so he converted his fury to mockery at her silence.

'My uncle will think I am having affairs with middle-aged ladies,' he sneered.

'You're such a fool,' she scoffed at him. 'But that is not my problem. That is yours. I am only interested in the box you stole. It is of no use to you. Where is it?'

Her intensity caught him offguard, and he withdrew a step. 'Somewhere. I don't know.' His eyebrow raised, possibly indicating the dawn of a new thought. 'It's nothing but junk. What's the big deal?'

Anjali tried to control her own temper. 'The big deal is that you're going to give it back.'

Dev started to smile, but she cut him short.

'Oh, yes. You will return it. And just maybe, I can get them to drop charges.' She detected a glimmer of interest on his part. 'That way I can help Raj Patel. He's had a fright. It might stick in his mind.'

'You're crazy,' Dev berated her. 'You come here handing out orders like a man. I don't need to listen to this.'

'Would you rather your uncle did?'

His temper flared, and he moved his body closer to hers. 'My uncle is a man of position in this community. You are nothing,' he growled. 'Trash! No one will listen to trash.'

Suddenly he seized Anjali by the throat and tightened his grip. Just as quickly she turned the tables on him. It was actually a simple, basic move she had practised hundreds of times in the self-defence classes she had taken after promising herself never again to be at the mercy of an assailant, as she had been that night now seemingly long ago. Yet the haunting memory of being overpowered had acted as a vaccination, so that she developed in her slim body the antidote to combat an attack of brute force.

45

In this instance the brute was immediately brought to his knees, his hand caught in the vice of her grip. It was elementary, though totally effective in both outwitting and immobilizing him.

'Your uncle need not know,' Anjali told him in an even voice, making no effort to torture him with greater pain. 'All I am asking you is to stop – and reconsider . . .'

The sound of a horn was blaring outside, summoning Loach and Noreen to the office window. Outside, they could see the driver in the Porsche, apparently getting impatient, pressing long and hard on the horn. Another blast heralded the lovely, long-legged Michelle rushing from the office and the garage into the waiting car. Her door had barely closed before the racing-car spun round and squealed out of the yard.

For once, Bob and Noreen Loach were laughing in harmony as they watched from the window. He mimicked Michelle's mindless voice: '"Can you tell Dicky I can't make it tonight?"'

That broke them up laughing again. 'Or any other night, I fancy,' he mused. 'Poor Dicky.'

Again they laughed together. As they did, they slowly faced one another, and gradually fell silent. He caught hold of her hand.

'You know, it's good to laugh at the same things, Noreen.' He wished he had the gift of eloquence, or even flattery, but he couldn't seem to sustain that mood.

'Flippin' 'eck! Just think of Dicky's face when we wind him up over this one.'

For the first time in ages they looked at each other without animosity. 'Like a cup of coffee?' she offered. That hadn't happened in a long time either.

'Great.'

She picked up two mugs, went to the coffee machine, filled each mug with black coffee, then added milk.

'Two lumps, luv,' he gently reminded her.

'I do know, Bob,' she lectured, though still sweet.

Shaking his head, thinking back, Loach had to laugh one more time. 'Michelle as a courier? Oh dear, oh dear! Thank God we've got you as back-up.'

Noreen, having set the coffees down on his desk and holding the carton of sugar cubes at the ready, stood up straight. Her reply was sharp (although he may not have detected the change in her intonation to C sharp until it was too late).

'You've got me as *what*?'

'Doing the courier job on the Stratford run.' Seeing the lump of sugar in her hand, he tried to draw her attention to it. 'Two lumps, ta, luv.'

Noreen nodded, and threw a lump into his cup, half the contents exploding on to his desk. He jumped back. Then two, three, four, five, six sugar bombs were plopped into the dwindling coffee.

The truce was over. The Hundred Years' War had restarted, entering its second century.

14

The mother of the abandoned children had regained control of herself and made tea for them all on her spotless stove. Back in charge of her nerves, she was explaining to Viv – and incidentally to Miss Brownlow, who had doubtless heard the whole story – the series of misfortunes that had led to the near-disaster.

'Sid – that's my husband – was working in Wales. He couldn't get a job around here, you see.' Viv could surely understand that fact of life. 'Anyway, he had an accident on the building site. His ankle got broke. It wasn't all that bad, but I got a message saying it was serious.'

She paused to recall the worried state of her mind at that turning point, then continued. 'Well, my Mum's up in Carlisle, so Sid said his sister, Rosie – she stays with us – that Rosie could look after the kids.'

Her expression hardened after mentioning the name of her sister-in-law. 'She's back now. The Police picked her up at Birmingham Airport.'

Viv couldn't help shaking her head in disgust. 'She needs locking up, you know that. Where is she?'

'Rosie?' the children's mother called out. After waiting for an answer, she called again. 'Rosie?'

Across the room a door opened slightly and remained ajar. Soon a shadowy face peered through the gap. Presumably Rosie.

'What d'you want?' she asked sullenly.

The young mother spoke to her sister-in-law in a stern tenor. 'There are people wanting to see you. So get in here.'

The door opened wider, and Rosie slouched into their presence, hugging herself, perhaps holding herself together in one piece. She looked as if she had fallen down a mine-shaft. In fact, she was the slattern Viv had expected to see when the children's mother first opened the door.

Rosie must have taken note of Viv staring at her lumps, bumps and bruises. 'I walked into a door,' she scowled in non-explanation.

Unimpressed, Viv went straight after her. 'Why'd you do it? Leave two small kids in a supermarket?' She still couldn't believe anyone would do something so stupidly dangerous, let along idiotic.

Rosie shrugged lackadaisically, absolving herself of any responsibility or blame. 'I thought they'd be all right. Lots of people to look after them.' Abruptly her vindication became vindictive. 'How was I to know not one bugger would lift a finger? Bloody nice that is!' The rest of the world was at fault, not her.

Viv was speechless, although her mouth was open. She kept staring as if Rosie were a zombie from outer space.

'It's all very well you looking at me like you was the Virgin Mary, but what would you have done?' she asked Viv rhetorically.

'What would I have done if what?'

'If you'd been offered a free trip to Torremolinos with the likes of Bill Braddock . . .'

Confused, Viv couldn't quite understand what Torremolinos or one Bill Braddock had to do with anything germane to their discussion. Perhaps Rosie would clarify her statement.

'You could wait a thousand years to meet a man with a body like that!'

Oh, thought Viv, so that was the reason she deserted the children. And worse, she was serious . . .

The expensive drilling bit had been returned to the Byron-Newman engineering works, and the manager had agreed to talk with Special Constable Anjali Shah. They met outside the entrance.

'I don't know how you did it,' he shook his head back and forth. 'And I'm not asking why.'

'You got your property back?' she asked him to confirm.

'Late this afternoon,' the manager acknowledged.

Anjali reflected before going on, speaking slowly, impersonally, unapologetically. 'What about charges?'

The manager gave her a searching look before conceding to her terms. 'I won't be pressing any.' Yet he didn't drop his judgmental gaze, and she realized he was trying to relate to her on some deeper level.

'I suppose you have to look after your own. And far be it from me to damage race relations,' he went on. Sadly, Anjali could sense the signals that he was about to deliver the same tired old sermon. 'But listen, I've been to India. On holiday, Taj Mahal and all that guff. I know India.' And how naively, casually, baldly he revealed that he knew nothing of the land at all. 'Whether I press charges or not, it won't make any difference. You know that. I know that.' As if she were his co-conspirator in keeping the bloody wogs under control – and as if it were a privilege for one of her kind to be taken into his confidence.

As smart as they might be, some people would never learn. What he had assumed he had won, yet had just as surely lost, was her respect, though unnoticed and obviously of no importance to him.

Freddy Calder was chatting with two young Specials as a group of them were returning from duty to the Division 'S' entrance later in the evening. One of them had a lead on a place that could be ideal for him.

'. . . Nothing fantastic, mind. Just a small bachelor flat,' Freddy coaxed them, envisioning this private paradise in his daydreams, and, best of all, *not* envisioning his mother living there with him. 'If you see anything, give us a bell, huh?'

Spotting Loach just inside the building, Freddy shifted into overdrive and accelerated into the station. 'Bob . . . ?'

Meanwhile, Viv Smith caught up with the two young Specials Freddy had left behind. 'Forget it. He's always looking for a place. He never ever follows any of them up.' This function also fell under the heading of duty: educating the new recruits.

Hearing Freddy's cry, Loach halted at the door to the parade room, where Freddy buttonholed him with a wink and a grin.

'Going up to the 4th?' Freddy inquired.

'Sure. After I've seen the troops in.' Only then did Loach think to question Calder's motives. 'Why?'

49

Freddy sidled up to Loach and spoke to him in the stage whisper reserved for confidential consultation. 'Well . . . I have a sensational announcement of a sexual nature to impart.'

His hand always quicker than the beholder's eye, Freddy whisked MacFoxy the puppet out of his pocket. The old furball, inspired by his master's hand, undulated in the most highly suggestive manner to relay his not-so-subtle message.

'It'll make your pants dance, Loach.'

A conniving wink, and Freddy was off.

'What? Now just hold it a sec, Freddy?'

Before Loach could stop him, Freddy had already disappeared deeper into the inner labyrinths of the building.

A few minutes later up at the Pub on 4th, Loach was keeping an eye out for Freddy and his puppet companion while sipping on a well-earned pint. Looking around to check the door, he saw Sergeant McAllister moving toward him with a tall fellow in tow. Just behind them were Anjali Shah and Toby Armstrong.

McAllister walked up to Loach's table and presented his guest. Loach stood up to meet them.

'John Redwood – this is Section Officer Bob Loach.' Andy turned to Loach. 'Mr Redwood is a budding Special, Bob. Could be under your wing any day now. Isn't that right, John?' When his gaze returned to Loach, he raised an eyebrow, disclosing a fly in the ointment. ''Course, that depends on whether he reaches the very high standards needed to join your merry men.'

Disregarding his irony, Loach couldn't fail to notice that Redwood certainly had the physical framework to handle the job his monicker implied, resembling nothing less than a giant sequoia from California.

'You'll get a friendly reception here,' Loach offered, shaking his hand firmly, eager to get started on the right foot.

'You bet,' McAllister agreed, motioning them to be seated. 'We're so understaffed we'd accept trained penguins.'

Loach and McAllister chuckled among themselves at that one. Only a trace of an amused smile crossed Redwood's stiff upper lip, putting a dampener on McAllister's jovial mood. In its place appeared a passing cloud, and he hesitated before giving Bob the weather report.

'However, Bob . . . that's not the reason I brought John up here.'

No? Loach silently asked, lifting an eyebrow at the trepidation in Andy's official announcement.

'No, I should've told you that Mr Redwood's also a solicitor . . .'

'Really?' Loach didn't have a clue as to what the sergeant was getting at or where he was heading.

'Aye . . .' There was no escape, so Andy might as well give it to him straight. 'He's handling the defence for Big Jess.'

For a moment, Loach didn't quite comprehend what was being said or where the reference to Big Jess was coming from. The confusion must have registered on his face, as McAllister tried to humour him.

'Joke, isn't it? A prostitute on Legal Aid.'

Loach stared at John Redwood, solicitor and would-be blooming Special. He appeared to be the strong silent type. Again McAllister was compelled to blunder into the silence between them.

'I did tell him that on one thing we are agreed. Big Jess is one hundred per cent guilty.'

Evidently that was not precisely Solicitor Redwood's conclusion. Nonetheless, he stated his case, and minority opinion, quietly.

'I believe that my client suffered a contusion of the jaw.'

That was it for Loach. The giant sequoia had outlived his prehistoric purpose. To make his point short and sweet, Loach showed the solicitor his bandaged thumb, feigning a thrust that might just accidentally stick it up his nose.

'And I didn't have a bust thumb before I met Big Jess.'

Redwood seemed unperturbed, merely formed the hollow smile of the bureaucrat's mask. 'Well, I hope you agree that everyone should have his or her day in court.'

McAllister almost blew a gasket. 'Even when it's a waste of the taxpayer's money?' He couldn't conceal his contempt, nor his bewilderment.

Loach was getting ready to stick his still healthy and unfractured other thumb in the solicitor's face when suddenly there was a commotion over by the piano. Momentarily, all eyes were distracted from ongoing business to find out what the fuss was all about.

Sure enough, it was Freddy Calder, trumpeting his grand entrance onstage. 'Ta-ra!'

Scattered applause, laughter, hissing and heckling greeted Freddy's fanfare for the common man, as he turned to wave a prearranged signal to Briggsy the barman. Briggsy then moved to a nearby panel of switches and instantly the entire pub was plunged into darkness.

51

Above the sudden gasps and surprised shrieks sang the stentorian tones of Freddy Calder, Master of Ceremonies. 'For your delectation, ladies and gentlemen – the very latest from North Korea –' he held their breath '– *bra and panties that glow in the dark!*'

Somewhere in the darkness where he was standing, Freddy removed his coat, revealing fluorescent glowing pink knickers and brassiere. By somehow wiggling his middle, the shocking pink lingerie was dancing in the dark.

In spite of the laughter and uproar, the mighty voice of thunder drowned out every other sound.

'MR CALDER!'

The raucous noise was instantly reduced to hushed murmurs. After a short delay, the lights were switched on again.

Freddy was wearing the pink knickers and bra over his trousers and shirt, and that sight brought the house down in renewed laughter. Trapped as the fool with the house-lights on and the curtain still up, he looked in vain for the tyrant with the thunderous voice.

Sneaking up behind him, Sergeant McAllister, cloud-busting Zeus in the flesh, lowered his voice so that only Freddy could hear.

'A word in your ear . . . darling.'

15

As usual, Bob and Noreen Loach had eaten breakfast in silence, each reading separate sections of the *Birmingham Post*. In No Man's Land, the small table between them, rested the final remains of their individually prepared petits déjeuners. The telephone ringing provided a welcome interruption from the monotony, and Loach took the call.

It was Jim, one of the Specials, reporting an attack of the 'flu. 'Yeah, I hear it. You sound terrible. Well, look, lad, you stay put.' Loach turned his back toward Noreen to provide some vestige of a private conversation. 'Don't worry. It's not the end of the world . . . or the end of the Specials that you've got the 'flu. Better you stay put. I don't want the rest of us catching it.'

Making his farewells and wishing Jim a speedy recovery, he banged the 'phone back on its cradle.

'Flippin' 'eck! That's another one off the list.'

When he looked around, Loach realized once again that he was talking to himself. Noreen was stacking the breakfast things into the dishwasher. When he didn't want her to listen, she listened; and when he did want her to listen, perchance to add to the discussion, she wanted to be elsewhere.

In one of her daytime uniforms, a close-fitting one-piece swimming costume, Anjali Shah was working with Mrs Pearce in the hydrotherapy pool at General Hospital. The middle-aged woman was lying against a support which held her at a 45-degree angle, allowing her to stretch her legs in time to the music playing softly in the background.

'Very good,' Anjali soothed her. 'Now rest, and then we'll try it again.'

Mrs Pearce heaved a sigh of relief, trying her best to relax. She looked out of the window, which occupied the entire space of the opposite wall. Beyond the thick glass she could distinguish the hazy forms of nature: healthy green shrubs, thriving infant trees . . . and a shadowy figure moving through them! She nearly jumped out of her skin, tried to scream, yet couldn't emit a sound from her throat.

The figure reached the window, making erratic, hysterical gestures. Finally Mrs Pearce turned Anjali's attention to the raving maniac at the window behind her.

Quickly Anjali looked back over her shoulder, but it was only Uncle Ram outside the window making a complete fool of himself – hardly a rare occurrence in her experience. She wouldn't give him the satisfaction of acknowledging his presence, let alone his jumping around like a monkey outside the hospital where she was employed, so she paid him no mind and returned to working with her patient – realizing, of course, that ignoring his bizarre attempts to contact her would infuriate him even further.

Mrs Pearce could not even begin to figure out what was going on between her therapist and the lunatic outside. Now mad as a bee, he was waving frantically at her.

'Try and keep your right leg straight, Mrs Pearce.'

The crazy man was rapping on the window with all his strength and fury, but its thickness prevented any noise from getting through: he might as well be hammering the glass with a rose petal. Still, his desperate efforts were frightening Mrs Pearce, and she was helplessly bewildered.

'Don't you think it might be something important?'

Anjali saw that Mrs Pearce had a kind heart, and calmly reassured her. 'Believe me, Mrs Pearce, I know the man well, and there's nothing important he has to say to me.'

Her patient still perplexed, Anjali tried to explain in as few words as possible. 'He's . . . he's a bit eccentric. Now, can we try and raise the leg a little higher? That's it . . .'

No longer quite so agitated or alarmed, nevertheless Mrs Pearce was entirely captivated by the blurry figure outside, as he implored heaven for an Excalibur to smash through the heavy glass window. Her fascination increased when another figure came into the scene, someone in uniform, perhaps a security man or even a policeman. While she couldn't hear what they were saying, she could see that their conversation was clearly heated and getting hotter by the second.

'Oh, dear, I hope he's not going to be arrested.'

Anjali turned sharply just in time to see a querulous Uncle Ram being led away by a security guard. Stifling a bubble of laughter, she left the hydrotherapy pool and went over to an internal telephone, leaving behind a somewhat flustered and befuddled Mrs Pearce.

The security office in the hospital was a tiny, cramped room, sparsely furnished apart from a utility table. In a grim frame of mind Uncle Ram glowered at the security guard across the table, although the guard was completely unaware of being scrutinized, his nose buried deep in the *Sun*.

Abruptly Uncle Ram was startled when the only door in the room opened, and his daughter – rather, his niece – entered. At least she was dressed in normal clothing, though much too modern, covering much too little.

The security guard winked at Anjali and left her alone in the room with Uncle Ram, who waited until the door was closed before reproaching her for the terrible way he had been treated. Finally she had gone too far. Much too far.

'Now look here, Anjali. You are a wicked woman!' He shook his head sadly. 'May Shiva hear me. I shall never forgive you this day.'

But Anjali was not buying his damnation today, any more than she would any other day. 'What rubbish you talk, Uncle Ram. I am at work with patients, and you believe I can drop everything?' He seemed confused rather than enlightened by her argument. 'And what kind of foolishness is it that you creep around the hospital?'

Ram took this as an affront; responding directly to the insult would be beneath him. Yet he felt wounded, anguished by her insolence.

'You have no feelings any more for your family.'

Anjali sensed he was being serious, not simply foolish. 'That isn't true, and you know it.'

Faintly, just perceptibly, there was a small kernel of a notion he thought he detected in her attitude, the layers of her bitterness peeled away for a brief moment, revealing a trace of old roots she had so long and fervently tried to bury. Even in this 'modern', rebellious woman perhaps there was yet a glimmer of hope for the ultimate flowering of family honour and tradition.

'Ah, so you agree that the family is important?' he ventured, careful not to invest too much hope at this point.

'Of course.'

However, she didn't seem to care much, not really. He decided to accept her contrition for what it was worth and try to guide her further along the right path, if only for the sake of his sister and the sacred responsibility she had entrusted to him upon the death of her husband.

'I'm glad to hear it.' Yet he couldn't resist making a slight comment under his breath. 'The way you mix out of your culture, it wouldn't surprise me.'

As usual these days, she was much too impatient with him. 'What are all these questions?'

'Things which are important to me,' he solemnly replied. 'And now your father is dead, it is my duty to see you do not let outside things interfere with your religion and culture.'

Her eyes were still sceptical, unaccepting. 'Then I'm surprised you need to ask. They are just as important to me.'

Again he might have interpreted her response as positive, though expressed from a contrary stance. 'Well, at least it is good that you have not forsaken your background . . . that the family is important to you.'

For some reason, that remark seemed to make her suspicious. 'Uncle Ram? You didn't come here to discuss race relations. Get to the point.'

She might have an occupation and a government uniform, but

she would never be a diplomat. 'Very well. We are having a very important meeting tonight. And by we, I mean the whole family.' He looked directly into her eyes. 'Which includes you, Anjali.'

'Uncle Ram, I can't. I am on duty tonight.'

'No, no, no, no, no!' How could she so misunderstand the meaning of the word 'duty'. 'It has been arranged,' he insisted. 'And did you not just tell me the family is important?'

Anjali could understand the significance of a family gathering to Uncle Ram, yet she also realized how futile it was to try to relate her feelings of responsibility for her brother and sister Specials, and for the human family, as pompous as it might sound to him.

'Uncle Ram, you're asking me to let a lot of people down. People who rely on me.'

'Your family also rely on you. This is a matter of great importance,' he repeated, trying to persuade her to accept his words on sheer faith for once.

'All right,' she conceded at last. 'I will cancel the Specials.'

'Praise be. That is the first sign of wisdom you have shown.'

He wished that now she would meet his wonderful surprise with innocence and not cynicism, with eagerness and not antagonism. However, she was barely showing any curiosity at all.

'But what is so important?'

He allowed himself a gentle sigh. 'Tonight, it is *you* who are going to meet someone special.'

'Who?'

He hesitated one more time, wanting to remember forever the look in her eyes when he told her.

'Your future husband.'

'My *what*?' she shouted, her face aghast.

Uncle Ram was distressed at her outburst and the unpredictable eruptions of her temper. What was he to do with such a spitfire?

16

Noreen was deep in the invoices and account ledgers when her husband came into the office, hands black with grease, headed for the small annexe where he could wash them.

'One of your fancy ladies called.' She raised her voice sufficiently so he could hear. 'One Anjali Shah. Special, she said she was.' Momentarily she lowered her voice. 'Aren't we all, I told her.' Then she shouted to Loach once again. 'Anyway, she can't make tonight.'

He reappeared, drying his hands, his face as long as the Queen's speech. Noreen began again in a normal tone.

'She's got family problems. I think I got that right. But I didn't like to pry,' she added. 'One woman's misfortune is another man's one-night stand, as they say.'

Loach slumped down at his desk, looking glum indeed. 'Oh very funny, Noreen, Bloody headaches is all I get. With this kind of pressure, you'd think I was the SDO and not just the SO.'

Noreen concurred with bitter sympathy. 'Not to mention S.O.D . . . R.A.T . . . and S.H. –'

'I get the picture,' Loach surrendered. It wasn't worth fighting about.

Before she could gloat in her little triumph of the moment, the outer door of the office opened, and young Kevin stumbled in, running at the mouth.

'I tried to tell her, Mr Loach, but she wouldn't . . .'

Before he could complete his explanation, Kevin was bundled aside by the mammoth hand of an enormous woman – Big Jess. She barrelled her way past him as an elephant would a wayward branch while trudging through the jungle.

'That's okay, Kevin,' Loach reassured the lad, sending him off to his chores.

As the young assistant moved out of her path, Big Jess made her move on Loach, her gargantuan breasts threatening to arrive well in advance of the main body. Loach held up his thumb as if to ward off vampires in general and this oversexed succubus in particular.

'Take it easy now, Jess. I don't want my thumb bitten again in another wrestling match.' Especially just when he had got over the first round.

When Big Jess laughed it seemed as if the desks and even the breeze blocks trembled. 'I'm not here to get even.' She glanced at Noreen, pointing to a light bruise on her jaw-line. '*He* did that. Arresting me for drunk and disorderly. I was so Brahms and Liszt I didn't know I was chewing his thumb.' She shrugged it off. 'Anyway, it only took a couple o' tricks to pay the fine I got.' On second thought, she shook her head. 'No, I like a man who can fight back.'

57

A grin started to curl the corner of her mouth. 'Mind you, if I'd been sober . . .' To illustrate her point, she pushed two fingers forward like a prong up close to his pupils. '. . . I'd've given him eye surgery.'

'Fascinating,' Noreen mused, her voice dripping with sarcasm.

Big Jess thumbed at Noreen, then turned to Loach. 'Can she take a hike?'

'Uh . . . this is my wife . . . Noreen.'

'Oh . . .' Big Jess was a bit taken aback. 'That's all right then.' She turned to Noreen with a friendly smile. 'I'm Big Jess.'

Noreen was about to make another comment, but Big Jess had already returned her attention to Loach. 'No . . . reason I'm here is I need a favour from you.'

If possible, Loach became even more uncomfortable. 'A favour? From me?'

Big Jess was rubbing her jaw, as if contemplating theoretical physics. 'I think you owe me one . . .' Then she deflected the focus away from herself. 'It's not for meself. Understand? It's for Jackie.' She took Noreen into her confidence. 'She's on the game like me,' she winked. 'Know what I mean?'

Rather than explain, she bawled in the basic direction of the door. 'Jackie? Get in here.'

Through the door edged a slim woman with a fragile prettiness and pale complexion. She was probably a great success in her field but right now Jackie was evidently one very scared prostitute. Protectively, Big Jess settled her in the chair beside Loach's desk.

'You sit there, luv . . . Just explain it like I said.'

Big Jess assumed a mountainous position behind her. Conscious of the looming presence of the Amazon to her rear, as well as the complete strangers in front of her, Jackie spoke up hesitantly.

'I've got to get a message to somebody . . . And I can't do it myself.'

'Too bloody true,' Big Jess confirmed, encouraging her to continue.

'And Jess said you could help me. It's a Detective Inspector . . .'

'Dutrow. That's 'is name,' Big Jess offered, trying to be helpful.

'Jess said you could get a message to him for me . . .'

'Sure,' Loach agreed, picking up the telephone on his desk. 'What's his number? I'll get him, and you can speak to him.'

A solid lump of meat, familiar to Loach as Big Jess's right hand, firmly pressed Loach's hand – clutching, then releasing the 'phone back down.

'Wait,' suggested Big Jess. 'Listen to her.' Loach was inclined to comply with this request.

Looking down and wringing her hands, Jackie struggled to find the right words. 'You see, I've been of some help in the past . . .'

'She's a Police Informer,' Big Jess said simply.

'Je-ss!' Jackie pleaded with her to be more discreet.

'Well, it's right, innit? It's not your fault you put your leg over the wrong bloke, Jackie.'

The hostile looks they exchanged spoke volumes.

'Trouble is,' Jackie confided, 'I've found out there's some scumbag in Dutrow's division selling information to Diesel . . .'

Big Jess stepped in once more to expand and elucidate. 'A real nasty turd, is Diesel. He's a pimp who's inna everything – drugs . . . you name it. Fancies Jackie rotten . . .'

That provoked a sharp response from Jackie. 'Oh yeah, he fancies me. With a razor in one hand and you know what in the other. He fancies me all right.'

Out of the corner of his eye, Loach noticed Noreen both fascinated and cringing at the same time.

Big Jess picked up the loose ends of the story. 'She wants out, but she's got something heavy on Diesel that Dutrow'll pay a lot to get.'

Jackie squirmed in her chair, apparently with some concerns regarding the policy being unveiled and interpreted by Big Jess, who sensed her discomfort and tried to bolster her self-assurance.

'Well . . . it's only right you get some big ones in your bin. The Police has got enough freebies out of you, gal, as it is.'

Loach was still trying to make some basic sense of it all. 'Are you saying there's somebody at Dutrow's division who's passing on Police information . . . taking money from this . . . Diesel? And that's why you can't approach Dutrow direct?' The plausibility of her story was hard to swallow.

But Big Jess had no doubts whatsoever. 'That's it. Right on the money. Figure it for yourself,' she challenged him. 'Wouldn't she look a real tart standing outside a police station?'

'I can risk anything,' Jackie warned vehemently. 'If Diesel got a sniff of it . . .' She shivered at the thought. 'No. I want out.' She looked up to Loach. 'And I want Dutrow to see me at the usual time tonight. Awright?'

Loach's eyes connected with hers. 'I can try. But why come to me?'

Again Big Jess answered for her. 'Because I told her you was straight. And that you're not a real policeman . . .'

Involuntarily Loach winced, and Big Jess must have noticed.

'. . . Well, you are a policeman, but you're more like us, if you see what I mean.' This time Noreen winced. 'And you can talk to them more than we can . . .' That didn't help much either.

'Anyway, I couldn't think of anyone else.' Aha, the real reason. 'And Jackie can't chance it on the 'phone, cos she don't know who the motor-mouth is down there, or anywhere else come to think of it.' She paused to collect her thoughts, such as they were. 'You get hold of Dutrow, personal-like, and give him Jackie's message. Right?'

A sudden rat-a-tat on the door interrupted and startled them. All heads instantly swivelled toward the ominous sound. Then weird, alternating, high-pitched voices spoke through the crack in the door.

'Knock, knock. Who's there? Foxy.'

A ridiculous puppet poked its head around the opening door, obviously soon to be followed by Freddy Calder.

'Foxy who?'

The rest of Freddy popped into the office singing the punchline. 'Fox 'e's a jolly good fella . . .' He laughed at his own joke. 'It's me, folks!' Then he saw the visitors, and stepped back in embarrassment and wonder. 'Oh, I'm sorry. I didn't know you had . . .'

Not giving him a second to finish his apology, Big Jess bounced up, pulling Jackie to her feet as well. 'That's all right. We was just going.' As they crossed to the door, Big Jess stopped to tickle Foxy under the chin (or finger, as it were).

'He's a real sexpot, innee?'

Gratefully Freddy let them pass, but seeing the way they were dressed he simply couldn't resist pushing a bit of business. 'I don't suppose either of you ladies would be interested in the latest in lingerie? At a special discount. The finest underwear a woman can put on,' he teased.

'Sorry, luv,' Big Jess consoled him. 'Most of the time we're taking it off.' They made their way out.

When their backs were turned Freddy did a comic double-take. Loach caught sight of Noreen's face, lacking any sense of humour, and tried to stall the words he knew would soon be coming from her lips.

Yet he spoke hesitantly, at least careful to respect her sense of decency. 'Big Jess is pretty forceful. She's . . . well, like she said . . . a prostitute.'

'I guess someone has to do it, Loach,' she said.

Apparently oblivious to their banter, Freddy was in the corner at the low filing cabinet that doubled as a table for the filtered coffee-making machine. Pouring himself a coffee from the beaker, he swallowed a good belt, then muttered to himself. 'It's only eleven o'clock, and I'm legless.' Looking down at the puppet, he answered himself in Foxy's squeaky voice.

'That's okay for you to say. I'm always legless!'

Then Freddy faced the Loaches with a repentant yet bull-in-a-china-shop smile. 'Hey! I'm sorry 'bout crashing in like that.'

Noreen looked dryly over to Loach as if to say: Does he ever do anything else? But Loach had other things on his mind.

'Forget it. Look . . . I hate asking this, Freddy. I know this is your evening off . . .'

Freddy piped in, speaking in Foxy's voice. 'Then don't ask.'

Loach had to remember to use his normal voice rather than talk back like Mickey Mouse. 'I wouldn't ordinarily, but we're really short. Anjali's had to pull out . . .'

It was almost a shock to hear Freddy as an adult, worry and weariness in his low voice just like everyone else. 'Oh, boy. Am I gonna be in deep trouble.'

'Heavy date, Freddy?' Noreen needled.

The burden weighing upon him, Freddy thought to himself. 'I guess you could say that.'

Loach understood that somewhere in his world Freddy was making a personal sacrifice. 'Thanks, Freddy.'

17

Freddy's Sierra purred to a perfect halt by the door of his terraced house. Grabbing his sample case as he got out, he happened to notice some flecks of grime on the panelling of the car, and wiped it clean with a handkerchief. Still looking for dirt and other invisible flaws, he moved to the back of the car and checked to make sure the boot was locked. After all, he and this baby had a long-running love affair – perhaps, more than he was willing to admit to anyone but himself, the only satisfying relationship of his entire 38 years.

Just as he cleared the car and reached the pavement, a little girl from down the block came walking by, dragged along by a small terrier. Freddy froze solid, panicked, then scrabbled to put the car between him and the animal.

'What's the matter, mister?' the little girl asked him oh-too-cutely. 'Don't you like Rambo?' Where were her parents? he wondered. And why weren't they as mean disciplinarians to her as his mother had been to him?

When he entered the house and went into the sitting room, Hilda Calder was standing in front of a wall mirror checking her appearance. She was dressed in her Wednesday best, although the *Birmingham Royal Ballet* crowd might not consider her bargain-basement style quite the height of fashion. She appeared to be having a fit of impatience trying to determine just where to place her floral brooch when she saw Freddy's reflection in the mirror.

'What kind of face is that to bring in the house?' she asked.

'I'm sorry, Ma,' he answered, meaning it this time.

She must have sensed something wrong. 'Sorry for what?'

'Tonight. There's a crisis.' He tried not to look into her eyes. 'I've promised . . . to help out . . . down at the station.'

Either she wasn't hearing, or heeding, what he said. 'That's as may be. I was under the impression that you had a previous engagement. With your mother. It is Wednesday, isn't it? I haven't gone and lost a day?'

'No, Ma,' he submitted. 'It's Wednesday. I'm really sorry. I know how you feel about us going out.' He battened down the hatches and prepared for a nasty blow of stormy weather.

'Keep your sympathy. You don't give a tuppenny damn what I feel. When did you ever think of anyone but yourself, Freddy Calder? You're just like your father . . .'

What seemed to gall her most was that, in spite of all his father's foibles and indiscretions, Freddy should still remember him so fondly. For that paradox of loyalty and disloyalty, she would never forgive him.

'The years I sacrificed for that man, working my fingers to the bone . . .'

His father had passed on rather suddenly back in '69. While washing his own sporty automobile, he had somehow contrived to touch the battery terminals. What with standing in a puddle of soapy water and, as the inquest later reported, having a weak heart, he had suffered a quick demise. In the past few years Freddy had begun to wonder whether it had really been an accident at all, or rather, if perhaps Alex Calder had duly considered the prospect of eternity in hell with his wife, Hilda, and decided instead to go over the hill, to take one last ride with his first love. All this when Freddy was only 16 and just beginning to take a shine to cars himself.

'And what do I have to show for it? You, Freddy Calder. Your father's spitting image. And just as selfish. As long as you get what you want, like playing at being a policeman.'

In her eyes he was forever a child, locked in time, perhaps in a period of obedient youth before he had grown to disappoint her. So now she accused him of 'playing' policeman. Why should any of his acquaintances be surprised to find a grown man still playing with puppets then?

'Do you ever think of me waiting for you to come home, not knowing if it's going to be in a box?'

She was close to tears, Freddy noted, a sure sign that soon she would be tugging on his heartstrings.

'I haven't many pleasures in this life, but one of them is going out on Wednesday nights. You know how much I look forward to the boiled ham at the Royale Restaurant.' Yes, but he didn't know why: after all, it wasn't Jonathan's, or Days of the Raj, or New Hall, or Plough and Harrow! 'I never thought I'd see the day you'd even take that away from me.'

In spite of his awareness of her usual routine, he had only managed to build up a limited immunity to her invective over all the years he had lived with his mother. Understanding what she was doing to him didn't make the lamb any less vulnerable to the slaughter.

'Wednesday night is a precious thing to me, Freddy Calder. It's my only night out except for Friday down at the bingo with Irene next door.' Irene was the only person left who would bother to listen to her.

'And if this is how much I count, then I'd be better to put my head in the gas oven!'

She cast the floral brooch into the back of the desk drawer to dramatize her imprisonment. In anguish, she collapsed into the nearest easy chair, her bosom suddenly heaving as if she might be suffering palpitations.

Frightened, Freddy anxiously rushed to her side and knelt by the chair, fearing she might be having an attack of some kind. She resisted his frantic attempts to help and pushed him away.

'Let me die in peace.'

18

It was going to be one of those nights. At Division 'S' the usual Specials were milling about the parade room as Loach was concluding his nightly sermon while dialling a telephone at the same time.

'CID want you to keep your eyes peeled for a couple of plates –' He read from the page: '– F311 YEP and E606 NWN – so add these to your list of stolen cars.' That was the last item on the agenda, as he dialled the final digit in the 'phone number. 'That's the lot then, troops. Any problems?' It was a rhetorical question, and there were no takers tonight. 'No? Okay . . . let's make it a good one.'

The telephone connection was made, and he lowered his voice, anxious to keep this conversation private.

'. . . uh . . . hello. Detective Inspector Dutrow . . . He's not in yet? Damn!' Where *was* he? 'Yeah! This is Section Officer Loach. I called a couple of times already.' That was putting it mildly. 'No. No message. I'll try later.'

Dismayed, Loach was about to replace the telephone when he looked up and froze. In the open doorway was a man in the uniform of a Sub-Divisional Officer in the Special Constabulary: SDO Rob Barker.

What the hell's he turned up for? Loach asked himself. As the Specials were leaving the parade room, Barker was nodding here and there in recognition of the familiar faces, yet by now there were also a few recruits who were total strangers to him. His eyes searched the room, finally locating Loach and joining him. They shook hands, although Loach felt a bit wary of the return of the prodigal son, still officially his immediate superior.

'Loach. Uh . . . good to be here again.'

'Sir?'

He seemed a little nervous, unsure of himself. 'Now, look . . . Just carry on with the parade . . . I'm a bit out of practice . . .' He squirmed in his stiff uniform.

'The parade's done. They're about to get stuck in.'

Standing with Freddy Calder while trying to ignore him, Viv Smith couldn't help but overhear some of the conversation going on between Section Officer Bob Loach and SDO Rob Barker in one ear and some of the conversation going on about *them* among the newer Specials in the other ear.

'Who's he? Visiting fireman?' asked one of the young Specials out of the corner of his mouth.

'*That* is our "now you see 'im, now you don't" Sub-Divisional Officer, SDO Rob Barker,' another Special informed him.

'Where's he been that I haven't seen him?' inquired the young one.

'Who knows? But I bet it's put a bee up Loach's left nostril.'

So much for that conversation, she thought to herself, turning away from them and instantly facing the fact that she would once again be spending an entire evening with plump Freddy. 'Stuck with you again?'

'You love having a hunk like me,' Freddy boasted. 'Admit it.' Yeah, maybe a few billion years from now when the next Ice Age arrived.

She decided it was time to change the subject back to life in the real world. 'D'you see what the cat's dragged in?'

'Barker, you mean?' As he invoked Barker's name, Freddy peered out of the corner of his eye at the SDO, who was talking with Loach. At that moment, Barker happened to glance at Freddy and Viv watching him. Freddy nodded, Barker acknowledged. 'Must be two months since he last showed.'

'I'm not surprised,' Viv murmured with a knowing smile.

'What's that supposed to mean?' asked the naive puppeteer.

She spoke in undertones, the lower register reserved for gossip. 'It means that when you've a little wife back home and a piece on the side, you don't have much time for anything else.'

Freddy and Viv were the last of the Specials to leave the parade room. Rob Barker seemed to breathe easier, drop some of the formality and try a friendlier tack with Loach.

'I'm sorry I've lumbered you with the work.'

'I enjoy it,' Loach was too quick to admit.

Rob eyed him more closely. 'Yes? . . .' Abruptly he shifted to another topic. 'Well, I kept meaning to let you know why I couldn't come in, but I never seemed to find the time . . .' He hesitated. 'It's the wife. She hasn't been feeling too good lately. Nothing serious, you understand.' An insincere smile appeared, then vanished. 'But worrying. You probably think I'm being over-protective, but I wanted to be close to her . . .'

'That's understandable,' Loach sympathized. But then, if Rob's having his troubles at home, why doesn't he pass the baton to Section Officer Bob Loach, now that everyone could see that the baton would be in good hands? He wanted to appreciate Rob's problems, but he had to admit there were other things he wanted as well. He made no secret of wanting to be the first millionaire Special (and he hoped he was on his way with Cougar Coaches); but he also wanted, and deserved, that promotion to SDO. In that case, perhaps Barker wasn't the obstacle but rather the opportunity.

'Does this mean you'll be packing it in? The Specials, like?'

'What? Oh no, no. Why would I do that?' Barker inquired, his voice having hardened a few shades. He didn't turn away from checking the roster sheets. 'We're a bit short tonight, I see?'

'Oh, nothing I can't handle.'

Barker gave him a calculating glance. 'Maybe it's just as well I came in tonight.'

Loach's brow raised a question mark.

'At least we can find something better for you to do, eh, Loach?'

What was he thinking? 'Ah . . . well, I've still the paper work to do . . .'

'No. That's my job, remember? I haven't forgotten how to do it.'

Damn, what had he stepped in now? Loach kicked himself for being such a clod. 'I wasn't suggesting –'

'– 'course you weren't,' Rob granted, a smug curl in his smile. 'So let's not waste any more time, mm?' He ushered Loach toward the door. 'Sergeant McAllister is probably down there looking for spare bods to go out on panda duty,' he explained.

Barker opened the door.

'Always remember something, Bob. We're all expendable. And the paperwork on this job doesn't need a Ph.D.'

Bob Loach did not enjoy being shunted around like this. There was a little something about it that he decided to tell Barker in no uncertain terms.

'There's nothing else, is there, Bob?'

He was sorely tempted. He knew more of what was going on right now than Barker did, or ever would, and he could damn well say so to the wee dictator's face.

. . . But that would be insubordination. Whether he liked it or not he had to respect the SDO's rank. That was the cornerstone of any police organization, regardless of his personal judgment.

He shook his head and left. The lion would live to come out another day.

When the door closed, Barker was left in the parade room alone. As it should be, he reasoned.

Thought the job was all yours, eh, Loach? he smiled to himself. Not quite yet. And maybe not even then.

19

Walking along the rough pavement through a part suburban, part light industrial estate with Freddy, Viv looked around and decided that now was as good a time as any. She came to a halt near the alleyway.

'I've got to have a quick puff, Freddy.'

'Thought you were trying to give it up?'

'I'm trying,' she attested, adding the main reason. 'Ginger doesn't like it.'

'Ginger? Who's Ginger?'

She brightened at the prospect of talking about her amour, even to Freddy. 'He's a PC. With "Z" Division. He's a *real* hunk, Freddy.' Poor Freddy wouldn't know one if he saw one, she mused.

'But – he doesn't smoke. Hates it, to tell the truth.' She inhaled the smoke of her own cigarette. Funny to be talking about this now, she thought. 'His mother used to puff like a chimney. You know the kind?

Fag dangling from her mouth, and the ash falling in the Sunday salad. It's easy to understand that he's got an . . . aversion, you might say.'

That was one of the recurring nightmares in her long procession of failed relationships: there was one something about Viv that her boyfriends didn't like. One stumbling block. And she was always willing to try anything to save the relationship. As a young girl just becoming enraptured with boys, she often used to think that maybe she tried too hard, talked too much, drove people into corners where they would rather chip their nails on the walls trying to escape than stick around in her company. So it was no wonder she would try to put that tenacity to some good use by kicking the smoking habit for Ginger. She hoped he was worth it.

'Anyway, we've got the kind of relationship where we don't hold anything back. And I can understand a fella not wanting to kiss an ashtray.'

Freddy's own lips recoiled at the thought, to his fantasies a particularly repugnant notion. 'That's disgusting.' His eyes roamed the broadish street, seeking some worthy quest, or anything that would get him away from further discussion of the sensual pleasures of oral intimacy with common ashtrays. 'Look, while you put another nail in your coffin I'll check that lot over there and join you back here.'

He didn't wait for her permission but set sail under his own wind for the small warehouse and builder's yard on the opposite side of the street.

Soon after Freddy had crossed the street Viv became aware that he had forgotten and left the radio with her. She was about to call out to him when she thought better of it. Why disturb the peace? It's only for a couple of minutes anyway, she told herself.

As PC Toby Armstrong cruised slowly down the suburban street, Loach was in the passenger seat concentrating on the layout ahead and figuring out how to make his obvious intention seem more subtle and unobtrusive.

'Did Anjali say why she couldn't come on duty?' Toby queried.

'Some family matter, I think,' Loach answered absent-mindedly.

'Oh.' Toby seemed to be waiting for Loach to take the lead in conversation, a skill that was not his forte.

'Mind if we take a left here?' Loach pointed.

'What?' asked Toby in mild surprise.

'I have to get a message to somebody in "X" Division.'

'I don't remember that being mentioned . . .'

Loach at once admired and cursed Toby's sense of proper protocol. 'No. I'm doing somebody a favour.'

Toby glanced at Loach, then returned to watching the road through the windscreen in front of him.

'I know it isn't according to the book.'

Not saying a word, Toby simply let out his breath in a sound conveying full comprehension that this would be a dangerous mission. He glanced again at Loach, held his gaze, and Loach looked him in the eye. Toby went back to watching his driving, and turned left.

'Thanks.'

Toby shook his head in reluctance. 'If McAllister hears about this, it's going to be your guts for garters.'

Freddy rattled the padlock on the warehouse doors, just to make sure it was secure. Then he went to check the side door before walking on.

He didn't mind being alone, really. That was the story of his life. At this stage in his adult life, he was more comfortable by himself, or at least that's what he repeated over and over and over again. Perhaps he ought to reconsider his position.

Arriving at the builder's yard, he tested the gate. To his surprise, it creaked open. Frowning, Freddy swung the gate inward, switching on his torch.

The light flickered over piles of sand, bricks and other materials of the building trade. Nothing out of the ordinary, until he saw a slight movement, a glimmer of reflected light in the shadows. Something – somebody – was there.

A scurrying motion raced from the shadows toward Freddy, although he couldn't catch it with the torch. As the beam searched deeper into the black void, he heard a low growl emanating from the darkness directly ahead. He snapped the torch to meet the noise, and there in the shaft of light were two narrow, hungry eyes of a hound from hell.

Sweating hard, Freddy slowly reached for the radio. It wasn't there! Suddenly he remembered – it was back with Viv. Meanwhile, the canine cannibal was snarling, looming toward him. Paralyzed, he tried to shout or scream, but his tongue was stuck to the roof of his mouth. In turn he was staring into the drooling mouth of an Alsatian beast.

20

Toby waited in the panda in front of the Division 'X' building, as Loach climbed the steep steps leading up to the entry doors.

Pushing through the swing doors, Loach crossed to the reception area and found a civilian on duty.

'Hi.'

No answer. The civilian was preparing a cup of coffee for himself. With seemingly exaggerated slowness, he managed to switch on the electric kettle, apparently a major accomplishment. His attitude suggesting a Jack-the-lad, he looked at Loach coolly, throwing him off-guard.

'Detective Inspector Dutrow . . . ?'

'Yeah?'

'Is he in?' Loach clarified for him.

'Search me.'

Loach practised his patience, counting to ten . . . actually to eight. 'But you could find out?'

'I guess.' Lazily he checked a large notebook, slowly fingering his way down the columns.

Outside a horn beeped: undoubtedly Toby. Loach went over to the swing doors and bent down to peer through them, motioning him an I'll-be-right-there signal. Off to his right, his attention was drawn to an activity going on in the yard. He moved to the window to take a closer look.

In the yard, a police constable was showing a group of Specials various transgressions to watch out for in a vehicle. Among the Specials was a face fresh in his memory: the solicitor, Loach reminded himself, although it didn't appear that the solicitor was being favoured in any way at the moment.

The lackadaisical voice of Jack-the-lad brought his thoughts back to present company. 'Got 'im. Two . . . two . . . three . . . seven . . .'

After dialling the number on the internal line, the civilian waited, offering Loach a sugary, confident smile.

'Dobson, front desk here. Got someone for Detective Inspector Dutrow . . . Hang on, I'll ask him.' Jack-the-lad cupped his hand over the mouthpiece and addressed Loach directly. 'Forget to get your name, didn't I?'

'Section Officer Loach.'

He reached out a hand for the phone, but Jack drew back out of range. 'It's . . . you heard it, did you?' He smiled at Loach, listening to the voice on the other end. 'Yeah . . . uh-huh . . . uh-huh . . . I'll ask him.' This time he didn't bother to cover the mouthpiece when he addressed Loach. 'Dutrow's out and about. D'you wanna leave a message with somebody else?'

Silently Loach debated with himself before making a decision. 'No. I'll call again.'

'He's gonna call again. That's what he said. Okay. Bye.' He replaced the telephone and returned to Loach with a satisfied smile.

'D'you have some paper and an envelope?'

The smile disappeared, and Jack breathed out with a vehemence to suggest the enormity of the task assigned to him. 'Phew!' Then he proceeded: 'Let me see . . .'

At that moment Loach could've strangled Jack-the-lad with his bare hands and taken his scalp to make sure Jack's spirit would never be set free.

On one side of the sitting room was the groom's family: his father and mother, two shy sisters under twelve, three elderly aunts and a matriarchal grandmother. Facing them were the representatives of Anjali's family: a bored Sanjay, who kept checking his watch, and an odd assortment of minor aunts and uncles and nieces and nephews hurriedly drummed up for the occasion.

Despite all their social pretending, the true centre of attention was divided between only two of them: Anjali, in her dress sari, and her intended groom. He was a thin young man with an unusually large nose; to make it worse, he appeared to have a perpetual sniff, and a noisy one at that. Anjali desperately wished that Uncle Ram and her mother would get in here and get this agony over and done with so that all these people and the nausea in her stomach would go away.

In the kitchen, Mrs Shah was preparing a tray of drinks and sweet nothings, while Ram poured himself a glass of whisky. She was nervous, and felt she had to confide in her brother, although he too seemed to be walking a tightrope.

'I tell you she's too quiet. She has always been a stubborn girl. She does not like having her mind made up. You know that.' As if he needed reminding.

He swallowed his whisky. 'All I know is, she's got opinions about everything. It is not womanly, sister.' He tried not to reproach her, yet rather her daughter. 'It is bad enough that she is a part-time policewoman. What kind of business is that for a well-brought-up Hindu girl?'

His sister tried to hide her eyes from him. He reassured her as best he could. 'I know she hoodwinked you. She told you she would be doing clerical work, and making pots of Darjeeling.' He scoffed. 'Now what do we find? She prowls the streets at night . . . in a car . . . with a man!' He shook his head, as his sister wiped a tear from each eye. 'Only one thing could be worse, and that is walking the streets and picking up a man.'

She uttered a sharp cry and buried her face behind her hand. He hadn't meant to accuse her but her daughter. 'Now look here. I blame myself. If I had not been in Bombay, this nonsense would have stopped before it ever started.'

Ram moved to comfort his sister for the stinging words, but before he could reach out to her Sanjay barged into the kitchen, an irritable look on his face.

'Are we to wait all night? I have plans, you know.'

Impatiently Ram waved him away, then had a second thought. 'We are coming. But now you're here you might carry the tray for your mother.'

Sanjay was evidently not pleased to be asked to perform a favour, let alone his simple duty to the family. He picked up the tray awkwardly, with neither grace nor any concentration. His mind was elsewhere.

Jack-the-lad spooned some Maxwell House into a mug, then tipped in a precise dash of milk, executing each task methodically and monotonously, Loach sealed the envelope and waved it for Jack to notice.

'Will you see that Detective Inspector Dutrow gets this immediately he comes in?'

'Important, is it?' the lad deduced.

'I think it is.'

'Then say no more,' said Jack-the-lad. 'I'll see to it personally-like.' He even went so far as to leave behind his coffee preparation momentarily to fetch the envelope from Loach.

Just then the group of Specials who had been out in the yard trooped through the reception area, the police constable in the lead, and Loach moved aside to let them pass. The PC activated a multi-button lock near an inner door.

'Drinking time, is it, George?' Jack-the-lad called out to him. The constable reacted with disdain.

Loach's eyes connected with those of the solicitor who had joined the Specials, yet whose name suddenly slipped his mind.

'It's Redwood. John Redwood.'

Recalling the entire pathetic tale, Loach snapped his fingers. 'Big Jess! You're her solicitor? I'd forgotten you were doing this,' he fibbed. 'How goes it?'

A slight smile crossed the other man's lips. 'There's more to it than people think.'

Loach nodded in mock sympathy. 'Yeah . . . well, this is the easy part.'

'So they tell me.' Redwood certainly played his cards close to the vest.

'So we might be seeing you at "S" Division, then?'

'Perhaps.' Behind the façade, Redwood seemed to be labouring to figure out where Loach was headed.

'Give me a chance to get back at you.' He parodied the solicitor's stern courtroom manner: 'Just answer yes, Mr Loach.'

Apparently he didn't have much of a funnybone either. 'A good solicitor doesn't play favourites.'

'No . . . suppose not. Anyway, you didn't win, did you?' he goaded.

'I think my client was satisfied. The court was quite lenient.'

Loach let out a laugh. 'Thank God! I'd have a white stick and a guide dog by now if they hadn't.'

Redwood's quizzical expression indicated that he didn't understand Loach's reference. 'Your client – Big Jess? Not to be messed with.' Redwood was still puzzled. Loach decided it wasn't worth getting into the part about Big Jess plucking his bleedin' eyes out of his head. 'Don't worry. It'd take too long to explain, Mr Redwood.'

There was an echo from the side. 'Mr Redwood?' The constable had a pleading look on his face. Redwood held up a placatory hand to stay the order momentarily, then shrugged at Loach.

'As I said. See you around.' Redwood nodded, and joined the constable.

As Loach turned to leave, he almost fell over Toby Armstrong coming in the front door.

'Dammit, Loach,' he cursed in an angry whisper. 'We've got a call. Move it!'

Before leaving with Toby, Loach turned back to the civilian and waved meekly, reminding him of the errand.

Jack-the-lad waved back, his hand holding the letter.

21

Freddy couldn't move a muscle. There was a bit more light now so that Freddy could better see the glistening teeth of the ravenous beast. Flanking him were two men who conceivably might speak in a human tongue, perhaps even the Queen's English, albeit their style of fashion was strictly for Yob's day-out.

'I'm asking you politely. Call off your dog.'

'Oh, yes?' wheedled Number One, to the left of the monstrous mutt. Freddy looked over to his right at Number Two, who wasn't smiling or sweet-talking at all, even in fun.

'Yes. And what the hell are you doing here at this time of night?'

'What do you think we're doing, officer?' queried Number One. 'Giving somebody a quote for double-glazing?' A roaming band of criminal comedians, no doubt.

'Listen. I'm not in the mood for games.' That was an understatement, though one of the few times in his life it was true. 'Instead of making it worse for yourselves, call off your animal. Right now!' he added for emphasis. 'And show me some identification.' He crossed his fingers and prayed.

Behind him, a hand descended on his shoulder. Freddy jumped like a scared frog.

It was Viv. 'I wondered what had happened to you,' she whispered.

Freddy couldn't believe his eyes.

'What's all this?' Viv asked Number One and Number Two, staring hard at the men. Her hand hovered over the button on her radio, and Number One seemed to notice. Instantly his tone became more affable.

'Your partner seems to have us down as villains.'

'Maybe he's up for promotion?' smirked Number Two.

Viv gave Number Two the fish-eye, as the canine decided to lollop toward them. Freddy couldn't breathe. He jerked his head back but it wouldn't go any farther. Closer and closer came the carnivorous cur, his tongue hanging out in grotesque anticipation of the raw meat embodied by Freddy . . .

Instead the dog trotted past Freddy and went to Viv. Bending down, she rubbed through the fur on the back of its neck.

'Just so happens, we're security,' declared Number One. He pulled out a greasy wallet, extracted a card and handed it over.

Freddy took the card. His lips were dry, but when he licked them he was even more intensely aware of how close to his own throat were the dog's jaws. He squinted at the card: it was official, all right, although his vision was blurred by a waterfall of perspiration streaming down into his eyes. Number One appropriated his card from Freddy before it got drenched.

'Security?' Viv quizzed, petting the Alsatian.

'We don't all wear uniforms, you know,' Number One reasoned. 'I mean . . . Just look at the state of this dump.' He had a point, Freddy had to admit. 'Anyway, read the collar.'

Viv checked the Alsatian's collar: there was a brass strip on it. Engraved on the plate was the word 'BAS' and a telephone number. 'B.A.S?'

'"Builders' Associated Security,"' responded Number One. 'Ring the number if you like.'

Viv got to her feet and checked with her partner. 'I don't think that'll be necessary. Do you, Freddy?'

Jack-the-lad stirred a spoonful of sugar into his coffee mug, then sipped it slowly. Carefully, he passed the letter from Section Officer Loach over the steam still rising from the kettle.

Sanjay Shah hurried through the motions of dispensing drinks to the guests. Yet finally when he had finished his last delivery there was an awkward silence, everyone giving all their attention to the drinks in their hands. No one stepped forward to offer a toast.

'This is a very nice room,' announced the intended groom's father, breathing out loudly. His side of the room nodded and murmured in total agreement.

'That is so . . .' concurred Uncle Ram. 'The cabinet in the corner is one of my personal possessions . . . as is the fine chair you are sat on.'

With a start, the father of the intended groom moved to vacate the fine chair, but Ram gently restrained him. 'No, my dear fellow, stay there. You are our honoured guest, and deserve the best chair.'

When the father of the intended groom was returned to the chair, and Uncle Ram returned to his, he resumed. 'But you were saying?'

'It is a very nice room –' the father repeated, 'and may I say the young lady is very pleasing also.'

'And healthy,' Ram added, doing his finest to emphasize her better qualities.

'I have all my own teeth,' Anjali submitted.

Uncle Ram closed his eyes in resignation. What was he to do with her? He opened his eyes to the intended groom's father, who gave him a wan smile. 'She likes to joke, you know,' Ram offered weakly.

'A sense of humour is good . . . now and then.'

The thin young man with the very large nose sniffed a long and wet snuffle. Anjali handed him a Kleenex.

Specials Viv Smith and Freddy Calder were just passing in front of the high wall enclosing the builder's yard. At last he could begin to breathe a little easier and try to calm down and relax.

'All this time, and you never mentioned you had this thing about dogs.'

The hair on the back of Freddy's neck stood up again. 'I don't want to talk about it,' he shuddered. 'And just . . . don't say . . .' But he caught himself short.

'Dog?' Viv obnoxiously and insensitively suggested.

'. . . that word,' he concluded. 'Okay?'

Viv gave thoughtful consideration to his soulful request, remembering his state of terror only a few moments ago.

'Well . . . we almost made a dog's breakfast of it back there.'

* * *

On the other side of the wall in the builder's yard, two chaps were loading brick on to a small lorry.

'You know . . .' began Number Two, 'one of these days we'll pull this trick once too often.'

'Naw. It works the oracle every time.'

'What'd you show 'im?' asked Number Two.

'National Insurance Card,' he chuckled, shaking his head at the sucker born every minute. 'Listen. He was so scared of the dog, I couldn't shown him the *Daily Mail*. Anyway, that'll do for the night.'

After completing the job, Number One turned and whistled softly into the night.

'Where the bleeding 'ell is that dog? 'Ere boy. Come 'ere, Bas.'

The Alsatian came running, jogging happily to the lorry.

'Good boy, Bas.'

22

Manning the control room, WPC Sheila Baxter leaned in on her microphone. 'Panda Victor. What is your E.T.A.?'

Driving the panda, Toby gave Loach a sour glance, nodding that Loach should answer the call.

Loach buttoned the car radio. 'We'll be there in a couple o' minutes. Over.'

'A couple o' minutes?' jeered Sheila's voice from the radio. 'You said that ten minutes ago. What you got in your tank – a tortoise? Our complainant is getting very stroppy, chaps.'

Toby wrenched the gears in a misguided effort to dodge the traffic and get there faster than humanly possible.

Even though her voice was coming through the radio, it was clear she was speaking in a confidential tone. 'Oh, by the way, Loach. I tried to raise Dutrow, but no luck so far.'

As if he didn't have enough to worry about without trying to go outside the proper channels to get a message to Detective Inspector Dutrow from a prostitute. Avoiding Toby, he stared out through the windscreen at the dark road ahead, wondering at his own willingness to travel to the ends of the earth to lend a hand to someone who had nearly chewed his thumb off of it.

*   *   *

Time had stopped. Anjali worried not only that the antiquated ritual of two families negotiating her future would never end, but that their great expectations were to make this merely the prelude to an eternity of such occasions. She could not help but study the thin young man they had chosen to be her husband, and her lover, trying to imagine a lifetime of intimacy with this stranger. Did he ever stop sniffing, even when asleep? She noticed that he had reduced the Kleenex to confetti, prompting her to venture a question during the next inevitable lull in the conversation.

'Speaking about health . . . Does your son have an allergy perhaps?'

A deathly silence permeated the sitting room crowded with otherwise supposedly living persons. Her intended husband's father did not respond to the question – perhaps pretending that no one had heard it, and therefore it had not been spoken – and instead pressed on with unyielding determination, staring doggedly at Uncle Ram.

'A substantial dowry was mentioned, I believe.'

Anjali feigned innocence as well, though at an awkward moment. 'I only ask in case there is something in the room which may be affecting his sinuses.'

Her interruption made it somewhat more difficult for everyone to ignore her. Nonetheless, Uncle Ram struggled to control his natural emotions and maintain his concentration as well as respect, and follow the age-old custom to the degree possible in a decaying modern society where unruly children didn't know their place.

'We are not a poor family, but neither are we rich,' Ram responded evenly, attempting a return to diplomacy.

Again Anjali interrupted, her mind obviously in another world. 'Of course, he could be allergic to *me*. And that would certainly pose a problem for our future happiness.'

Her intended husband's expression changed from disoriented to dumbfounded, although the sniffs continued unabated. The remaining members of his family were struck dumb as well, except for his father. Manfully shouldering his burden in the face of unanticipated opposition, he ploughed on once more.

'My son has a good job with good prospects.'

'Doing what?' Anjali asked, seeing Uncle Ram bridle out of the corner of her eye. 'Am I not allowed to ask?'

Sanjay giggled behind his hand, enjoying her every calculated blunder. Meanwhile, the mystified relatives of her intended husband were becoming restive.

Uncle Ram cleared his throat to restore order, both internal and external. 'A good job with good prospects is . . . very good indeed . . . And no doubt he is a good worker?'

The father nodded humbly and proudly. 'My son works in a supermarket.'

'Not in the Delicatessen, I hope,' Anjali remarked more to herself than the assembled witnesses.

'He earns nearly eight thousand pounds,' the father boasted.

She nodded as though impressed. 'Really. Let me think.' Her eyes rolled upward, searching her memory. 'What do I get for my job, Uncle Ram? Do you remember?'

Uncle Ram burrowed deeper into his chair.

'Oh, yes,' she answered herself. 'Twelve thousand last year, I think it was.'

That was the final blow. A grim hush descended upon them all, perhaps out of respect for the dead. With quiet reserve, the now-unintended groom's father addressed Ram in a formal manner, cold as a cadaver. 'I think your niece makes fun of me and my son.' When he arose from Uncle Ram's chair, his entire family stood up, including the former groom, followed by all of Anjali's aunts and uncles and nieces and nephews.

'She is too wise, perhaps . . . too old . . . for my son, I am thinking. My son needs a more . . . *traditional* girl, you understand.'

Mute, speechless for perhaps the first time in his life, Ram could do nothing but watch the father, his sniffing son and the rest of his family slowly depart from the sitting room – and from Anjali's life forever – their contemptuous noses in the air. He paced to and fro, marshalling his thoughts among the members of his own family milling about, until the ill-fated groom's family was gone. The sight of his heartbroken sister, her eyes about to dissolve into tears, brought him to a halt. He placed a comforting hand on her shoulder and stared at Anjali as if she'd turned green.

'Look at your mother. My sister was once a beautiful woman. Now see the lines on her face. Every one has been placed there by you, her ungrateful daughter.' Frustrated to tears and anger himself, he tried to appeal to her one last time with his words. 'How can I make you understand?' he pleaded with her. 'You are twenty-five years old. You need a life-partner!'

'And be the slave to a stove? Have a husband tell me how much of my own money I should give to the Temple?'

There was so much she didn't know. He tried to reason with her, shifting his strategy hoping he might catch more flies with honey than vinegar. 'Anjali? Marriage is like a tray of candies – sweet!'

She scoffed. 'The kind that gives you indigestion.'

At the end of her endurance, Anjali's mother burst into sobs. Watching her grief, Uncle Ram and the others consoling her, Anjali didn't know how she could live her own life without bringing disharmony and disappointment to theirs . . . except for Sanjay, amused by her embarrassment, who seemed to enjoy her in the role of family misfit for all seasons.

23

The panda was parked on a well-to-do suburban street in front of a posh house where Toby and Loach waited at the door. Toby decided to ring the doorbell again, but before he could the door was flung open by a diminutive gentleman, apparently the houseowner, a short barrel of spleen.

'Well, about high bloody time!' The houseowner jerked his thumb toward the equally posh residence next door. 'It's been like World War Three in there.'

'Can we come in, sir?' Toby asked politely.

'What for? It's next door you want to sort out.'

'I appreciate that, sir, but I'll need to get some particulars down. What is the nature of the complaint? And I'd rather we did that inside, and not out here on the doorstep.'

The houseowner appeared to debate the suggestion mentally, although he gave in with ill grace. 'Oh, all right. Bloody red tape. Come in.' As they passed him, he called to someone inside. 'It's the police, luvvy. They want to come in.' Closing the door behind them, he added in a muffled voice: 'But we're only wasting time . . .'

When Toby and Loach reached the doorway of the sitting room, they were met by the houseowner's short barrel of a wife, obstructing further progress. Bringing up the rear was the houseowner, pinning the Specials between them. There was no way they were going to be allowed to sit down.

'It's been two hours . . . isn't that right, luvvy?' His wife agreed, though in stone-faced silence. 'Two hours of continual din . . . smashing and crashing . . . It's like living next door to Beirut.'

'Seems quiet enough now, sir,' Toby suggested.

'That's probably because someone's had their head bashed in. I'm telling you it wasn't somebody just making noise. This was frightening. Wasn't it, luvvy?' The stone-face didn't move an eyelash. ''Course, we've been expecting something like this . . .'

'Why's that, sir?' Toby inquired.

The houseowner was exasperated, perhaps as much by the question as by the answer. 'It's the kind of people they are. Young couple . . . you never know if they're married these days . . . he's some kind of dealer . . . but I think he was a market trader . . . acts like one, anyway . . . I mean, what kind of person cuts down trees? Turns his back garden into concrete? The view from our bedroom is a disgrace, isn't it, luvvy?'

A gaping maw opened in the great stone-face, as if she were going to be ill. Taking no notice, her husband continued on down the concrete garden path. 'They had a plum tree . . . juiciest fruit you ever ate . . . chopped it down . . . I mean *chopped it down!*' he fairly shouted at them before cooling to a simmer. 'There really ought to be a law.'

Good grief! Loach brooded, cursing SDO Barker for putting him out on the street: *he* should be stuck here and have to put up with such nonsense.

This early in the evening, Rob Barker was the only person in the Pub on 4th besides Briggsy the barman. The way he was checking his watch every few minutes, it was obvious he was waiting for someone, impatiently.

'Another drink, Mr Barker?'

Shaken loose from his thoughts, Barker tried to focus on the barman's query, but abruptly he was distracted by that someone. Sandra Gibson came in, saw him, and crossed to the bar.

She appeared to be expecting a kiss, but he held back, taking her hand instead. A frown of doubt flickered across her brow for an instant, before her familiar, if somewhat uncertain smile returned.

'A drink?' he suggested.

'Sure. The usual, Briggsy.'

'One gin and tonic coming up.'

'I'll have the same.' He led Sandra to a table away from the bar and out of earshot for Briggsy. Still, when they were seated next to each other, he spoke to her in a low voice.

'I'm sorry I wasn't able to keep our date night before last.' He looked at her with his little boy eyes and lashes.

'The last three dates, Rob.' Already she was having trouble hiding her bitterness. She didn't know if she could calm down and stay afloat before getting in over her head. Of course, that had always been her problem.

'Well . . . yes, I know,' he conceded. 'I tried to explain on the phone. That's why I thought it better we meet.'

Sandra surveyed the empty pub. 'Isn't this a bit public for you?'

His nerves belied his words. 'No. People wouldn't read anything into it. They know you're the Admin Secretary for the Specials. It would be natural for you and me to have a get-together here.'

At the bar, Briggsy arranged the drinks on a tray, trying not to listen, or at least not to hear anything specific that could become the next hot gossip if he were, even in a moment of weakness, other than the soul of discretion. Nevertheless, he had their relationship well and truly pegged.

'Maybe we should come right out and tell them,' she said in a much too loud voice. 'Rob Barker and Sandra Gibson are doing it! Isn't it wonderful?'

He was not amused. 'For pity's sake, Sandra . . .'

Quickly he alerted her with his eyes that Briggsy was coming with the drinks. At least she held her tongue for the time being, so he could cover for them. 'Thank you, Briggsy. All work and no play, I've been telling Sandra.'

'Oh yes?' Briggsy asked rhetorically, not waiting for an answer before leaving them alone.

He waited until Briggsy was out of sight, then became serious again. 'That isn't the way we planned it.'

'Oh, that's right, we had a "plan", didn't we?' So gullible in the past, her cynicism now betrayed her. All she could see behind her was two wasted years of her life waiting for this sorry man to sort himself out. That had been the 'plan', hadn't it? To offload a wife who thought more of herself and her infirmities and less of Rob's career as a draughtsman and his happiness? What was any different now, other than Sandra's unhappiness as well?

'And here we are – two years down the M6 – and I'm still waiting to hear what's changed in all that time. You had a wife you didn't love. And she couldn't care less what you did.' His eyes didn't contradict her, but he was helpless to escape her conclusion. 'Well, you still have the same wife, don't you, Rob?'

His expression begged her not to burn their bridges behind them. 'She's the reason I couldn't get to see you. She's ill, Sandra,' he implored her for the hundredth time. 'Wants to go back to Scotland.' By this he seemed to be holding out a ray of hope, despite appearing to withdraw from the spotlight. 'It's been very difficult for me.'

'What do you want, Rob? My sympathy? It's in short supply right now.' *Her*, of all people – known far and wide as the Mother of all Midland Specials, whose entire life had become consumed by a job that demanded sympathy and concern and attention for many, many people – drained of her capacity for loving or caring for anyone by one man. 'I get the feeling this is some kind of risky adventure for you. A bit on the side that got serious, and you don't know how to handle it.' He winced. Touché. 'Well, I'm sorry. I've had enough of backstreet affairs.'

To her their love had been a series of meetings, arranging their future on maps endlessly sketched, redrawn and reconstructed. Alone, he made love to her openly; yet when they were not alone intrigue seemed the compelling force in their relationship, at least on his part.

'I just need time,' he sighed, his standard refrain. 'To sort out the whole mess. It's bloody hard telling an invalid you want a divorce.'

The same old story, the story of her life, only different. But a sick feeling of impending separation reminiscent of the other one . . . other ones . . . who got away. She blew the air out of her cheeks, giving up the ghost.

'I need your help,' he pleaded. 'What do you want me to do?'

She felt weak in the stomach. 'To grow up.'

Toby and Loach weren't getting anywhere with the houseowner or his stone-face wife. 'Unless we know for sure, we just can't barge in next door,' Toby was telling them. 'We'll need a warrant.'

In the meantime, the vehemence of the houseowner's neighbourly animosity has not diminished one iota on the tantrum gauge. 'I don't believe it! Are you saying you have to wait for the blood to leak out under the front door before you'll do anything?'

Suddenly a series of horrendous crashes exploded in their ears, coming from next door. Loach and Toby exchanged startled glances, then raced for the door. The houseowner mocked them with a told-you-so smile: 'I could do with a nice cup of tea . . .'

Toby pounded on the door of the next house, Loach backing him up. After a few moments, the door opened slowly.

Alert to any possibility, Toby was shocked into alarm by the young man standing in the doorway. Appearing exhausted, his shirt and pants in disarray, the young man was leaning on a long-handled axe, as if he'd been chopping wood for a long winter or impersonating Lizzie Borden.

Instantly Toby rushed the man and disarmed him, taking possession of the weapon. The young man frowned, but didn't block or resist his move in any way. 'Can we come in and have a chat, sir?'

Though confused, the young man shrugged. 'Sure. Why not?'

When Toby and Loach reached the main room inside the house, they discovered a scene of cataclysmic devastation. The place was a total shambles: furniture all smashed, pictures and knick-knacks shattered to smithereens, the carpet mottled with shards of vapourized porcelain and pottery. Simultaneously apprehensive and baffled, they viewed the scene like virgin soldiers sickened at their first sight of mass destruction.

'Is your wife here, sir?' Loach asked him.

The young man gave him a cool nod.

'Then we'd like to see her,' Loach informed him warily.

For the first time, the young husband was truculent. 'You'd better find out if she wants to see *you*.'

Toby tried to correct the young husband's apparent misconception. 'You don't seen to understand, sir. We want to see your wife . . . *now*.'

'Listen. What my wife does is her choice. Okay?'

'No, it isn't okay,' Toby admonished him. 'You're going to be in serious trouble if we don't see your wife pretty sharpish.'

'What for?' said a woman's voice behind them, and as they turned around, a young woman – obviously the husband's wife – walked between them into the room. In her hands was a sublime blue vase,

84

and on her face a look of blue thunder not the least sublime.

'What the hell so you want?' she inquired, pitching the vase past them. Instinctively they ducked, as a blue streak disintegrated against the wall behind them.

Loach looked at Toby, and Toby looked at Loach, silently asking each other what the hell was going on here. Had they somehow wandered into the psychiatric ward?

An unlit cigarette dangling from his lips, the young husband searched his pockets for a match. The young wife happened to notice him, looked through the debris and unearthed a small jade object. Retrieving it from the rubble, she flipped it at her husband.

By now a bit gun-shy, again Loach and Toby ducked. The young husband caught the lighter easily and lit his cigarette.

'It's them next door, isn't it?' griped the young wife.

Their failure to answer confirmed she was right.

'Well, you can tell Mr and Mrs Snoopy that we're having a divorce, and we don't particularly care who hears it!'

The young husband picked up a cuckoo clock, the cuckoo bird hanging from a spring like a strangled chicken. He turned something and made the clock 'point' forlornly before he dropped it back into the rubbish all over the floor. He sighed.

'We can't agree on anything . . . politics . . . my job . . . her job . . . sex . . . not even this lot . . .' He gestured to the remains littering the room beneath their feet. 'So we thought . . . sod it . . . if we can't agree who owns what, then neither of us is going to get anything.' On this, and perhaps on this alone, his young wife seemed to agree.

Loach thought he'd heard it all, but this one had to take the cake. Stunned by their lunatic display, he leaned back against the only object left standing in this universe – an antique table. It crumbled under his weight, taking him with it. After hitting the floor hard, he struggled to climb back up while looking at the young couple with what he was sure appeared to be a sheepish and apologetic grin. 'Oh well. I've saved you doing this one.'

Yet they did not seem to be sharing his amusement, their mood having suddenly changed. Once again, they agreed. And in fact, they were appalled.

'You bloody barbarian!' the young wife spat at him.

'You know what you've done?' her husband demanded.

'What?' Loach asked rather innocently, though with considerable apprehension at this point.

'That was a Georgian table, you cretin!' the young wife informed him.

There was cold anger in the husband's intonation. 'I hope you've got good insurance cover, guy. Because you'll need it before I'm through. And right up front, I'll have both your numbers.' He looked down, aiming his gaze at Loach. 'And I want your name most of all, Sunny Jim . . .'

Helpless and hopeless, Loach exchanged glances with a grim-faced Toby. Another fine mess he'd gotten them into.

24

The Pub on 4th was busy later that evening with a full complement of both regular Police and Specials. At one of the tables Viv Smith was having a drink to pass the time while waiting with Freddy Calder and a group of PCs and other Specials. When a PC with distinctive ginger hair entered and started to look around the room, Viv shrieked, jumped up, and, in her haste to join him, upset and nearly spilled the table and its contents into their laps.

'What's going on?' asked one of the PCs at the table.

'Ginger . . .' Freddy answered, as he watched Viv possessively embracing the object of her affections. Now *that's* the proper way to treat the chap in your life, he secretly smiled, happy for Viv in his own way. 'The walking no-smoking zone,' he added, also a bit jealous of Ginger himself.

The PC kept his eyes on Viv. 'By the way,' Freddy interrupted his reverie, trying to distract him from Viv, 'you seen anything on your travels of a nice bachelor flat?' It was time for him to think about making plans for his own paramour . . . should he ever be fortunate enough to find her.

The PC gave Freddy the same old-fashioned look of mild disbelief, followed by a patronizing smile. 'Give over, Freddy, and pull the other one. If I'd a quid for every time you've asked me that, I'd . . .'

'Okay, fair enough,' Freddy surrendered, raising his hands. 'I'd hate to put you to any trouble.'

Freddy ignored the PC rolling his eyes and once more gazed at Viv and Ginger. In the doorway, beyond, a burly fellow looked over the pub. Apparently not finding what he was searching for, the man walked over to their table and barged between Viv and her obsession. After a brief discussion, Viv pointed him in the direction of the bar.

Nodding his thanks, the burly fellow ambled over to the bar counter, where Loach was chatting with Toby Armstrong.

'Loach?' inquired the burly.

'That's me.'

'I'm Detective Inspector Dutrow . . .'

Loach's eyes widened. This wasn't quite what he had expected.

'Now what the hell are these messages I've been getting all over town?' Dutrow demanded, his own eyes narrowing. 'Who the hell are you?'

Loach was confused. If Dutrow didn't know him, how did he know enough to find him?

'You got my note?'

'What note?' asked Dutrow, plainly ignorant of whatever Loach was talking about.

Queasy all of a sudden, Loach had a sick feeling deep inside. He looked up at the clock above the bar counter. It was the witching hour . . . which he had almost been able to make himself forget.

The pedestrian underpass was dark, almost always empty, always lonely. No doubt that's why it had been chosen as a rendezvous, but that was no help to Jackie. The cement walls covered with graffiti gave her no refuge. And Dutrow gave her little assurance, not much of a straw to grasp. But she needed to hang on just a while longer, to make the connection. He would understand right away – after all, he wasn't that stupid – and he would pay in order to get Diesel. Then she could get out of here, get away, find something else. At least she wouldn't be trapped in this desolate black hole, a walking target in a deserted underpass waiting for a fat cop to rescue her. Fat chance.

As the last chimes of the church clock died away, she heard footsteps in the distance . . . one set of footsteps. For the first time that night she allowed herself a small sense of relief, closing her eyes in thanks to the spirits of the darkest hour. She straightened up, ran a quick brush through her hair, and tried to make herself look nonchalant, like a slut who didn't give a damn about anything.

When he got closer, her composure disappeared instantly, overcome by complete horror. It wasn't Dutrow. It was Diesel. The wrong man.

Sheer panic paralyzed her. No place to run, no place to hide . . . he was coming after her, taking his time. What could she say to him? She had to think of something, fast. She had to put her face back together, stop shaking, try to smile, think of something to say, anything.

Maybe Dutrow was on his way, maybe he would get there in time to save her. She had to stall Diesel. She had to come up with some kind of a story, just to hold him off for a few seconds until Dutrow got there. Fast! She had to think, *think!* Up until the last moment, her mind was a blank: she couldn't think of anything at all.

A shadow loomed over her. Above her, alone with her in a lonely place, stood the nightmare she dreaded, in the flesh, a lop-sided grin on his grotesque, pitted, sadistic face.

'Not thinking of running out on me, are you, Jackie?' inquired the beast who had sexually abused her time and time again.

The blood drained from her face, and she was afraid she would pass out before she could think of an excuse to stall him just a little longer.

'I don't know what you mean, Diesel . . .'

''Course you do,' he soothed her. 'I need you, Jackie. In fact, I can't live without seeing your pretty face on the pillow next to me . . .'

Jackie closed her eyes.

25

In the kitchen the next morning Anjali had breakfast in the presence of her mother and Uncle Ram, though in total silence. Yet she knew him well enough to know he was building up to something. After he had settled in with his tea, he began to fold the newspaper he had been reading (or failing to read, more likely) in half, then again, and again, until he finished with a neat square. Finally he looked at her.

'I have come to a conclusion regarding last night.' He paused once more, deliberated, then resumed. 'I may have made an error of judgement regarding the young man we met. It struck me at the time that he was most definitely not a wise choice: agewise or classwise. After all, what is he? No more than a purveyor of baked beans!' He went no further; that was his speech.

Anjali arose from her chair at the table and went to his side, kneeled next to him and gave him a kiss. Sometimes, she had learned, when personalities in a family were unalterably opposed, the only answer was love, however irrational. Uncle Ram made a fuss of pushing her away, but it was crystal clear to her that he enjoyed this moment of being loved by the niece he had sheltered as his own child, whatever their differences. She resumed her place a much happier individual.

'I'm glad, Uncle Ram, that you accept that my private life is just that – private.'

The cup froze on Ram's lips. 'That is not what I said. If you ask me what I said, I will tell you what I said.'

She groaned in anticipation of another petty dispute. 'So what was it you said?'

Ram cleared his throat and assumed his full dignity. 'It is still my responsibility to see that you are married. But I realize I will need to do things differently.' He made a small, deferential nod in her general direction. 'Clearly, what you require is an older man, a father figure.'

Anjali growled, too annoyed to put her immediate reaction into kinder words. Ram simply ignored her.

'And there is something else.'

By now she was numb. 'Something else?'

His duty done, Ram now returned to the sore subject of a prior insult in a different matter entirely, yet a grievance he could not forget, not let go unspoken, and thus unpunished. 'I am thinking about sueing your hospital for being manhandled and suffering loss of dignity.'

Anjali wavered between laughing aloud and barely retaining her temper. 'Oh really. Then let me warn you.' She was galled by his utter gall. 'You were very lucky not to be arrested. The very idea that you think you can peep through windows at middle-aged ladies wearing no clothes!'

Stunned, Uncle Ram's mouth opened and shut like a soundless

goldfish gulping water. Her mother was horrified.

'Ram? Is this true?' she asked in fearful shock.

Continuing his fish impersonation, he floundered.

Holding a wrapped bunch of flowers, Bob Loach walked slowly along the corridor looking for one particular ward he didn't particularly relish the thought of finding. Just up ahead he saw something – or, rather, someone – and his progress became slower. Sitting in a chair was Big Jess, as if she were a dead load dumped in place, a pile of leftovers in the waste bin.

He approached her tentatively. Appearing to be heavily drugged, she looked up at him without recognition. Still, he recognized her, regardless of her appearance. Yet he didn't know how to say what he felt must be said, by him, to her.

'I screwed up. It may not mean much, but . . .' He had to force himself to go on. '. . . I feel sick to the pit of my stomach.' He struggled for strength one more time.

'I'm sorry.'

Big Jess gave out a weary laugh, raising her clawed hand. 'You know . . . last night I'd've pulled your heart out. But somewhere in the wee small hours, I said "what the hell!" You can't stay angry all night, Loach.' She noticed the flowers, and noticed soon after checking his face that the flowers were not for her but for her friend. Nonetheless, a tired smile lifted a few of her sagging facial muscles for a brief respite. 'Anyway . . . you've the bottle to turn up,' she reminded him, referring to the flowers. 'There's not many would do that for a brass.'

He reached out to touch her, but quickly and clearly her eyes signalled that he shouldn't, and he respected her wishes. Her eyes then motioned his to the side ward just off the corridor.

'She's going back to Newcastle . . .' Her mind seemed to wander. 'Who knows? Maybe her old boyfriend might have her back. Even considering . . .'

She never finished the sentence. He learned why in the side ward. Lying in the solitary bed was Jackie, or what was left of her. He couldn't see much really, as most of her head and upper body was swathed in bandages. What yesterday had seemed such a fragile, delicate beauty had been fractured and torn to pieces . . . and partly, at least, because this ephemeral creature had trusted him.

Over by the window, Detective Inspector Dutrow was standing

90

with a nurse. 'She's asleep,' he said softly.

Awkwardly, Loach handed his bunch of flowers to the hovering nurse, and Dutrow gestured that they leave the room. Loach was grateful to accept the suggestion, since there was obviously nothing he could offer Jackie anymore.

In the corridor they passed Big Jess, who ignored them. Loach tried to think of what to say to Dutrow, something that wouldn't be embarrassingly inappropriate . . . anything, in fact.

'Jess tells me Jackie's going back to Newcastle.'

'That's good.' They walked on in silence for a while. 'If she stays, the likes of her could well be dead by this time next year.'

The thought of her further suffering and early death depressed Loach to the point of tears. He desperately tried to hold them back, though without knowing why, except that he was with a fellow officer, so he must not surrender to grief or self-pity. Like a robot, he followed Dutrow to the lift, which they entered in silence.

'I've another visit to make,' Dutrow announced on the way down. 'I'd like you to come with me.' Loach wondered what was next, but didn't say anything, rather accompanied the Detective Inspector mechanically.

In some other ward, in some other bed, Dutrow showed him another mummified patient, wrapped in bandages and tape, who appeared to have broken every single bone in his or her body.

'You may not have heard, but there was a nasty accident last night at my Division. You know the front steps there are pretty dangerous. We've all complained about them. Just shows you. They tell me he's in a worse state than Jackie upstairs.'

Loach looked down at the bandaged body manifestly unconscious and oblivious to his sympathy. 'Is he one of your constables there?'

'No, no. I thought you knew him.'

Perplexed, sceptical, Loach shook his head. 'How could I? There's no way I'd know him through all those bandages.'

'True . . .' Dutrow gazed at the motionless form on the bed. 'Anyway. He's the civvie on duty at the reception. You know?' He turned to Loach. 'The one you gave the letter to? For me? I hear he was a nice lad. Pity it hadn't happened to that punk Diesel, eh?' he nudged Loach. 'But you never know your luck.'

26

John Redwood and two other Specials, another man and a woman, were clambering on board a single-decker bus to quell a burgeoning riot among twenty football supporters turned into a mob of hooligans. Brandishing beer bottles and lager cans like weapons, the heaving mass of sweaty bodies came in full battle uniform: knee-length scarves, jaunty caps and rosettes; more like a party gone wild than a mob gone berserk, each hooligan intent on showing he could laugh, shout or sing louder than the next, all showing exaggerated signs of public drunkenness.

'Here we go, here we go, here we go,' some of the wrestlers were singing. 'Way the reds!' bawled others.

Hand waving aloft to calm the situation, Redwood soon had to bring them down to protect his own midriff from two thugs brawling nearest to the door. He tried to deal with them firmly, yet quietly, and with professional courtesy.

'All right. Can we settle down – please.'

The two thugs stopped brawling and aped his 'please' with raucous laughter. Another thug grabbed the woman Special and bounced her on his knee.

'Hullo darling.'

Restoring order, Redwood tried reasoning with them. 'Now listen, everyone. I'm sure you don't want to miss the final.' A few hoots and hollers came from the hecklers who were not otherwise occupied punching out somebody next to them. 'But we have a job to do. And we need your co-operation . . .'

The mob gave him a sing-song reply: 'Two, four, six, eight – why should we co-operate?'

One of the thugs snatched Redwood's cap and hurled it like a frisbee the length of the bus. 'A hundred and eighty!' he boasted.

'Come on, now,' Redwood endeavoured to caution them. 'Let's be sensible . . .'

But the mood on board the bus was getting angrier and uglier, more disorderly by the second. Some of the mob were crowding around Redwood, surrounding him, pushing and shoving every which way.

Just when it seemed as if he might be swamped, a loud voice shouted from the back of the bus. 'No, no, no! Hold it!'

Everyone stopped wrestling, and hostilities vanished in an instant.

The irritated voice belonged to Sergeant Crombie, who had been observing the drill from the back seat of the stationary bus at Tally-Ho, the Police Training Centre where Specials and police alike are trained. The hooligans were not supporters of the *Birmingham City Football Club* or the *West Bromwich Albion Football Club* or the *Aston Villa Football Club* or any other for that matter. They were simply off-duty policemen thoroughly enjoying the academic discipline of teaching new Specials the ropes.

Sergeant Crombie was a large, imposing figure whose aggressiveness seemed heightened, if possible, by the brevity of his hair. His iron stare had already singled out Redwood for a dressing-down, and the others moved away from the eye of the storm.

'Who's the ringleader? Him?' Sergeant Crombie badgered Redwood, pointing to one of the pseudo-thugs. Redwood nodded, which only seemed to aggravate the tough sergeant. 'Then collar him! Be physical! Or you're the one to go outa here feet first. These are militant drunken louts looking for trouble. The fact that they're off-duty policemen having a lark for your sakes is neither here nor there. You're not here to play games. Get stuck in!'

Meanwhile, the mob surrounding them had dropped all pretence of aggression. Newspapers magically appeared, now being read by the former hooligans lolling in their seats. The woman Special had been restored to her feet. Someone tossed Redwood his cap.

Unable to ignore his education as a solicitor, however, Redwood was not entirely satisfied with the methods he was being taught, a few knotty questions still lingering in his mind.

'Shouldn't we first establish . . . uh . . . ascertain who's responsible? We don't know who's guilty and who's innocent.'

Sergeant Crombie did not seem overly concerned with the finer points of the law at a moment when mob violence could be imminent. 'Ascertain? You've already *ascertained*, and you'll get a broken bonce if you ascertain any more. Maybe I should remind you . . . uh . . . ?' He was searching for the name.

'John Redwood.'

'*Special* Constable Redwood . . . of what goes on in the real world.' As Sergeant Crombie held up and counted his stubby fingers, many of the off-duty police veterans in the mob joined him in reciting the code of the west.

'Ask 'em . . . tell 'em . . . lift 'em.'

Sergeant Crombie turned and addressed the chanting mob sweetly. 'With your permission, gentlemen . . .' Then he turned on Redwood, and the hard edge returned to his voice.

'Now let's get at 'em, shall we?'

That attitude, John Redwood contemplated and remembered, personified the tone and spirit that pervaded the entire training regimen prescribed for the recruited civilians who volunteered to serve as Specials. They weren't given any special treatment, at least in the sense of mollycoddling. Yet they were given very special treatment in being afforded the same training opportunities as the PCs: what the police constables had to do, the Specials had to do.

Redwood specifically remembered the hardships of strenuous physical conditioning. Not that he was in such bad shape, but he felt all of his 42 years after several laps around the grassy perimeter of the running track. He recalled the camaraderie among these volunteers, when one of them had faltered on the track and others had given him a helping hand and encouraging words to keep going; and when the same had nearly happened to him, as he was winded and barely ploughing along under the stress: the encouragement had been for him that time. As a private, reticent, even shy man, to whom social relations and friendship had never come easily, he was getting something more out of this experience than he had expected, and it was making a deep and lasting impression on him.

Certainly he was learning skills he had never expected to acquire or need in his profession, such as how to apprehend a hostile suspect, or how to disarm a potential attacker. For a time he had been confused about such technical issues as whether his adversary's arm should be bent up in front of or behind the body. Once he had stepped forward to face the instructor, confidently ready to spring into action and demonstrate the manoeuvre he had been shown, only to be sent flying effortlessly by the instructor.

All this in preparing for the worst, as Sergeant Crombie constantly reminded them. 'Just because you've been vetted by the police, in your homes and workplaces, doesn't mean you're fit to undertake the duties and responsibilities of being a Special Constable,' he had said, simultaneously warning them about and explaining the rationale for the extensive training, mental as well as physical. 'You'll learn what it's like out there on the streets. And we'll learn whether you're competent to wear the uniform. Because you're there to assist the police, in the full knowledge that you're under their command, control and discipline at all times.'

Those were the kinds of ideas Redwood could respect, and wanted to hear. At least that's what he had thought prior to one particular afternoon when he and several other Specials were in a classroom with Sergeant Crombie. On the blackboard behind him were some of the buzz-words relating to the Specials under the heading: Duties and Responsibilities. Below that were the words Code of Practice, and under that, indented to the right, each on a separate line, such phrases as Stop and Search, Obstruction, Restraint, Intimidation. Sergeant Crombie had referred to them by pointing his thumb at the blackboard over his shoulder.

'Okay, that's the theory,' he had said. 'But out on the street nobody's gonna make any allowances because you're a Special. The fuzz is the fuzz . . . even though *you* don't get paid for it.'

A cheeky-faced young woman held up her hand, and Crombie had nodded for her to proceed. 'Sir? I thought we got a quid a year?'

Although her observation tickled the Specials in the classroom, Sergeant Crombie appeared soured by her notion. 'I've always thought that too generous.' Polite laughter greeted his rejoinder.

'But you'd better be damned sure you know why you've signed up to be a Special.' At once, Redwood had never seen him more serious (though Crombie was a teacher who never even smiled). 'And, of course, all of you sitting there think you know.' Before they had a chance to think about it, he pounced. 'Hands up, the ones who want to help society . . . clean up the streets . . . save the delinquent . . . ?'

One of every pair of hands was raised high in the air, including Redwood's.

The singular motivation for his wanting to become a Special was a painful memory. It was over a year ago, two years after his wife, Anthea, had died of a cerebral haemorrhage at the age of 36. At the time he had thought her death – so swift, so harsh – was the worst moment of his life. But then their son Simon, their only child, just 16, had been mugged. Pursued by a gang of young thugs, trapped on a pedestrian bridge over an inner city freeway, Simon had fallen from the walkway. His back had been broken, he'd suffered severe head injuries, it was touch-and-go whether he would survive. As a father called by police to identify the shattered body in the hospital bed, his first feeling had been pure hatred, a raging fury that God had singled him out again. He would have turned his back on life had his son died that night.

Confined to a wheelchair, Simon continued to suffer from the after-effects, emotional as well as physical, of the mugging, as did his father, Yet his father was an adult, capable of taking responsibility, and taking action, and he was not held back by a wheelchair. He felt that he must *use* his hatred, channel and focus it on something *positive*, something that would demonstrate – in actions rather than words – his protest against the savages, and the savagery, guilty of crippling his son. Something had to be done, he told himself. Some good had to come from this evil, some way to right the wrongs, to stand up for justice and humanity and life itself at a time when they were being threatened. And so he had joined the Specials . . .

'Liars!' shouted Sergeant Crombie, so rudely interrupting the noble thoughts of the volunteer peacekeepers and holy crusaders sitting in the classroom before him. For once in a lifetime he smiled at them, even as their smiles disappeared, and he cheerfully bullied them in a bantering tone.

'Deep down . . . don't you want to tell people what to do? Be Jack-the-Lad in a uniform? Be the Last of the Vigilantes?'

To his chagrin, Redwood realized that he, too, had a hidden agenda. Not that he really saw himself as an avenging angel, but he had often thought, in his words, 'by being out there, I might see something, hear something,' and often wondered what would happen if he were ever to meet face-to-face the muggers who had battered Simon. At this point, only God or a Jesuit could answer that question, but he had to admit to himself that, God help him, revenge was one of his primary motives.

A voice from the back of the classroom once again disrupted his thoughts, answering Sergeant Crombie's nasty accusations: 'No. I'm doing it for the money, Sarge.'

Laughter returned to the faces of the Specials, just as Crombie's visage reverted to its normally dour form. 'Comedians is what I get!'

Redwood had laughed along with the others, and that hadn't been the first time. He fondly recalled a few other occasions when a wisecrack during one of the humourless training sessions, at an awkwardly inopportune moment, had nearly brought tears of laughter to his eyes. Whenever *was* the first time with this group, though, it had probably been the first time he had laughed aloud since Anthea was alive. Of course, he didn't tell them about that. They didn't know him, really.

But in a very real way, he was beginning to see that they did know each other. They were all in this together, all in the same boat, and each of them, man and woman, held an oar to pull. Despite the disbelieving scorn of Sergeant Crombie, there was something all these people cared about, in addition to each other. Yet it was the addendum that was affecting him and surprising him most. After a long, self-imposed solitude, he was, little by little, finding friends.

It wasn't just a shared laugh or cup of coffee, all play and no work. There were serious and solemn occasions that brought them closer together as well.

Like the day of the final ceremony at the parade ground. Redwood's own iron constitution harbored a secret weakness for pomp and circumstance (as, apparently, did Sergeant Crombie). He loved the proud music blazing forth, the synchronized rows of smart uniforms marching in precision to the pulse of the police band, filing past the highest-ranking officers, the dignitaries, and the Chief Constable, his uniform encrusted in braid . . .

. . . And finally coming to a halt in front of Sergeant Crombie. In spite of the stern demeanour the short-haired goat was trying to maintain, Redwood noticed (twice in a lifetime) a smile tugging at the corner of Crombie's mouth.

'Right, you lot,' he stated, looking over the lot of them, one at a time, before going on. 'Here endeth the lesson. Just remember . . . We live in iffy times.' He was surely no good at sentimentality, which, naturally, Redwood regarded as one of Crombie's most appealing qualities.

'Good luck . . . You'll need it.'

A loftier speech would have had less of an effect on his audience, but the Specials felt the full weight and burden of what he didn't say. Now they understood how it felt to be police.

In the magistrate's court as the day's business was about to begin, lined up before the bench was a neat row of Special police constables in new, knife-creased uniforms. Facing them, in front of the bench, was Sandra Gibson, Mother of all Midland Specials. On the bench, the magistrate read the 'swearing-in' from a card, the Specials echoing each phrase of their pledge.

'I do solemnly and sincerely declare and affirm . . .'

'I do solemnly and sincerely declare and affirm . . .'

'. . . that I will well and truly serve . . .'

'. . . that I will well and truly serve . . .'

'. . . our Sovereign Lady the Queen . . .'

'. . . our Sovereign Lady the Queen . . .'

'. . . in the office of Special Constable . . .'

Mumbling the words, John Redwood looked down at the warrant card in his hands, the magistrate's resounding tones becoming indistinct.

'. . . faithfully according to law.'

It was over as suddenly as it began. For a few moments, there was an awkward silence, a time for introspection and personal reflection perhaps. No one had really been given permission to move as yet.

The magistrate broke the tension unceremoniously. 'Well, that's it, ladies and gentlemen. I have a court to run.'

Officially acknowledged, authorized, warranted and sanctioned, as well as dismissed, the Specials breathed a sigh of relief, warmly congratulated one another and walked from the courtroom with shiny new haloes over their heads.

In the meantime, the magistrate leaned over the bench to detain one of the Specials. 'Oh, Mr Redwood?'

'Sir?' Redwood replied, turning from his departing friends to the looming magistrate.

'I see you've put yourself in the curious position of being sworn in as upholder and defender of the law on the same day.' Redwood was about to change hats and present a case before the magistrate's court that morning. 'This may cause you some difficulty in the days to come. Policemen need to know the law in order to act upon it. Whereas it is a well-known fact that lawyers are the only people whose ignorance of the law goes totally unnoticed.' His wit, alas, was apparently unappreciated.

'However, I'd be obliged if you would slip into something more appropriate for a defending counsel . . . since I believe your case comes before me in thirty seconds.'

27

At Police Administration Headquarters, the office of Sandra Gibson, Administrative Secretary for the Specials, occupied a large, airy square with two walls of cupboards and filing cabinets and two desks, the smaller one for her assistant, who was absent, as usual. At her larger desk, Sandra sat watching and helping Section Officer Bob Loach fill out the official report of his grievous injury.

'"Occupation?"' he read from the document. 'I suppose I put down managing director like?'

Poor Loach. All grease and few graces, she mused. 'Well, let's think about that,' she reasoned with him rather as she would with an older child. 'They could say that the injury you suffered in the line of duty didn't hinder you in your capacity as a managing director. Let's face it: managing directors mainly sit on their bottoms all day. And it was your thumb and not your bum the lady bit, wasn't it?' Loach didn't seem to take her attempt at comic relief too kindly. 'Why don't you put bus mechanic to be on the safe side.'

He shrugged. Some people just never understood, so you had to treat them like children. 'Managing directors have to be able to sign things, Sandra. And if you've got a dodgy thumb, it doesn't make much odds if you're using a Bic pen or a number six box spanner.' She didn't seem to understand that either.

'It's up to you,' she yielded to his obstinate whims. 'By the way, how did the woman . . . what's-her-name?'

'Big Jess.'

'Uh-huh. How did she manage to bite your thumb?'

'With her teeth . . . What else?'

A stout heart, strong muscles, an exemplary Special, but not much power upstairs, she concluded. 'No, I meant . . .' Never mind. 'Oh well, it'll be in the police report.'

'That's it then. Where do I sign?'

She leaned across the desk to show him exactly where. 'There . . . and at the foot of the page.' As he was signing the form, the telephone rang and she picked up the receiver.

'Good morning! Sandra Gibson of the infectious smile speaking.' It was an unfamiliar voice. 'Yes, this *is* Sandra Gibson.' Someone unfamiliar with her voice as well. 'Uh-huh, Administrative Secretary for the Specials.'

He had just become a Special, wanted to speak with her, wanted to know if he should bring along his companion, an off-duty policeman. They were in the reception area downstairs. 'Uh-huh, I see. Well, you'd better both come up. Security'll point you in the right direction. All right? Bye.'

During the 'phone conversation, she had stood up and wandered over to look out the window at the parking area, her lovely scenic view. After she replaced the receiver, she was still looking out of the window for something she couldn't find.

'Where's the famous white Jag then?' She had to hand it to him, though. Everyone's immediate association with Loach was a fancy white Jaguar. Not bad. 'Or are you parked somewhere else?'

He appeared strangely discomfited and evasive. 'Er . . . I don't have the Jag today. It's . . . on hire . . . for a wedding.'

She was somewhat startled and incredulous as to what some people would do to make money. 'You've hired your car for a wedding? Aren't you taking this millionaire Special thing a bit too far, Bob?'

'Flippin' 'eck, what d'you take me for? If you must know, someone got let down . . . at the last minute. I don't like to see folk disappointed.'

Try pulling the other one, she wanted to say. He didn't go on, he didn't go out. She looked at him expectantly.

'Was there something else, Bob?'

Still he seemed ill at ease. 'Well . . . now you ask . . . I did have another reason for coming here, Sandra. There's something going on . . . and you're the only person who might give me a straight answer.'

Something in his hesitant manner aroused her suspicion. 'That'll depend on the question.'

He contemplated, then decided to go ahead. 'All right. It's about Rob Barker – my Sub-Divisional Officer.'

Her fears confirmed. Winter came early, as her blood froze into ice.

Meanwhile, Loach was oblivious to the drop in room temperature. 'What I want to know is . . . whether he's coming or going? Viv Smith tells me he's been into her Building Society making plans about selling his house.'

'Selling his house?' she asked bleakly.

'Aye. What I want to know is if you've heard anything. Officially or unofficially. Is the man resigning or not?'

Before she could think of a hedge to put him off, there was a tap on the open door to her office. Standing there awkwardly was the young Special who had called from the reception area accompanied by the off-duty policeman, who appeared vaguely familiar to Sandra.

'Sorry to trouble you,' the young Special apologized.

'That's what I'm here for,' she assured him with her best motherly smile.

The off-duty policeman spoke up. 'I told him to touch base with you, Miss Gibson. Before he saw the lot upstairs. I'm Police Constable Leadbetter, by the way.'

Sandra nodded welcome, and Loach acknowledged him as well.

The young Special was eager to jump in. 'I wanted to know what I'm expected to buy for meself. When I become a Special. How much am I gonna be in for?'

'That's easy,' she grinned. 'Nothing. You'll be supplied with everything you need free of charge. You're not expected to buy anything.'

The young man frowned. 'But I heard . . . Well, what about other things . . . like handcuffs?'

It was Loach's turn to field that one. 'Uh . . . Somebody should've told you. A Special isn't allowed to use cuffs.'

'He's right,' Sandra was happy to concur. 'This is Bob Loach. He's a Special as well. A section officer.'

'Nobody can stop you buying them,' Loach conceded, qualifying his earlier admonition.

Leadbetter snorted. 'Bloody stupid, if you ask me. 'Ere we got young lads like the lad 'ere who volunteer to be Specials, knowing they've gotta stand in line and take the same bleeding punishment a cop like me has to. For what? They don't get paid. I got cuffs. They should be given cuffs. You can't stand about like a bleeding football and have your head kicked in. You can ask 'em, tell 'em, but I'm buggered if I know how a Special's going to lift 'em without cuffs.'

As if that extensive exposition weren't sufficient, he added one more item to the wish list for good measure. 'And another thing, they should be paid. Like the rest of us in the force.'

Loach was genuinely moved by his emotional support for the

Specials, including the young man beside him. 'I wish more policemen felt the same as you do. And I'll tell you, there's not many would give the time of day to help out a young Special the way you're doing.'

Leadbetter just shrugged and smiled. 'Got to, haven't I?' He put his arm around the young Special's shoulder.

'I'm his dad.'

Redwood's combined office and residence was a modest house with a minute garden fronting it, the only outward sign of his existence a burnished brass plate fixed to a wall pier and bearing the legend: 'John Redwood, Solicitor and Commissioner of Oaths.' Stella, his secretary, who had been with him since the time when his dear wife was still alive, was fluttering at the window, waiting for him, when she saw his car pulling up. In a twinkle she flew to her desk, where a plate of savouries awaited, along with a bottle of champagne cooling in a flower vase. She carefully picked up the champagne and got ready. When she heard him enter the house, she started counting to herself.

Just as he opened the door to the office, she popped the cork in his direction. Momentarily startled, he put his hand over his heart and staggered toward her.

'God, Stella, I thought you were a dissatisfied client.'

He dropped his briefcase on her desk and noticed her preparations. Slung over his shoulder was a plastic suit-carrier enclosing his uniform, tying up one arm.

'Congratulations, John.' She pushed a glass toward his lips, then pretended to snatch it back. 'Wait. Are you allowed to drink on duty?'

Finally smiling and tolerant, he accepted the glass. She took care of the suit-carrier, transferring it to the cupboard. Just before doing so, however, she removed the cap. Taking it over to him, she playfully set the cap at a jaunty angle on his head, embarrassing him with her teasing. She tilted her head to one side, in parallel with the cap, and studied him.

'Well, I am impressed.' She gave him a cocky salute. 'Evenin' all.'

They clinked glasses and tasted the champagne. He sneezed on the bubbles.

'Dammit. Just remembered . . . the conveyancing for 15 Sydney Street? Is it done?'

Stella was a bit piqued by his anxiety. 'Of course it is.' Now that he brought it up, she was irked that business was intruding on her

102

carefully arranged mini-party, so she forestalled his next query as well. 'And what's more, I got the deposit cheque.'

She leaned over her desk to retrieve a document, then watched in amusement as he tried to read it: squinting at it, tilting it sideways to catch the light from the window. Her reaction to this foible was more good-natured. 'How did you pass your police eye-test, John?'

'There isn't one.'

'And I see you've forgotten your glasses. Again.' She shook her head in wonder. 'The vanity of some men.' In truth, that was one of the foibles she liked very much about him: that secretly, buried somewhere beneath all that reserve, he still knew what a formidable, virile, attractive man he was. On the other hand, perhaps he had inadvertently revealed the source of her dilemma as well. Why did he overlook the obvious solution she offered to his loneliness? How could he fail to take any notice of the signals she was sending him constantly? Perhaps he was simply blind, literally as well as figuratively.

'What?' he asked absent-mindedly, engrossed in the papers instead of in her.

The door to the office rattled as if struck by something heavy. Surmising that it was probably a certain 16-year-old paraplegic in his wheelchair, Stella opened the door.

'Simon! You're just in time,' she smiled at him.

Framed in the doorway, the wheelchair didn't move. Simon confronted his father with a hard stare, open mockery on his face.

'Hello son . . . We were . . .'

Abruptly, out of the corner of his eye, he must have caught sight of himself in the wall mirror with the police cap still at a rakish angle on his head. Immediately he stiffened, removed his cap and returned it to the cupboard with the rest of the uniform.

Worried the fun might be spoiled for John, who had surely earned his moment of harmless celebration, Stella looked from father to son, desperately wanting to strike the right note between them and keep the party going.

'Simon? A glass of bubbly. To toast your Dad.' She had poured a glass for him, but he rejected it.

'Sorry. I thought you wanted me to fix your database programme,' he reminded her, his voice dripping with sarcasm. 'I didn't know it was party-time.'

In all the excitement of getting ready for the homecoming

celebration she had totally forgotten the peace proposal she had negotiated with Simon. She felt awful.

'All right, Simon,' his father stepped in. 'I think you've made your point. But Stella doesn't deserve that kind of remark.'

'No, it's just as much my fault,' she conceded. 'Simon has a physio appointment at half four. I thought he might save me making a hash of things. You know – crashing the computer.'

Silence was closing in around them when there was a ring from outside. Saved by the bell.

'That'll be Mr Dawson.'

With a quizzical expression, he asked who Mr Dawson might be. She indicated the document he was holding.

'15 Sydney Street.'

With a tender smile at the man who needed her, she went to answer the door, hoping he wouldn't notice the tear in her eye. Yet why would he notice that and nothing else about her? And, as she stepped lightly around Simon's wheelchair, she recognized that although his father might not notice her feelings, Simon hardly noticed her at all, other than as the woman who worked as his father's secretary.

28

Freddy Calder drove his 'classic' blue Sierra into the Cougar Coaches yard and parked next to Noreen's Renault 25 in the spot usually reserved for her husband's white Jag. Before heading for the office, he picked a few of the pulverized bugs off the body of his beloved Sierra, spat on his finger and rubbed the hardened insect entrails from the smooth polished surface.

Sure enough, when Freddy entered Noreen was the only one in the office. She didn't bother looking up from her work to see who it was. 'Must be four o'clock. I'll give you one thing, Freddy, I can set my watch by you.'

He went to the coffee dispenser and poured himself a cup. 'Part of my charm.'

'Really? Why haven't I noticed the rest of it?'

Freddy rewarded her with a thin laugh. 'Where's Bob? Didn't see his feet poking out under a bus out there?'

This time she did look up at him. 'With a woman. Where else?' Then, looking straight at Freddy, she suddenly remembered something, and started hunting through her bag.

'Really! Anyone I know? . . . intimately?'

'Sandra Gibson.'

'Ah! The Mother of all Specials. She who clasps us Hobby Bobbies to her warm bosom.'

'Hmm?' She looked up again. 'Is that why Bob was in such a hurry?'

Noreen seemed so hypersensitive lately. '*Figuratively*, Noreen. I was talking figuratively.'

She had apparently found what she had been searching for in her bag, and proffered what seemed to be a tissue to Freddy. 'I knew I had it somewhere.'

He swallowed the rest of his coffee and put the cup down. Gently and humbly accepting the tissue from her hand, still he had absolutely no idea what he was supposed to do with it, other than blow his nose or clean his ears or something else perhaps.

'You asked me if I knew of any flats going. Somewhere that would suit you . . . Somewhere cheap?'

He clapped a hand to his forehead, unable to fathom the depths of his sudden good fortune. 'Sorry. Wasn't thinking. A flat? Right.'

The public sleuth brought the object up to his private eye for closer investigation. There, bleeding through the tissue because it was written in eyebrow pencil, was a barely discernible address. Straining to focus, he tried to read the number.

'"Forty-Three Gladstone Way." Right.'

Turning the tissue over, he found the red-imprinted cultural icon of a pair of woman's lips. Noreen noticed, and blushed, as they exchanged glances. Suddenly hearing someone coming, she spoke to Freddy in a lower voice. 'Sorry. It was the only thing I had.'

Freddy stuffed the tissue into his breast pocket just as Loach entered the office and caught him in the act.

'What's this then? Love notes?'

'My lips are sealed,' Freddy smirked. He kissed the back of Noreen's hand, then flicked MacFoxy the glove puppet from an inside pocket to bid her farewell.

'See you at the compost convention, dear lady,' waved Foxy on his way out, leading Freddy by the hand.

Satisfied he had gone, Loach turned his attention to his wife. 'What was that all about?'

'Freddy being Freddy,' she quipped.

'No . . . The piece of paper.'

Noreen studied her husband through veiled eyes. What was he really saying? 'It can't be jealousy. And you can't be worried I'm giving Freddy the trade secrets of the company.'

He pulled a face, the one he usually used on these occasions. 'Just for once . . . Why can't you give a simple answer to a simple question instead of going round the houses? It's like pulling teeth.' He was getting nowhere. 'Aw, forget it. Who's interested?'

'Well, you are for a start.' She considered whether he even deserved her honesty any more. What difference did it make whether she were true or false, or whether he believed and trusted her or not? 'If you must know, he's looking for a flat, and I happened to hear of one coming on the market.'

Loach started laughing so hard he couldn't stop. 'You found a flat for Freddy?'

She wrinkled her nose at his antics. 'Yes, I found a flat for Freddy. What's so all-fired funny about that?'

'Listen,' he confided between chuckles, 'there are three kinds of liars: liars, bloody liars and Freddy Calder.' It took him a while to get his funny bone back in the socket. 'For as long as I've known the bloke, he's been going on about looking for a flat.' He pressed his advantage for once, sensing her discomfort and naiveté. 'He wants one like you need a hole in the head.'

Though sceptical, her curiosity was aroused. 'All right. What do you know that I obviously don't know?'

His ironic smile scarcely warped the shape of his mouth, as he shared the inside joke with her. 'I know his mother, Mrs Hilda Calder, for a start . . .'

Clearing the tea things from the table, she saw Freddy hovering in the doorway wearing his dark coat, obviously coming to inform her that she was going to be home all alone for hours again tonight while he ran out to play. Just like his father.

'Got to be going, Ma. Duty calls.'

Parade duty perhaps. Or maybe something else entirely that had nothing to do with duty, and his cover story was just a ruse to escape from home to play some other game every night. 'You're hardly in the door when you're going out again. You'd think you were in charge of every investigation in Birmingham.' Her son, like his father before him, often exaggerated his own status and prestige.

'If only we were that important. No,' he protested. 'We're the ones who wipe noses and help old ladies across the street.'

She knew exactly what he was insinuating with that kind of talk, and he might as well be disabused of that notion right that minute. 'You'll never need to do that for me, Freddy Calder.'

Palpably impatient to leave, and leave her behind, he seemed happy, for some unknown reason. 'Humph . . . Sometimes I wonder if it is the police station you're off to in such a rush?'

As if to prove his adolescent manhood, as well as paramilitary pedigree, Freddy began to unbutton his coat so that, once again, he could show off his uniform underneath.

'That's supposed to make it gospel, is it? Huh!' Anybody could wear a mail order uniform. He had a guilty conscience, she could see it written all over his face.

'I've got to go, Ma.'

She swept him away with an imaginary broom. 'Go, go. Who's stopping you?'

He hesitated before leaving. Now, she thought, *now* he remembered what he had said to hurt his mother's feelings, now that it was too late. She couldn't wait for the day he would come to her for love and protection, begging to stay rather than leave, and she would remember each and every one of these petty humiliations.

In the end, he did leave, abandoning her again to this shabby prison. Slowly she crossed to the window and pulled back the curtain. She saw Freddy reach his precious car, then turn and notice her in the window. He gave her a small wave. She sniffed indifferently, dropping the curtain back in place.

29

With the Specials gathered in the Division 'S' Parade room, Bob Loach was between Freddy Calder, John Redwood and Tom Fields as they listened to SDO Rob Barker taking the parade. Probably a little rusty, Loach figured. Barker began by clearing his throat with a dry laugh.

'Got your pencils sharpened?'

Surveying the faces in the parade room, he must have noted that his heavy attempt at humour raised but a few wan smiles. 'Because you've been invited to put your names down for a "special" cause, I advise only the physically fit to apply.' He tried another dry laugh, then gave it up. 'But to more serious matters . . .'

His tone and expression indeed became more serious, as he frowned at the face he was holding in his hand. 'The Inspector has given me an identikit picture, which I'll pass around. It's a man in his mid-thirties who drives a light-coloured car whose registration number includes a five, a six and a three.' He shook his head. 'Sorry, that's all we've got to go on. He has sexually assaulted three women to date. His method is to force them into his car. He's dangerous, so do not approach him.'

As Barker was moving on to more mundane matters, Fields tapped Loach on the shoulder. 'Been demoted again, have we?'

'Very funny, Tom.' Barker's words became indistinct.

'Looks like Barker's back, doesn't it?'

Loach didn't take his eyes away from watching Sub-Divisional Officer Barker. 'Don't count his chickens.'

'Oh,' Fields wondered aloud, 'something I should know?'

'When the time comes . . .'

Barker's voice faded back into Loach's consciousness. 'Right . . . As far as the tours of duty are concerned . . . Special Constable Redwood? You'll be out in the panda with WPC Morrow.'

Some feral hound in the pack gave her a wolf whistle.

'Now, now,' Barker scolded, 'let's show more respect for WPC Morrow.'

The wolf howled.

Another anonymous wag agreed with the wolf. 'Can't get more respect than that!'

'That's the drill for tonight. Good luck, everyone . . .' As the Specials filed out, he picked out a face in the crowd. 'Ah, Special Constable Redwood . . . ?'

Redwood nodded, waiting for Barker to join him. In the background, Loach watched with a speculative eye.

'Can I have a word?' Again Redwood nodded, remaining behind

108

the others. Rob spoke to him in a lower, confidential voice. 'It's rather noisy here. Perhaps we can go up to the Club. It'll be quiet at this time of the evening, and Loach can manage the store.' He signalled to Loach to stay and take care of business while he was gone, then turned to escort John Redwood from the parade room.

Freddy looked for Loach's reaction. 'The new boy's getting a lot of attention?'

Loach shrugged. 'You on your own, tonight?'

'Looks like it,' Freddy affirmed, not looking forward to pounding the beat by himself.

'Is it Viv's night off?'

Equivocating, Freddy scratched his chin. 'That's debatable, if I know Viv . . .'

Her bedroom looked like a boudoir straight out of Cosmopolitan, and that was just what Viv wanted. Standing in front of the make-up mirror in her fluffy, comfy robe, she was generally pleased with what she saw while slowly applying another layer of eye-shadow. She would do.

A buzz on the door-intercom startled her, and she frowned, smearing some of the eye-shadow. She wasn't expecting a certain visitor . . . not just yet anyway. Walking into the small sitting room, she went to the door and lifted the intercom telephone.

'Hello? . . . Ginger? But I thought . . .' Didn't he remember the time they set? 'Of course you can come up. It's just I didn't expect you for another hour. I'm not decent . . .'

Neither was his response.

'Ginger, you've got a dirty, horrible mind . . .' she half-smiled.

'I know it's a bit late in the day, but congratulations,' Barker declared, once they were settled at a table in the Pub on 4th and Briggsy had served him a mug of brew, which he offered in solitary toast.

'Thank you,' nodded the modest John Redwood. He had declined having to drink.

'It's good to see professional people like yourself joining the service,' Barker began. 'When I became a Special, more moons ago than I care to remember . . .' he winked, '. . . well, the quality of intake was, shall we say, lower down the scale. Conversation was on a par with the corner pub.' He took a sip of the brew.

Redwood raised an eyebrow. 'What's more important, surely, is if a man or a woman can do the job well? I don't believe their background makes any difference.'

Barker wasn't about to argue if Redwood were going to make an egalitarian issue out of an innocent pleasantry. Already he could see the man's tenacity in defending a moot point, which was, after all, an encouraging sign.

'True. Very true, John . . . I can call you John?' Redwood indicated his assent. Barker smiled, then assumed a more confidential attitude. 'The reason I wanted to have a chat with you is not so much that you're a fellow Special – although that's important,' Barker reassured him. 'No . . . it's of a more personal nature, if you follow me.'

From the look on his face, Redwood did *not* follow exactly, seeming uncomfortably uncomprehending. 'As a solicitor, you must get a lot of people chewing your ear . . . needing advice . . . You probably hear all kind of things . . .'

Redwood mumbled something noncomittal. Barker breathed deeply, and ploughed on. 'Not putting too fine a point on it, life's a bit of a bind for yours truly at the moment . . .'

'I'm sorry to hear that, but perhaps –'

Barker cut him off before he could raise some technical objection or other. 'My wife's been ill – still is – and, well . . . I don't suppose I'm any different from other men at times like that . . . I was lonely . . . looked around for . . . relief, if you get my meaning.'

Redwood winced. 'Do you really want to –'

Barker cut him off again, presuming the question and the answer. 'Like they say on Mastermind, I've started so I'd better finish.' He looked down at the suds in his mug. 'I suppose it all sounds foolish, but . . . before I knew it I found myself stuck in the middle of an affair . . . that became serious.' Quickly he amended his statement. 'Not on *my* side . . . Good Lord, no! But what worries me now is the thought that it could turn nasty. "Hell hath no fury like a woman scorned,"' he quoted.

'Mark you, there's nothing in writing . . . made damned sure my letters couldn't be construed as anything more than business-like . . . typed by my secretary at work, as a matter of fact . . .' He appealed to Redwood's eyes for sympathy. 'But you hear of other men being taken to court . . . which would absolutely destroy my wife . . .' Halting, he couldn't let himself continue along that line of contemplation, and took a step back in his reasoning.

'It doesn't bear thinking about, but sometimes you have to be pragmatic, and . . . well, you've probably been through this a hundred times . . . frankly . . . what's the bottom line . . . How much could I be liable for? Give me a number.'

Barker could almost see the wheels turning, as Redwood thought to himself a moment. Then he pulled out a small notebook, flipped though the pages to find a fresh one, and rapidly scribbled something on the paper, which he then tore from the notebook and handed to him. Shrugging, Barker took a deep breath, girded his loins and looked at the note. He was utterly baffled.

'I don't understand . . . This is a *telephone* number.'

'My office phone. Ring my secretary. Tell her who you are and she'll fix you an appointment.'

'But . . . ?'

Redwood stood up. 'Now, if you'll excuse me. I have a WPC sitting in a panda wondering what's happened to me, and, as my superior officer, I'm sure you don't want me holding up our tour of duty.'

'Of course not . . .' Barker meekly acquiesced, and watched Redwood leave. What nerve and snobbery those solicitors pretended. He crabbed to no one. He scrunched up the note and tossed it away.

30

As soon as his lips touched and pressed into hers Ginger's passion was intense, kissing her over and over again in rapid succession, searching for an opening, already caressing her neck and shoulder with one hand, the other moving down her lower back. Viv didn't know how he could be everywhere at once, because she certainly couldn't. Yet his mouth, and his hands and fingers, and his tongue were most urgent, insistent, hungry . . .

Not quite ready to be devoured, she pulled away from his lips, gently turning her own into a coquettish smile at his confusion. 'It takes me two hours to do my face and hair,' she explained, knowing he would never understand what she had gone through for him, nor accept this as any excuse for her non-co-operation. To mollify his sexual frustrations somewhat, as well as confuse him thoroughly, she came closer once more, nuzzled his neck, and sniffed the sweet scent. 'Mmm . . .' she purred. 'Like the aftershave.' That should hold him for a while, she mused, pushing herself away.

Ginger strutted as much as he could in the cramped sitting room before sprawling on the sofa, casually beckoning her to join him there. Instead she played coy and went over to the drinks cabinet.

'I've got to get dressed.'

'Dressed?' he leered, his lust evidently undiminished. 'You're crazy.'

'Ginger . . . behave yourself,' she chided him. She held out a glass. 'Scotch?'

'Uh . . . no.'

Viv poured herself a vodka and orange, wondering what the explanation he was groping toward would be this time.

'Not for me, luv. Listen, I don't know how to say this except . . . to say it.' Here it comes, she thought. 'I'm on duty tonight.'

She almost spilled her drink – *that* was a possibility she hadn't anticipated – and lost her temper. 'What? But Ginger, we had a date!'

She got another surprise when Ginger seemed untroubled and unapologetic. 'I guess you, of all people, know how the police works in its mysterious ways . . .'

'Dammit!' she cursed them. 'It isn't fair. I haven't seen you for a whole week. They can't keep you working like this.'

Ginger pulled Viv down beside him on the sofa, her graceful descent thwarted to some degree by the glass in her hand. Increased her annoyance, some of the vodka and orange spilled on him as she was setting her glass down on the side table. But once free of responsibility for the glass, she tried to relax a little, and let him draw her closer.

'Come here, luv.'

She allowed herself to be embraced by him, and gave him a tender kiss. He showed her, impulsively and a bit roughly, that he wanted more, but she was feeling romantic rather than lustful, and now disappointed as well.

Getting up, she grabbed her glass and stood by herself, sipping moodily. 'I'm sorry. I'm just not able to concentrate on the other. Damn! You can't blame me for being cheesed off.'

Ginger shrugged. 'I don't make the rules.' Impatient, he pointed to his watch. 'Look, I haven't got a lot of time, Viv.'

She has started pacing, but that line pulled her up short. Looking down at Ginger in a new light, she could feel the beginnings of bad vibes twisting in her guts. He was taking off his uniform jacket when he paused mid-elbow to give the sofa an intimate, inviting pat.

Viv put on her seduction smile to stall him. 'I . . . must powder my nose.'

The oldest line in the book, and it still worked on the adult male of the species, she rattled to herself as she slipped away toward the bedroom. She closed the connecting door firmly behind her, then went to the bedside phone. When the call went through, she spoke in a low voice.

'Hello? Can you put me through to WPC Baxter in Control? Tell her it's Viv Smith.' She had a fleeting awareness of what someone calling the Specials in a hurry must feel like. 'Yes, I'll hang on . . .'

Ginger must be looking at his watch by now, she thought. She could just see his rugged face screwing up in irritation, looking in the direction of her bedroom door . . .

By that time, she had got the quick answer she needed. 'Thanks, Sheila . . . No, no, nothing's wrong. Put it all down to strong aftershave. Bless you. I owe you one.'

She had no sooner replaced the receiver when the bedroom door opened. Ginger entered, his impatience plainly growing as he dumped his uniform jacket on a chair and started undoing his tie, making sure she saw his chest heave and swell. Yet he made no effort to disguise his petulance. 'I'm worried about my time.'

'Why?' It usually only takes you thirty seconds,' she snapped tartly.

That punch rocked back on his heels as if she'd struck him physically. In response, his jaw-line hardened. 'What's that supposed to mean?'

'It means you're getting it somewhere else, you dirty git!' she accused him. 'And what does that make me? The prawn cocktail before the main course? Is that it?' She refused to let herself be humiliated, although she was.

Naturally Ginger feigned complete innocence. 'What are you talking about?'

She glared at his little-boy-blank expression. 'I'm talking about "no duty for PC Ginger Stokes" tonight. Or last night, and all the other bleeding nights, for all I know!'

Cornered by the truth, he spat back at her. 'You been checking me out? Is that it? What right you got to check me out? We're not bleeding married, you know?' Turning on her and blaming her for everything, he was rapidly talking himself out of the door. 'I thought we were having a good time.' He picked up his jacket, then rose to face her, giving it one last try.

'I'm here, so what's your problem?'

For someone ordinarily a soft touch, she could hardly contain the fury exploding inside her. 'What's my problem? What the hell do you think I am? A bottle of Martini – anywhere, any place, any time?'

Some idiotic game show theme-tune was playing on the television when Hilda Calder switched it off. There's nowt but rubbish on these days, she said to herself in disgust. It left her nothing to do but retrace the same beaten path through her house, haunted by the same old memories. Absent-mindedly she picked up a photograph of Freddy from the bookshelf and gave it a wipe on her cardigan. And that got her thinking about Freddy again, though at this stage in both their lives there wasn't much she could do any more to straighten him out. Then again, perhaps no rod can rectify a twisted trunk, she remembered, trying to forgive herself.

Wandering into his bedroom, she looked around at the mementoes of Freddy's life spread everywhere – photographs of a beaming Freddy along with 'business associates' under banners shamelessly proclaiming such-and-such lingerie houses; a finely head-crafted model boat he had diligently constructed at the age of twelve; two ancient posters for famous magicians at theatres now long departed; car magazines of every sort; several miniature racing cars . . .

His sample case was lying on the bed. Glancing behind her to make sure Freddy hadn't mysteriously reappeared from hiding somewhere, she went to the case and opened it. The pair of knickers she lifted out were utterly beyond the bounds of imagination, let alone civilized decency: practically nothing at all, and, what there was of it, completely see-through. Just the sight of the ghastly things made her nose curl. Disgustedly, she thought to herself; they'd be as well to wear nothing, the trollops . . . although she couldn't help wondering if Freddy actually came into direct contact with any of the customers who would purchase and even *wear* such lewd and provocative items.

The same old refrain – nothing she could do about it now. With a sigh, she shook her head at Freddy's suit sprawled over the bedside chair. Putting the trousers on a hanger, then fitting the jacket on top, she happened to notice a piece of paper sticking out of the breast pocket. She gently tugged it out for a closer look.

It was a tissue. On one side was the red satin of a woman's lips; on the other, an address inscribed with an eyebrow pencil.

As if suddenly kicked in the stomach, she had to sit down to catch her breath, while wondering if her heart would stand the shock.

31

Loach poked his head into Police Sergeant Andy McAllister's office. 'You wanted me, Sarge?'

'No! I wanted Obiwan Kenobe, but I guess you'll do, Loach.' His body followed his head into the office, as Andy revealed a rare smile. 'We've had a complaint from a lady about a prowler. And you're it.'

Loach threw up his hands. 'What am I supposed to do? get on my bike?'

'No,' Andy grinned, 'you're in luck. The address is just around the corner. Her name is Miss Dowty.'

'I suppose there's no doubt about that, Sarge?' asked Loach.

But McAllister's expression had reverted to form, and this time it didn't change. 'Very good, Loach. Shows your brain is still functioning.'

On a suburban terraced street on a cold and bitter night, Hilda Calder checked that the name of the street coincided with the address on the tissue in her hand. Gladstone Way. Then she walked down the road until she was outside the house number she was seeking. Forty-three.

The small house had been split into three flats, and there was a separate bell-push for each tenant. Two were clearly male, but the third brought a scowl to Hilda's face: the name was Rita Loosemore.

She pressed the bell-push, paused, then tried again. After a long wait, a third stab on the button convinced her there was no one at home.

Finally, she took up an observer's post from a darkened shop opposite, pulling her coat collar tight around her throat.

His head back, Loach looked up at the tallish building, which boasted the convenience and security of a remote door-unlocking system. A woman's voice issued from the grille loudspeaker.

'Hello?'

'Miss Dowty? This is Section Officer Loach . . . You called the station about a prowler?'

'Oh yes,' said the voice. 'Do come up, Officer. I'm on the fourth floor.'

He paused outside Miss Dowty's door, fixed his tie and smoothed his hair in the mirror, then faced the small fishbowl marble to allow himself to be viewed. He showed his warrant card to the glass eye.

The door opened to reveal Miss Dowty: in her early forties, wearing casual but fluffy clothes, her blouse the kind that tended to gape, her skirt split to just above the knee. She ushered Loach inside, standing so close that he had to struggle to keep his distance. Her flat was elegant in its own modern, tubular way, graced by a tall, majestic window leading to a walk-on balcony. Closer to hand, she indicated a small table bearing a tray with coffee and all the trimmings. Her voice was confidential, for him alone.

'Do sit down, Officer . . . ?'

'Loach, miss.'

'I was just pouring myself a cup of coffee.' There were two tiny demi-tasse cups. 'Do join me. It's Blue Ridge.'

She offered him one end of a two-seater sofa, but he thought better of the idea and sidestepped it, choosing an empire-style chair instead. Bowing to his Pyrrhic victory, she poured the coffee.

'Now this prowler, miss . . .'

She offered him a demi-tasse. 'Your coffee, Officer. Cream? Sugar?'

More accustomed to mugs, he feared he might crush the delicate little toy teacup. 'Milk – no sugar.' A little sugar, and there would be no room for coffee or milk. 'Thank you, miss.'

He swallowed the cupful in one go. Miss Dowty blinked. Uncomfortable, he got up and replaced the fragile, tiny cup on its tray. 'I'd better get some information on this prowler of yours, Miss Dowty.'

Her fortyish face taking on a girlish expression, Miss Dowty brushed her slender hand ever so lightly on his knee. 'Oh, he's not *my* prowler, Officer.'

'Of course not,' his voice cracked. He cleared his throat, and tried to make some sense out of what he was saying. 'But where –?'

'– did I see him? Oh . . . from the balcony.' She pointed toward the balcony window, and he went over to see.

Sliding the window open, he stepped onto the small patio. He looked over the edge down into a cemented open area, well-lit and bordered by private garages. A black cat would feel exposed down there.

She joined him on the balcony. With a coy shiver, supposedly from the cold, she leaned in toward him. There was no room whatsoever for retreat of any kind; he had to hang out his arm so that she couldn't nestle in it.

'Exactly where, miss, did you see the prowler?'

She pointed down vaguely, 'Somewhere down there. He was there one minute, and the next he was gone.'

'Could it have been someone who'd just parked their car – a neighbour, perhaps, and you mistook him . . . ?'

'I suppose it's possible.' She affected a shy smile. 'Oh dear. Now you'll think I'm afraid of my own shadow.'

'No. Not at all. Better be safe than sorry.' Which made him consider his own advice. 'Maybe we should go back in. It's cold out here.' Hot as a coal furnace, actually.

She looked out into the darkness with a small sigh. 'Such a pity it's so cloudy. There's a full moon tonight, you know?'

His eyebrows arched, looking down rather than up. 'Is that a fact?'

The cow could jump over the moon at the moment, for all he cared. How did he ever get into this cliffhanger? And how was he going to get out?

Shivering miserably in the night air, Hilda Calder heard the telltale clip clop of high heels coming down the street. Peering towards the sound, she saw a woman approaching, a bottle-blonde she appeared to be, at least in her thirties or more, striding down the street with a confident swing as if she never had a care in the world.

The woman paused outside the house Hilda had under surveillance.

Hilda watched and moved cautiously. When the woman opened the door, Hilda loomed behind her. The woman jumped.

'Am I talking to Miss Loosemore?'

'You are.' Her eyes knew she was trapped.

'Then I want a word with you, madam.' She tried to barge past the woman, but the bottle-blonde was too tough and held her at bay.

'Just a minute,' the woman demanded. 'Where do you think you're going? Who *are* you?'

Hilda stood erect, and acknowledged her identity to the vile hussy in no uncertain terms. 'I am the mother of your fancy man.'

'My what?'

Hilda raised her voice in anger. 'If you want the whole street to hear what I have to say, then so be it!'

Both anxious, WPC Morrow was driving and SPC Redwood 'riding shotgun' in the passenger seat as the panda car bore down on Freddy Calder walking along a quiet street, pulling up alongside him by the kerb, stopping him in his tracks. His face a wide questionmark, Freddy had to bend down to peer in through the driver's side.

'Uh . . . they want you back at the station,' announced WPC Morrow.

'What's up?' he asked, unsuspecting.

WPC Morrow exchanged glances with Redwood, her expression pleading that he inform Freddy.

'I asked. What's up?'

Redwood looked him in the eye. 'The Sergeant had a call from your next-door neighbour – Irene?'

Freddy nodded, his pasty face sagging.

'It's your mother,' Redwood confided. 'She's been taken ill.'

'It's not serious, so don't get all het up,' WPC Morrow quickly added.

Redwood gave it to him straight. 'They think it best you take the rest of the night off, Freddy.'

Again WPC Morrow had to smooth over Redwood's blunt approach. 'Just in case . . .' And she grimaced when she realized what she'd said. But there was no taking it back, as Freddy got into the car.

* * *

118

Loach was making his report to Police Sergeant Andy McAllister, and making a conscious attempt to keep his recitation as professional as possible.

'I think she's a Miss Lonelyhearts – jumping at shadows.' He shrugged. 'There was nothing there I could see. Anyway, she's four floors up.' Which prompted him to recall his comment to Miss Dowty. 'I told her it would take Spiderman to get to her flat.' He quickly erased a smile, as McAllister glowered at him. 'I got out before she perked more coffee. I said we'd check the parking area during the night so she could rest easy.'

Loach checked McAllister, who was not resting easy. Irene brought a cup of cocoa to Hilda Calder, sitting up in bed, who coughed and sniffed at her approach.

'Irene, you're a good friend,' she said weakly.

'What are neighbours for? Now you drink this cocoa, mind? You're lucky you didn't catch your death.' She didn't really feel like patting Hilda's forehead, so she backed away and started to make her exit. 'I'll pop in tomorrow. See how you feel. Anyway, Freddy should be back any second . . .'

Hilda's eyes widened in sympathy for herself. 'It was for his own good, Irene.'

'What?'

'I know you think I'm possessive . . .'

'I said nothing of the kind.'

'I get frightened for his sake,' she explained. 'He's all I've got.'

Irene tried to comfort her with a recognition of how much she did have to live for. 'That's more than some, Hilda . . .'

A door slammed in the other room, and Freddy's voice called out. 'Ma? Ma?'

Hilda clutched hold of Irene. 'Tell him nothing! Say nothing.' Then she stared at the door, waiting for him to come to her.

Irene met Freddy as he was crossing the sitting room to go to his mother. 'Ma?' Raising a finger to her mouth, she shushed him.

'Not so much noise, Freddy.'

'Ma's all right, isn't she, Irene?' Freddy asked her anxiously.

'She's caught a bit of a chill, but she'll be fine. What can you expect if she's out on the streets at this time of night?'

Freddy's mouth dropped open before he spoke. 'What was she doing out?'

119

Irene shook her head as a way of explaining there was no way to explain. 'You know your mother – mind all her own.' She shrugged. 'Anyway, I'll get back next door. I've given her some cocoa.' Grasping his arm, she gave him a brave smile before departing.

When Freddy arrived, his mother was lying helplessly in bed, eyes closed, her face pale in the glow of the bedside light. He sat down at the edge of her bed.

'Ma?' he whispered.

Like a dead woman, her eyes remained shut. He dropped, and at a moment, her eyes opened more like a roused bird of prey. Freddy clutched her hand impulsively, but she shook him away.

'I may die of pneumonia, Freddy Calder, but I've put a spike in your little trollop's game.'

'What are you talking about?' Freddy asked her.

She thumped a crumpled, messy tissue into his hand. 'There were to be no secrets, Freddy Calder! You promised. But it's your father all over again,' she wailed.

Smoothing out the tissue, he recognized it for what it was. 'My God, what have you done?'

'Told the hussy some home truths,' his mother replied. 'I told her the house was in my name. And the savings in the Abbey National as well.' Freddy was aghast.

'Oh, she pretended well enough. Put on an act she didn't know what I was talking about. Hump! She'll know me well enough in future by the mark I left on her face.'

He couldn't bring himself to believe his mother had gone off her head and attacked a stranger. 'You slapped her?' She didn't deny it. 'Ma,' he shook his head back and forth, 'you don't know what you've done. My God! If this gets in the papers . . . if she sees a solicitor . . .'

Freddy was on the verge of tears. 'Ma! I don't *know* this woman! She doesn't know *me* . . .'

At first she looked at her son askance, as if to say pull the other one. Then, seeing his unwavering sincerity as he looked sadly into her eyes, a seed of doubt crept in, and a quiver of alarm crossed her mind.

32

'You see what I see?' asked WPC Morrow, bringing the panda car to a halt. A quick glance at Redwood, his brow furrowing as he peered ahead through the windscreen, confirmed that he did.

Approaching them on the opposite side of the perimeter road skirting the public park was an older man of about 60 wearing no trousers – just a shirt, underpants, socks and shoes. Half-walking, half-running, weaving erratically, he reached the park entrance and lurched to his left into the park, disappearing into the foliage.

Without a word Redwood jumped out of the car and went after him.

'I'll drive round to the other side and cut him off,' she shouted to him, engaging gear and pulling away.

Freddy had dreaded this moment of truth. But it had to be done, if only because now it was a matter of honour.

Bracing himself, preparing himself mentally, ready to meet whatever happened, ready to react to any contingency without losing his nerve, he cautiously poked the doorbell at 43 Gladstone Way.

Within a few moments he heard a window being raised above, and a woman's voice called out to him.

'Who is it?'

He took a backward step and craned his head up to see where the voice was coming from. There she was. The woman leaning out of the window looking down at him must be . . .

'I wonder . . .' Freddy stumbled. 'Can I have a word with you, Miss Loosemore?'

Not getting an immediate answer, he moved further into the light cast by a street lamp, puffing his chest as he looked up so that his raincoat would open a bit more to reveal that he was wearing a policeman's uniform. He hoped this would reassure rather than arouse suspicion.

Up at the window, Rita Loosemore debated with herself. Her first impression was that the uniformed stranger didn't appear to be dangerous or mad, and she was rather a creature of impulse herself.

'Just a second. I'll be right down.'

Her face disappeared from the window. She didn't seem such an unpleasant-looking wench, Freddy told himself; perhaps even somewhat *foxy*, in her own way. At least in the dark.

With a wary eye and a quiet step, Special Constable John Redwood pursued his investigation further into the darkened park. The winding path took a turn and cut through a mass of bushes, opening out into a large oval area. In the centre of the clearing was a bench, and on the bench reposed the huddled form of an old man. Casually and slowly, so as not to frighten him, Redwood walked across to the bench in plain view.

'May I?' Redwood asked the trouserless old man, gesturing to the bench.

'Certainly.'

Redwood removed his coat and gently covered and wrapped the old man's bare legs as he sat down next to him. 'It's a cold night,' he offered by way of explanation.

'It is . . . but don't you think the temperature is above normal for this time of year?'

Redwood kept a straight face but was nonetheless mildly surprised at the rational observation of an old gent who had lost his pants somewhere. 'I haven't thought about it.'

'One always wonders . . . you know . . . all this talk about the Greenhouse Effect. It could all be psychological, that we *think* the climate has got more temperate. After all, we're only talking about a few degrees.'

Yet the cold wasn't simply imaginary; Redwood could feel a chill coming on. 'It's still a cold night . . .' He tried to ease gingerly into his overture. 'Can I be of some help? I have a car. Perhaps I could see you home?'

Unsmiling, the old gent nodded. 'That would be most kind.' His frown deepened. 'Trouble is: I can't remember where I live. I'm sorry to put you to any trouble . . .' He tried to manage a brave smile. 'And to make things even worse, I must confess: I don't know who I am.'

Once again Section Officer Robert Loach marched into the swank edifice housing Miss Dowty's fashionable flat, this time in a different frame of mind. This time there was no checking in the mirror on the fourth floor. There was no presumption of innocence either, at least not from his experienced point of view.

This time she met him at the door in a negligée. A most revealing negligée. Satin and lace, and not much else. Black, elegant, infinitely smooth, though artificial and coarse next to her perfectly creamy alabaster skin.

She didn't say a word. Neither did he. She waited, obviously expecting him to come in. There was really nothing else he could do. With reluctance, remembering how hard it had been to extricate himself the last time, he entered her flat.

What Loach failed to notice was the predatory smile on Miss Dowty's face as she closed the door behind them.

Swaddled in a blanket, with a placid, vacant look in his eyes, the old man sat at a table in the Division 'S' Interrogation Room. Half-watching him over by the door, Police Sergeant Andy McAllister and Noel Weaver, a CID man, spoke in undertones interviewing WPC Morrow and Special Constable Redwood.

'You found him in the park, you say?' Weaver queried.

'That's right, sir,' answered WPC Morrow.

'But you haven't booked him?' asked McAllister, one eyebrow raised.

'Well, no,' she admitted. 'We can't have him for breach of the peace, since no one's made a complaint. We brought him in because he doesn't know who he is or what's going on,' she explained, then looked over at her partner. 'Special Constable Redwood wondered if he might be suffering from amnesia?'

McAllister seemed to consider the possibility doubtful. 'Hmm . . . In all my years in the Police, I've yet to see a genuine case of amnesia . . .' Weaver, the CID man, nodded in amused agreement, even less disposed to take the notion seriously.

'He does need to see a doctor, Sergeant,' Redwood quietly insisted.

McAllister shrugged. 'Don't fret. He's on his way,' the veteran recited in a routine monotone. He nodded to Noel Weaver, and they walked over to the old man, leaving WPC Morrow and SC Redwood behind.

Weaver leaned over and spoke in a loud voice, as if talking to someone who was hard of hearing. 'Now then, sir. I hear we're having problems remembering who we are? Anything come back yet, sir?'

The old man winced at the volume of the CID man's questions, but shook his head in reply.

'Any idea what happened to your clothes?' McAllister asked somewhat more gently.

Still the old gent shook his head. 'I do apologize. Believe me, if I could answer your questions, I would do so.'

'And you've no idea where you live, sir?' Weaver shouted.

'In a house,' the old man promptly responded, but then the flicker of light in his eye vanished and he hesitated. 'I have a hazy recollection of a largish house.'

McAllister was sceptical. 'That's not exactly helpful, sir. An address was what we had in mind.'

'It's curious.' The old man seemed genuinely puzzled. 'I can understand your questions, and marshal my thought processes with no trouble. But when I try to concentrate, I find myself looking at a complete void.' He stared into the empty space ahead. 'Oh, it's not frightening – curious, just curious.'

There was a tap on the door, and a PC entered with a cup of tea for the old man, who smiled warmly as he accepted it. Sergeant McAllister and Noel Weaver drew back for a private conference beside Redwood and Morrow.

'What d'you think?' the CID man asked McAllister.

'I think he's pulling a fast one,' the sergeant scowled.

Redwood couldn't keep a whisper of irritation from escaping, and McAllister was quick to turn on him.

'You don't agree, Mr Redwood. How do you read it?'

'If he's fooling us, as you suggest . . . then why? For what purpose? I look at him, and I see a confused old man.' Rather than oppose them, he tried getting them to grant the daft old codger the benefit of the doubt. 'Isn't it just possible we may always look first for the worst – and assume things from that point of view?'

'Aye, that's a possibility. Working in this place can make us all a wee bit cynical,' McAllister conceded, though in a patronizing tone. 'But supposing, Mr Redwood, that you're not in full knowledge of all the facts?'

Redwood gave him a wordless look asking what McAllister knew that he didn't.

The sergeant smiled benignly, yet like a magician with a trick up his sleeve. 'Earlier this morning, somebody torched a pillar-box . . . and the modus operandi is of particular interest.' The glint in his eye brightened. 'The computer has come up with three similar jobbies in the last two years.'

'That's right,' Weaver certified with smug satisfaction.

'Aye. You see . . . whoever sets fire to these post-boxes always uses a pair of trousers soaked in petrol to do it.'

Mocking his supposed gullibility, Noel Weaver pretended to take Redwood into his confidence. 'Better keep a close eye on Rip Van Winkle. He could be our nutter.' With a farewell grin, Weaver joined Andy McAllister, and they left the Interrogation Room together.

Morrow and Redwood exchanged looks, then turned to regard the trouserless old man. He smiled at them angelically, sipping his tea.

'I don't believe it,' WPC Morrow persisted.

Silent John Redwood, too, was having some misgivings as to whose side he should be on.

The empire chair he had escaped to the previous evening had mysteriously disappeared. By now Miss Dowty had progressed to pinning him on the two-seater sofa, using her delectable body to wedge him in tight. And by now his own resistance was weakening: stubborn, principled, and married as he was, no man could dismiss temptation from his mind forever. Or anyway, Loach warned himself that *he* probably couldn't last much longer. He, not she, was the one in danger.

'I do feel much safer with you in the flat,' she soothed him.

'Look, Miss Dowty . . .'

'Please call me Annabel.'

Briefly he wondered where this left official etiquette, but observed: 'I've checked the whole building. There's no sign of a prowler. Anywhere.' No sign of a cat, let alone cat burglar. 'You've absolutely nothing to be frightened of.'

He was also hemmed in by the sheer power of her negligée, especially as it kept sliding up, gradually revealing more thigh. What made it worse was that she, Annabel, was an extremely tactile person, and her right hand seemed to be creeping perilously close.

At the last moment, he made a move to rise to his feet, but she caught his hand and held it near to her bosom . . . so near he could feel her heart or his own heart beating madly, he wasn't sure which. 'Oh please . . .'

125

Loach not only found himself being pulled gently down again on to the sofa, but discovered his annoyance diminishing as well, and he was not sure he really minded, except that it was an unforgiveable waste of time, considering he was on duty. Now that she had hold of his hand, she showed no inclination to let go.

'A woman on her own is so vulnerable, don't you think . . . ? It was different when Geoffrey was here . . .' she continued with a faraway look.

Alas, his spirits drooped, sensing he was in for a life-story.

'He was in the services . . . the Army actually . . . course he's retired now . . . went back to Cornwall . . . his family came from there . . . You ever been to Cornwall, officer?'

'No.' He looked at his watch.

'I'd like to go to Cornwall . . .' she murmured wistfully '. . . but Geoffrey has things to sort out . . .' When her eyes met his, she was immediately back in the present. 'You're a lot like him . . . You know . . . always bustling . . . I suppose it's the uniform . . .' Her other hand began fiddling with his buttons. '. . . You know . . . men in uniform have a sort of inner authority. Quiet, but it's there. Women like that . . .' Her hand moved from his buttons to the sleeve of his jacket, and started to rise. '. . . Well, I do . . . Makes you feel secure.' Her right hand squeezed his. 'Have you been a policeman long?'

Slowly, her finger traced a path up his arm, and he began to realize that she would be bragging to her rich and supercilious friends that she could push him over with one finger. It was now or never.

'Well, actually . . . I'm not a policeman.'

'What?' she asked startled.

'I'm a Special. See?' He pointed out the badge on his upper arm just above her finger. But the badge simply intrigued her, and she traced *that* with her finger, as her breathing came harder.

'Special? You mean a *special* kind of policeman?'

'Er . . . No!' he exclaimed as she touched upon a sore spot. 'Not exactly. More like a . . . *reserve* . . . policeman.'

She was unable to conceal her disappointment. 'A reserve? I don't understand.'

'I'm a . . . part-time policeman,' he declared, at last finding the way out from under her thumb. 'I suppose you could call me a . . . temp.'

126

'A temp?'

She leaned away from him in disgust. Loach took her glance to mean he was off the hook.

33

Left alone in the Interrogation Room with Redwood, the old man seemed to want to tell him something, although he couldn't quite bring himself to say it. Agitated for some reason, he pointed to the double cassette recorder on the wall.

'Am I correct in assuming that's some kind of taping device?'

Redwood discerned that the old man was afraid the machine was listening and remembering whatever he would say. 'Yes. But its main purpose is to *protect* the individual . . . to show he hasn't been treated unfairly during interrogation.'

The old man spoke directly to the tape recorder in a loud voice. 'Everyone has been very polite and kind.' He winked at Redwood, and resumed their conversation in more confidential tones. 'There . . . that should go down well, don't you think?'

'Indeed it would . . .' Redwood agreed, 'but it's not turned on.'

The old fellow feigned disappointment, still it was clear he was relieved. He looked at Redwood, then glanced over at the door to make sure no one else was listening or recording, before redirecting his gaze back to Redwood. 'I'm puzzled. If you don't mind me saying so, you seem to be different from the other policemen.'

Seeing this as a compliment, Redwood gave him a shy smile. 'Oh dear. I hoped it wouldn't show . . . but I'm a new boy . . . And this is my first day on the job,' he confessed.

'That accounts for it,' the old man concluded. He searched Redwood's eyes before coming to some kind of decision.

'Look, I feel I can trust you, and it's imperative that I trust someone. But one has got to be so careful these days.' He looked around again, then became more secretive. 'Even those in authority might well be one's enemy. By telling you, I could be jeopardizing my life, and the lives of many people.'

His eyes were pleading. 'May I have your solemn word that what I am about to say goes no further than the walls of this room?'

Perplexed, Redwood nodded his assent.

The old man became reticent for a moment, then proceeded to tell all.

'They are quite right . . . your associates. I did set fire to what they charmingly call a post-box. Only, it isn't the innocent device they think it is. Oh, dear me, no.'

He leaned closer to Redwood, the inner flame burning hotter. 'It is something much more pernicious than that,' he warned. 'It is a drop-off point which enemies of the State use to disseminate the propaganda.'

Suddenly his voice became stronger and more urgent. 'My name is Walter Deighton. I am, and have been, for many years, an agent for MI6.' Redwood must have appeared a bit sceptical. 'Whether you believe it or not is immaterial. But what you must believe is the existence of foreign agents in our midst.'

Squeezing even closer to Redwood, the old man made a heartfelt appeal. 'I beg of you. Let MI6 know of my predicament.' He shared an ironic smile with his co-conspirator. 'Being apprehended was not part of my mission,' he explained apologetically.

Redwood stared at nothing, his thoughts confused by his feelings, as well as shock. Where to begin?

The door opened. Sergeant McAllister and the CID man Weaver, ushered a quiet, dignified lady over to the old man. She sat beside him, and affectionately gathered his hands in hers. He recognized her, looking at her with great pleasure evident in his tired eyes and face.

'Letty.'

'Walter? I was so worried.'

The old codger patted her hand in reassurance, then confided his weary burden to her. 'I hate carrying out these dangerous assignments, Letty. But someone must do it.'

'I know, I know,' she sympathized. 'Now. Do you feel strong enough to come back with me to the Institute?'

He nodded fervently, and she helped him to his feet, directing him toward the door. But first he stopped to conclude his business with Special Constable Redwood, and spoke directly into his ear in a low voice.

'Letty calls it the Institute. It's what we in the trade call a "safe house".' He patted Redwood's shoulder. 'You've been most kind, and I've enjoyed your company. We have a secret, you and I,' he whispered.

Letty guided him to the door and beyond, accompanied by Noel Weaver. McAllister stayed behind a moment, studying Redwood.

'It's a funny old world, Mr Redwood.'

He felt sheepish. A capable solicitor he was, perhaps, but still very much an *amateur* sleuth. 'I think I owe you an apology, Sergeant McAllister. I spoke too quickly when I seemed to criticize your judgment earlier.'

'If you did, I didnae notice it, man.'

However, Redwood didn't let himself off quite so easily. 'I made the error of assuming too much from too little.'

'Well, the Police are always getting stick for that too,' McAllister allowed, emphasizing their common bond. He shook his head, thinking back to the trouserless crackpot just departed. 'You know, the old man ups and does a bunk from the Institute every so often, when the urge is on him. And what's really weird is – it's always post-boxes he sets fire too!'

Unable to answer the larger questions, McAllister kept shaking his head in perpetual wonder as he started to leave. Redwood couldn't resist one final curiosity, and stopped him for a last word.

'There was one other thing, Sergeant.' McAllister cocked an ear. 'Did he . . . did the old man ever work, do you know, for security in some way?'

McAllister let out a boisterous belly laugh. 'Lord no! Why should you think that? No! He was some high-up in the Post Office . . .'

For once Freddy Calder couldn't believe his good luck, his own incredible domestic adventure. How many of today's women knew the first thing about preparing epicurean delights? Lightning had struck, he had discovered the one in a million! As they left her flat, she even helped him put his coat on.

'I've eaten you out of house and home, Rita.'

'It was only a sandwich, Freddy,' she replied ever so modestly.

'But – dee-licious!'

'I'm in catering,' she added. 'I should know how to make a decent ham sandwich by now.'

At this, sly old Foxy practically jumped out of Freddy's pocket. 'Takes one ham to know another!' he hammed it up in his best MacFoxy impersonation.

Laughing, Rita tickled Foxy's fuzzy nose, making Freddy bashful again. He banished Foxy back to his cave, and spoke to Rita in his own voice.

'Listen, I'm keeping you out in the cold. I only came to . . . well . . . you know . . . my mother and . . .'

Rita reached out a comforting hand to him; he didn't have to finish.

'There's no need. It's all forgotten.' The fair maiden searched in his eyes. 'I think you're very brave to keep your mother with you . . . at home. These illnesses old people get can make it so hard on their family.' She must have had a mother herself.

Again inwardly thrilled by his good fortune in finding a woman whose heart was in the right place, Freddy made his expression suitably distressed. 'That's true. You're very understanding. Some people can't make allowances for illnesses.'

'I don't know how you do it, and still have time to be a part-time policeman.'

'Special,' he gently corrected her.

There was an awkward pause while he rummaged around for the keys to his chariot.

His voice dropped to a lower pitch. 'I hope you didn't mind me bending your ear. Sometimes I do go on and on. It comes with the job, like,' he chided himself. 'Difficult to be a salesman and keep your mouth shut.'

Her face was lit by a beatific smile. 'Don't apologize. I enjoyed your company.'

Freddy nodded ecstatically . . . and shook her hand. All that build-up, all of that preparation, all of that warmth and sharing and understanding and repressed libido, and all he had the nerve to do was shake her hand! What a fool he was!

'Then goodnight, Rita. Maybe I'll see you . . . around?'

'Not here you won't.'

Freddy was suddenly apprehensive. 'Oh?'

'I'm moving.' He was crestfallen. 'I'm giving up this flat . . . remember?'

Ah yes, how the entire adventure got started in the first place. ''Course you are . . . well . . . sorry you missed the movie on telly.'

'Oh, it'll come round again. They always do. Drive carefully.' And she blew him a kiss.

Freddy wasn't sure that driving carefully was remotely possible right now, but he didn't really care. Whistling 'Zippity-Doo-Dah' and with a lightness in his step, he stopped to unlock the door of the glorious sapphire carriage that had brought him to this enchanted isle.

The Pub on 4th was fairly quiet, a few PC's and Specials sitting at tables and talking among themselves. Bob Loach stood at the bar having a soft drink when Sergeant McAllister came in and joined him.

'Orange juice, Briggsy.'

'Single or double, Sarge?' joked the barman.

'A single, lad.' Then he turned his eye to Loach.

'That woman called again,' he teased.

'Flippin' 'eck . . . not that Miss Dowty again!' He was livid. 'I don't believe it! I don't care what you do, Sarge, I'm not going round there again looking for the invisible man,' Loach vowed.

'Och, ye needn't bother yourself about that.'

Briggsy set down an orange juice in front of the sergeant, who took a long, noisy sip. Loach was still muddled about McAllister's reply, and waited for some further elaboration.

'Man, Loach, ye must have been an awfie disappointment to the poor lassie.'

'What do you mean?'

'Well . . . she asked me to send a *real* policeman this time, and no the substitute crater I sent before.'

34

What better way to spend an evening? His old Jaguar comfortably parked across the street from the gracious home of Miss Iris Davies, Ronald Hyde-Thompson picked up the large bunch of red roses lying on the passenger seat and breathed in their aroma. *Greensleeves* played on the car radio, he whistled quietly the bass harmony he had learned as a boy. He had always had a voice at the lower end of the register – yet a face that seemed young – for his age. Even now at the age of 42 . . . well, 44, actually . . . women often told him that he looked to be in his late 30's. It was his mind that had gone to seed, rather like the Jag.

Slowly approaching the Jaguar, two joggers bobbed along the

broad pavement, the male half of the pair shielding his eyes from the glow of the female's bright yellow track suit.

'Will you stop doing that?' she panted.

'Doing what, lovely?'

'*That*!' she grunted. 'Plus the snide remarks.'

A stone in his trainer, the male slowed down, while she kept jogging on the spot. 'All I said was you look like hot buttered sunshine, lovey.' He took the trainer off and shook out a pebble. 'What's wrong with that?' Losing his balance, he leaned on the Jaguar for support while putting his shoe back on.

Outraged at the brazen bum reclining on the bonnet of his car, Hyde-Thompson decided that this thoughtless, self-righteous health-nut needed to be taught a lesson. With an evil grin, he jammed his hand down on the horn.

The jogger leapt back from the bonnet, then glared angrily into the dark recesses of the Jag before joining his partner and jogging away, mouthing curses.

Coming from the other direction, Specials Bob Loach and Anjali Shah heard the Jaguar's horn and saw the jogger's reaction: he still had a sour look on his face when he jogged by with his partner.

Anjali noticed Bob scowl at the man before they turned their attention to the parked Jaguar.

As Hyde-Thompson glanced in his driving mirror and saw two uniformed persons on his tail, he quickly ducked forward and leaned across the passenger seat, pretending to be looking for something in the glove compartment. 'Toddle off, then . . . toddle off . . .' he sang softly under his breath.

Anjali and Loach took in the parked car as they walked by, noting the figure that crouched conspicuously low behind the dash. They walked past, careful not to arouse the suspicions of the occupant as he had theirs.

'Did you see that?'

Loach's silence indicated that he had. 'Let's go round the block. If he's still there when we get back . . .'

She nodded.

'Never trust a bloke with a Jag . . .' Loach chuckled.

WPC Sheila Baxter was trying to line up a sheet of paper on the photocopier while an anxious Freddy Calder hovered over and behind her, apparently bent on driving her batty with his impossible requests.

'Rita what?' she asked again, trying to get it straight this time.

'Loose something.'

She gave it up. 'Try the phone book. Let your fingers do the walking.'

'She's just moved out of her flat,' Freddy patiently explained.

'So?'

'So I don't know where she's moved to.'

Quite unconcerned, Sheila activated the photocopier. Her behaviour seemed so out of character: after all, he knew she liked him well enough. But now he hesitated to ask another favour.

'I thought . . . I might be able to use the computer.'

'Forget it, Freddy.'

'Nobody'll know.'

'Forget it.' She pulled the copy out of the tray.

'What if she's got a record?' Freddy persisted. 'You wouldn't want me to go out with someone with a record?'

'You're incredible. You met this woman once, and now you're planning a life together with her. With a bit of help from the police computer.'

'So what are you saying?' persued Freddy the Fearless. 'Romance is dead? Is that what you're saying?'

She wasn't sure whether he was being serious or what made him anxiously fiddle with a bit of scrunched-up tissue. 'What's that?'

'Nothing. Her old address, that's all.' He held out the tattered tissue for her to examine.

'Don't give it to me. I might catch something.' She put another sheet of paper on the glass, re-activated the photocopier, then took the tissue and gave it a closer look. 'Why don't you ask McAllister to get it genetically fingerprinted?'

Freddy was nearing exasperation. 'It's not her tissue. It's just got her address on it.'

'You've lost me.'

Just then WPC Morrow arrived to the rescue, breezing through while picking up her partner and dragging him along.

'Move it, Freddy. We're out of here.'

'Coming . . .' Yet he eluded her grasp, and tarried behind one more moment with Sheila.

'Don't think I don't know the real reason you won't help me.'

133

'Freddy!' his partner warned.

But Sheila was curious. 'The real reason?'

'You're jealous,' he declared, having finally figured out the solution.

'What?'

'It's obvious.'

Sheila stared at Freddy as though he were a foreign substance then motioned to his partner, WPC Morrow. 'Get him out of here.'

WPC Morrow proceeded to leave, followed by her deluded partner.

'Freddy,' Sheila reminded him.

'What?'

'You forgot to bag the forensic evidence.' Tentatively she held up the tissue between her thumb and forefinger and waved it in front of Freddy's face. Being very careful not to tear the tissue, Freddy took it from her and walked away with a shrug.

In the corridor outside Control, his partner was kicking her heels. But Freddy had a strangely dispirited look on his face and a flimsy tissue in his hand, prompting a reluctant twinge of sympathy.

'Sorry,' he muttered.

She took out a mini-pack of tissues and offered him one.

'What's this?'

'I thought you might like a clean one.'

Abruptly, a voice barked out from behind them. 'Report your positions.' They turned to find tonight's Despatcher, WPC Sheila Baxter, framed in the doorway, having just received a late report on the radio.

'I've got a job for you two . . .'

Outside some nondescript park gates, Bob Loach and Anjali Shah stopped to observe the Jaguar still parked in the same place. It was time for them to take the next step.

Meanwhile, Hyde-Thompson checked his wing mirror and noticed the same two uniforms coming his way. 'Are you two in orbit or what?' he said to himself, again leaning across the passenger seat and pretending to be looking in his glove compartment.

Loach looked at the rear inside tyre of the Jag. 'Bald as a coot.'

Hyde-Thompson was still pretending to hunt through the glove compartment when there was a sharp tap at the window. Trying to appear unalarmed, he turned slowly to see the uniformed gorilla smiling at him. He returned a most charming smile as he rolled down the window.

'Still not found it, sir?' Loach asked.

'I'm sorry?'

'You were looking through your glove compartment when we came by the first time.'

'Was I?'

'Is there a problem, sir?'

The man frowned a bit, as if reflecting. 'Well, nobody's life is without its ups-and-downs.'

'I meant with the car,' Loach corrected him. The man's eyes seemed to glaze slightly.

Hyde-Thompson peered out at the uniformed woman standing by the bonnet staring in at him, as though he were a fishbowl.

'You okay?' asked the uniformed man at the side window.

'Fine. Yes. And you?'

Having had more than enough chatter, Loach stood back. 'Would you mind getting out, sir?'

Without any protest the man got out of the car. 'Could I see your licence?'

'Yes. Why not?' He stared searching his pockets, eventually finding his wallet, extracting his licence from it, and handing the licence to Loach.

'Mr Hyde-Thompson?'

'When I last looked.'

'Is this your current address?'

'The car?' Hyde-Thompson chuckled at his own wit. The woman slowly grinned, although her mate remained impassive.

'I meant the address on the licence,' he said.

'Absolutely,' Hyde-Thompson proclaimed. 'I'm not some rootless vagabond, you know.'

'Can I ask what you're doing here?'

Immediately Hyde-Thompson became more diffident. 'I . . . wish you wouldn't. It's very delicate, you see.'

The gorilla didn't blink. In the meantime, his mate was spying into the car. Hyde-Thompson had to think fast.

'Oh – very well then. It involves a lady.' He went over to the woman at the car. 'I notice you've seen the flowers. That's who they're for. The lady, I mean.'

135

'They're lovely,' Anjali acknowledged.

Hyde-Thompson opened the car door, leaned in, and lifted the roses from the passenger seat. Removing one from the bunch, he offered it as if to a maiden.

She accepted his gesture as graciously as was appropriate under the circumstances, simultaneously observing that Section Officer Loach did nothing to disguise his expression of disgust.

'So this lady could verify . . .' Loach resumed.

'No! No, she couldn't,' Hyde-Thompson protested. 'That's the whole point.'

'I thought you said . . .'

'We've never been introduced, you see.'

Loach looked over to Anjali, only to find her eyes fixed on him. He frowned, beginning to realize how far short of old Sherlock's were his own modest powers of reasoning. 'Let's get this right. If she doesn't know –'

'I'm smitten,' Hyde-Thompson abruptly confessed, and instantly appeared to regret the indiscretion. '. . . That's what it boils down to. I've been reduced to worshipping from afar.' Around the edges he seemed to be cracking a bit, his eyelashes ever so slightly atremble. '. . . That it should come to this . . .'

'I'm still not sure . . .'

'I've been sitting here trying to pluck up courage to walk across the road and thrust these into the porcelain hands of the lady who lives there,' he stated directly, gesturing across the road to a rather large detached house.

He softened his appeal to Anjali. 'What would you do if you were me?'

She returned an enigmatic smile. 'I don't think you need advice from me.'

'I don't fool you for a moment, do I?' he inquired with a charming grin that would melt a taxman's heart.

Loach, however, was cut from a different cloth, more an unyielding serge. 'Did you know your tax disc is out of date, sir?' He had moved round to the other side of the Jag.

'Oh no. Surely not. It seems only yesterday I renewed it.'

'And you've got a bald tyre.'

'My MOT's due next month,' he offered by way of explanation. 'I was going to get everything done together.'

136

'You do have an MOT certificate, then?'

'Oh yes. I'm a great believer in all that,' Hyde-Thompson assured them without much conviction. 'That's why I'm simply stunned to learn my tax disc is out of date.'

Oddities, nuances of manner and speech, kept whispering to Loach that something about this would-be gentleman was amiss. Moving to the Jag, he aimed his torch inside, scanning the surfaces and corners.

On the back seat, protruding from under a tartan rug, as if it had been purposely concealed, was what appeared to be an oilskin package of some kind.

'What's that?'

'A rug. You never know when you might run out of petrol on the Pennines.'

'Under the rug,' Loach jogged him.

'Just some bits and pieces . . .'

'Such as?'

'You know – bits and pieces.'

'Do you think we could have a look?'

With great distaste and reluctance, Hyde-Thompson opened the back door, reached in, and retrieved the oilskin package.

'On the bonnet, sir,' Loach instructed.

Hyde-Thompson placed the oilskin package on the bonnet and stepped back, Anjali watching from behind him, as she had been trained, although she could hardly imagine him as someone who might be physically dangerous. Still, her job was to be prepared for any eventuality.

Warily, Loach unwrapped the package. Inside there were all sorts of implements – screwdrivers, hammers, glass-cutters, putty, jemmies – an awkward halfway house somewhere between the contents of anyone's toolbox and a burglar's kit.

Anjali couldn't hide her disappointment from Loach, nor did she try. What a shame, was all she could think at that moment.

'Some interesting bits and pieces,' Loach remarked.

Sorting through the tools laid out on the bonnet of the Jag, Loach picked up the glass-cutters and held them in front of Hyde-Thompson, who merely seemed ignorant of their purpose, as well as of their presence in an oilskin package that had been concealed under a rug in the back seat of his aging automobile.

137

'Yes – what is that?'

'Don't you know?' Loach queried.

'Not really,' Hyde-Thompson shrugged. 'It was in with all the other things,' he explained.

'A glass-cutter,' Loach enlightened him.

'Really! Well, you do surprise me.' He presented the roses to Anjali for safekeeping, then took the glass-cutter from Loach for closer examination.

In the meantime, Loach turned up the pressure. 'You see, sir, a suspicious mind might wonder whether you might be waiting for this lady to go out.'

'Go out where?'

'Anywhere.'

Hyde-Thompson appeared puzzled, not seeming to get the drift. 'Why would I do that?' he scoffed. 'I can hardly stuff the flowers through the letter-box.'

Clearing her throat to get Hyde-Thompson's attention, Anjali interjected a simple translation. 'I think he means it might be easier to gain unlawful entry to a place that's unoccupied,' she stated, unsmiling.

'Then he must think I'm . . .' Hyde-Thompson fell back theatrically against the Jag, as if he had just been administered a mortal blow. 'Oh, my dear fellow,' he moaned, 'if only you knew how hurtful . . . to be accused of *that* . . .'

'I'm not accusing you of anything, sir.'

His narrowing eyes gave the lie to Loach's official courtesy. 'So you think these beautiful blooms are nothing more than subterfuge then? That their only purpose is for such an occasion as *this*?'

Loach's expression suggested: Well, you said it.

Hyde-Thompson seemed incredulous that anyone should suspect him of all people. 'Do I look like a burglar? Do burglars dress like this?'

'They come in all shapes and sizes,' Loach informed him.

Nonetheless, the courtly Hyde-Thompson, rising to the occasion in well-pressed, innocent-looking clothes pleaded his case. 'I admit to being careless in matters of the road . . . tax discs . . . balding tyres. But I think you'll find in all other matters . . .' Judiciously he left the thought unfinished. 'Check for yourself. You have records. See if you can find one single black mark against the name of Ronald Hyde-Thompson.'

As if to call the witness who would clear his good name, he took several strides out into the road, then spun around to face his accusers.

'Well, come on, then. Let's ask the lady herself.'

This time Anjali was first to inquire. 'Ask her what?'

'If she knows of me.'

Immediately Loach jumped on the contradiction. 'You haven't been introduced – remember?'

'I said if she knows *of* me,' Hyde-Thompson corrected him. 'There's a difference,' he insisted. Then he turned and crossed the road to the house he had previously pointed out, Anjali and Loach following close behind.

35

WPC Morrow and Special Constable Freddy Calder climbed out of the panda car, and she quickly looked around, trying to get her bearings.

'This is the *top* end of Theobald Road?' she asked in a sceptical tone of voice.

'Well, it's not the bottom end,' he assured her once again, as it was unfamiliar territory to her.

Unfortunately, there appeared to be only one residence at the top end of Theobald Road that could possibly fit the address, and it was looming in front of them. Together they ascended the steps of a genteel Victorian house much in need of rendering and lick of paint.

Filled with righteous indignation, Hyde-Thompson glared at Loach as he rang the door-bell to the detached house. Anjali still held the roses.

'You can apologize now if you want,' he advised them in a low voice. 'It'll be less embarrassing than having to do it in front of the lady.'

The front door opened, and the lady herself appeared: a plainly miserable-looking, fifty-something hag wearing an ill-fitting coat salted with flakes of dandruff. Her queasy expression suggested one suffering from a chronically upset tum.

'Sorry to bother you, madam,' said Loach. 'We were just –'

'Mr Hyde-Thompson, isn't it?' the lady interrupted.

'Indeed it is!' he warmly confirmed with an audible sigh of relief, clutching her hand.

Loach seemed a bit miffed, Anjali thought. He spoke to the woman at the door. 'You know this man, uh . . . ?'

'Miss Davies . . .' Hyde-Thompson interjected. Then he looked at her, and his voice mellowed into a pleasant baritone. '. . . Iris.'

'Well, I know Mr Hyde-Thompson,' Iris Davies answered. 'He's usually at bingo. Of course,' she added, 'we haven't been formally . . .'

'Introduced?' Loach offered.

Lowering her eyebrows, Miss Davies began asking her own questions. 'What's he done? Why is he . . . ?'

Interrupting the proper order, Hyde-Thompson was quick to enter his version of a confession. 'You see before you a guilty man. These good people have found fault with my tax disc.'

'They're arresting you just because of your tax disc?' she inquired in disbelief.

Anjali tried to clear up her misunderstanding. 'We're not arresting –'

Miss Davies cut her short. 'I would've thought you'd prefer to go after real criminals,' she lectured them. 'Still what do I know?' She turned to Hyde-Thompson almost wistfully. 'You won't be at bingo tonight, then?'

'Alas – no.'

'Tonight's your bingo night?' Loach asked.

'Every Wednesday night,' Miss Davies affirmed.

Her answer suddenly rekindled his suspicions. 'So Mr Hyde-Thompson would've known tonight is your bingo night?'

'I haven't missed a night in three years,' she proudly claimed.

'Which is why I'm here,' Hyde-Thompson jumped in. 'To see if Miss Davies . . . Iris . . . wanted a lift.'

Gently taking the roses from Anjali, he gave them to Iris, his face beaming with hope and uncertainty.

She was stunned. 'For me?'

'For you.'

Loach unclipped his radio and aggressively buttoned it to sound, pointing to the Jag. 'No one's going anywhere in that thing – it's a death trap.' Then he spoke into the radio. 'Loach to Control. Over.'

Iris Davies stepped boldly forward. 'Then let me do the honours,' she proposed.

'He's not going to bingo,' Loach gently explained. 'He's coming down the station with us.'

'Control – over,' said WPC Sheila Baxter.

Loach spoke back to her into the radio. 'Request car to bring suspect to station. We're at . . .'

'You don't need a car,' Iris Davies interrupted again. 'I'll give you all a lift.'

Letting Miss Davies drive them to the station might be a bit unorthodox, Loach reasoned, but in this particular case it might just be the perfect solution. The whole affair might be cleared all the more quickly.

Hyde-Thompson was still gaping at his guardian angel. 'But you'll miss the first card . . .'

At times so dominant a force, Miss Davies now ducked behind her screen of diffidence once more, looking up into Hyde-Thompson's compassionate eyes. 'I can't go to bingo knowing you've been thrown into some damp cell . . .'

Loach spoke into the radio to WPC Baxter. 'Scrub that, Sheila. We're getting a lift.' But he wasn't especially pleased.

36

The monumental, ramshackle Victorian house on Theobald Road seemed an unlikely setting for a party gone wild enough to cause complaints. Indeed, the only sound drifted through from the conservatory, where the strains of *Eine kleine Nachtmusik* emanated from a record-player.

In the small, threadbare sitting room, Special Constable Freddy Calder was calling on Mrs Tovey – a tiny, fragile Miss Marple in her eighties with eyes as bright as a starling's – while WPC Morrow looked on in bewilderment as the elderly woman bewailed the mob riot supposedly taking place at that very moment in the conservatory only a few yards away.

'They just won't leave,' she complained. 'And they've drunk all the blackcurrant cordial.'

Freddy clucked and shook his head in an exaggerated expression of sympathy generally reserved for tiny tots (with whom he also seemed to have extraordinary rapport, WPC Morrow recalled).

'That's when I phoned you,' Mrs Tovey explained. 'I didn't want it turning into one of those acid-drop parties.'

WPC Morrow had to stifle her laugh. Freddy merely smiled. 'Don't you fret. Leave it to us.'

Nonetheless, she did fret. 'But I'm worried about what the neighbours might think.' The frail old lady began to break down, her hands trembling, her bright eyes clouding over and watering. 'I get frightened. I live here on my own, you see.'

Freddy cupped his hand over Mrs Tovey's, reassuring her in a calm, affectionate voice, as if bringing solace to the mother he never had. 'You know, you just have to pick up the phone, and we'll be round straight away.'

'It was meant to be a quiet birthday party . . . although I like people to enjoy themselves.'

Her birthday: a gathering of lost souls now completely unhinged by blackcurrant cordial and dancing in wild abandon to the tunes of Mozart on the record-player in the conservatory, raising a rumpus to wake the dead.

'It probably got out of hand when they couldn't agree who was going to have the next dance with you,' he intimated coyly.

'Oh my goodness – do you think so?'

Unable to distinguish between Mrs Tovey's fantasy and reality, the more pragmatic and prosaic WPC Morrow tried to elicit the basic facts. 'Who exactly are we talking about?'

Despite Freddy's gestures of silent protest, Mrs Tovey answered as if making an apology. 'Some friends of my husband.'

'Then why can't your husband –'

Mrs Tovey cut her off. 'Don't be silly, dear. He's been dead for donkey's years.'

A bit stunned by her announcement, WPC Morrow walked over to Freddy and put a short message in his ear.

'Can I have a word with you outside?'

He stopped her with one look.

'It'll have to wait. We've got these people to deal with first.'

As he turned toward the conservatory, the totally confused WPC Morrow started to follow him, until she felt a tug on her uniform.

142

Pleading with her was the withered old face of experience, still caring enough for the young and lively to pass along her hardened wisdom.

'This is a man's business, dear. There are some things a young girl like yourself shouldn't see. And men in that state is one of them.'

To WPC Morrow's added surprise, Freddy nodded his agreement. 'That's right, Morrow,' he said solemnly, 'You're too young for this sort of thing.'

Inflating his chest, squaring his jaw, Freddy faced the conservatory door, opened it with a bullfighter's flourish, and bravely advanced through the portal to confront the chaos within.

Once inside, he closed the door behind him. As he had suspected, the room was filled with nothing, except an old basket chair next to a cane table, upon which rested a portable gramophone and a forlorn bowl of African violets. Perhaps this is the eye of the storm then, he reflected with a smile.

Outside the conservatory, Mrs Tovey stood listening by the door. Yet WPC Morrow could hear Freddy's every loudmouthed word from where she stood back in the centre of the sitting room. All of a sudden the possibility flashed through her mind that a couple of trouble-makers *could* be crashing the old luv's birthday.

'Party's over, gents!' Freddy's voice asserted. 'Time to go home. Mrs Tovey wants to turn in . . .'

Abruptly there were some rumbling or scuffling noises from the conservatory, silenced by Calder's commanding order.

'Now then, sir, we'll have none of that! You wouldn't want me to start taking names . . .'

Then the music stopped, and there was quiet. Quickly WPC Morrow moved across the room with long strides, her path to the conservatory cleared by Mrs Tovey cowering back. But just as she reached for the door, it opened.

Freddy emerged the soul of tranquillity and calm, moving to pacify the hovering Mrs Tovey. 'I've made them go out the back way,' he assured her. 'We don't want the neighbours talking.'

Timidly, step by step, tiny Mrs Tovey approached the conservatory and peered inside, as did WPC Morrow. Then they went through the door into the empty room.

'Just look at the mess,' she lamented, surveying the spotless walls of what had once been a sumptuous conservatory but now lay bare as the last shadow of dusk. 'It'll take me days to get all this sorted out.'

WPC Morrow rolled her eyes at Freddy, while Mrs Tovey approached them with a sweet smile restored to her timeworn face. 'You'll both take a small glass of sherry?'

He gave her his warmest smile. 'I think it'll be all right, seeing it's your birthday. Don't you, Constable?' he inquired, turning to grin at WPC Morrow.

On a bench in the Division 'S' corridor outside the Interrogation Room, the widow Davies – Iris – sat and waited forever, clutching her roses, sniffing them, looking dreamily into the air specially perfumed for her pleasure.

Inside the Interrogation Room, an oilskin package was lying open and cluttered with tools on the table that separated Hyde-Thompson from his blunt, no-nonsense interviewer, Police Sergeant Andrew McAllister. The latter was doggedly sceptical, the former defensive. Standing by the door witnessing the interrogation were Special Constable Anjali Shah and Section Officer Bob Loach.

'I'm not convinced,' McAllister finally pronounced, shaking his head.

Hyde-Thompson appeared to be near his wit's end. 'Yes, yes, I see that. And I did so want you to believe me.'

'Maybe if you could remember the name of the man you borrowed this little lot from?'

For the hundredth time, Hyde-Thompson shrugged his shoulders. 'He was just a chap in my local. I never thought to ask his name.' McAllister raised a cynical eyebrow. 'Well, you don't, do you?' Hyde-Thompson went on. 'Not when you've just got chatting.'

McAllister sighed and went over the same story again. 'And he lent you this little lot so that you could repair a broken window in your flat?'

Hyde-Thompson nodded, a faint smile on his lips. 'Salt of the earth.'

'Someone he's just met?' Andy queried. 'I mean, what was to stop you walking off with all this?'

'That's what makes it so remarkable,' Hyde-Thompson reflected. 'The fact that there are still people out there willing to trust others on the basis of little more than a passing acquaintance.'

'I find that remarkable too,' Andy observed drily.

Hyde-Thompson was too rattled to notice. 'I was going to return it to him tonight.' McAllister didn't bite at that one either. 'In case he was in the pub . . . That's why I had it in the car,' he concluded, stitching the patches into a crazy quilt.

'You've mended your window then?' Andy prodded.

'Yes. Most satisfactorily.'

McAllister picked up the jemmy. 'I suppose you used this to spread the putty.'

'I didn't need to use that. It came with the . . . tool-kit.'

'A tool-kit? Is that what it is?'

'Look. I'll have to be toddling along soon,' remarked Hyde-Thompson, as fidgety as could be.

'Is that so?' McAllister asked. 'Why?'

'Well, we've still got time for a few more cards if we hurry.'

'Cards?' Andy asked him.

'Bingo,' Anjali offered in explanation.

McAllister nodded, then fixed Hyde-Thompson with an unblinking stare and gave his decision. 'Well . . . you'd better toddle along, then.'

'I'm not being booked?'

'You think you should be?' McAllister asked him soberly.

Without a word Hyde-Thompson arose to go and join the waiting Iris.

'Don't forget your . . . tool-kit,' McAllister reminded him.

Bob and Anjali were left open-mouthed as, hastily wrapping the oilskin package, Hyde-Thompson turned to leave. McAllister blocked his path, though.

'I want you back here first thing tomorrow. With driving licence and insurance and MOT.'

'Depend on it,' said Hyde-Thompson and made his escape as McAllister stepped aside.

'You're letting him walk?' asked Loach in disbelief.

McAllister held up his hands in surrender, as if there were no other choice and explained the facts of life to Section Officer Loach.

'You caught him in the act of sitting in his car. I sit in my car sometimes, too.'

'But he's as guilty as hell!'

Andy simply smiled and sighed. 'Guilty of what? Thinking on his feet?'

The oilskin package bundled unobtrusively as possible under his arm, Hyde-Thompson emerged from the Interrogation Room and immediately went to Iris, who welcomed him with open arms.

'Was it awful?' she asked, looking up to him as if he were a returning POW who had bravely endured days and nights of torture for her sake.

He gave her a quiet smile, playing his role to the hilt. 'They had your best interests at heart. That's all that matters.'

Gathering her roses and preparing to leave, Iris tucked her arm through his. For a second he seemed surprised, then lifted his shoulders, accepting her gesture with good grace.

37

An irritated WPC Morrow stood by the panda in front of Mrs Tovey's house on Theobald Road waiting for her partner. Meanwhile, on the steps of her dilapidated castle, the octogenarian duchess was holding onto Freddy and saying her fond farewells.

'Guess,' she teased him.

'Sixty?' he ventured.

'I'm eighty-five,' Mrs Tovey proudly blushed.

'You're not!' he bantered.

'Today was my eighty-fifth birthday.'

'You could've fooled me.'

His partner's voice called to him from below. 'Let's go, Freddy.'

He kissed her gnarled hands. 'Got to go, love. You take care of yourself.' He blew her another kiss and went on his way.

Freddy came down the steps, waving back at her; and Mrs Tovey returned the wave, then disappeared into her ancient castle.

WPC Morrow finally had the story all figured out. 'You've been here before,' she accused him pointblank.

He didn't deny it. 'A couple of times. In fact, every time she has a birthday.' His straight face started to crack.

'I suppose it would've spoilt your little joke to tell me.'

'You should've seen the look on your face!' Freddy burst out laughing, till she clipped him on the back of the neck with her shoulder bag.

'Watch it!' he warned. 'Don't blame me if you didn't get his autograph back there.'

'What autograph? What're you talking about?'

A serious look on his face, Freddy went down on one knee, still looking up at her. 'Mick Jagger's!'

'Mick Jagger?' she repeated in amazement.

'Mrs Tovey throws some wild parties,' Freddy confirmed, then fell about, helpless with laughter. WPC Morrow was not amused.

The discussion was still going on when Freddy and Morrow returned to the Division 'S' building.

'Who gets to write her up, then?' Freddy taunted her. 'You or me?'

'She'll end up being sectioned if I do it,' replied the unrepentant Morrow.

'Not if you use invisible ink,' Freddy suggested.

Suddenly a booming voice called out to him from the rear. 'Mr Calder?' The severe Police Sergeant McAllister stood behind the desk at the back of the entrance office.

Freddy shared an anxious look with WPC Morrow and muttered: 'If Baxter's dropped me in it . . .'

When he got into McAllister's office he saw that the sergeant had evidently just interrupted a conversation and hung up the telephone.

'Before you say anything, Sergeant, I never actually used it.'

'Used what?'

'The computer.'

McAllister stared at him as if he were mad as a programmer, then changed the subject.

'I've got something to show you.' He beckoned the mystified Freddy and led him through into the cell area.

Down the corridor at the door to one of the Interview Rooms, McAllister stopped and pointed to the glass.

'Have a look at them.'

Freddy peered through the glass. 'Ring any bells?' asked McAllister. Freddy recognized two familiar faces: Number One and Number Two from the builder's yard.

'The security men. Came across them patrolling this builder's yard up on the industrial estate a few weeks back.'

McAllister's mouth turned into what passed for a smile. 'If they're security men, I'm your Aunt Mary.'

'What?'

'They were helping themselves to building materials when you came across them,' McAllister informed him.

Aghast, Freddy peered into the cell once again, seeing the pair in an entirely different light.

'It's their gimmick,' McAllister continued over his shoulder. 'If they run into trouble, they just tell everyone they're security men. You can't beat a nice bit of protective colouring. Ask a chameleon.'

Freddy shook his head. 'I knew something wasn't right about them . . .'

'And what about the dog?'

'The dog?' he said, with all the nonchalance he could muster. 'Oh yeah. Right. The dog.'

'People tend to be less diligent in pursuit of the truth when they have a slobbering great beastie sniffing at their private parts.'

Swallowing hard, Freddy kept a brave face. 'I wouldn't let a dog put me off the scent . . . Off the scent – geddit?'

McAllister nodded. 'So you won't mind identifying the dog, then?'

Freddy's heart sank like a stone. 'You mean . . .'

A happy man at last, McAllister nodded and let out a piercing whistle.

From around the bend, Bas, the Alsatian hound from hell, came lolloping down the corridor at Freddy, who jumped out of his skin through one of the cell doors, clanging it shut behind him.

McAllister rubbed his eyes: Freddy had vanished. Bas wagged his tail as he obediently awaited him outside the cell door.

An evil grin on his face, McAllister walked over, kneeled down and gently patted the animal. Then he stood up, stepped in front of Bas, and tapped at the cell door before going in.

Freddy was a pile of quivering jelly that didn't look up to greet him.

'Dog's made quite an impression on you, I see. I take it this is a positive identification?' He even smiled.

38

Every day Anjali was finding it more difficult to relate to the members of her family when they were all together. This morning her mother and her Uncle Ram sat side by side at the kitchen table happily cooing over the picture of Rani, who was to be Sanjay's intended. Yet in the meantime, Sanjay himself picked at his breakfast with the same old nonchalance, pretending not to care in the slightest about this woman chosen to be his wife. It was this kind of attitude in Sanjay that drove Anjali to distraction, try as she might to keep herself from turning against her own brother.

'So very beautiful,' Mrs Shah sighed, admiring the picture of Rani, her eyes glistening with hope for her only son. 'Oh, Sanjay, you can only find happiness with such a girl as this.'

Sanjay paid no attention to her, concentrating instead on scraping the charred flakes from his burned muffin.

'There is so much to do,' Uncle Ram enthused, excited by his own central role in the process. 'The betrothal will be on us before we know it.'

Irritated, either by the food or the conversation, Sanjay pushed his breakfast away. 'There's plenty of time.'

'Everything must be in readiness,' Uncle Ram counseled. 'If everything isn't in readiness, matters will badly back up on us and bring shame to the family.'

Just then Anjali rushed into the kitchen doing up her coat, in a hurry to get to work. Right away her mother was upset.

'You miss breakfast again, Anjali. You never sit down and eat with your family anymore.'

'No time. I'm late.' She quickly poured some coffee and swigged it back.

'You don't get enough sleep. You come in late again last night . . .' She threw up her hands helplessly.

'It's because she does two jobs,' Uncle Ram started in. 'She's not content with one job. She has to do two.'

Anjali sat down on the edge of a chair to slip on her shoes, as her brother looked down at her with disdain.

'My wife shan't work.' His arrogance was deliberate.

'Does she know that?' Anjali threw back.

'I'll forbid it. It's the man's role to work. Women satisfy his needs and see his food is prepared.'

'You might find she has other ideas.'

Sanjay stood up, fuming. He took two steps toward her, threatening, as she backed away.

'She'll be kept away from you!' he warned her. 'Forbidden to come near you. Women with your ideas should be strangled at birth.'

'How do you know which babies will develop bad ideas?' she taunted him. 'By the way they cry?' She gave him one last defiant scowl and marched out.

Behind the cash desk in the main office area of the Bromsgrove Building Society, Viv Smith was serving a customer who was just another number.

'How would you like the money? Tens?'

The customer nodded, and she counted out three ten pound notes, sliding them under the glass with his passbook. The transaction was entirely impersonal, and she felt a bit like an industrial robot.

The customer walked to the door, then held it open for someone coming in . . . but this was someone she knew – Rob Barker, her Sub-Divisional Officer.

Tensing up in spite of herself, she noticed that Rob Barker smiled nervously at her, as if hesitant about going to her position.

'You're stuck with me, I'm afraid.' Viv pointed at the light over her position, and he came forward.

'How are you, Viv?'

'Fine. And you?'

'Oh – you know,' he muttered noncommittally.

'Putting it in? Or taking it out?'

That woke him up, but his face was a blank. 'I'm sorry?'

'Money.'

'Oh – I see. Neither.' He looked beyond her. 'I'm here to see your Mr Maynard.'

Viv left her position and came round the door at the side, unlocking it for him.

'Actually I might well have taken out a few quid if I'd remembered my passbook.'

'A bit extra for the weekend?' she smiled slyly at him.

Again he put on a blank expression. 'What?'

'Lunch at *The Game Bird* must leave you short,'

150

'*The Game Bird*?' Still feigning ignorance. At least he could admit the dalliance if someone clearly knew where he had been dilly-dallying.

'I thought I saw you in there last week. With Sandra Gibson,' she teased.

He shook his head after a moment. 'I don't think so, Viv. *The Game Bird*'s not my sort of place.'

She smiled to herself, but didn't contradict him. The customer was always right. Standing aside to let him through, she then shut and locked the door.

A coach backing out of the garage area nearly ran over a smallish man coming into the yard at Cougar Coaches. He dodged out of the way and shouted up to John Barraclough in the cab.

'Mr Padgett?'

'I don't think he's in yet.'

Barraclough resumed backing the coach, as Bob Loach, in his overalls, walked over from the garage to see what he could do for the perplexed stranger.

'Can I help?'

The smallish man looked round. 'I have to talk to Mr Padgett.' His diffident manner seemed to combine timid and stubborn in equal measure.

'He's not coming in today.'

'Do you know where he is?'

'Well . . .' He wasn't sure what to say.

'He will want to speak to me. I promise you.'

Loach thought a moment, then motioned to the stranger to follow him, and started back towards the office.

Back at the coach, John Barraclough got down out of the cab, then walked a few steps staring quizzically in the direction Loach had taken the stranger. Barraclough knew that man: it was Timson.

Rob Barker . . . Rob Barker . . . Barker . . .

Mr Maynard hadn't found a moment to brief himself in advance, so now he had to hunt through a thick file on Barker while keeping up his end of the conversation. Barker was sitting on the other side of the desk.

'You're moving to Edinburgh?'

'My wife's idea. She was brought up in Edinburgh.'

151

'Let's see now. The house has been on the market for . . .'

'Three months.'

'And the house is in your wife's name?'

'Yes.'

'And the flat . . .'

'. . . is in my name.'

At last Maynard stumbled on the section of the file for which he'd been searching. 'And now you want to sell the flat?'

'The flat too,' Barker amended. He happened to catch the eye of Viv Smith looking at him from the main office area. Coincidence or not, that left him no alternative: he would have to come clean.

'This is going to sound strange . . .'

'Strange?'

'I don't want my wife to find out about the other property. The flat, I mean.'

Not batting an eyelid, Maynard went back to what he had been reading. 'As you wish.'

'I realize there's not much chance of her finding out in the normal course of events. But there'll be a lot of correspondence going back and forth over the next few weeks, and . . .'

'Put your mind at rest, Mr Barker. The sale is on your property. Your wife won't know.'

'I wish it were as simple as that.'

Maynard looked up at him once again. 'How do you mean?'

Rob hesitated, then sighed. 'It concerns one of your staff.'

Maynard was unprepared for this development. 'My staff?'

'Don't get me wrong. Viv's a lovely girl and all the rest of it . . .'

'Viv? Viv Smith?'

'I'd rather she didn't know more than is absolutely necessary about my private affairs . . .' He could feel Maynard staring into his skull. '. . . for reasons I'd rather not go into at this stage.'

'I'm not sure . . .' Maynard began.

'She talks, Mr Maynard,' he said bluntly, reminding himself again that this precaution was absolutely essential. Closing his eyes a moment, he lowered them to the desk, and forced himself to go on.

'Viv tends to make shortlived liaisons with all sorts of people . . . and she's not exactly the soul of discretion.'

'I assure you, Mr Barker, the society prides itself on client confidentiality.'

'I'm sure the society does.'

'Very well, Mr Barker,' said Maynard after a pause. 'I'd better make your file off-limits to our Miss Smith.'

Rob breathed a sigh of relief and avoided any further visual contact with Viv.

Back behind the cash desk, Viv sat pensively, staring into space and wondering what was going on between Rob Barker and Sandra Gibson . . . or Rob Barker and his wife for that matter. She shot another staple onto the counter. Business was slow today.

39

In the office of Cougar Coaches, the smallish man stood above the desk talking on the telephone to Dicky Padgett. Listening in, Loach was rinsing his hands at the sink in the alcove.

'Just make sure you're there, Mr Padgett. I've had enough wild goose chases for one day . . . No – make it one-thirty. I've got a lot of people to see and I'm running late.' No goodbyes – just slammed down the telephone.

Loach emerged from the alcove wiping his hands on a towel. 'I'm his partner. If this is something that concerns the company –'

The smallish man cut him short. 'I'm sure Mr Padgett'll be able to tell you that.' He picked up his case and walked to the door, turning and looking back at Loach. 'Thanks for the use of the phone.'

John Barraclough came into the office as the little man left. He slowly shook his head. 'He's the last person I expected to see here.'

'You know who that was?' Loach asked him.

'Timson. He's the competition.'

'The competition?'

Barraclough nodded. 'He works for Redbird Express. He's their Financial Director.'

Not much of a recommendation – the money man in a losing operation.

Viv Smith watched Mr Maynard unlock the partition door for Rob Barker and usher him through the customer area, finally shaking his hand and bidding him farewell. Briefly Rob looked across at her, showing a weak smile before leaving. Mr Maynard was still looking in her direction. She didn't care for his expression either.

Freddy fluidly wheeled his classic Sierra into the parking lot of the large department store and into the bay marked by a white 'RESERVED' placard: 'MANAGING DIRECTOR ONLY.'

Getting out, he removed his sample cases and laid them on the ground, leaving the curvaceous cut-out, Salvador Dolly, though barely covered over her target areas, lying on the back seat. He locked the car and, late though he was, stopped long enough to apply a little spit and polish with his hanky to a smudge on the sapphire bonnet.

On the far side of the lot Freddy spotted a security guard – only the top half of his burly body showing above the other parked cars – and he thought the security guard spotted him as well. Oops, time to get moving. Bending over to pick up his sample cases, he was summoned by a very loud and insistent voice.

'Hey you! Stop right there!'

Nonchalant, Freddy waved at him cheekily, then grabbed his cases. 'Yeah, yeah, yeah!' He turned to leave.

The voice shouted even louder. 'I told you to stop!'

Freddy halted, with exaggerated weariness, and turned to face old Georgie. 'Look! What's your prob –'

The blood drained from his head. It wasn't old Georgie, but a new, younger replacement. And that wasn't the worst of it. Now in the open, having cleared the other cars, the new security guard revealed that he also had a powerful new *dog* straining at the leash.

'Identification!'

'Awe, Goddammit!' Freddy was sweating hard and shaking.

'You've parked illegally. You're carrying suspicious cases. I need identification, sir.'

Freddy was exasperated as well as terrified. 'Look! You must be new. I'm a salesman. I always park here,' he explained carefully so as not to disturb hungry doggie. 'Is this really necessary?'

The security guard nodded in the direction of the reserved parking bay. 'Oh! You make a habit of this then?'

The guard's growl seemed not unlike his overgrown dog's, surely an evil omen.

*   *   *

154

Its rear door open, the bus rested in front of the entrance to the General Hospital. As Simon Redwood positioned his wheelchair on the raised platform, a male nurse moved closer to help, but Simon raised a restraining hand, backed up by a surly stare.

'So what's the programme today?' he asked with a heavy load of sarcasm. 'Ten laps round the hospital grounds? I know,' Simon decided, 'why don't I sit here, and *you* do the exercises?'

Walking by, Anjali Shah heard the last remark.

'It's all a bloody waste of time.'

Although she was almost sure he recognized her as well, he offered no sign of it. As soon as he reached the ground, he rolled himself quickly toward the hospital entrance.

Anjali turned back to the bus and watched as the nurse prepared one of her elderly patients to alight. She waved cheerily to him, calling to him in a loud voice. 'Hullo, Mr Worthington! See you in a couple of minutes, alright?' He saw her, and moved his fingers in a valiant attempt to wave back.

A world of difference. A young man with all the time and nothing to live for; and old man with not much time and everything to live for.

John Redwood rummaged through the papers on the desk in the office of his home, then yelled for Stella.

'I've had Spencer on the phone to me again,' he said with barely concealed irritation when she arrived. 'He says he hasn't had the deeds yet.'

'I got them off in the post this morning.'

'You'd better ring and tell him.'

She went to leave, when he found that he couldn't refrain from having a word with her about Simon and getting the resentment out of his system.

'You're not his housekeeper, you know.'

'Sorry?'

'You've been tidying Simon's room again.'

Though pinned, she remained elusive. 'I thought now'd be a good time. While he's down at the hospital.'

'It's not your job,' he reminded her. 'In fact, I'd rather –'

Quickly she interrupted before he could forbid her from ever doing it again. 'It's just that your cleaning lady refuses to go in there.'

'Only because he's so bloody rude to her.' Looking at Stella, he appraised her capacity to put up with the behaviour of his son. 'You'll get the same treatment if he realizes you've been poking around in his room.'

Stella offered an alternative explanation. 'I don't think he likes her. She treats him like a yob. She doesn't see the wheelchair anymore.'

'Good,' he nodded. 'That's the last thing he needs. To be constantly reminded he's in a wheelchair.'

'But she's so . . .'

'He's got to come to terms with it,' his father insisted, clumsy at hiding his concern. 'We can't pack him in cotton wool! If we keep making allowances . . .'

'I think,' said Stella tentatively, 'I think he misses . . .'

'What?'

'His mother.'

'I only wish his mother was here. But she isn't. End of story.'

'It's just that for something like this to happen at his age . . .'

'I know what happened to him, for God's sake!' He controlled himself and continued. 'He's got to make an effort, too. That's all I'm saying. He's got to meet the world halfway.'

'I don't know how you can be so calm,' Stella protested. 'The people who did that to him are still free. They're still out there.'

'So what do you want me to do about it?'

Tired of paternal responsibilities, he slumped into the chair behind his desk. 'I'm sorry. I don't mean to take it out on you.'

'I don't mind,' she said.

'You better ring Spencer.'

40

The stark, unartistic photographs on the table in the Division 'S' parade room simply documented vandalized playground apparatus – knotted chains on swings, rungs on the ladder for the slide hammered out of place, that sort of thing. Yet the cumulative effect made the message clear enough. One of the fundamental amenities of a civilized society – a proper place for young children to play – had been denied to the very people it was intended to serve.

Section Officer Bob Loach was taking parade, and he was indignant about this one, as it involved damage concentrated in a single location, clearly a case of intentional destruction.

'The Lancaster Street play area.'

'Looks more like a breaker's yard,' observed Special Constable Wally Harris, a middle-aged madcap of substantial bulk.

'It does now,' Loach agreed. He looked out at their faces – Anjali Shah, Freddy Calder, Viv Smith, John Redwood, and the others . . .

'Some of you will be on stake-out up there tonight. Just in case whoever did this decides to finish the job.'

'Is that likely?' Viv popped up.

'Is what likely?'

'That he'll come back.' She seemed dubious.

'You tell me,' Loach answered. He started to collect the photographs. 'Okay – two teams of two. Tommy Rose and Steve Northcott in one. And Viv Smith and John Redwood in the other.'

'Watch out for Viv in the bushes,' sniped Wally Harris.

'Very funny!'

'Wally's group leader,' Loach continued. 'He doesn't want to see any of you. Stay well out of sight. It's just Wally and the night and music . . . and his dog, of course.'

'Dog?' queried Freddy, instantly tensing.

Wally Harris saw the issue from a somewhat different perspective. 'Mr Redwood gets Viv, and I get a dog. Does that tell you anything?'

'This dog's not called "Bas" by any chance?' asked Freddy.

'You're not playing, Freddy,' Loach reminded him. 'WPC Morrow's your child minder for the night.'

'Again?' he whined.

'She's not exactly over the moon herself,' he remarked with a smile.

Police Sergeant Andy McAllister was doing a slow circuit of the Interview Room, retracing a series of possibly related events and information that might form a criminal pattern. His attentive students were Bob Loach, standing like a soldier, and Anjali Shah, sitting and looking at the file (although, he had learned from experience, always listening as well).

'What pattern?' asked Loach, curious.

'Someone's going round specializing in lonely women. That's all we know.'

157

Not a quick thinker, perhaps, Loach nonetheless learned his lessons thoroughly, methodically. 'And you think our friend Hyde-Thompson might be that someone?'

'Let's put it like this. We've come up with two other victims who went to the same bingo hall.'

Loach snapped his fingers. 'I knew it. He didn't strike me as the type who spends his spare time playing bingo.'

'He's also done a tour of some of the other clubs in the area,' McAllister added. 'Or someone very like him has.'

'He's done his market research,' Loach remarked, giving the devil his due.

Anjali looked up from the file, a frown disrupting her usual composure. 'He couldn't have done all this,' she concluded. 'He's just not good enough. Look what happened last night. He didn't even get as far as the front door.'

Loach offered the easy explanation. 'He's had a run of good luck, that's all.'

'Maybe he'll come up smelling of roses, who knows?' Andy asked rhetorically, obviously not believing the possibility for a moment. 'In the meantime, this Miss Davies has a right to know what's been going on. Let her be the judge.'

'Shouldn't CID . . . ?' Anjali started to suggest . . .

'She's met you two,' the sergeant answered simply. 'A visit from CID might put the wind up her.'

Anjali shut the file and pushed it away. McAllister saw the gesture, picking up on her scepticism. He tried to explain why precautions were necessary.

'He might decide to put her on his list for a later date.'

Apparently she was in no mood to hear his sage counsel. 'Do you really think he'd be so silly as to . . . Sorry,' she concluded on observing his sharp, stern look.

Dressed in plain clothes for their undercover operation, Specials Viv Smith and John Redwood walked along the edge of the Lancaster Street play area, although they didn't make much of a pair. It didn't take much to see that he was tense, preoccupied. She wondered if there were any hope of this strong, silent type ever being playful.

'We don't exactly look like a couple out for a stroll.'

158

He smirked, remembering all the couples he had known. 'Oh, I wouldn't say that.'

'I suppose we might pass for a couple who's just had a row,' she suggested.

'Well, let's build on that, then.'

Viv stopped suddenly. 'I take these things personally, you know.'

'Take what personally?'

'The fact that you look as if you'd rather be anywhere than here.'

'That's not because of you.'

'Oh yeah?' She tossed him a cynical grin over her shoulder and walked on.

Caught by surprise, he had to quicken his step in order to catch up with her. 'Honestly. It's not because of you.'

She stopped again, looked him over, smiled and offered him her arm.

'Maybe we ought to try to look like a couple.'

'A couple who've just made up,' he added with a grin. He put his arm through hers, and they carried on walking.

41

Slumped lethargically in the seat of the cruising panda car, Freddy stared out of the window. Though at rest, his mind was as alert as a karate instructor's, and suddenly he jolted forward.

'Pull over!'

'What?' asked WPC Morrow, her state of alertness obviously not on the same level with the karate instructor's.

'*Pull over!*'

She hit the brakes, and the panda squealed to a halt alongside a parade of shops on High Street.

'What did you see?' asked WPC Morrow, now on her toes and ready to leap into action.

'A doner kebab place.' He started to get out, then remembered his manners. 'You want anything?'

'No.' An Uzi perhaps, loaded.

'Sure?'

'Positive.'

159

He got out of the car. She shut her eyes and rested her head against the wheel, heaving a long sigh as she imagined the scene where she blindfolded him and offered him a last cigarette.

Viv Smith sat on a park bench with John Redwood in the children's play area talking quietly. Her conversation had been anything but puff and pastry, and he actually listened to her ideas, a compliment most unusual among men, in her experience.

During a lull in her chatter, she dropped a pebble into his pool of silence: 'I don't imagine you go in for this much.'

'What?'

'Sitting on park benches with women at this time of night.'

She coaxed another smile out of him, although his eyes were far away.

'I was young once, you know. I know it's hard to believe . . .'

'You're not old,' she ventured, flirtatiously. She found him a bashful boy.

'Usually get treated as if I am, though. I suppose it comes with the job.'

'With being a Special?'

'Being a solicitor.'

Ah, money talks. Probably well set financially. A lonely gentleman, needing someone to share his home and wealth . . .

The barking of a small but loud dog interrupted her reverie. The little mongrel bounded up to her and licked her leg, pursued by Special Constable Wally Harris, also in plain clothes.

'It's off,' Wally called out, abruptly announcing that the mission had been scrubbed.

'Why?' Redwood asked.

'Mine's not to reason why,' said Wally with a shrug.

'We haven't been here an hour yet!' Viv protested. And just when things were going so well . . .

'By the way – there's no van,' Wally added. 'It's Shanks's pony, I'm afraid.'

'Great,' Viv sighed.

'What about me?' complained Wally. 'I've been walking the pooch around all this time. I'm not used to so much exercise.' His girth confirmed the truth of his statement.

Nonetheless, off he went across the park with the mongrel, while

Viv and John headed in the opposite direction. When they got to the roundabout, she couldn't resist and decided to have a go, hoping a special someone might join her.

She pushed as fast as she could, then jumped on and rode round, shouting to him: 'Come on! Let your hair down!'

He cupped his hands and shouted back. 'I'll pass.'

'Chicken!'

'I'd get dizzy.'

Viv let the roundabout slow down slightly before she leapt off. Not slow enough – centrifugal force threw her off balance and she landed flat on her back in the dirt.

He rushed over to her. 'You alright?'

'No bones broken,' she said, battered and bruised though she felt – and more than a little embarrassed.

He helped her up, and she brushed herself down. Yet he appeared angry with her.

'That was a silly thing to do. You could've hurt yourself.'

'Kids like me never get hurt. Kids always bounce back.'

The flash of pain that passed across his face instantly informed her that she had just committed the worst possible blunder, bringing back the memory of his crippled son. She was mortified at her unintentional cruelty to someone she had the least desire to hurt.

'I'm sorry. That was a dumb thing to say. I didn't mean . . .'

He dismissed her apology with a weary wave of his hand, as if it were unnecessary. 'It's time we were getting out of here.'

He walked away. Damn! She had just blown whatever rapport they had been developing. Already she was feeling the loss.

Bob Loach and Anjali Shah stood before the front door of the large detached house of Miss Iris Davies. He rang the bell again and looked at the upstairs windows.

'Maybe it's not working,' she conjectured. 'I didn't hear it ring.'

'Or maybe she's gone to bingo.'

The door now opened, revealing Iris Davies, although she was a different woman altogether. Gone were the baggy clothes, the greasy hair and flakes of dandruff, the scrubbed face. In their place were the features, cosmetics, and accoutrements of a woman who, though still in her fifties, looked quite elegant, as if she'd gone to work on herself.

She greeted them graciously, although her frown suggested they vaguely recalled to her mind some unpleasant association.

'Sorry to bother you again, Miss Davies,' Loach began. 'Only we've had some more information through on a series of burglaries in the area. And as we believe you were almost a victim of one of them . . .'

Her frown deepened, yet the door opened further. 'Won't you come in?'

They entered, and followed her through the hallway to the living room. In the meantime, Loach was trying to apprise her of the facts as they were now known.

'The thing is, Miss Davies, we're fairly certain that this Mr Hyde-Thompson is in some way . . .'

He dried up. Directly before them was Hyde-Thompson himself, ensconced in front of the TV: tie loosened, top button undone, jacket off, looking much at his ease.

'Well – hullo there!' he greeted them with a chuckle.

With utter distaste, WPC Morrow watched Freddy Calder, sitting in the passenger seat next to her, chomp on his doner kebab. Pointedly she rolled down her window to allow the smell to escape, although it would have to wend its way past her nostrils in the process.

Whether she personally had a taste for the food Freddy ate was of no consequence: he always transformed the meal into a shared experience anyway.

Specials Bob Loach and Anjali Shah sat bemused in the living room as Hyde-Thompson poured tea for them, Iris Davies looking on proudly. Seeming to be in his element, Hyde-Thompson dominated the conversation with a certain glib charm.

'So basically, this fellow's going round robbing lonely women?'

'Something like that,' Loach confirmed.

'Astonishing. Truly astonishing.'

Iris gazed upon her newfound protector. 'Well, he'd better not try anything with Ronald here.'

'Don't worry, my angel. I'll give him a bloody nose if he turns up.'

Having poured the tea, he resumed his place in the best chair, Iris sitting next to him on the arm, and launched into a lecture on contemporary morality. 'What's wrong with people, eh? The world today . . . grab . . . grab . . . grab. Everyone'd be much happier if they listened to that still, quiet voice inside them.'

Loach remained sceptical. 'And what does your still, quiet voice tell you, Mr Hyde-Thompson?'

'That money and possessions eat at the soul and leave a big, empty hole inside you.' Loach, he noticed, looked unconvinced. 'Hardly an original notion, I know, but I find it's worth taking out and dusting down from time to time. There are, after all, just more important things in life.'

Placing a protective arm round Iris, he put his feet up on the coffee table, but she would have none of it.

'Feet off the table, Ronald.'

He complied in an instant, quite unabashed.

Freddy rammed the carton that had contained his doner kebab, plus all the slime and goo that came with it, on to the dashboard, then wiped his hands on the cheap paper napkins.

'That was rubbish,' he declared.

'I noticed you finished it,' observed WPC Morrow, turning up her nose.

'I was hungry,' he said simply. Then be belched, leaking toxic fumes into the atmosphere.

Grabbing the kebab carton, she climbed out of the car, walking from the panda to a nearby wastebin. After making a big show of stuffing his garbage into the bin, she started back, but her attention was distracted by the sight of a young man weaving drunkenly from the pub opposite to its adjoining car park.

'Freddy!'

He got out of the panda and came over to her.

'It's breathe-in-the-bag time,' she told him, indicating the drunk on his way to the car park.

The suspect was somehow familiar to Freddy. He stared at the man, studied him . . .

Then he recognized him. It was the burly security guard from the department store parking lot! The new one with the nasty attitude. The one with the dog.

Freddy wiped his mouth, leaving a greasy smile on his lips.

'Definitely.'

42

Special Constables Viv Smith and John Redwood walked in silence down a dark roadway past a complex of warehouse buildings in an industrial estate. While there wasn't a soul in sight, nor had they heard a pin drop, still the power of imagination set their nerves on edge.

'I promise you it's the quickest route,' explained Viv, a bit apologetic.

Suddenly they both saw a dim light flickering inside one of the windows of a warehouse shed, identified by a sign proclaiming Exarco Chemicals Plc.

'Security guards?' he wondered, his voice in a whisper.

'So what's wrong with the light switch?' she asked, the next logical question. Something looked peculiar here.

Just then his eyes were drawn to a panel truck jutting out from behind the building. A shadowy figure jumped into the back.

'I'll radio in,' Redwood whispered, unclipping the instrument and buttoning it to sound.

Fumbling with his keys, the inebriated security guard stood by his battered Capri in the car park adjoining the pub he had just stumbled out of, as WPC Morrow and a grinning Freddy Calder came up from behind to watch.

'How much have you had to drink, sir?' she asked the burly guard.

The question didn't disturb him much; it was the keys he couldn't figure out, occupying most of his concentration.

'Just the one.'

'You won't mind taking a breathalyzer test in that case,' she said.

'Get knotted!'

Freddy took a step toward him and reached for his arm when he noticed something else – framed in the car window was the snarling guard dog who had been the security man's companion when they met the first time. Freddy froze.

The security man smirked at Freddy, wobbled backward, and waved his fingers at the mad doggie in the window. The dog put up a paw and scratched at the glass, yipping to join him.

At that moment Freddy realized the canine monster was locked in the car and couldn't get out, so he unfroze, and turned to the guard.

'You make a habit of this, then?' he said with obvious relish, savouring his revenge.

The befuddled guard stared at Freddy with a strange expression, as though recognition was just about to dawn on him.

There was always the chance that the gang could pack up and be gone before the police arrived, so John and Viv agreed that they would have to get close enough to see the number of the van. They moved gingerly, creeping quietly into the warehouse complex, keeping close to the wall. Finally, worried about being detected, Redwood grabbed her.

'That's far enough.'

'I can't clock the number from here,' she whispered.

'We don't need to clock it. If the cavalry are about to arrive . . .'

'If this lot aren't gone first . . .'

Peeking out from behind the corner, they saw a moving figure walk to the van and climb into the cab.

Viv pulled John back flush against the wall.

'Did he see us?' Redwood asked her nervously.

The man in the truck thought he saw something over by the far corner of the warehouse. He wasn't sure, maybe it was nothing, but he was spooked anyway. Taking a torch from the glove compartment, he decided to have a look. He opened the door and got out of the van, taking a crowbar along with him just in case.

'Great,' Viv muttered. Now they were in danger of having their heads stove in.

Thinking fast, she tore at the buttons of her blouse. 'Give me your hand,' she urged him. 'Do exactly what I say!'

The look-out man slowed to a crawl. He thought he could hear something, but so far the beam of the torch revealed nothing out of the ordinary. He stopped short of the corner of the building to listen. There *was* a noise, a rustling of some kind, a groan. Something was there. He gripped the crowbar.

Jumping to the side, he turned the beam into the corner to catch whatever it was by surprise.

The beam of the torch caught Viv and John in flagrante delicto

– his hands clutching at her breasts, her naked leg stretching around his waist – moaning breathlessly.

On the other side, hidden from the beam of the torch, Redwood's thunderstruck face pressed tight against Viv's, as he prayed for them to get away with the ruse.

'You two! Go and bonk somewhere else! This is private property!'

Awkwardly they started to unlock and pull back, averting their faces and trying to move away.

The man with the crowbar permitted himself a lecherous grin as he picked out another glimpse of her unbuttoned blouse with an exploring stab of his torch; then he switched it to his own path and hurried back to the van.

Half-running from the warehouse complex back to the road, Viv and John were laughing noiselessly, out of breath, both mightily relieved. As they reached safety, four squad cars glided silently toward them and the gate of the warehouse complex. Suddenly their headlamps blazed on, transfixing the 'lovers' once again in a broader, brighter beam of light, although Viv's blouse was not quite so open to the elements as a few moments ago.

The police cars pulled up just in front of them. A uniformed officer came over in a hurry to get the basic facts, then motioned to the others. Soon they were springing from the cars and running toward the warehouse.

As he was on his way to join them, the officer stopped to have a quiet word with John. 'Oh, Mr Redwood – I'd clean up that face if I were you . . . because if that's not lipstick, you'll bleed to death.'

Blushing red herself, Viv turned to John to check how flagrant he really was. Sheepishly looking after the departed officers, he wiped his smeared mouth with the back of his hand.

43

At the Pub on 4th, WPC Morrow stood at the bar pouring tonic into the gin Briggsy had just brought her. Letting the liquids blend, she looked round the room that was beginning to get busy and saw Freddy sitting alone at a table. Now that duty was done for the day, she decided it was about time for her to forgive him for being what he was. If the world had to have its Freddy Calders, the real one had some unexpected qualities that, even she had to admit, sometimes proved surprisingly helpful. There was, after all, something to be said for Freddy: a man like him volunteering his time as a Special said a lot. Indeed his genuine concern for those who were most helpless was an endearing virtue, despite all his foolishness.

So she picked up her drink and a beer bottle and walked over to the table where Freddy was sitting.

'I got you a drink.'

A look of incredulity flickered across his face. 'I'm on non-alcoholic. I'm driving.'

'I've got you non-alcoholic,' she announced in triumph, sitting next to him and setting her drink on the table. 'Is this your glass?'

'Yes.'

With slow application, she pantomimed pouring beer from what was, alas, an empty bottle into his empty glass, even adding the glug-glug-glug noises higher and higher as the glass supposedly filled up. Then she handed him the full empty glass.

'What's going on, Morrow?' he frowned, not quite sure how to take it.

'It's a special. A special for a Special.' She raised her own glass. 'Enjoy! The old lady's guests drink nothing else.' It was her turn to laugh.

Freddy twigged . . . then allowed himself a grin, clinking his empty glass against hers.

'Cheers.'

Redwood followed Viv into the Division 'S' parade room like a skittish puppy worried about supper. She, on the other hand, was on top of the world, cool and rather amused, as she sipped on a warm coffee. She guessed what was on his mind – thought she might wind him up a bit.

Even the silent type couldn't hold out forever. 'So how are you going to write this up?' he blurted at last.

'How do you mean?'

It pained him to find and say the words.

'Well, one of them actually spoke to us.'

'He did – yes. Rude boy.' Little Miss Innocent hunted through her bag, seemingly paying no attention to him. 'Got any matches?'

'I don't smoke.'

This was trouble. She really couldn't find any matches.

Still, he hesitated. 'Will we actually write what he said, or . . .'

'Or what?'

'Or doctor it slightly.'

To her surprise, his worry was serious. She grinned coyly at him. 'You're not suggesting we tamper with the truth?'

'Well no but . . . we could say he didn't *actually* see us . . .'

'But he did see us. He said –'

'I know what he said!' he interrupted.

Must not want to think about it, she thought, or even hear the words. 'And you a solicitor too,' she teased him. 'Shame on you.' After further chaotic rummage she finally found some matches and lit her cigarette.

'I'll make it sound convincing. Whatever I write.'

The grin spread across her face as the gin-and-tonic she spilled spread on her sleeve.

The Pub on 4th was quite full and hopping with activity and conversation. All sitting at a table near the door, Bob Loach, Anjali Shah, Viv Smith, John Redwood, and Andy McAllister were engaged in a lively discussion, as usual, talking business. Loach was leading the debate, expounding on his vast ignorance and confusion about the gentler sex.

'All I'm saying is that I'm surprised she fell for it. No way is this Hyde-Thompson interested in her.'

'She's interested in *him*, though,' Anjali countered.

'She should have more sense,' he scoffed. Surely an old girl must have enough brains to ask herself why a smooth operator was trying to sweep her off her feet, he reasoned.

'How do you know she can't see right through him?' Anjali asked.

'Then why . . . ?' Loach started.

'Maybe she's prepared to take the risk,' Anjali suggested. 'What did she have before? Bingo every Wednesday night. At least she's got someone now.'

Andy McAllister – Old Reliable – was the official sceptic as always. 'Until he disappears with her life savings in his body-belt. And guess who she'll come running to then. Us, that's who.'

Loach disagreed, preferring his own scenario. 'He's made a tactical withdrawal, that's all. He's keeping his head down for a while.'

Redwood spoke up for once. 'Or maybe he's just . . .'

As everyone stopped to listen, he stopped talking. At that moment across the table, Viv was extracting from her bag the slightly scrunched-up report she had prepared. She then turned to Andy McAllister next to her and stuffed the report in his hands.

'What?' Loach asked.

'Doesn't matter,' Redwood shook his head. He had forgotten what he was going to say anyway.

Dismissing the distraction, Loach resumed his diatribe. 'Well, she deserves all she gets, that's all I can say. She's as bad as him in my book. Anyone who can go for Hyde-Thompson badly needs her hormones MOT'd.'

This was the typical male attitude that most annoyed Anjali, or maybe it was just the male of the species in general. 'Men have no idea what women find attractive. It's not always Paul Newman, you know.'

'That's right,' Viv chimed in. Out of the corner of her eye, she saw Noel Weaver, the CID man, about to weigh into her for defending her sister feminist. 'Maybe,' she pursued, 'a woman might prefer someone like him to the company of some . . .'

Weaver's rough hands came down on her shoulders, as he stood immediately behind her, but she ploughed on regardless: '. . . of some boring macho males I could mention.'

'So did these guys at the warehouse see you both or what? I'm hearing conflicting stories,' Weaver put in.

'No,' said Redwood; 'Yes,' said Viv – simultaneously.

McAllister was first to pounce. 'Get your alibis sorted, boys and girls.'

'And they didn't carve you up?' Weaver inquired with tactful professional concern.

Redwood floundered. 'Well, they did tell us to clear off.'

'To clear off, eh?' Weaver queried with a derisory snort.

'That's not exactly how it happened,' Viv stated.

Weaver looked at her. John looked at her. Everyone looked at her. 'So how did it happen?' Noel inquired.

'You wouldn't believe me if I told you.'

Redwood winced.

'Try me,' Weaver offered. 'One day we may need your expertise.'

She ignored his sarcasm. 'We took "evasive action".'

Looking at the floor, Redwood started moving his hand up slowly to cover his face.

'Evasive action?' Weaver led her on.

She paused, making sure they were all hanging on her every word, especially John.

'We threw caution to the winds and made mad, passionate love. Just like in *Body Heat*. It somehow made our reason for being there more . . . convincing.'

They all turned to a speechless John Redwood, who showed every sign of wanting to crawl into a hole and die.

Weaver laughed in total disbelief. 'With him!? What're you trying to tell us? This guy's Tom Cruise?'

The entire gathering laughed. It seemed as if the entire pub full of PC's and Specials laughed. Redwood sank deeper into the hole.

Viv gave him a loving smile. 'Don't let appearances deceive. You know what they say. It's always the quiet ones.'

Sergeant McAllister had opened the report and was scanning the pages for the relevant section, anticipating the discovery with a heavy frown.

'I hope you haven't cluttered this up with these . . . fantasies,' he growled.

'Ah well, you see . . .' She glanced across at Redwood, his eyes pleading with her to show him some shred of mercy '. . . I guess we just got lucky,' she confessed.

Only John Redwood caught her sly wink, as he recovered from his second brush with death that evening.

II

•••••

Ask 'em, Tell 'em, Lift 'em

1

Shoppers drifted through the open-air mall in their never-ending search for bargains. Denzil looked at only one store, and although the shop was having a sale on hi-fi's and CD players and all sorts of gear to reproduce the music he loved, he could only afford to look. He was 18, of West Indian extraction, and hearing his music had much to do with the way he experienced life. Music was just about all he had, and he didn't have much of that.

Wondering how much time he had left before he had to go home, Denzil checked his watch. It didn't move. He shook his wrist, hard. His watch was dead. He scouted around for a nearby clock instead.

Elsewhere in the crowd, a weedy teenager was eye-balling the same window, though not for the display of discount placards as loud as the shop's ghetto-blasters. He was looking for something, and someone, else.

His gaze flicked through the shoppers in the area, then locked on two punks, male and female, lolling indolently but ready to spring into action. A silent signal passed among the three, and they switched their attention to the fourth, who was also a teenager, this one black and female, although you'd scarcely know her sex from her hair-style and clothes.

An inclination of her head pointed to a well-dressed Asian woman laden with packages walking in the crowd: their next target. She checked that all of them were in position to execute their individual assignments, but abruptly there was a delay, since the target had been detained by another shopper.

Denzil asked the woman the time, and she reacted as if he had asked for the moon. She had to shift her packages in order to look at her wrist-watch, and she had to let him know that he was wasting her valuable time as well.

Denzil was none too bothered by the old woman, and went back to his window-gazing. The woman shifted her packages again and moved on.

At this point the quartet lunged from the crowd to descend on their prey. Bystanders were blocked, the Asian woman was smacked, and the handbag was ripped from her fingers – all in one coordinated motion.

In a flash they were gone, already melting into the crowd.

The Asian woman was down on her knees screaming. To many of the bystanders, this was the first sign that anything was even amiss.

Not far away, a PC and a WPC heard the screaming. When they got to the victim, she was surrounded by curious shoppers. She was staring wildly at the surrounding bystanders, and they were all a multiple mirror image of her. As she was being helped to her feet by the WPC, she recognized a face in the crowd and screamed once again.

'That's him!' she shouted, pointing at Denzil.

At first he froze. On second thoughts he streaked away like a cheetah, darting through the puzzled crowd and breaking clear.

Denzil had a way of running on the balls of his feet, a fluent motion that seemed to terrify ordinary people, especially whites, with his cockiness: people tried to get out of his way.

Racing to freedom, he flew from the crowd behind him and finally turned the corner, only to plough into the arms of two constables running to the scene of the crime from the other direction.

When he realized he'd been caught, he resisted with all his might, twisting and tugging, but his struggles were of no use. The two constables wrestled him to his knees.

Stella helped Mrs Taylor through the corridor of John Redwood's home into the waiting room to his law office. Struggling with two heavy plastic bags, which she insisted on carrying herself, and clutching a wrinkled piece of paper with an address scribbled on it, the distraught Mrs Taylor was anxiously complaining in a strong West Indian accent.

'I gotta see the man. You know. The man written on the piece of paper. They said I should come here.'

'Of course,' said Stella soothingly. 'Well, look . . . come on in, and I'll see what we can do. Let me help you with those.' Stella relieved the woman of her shopping bags and placed them firmly against the wall in plain view where Mrs Taylor could keep her eye on them. Then she showed the woman to a chair beside her desk.

'The people down at the court said I should see Mr Redwood. But I tell them I don't have no money. But they say you go see Mr Redwood.' She talked faster than most people could run.

'That's quite right. Mr Redwood is a Legal Aid solicitor.' Stella reached for a notepad and pen. 'Now, I'll write a few particulars. To begin with, I need your name.'

'Me? Oh, my name is Verna Taylor.'

'And why do you want to see Mr Redwood, Mrs Taylor?'

Immediately she became defensive. 'Oh, it's not for me. It's my son, Denzil. He been arrested by the Police. But he didn't do nothing . . .'

'Of course . . .' Stella tried to sympathize, but also tried to stop the woman's chatter in order to pin down the basic facts, such as her son's full name, age and so forth.

'. . . I come from the islands thirty years ago. We never had any trouble with the Police . . .'

The door to the office opened, and John Redwood appeared, shepherding a client out of the room. Mrs Taylor acknowledged his presence, but kept on talking, evidently not wanting to lose Stella's attention.

'I been working at the railway station for twenty years. I'm a cleaner, you know . . . Denzil's father, he died. He was my first husband. An' my second husband . . . he and Denzil don' exactly get on, if you know what I mean?'

Stella attempted to postpone Mrs Taylor's life story for a moment, as John joined them. 'Excuse me, Mrs Taylor.' She took him aside for a hurried, whispered conversation to let him know she hadn't learned much of anything other than what he had just been hearing.

John went over to shake Mrs Taylor's hand. 'Mrs Taylor, I'm John Redwood. Your son – Denzil? – is in some difficulties, I gather. Do you know what he's being charged with?'

She put her face in her hands. 'They sayin' he stole something from a woman down the Arcade,' she said, shaking her head in denial. 'But I tell you, Mr Redwood, he's a good boy.'

175

He reached out to touch her shoulder, urging her to rise. 'Let's go into my office, Mrs Taylor, and we'll sort it out.'

'He never been in trouble,' the upset mother continued as he ushered her into his office. 'An' it's not his fault he out of work, Mr Redwood. He used to 'ave a good job down at the carpet place, but Denzil and half the people were sent home. I swear you . . . I know my child . . . he not a thief, Mr Redwood.'

He nodded. 'I'm sure he isn't . . .'

And he wondered.

2

Lying on a pallette, young Kevin adjusted his body, then signalled to Loach, who helped slide him under the bus. He was teaching the lad about lubricants and hydraulics, while works manager John Barraclough, leaning against the bonnet and chewing his lip, was giving Loach a status report at the same time.

'I don't think the Daf'll be ready for a week, Mr Loach.'

'Tsk . . . damn!' Bending down, he guided Kevin with a patience he didn't feel. 'Can you see it, Kevin? It looks like a big nipple . . .' That ought to hold him.

'I'm looking, Mr Loach,' Kevin called out, eager to succeed.

When he stood up, Barraclough met him with other problems. 'I think we'll cover the bookings we have. Any more and we'll have to get the spare pans from old push bikes.'

'Aye . . .' he agreed, though shaking his head no.

Behind them, a young man wearing a backpack strolled into the yard at Cougar Coaches, scouting around before catching sight of the two men by the bus.

Barraclough narrowed his eyes at the young man approaching them. 'Is that Derek?'

Loach turned to look. 'Aye, it is!'

Delighted to see his younger brother, he rushed to greet him, and just as they were about to embrace, instead they clutched one another by the forearm. Recognition of the distance in their close relationship always awakened in him the same twinge of wistful regret.

'Surprise, surprise, Derek!'

''lo, Bob.'

'I didn't hear you say you were coming?'

Derek nodded to John Barraclough as someone he knew. 'Mr Barraclough.' Then he returned to his older brother. 'I didn't know myself until a coupla hours ago, to tell the truth.' He tapped the side of the bus and grinned at Barraclough. 'Still sticking them together with Sellotape, I see.'

'Aye, and you're still as cheeky as ever, young Derek.'

'It's what they teach them nowadays at Police Academy,' Loach let drop with a bit of pride.

Kevin's voice called out from under the bus. 'I think I've found it, Mr Loach.'

'Well . . . whatever you do, Kevin, don't –'

Too late. They heard a coughing wail, immediately followed by Kevin shooting out from beneath the bus, his face and the upper half of his body drenched in dirty oil. Hiding his smile, Loach thumbed toward the oily mess. 'That's Kevin. Latest member of the firm. If you can still hear me Kevin, this is my younger brother, Derek.'

Tilting his head in the direction of the office, he led Derek away.

'See you later, Mr Barraclough,' Derek waved. 'Nice meeting you, Kevin.'

Barraclough stared down at the miserable lad trying unsuccessfully to wipe his face clean. 'Well, well, well. Let this be a lesson to you.' He shook a finger at Kevin. 'Never lay your hands on anything that looks like a nipple unless you're damned sure you understand the consequences.'

Seeing his brother again after a time always brought some satisfaction to Bob Loach, along with the bittersweet memories that came back with him. They had come a long way from a poor background and a tough childhood for Bob, and then for Derek. He never wanted to see brown paper on his windows again, or live in 'back-to-back' street housing, or share wash-houses and lavatories with the neighbours, as he had in his father's day.

Their father, Reg – Reginald Chadsey Loach – had been a tool and die worker, never more than a basic artisan, although he kidded himself that he was more skilled than his employers ever gave him credit for. So he lurched from job to job, and bar to bar . . .

Nevertheless, he had instilled in Bob a love of all things

mechanical. Yet lung cancer prevented him from staying around to witness the blossoming of Bob's engineering skill, or his climb out of poverty.

And so, at the age of fourteen, Bob found himself a surrogate father to Derek, a toddler of two. Their mother never quite recovered from the death of her husband. She would go shopping in her carpet slippers, or wandering on bitterly cold days in a thin print dress. The Police were frequent visitors, escorting her back home.

One sergeant in particular took it upon himself to protect their mother from mockery, as well as try to keep her out of a state institution.

A few years later, she died. Bob was eighteen, He had been a grease monkey in a garage for two years. Derek was six.

By that time, they both called the sergeant Uncle Dave. He figured in both of their lives until his retirement, when he moved out to the West Country, and Bob still felt guilty about losing touch after all these years.

They had grown apart. Uncle Dave was bitterly disappointed when Bob rejected his advice to join the force and let his 'hands be dirtied with diesel' instead. He resented Bob's basic motivation to get along in life and 'make a million,' while still fulfilling his responsibilities as a concerned citizen. It was only a minor victory for Uncle Dave when Bob was eventually inducted into the Specials. From Uncle Dave's perspective, the real and only hope was always Derek.

At long last, it was finally about to happen. Derek would soon fulfil his dream and graduate from the Police Academy. The very thought of it unloosed a torrent of memories, doubtless in both of the brothers.

As soon as Noreen saw Derek come into the office, her face lit up, and she ran to embrace him. 'Derek!'

'They gave him a few days off before the big examination,' his big brother explained. 'I told him we could pitch a tent in the garden for him.'

Noreen unclasped Derek and let him breathe. 'I've got my fingers crossed. Though why anyone wants to be a policeman these days is beyond me.'

Derek raised his hand to his face and crossed his fingers as well. 'I still have to pass first.'

'You'll pass,' she assured him. 'At least someone in the family has brains.'

'You're right, Noreen,' said her husband. 'He got the brains. I got the looks.'

'Pity you left them out in the rain.'

Derek shook his head with a grin at his elder brother, who pretended a crestfallen look as if to say: You can't win against *her*.

Noreen turned her attentions to his younger brother. 'Derek, you must be famished.'

He made a move to protest.

'Don't shake your head. The Loach family is always hungry for something.' She addressed her husband directly. 'Why don't I take Derek back to the house?'

'Good idea. I've got a few loose ends to tidy up, and then I'll come join you for tea.'

'Listen,' Derek finally interjected. 'I don't want to take you away from your work.'

Noreen had got all her things together, and she wasn't about to be dissuaded. 'I've been waiting all day for my Prince to come and take me away from all this, so don't start.' She tucked her arm through her brother-in-law's. 'Come on, Derek. Let's make a few tongues wag.'

On their merry way out the door, they bumped into Dicky Padgett on his way in. After an awkward readjustment, Dicky grabbed Derek's hand.

'Hullo, Derek. You Chief Constable yet?'

'Gimme a year,' he grinned.

'Hello and goodbye, Dicky,' quipped Noreen, moving past him.

With a smile, Dicky checked his watch. 'You going, Noreen?'

'You betcha. Watch my smoke.'

He stepped out of their way, watched them go, and shut the door behind them. 'He's a likeable chap, is Derek,' he offered by way of conversation.

Loach nodded, waiting for his partner to come to the reason for his rare visit.

'I see you've a new lad in the yard.'

Frowning, Loach shook his head no.

'Black chap. I just saw him with Barraclough.'

The penny dropped. 'No . . .' he chuckled. 'That's Kevin. He's finding out that buses need oil.'

Padgett didn't budge a smile. There was a pause, as he picked his moment.

'I may have landed us something really big, Bob . . .' he began slowly. 'A Spanish company . . . in Barcelona.' (*Barthelona* he said.)

'Oh aye?'

'They're talking fat contracts if we can show them we're big enough to handle their business,' said Dicky casually.

He scribbled a number on a notepad, ripped off the top page, folded it, and pushed the paper across to Loach.

Pretending to be a bit indifferent, he picked up the paper, unfolded it, read it, somehow managed to keep his eyeballs from popping out of his skull, and flopped back in his chair, electrified.

Satisfied with his reaction, Dicky released his own pent-up triumph with a little chortling. 'Pretty good stuff, eh? What price now you making it as the first millionaire Special?' He smacked the table with an open palm.

'Flippin' 'eck!'

Abruptly Dicky turned and stared out the window into the yard. ''Course we need to guarantee we have the capacity.'

The alarm clock tripped off in his head, alerting Loach to another set-up by his so-called partner. 'What?'

'We need to accommodate a thousand bums for starters.'

Loach sagged in his seat, and his heart sank. 'That's not on. I've just been speaking to John Barraclough. We're up to our eyebrows already. We're cannibalizing coaches to keep others on the road.' He shook his head back and forth. 'And do you know how long it takes to get new stock – let alone raise the finance? I'm still waiting to take delivery of that supercoach we ordered.'

'We can't wait for new stuff. Look . . .' The partners faced each other. '. . . I'm not an idiot, though you sometimes think I am. I've done my homework on this one . . .' A twinkle appeared in his eye. 'Let me run a name past you – Redbird Express?'

'They're crap. What about them?'

'Something a little bird told me.'

Loach snapped his fingers. 'Of course. That guy Timson who was looking for you. Isn't he their accountant?'

Dicky brushed the reference aside. 'It never hurts to have the inside dirt, Bob. Anyhow . . . the word is that Redbird Express're going down the toilet. Bust. Caput. Only a matter of time.'

180

'No wonder. Their vehicles are clapped out junk!'

'I can get them cheap.'

So Dicky had it all figured out, Loach thought. All the ducks were in order . . . except the partner.

'You don't hear me, Dicky. I said they're only fit for scrap.'

As it turned out, Dicky was every bit as frustrated with Loach's conservative stance: long-buried hostility resurfaced, only thinly disguised by his voice. 'Bob? Listen to *me*, Bob, for a change.'

He paced around the small office. 'You and Barraclough are magic with your hands. That's the difference between us and Redbird Express. It's your know-how that got me into this crazy business in the first place.'

Dicky stopped in his tracks, then sat immediately opposite Loach, staring into his eyes. 'Listen. I want this contract. And I think you want it just as badly. Don't make your mind up now. Sleep on it.'

Then he leaned closer. 'But, Bob . . . I don't want to lose this one.'

3

The old Victorian building where Division 'V' was headquartered, and where John Redwood, solicitor, was interviewing a client, stood in stark contrast to the modern Division 'S' headquarters, where John Redwood, Special Constable, based his efforts to apprehend suspects such as the one now sitting across the table in the Interrogation Room.

Truculent, angry, aggressive, Denzil Taylor was a black man caught in the gears of a pervasive white society. He was being defended by a white solicitor, and as much as Redwood tried to understand and sympathize with this young man, he knew that there was infinitely more he would never understand.

Still, for this seething young black man, Redwood was his only hope, the one chance he had, so the solicitor must do the best job he possibly could. Part of that job was telling his client the hard truth, and in this case, the situation looked bleak, especially considering the defiant, uncooperative attitude of the defendant.

Redwood avoided his eyes, fingering the file lying on the table.

'The Police will ask you to answer certain questions. You're not obliged to say anything that might incriminate you.'

Denzil was of no mind to consider bureaucratic procedures. 'Hey, man. How many times do I have to tell you. I didn't do nothing. I'm looking in a shop window. The Paki lady screams. I go to see what's happening. End of story. You understand, or am I talking too fast for you?'

At least he had some brains, some ability to reason. 'The Police say you were running away from the scene of the crime . . .'

'Cos I'm the only black face in the place. And the Paki's screaming at me.'

And his reasoning made some sense. 'Well . . . my job right now is to get you bail so you can go home. I don't need to tell you how worried your mother is.'

At the mention of his mother, Denzil exhaled a world of troubles; distress momentarily replaced contempt in his eyes.

'I know . . . But I can't pay no bail.'

'Leave that to me.'

'I don't take no charity, man.'

'It's your right. There's no charity involved.'

For once, Denzil seemed to digest a morsel of information. He paused to consider. 'Then what happens?'

'They'll set a date to hear your case.'

He scoffed, the closest he could get to a sense of humour. 'That's gonna be a joke.'

'Not if we get our facts right, and put on a damned good show.'

Denzil merely aped him. '"A good show?" Oh, I get it. You want me to put on a suit, and a tie; get my hair cut; don't wear sneakers; don't look cool – belly up like a good white boy? Yeah?'

Redwood smiled at his own whiteness, and shrugged. 'Everything helps.'

'That's not what it's about, man. The magistrate? He looks at me an' sees right through all that crap. It don't matter I didn't do it. I'm black. That's all they see.'

While Redwood might agree in principle, there was nothing he could do about that. Rather, he concerned himself with what *could* be done, particularly if Denzil were innocent, as he, quite sincerely and credibly in his own way, maintained.

He checked his pad. 'The Asian woman – Mrs Nazur – made a

positive identification. She says you were one of the gang who assaulted her, and stole her bag.'

Denzil was running out of rope, and he seemed to know it. 'What else is she gonna say? . . . Listen, man. There's tricks you guys can play.'

'Tricks?'

'Yeah!' Denzil insisted. 'Like telling the magistrate the police didn't treat me good, man.'

Suddenly Redwood reacted as a Special, rather than as a solicitor, taking offence at his client's suggestion.

'Are you saying you've been badly treated here?'

Denzil saw that his solicitor was not going to cooperate in using his influence to set him free, and his impatience grew, along with his mistrust. 'Let me try to tell you one more time. I didn't do it. But that won't stop them stitching me up.' He turned on Redwood, seeing him as part of the white problem, not the solution.

'Know something? You're givin' me a headache, man.'

Bob, Noreen, and Derek Loach sat around the small kitchen table upon which rested the remains of their tea. The man of the house was cramming a piece of bread and jam into his mouth while bolting down his tea, trying to talk to his younger brother at the same time.

'You're coming down to the club tonight, I hope?' By which he meant the Pub on 4th at Division 'S' headquarters.

Derek looked from Noreen to his brother, then nodded. 'Sure.'

'The Super'll want to have a word when he knows you're in town . . .' By whom he was referring to Frank Ellsmore, Division 'S' Police Chief Superintendent.

'At least you can talk to Ellsmore,' Derek acknowledged.

That reminded Loach to check the clock, and abruptly he lumbered to his feet. 'Oh, damn, look at the time. I'm going to be late.'

Noreen winked at Derek. 'When the Specials call, your brother is off faster than a bride's nightie.'

Trying to ignore her, he explained his rushing off to Derek. 'I'm taking Parade tonight. I've got an SDO who swans around. Most times he never shows, then up he pops like a bad penny.'

'Is that Barker?'

He nodded, getting ready to go.

'Didn't you tell me he was leaving?'

'Just rumours so far. But I'm gonna make it clear my hat's in the ring. It's that important.'

'A policeman's work is never done,' Noreen droned.

Now was the wrong time for her attitude. 'For once, try to understand, Noreen.' He turned to his brother for some sympathy. 'Derek understands, don't you, Derek? You don't mess around when it comes to duty.' He drained the last dregs of tea from his mug.

'I've never understood, you see, Derek,' she continued mischievously, 'but I'm sure you'll be able to make it crystal clear.'

'I don't want to be piggy in the middle. But he's right, Noreen. Duty comes first . . . with the Police, certainly.'

Noreen blew a soft raspberry at her husband, who turned in annoyance at his brother. 'What's that supposed to mean? That what goes for the Police doesn't go for the Specials?'

'Oh, come on now, Bob,' his wife scolded, 'don't get all het up.'

He looked at Derek. 'Well . . . ?'

'Bob, I didn't mean it that way.'

'Then what way did you mean it?'

Noreen interrupted their quarrel. 'God, if I'd thought I was going to start a war . . .'

But Derek was nettled. 'Sometimes, Bob, you make too much out of the Specials. Surely no one expects them to bust a gut turning up.'

''Course you'd know all about that, being in the thick of things at Police Academy. Well let me tell you something: my troops . . . my lads take it bloody serious-like!'

'For God's sake, Bob. The lad's only been here a couple of minutes, and you're jumping down his throat.'

'I get enough rubbishing from other people. I don't need it from my own brother.'

His brother coloured crimson. 'Ease up, Bob. We joke about it at School, but everybody I know realizes how much the force needs the Specials.'

'There. Satisfied?' said Noreen. 'You'd better be . . . It could be last chance to mouth off at Derek.' Both of them looked at her, slightly mystified at her meaning. 'You, Bob Loach, will have to watch what you say to your brother in future.'

'What are you on about?'

'Once he passes his examination, and correct me if I'm wrong

'. . . but won't Derek, as a regular policeman, outrank not only you, but all your merry men as well?'

While Derek covered his mouth to hide a grin, his brother was furious.

'The more you open your mouth, Noreen Loach, the less I like it. Especially when you talk about something you don't understand.'

Going to the door, he turned to his brother. 'I'll expect you down at the Club later.'

He walked out. There was a long silence before Noreen began to clear away the tea things. Derek seemed embarrassed.

'That was out of order. Why do you let him talk to you like that?'

'Maybe because I talk to *him* like that.'

Derek shrugged his shoulders, trying to manage a smile. 'As long as I live, I'll never understand the pair of you,' he told her, though with affection. 'You fight like cat and dog. It's been like this ever since I've known you.'

'That's not true,' she reacted defensively. 'It just seems that way. Relationships change from day to day, I suppose.'

'Maybe you two should've had kids.'

'Don't you start. Why is it that everybody thinks that having kids will solve everything? It doesn't. And you're also forgetting something else. When I first met Bob, he was trying to bring you up.'

He started picking up the cutlery. 'Don't I know it. He hasn't stopped since.' 'Flippin' 'eck!'" he mimicked, '"The only reason you became a Police Cadet was because I became a Special."'

Noreen smiled wanly, and Bob thoughtfully conceded: 'I don't suppose it was much fun having a snotty-nosed kid around when you married Bob.'

'It didn't do our love life much good,' Noreen admitted candidly. She recalled her first meeting with Bob's adolescent brother: 'The first day I clapped eyes on you, I said: "There goes a real cheeky kid."'

'And now?' he asked seriously.

'I'd say you've improved.' She dropped her eyes, and tried to change the subject. 'Which goes to show that Bob must've made a good job of you, Derek. Don't knock it.'

He held up his hands in mock surrender. 'Hey! We're on the same side.'

185

Accepting his truce, she resumed clearing up the tea things, and he began to help.

'Right. Who washes and who dries?'

She merely opened up the nearest appliance. 'Don't be daft. Shove them in the dishwasher.'

Apparently, for him, it wasn't all that simple. 'I don't know if I approve. A lot of problems used to be settled over the kitchen sink. You know . . . washing and drying. Dishwashers could have a lot to answer for,' he concluded.

Noreen had to laugh. 'My God! I thought you were going to School to become a policeman, not a marriage guidance counsellor!'

4

Most of the usual Specials had already gathered in the Division 'S' parade room as a few latecomers drifted in. Viv saw John Redwood enter and went over to join him.

'Did you get the message?' she asked.

'What message?'

'Sergeant McAllister. He wanted to see you immediately you came in.'

He nodded thanks as he turned around and went back out.

'I'm telling you . . . it's only costing me ninety-nine quid,' Special Constable Julie Deane was telling her circle.

'For a week on the Costa Brava?' Mike Sullivan asked.

'Full board,' she confirmed.

'Well, that accounts for the bed,' chirped Phil Warren.

Their chatter was interrupted by Section Officer Loach. 'Okay . . . can I have shush.' He waited for absolute quiet, as tonight he was feeling a shade edgy.

'Right! Before we get down to basics . . . a word about some of the reports I've been getting lately.' He ran a beady eye over his troops. 'If you wanna write a novel, don't ask me to read it, and . . . oh yeah, another thing . . . and I mention no names . . . but d'you honestly expect anyone to believe some villain held up his hands and said: "It's a fair cop, guv!"'

186

Before anyone could answer, the telephone rang, and he was the one who had to answer.

'Hullo . . . Who . . . ? Just a second.' His eyes roved over the group, picking out Anjali Shah. He pointed the phone at her. 'It's for you. Don't be long.'

While Loach carried on with Parade, Anjali covered one ear and put the phone to the other. 'Hello? Yes . . . this is Anjali Shah. Who is this?'

'My name is Gupta, Miss Shah, I know your Uncle Ram very well.'

'Oh yes?' she replied guardedly.

'May I come and see you, Miss Shah, at the police station?'

'That won't be possible. I'm about to leave any moment. Why do you want to see me?'

Gupta lowered his voice. 'It is an embarrassment. But I have a document . . . It came in a brown envelope . . . and I need to know what I should do. It is all very urgent.'

She could hardly hear him with Parade going on, but she didn't want Uncle Ram's friends coming to headquarters to pester and delay her on a matter of astrology. 'Perhaps you could read it out to me, Mr Gupta?'

'Uh . . . no. That is not good. I must come and see you.'

'Well, I could meet you tomorrow after work.'

'Then will be too late. I shall come and see you right away.' Before she could refuse his invitation, he hung up.

'Mr Gupta? Mr Gupta? Are you there?'

In a Division 'S' cell area, Police Sergeant McAllister took his time before having his say with the New Special, John Redwood, giving him a while to squirm and wonder what this little conference was going to be about. Eventually, he decided the solicitor's discomfort had reached a sufficient intensity, and he attacked: 'I know you're handling the Denzil Taylor case. And I know you'll do your damnedest to show us poor Bobbies as hounding another poor wee innocent black laddie.' He cut off Redwood's denial.

'But maybe you should have a gander at this.'

He handed Denzil Taylor's charge sheet to Redwood, cataloguing numerous appearances in front of Juvenile Court, including petty theft and grievous bodily harm, with some assault and battery thrown in. Andy watched the solicitor scan the long list. 'He's no angel, Redwood.'

'No! But he's still innocent until proven guilty of this latest charge,' he argued.

'I'm not disputing that, man,' McAllister granted him. 'All I'm saying is: Don't use the Police as a punch-bag to get your client off the hook.'

Keeping it to himself, Redwood felt that he neither needed nor deserved the warning.

Bob Loach looked over the group, now thinning out, and found Anjali. 'I'd like you, Anjali, to link up with John Redwood . . . Plain clothes down at the Lancaster Park Kiddies' Playground. Redwood's already done it, so he can fill you in . . .' Looking around again, he realized that Redwood was nowhere to be seen. 'Where the hell is he? Flippin' 'eck! He hasn't been here a week and he's doing a Freddy Calder!'

Freddy himself spoke up, only in the high falsetto voice of Foxy. 'Somebody call?'

Amidst the few titters, John Redwood hurried into the room. Angered, Loach gun-pointed a finger at him.

'I know you're a busy man, Mr Redwood, but when you put your name down for duty, I expect to see the colour of your face on Parade on time! Is that understood?'

'Absolutely,' answered Redwood, 'but –'

'No buts . . .' Loach ordered. 'Is it understood?'

Without further dispute, Redwood accepted the censure. Only then did Loach realize that Special Constable Redwood was in uniform.

'You do have your civvies with you, I hope?'

'I was led to believe I was on the beat with Viv.'

'Never make any assumptions on this job,' sighed Loach. 'You're with Anjali down at the Playground. While you get yourself organized, you can give her the low-down on what's been going on there.'

Viv Smith came up to Loach, as John Redwood and Anjali Shah were drifting away, and Parade was breaking up.

'You were a bit rough there, weren't you?'

'Don't stick your oar in,' Loach advised, his nerves frayed at the moment.

'Got the worst of Noreen, did you?'

Viv's insight irritated him. 'You're pushing your luck, Viv.'

'He was in the building, you know?'

'What?'

'Mr Redwood. The Sergeant collared him for something.'

'Then why didn't he say so?'

'You didn't give him much of a chance, luv.'

5

The suburban street outside was peaceful and undisturbed. There were no strange sights or sounds to suggest anything in the least out of the ordinary. While there was still light in the sky, the quiet middle-class box houses lined up in rows on either side of the darkened street seemed to be all one happy family: there was nothing to suggest that inside one of these boxes, one of the family had just experienced a disaster.

Special Constables Viv Smith and Freddy Calder had less important matters to discuss, though perhaps not to them, and certainly not to Freddy, for the sudden discovery and disappearance of Rita LooseSomething was the tragedy of his life. Until now, he had never met anyone like her, nor seen anyone vanish from his life so quickly either. Boy meets girl, boy forgets to note her new number, boy loses girl, end of story.

'You are a plonker, Freddy Calder, and no mistake,' Viv laughed. 'You find a woman you like, and then lose her. That sounds like a wally to me.' She couldn't help teasing him after all the times he and Foxy had needled *her* about boyfriends.

'I didn't lose Rita,' Freddy expostulated. 'By the time I looked her up, she'd moved out of her flat. No telephone number; no forwarding address. I didn't want to look pushy. And how was I supposed to know it was her flat that was on the market?'

At that moment a young woman burst out from the bushy gateway to her house and crashed into Freddy, nearly sending him sprawling.

'Gracious! . . . You're the Police?'

Freddy brushed himself down. 'It's the uniform that gives us away, miss,' he said with a straight face.

The woman gave him a blank stare. Then abruptly burst into tears. Viv pushed Freddy aside to reach out to the woman, gather her in and comfort her.

'Sometimes, Freddy . . .' She looked into the face of the woman. 'Can we be of help?'

'He's going to kill me,' she said through her tears.

Freddy was suddenly all attention. 'Who is?'

'When he finds out . . .'

'Excuse me?' Freddy coaxed her.

She looked up at him, though now her eyes were vacant. 'What am I going to tell him?'

Viv tried to shelter her from Freddy's prodding concern. 'Look . . . can we see you home? This your house?'

The woman gave her a weepy nod.

'All right. Take your time.'

Viv pulled gently, but the woman appeared to want to tell her something.

'Don't try to say anything just yet.' She turned around. 'Freddy? Give me your handkerchief.'

The three of them entered the house and Mrs Coleman pointed distraughtly toward the door to the kitchen, which was standing open.

Admiral Freddy Hornblower discovered the kitchen floor awash in a lake of fresh water, the level rising by the second.

'It's all my fault . . .' Mrs Coleman was crying. 'I thought I would do somebody a good turn . . . Now look what's happened . . .' Like Alice, her tears threatened a flood of their own.

Freddy shook his suddenly weary head. 'Well, first things first. You any idea where the stopcock is?'

'I'm not too good at this sort of thing, Officer,' she trembled.

'No? . . . That's a pity.'

'They're usually under the sink, aren't they?' Viv mildly suggested.

He looked down at the water with a sinking feeling. 'Bloody hell,' he muttered in an undertone.

He hoisted up his trouser legs, then tiptoed gingerly through the water to get to the sink unit. Opening up the cupboard underneath, bending cautiously in case he accidentally sat in the water, he tilted his head down to examine the interior. His cap fell into the pond. He stifled a curse as he cleared away some cleansing items to reach the stopcock. Between it and the sink tap was a broken canister that had come adrift.

Meanwhile, Mrs Coleman had not stopped the torrent of her explanations. 'You see . . . they told me at the Voluntary Services Organization . . . I help out down there in my spare time . . . it's not much, but one has to do something . . .'

'Anyway, they said Mr Piggott was a good plumber . . . He'd been in prison, you see, and was having problems getting work . . .'

Freddy's eyes rolled skyward. Finally he succeeded in turning off the tap.

'Richard . . . that's my husband . . . decided we should have a water filter put in. And he knew a firm who'd do it for three hundred pounds. Mr Piggott said he could do it for two fifty. He said he knew a man who could supply the filter wholesale . . .' And now her charity was floating down the river that drowned two hundred and fifty pounds.

'You try to help people, and this happens!' her grief suddenly turned to anger. 'The first time I turned the tap on . . .'

'Probably the pressure did the filter in,' Freddy surmised. 'Didn't this Mr Piggott . . . this plumber of yours . . . didn't he test it while you were here?'

'No. To tell the truth, I was glad to be rid of him.'

'I don't suppose you've anything on paper, Mrs Coleman?' Viv asked.

She shook her head, yet answered to the contrary. 'Just a receipt. I needed that to show Richard.' Just then she seemed to remember something else. 'Mr Piggot wasn't too keen . . .'

'I'll bet he wasn't,' concurred Freddy sarcastically, imagining the villain's reluctance to leave a paper trail.

'Richard's coming back tomorrow. What am I going to do? It seemed a good idea at the time. I was saving Richard money . . . and I was helping someone who was in trouble . . .' She searched her soul and their faces for the reason.

'There's no easy answer, Mrs Coleman,' Viv sighed.

Freddy's eyebrow went up. 'Can I see the receipt?'

Mrs Coleman picked up a scrappy piece of paper from the work top and handed it to Freddy, who studied it carefully. Viv gave it only a cursory glance before turning to advise the victim of her rights.

'There's one consolation, Mrs Coleman. You can swear out a complaint, and let the courts decide.'

'But that could take weeks.' Her eyes pleaded.

Abruptly Freddy looked up from the receipt. 'Hang on. There might be another way.'

He smiled. 'Mrs Coleman is going to drive us round to . . .' He held Piggot's receipt up to the light: '. . . sixteen Yalding Terrace . . . and pay her neighbourhood plumber a friendly call.'

6

Standing in the sitting room waiting for John Redwood to change out of his uniform and into his civvies, Anjali was flipping absently through a solicitor's journal of some sort when she was startled by a clatter in the doorway behind her. She turned to find Redwood's son, Simon, entering in his wheelchair.

By the time he saw her, he couldn't turn back. He looked up, pointed at her in recognition, and she pointed back.

'You work in Physio, don't you?'

She remembered the last time she had seen him, getting down from the bus outside the hospital entrance, and how he had seemed, or pretended, not to recognize her.

'I knew I'd seen you someplace. I'm Anjali Shah.'

'Simon. Simon Redwood.'

Both a bit self-conscious, they shook hands awkwardly.

'But what brings –' Simon started . . .

'I thought I –' she began at the same moment . . .

'I'm sorry . . .' Simon deferred to her.

'No, that's all right. I was going to say that I should have made the connection.'

'Sorry?' he wondered.

'Nancy told me your name was Redwood.'

'So you know my father?' he asked, then immediately corrected himself. 'That's a dorky thing to say . . . course you know my father, or you wouldn't be here.'

'I'm waiting for him . . . to change . . .' She noticed him frowning. 'We're undercover agents tonight . . . top secret . . . out of uniform.'

A puzzled expression on his face, he appeared to be confused by her story. 'I don't believe it. You can't be a Special . . .'

Behind Simon, his father returned to the room, having changed to casual clothes. 'Ah . . . I see you two have met.'

She and Simon looked at each other. 'We met down at the hospital,' she said shyly.

Redwood nodded with paternal understanding, but Simon immediately spun his wheelchair around to face the doorway so he could go out the same way he had come in.

'Well, I got a programme to debug,' he mumbled in a low, bleak voice. 'I guess I'll see you sometime.'

Head down, he rolled from the room, and in another instant he was gone, leaving his father a little flustered. Anjali was aware of his discomfort, and her heart went out to him.

'He eats, sleeps, and drinks computers,' he explained, avoiding her and looking after his departed son.

In the yard, Kevin Piggott was painting his name and profession on his new, though battered, van as day was turning to night. He could still see well enough under the dim light to finish the lettering. Not that he had much of a hand as a painter – that's why the lettering spelled out plumber – but it would do for the next couple of weeks or so.

Freddy Calder, Viv Smith, and Mrs Coleman walked together toward the open corrugated iron gates to the yard, and Piggott's light was sufficiently bright to discern his rough features in the distance.

'Is that him?' Freddy asked Mrs Coleman.

'Uh-huh.'

'That his van?'

She hesitated. 'I don't know. This morning he came on a bicycle.'

Nodding his head in understanding, Freddy pushed on ahead to confront Piggott. As they approached, Piggott looked up at Freddy, then to the women just behind. When he recognized Mrs Coleman, the first tremors of nervousness started to show in a lumpy face that otherwise lacked expression.

'Evening, sir,' Freddy smiled, gesturing a tip of his cap. 'It is Mr Piggott, isn't it?'

The hulk responded with a shifty, sickly nod, none too sure whether he should agree or not.

In the meantime Freddy proceeded with the introductions. 'Special Constable Calder; Special Constable Smith; and, of course, you know Mrs Coleman.'

Walking back and forth, he studied the van, with Piggott in close attendance trying to shield his vehicle from scrutiny. 'I hope you don't mind me getting right down to the nitty-gritty, but . . . we've just come from Mrs Coleman's kitchen . . . You made a real pig's breakfast, didn't you, Mr Piggott?'

Piggott let out a nervous laugh.

'I don't think Mrs Coleman finds it in the least bit funny. Her kitchen is knee-deep in water.'

'When I left, everything was okay,' he excused himself.

'I studied your handiwork, Mr Piggott. The filter was probably second-hand when I was in short pants. It sort of died of old age when Mrs Coleman put pressure on it.'

'She must have done something to it.'

'She certainly did, sir. She turned on the tap.' He paused for another disarming smile. 'Now I suggest we sort this out like reasonable people. Mrs Coleman paid you two hundred and fifty quid. As I see it, Mr Piggott, you owe her two hundred and fifty for a botch-up. So . . .'

'Hang on,' Piggott interjected. 'I don't see why I owe her a cent.'

'You don't? Well, that leaves us with a serious problem, Mr Piggott.'

'It ain't mine. That's for sure.'

Nodding slowly, Freddy moved on to the next topic. 'This is your van, Mr Piggott?'

'Yes.'

'Just got it, have you?'

Piggott started wondering what he was getting at. 'As it so happens . . .'

As Freddy made his voyage around the vehicle, Piggott trailed immediately behind, tripping on his heels. 'Viv? Got your notebook handy?'

Quickly she took out her notebook and a fresh pencil and started following in the parade behind Piggott.

'Left-front tyre tread almost invisible. Right front tyre . . . bald as a soft-boiled egg.'

When he rattled the side of the van, a drizzle of rust made a line on the ground.

'Rear light . . .' Accidentally on purpose he leaned a hand on a loose fitting, and, surprise, it fell off '. . . Oh dear, oh dear, oh dear!' He turned from the fallen fitting to Piggott's stunned reaction. 'Unless I'm much mistaken, Mr Piggott, you're definitely the one with a serious problem. Not even if this vehicle was driven by Madonna's knicker elastic would it move from this spot.'

Piggott opened and closed his mouth like a drowning goldfish. Apparently, however, he knew a brick wall when he saw one. 'Look . . . I gotta problem . . .'

'And what's that, Mr Piggott?'

'I don't have the money. I used the lady's dosh to buy . . . the van like.' He thumped the vehicle with a touch too much zest and winced when the wing mirror dropped off.

'Where did you buy the van, Mr Piggott?'

The plumber was beginning to fade under Freddy's withering pressure. 'El Supremo Cars . . . It's just around the corner.'

'Thank God for that. You get in the van, and we'll follow you.'

Piggott's perpetual blank look had returned and settled once again. 'Where?'

'To the El-what's-its-name.'

Fear began to suffuse through the blank lumpy face. 'But that's Grouty's place!'

'So?' smiled Freddy.

Dreaded anticipation had suddenly galvanized his resistance to where Freddy was taking him.

'He . . . he sells vehicles. He doesn't take them back, if you know what I mean.'

Unfazed, Freddy ushered Piggott to the door of his van as if they were off to a teddy bear's picnic.

'We'll make him an offer he can't refuse.'

Anjali and John Redwood had taken up a surveillance position in an arc of shrubs and bushes half-encircling the Lancaster Street children's play area. It seemed impossible to understand why any madman would choose to destroy a carousel, or swings, or the slide, or the adventure boxes . . .

Anjali was more upset than she thought that she should be. 'God knows why people vandalize things which could injure a child. It's just mindless.'

'I wish I could give you a measured judgement, but I can't.' His voice was low, steady. 'Maybe they don't think of the consequences of their acts. Like a drunk at the wheel. Never crosses his mind he might maim or kill.'

She hesitated before asking the next question, but it seemed inevitable that she would, so she ventured ahead with caution and, she hoped, sensitivity.

'Was that what happened to Simon?'

He appeared distracted, unable to focus on the question. 'I'm sorry . . . ?'

'A drunk driver . . . hit and run?'

'No.' His eyes gazed ahead, unseeing. 'It wasn't . . .'

'It was an accident, then?'

He allowed himself the indulgence of a dry laugh. 'You'd make a good lawyer.' His eyes refocused on her.

'My brother says I'm a snoop. I'm sorry, Mr Redwood.'

'Don't be . . . and it's John, by the way.'

This time she looked away, and they lapsed into silence. Anjali surveyed the quiet playground, waiting for him, not pushing him any harder.

'He was mugged. About two years ago. He was set upon by a gang. Simon tried to get away. There was a scuffle, and he fell from a pedestrian bridge. His back was broken . . . but you know that.'

Then he stopped, and that was all there was to say.

'Did they get the people who did it?'

'No . . . Not yet,' he answered, his voice weakening. 'We live in hope . . .'

His thoughts were trailing away when she suddenly gripped his forearm.

'What is it?' he whispered.

'To your right,' she whispered back. 'Among the shrubs. There's someone there.'

She motioned for him to go one way, as she began creeping in the other.

Reaching the cover of the shrubs and ducking low to hide behind them, he edged forward without making a sound, slowly approaching a shadowy figure who could not possibly see him coming.

The man gave a start when Redwood sprang out and suddenly loomed over him.

'Stay where you are, sir. Police.'

Instantly terrified, the man raised his hands in surrender.

'Please . . . I am –'

He got no further – Anjali swooped down on him from behind, pinioning the man in a tight arm-lock.

'What is your name, and what are you doing here, sir?' Redwood demanded.

'My name is Gupta . . . and I am looking for Anjali Shah.'

Astonished, Anjali set him free and came around to face the terrified man with her questions.

'You are Mr Gupta? And you called me earlier?'

Bob and Derek Loach toasted the younger man's impending graduation from the Police Academy with a quiet drink at the Pub on 4th. After a pause, Derek decided to use the occasion to bring up a subject he had been wondering about all night.

'I was having a long chat with Noreen tonight.'

'Oh aye?' the elder asked warily.

Reluctant to say the words, nonetheless he pushed them out. 'It's a bit late in the day, but . . . well, I suppose I never thought about it until now . . .'

His older brother made a winding-up movement. 'What?'

'It's about when I was a lad . . .'

'Flippin' 'eck. We're not going back over that business about the rabbits?'

Derek looked at his brother slightly mystified. 'No. Something Noreen said.' Skipping the strange reference to rabbits for the moment, he plunged into the breach, though stammering and halting once he became immersed.

'Well . . . was it because . . . I was around . . . that you and Noreen didn't have kids of your own?' At last the cat was out of the bag.

'It's taken you fifteen years to think of that? God help us.' But he could see Derek was serious. 'No, it had nothing to do with you. We didn't live in one room, you know, Derek. Anyway, I used to lock our bedroom door when we . . . you know . . .' Somehow he couldn't finish.

Derek sipped his drink, the smile on his lips faded, the mystified expression returning. 'What business about what rabbits?'

He was saved a reply when he spied Division 'S' Police Chief Superintendent Frank Ellsmore and Peter Whittaker, District Commandant of the Specials, coming into the pub. He got to his feet and motioned to catch their eye, and a moment later Derek stood up to be seen as well.

'Evening, sir . . .' Loach greeted Ellsmore, and 'Sir,' he acknowledged Whittaker.

The Superintendent shook Derek's hand, then turned to Whittaker to introduce them. 'Have you met Derek, Peter?'

Whittaker reached for Derek's hand.

'Derek, this is Peter Whittaker, District Commandant of the Specials . . . Sees your brother toes the line.'

Whittaker nudged the brother in uniform. 'We run a tight ship, don't we, Bob?' Then he regarded the younger sibling. 'But we're always on the look-out for new faces.'

'Ah, you're a bit late there, Peter,' the Super chided him. Whittaker smiled his puzzlement. 'Derek's got his eye on my job . . . When's the big day, Derek?'

'Next Tuesday, sir.'

'Well, it goes without saying . . . good luck. And think about us at Division "S" when you're deciding your future.'

The elder brother pinched his nose at this suggestion. But the Super then gestured to the younger brother to resume his seat.

'Sit down. Let me buy you a drink.'

Derek reached for his wallet, but Ellsmore waved it away. 'Well . . . just a small half . . . of bitter.'

'What about you, Peter?' Ellsmore offered.

198

Whittaker checked his watch with a frown. 'Can we make that later? I should've been at the Community Centre ten minutes ago.' He turned to say goodbye to Derek – 'Nice meeting you . . .' – and nodded to his older brother as he took Frank Ellsmore aside – 'Bob . . .' After a brief private consultation, the brass parted ways.

'We'll see you later, Peter,' Ellsmore called to the Commandant leaving the bar. Then he returned to the table. 'He's a good man, Peter . . . Now, where were we . . . ?' He pointed at Derek. 'Half of best bitter . . . right?' Derek nodded. 'And Bob?'

'Nothing . . . but if I could have a quick word, Super.' He walked to the bar with Ellsmore.

At the bar, the Super signalled to the barman, speaking to Loach from the side of his mouth. 'What's the problem?' Before he could answer, the barman arrived. 'Half of best, bitter, Briggsy. And a single Dewars.' Ellsmore checked once again with Loach. 'You sure, Bob?'

'Positive . . .' Now that he had the Super's ear, there was no point in wasting time. 'Look, I don't want to jump the gun, but . . . I'd like my name on the record if there's going to be a vacancy for SDO.' It looked as if he might make Sub-Divisional Officer before he made his million, after all.

The Super seemed baffled. 'SDO?'

'I believe Barker is resigning?'

'First I've heard of it.' Ellsmore frowned. 'If I remember rightly, Bob, you were the first Special ever to ask for promotion when you got upgraded to Section Officer.'

Slowly sinking under the weight of the Super's censure, Bob took on a hangdog expression. 'Well . . . I suppose . . . when opportunity knocks, you know . . .'

'It's one thing to knock on the door . . . but quite another to kick it in,' the Chief Superintendent scowled.

Anjali mildly but firmly chastised Gupta for spying on them, while Redwood squinted under the available light to see the document the man had produced.

'Mr Gupta, this is a foolish thing to do . . . to follow us here . . . It could have been dangerous,' said Anjali.

'I did not know what else to do.'

Redwood stepped back into the conversation after he had read through the document. 'My advice to you, Mr Gupta, is to be at

199

the Magistrate's Court first thing in the morning, and pay what you owe. Didn't you see here that you can be given a prison sentence if you don't?'

Gupta was alarmed by this news. 'I can go to prison?'

'If this remains unpaid,' Redwood assured him.

Her questions yet unanswered, Anjali remained upset with Gupta. 'I still don't know why you couldn't tell me over the phone. Why did you insist on seeing me?'

Despite his shame, Gupta told her the truth. 'So that *you* could *read* it to me.'

'What?'

He smiled sadly. 'I cannot read or write, Miss Shah. I did not want my family and friends to know. That way I would lose face. I had no one to turn to. That is why I followed you . . .'

Anjali and Redwood were no longer listening to him. They were staring intently toward the far side of the playground at a ghostly figure in a hooded anorak sneaking through the dark. Using silent signals, the Specials instructed Gupta to stay where he was and keep hidden, then checked with each other before taking off rapidly in opposite directions.

The ghost in the anorak made sure there was no one wandering through the playground at this time of night, then moved cautiously from the periphery into the open. The target chosen for this evening's ceremony was a rope climbing frame.

Gloved hands holding a long pair of wire cutters twisted angrily at the wire links that provided support to the ladder-like ropes. As each wire parted, there was a sharp snapping sound.

Suddenly, before the ghost saw them, Redwood and Anjali dashed from the protective shrubbery and seized the ghost from both sides. The ghost wriggled and struggled to break free, but was soon overpowered by Anjali's restraining arm-lock.

During the struggle, the hood of the anorak was dislodged sufficiently to reveal the face of a woman: forty or younger perhaps; bitter and contemptuous; slight in figure, as though anorexic. Though gradually resigned to her fate, she didn't look into their eyes, but rather stared icily at the toys of childhood on the playground.

8

For a start, Mr Grout, rather an aggressive chap – proprietor of the El Supremo Car and Van Company second-hand car lot – was el supremo giant, substantially larger, taller, heftier, and obviously stronger than Freddy. Yet Freddy was standing his ground in the early going, as Viv Smith, Mrs Coleman, and Kevin Piggott stood to the side in awe of el supremo.

Nonetheless, Grout was poking a hole in Freddy's chest like an oil rig pounding the drill home over and over again. 'And I don't care if you're the SAS. I don't accept any liability for the return of goods.'

Grout wasn't going to be the pushover Piggott was. 'I warned him,' Piggott reminded the ladies. 'Grouty is a pig.'

'Then maybe we'll need you as an interpreter,' Viv suggested.

Yet Freddy wasn't taking this threat lying down. He stood up to Grout as David to Goliath. 'Mr Grout . . .' Then his mouth assumed his old salesman's smile. '. . . Let me say straightaway that I understand your position.'

'Great. And you'll also appreciate that I'm a busy man, so I'll say goodnight, Constable.'

Freddy jumped to block his passage. 'And a busy man doesn't want the Police poking their noses in every minute of the day.'

'Too bloody true, he doesn't . . .' Then Grouty's eyes narrowed in suspicion. 'Hey! What's that supposed to mean?'

'Nothing,' Freddy shook his head. 'But a word in the wrong ear . . . you know . . . the Drugs Squad, that some kids are using your place to hand out crack . . . of course, without your knowledge . . .'

'You trying to threaten me?'

'Certainly not. Give me your hand.'

'What?' Before Grout could think of a good reason to refuse, Freddy simply took the big man's colossal paw into his own. 'You could probably squeeze my head like a lemon with that hand.' He gave the hand back. 'Mr Grout . . . you're a strong man . . . but I also think you're something else.'

'What else?'

'A good business man who would never pass up a good deal.'

Again Mr Grout couldn't think of any reason to disagree. ''Course not.'

'Well, I think I can interest you in just such a deal, Mr Grout.'

In spite of himself, Grout leaned closer to listen to Freddy's offer.

'Mr Piggott paid you two fifty for the van. Right? Right! And you made a handsome profit. Right? Right! I don't want to know what it was. That's not my affair. That profit is yours.' The giant grew more restive at mention of his profit. 'No! What I'm going to do is sell this van back to you . . .'

Viv could see Grout starting to bridle.

But Freddy ploughed on stubbornly. 'Sell it back to you *at a lower price than you sold it*!' El supremo was more confused. 'Right, Mr Grout. You give me two hundred quid – and the van's yours! Remember, you still have the profit you originally made, and you've still got the van to sell again. You don't need a calculator, Mr Grout, to tell you this is a sweet deal, do you? And it isn't every day you can tell your pals you made a sucker out of a policeman, is it?'

Freddy laughed heartily. And finally, after some reluctance, Grout finally echoed his laughter.

A sly grin remained behind on his face. 'Maybe if you was to make it one seventy-five . . . ?'

'Two hundred's the best I can do, Mr Grout. Leave me my underpants, eh?' That one finally brought a grin to old Grouty's sourpuss features. 'But wait . . . there is something else I can do to sweeten the pot . . .'

Freddy whispered something in Grout's ear. To everyone else's surprise but Freddy's, Grout fairly beamed at his kibitzing. Then, reversing the gesture Freddy had made previously, Grout took Freddy's little paw into his own huge shovel of a hand, undoubtedly cutting off the blood supply to the Special's fingers.

A moment later Mr Grout was banging fivers into Freddy's pained palm.

Viv and Mrs Coleman were shocked. 'I don't believe it!' wailed Kevin Piggott.

A few minutes later, Freddy was counting out the fivers from Mr Grout's giant hand into the slender hand of Mrs Coleman in her kitchen while Mr Piggott and Viv looked on in wonder.

'I've lost me van, and you want me to do *what*?' cried Piggott.

Freddy counted the last of the fivers and placed it firmly on the pile. 'Two hundred. It's the best I could do, Mrs Coleman.'

'Maybe it's worth fifty pounds to learn a hard lesson,' she admitted, grateful to get back what she could.

'Well, Mr Piggott here is going to have to remove his joke of a filter, and mop up the kitchen to your full satisfaction. Maybe that's worth the money you've lost.'

'And who's gonna make me do all this? You? The Police? I'm sure the papers'll be delighted to hear how the Police lean on innocent people.'

'You're walking on thin ice, Piggott, going around telling respectable people you're an ex-prisoner who's up against it . . . playing on their generous natures like that.'

Piggott was clearly suspicious of how much the Special Constable could know. 'What are you getting at?'

'Oh, you may have skated close, but you've never been inside in your life. So give that one a rest in future.'

The mountebank was amazed. 'Well slap my wrist . . . Officer!'

As he was about to turn away with Viv, Freddy had second thoughts, which he expressed to the lady of the house while keeping watch on Piggott out of the corner of one eye. 'We'll be back here before we call it a night, Mrs Coleman, to see everything's ship-shape.'

'Just a damned second! You can't force me to do one picking thing! Not you or anybody else.'

Freddy's smile widened. 'I wouldn't be too sure of that.'

'No?' Piggott challenged him.

'No. Somebody else will be very annoyed if he finds out you didn't co-operate.'

'Yeah . . . who?'

'Your friend Mr Grout.'

Piggott's face paled as the blood in his formerly pink cheeks drained to his toes. 'Grouty? What's he got to do with it?'

'Didn't I tell you? Sorry. You see . . . part of the deal with Mr Grout was that he kept an eye on you.'

The blood suddenly reversed and rushed back to Piggott's face. 'You bas –'

Freddy raised a finger to caution him against profanity in the presence of ladies. 'Uh-uh. There's more.' He was positively grinning by now. 'What really clinched the deal was that I told him you'd paint the van any colour he wanted – seeing you'd already begun to do it like. He's expecting you tomorrow morning, Mr Piggott. With your paint-brush.'

Leaving the would-be plumber with his mouth hanging open, Freddy turned and walked away with Viv, whose eyes were glowing in admiration.

'You never cease to amaze me, Freddy Calder.'

With that, she pulled him to a halt, and before he could protest, kissed him soundly.

'Mind you . . . you'll never be the man your mother was . . .'

9

Dejected more than defiant, the thin, anorexic woman apprehended at the Lancaster Street playground sat in an open Interrogation Room in the Division 'S' cell area, her eyes downcast and vague. No longer a danger, the vandal was now merely a pathetic figure in the custody of the Police.

Noel Weaver, another CID man, and WPC Holt entered the Interrogation Room and closed the door behind them.

Down the corridor, Special Constables Anjali Shah and John Redwood were conferring with Police Sergeant Andy McAllister. 'She's a sad woman,' said the latter as he shook his head ruefully.

'Do they know why she did it?' Anjali enquired.

Andy told them what he knew. "No" the whole story. She had a child of her own. She's not married, and the father left her before the child was born. The child died . . . It was an accident.'

'Not in the playground?' she asked.

'No, lassie. Not as pat as that. We've talked to a neighbour. The child was a cot death.'

'But I don't understand . . . ?' Anjali wondered.

'Doing these things in a children's playground?' He measured Redwood with a questioning look. 'Maybe John Redwood is better qualified to answer that. There are some folk never get over their grief . . . Some try to steal another's baby. Maybe this one hated to see other kiddies enjoying themselves. What do you think, Mr Redwood?'

Whatever he was thinking to himself, it was buried deep, although the furrows in his brow showed that this experience had triggered his own earthquake within that had exposed old wounds.

'I wouldn't presume. It's all too sad,' was all he could say.

'Aye, it is that,' McAllister agreed. Then his usually gruff and gloomy manner took a surprising turn for the better, with a glimmer in his eye and the trace of a smile as well. 'But just in case no one has mentioned it . . .' He looked at each of them in turn. '. . . Well done.'

The Pub on 4th was hopping, as more off-duty Police, Specials, and guests poured in to share a pint and a chat before heading home at the end of the evening.

With Briggsy the barman as an occasional, puzzled eavesdropper, the brothers Loach had been standing and talking at the bar a long while, a few empty glasses still littering the counter before them. It was getting late . . . time for Bob to tell Derek the facts of life before his little brother graduated from Police Academy next Tuesday.

'Listen. Let me explain. You remember the chinchilla rabbits?'

'Yes,' Derek faintly recalled.

'Well, your big scheme was to breed them to make gloves.'

'Dammit, that's right! I'd nearly forgotten that.'

'Aye, but what you didn't know was that you'd have to be the one to turn the baby bunnies into gloves,' he said, illustrating his point by making a chopping motion with the back of his hand.

'Nasty,' Derek shivered.

'That was when I cheated you,' the elder confessed.

'You did?' he asked, not quite believing.

'You thought you had a mummy and daddy rabbit.'

'I did?' he puzzled, not quite remembering.

'You didn't. I switched one. You had two lady rabbits. You cried your eyes out when there were no baby bunnies. But I had to do it to be kind, Derek.'

No longer an innocent boy, Derek looked at his brother with mock hatred. 'I'll never forgive you for that, Bob, as long as I live.'

The older brother hung his head. 'You had to know the truth.'

That's when Briggsy chose to stop by, and the confusion on his face indicated he wasn't sure whether he should interrupt the family feud. The elder brother saw him, and turned to the younger. 'Same again?' The younger nodded. 'Same again, Briggsy.' The barman scratched his head and left them to their heart-to-heart.

Meanwhile, at one of the busiest tables, Freddy Calder was basking in the glow of his triumph, as a well-lubricated Viv Smith had been relating his noble saga to anyone who cared to listen.

'He was so commanding, you know. He took that Piggotty plumber, and . . .'

Abruptly her voice stopped cold and her face frosted over. Julie Deane and the other women Specials at the table all turned their heads to see what had stopped Viv in her tracks.

Just entering the pub was PC Ginger Stokes, Viv's former paramour, leading his WPC paramour of the moment, who happened to have been blessed with matching red hair.

Viv drained her glass of vodka-and-orange and rose unsteadily to her feet, as Freddy tried to hold her back.

Across the pub, Ginger and his WPC redhead moved to a corner seat. Sitting at the next table were District Commandant Peter Whittaker and some of the brass from London.

Viv took no notice of Whittaker: she only had eyes for Ginger and the other redhead. He saw her coming his way, and watched her approach with rising apprehension.

Finally Viv stood right in front of their table and stared at both of them. 'I'll say one thing. At least the colour of your hair doesn't clash.'

'Look, Viv . . .' Ginger began. 'Get off my back. Let it be.'

She swung her attention to the other redhead at the table. 'I suppose bumping up and down in the squad car, night after night, did it, eh, luv? Wham bam, ta very mooch in the panda, like.'

Ginger got to his feet, motioning to his current beloved. 'Let's get out of here.' Without another word, they walked out.

Viv couldn't let it be, calling after them. 'What you didn't know, of course, was that he was hopping round to my place for a bit of afters . . .'

But they were gone, and everyone else was looking at her, not them. Hiding her face behind her hand, she slumped down onto Ginger's vacated seat.

As the rest of the crowd went back to their own business, DC Whittaker got up from his table and moved over to Viv's, leaning down next to her.

'Don't tell me. I made a right prat of myself.'

206

'No . . .' he said quietly. 'What I have to say is this: Either get over it, now, or get out. We're not running a Lonely Hearts' Club, Viv. We're here to support one another.'

Viv reacted to her second rebuke with more grace, simply by keeping her mouth shut, hiding her face again, and nodding to her superior that she understood. But she was a mess.

Across the pub at a popular corner table were a pensive John Redwood and Anjali Shah, surrounded by her usual coterie of Romeo PC's and Specials, ostensibly discussing the daring capture of the playground vandal.

'You were dead lucky with that crazie, tonight,' remarked PC Larry Fowler.

'I'll say,' agreed SC Steve Northcott. 'Dead jammy, Anjali.'

Anjali frowned, unsure whether to push this any further to learn what she didn't yet understand. 'I know this is a mistake . . . but what are you talking about?'

'For starters,' PC Barnes interrupted, 'the woman could've had a knife like Crocodile Dundee, and fisshht –' He slit his throat in pantomime. 'Bye, bye, Anjali and Redwood.'

Frowning, Redwood looked to his partner, and her throat. 'I guess we didn't stop to think about that.'

'None of us do,' said Barnes, moodily drinking from his glass.

Steve Northcott leaned over to confide in Redwood. 'He got a knife in his back trying to sort out an argument outside a pub. That can make you think twice.'

'Okay!' snapped Larry Barnes, having overheard him. 'Change the tape, shall we?' He lifted his glass once again.

During the lull that followed, Anjali took the occasion to stand up. 'I must go. And don't . . .'

'You wanna ride, Anjali?' asked PC Calvin Elwell.

'What?' Steve Northcott protested. 'In a red Reliant Robin? Get lost!'

Redwood got up to join Anjali. 'I'm leaving as well. Let me drive you home.'

Knowing looks quickly passed around the table, compounded with broad winks at each other and Redwood.

'It's not too much trouble?'

The knowing smiles were knocked off the dumbstruck faces of the many oft-spurned Romeos.

'Not in the slightest,' Redwood answered with his own knowing smile.

'Brilliant,' she responded in her turn. Simultaneously they acknowledged the Romeos at the table before leaving.

'Night . . .'

As they walked away together, a vacuum of stunned silence remained behind them at the table of Romeos. There were no words that could express their collective shock.

On their way out, Anjali met Chief Superintendant Frank Ellsmore in passing, and he stopped to shake their hands and say a few encouraging words before strolling across to the table of the other hero of the night, Special Constable Freddy Calder.

When the others at the table noticed his arrival and fell silent in his presence, the Super turned to Freddy, the fixer.

'Well, Calder, I have to hand it to you. I've never heard of anyone getting the better of Grouty.'

The other Specials and PC's at the table raised their glasses in salute, accompanied by a few good-natured taunts and chuckles along with the cheers and toasts of 'Way up, lad!' An uncharacteristically bashful Freddy tried to disguise his blushes behind a long swallow of non-alcoholic lager.

'And I hear you sorted out a plumber, was it?'

'Piggott,' Freddy modestly corrected him. '. . . Sir.'

Ellsmore let out a deep sigh. 'Quite a night you've had.'

He shook his head with a patronizing smile and turned away. The noise at the table picked up again, the jeers and taunts getting thicker by the moment. But the atmosphere quieted once more as the Super turned back to Freddy, motioning to bend his ear because he'd had another thought.

'But . . . can I give you a piece of advice, lad. Always remember we're here to keep the peace, not to enforce the law like a vigilante.' Any trace of a smile had vanished from his stern visage, and there was absolute quiet from the table of PC's and Specials.

'In future, follow procedure. In other words . . .' and he looked around at all of them, '. . . don't do it again.'

10

Sun filtered in through the frosted glass windows of a cramped, street-corner pub. Percy, an erect, young-looking gentleman of 73 was just coming out of the loo when his eye was caught by the television news. 'The most troubling statistic in what is overall a devastating set of crime figures,' he heard, 'is the eight percent rise in property offences in the first quarter . . .'

The barman interrupted his thoughts, pointing to the corner table where his friends were sitting. 'They've already got 'em in, Perce,' he said, referring to the drinks he had delivered while Percy was in the loo.

Percy looked quizzically at the barman. 'Wasn't waiting to be served.'

He crossed the pub to the table he and his friends had made their own. Playing dominoes were his cronies, Dave and Walt. Roughly the same age, Dave had let himself go, Percy had stayed young, and Walt had remained the bohemian of the trio, sporting long, silvery hair.

'It's your go,' Dave offered Percy.

His offer was met with a sneer. 'Dominoes. We're turning into professional pensioners.'

'What do you mean?' Dave asked him. 'We haven't played for ages.'

So Percy sat at the table and looked, then put down his domino.

'That's not a five,' said Dave.

'It's the five with the dot scratched out.'

'I've got the five with the dot scratched out,' Walt spoke up, sipping his ale. Then he looked into the glass and frowned. 'Bit cloudy.'

Percy picked up the disputed domino and slapped down a replacement. 'Now tell me that's a three with two extra dots painted on.'

After a long look, Walt shook his head. 'Can't go.'

At the moment Percy was more interested in the news report on the TV over the bar. 'I remember when they had a copper on every street corner,' he muttered under his breath.

'What?' said Dave.

'Nothing.'

The barman switched channels but Percy caught him in the act. 'I was watching that.' The barman scowled and switched back. In the meantime, Dave reached a hand in front of the rapt Percy's face and clicked his fingers.

'Anyone in?'

'We'll be going on coach parties next,' Percy grumbled, still trying to keep an eye on the telly. 'Along with all the other professional pensioners.'

Reluctantly, almost without looking at what he was doing, Percy put down his domino.

Walt picked up Dave's beer and checked to see if it were cloudy, too.

'Yours is okay,' he pronounced.

'I didn't have the same,' Dave explained.

The TV report went on: 'The truth is that crime statistics are a barometer of society's health.'

Percy scoffed. 'Baloney. The police don't get any support from the public any more. That's why the figures are up.'

Dave put down another domino then waited for Percy. 'Look – are you playing or watching that?'

'I can do both.'

'Prison doesn't mean prison anymore,' growled Walt. 'That's the problem. They all have colour TV's in their cells now.'

Percy gave him the real story. 'There's no respect for the police. Bits of kids in uniform. Bum fluff round their chops. They can be chief inspector at 25 now.'

'What are you on about?' Dave moaned.

'We came up the hard way in my day,' declared Percy, reminiscing.

'In your day?' asked Dave.

'I thought he worked for the Council?' Walt said to Dave.

'You were in the police?' Dave pressed him.

'Well . . . sort of.'

Dave dismissed that notion with a shake of his head. 'Either you were or you weren't.'

'I was a Special. There's regulars and there's Specials. I was a Special . . . S'pose I still am. I never really retired.'

'No wonder they never caught Jack the Ripper,' Walt quipped.

Suddenly looming above them, the barman banged down a cleaner-looking pint of beer in front of Walt. 'Try drinking it instead of analysing it.'

*   *   *

In the Parade Room, Loach read from a clipboard to the dozen Specials gathered round. 'A red Renault 18 Estate. Nicked from the car park of Zeeland Mouldings.'

'It'll be miles away by now,' Viv Smith reckoned.

'Maybe not,' Loach disagreed. 'Witnesses saw some kids hanging around.' He checked the roster. 'Okay – more or less the same as last night. Anjali on car patrol with Toby Armstrong . . .'

'No wonder people are talking,' Viv commented.

Anjali didn't share the group's humorous reaction to Viv's wisecrack, especially since Toby was still going through a difficult labour with his wife, Shirley, and had been away from the Specials for some time. The joke struck her as being in poor taste, although she didn't want to make a big fuss about it.

'Special Constable John Redwood,' Loach announced, then turned to face him. 'You've drawn the short straw. You get Viv in the absence of Freddy.'

'Charming,' she approved.

He returned her smile. 'I'm sure we'll get on famously.' She put an arm through his, though he looked a bit nonplussed at this.

Anjali felt a tinge of jealousy, though she tried to tell herself it was imaginary.

'I'll look after him,' Viv promised, hanging on to his arm.

'That's what I'm afraid of,' Loach remarked. Just then through the open door he saw DC Peter Whittaker pulling a coffee out of the corridor vending machine and walking off. Now was the time to catch him. 'Okay. Let's hit those mean streets.'

Parade disintegrated, fragmenting into small groups. Loach looked back toward the door, as Viv interrupted his thoughts.

'Maybe they were just there.'

His mind was still on Whittaker. 'What?'

'These kids,' Viv reminded him.

Loach dismissed her with a nod, then sprinted out through the door.

'Didn't realize I was such a riveting conversationalist,' she mumbled.

In the corridor, Whittaker was slowed down by his effort not to spill a drop of the coffee. Loach caught up with him.

'Can I have a word, Mr Whittaker?'

The Commandant turned slowly then narrowed his eyes at Loach.

'Surely.'

Yet there was suspicion lurking in those eyes.

Percy's eyes wandered over the cluster of photographs on the sideboard in his bedroom, focusing on one of himself: a much younger man, his hair completely blond, standing proudly in his uniform. He picked up the photo, and placed it at the front.

From the top of the utility wardrobe he pulled down an old suitcase and put it on the bed. Without dusting it off, he opened it. Inside, lay a neatly folded uniform as crisp and clean as the day he had put it away too many years ago to count. Carefully he took it out, unfolded his jacket, and held it up to his chest in the wardrobe mirror. It was as tight a fit as ever.

11

Loach had managed to corner DC Peter Whittaker in the corridor by a pair of swing doors constantly in use by Specials and PC's going in and out. Maybe if Whittaker failed to understand him it was because he couldn't hear what he was saying.

'The SDO's job?'

'I wanted to know if you'd second me,' Loach repeated, this time a bit too loudly.

'Didn't know there was a vacancy.'

'I thought Barker was resigning.'

Whittaker shook his head. 'Barker? He hasn't said anything to me.'

'I understood . . .'

With a deliberate look, the Commandant interrupted him. 'Tell you what. I'll . . .' A flying PC coming through the swing doors nearly sent Whittaker's coffee flying. Flustered, he seemed to take his irritation out on Loach.

'I'll let you know when he's resigning, and not the other way round. He's more likely to hand his resignation in to me, you see.'

Not waiting for a response, he went off with what was left of his coffee. Loach was puzzled. What was going on with SDO Barker? Leaving or staying? Why wouldn't anyone tell him?

* * *

Looking chipper in his newly pressed (though perhaps a bit antiquated) uniform, Percy emerged from his house a new man. He double-locked the door behind him, then strolled off down the street, hands behind his back, just as they always were.

He was back on the beat.

Viv Smith and John Redwood walked along the suburban street, chatting now and again, occasionally gazing into the shop windows. After a time when he seemed lost in silence, she tried once more to strike up a conversation.

'I thought you'd get enough of this during the day.'

'Enough of what?'

'The law.'

'Different side of the street.' He stopped walking to explain himself. 'I suppose I wanted to see things from another point of view for a change. You know – hand in my pit deputy's badge and do a few stints at the coalface. I don't know. There are so many reasons we do anything that every time we analyse ourselves we only pick out the motives that'll give us Brownie points.'

'Brownie points?'

'Am I being pompous?'

Frowning, sensing he had discerned her answer, he turned and walked on. She hurried after him.

'No. No. I don't think you're being pompous. It's just that . . .'

'What?'

She felt a bit sheepish. 'I haven't a clue what you're on about.'

As Percy was watching a couple of wayward youths up to no good under a railway bridge, he saw one of them throw down a fish and chip bag. That was just about all he could stand, and he called across to them.

'Now pick it up!'

The youths looked back at him incredulously and laughed.

'I said . . .'

But they merely ran off under the bridge, cowards that they were. With a sigh, Percy walked over to the offending wrapper and picked it up himself, saving it for a waste bin somewhere.

* * *

213

In the shopping mall, the shopkeeper was putting up his shutters for the night when he seemed surprised to see Special Constables John Redwood and Viv Smith walking down his street.

'Can't move for you lot tonight.'

The Specials looked at each other with quizzical expressions.

'Just like buses. Nothing for hours, and then three come along together.'

It was Viv's turn to seem surprised. 'Somebody's already been down here?'

The shopkeeper nodded vigorously. 'Oldish bloke. Not ten minutes ago.'

'When you say oldish . . .' Redwood began.

The shopkeeper cut him off impatiently. 'He was off before I could get a good butcher's.'

He went back inside his shop, as Viv and Redwood looked at each other trying to figure out who could have been there before them.

Michael and Geoffrey were legging it down the empty street just as fast as they could.

'It's coming after us!' screamed Michael, looking back over his shoulder.

Geoffrey was too terrified to look; all he could do was run. 'Where?'

All of a sudden Michael walloped straight into Special Constable John Redwood, who quickly bounced back and grabbed him. The boy, no more than eight or nine, vainly tried to wriggle free, but the towering Redwood was way too much for him.

'Get off!'

'Take it easy,' Redwood steadied him.

Viv chased after the other boy, grabbed him from behind, and tussled with his squirming arms.

'What's the hurry?'

Her captive screamed. 'Ghosts! Let go! Ghosts!'

'What!?' asked Viv, not believing her ears.

'It's okay.' Redwood tried to reassure them.

'We weren't doing nothing,' Michael protested. 'We were just playing in the garden.'

Redwood relaxed his grip, though still holding the boy's arms. 'You're not making any sense, sonny. Just slow down.'

Viv relaxed her hold on the other boy as well. 'What garden?'

'Don't tell her!' Geoffrey warned Michael.

But Michael was more afraid of ghosts than police. 'The house in Dennison Avenue.'

'What house is that?' Redwood asked him.

'The big empty place,' he answered.

'Trying to break in, were you?' Viv guessed.

'No!' shouted Geoffrey, tugging to break loose.

'His face was yellow,' the first boy told Redwood, clearly afraid of what he had witnessed.

'Whose face?' Redwood inquired gently.

Michael didn't want to answer, trying to avoid the policeman. But he had to tell someone what he had seen. 'The face at the window. All yellow.'

His words jogged young Geoffrey's recent memory as well, and he shivered.

'It was a ghost! I know it was!'

12

Percy walked by the police station without thinking. But then, when he had already gone well past the entrance, he did think about it. He stopped, turned around, and looked back. Should he? Or not? He couldn't decide.

Then, on pure impulse, he decided he might. Pulling his coat smartly round him, he started walking back the way he had come.

Redwood knocked at the door of a house in bad repair. The rotting window-frames sagged like pouches under tired old eyes, and the door itself threatened to cave in if he knocked too hard. Viv held the two kids, each by one wrist, in case they tried to do another runner.

'He'll kill us,' worried Michael.

'Don't be daft,' Viv scoffed.

The door opened, and a bald, middle-aged gnome glowered at them.

'Okay – what have they done?'

'Do you know these children, sir?' Redwood inquired.

'So?'

'Do you know them?'

'I'm their father,' he announced irritably. 'Okay? What have they done?'

'Nothing,' Redwood answered, starting to bristle. 'They were just out rather –'

'Inside!' the father ordered his children, ignoring Redwood. As they passed, he cuffed Michael on the back of the head.

Having seen it all before – or at least the consequences of abusive parents – he resumed wearily. 'Isn't it rather late for them to be out on their own?'

'You got kids?' the father challenged him.

'Yes.'

'So you're the perfect parent?'

'No. No, I wouldn't say that.'

'You just expect me to be.'

'The point is that they were frightened.'

'Yeah. Frightened by *you*! Why don't you get out there and catch a few child molesters instead of scaring my kids half to death?'

Incensed, Viv couldn't hold herself back. 'They're probably more frightened by –'

The father stepped back inside and slammed the door, as Viv's voice trailed away. '. . . by the video nasties you bring home.'

Suddenly with nowhere to go, nothing to say, Redwood was upset with himself. 'I didn't handle that very well.'

'You didn't do so bad.'

'I lost control of it. I let him take over.'

She unclipped her radio and buttoned it to sound. 'Special Constable Smith to Control. Over.'

WPC Sheila Baxter's professional voice came back over the radio. 'Go ahead. Over.'

'There could be some hanky-panky up at the old place on Dennison Avenue. We're going to have a look. Will radio in if we need some assistance. Over.' She clipped the radio back on her tunic, then noticed that Redwood had gone thoughtful again.

'You fit?'

216

'Yes,' he smiled a bit wanly, coming back to life.

'Let's go ghost-busting, then.'

Percy stood at the front desk of the police station waiting to be seen. Sitting at the back of the reception area, Maggie, the rather prim civilian receptionist, happened to look up and discover him standing there, and she started to rise.

'Don't get up. Just popped my head round the door to report everything's quiet up at Union Street. So if you could let the guv'nor know . . .'

'I'll pass it on,' she said to humour him.

Nodding in acknowledgment, he saluted, then left.

Looking out to watch him go, Maggie noticed Bob Loach passing through.

'You see that old bloke who just went out?' she asked, pointing to the door.

'What about him?'

'He decided to pop in to tell us it's quiet in Union Street.'

'So?'

'Isn't that taking Neighbourhood Watch a bit far?'

'Don't knock it,' he suggested. 'It's difficult enough to get these schemes going without rubbishing them from the start.'

'I could've sworn he was wearing . . .'

'What?'

She shrugged and let it go. 'Doesn't matter.'

Loach nodded and left. But Maggie couldn't leave it alone, her eyes still gazing at the door, waiting for the old wizard to reappear.

Special Constables John Redwood and Viv Smith looked at the huge old house across Dennison Avenue. It was all rather eerie, looming in the dark, the bottom half boarded up. The estate agent's board was lying broken in the long grass.

'What do you think?' she checked with him first.

Instead of answering her, he started walking toward the house.

Crawling along in the panda car, eyes on the edge of the deserted shopping precinct, Toby was passing the time by telling Anjali his favourite story of the week. Only somehow, she wasn't getting the idea of why it was so funny. Maybe it was a matter of cultural differences, or maybe you just had to be there, although he had told the story to a few thousand people who happened to think it was hilarious.

'An air-gun pellet?' she asked with a quizzical frown, trying to unravel the details of what had actually taken place.

'In the bum!' Toby chuckled. 'A target that size probably proved irresistible. And the colour of her plumage helped. She was wearing one of those orange sari things.' He wasn't sure what it was supposed to be called.

'She was shot at?' Anjali asked again.

'It wouldn't have taken a brilliant marksman,' Toby laughed.

'So what if she was hit in the eye?' Anjali argued, still not getting the point.

'Well, she wasn't. She was hit in the bum.'

'That makes it funny, does it?'

Toby soured: she was impossible. 'You have to admit it's a *bit* funny.'

There was no change in her expression. 'I'm sorry. I just don't share your sense of humour.'

Sometimes, he reminded himself, she just goes too far. 'Lighten up, Anjali.'

She turned away and looked out the window again.

'It's going to be a long night,' he muttered under his breath.

Eyes and ears ultra-sensitive to any signs of life, Redwood and Viv came round the side of the big old house through the overgrown forest of a garden. He checked the door leading into the conservatory.

'Nobody's been through there lately.'

'Ghosts don't need to force locks,' she reminded him. As she crept forward, she tried to make certain that nothing spooky was immediately in her path getting ready to pounce on her and suck the blood out of her neck before Redwood could get himself unfrozen and pull the disgusting thing off of her. Just thinking of it and feeling her neck half-convinced her that nightmares could come true.

Coming to a corner, she stood up slowly, then stepped back to look up at the upper floor windows, one by one.

There was a face in the attic window!

She ducked down immediately. She didn't know if the face had seen her, but she was sure she had seen the face.

218

'John.'

She turned, but he was nowhere to be seen.

Slowly, cautiously, she stood up again, and leaned back slightly, looking, at the attic window. A disembodied face glowing in the dark window was looking down at her.

'John!'

She took off, heedless of the noise she was making as she fled, ran along the wall to the other side of the house, and finally careered into Redwood coming the opposite way.

'There's someone in there!' she whispered, panting.

'Kitchen door's been forced,' he told her. Turning around, he led her back to what he had found.

Already half-open, the kitchen door gave a little with each push he made. Finally he was able to squeeze through. An upended table had been placed in front of the door to obstruct entry, requiring a good shove to clear it.

Viv searched the room with her torch. The place had been ransacked.

'What a mess,' Redwood whispered. He edged to the hallway door, followed closely by Viv.

His torch moved across the living room. Drawers had been wrenched open, chairs ripped and the stuffing pulled out.

Viv looked anxiously up the flight of stairs leading to the attic. She checked to make sure John was right behind her this time.

'This is the bit I'm not looking forward to,' she moaned. Taking a deep breath, she climbed the first step.

As they approached the top of the stairs, she could see a fluttery light under the attic door. She turned back to her partner.

'Phasers on stun?'

'Let's do it by the book,' he suggested.

Positioning himself at the side of the door, with Viv crouching on the opposite side, he knocked three times.

'Police. Open the door.'

There was no answer, no sound. Redwood looked at Viv.

'Ready?'

She nodded, standing up. Redwood braced himself, turned the handle slowly, and suddenly lunged at the door and pushed through.

The flickering light was coming from a candle, distorting the face of the man who was holding it.

Suddenly he blew the candle out, plunging the room into total darkness.

13

An atmosphere had descended on the panda car sitting at the edge of the empty shopping precinct car park. Anjali rested her arm on the ledge of the open window, staring into the empty night, as Toby poured some tea from his thermos.

'Want some of this?'

'No.'

'It's Indian.'

She couldn't help but grin at him. Grabbing the thermos, she started to pour some tea for herself.

'Idiot.' It was easy to get mad at Toby, but often easy to laugh away her grudge as well.

All of a sudden the quiet was shattered by the wrenching, scraping sound of a metal shutter being torn down.

'What was that?' Toby snapped.

'It came from over there.'

Toby was already out of the car. Anjali didn't quite know what to do with the thermos, but she dumped it as soon as she could get out of the car.

She hit the ground running, and wasn't far behind Toby, who raced across the car park to an alley.

The two heavily built young men caught twisting the security screen off a small shop front turned to see Toby and Anjali running toward them, then dropped their tools and split.

Picking one, Toby was shifting course to pursue him when another one stepped out from inside the shop and hit him with an iron bar from behind. Toby stumbled and fell.

'Toby!'

The man was about to finish him off with the iron bar when Anjali flung herself at him, thrusting him down and forward on his face, her knee jammed into the small of his back.

'Bitch!'

Furious, the man loosened her grip and threw her off, catching her with a flailing blow on the face and driving her into the wall. Scrambling to change direction, he ran away without looking back.

Anjali rushed over to Toby, who waved her away.

'I'm okay. I'm okay.'

For a moment, she hesitated, as her rational mind told her not to rush into danger alone. But she was expected to go, and that was enough.

Toby staggered to his feet, blood cascading down his face and neck. He unclipped his radio, stumbled woozily forward, and dropped the radio to the ground. On all fours, he dragged himself over to the radio, picked it up again, and buttoned it to sound.

Now Anjali was running flat out down the street, chasing the fugitive, without being able to gain on him. Not much of a sprinter, but she had stamina and could keep going at this pace for another kilometre maybe, and he must be tiring too. And when he fell back, she would be there, and ready. At least she hoped so.

Finally she seemed to be gaining on him a little, but just as she began to build up her hopes that maybe somebody would come to her rescue, the fugitive veered off to a building site.

She followed him, out of breath, no reserve left to be ready for him.

Suddenly he was just ahead, climbing up a half-built wall. She almost had him. Throwing herself on the wall, she clambered up after him and made a wild grab for his ankle. He kicked her away, but when she managed to get a leg up on to the wall the unsupported structure collapsed under their weight and motion, caving in and falling away beneath them in an instant, bringing materials and debris crashing down on their heads and burying them in the rubble. Neither of them ran any farther . . . or moved at all.

Anjali regained consciousness inside the ambulance, lying on a stretcher-bed. She could feel a terrible ache by her left eye and cheekbone, and when she tried to reach up to feel it, a stab of pain in her shoulder prevented her from lifting a finger.

'It's dislocated,' Toby told her.

She looked over at Toby, sitting opposite her while holding a bloody wad of bandage to the back of his head.

'Did we get him?'

221

Toby nodded his head toward the door of the ambulance. 'See for yourself.'

Outside the ambulance was another stretcher, and somebody was lying on it. Anjali assumed it was the man she had chased, and closed her eyes with a smile.

14

The young man found in the house in Dennison Avenue was sitting at the table in the Interview Room. In his early twenties, he had refined, aristocratic features and all the cool confidence an expensive education could provide. Police Sergeant McAllister stood opposite him with Redwood standing ready by the door.

'You got a name?' the sergeant questioned.

The young man sat back in his seat with an amused smile on his face.

'Turn out your pockets,' McAllister ordered.

Complying without objection, the young man spilled the contents of his pockets on the table – keys, sweet wrappers, betting slips – but no identification or wallet. McAllister picked up one of the betting slips.

'A gambling man, I see.'

'Life gambles with me. I'm just returning the favour.'

McAllister sat down at the table, settling in for the long night. 'So what were you doing there?'

'You mean in an existential sense?'

'Just answer the question.'

The young man merely smiled. 'No – I don't think so. I really don't feel in a chatty mood.'

The sergeant tried to be patient. 'Did you smash the place up?'

'*Was* it smashed up? I couldn't see. It was too dark.'

McAllister questioned Redwood with a glance.

The solicitor catalogued the evidence. 'Drawers pulled out . . . stuffing ripped out of chairs . . .'

'Sounds smashed up to me,' Andy concluded.

'Depends on what you're used to . . . Let's just say I had every right to be there.'

This had Andy worried. Redwood stepped in with his own question.

'Why did you need to break in, then?'

The young man stared at his captor. 'It really is none of your business.'

PC Larry Fowler walked in and went immediately to the sergeant, whispering something in his ear. McAllister kept looking straight at the young man all the while, then abruptly stood and left with the PC.

McAllister came into the entrance office to find a gaunt, nicely dressed woman, in her mid-thirties, chatting with Maggie the receptionist at the front desk.

'Miss Hibling?' he asked.

'Yes.'

'Owner of 10 Dennison Avenue?'

'Yes. Look –'

He settled her down with a few nods, assuring her she was in good hands. 'Thanks for coming in. We weren't sure if we had the right one.'

'They mentioned something about a break-in on the phone.'

'I suppose you could call it that. It doesn't seem to be a classic straightforward break-in, though.'

Miss Hibling cocked an eyebrow. 'I don't follow.'

'This character hung around after he vandalized the place.'

'The house has been vandalized?' she inquired, aghast.

'Afraid so.'

'That's all I need,' she groaned.

'Was there anything of value there?' the sergeant inquired.

'What? No. Just a few old bits of furniture. The house belonged to my mother, you see. She died six months ago.'

'And there's no one living there now?'

'No. No, I'm trying to sell it,' Miss Hibling explained. 'It's not much fun having to pay tax on an empty property as well as your own place.'

McAllister's expression said that he sympathized, though Miss Hibling probably couldn't discern one of his scowls from another. 'It's just possible he's a squatter.'

She was quite surprised. 'A squatter?'

'He seems to think he's got some kind of claim on the place.'

'Claim? What claim? I don't understand?'

'Let's put it like this,' Andy shrugged. 'He's carrying on as if he owns the place.'

Returning to the interview room, Sergeant McAllister accompanied Miss Hibling past Redwood at the door. The young man had turned his back and couldn't see them.

'This is our man,' McAllister proclaimed.

The young man turned to look at the woman.

'David!'

'You know him?' Redwood asked her.

'He's my brother . . .'

McAllister and Redwood exchanged glances, as Miss Hibling glared at the young man.

'Where the hell have you been? Why didn't you get in touch when Mum died?'

He turned his head, brushing her questions aside.

'You didn't need to break in. The house is as much yours as mine.'

Hostility and resentment were seething inside David Hibling. He looked at her and shouted: 'Where've they hidden it?'

'There *is* no money,' she told him in exasperation, obviously not for the first time.

'Not in the bank – no.'

'There isn't any in the house. They'd spent it all.'

But her brother was unconvinced, and just as insistent. 'The nest-egg. Thirty grand. Salted away for a rainy day.'

Her eyes rolled back, as she tried to explain to him that the money was gone. 'They had their rainy day.'

'What?'

Her head shook sadly to and fro, her eyes looking into his. 'It all went on medical bills. Operations. The hospice. Mum wanted Dad's last year to be –'

'You're lying,' he said simply.

She glared at him. 'I'd have shown you the bills if you'd put in an appearance occasionally. They might as well have stuck with the NHS for all the good it did them.'

'You've got it,' David accused her. 'They gave it to you.'

'All I've got are two houses mortgaged up to the hilt. One mine. One ours.' Financial stress tightening the screws, her pain became unbearable, and she held back the tears. 'Oh, God – I put all this in the letter.'

Her brother showed no appreciation for her supposed concern. 'It's easy to say that now.'

Her tears were overcome by anger. 'What about you? Where've you been all this time? You never even tried to contact us. Not even once!'

Again he deflected her accusations, returning to the theme that was eating him alive. 'There has to be some money . . .'

'How many more times?' she shouted at him. '*It's all gone!*'

David leaped to his feet. Quickly Redwood stepped forward in case the young man needed to be restrained.

'I need that money, Alison! I'm in a lot of trouble!'

He was shaking from the outburst, and she appeared shaken as well. McAllister pushed some of the betting slips and markers across the table to her.

'He's not exaggerating, either.'

She stared at the betting slips, then looked up at her brother. 'Look, David, maybe I can manage a hundred pounds.'

David was incredulous, his nerves stretched to the breaking point. 'A hundred pounds? What good's a hundred pounds? These people are . . .' Again he turned away, unable to face her.

'I'm dead, Alison. I'm finished.'

15

A group of children came out of the school gate and walked by a lollipop lady who was chatting animatedly to one of their mothers. 'Apparently, the whole family was playing truant. The two boys . . . the girl . . .'

Something caught the mother's attention over the lollipop lady's shoulder.

'Who's he?'

'What?'

The lollipop lady turned around and saw an old man in some sort of military uniform halting traffic and ushering the group of children across the road. She was astonished at his impertinence.

'Right!'

Focused on her objective, the lollipop lady marched directly over to the old man in the uniform.

'Clear off or I'll call the police.'

Percy ignored her. 'I *am* the police.'

But as soon as she switched her attention to the children, he beat a hasty retreat across the road.

Watching the old man walk away, the lollipop lady turned on the children in a stern voice, warning them again in one of her most oft-repeated lessons.

'What have you been told? Stranger means danger!'

John Barraclough walked out of the garage area into the yard of Cougar Coaches to a man looking over one of the coaches as if he owned it. A stringy-looking fellow with longish hair, he appeared to have a permanent indolent smile etched on his face.

'Can I help you?'

'I'm meeting Dicky here,' was all the man offered. He wheeled away and went to have a look under the coach he had been inspecting.

Barraclough wiped his hands on an oily rag and headed for the office, where he found Loach and his wife at work: he adding some figures on his calculator, she looking for her kettle lid.

'Have you seen the –'

'Just a minute.' Loach paused to jot the subtotal on his blotter. 'Seen the what?'

'The kettle lid.'

He raised his head to look around when John Barraclough came in wearing his usual frown.

'We've got some bloke in the yard.'

'So?'

'He's looking over the livery.'

'What?'

'Says he's waiting for Mr Padgett.'

Loach got up to investigate. 'What the hell does *he* want?'

Noreen piped in. 'Probably a gin and tonic if he's a friend of Dicky.'

The string-fellow in the yard looked up and waved when he saw Loach and Barraclough bearing down on him.

'Loach the Coach – right?'

'Who are you?'

'Jake Miller.'

'*Jake* Miller?' Barraclough went back to work with a grin.

Miller had a question on his face. 'Name doesn't ring a bell – right?'

'Can't say it does.'

'That Dicky. Likes playing things close to his chest.'

'What's all this about?'

Before he could answer, the roar of a sports car distracted them. Miller just smiled. 'Why don't you ask him?'

Dicky Padgett powered his BMW into the yard, pulled up short, jumped out, and walked over to Loach and Miller.

'See you two have met.'

'What's going on?' asked Loach.

Dicky looked at Miller. 'You haven't filled him in yet?'

'Tried to.'

Putting his arm around Miller, Dicky smiled at Loach. 'Jake's Redbird's top driver.'

'I'm very happy for him.'

'Just the kind of man we're looking for,' Dicky remarked.

Loach was surprised: first he'd heard about it. But the name Redbird jumped out at him like an old family curse.

'Didn't realize we needed another driver.'

Dicky's delivery was casual. 'We'll need several if we're taking on extra capacity.'

'Hang on,' Loach warned him. 'Nothing's been decided.'

For a second, the old rugby rivals appeared to consider fighting it out, right there and then.

Finally, Dicky spoke up. 'Well, maybe it's time we did. Decide, I mean.'

'Office,' Loach nodded, and headed in that direction.

Miller's indolent smile changed to annoyance. 'I don't need this.'

Padgett tried to pacify him. 'Don't go away.' Then he followed Loach into the office.

Not only irate, but determined to tear his partner limb from limb, Loach stormed into the office pursued by Dicky Padgett. Caught in the middle, Noreen immediately sensed the ugly mood.

227

'*Jake* Miller? Got fed up of Jack, did he?' Loach raved. 'Or is he just a Country and Western fan?'

'Blokes like him don't come on the market every day. If we don't move fast, he'll push off to London and get a job there.' Belatedly he acknowledged Noreen. 'Hello, luv.'

'Dicky,' she greeted him as impersonally as possible.

'I don't like him. I don't like anyone who calls himself Jake.'

'What's that got to do with anything?' Dicky wanted to know.

'I don't trust him, then. I know the type. He's up there in the cab with Kris Kristofferson and his CB.'

'Give over,' Dicky sneered.

But Loach wasn't giving up: 'He's a chancer. The sort who'll try to cut twenty minutes off the London to Coventry run. He'll have us in court before he's out of the yard.'

Dicky went nose-to-nose with him. 'I rather like people who take chances. Pity I don't have a partner with similar ambitions.'

'Maybe you ought to team up with Jake, then.'

Noreen tried to step in between them. 'Cool it, you two.'

Dicky still wouldn't quit. 'Look. If we buy out Redbird, it makes sense we take their best drivers.'

'I'm still not convinced we should buy out Redbird.'

Up against a brick wall, Dicky's frustration was steadily building to a head. 'I'm getting sick and tired of this. We don't have forever to put a package together.'

'And I'm sick and tired of you doing deals behind my back. First Timson. Now this Jake Miller.'

'Fat chance of putting any deal together with you vetoing my every move!' Dicky spat, his voice rising.

'Maybe *I'm* just fed up with finding out about things after the event!'

'Right. After the event. That's you all over, Bob. Mr After-the-Event. Well, you better get your act together, mate! Find out what you want – to stay a piddling little provincial operator, or take on the big boys.'

Turning his back on Loach, Dicky walked to the door, then looked around once more.

'I don't intend to lie down and die just because you've lost your bottle!'

Dicky looked down apologetically at the woman married to the wrong man. 'Sorry, Noreen.' And he walked out.

Loach kicked the door shut after him.

His wife, if he had cared to notice, was growing unhappier by the minute.

16

In Traffic Control, two shortsleeved controllers, Leslie and Andrea, surveyed the banks of TV monitors in front of them. Blocks of traffic were appearing on each of them.

'What's going on?' he asked.

'It's called rush hour,' Andrea answered.

Leslie screwed up his lip. 'It's never this bad.' He picked up the phone and punched out a number.

'I think we've got a traffic light down on Threemile Road,' he said into the phone.

'Looks more like pilot error to me,' Andrea giggled.

Leslie gave her a withering look, and she shrugged. 'If you want my opinion.'

From Division 'S' Control, WPC Sheila Baxter was talking to Traffic Control on her headset, keying in the information on her computer screen.

'We've nobody down there as far as I can see.'

Meanwhile, out in the middle of the traffic jam, Freddy Calder sat absolutely still in his shiny blue Sierra sharing the non-ride with Foxy the glove puppet, lying on the front passenger seat and enjoying the hot sun. Unfortunately, Freddy had to do the driving, or non-driving as it were.

'What's going on?' he wondered to nobody in particular. He picked up the car-phone and punched out a number.

Back at Control, WPC Baxter was still talking on her headset to Traffic Control, trying to figure out what was happening out there to cause such a snarl.

'We'll get a panda down there.'

Her outside line started buzzing, and she lifted the receiver. 'Baxter.'

Freddy had made his connection. 'Sheila. My fantasy woman. I'm sitting in a queue of traffic as long as the Great Wall, and I'm bored . . . bored . . . bored.'

'You wouldn't be anywhere near Threemile Road by any chance?' she inquired curiously.

'You mean to say you want help from *me*?' The very thought made him giddy.

'Frightening, isn't it?' she admitted.

'I'd say the front of this queue's in Threemile Road,' Freddy duly informed her.

'So where are *you*?' demanded Sheila.

'Selly Park.'

WPC Baxter was not amused. She hung up.

Percy was still on point duty in the middle of the T-junction, although he was becoming a little flustered. His hands were shooting every which way. There were cars slewed across the road, half in and half out of the junction, effectively blocking off one of the main carriageways.

'Come on, then! Yes . . . *you*!'

He frantically waved on the car facing him, but as other vehicles were still coming fast in the opposite direction, the driver was reluctant to pull out.

'What are you waiting for, Christmas?'

The driver shouted something Percy couldn't quite understand, but his ears burned anyway.

A panda car pulled out into the main carriageway, and other cars squeezed over to let it pass. PC Douglas Thorburn got out of the panda, walked over to Percy, and looked him over up, down, and around, unable to figure out which planet he had come from.

'Who the hell are you?'

Percy was a bit sheepish. 'Right. I'll leave you to it, then.' And he backed away, and gradually melted into traffic on foot.

'Hey, you!'

Thorburn was about to give chase when he realized that he was being hooted and yelled at from all sides.

'Alright, alright!'

Driving along a stretch of dual carriageway on the outskirts of Birmingham, Freddy was talking on the car-phone. He cradled the phone on his shoulder and flipped through his sample case of transparent nothings garnished with lovely lace in every colour of the erotic rainbow.

'I got them in bottle green, yellow, and plum de ma tante . . . uh-huh . . .' He checked his imitation Rolex for his ETA. 'Well, I'll be there soon.'

After goodbyes, he hung up, then went through the usual routine – craned his head to catch his reflection in the driving mirror, checked his hair, looked for any new flaws. Then he breathed into his hand, and pulled a face when he smelled the result. Death of a salesman. That was something he would definitely have to do something about.

He slowed and turned into a large lay-by with a mobile diner, pulling up behind a juggernaut.

'Tube of mints,' he said to the woman behind the counter.

Then he took a closer look at her, and suddenly realized who she was (although she didn't seem to recognize who he was). RITA! He couldn't believe his eyes and wished he'd gone to heaven. RITA! Could this really be true, or was she just another look-alike? RITA!

'Twenty-two pee,' she said to him, not looking up.

He was just about to say something when she was distracted by a trucker coming up to the counter with an empty cup.

'Another of those,' said the trucker.

Rita was going to give the trucker his refill when she finally looked over and noticed Freddy beaming at her. All of a sudden, Foxy popped up behind the counter, speaking in his high squeaky voice.

'Remember me?'

'Freddy! Freddy . . .'

'Calder,' he reminded her in his normal voice.

'I didn't recognize you in those clothes!'

The trucker waiting for his refill had become absorbed in their conversation. Freddy beamed at him, flirting in Foxy's voice.

'I usually wear slinky little off-the-shoulder numbers.' Turning away, the trucker decided he would rather chase real women.

Her eyes laughed the way he remembered. 'So what are you doing here?'

He stepped back and gave the diner a quick, patronizing once-over. 'I could ask the same of you.'

'It may not be much, but it's mine,' she said defensively.

Realizing his faux pas, Freddy scurried to retrieve the situation. 'No. No. It's great. Really. Your own little business.'

Rita didn't know quite how to respond to this. Was he serious? Was he ever serious? Was he mocking her? And what about the puppet in his pocket?

He nervously fingered his tube of mints, and he was beginning to make her nervous, too.

'Did you want anything else, Freddy?'

'No,' he said, though leaving his mouth open to say more.

'Good job all my customers aren't like you. I'd go bankrupt in a week.'

It was those laughing, glistening, larger-than-life eyes that got him. Although it was difficult to suggest that her wonderful, wild garden of hair wasn't her most attractive feature, set off with her dancing earrings. But actually, if you got a bit closer, it was her lips, her mouth, that drove him crazy . . . just the thought of how her mouth would feel, and move. And for all that, there was how much more he couldn't see, only imagine.

'Except . . .'

She cocked her head. 'What?'

Surreptitiously he checked again to make sure the trucker was out of earshot.

'Do you, uh, fancy going out to dinner?'

There. He had done it. At last.

'Dinner?'

Oh lord, no . . . she can't believe I'd ask her . . . she thinks I'm a buffoon . . . she's about to laugh in my face . . .

'I'll understand if you're busy. I know this short –'

'When?'

It wasn't possible. It was possible? Could miracles happen? Because, if they could, one had just transpired on this very spot. This was unbelievable.

'Tomorrow?'

'Okay.'

He would live for tomorrow. He would die for tomorrow. 'Seven?'

'Fine.'

He wondered if she kissed with those magnificent bedroom eyes open.

'Great. Your carriage will wait.' Then he lowered his voice to her in confidence. 'That's my car.' Finally his beloved automobile had served its exalted purpose – to impress the woman of his dreams – and perhaps it would bring him the ultimate luck, and provide both opportunity and mobility for their tryst.

And yet, he saw one just like it pulling out of the lay-by. In fact, as he looked a little closer, it was exactly like his car . . .

Freddy was thunderstruck. This couldn't be happening. He had just fallen in love. Everything had been going so incredibly well. This was his worst nightmare.

'Hey! *That's my car*!'

17

Although Mr and Mrs Robert Loach were both in the same room – the office of Cougar Coaches – they were no longer on the same wavelength. He was on the phone to District Commandant Whittaker, talking while sharpening a pencil.

'Where? . . . Did he now? . . . No, I agree . . . Okay. Leave it with me.'

He hung up just as Noreen came out of the alcove.

'Whittaker.' She gave him a blank stare. 'The District Commandant.'

'Oh, him.' She seemed underwhelmed.

'Apparently there's some old bloke going around dressed as a Special.'

'He must be a glutton for punishment. That's all I can say.'

Putting on his coat to go out, he sighed and shook his head, after all these years realizing it was no use to tell her she wasn't funny. So he said nothing.

'Where are *you* off to?'

'Police Headquarters.'

'What about Dicky?'

'What about him?'

Noreen found it impossible to tolerate that his mind could be elsewhere.

'Hadn't you better smooth things over with him?'

'Dicky can wait. Right now I'm more concerned about daft old buggers going round making us look proper Charlies. The mileage the regulars'll get from this . . .'

'The way you go on you'd think it's your responsibility,' she said with disdain.

He was getting sick to death of it.

'Why don't we discuss this when I get back?'

'It's always the same,' she said wearily.

'What's always the same?'

She, too, was too tired to continue bickering, and too busy.

'Doesn't matter.' She picked up a couple of mugs and went back into the alcove.

He also realized that every time they left it this way, it got worse between them. So he didn't want to leave it like this now, although he couldn't see what else to do about her for the moment.

'I'll be back as soon as I can,' he called to her from the door.

'Okay,' she responded listlessly from the alcove.

He left in a hurry.

Rinsing the mugs in the sink, she leaned back and looked forlornly back into the deserted office.

Loach hurried through the yard to his waiting Jag. Climbing down from the cab of one of the coaches, John Barraclough shouted after him.

'Gear box mountings on number three are shot.'

'Talk to you later, John.'

As Loach's Jag squealed and sped out of the yard, John Barraclough was another of those unhappy to see him go. It wasn't like him to vanish when he was most needed.

Administrative secretary Sandra Gibson hunted through her cardex system, as Bob Loach leaned against the window ledge in her office.

'There are twenty thousand Specials in England alone. And you want me to find one special Special!'

'Let's keep it local,' he suggested, trying to be helpful.

'Great. We're down to a thousand.'

Loach thought he might narrow the possibilities a little more from what they already knew. 'He's getting on. Probably in his seventies.'

'So what? That doesn't tell us how long ago he joined.'

'And the uniform's out of date,' he reminded her.

'How out of date is out of date?' She wasn't trying to put him off, but to demonstrate how impossible it was to find a needle in a haystack.

'Buttoned-up collar.'

Ah, now that was information. She pushed shut one drawer of index cards and pulled open another. 'That's out of date.' She was going to have to dig still deeper.

Next they went to the files stores, towering rows of metal shelves crammed full of file-binders and folders.

Unerringly Sandra picked her way down one of the gangways followed by Section Officer Loach.

'How come he kept his uniform?' she wondered.

'You're asking *me*?' he laughed.

Her head back looking up, Sandra moved the ladder to the section she was interested in, while Loach regarded the potential sturdiness of the ladder.

'Do you want me . . . ?' he offered.

'It's okay. I know where to look.'

She climbed up about six rungs of the ladder, unintentionally revealing an elegant leg. Loach found it difficult to keep his mind on business without at least taking a glance while he had the opportunity. The latter argument was persuasive, although he couldn't bring himself to think of Sandra in that way. So he tried not to look.

'Mind if I use your shoulder?' she asked nicely.

That didn't appear as though it would help his dilemma much, but it was surely an offer he couldn't refuse.

'Be my guest.'

Sandra put a foot on his shoulder while she reached across to get the box file she was after. 'Gotcha!' she exclaimed as she grasped the box in her hand. Still standing on the ladder, she blew a cloud of dust off the box file.

Loach, looking up at the wrong time, took the dust storm full in the face, though to sneeze would have been to give the game away, so he held back until she was safely down from the ladder and her shapely legs were out of sight.

Back in her office, she separated out a few files on her desk and handed the select few to Bob Loach. As best she could, Sandra had whittled down the list of candidates to a reasonably manageable investigative task.

'They're you're best bet,' she concluded, indicating the files now in his lap.

'I don't suppose I can take these with me.' For him, there was still much work to be done.

Sandra was sympathetic, but that far she couldn't go, 'You know you can't take anything out of the office.' She started putting the remainder of the documents back in the box file.

'Can you photocopy them for me, then?'

'You know where the machine is.' What some men wouldn't do to avoid a clerical task, she smiled to herself.

'Doesn't matter,' Loach decided. 'I'll only need their addresses.'

And that confirmed her supposition: he would rather spend twenty minutes with a pencil instead of one minute with a machine. Of course, he probably didn't see it in terms of efficiency, as she had to.

While Sandra turned her attention to other responsibilities, Loach sat at an empty desk in her office and began to copy down the addresses of elderly Specials in the files. Surprisingly, just from a cursory glance at them, it didn't take long for him to discover a telling detail.

'I think I know why he's still got the uniform,' he announced, holding up one of the files.

'What?'

Loach smiled. 'He never retired.'

Among the Specials standing around in little groups waiting for Parade were Viv Smith and heartsick Freddy. He felt as though he shouldn't be here, as though there had been a death in his family, and if he hadn't given his word, he surely would be nursing his grief somewhere else. It was simply too much for one man to bear.

'Stolen?' said Viv in disbelief. She didn't know whether to laugh or to cry.

'In broad daylight.'

'So when was this?' she inquired like a relative asking about the heart attack.

'This afternoon. I'd just stopped for a minute.' The story got worse every time he told it.

'Was it locked?' Viv asked.

Freddy didn't answer immediately, but hesitated, then answered a different question. 'I didn't actually *leave* the car. It wasn't as if . . .'

'Was it locked?'

Again he hesitated. Then, finally, it came out.

'No.'

'Brilliant,' she pronounced, laying it on thick. This little morsel would feed the meat grinder for days.

'It could happen to anyone. Are you telling me you've never . . .'

Suddenly he broke off. Viv looked at him suspiciously. 'Never what?'

'Nothing.'

All of a sudden she twigged. 'You left the keys inside!'

Freddy tried to shush her, looking nervously over each shoulder. 'Keep your voice down. People'll hear.'

'You twit, Freddy.'

Eager to get out from under her tongue-lashing, he also wondered if there were some way he could utilize the resources of the Specials to find and to save his mean machine. 'Maybe I ought . . .'

He zig-zagged to the front of the room and cleared his throat. 'Could I have everyone's attention, please? I'd like to make an announcement.'

'You taking the parade tonight, Freddy?' wondered someone.

'What? No. This is more by way of a private announcement.'

'You're getting married.'

It wasn't easy for Freddy to convey the understanding that he was being serious, although they must have heard of his catastrophe by now. 'Could you all keep your eyes out for a blue Sierra?'

'How much are you willing to pay for it?'

All Freddy could manage was a rueful smile. 'Yeah. Side-splitting. You ought to be in the Specials.'

'So what do we look out for first? "A blue Sierra? Or a suitable flat?'

He ignored the scattered chortling and pushed ahead, yet couldn't help feeling the futility of it all. 'Licence number is D310 UCF. It was last seen –'

As soon as everyone saw Police Chief Superintendent Ellsmore enter the gathering, there was an immediate hush. The Red Sea parted, and his natural gift for taking command made them believe he could have walked on the water instead just as easily. In an instant, the mood had become dead serious.

'If I could just have a moment of everyone's time . . .' The Specials gathered in a little closer around him. No one was laughing now.

'Some of you may know, but, for the benefit of others, Special Constable Anjali Shah suffered contusions and a dislocated shoulder in the line of duty. However, I can report that her injuries are not critical, and she is well on her way to a full recovery.'

There was some applause, though sporadic and uncertain, when a few people could not contain the emotions they felt for Anjali Shah at that moment.

'We're very proud of her. She put herself on the line. If she hadn't, one young constable might well have had a widow this morning . . . So in view of all that . . .' The Super's eyes swept the room.

'. . . you'll be pleased to learn she'll be receiving a commendation for bravery.'

This time the cheers and applause broke out in full force. Every one of them knew why they wanted to be members of this privileged band.

18

Anjali was feeling trapped in the sitting room of her own home – able to walk, move, get about, but held back and made to sit still by her mother and her uncle. She had to admit that she didn't look such a prize right now, her face bruised and discoloured and her arm hanging in a sling, but she was more restless than disabled. And professionally, she simply knew it would be better for her to get up and get back into shape. Certainly it wouldn't be half as excruciating as listening to the constant harangues of her mother and Uncle Ram.

Her mother, in particular – tied to the ancient traditions – was perhaps more shocked and troubled by her injuries than even Uncle Ram. She thought her daughter's life was probably ruined, whereas her uncle was merely convinced she would wind up a poor, unloved spinster who brought immeasurable shame to her family. Yet her mother had not been so worried since Anjali's father had died and left them almost destitute.

'Hasn't enough misfortune been visited on us?' her mother cried. 'Anjali – fate is cruel enough without you provoking it.'

'I didn't provoke anything,' she objected.

Ram thought that was nonsense, although it was no laughing matter, but rather a personal tragedy for all of them. 'Just look at what's happened to you! This is what you get for being a policewoman. This is your reward. You could've been badly disfigured. And then you'd have had no prospect at all of finding a husband.'

'And what about the dislocated shoulder?' Mrs Shah brought up yet again. 'Dislocated shoulders are very worrying. Your aunt spends so much of her life in the Out Patients. And all because of her shoulder. Is that any way to live – a life spent in the Out Patients?'

'She's got a frozen shoulder," Ma,' Anjali protested wearily.

'Don't argue with your mother!' Uncle Ram yelled at her.

'I'm not arguing with her. All I'm saying is that frozen and dislocated shoulders are two different things. I ought to know. I'm a physiotherapist.'

Not that it was doing her much good now. And not that her profession in any way alleviated her very real soreness and pain. But sitting here was only making her problems worse.

She was about to let loose when the door-bell rang. Since she was already struggling to her feet, she started for the door. 'I'll go.'

But of course it was Mrs Shah who opened the front door. Standing outside were a man with a bandage round his head and a young woman who was very large with child.

'Hello. Is Anjali in? I'm Toby Armstrong. This is my wife – Shirley.'

Mrs Shah was surprised to see the policeman her daughter said had been hurt so badly – and, of course, a woman who was that close to term should not be out of confinement – yet her politeness was more than a formality. She was genuinely impressed to learn that they had made such an effort to see her daughter.

In the living room, Anjali visibly cheered up to see Toby and Shirley and receive their flowers.

'This is the first opportunity I've had to thank you. Properly, anyway.'

Poor Shirley could barely hold back her tears. 'He could have been killed if you hadn't been there.' Suddenly she reached out to Anjali and hugged her for all she was worth.

Embarrassed for both of them, Toby tried to make light of the situation for Mrs Shah and Uncle Ram. 'If she hadn't jumped in . . . a couple more whacks, and I'd have scrambled eggs for brains.'

239

Mrs Shah turned up her nose at this reference: although she didn't understand it, yet it certainly seemed unpleasant. But it did serve to remind her of refreshments.

'Be seated . . . please. You must let us offer you some tea.'

Anjali smiled. 'He drinks only Indian.'

Toby and Anjali laughed, while Mrs Shah and Uncle Ram traded baffled looks at their private joke. Shaking her head, Mrs Shah went to the kitchen.

Drying her tears, Shirley Armstrong tried to express her gratitude and appreciation to Uncle Ram for the courage of his niece.

'Anjali is very brave. You must be very proud of her.'

'Very proud indeed,' replied Ram, prompting Anjali to hide a smile. The words certainly weren't familiar to his mouth.

The door-bell rang again, and this time Uncle Ram rushed to get it. 'Sanjay has forgotten his keys again. Excuse me . . .'

When he opened the door he found two more police officers – Viv Smith and Freddy Calder – also bringing flowers.

The panda car pulled up opposite a row of terraced houses. Hanging on to his briefcase, Loach got out of the car and glanced back at the PC in the driver's seat.

'This shouldn't take too long.'

He slammed the car door shut and crossed the road to one of the houses, then rang the bell. There was a light on in the window, so he was pretty sure someone was in. He went to ring the doorbell again when the door opened slowly, revealing an old, overweight man.

'Mr Beasley . . . ?'

'This'd better be important. Do you know how long it takes me to get up?'

'Sorry to trouble you. We're –'

'You'd better not be selling double-glazing or anything. I've got all the glass I want.'

Loach noticed that Mr Beasley was leaning on a zimmer, and realized that he couldn't possibly be the elderly Special who was turning up everywhere in town directing traffic and helping those who needed no help. In the meantime, Mr Beasley had stepped out on to the street and gestured to his living-room window.

'See that? That's glass. That'll see me out. I don't want no more.'

'So I see,' Loach smiled. 'Well, I won't take up any more of your . . .'

Beasley went back inside and shut the door in Loach's face.

'. . . time.'

The living room of Anjali Shah's home had filled in only a few minutes. Standing at the kitchen door, Mrs Shah and Uncle Ram looked out upon a room containing not only Specials, but also neighbours, all mixing together.

'I hope this is an end of them,' Mrs Shah confided in her brother. 'I am running out of everything.'

Ram wouldn't hear of it. 'We musn't run out. It will look bad if we run out.'

'So many people,' her mother marvelled. 'She has so many friends.'

But Uncle Ram was no longer amazed; now he was taking it for granted. 'It is not surprising. After all, she is my niece,' he smiled.

The door-bell rang yet again. Ram gave his sister a despairing look as he went off to welcome more guests.

Freddy had managed to get himself thrown in with a young Indian whose name he couldn't pronounce, who reportedly knew a great deal about the world of automobiles as well.

'I understand you sell cars,' he ventured, after his other conversational ploys had played out.

'You want to buy a car?' he asked, a glint in his eye.

Freddy tried to explain. 'Not exactly. I was wondering if you could keep an eye out for a blue Sierra.'

'You want to buy a Sierra?'

Freddy shook his head slowly. 'No . . .' He wasn't quite getting the picture.

'I can get you a Sierra. In any colour,' the man offered him challengingly.

'Forget it.'

Abruptly Freddy realized that the room had gone quiet, and his last words were all anyone had heard. What's more, standing at the door with Anjali's Uncle Ram was Police Chief Superintendent Frank Ellsmore in full dress uniform.

The Super immediately picked up on the change in atmosphere since they knew he had entered. 'I seem to be the spectre at the feast.'

'No, sir,' Uncle Ram bowed. 'You are no spectre, sir. You are very welcome.'

Viv Smith sneaked up behind Freddy and put a word in his ear. 'We'd better make tracks. We're not meant to be here.'

'Right.'

A solicitous Uncle Ram ushered Chief Superintendent Ellsmore into the room, and he happened to pass an embarrassed Viv and Freddy on the way. He glanced in their direction as he passed, though ostensibly addressing nobody in particular.

'There must be a few villains tonight wondering what's happened to your much vaunted presence on the streets.'

Uncle Ram brought his embarrassed niece forward.

'So how are you feeling, Anjali?'

'Much better, sir.' She was unable to concentrate on the Super, being only too aware of her uncle beaming up at him.

'This is my uncle, sir . . . Chief Superintendant Ellsmore, Uncle Ram.'

At such a profound moment in his life, Ram was suddenly speechless. 'A chief . . .'

As Uncle Ram left them alone to confer with his sister, Ellsmore leaned over to Anjali. 'Well, Anjali, I was going to tell you the good news. I imagine it's already leaked, though . . .'

Ram and his sister watched them, bursting with new-found pride in Anjali.

'This is a very important man,' said Ram, equating Ellsmore with heads of state. 'A chief superintendent! Do you see in what high regard our Anjali is held?'

19

The panda car was parked on a street near the house of another suspect. Pressing the bell-push near the front door, Loach was tired of the hunt by now, though the PC driving appeared to be enjoying himself hugely at the expense of the Specials.

'Keep your fingers crossed,' said Loach, as this was the final primary candidate. Suddenly he noticed a young girl of about seven looking at him from the door of the next house.

'He's not in,' said the little girl.

'Isn't he?' asked Loach in what he hoped was a kindly Uncle Bob sort of voice.

'He went out,' the little girl reported.

'When?'

'He goes to be a policeman,' she said.

'Does he now?' said Loach with joy in his heart.

'Mum says he's as daft as a brush,' said the young innocent.

'I think she might be right about that, luv.'

Percy walked slowly along the pavement, tested a gate to make sure it was padlocked securely, and then walked on. Turning the corner, he strolled by an open parking lot behind a pub. He noticed that some youths had gathered round one of the few cars parked there. One didn't need to be a spring chicken to see that there was trouble afoot.

He watched for a few moments, and then heard a hard, snapping noise, as they broke the door open with a jemmy. Percy went after them. No time like the present, he told himself.

'Hey! You lot!'

The youths looked over in the direction of the shout, but they didn't seem to pick him out precisely. Instead, one pulled open the door and jumped in; another two piled in after him.

'Right!' barked Percy, walking as rapidly as he could toward the car.

The youth in the driving seat was bent forward trying to hotwire the vehicle into life. One of the youths in the back seat, watching the old man approach, was becoming anxious. 'Move it!' he shouted.

Suddenly the engine roared into life, and the driver mashed the car into gear.

Percy changed direction and hurried across to the narrow exit from the car park. Now the car was charging toward the exit as well.

The old Special won the race, at least the first one. He reached the exit and stood where he was. 'Stop!' he cried.

The stolen car accelerated racing now with death if the old man were unable to get out of the way. He loomed ahead, too old to move fast enough, yet not moving a muscle.

The driver held on to the wheel and aimed straight for the exit.

At the last moment, one of the youths in the back seat lost his

243

nerve and panicked. He flung himself over the driver's shoulder and yanked the wheel hard over.

The car braked but glanced off Percy as it changed course, and sent him flying before it skidded into a wall.

Percy's limp body lying on the ground was merely a sack of old laundry.

Loach was sitting back in the front passenger seat of the panda car looking dog tired as the PC drove through the night.

'So who are we seeing down here?'

'Nobody in particular.'

'What are we doing then?'

Loach leaned back. 'I thought we'd drive around for a bit. Take in the ambiance of the place.'

'We're not looking for this geezer *now*?'

The PC was still young, Loach began to realize. 'He's outside . . . on foot . . . in this patch . . . in a uniform that went out with PC49. Surely he can't be that difficult to find.'

'Control to Four. Over,' said the voice of WPC Sheila Baxter over the radio.

The driver buttoned the handpiece to sound. 'Four to control over.'

'Didn't know we were taking on OAP's these days. Over,' Baxter shot back.

Smiling, Loach took the handpiece. 'Tell me. Over.'

'They've got a granddad in a rather old Specials uniform down at the General. Over.'

The PC chuckled. 'He's probably on a recruiting drive.'

Ignoring him, Loach acknowledged the message. 'We're on our way. Over.'

In a small ward at General Hospital, Percy was lying in bed with facial injuries and his leg in plaster. His old friends Walt and Dave were sitting at his bedside, basking in his glory.

'At least you had a go,' Walt enthused. 'I'd have been out there with you if it hadn't been for my arthritic hip.'

Dave scoffed at his claim. 'Oh yeah? And who was whingeing on about having to come out here because it was way past his bedtime?'

'Didn't have much choice, did I? Not when the police turns up on your doorstep at half-eleven at night!'

Now calm and under sedation, Percy was sorry he'd caused them all to go to so much trouble. 'They asked me if I had any next of kin or anyone I wanted telling.'

'You just wanted to show off,' Walt griped.

'He's got reason to show off,' Dave boasted on Percy's behalf. 'He's put three louts off the street for a couple of months.'

Bob Loach's voice wafted through from the doorway, before they had seen him. 'Maybe. Charles Bronson he isn't, though.'

Three old heads turned to the door, as Loach walked over to greet them. 'Special Section Officer Loach.'

'Special Section what?' asked Percy.

Loach stood over his bed and smiled. 'No doubt the ranks were different when you were in the Specials.'

Dave stepped up to defend his old buddy. 'Pity there aren't more like him.'

'Oh, aye. He's been leading us a merry dance, haven't you, Mr Thorogood?'

Slightly embarrassed, Percy shook his head.

As sympathetic and respectful as he might be, Loach was also angry. 'You're fortunate you and your three louts aren't laid out in the morgue. It would've been a high price to pay for a bit of small-time thieving.'

'There was just thieving in our day,' said Dave angrily. 'None of this small- or big-time stuff. Just thieving.'

Loach smiled, remembering Freddy Calder's adventures earlier that day. 'One of my blokes had his car nicked this afternoon. But he didn't throw himself in its path, causing a pile-up and risking lives.'

Percy and his friends were suddenly quiet.

'Rule book's different these days.' Loach went on. 'We don't have a go unless it's the last resort.'

Too weak to be stubborn any more, Percy looked up at Loach. 'I was just keeping an eye on things, that's all.'

But Loach wouldn't let him off easy, not if the old guy still wanted to walk the beat and call himself a Special.

'Those kids could've spread you across the car park. Lucky for you one of them had a conscience. Usually the odds don't come down in your favour.'

Walt would have none of it. 'He knows what he's about. He was trained, too. Just like you.'

Loach shook his head with a smile. 'Life was simpler then. The conditions have changed. It's different now.'

Old Percy agreed. 'It's different alright. Everything's different.'

But Dave was still defensive, and proud of the courage his friend had shown in the face of danger. 'He deserves a medal for what he did.'

'I don't want no medal,' Percy complained. 'I didn't do it for medals.' He turned his head away, brooding. Meanwhile, the faces of Dave and Walt were filled with reproach.

'Now's not really a good time. We'll talk when you're feeling better. Is there anything you need?' He started toward the door.

'Hold up,' said Percy.

Loach turned to face him.

'Can you do something for me?'

'If I can.'

'In the cupboard there,' Percy said, indicating where he wanted Loach to go.

Loach opened the cupboard and found Percy's old uniform: for the first time, he had a hard time keeping a still upper lip.

'I want you to take it,' Percy told him. 'I should've handed it in years ago.'

'Leave it to me,' Loach assured him, feeling such a depth of kinship with this old knight that he couldn't speak.

Percy's voice started to waver. 'And maybe you could put it in the book that Percy Thorogood's resigning from the Specials. Effective from tonight.'

Bob Loach was not the kind of man who could fill others with inspiring words, like Frank Ellsmore. He knew he had no words adequate to this situation, and no idea what to say.

He just kept running his hand over the old uniform, hardly tarnished from the accident. Another fluke.

'This is a lot heavier than ours,' Loach said to him quietly, admiring the sturdy cloth that had served in good stead for so long.

'Made to last,' said Percy, looking up into Loach's eyes.

'You reckon?'

'And the buttons, lad . . .' For the last time, the old gent's fingers

246

brushed against these small symbols of a belief in human dignity.

'. . . They don't make buttons like that any more . . .'

20

At the Pub on 4th, Bob Loach carried his drink from the bar to a vacant table in the corner, sitting down and putting his feet back up on the opposite chair. Then he continued with his long talk to himself, taking stock, going over the evidence, making the logical deductions.

Maybe it was time for him to turn in his uniform as well, like Percy. Maybe he was getting a little old for playing policeman. He'd had a pretty good go at it, he'd performed a service. Now perhaps the best days were over, and it was time to get on with the rest of his life.

All the signs pointed in the same direction. Look at the old man; look at the rest of his Specials for that matter. You put in the hours, and what do you get for it? Run over. Hit by a pipe on the back of the skull; if your partner isn't there to back you up, maybe you get your skull caved in as well. Dislocated shoulder, and lucky that's all it was. Subject to the same perils as the regulars. And for what? Even they joined in to give you more grief.

For all the times you really help someone, there were just as many incidents that were trivial, comic relief for the real work.

Then there was the constant politics. There was no good reason he *shouldn't* be the SDO, with or without Barker. He was a capable and conscientious leader, and he never got much recognition for it.

As for his job . . . his real job . . . the business was at a crossroads. He could make a million, or he could lose a million. But he couldn't make much of a difference one way or the other if he weren't even there half the time. No, his fortune was in being a great mechanic, not being a great Special.

His marriage was a disaster. If he didn't pay attention to saving it, or at least trying, he might as well quit and give her her share of the business right now. What he had to find out was whether he had any love left for his wife.

So everything was added together into one big pile telling him to go home. Let it go. Hang it up.

But somehow, every time it came to this, he couldn't.

The people, that was why he couldn't. These were his friends. These were his colleagues, his peers, his cronies. These were the kind of people who would put their lives on the line for yours. They believed in what was right, and they were willing to act on their beliefs.

That's where Bob Loach wanted to be. These were his kind of people. Whatever their individual quirks, however imperfect their attempts, their hearts and minds were in the right place. They gave what they had to give.

It was no wonder they became so close to each other. Whatever happened in their separate lives, here they shared a common bond. Here they belonged.

And so did he.

But there were surely times when his loyalty and dedication were put to the test. Two of them were headed for him right now – regulars without a doubt trying to cause more trouble for his Specials.

'What's this? A delegation?'

'You haven't got any brochures, have you, Bob?' asked one of them.

'Brochures?'

'For the Specials.'

Loach didn't spare the sarcasm. 'You're not going to believe this, lads, but I'm right out of them at the moment.'

'Only I know someone who wants to join!'

'Oh aye?'

'My Gran,' he bragged.

'She shoots first and asks questions later.'

Their derision was interrupted momentarily by someone they saw over at the bar.

'Here he comes.'

'What are you two up to?'

But when Loach looked where the PC's were looking, he spotted one Freddy Calder. Sure enough, the two went up to meet him at the bar, sneaking up from behind.

'Freddy!' one of them shouted, and Calder nearly jumped out of his skin.

'Let me get you one, Freddy,' the PC offered.

248

'Now you're no longer driving.' The two PC's stifled their own laughter, but several other PC's and Specials nearby observed no such truce.

'Actually, I've already –'

'About your *car*, Freddy . . .'

'What about it?'

'Was it a Sierra by any chance?'

Freddy sighed. 'Yes.' He remembered it all so well. Goodbye comfy seats. Goodbye smooth ride. Goodbye Salvador Dolly. Goodbye Sierra.

'Blue?'

Immediately Freddy realized they were on to something. They knew something. He was afraid of getting his hopes up again, but he needed to believe in *something*. Without his beloved car – without the hope of a quick getaway – life just wouldn't be worth living . . .

'Registration number D310 ULF?'

Freddy was overjoyed. Lost and found!

'Oh, my God, yes! You know where it is?'

The PC smiled knowingly. 'Right here.'

He placed a little miniature model of a Sierra painted blue on the bar, and let 'er roll.

The bar broke out laughing. The two PC's practically fell on the floor.

Freddy didn't think it was funny. Specials had more dignity.

21

The open-air market was one culture in the midst of another, a branch of Asia transplanted into the urban centre of the Midlands, crowded with merchandise as well as bustling with people. Brightly coloured stalls overflowed with luscious blue and searing red silks; exotic spices, tasty pulses, fresh fruit and vegetables; wild shirts and simple footwear; plastic shapes and toys for children; and a multiplicity of brass and china bric-à-brac everywhere.

The stalls filled an open space enclosed by small shops, whose first and second floors were, for the most part, residential. On the first floor of one of the perimeter shops, which offered fancy goods, was a curtained window. The curtain opened, and the barrel of a pistol poked out. Slowly the gunsight began to search through the people wandering through the marketplace, until it came to rest.

Dressed in luminous purples, a rather heavyset Asian woman was haggling with the owner of one of the stalls over a length of material she brandished in his face. Yet she was a moving target: bobbing and weaving, never standing still, throwing her head and shoulders back to show the world she was being robbed blind. Then she dipped down to look for a cheaper bolt of silk, and for a moment she was motionless, her ample backside a stationary, tempting target.

The barrel of the gun lowered slightly. Abruptly the woman turned just as the gun recoiled with a jerk.

There was a soft whump. Immediately the woman screamed, grabbing at her neck below the right ear, and collapsed across the soft silks, to the astonishment of the stall-owner and the people around her. Rushing to her aid, several of them tried to help her to her feet. Some gasped at the blood seeping through her fingers. Others looked around frantically for the maniac.

Up at the window above the fancy goods shop, the curtains touched with no sign of disturbance. The barrel of the pistol had disappeared.

While Anjali's arm was still in a sling, her facial and other surface injuries were nearly healed. Yet although she was no longer confined to home, for the moment she was a captive audience to her Uncle Ram, who was pacing the sitting room and lecturing her about the madman with the air pistol who had been running amuck in the market lately.

'The community is demanding something be done!' he insisted. 'And quickly! This is the fifth time. And I know we are only talking about air-gun pellets, but this one was very serious. My friend, Dr Mahendra, said that an inch higher and the poor woman could have been struck in the eye.'

Anjali remembered saying almost the same thing not so long ago, just before she herself had been wounded, and the memory made her angry. 'I only wish you and the other men had shown as much concern all the other times.'

Ram appeared somewhat perplexed. 'What are you saying?'

It was while they were sitting in the panda car parked at the shopping precinct, she and Toby Armstrong, just before all hell had broken loose. He had been telling her what he thought was a hilarious tale about an Indian woman getting shot 'in the bum' with an air-gun pellet.

'I'm saying that you and . . . yes, some policemen I could mention . . . think it's so funny when fat women get shot in the bottom.'

'That is not a nice thing to say,' Uncle Ram objected.

'But it's true. If this had been taken seriously at the start, you and the community might not be so excited now.'

'All right,' he conceded. 'I admit we let those other occasions pass. But your precious police have done nothing either. Oh, they wrote things in their notebooks, and said they would look into it,' Ram scowled. 'I tell you, Anjali, our people are saying the police would do more if white persons were being shot.'

'Uncle Ram, white people accuse the police of doing more for the ethnic community than they do for their own kind.' She shrugged. 'We can't have it both ways.'

Uncle Ram remained staunchly unconvinced. 'Words get us nowhere. People want results. Before someone gets killed. Otherwise they will take matters in their own hands.'

To him, this was not a threat, but to her it was, and a threat that he could help to defuse. 'Uncle Ram, *you* must tell them to let the police complete their investigation.'

'The police have nothing to show us, Anjali. You cannot expect me to stand up before the people and ask for patience if I have nothing but empty words to feed them.'

While she sighed in frustration, she could see that he was sincere, and to some degree she could feel his frustration as well.

'The police should be made aware that there is much rage in the community,' he told her in a voice at once gentle and stern.

The clock on the wall inside the Bromsgrove Building Society clearly showed that it was five-thirty when Viv Smith finished her check-out. She was just getting her coat when she discovered Madge, the nice young trainee, standing beside her.

'Well, Madge . . . giving the town a whack tonight, are we?'

She returned a shy smile. 'You must be joking. I'm going down to Safeway for a Chicken Korma, and watch telly back home.'

Viv was in a good mood, and didn't mind sharing it with Madge. After all, she really hadn't had much of an opportunity as yet to give Madge a bit of attention and get to know her a little better.

'Tell you what. It's happy hour. Let me buy you a drink. I know just the place.'

'Ooh . . . I dunno really . . .' said Madge shyly.

Viv put an arm about Madge and marched her to the door, determined to coax a stronger, more confident smile out of her.

'Come on, Madge. Life wasn't meant to be all pickles and milk. Anyway . . . it's not far.' And off they went.

Behind them, with a wary eye and a raised eyebrow, Mr Maynard watched Miss Smith leave, taking the naïve young trainee under her wing. He wondered if Miss Smith might not threaten to become the one bad apple beginning to spoil the rest.

22

The small dolls in Viv's collection were everywhere in her tiny sitting room – including much of the space afforded by the cabinet and shelf unit that also housed a drinks cupboard – except for the stuffed chair and two-seater sofa. The exquisite miniatures provided a packed, polite, silent audience for any visitor who could fit into the cramped room along with them. Yet other than an occasional guest, they lived quietly amongst mementoes and souvenirs from vacation trips to Greece and Spain, although the dolls had never travelled anywhere.

Madge's eyes were filled with wonder at this small and precious world, as Viv handed her a vodka and orange and lifted her own glass. 'Cheers, Madge.'

'This is brilliant.' Madge sipped her drink, made a sour grimace, and tried to smile, yet all the while her eyes flicked round the room. 'D'you share?'

'Not likely. Been through all that. The smell of other people's nail varnish? No thank you.'

'I've three brothers,' Madge nodded. 'And the smell of odour-eaters!'

Viv found herself enjoying the role of older sister. 'Don't let it get you down, Madge. Keep thinking of the big day you'll move out.'

'Huh,' she shrugged. 'It's gonna be ages before I get promotion, and can afford to leave home.'

'You never know. Some of us old biddies could get put out to grass.' She was thinking of the disapproving looks Maynard had been casting her way of late.

'Oh, I didn't mean it that way,' Madge protested. 'I don't expect any –'

''Course you didn't,' Viv quickly replied. Perhaps she could tickle Madge out of being so literal, serious, and self-conscious. 'Anyway, there are other ways, you know, Madge. You could always go on the game.'

She gave Madge the 'once-over,' appreciating her curves from top to bottom. But once she returned to catch the younger woman's eye, she detected a look of wounded innocence, and immediately laid a gentle hand on her arm.

'Just a joke in bad taste, luv,' Viv apologized. 'Don't take me seriously. I've a mouth as wide as the Watford Gap. Come on, I want to show you the bedroom.'

With that, Viv pulled the reluctant Madge by the arm. Once she got into the bedroom, however, Madge was overwhelmed. Viv had said she'd copied her boudoir from *Cosmopolitan*, only a deal less expensive, but Madge had imagined nothing like this. All the luxuries – the special make-up jars and boxes, the china shepherdess that disguised the talc, the ultra-feminine bed with its pastel drapes . . .

'This is . . . brilliant.'

'I designed it myself,' Viv boasted.

'I'd give anything to have a room like this. And just be on my own.'

'You don't have your brothers in your bedroom as well, do you, Madge?'

She still couldn't grasp the humour. 'No . . . just my sister, Peg.'

'And she steals your tights? Don't tell me. I've been all through it.'

Dismissing that train of thought, she glanced at her watch and whistled. 'Better get my skates on. Look, Madge, I need to change.'

As Viv began to usher her to the bedroom door, Madge swallowed the rest of her drink too fast, resulting in a loud gulp. 'You want me to go –'

'No, no. I'll only be a coupla ticks. Help yourself to a drink. You know where everything is.'

'No ta very much. But could I use your toilet?'

'Sure. It's free of charge.' Viv pointed out the bathroom before ducking back inside the bedroom and closing the door most of the way.

Madge was delighted to find that the bathroom echoed the soft, feminine touch of Viv's bedroom. After tipping her unfinished drink into the toilet, she began to nose around, sniffing a few of Viv's smellies. Some she rated as slightly old and over-sweet. A couple she liked, and dabbed on her wrists and neck.

Above the wash-basin was a cabinet that looked intriguing and she couldn't resist, opening it just as she glanced furtively over her shoulder. Among the miscellaneous items in the cabinet she came upon a toilet accessory bag, and a quick look inside revealed a man's shaving gear, among other dead giveaways, that brought a more confident smile to her face after all. Closing the cabinet, she checked her face in the mirror, then flushed the loo before leaving the bathroom.

Meanwhile in the bedroom, dressed only in her undergarments, Viv was applying a light touch of make-up to her broad mouth and the brows and lashes above her wide-set eyes. It was the smile that made her best face, she thought, and not too much at that.

'You okay, Madge?' she called.

'Oh yeh, fine,' Madge called back from the sitting room, keeping a wary eye on the bedroom door in case Viv should appear unexpectedly. She began cautiously to poke about, feeling a surge of envy at each new discovery.

'It's really a lovely flat, Viv. It must cost a fortune. How d'you manage?'

'Oh, the usual . . .' she responded from the bedroom. 'A tidy mortgage, ta very much to the Bromsgrove.'

'But the payments . . .' Madge wondered, '. . . 'cos let's face it, the Building Society pays peanuts.'

'Well . . . I don't have a sugar daddy, if that's what you're thinking,' Viv laughed, confiding in a loud voice to someone whose reaction she couldn't see, as if to herself. 'Let a man have a key to the front door, and you'll end up washing his underpants and darning his socks.'

Madge was obviously sceptical about Viv's remark, as she peeked into the top drawer of a sideboard. 'Viv . . . I really don't mean to pry.'

'Forget it, luv,' Viv answered, considering which excuse to try next. 'I'll let you in on a secret. I'm a gambler, Madge.' Choking off a chuckle, she pulled on her dark skirt while noting the burgeoning derriere in the mirror.

What she couldn't see was Madge's eyes open wider, taking in all of Viv's commentary at face value. 'My Da does the pools . . . never won a thing yet.'

'Well there you go,' Viv mockingly chided her. 'I play the gee-gees.'

Madge frowned. 'But . . . supposing you lose.'

'Oh, a bit of petty theft comes in handy,' Viv called back from the bedroom.

'You're having me on . . . aren't you?' Madge suggested uneasily. In the same breath, she noticed the expensive TV set above the VCR with all sorts of gadgets on it.

Suddenly Viv appeared from nowhere blowing her own horn: 'Ta-daah!' Flushed with guilt, Madge swung round to face her, only to find Viv draped in the doorway in an incongruous pose, as she was dressed in a police uniform.

'Like it?'

Madge was nearly dumbstruck. 'I . . .'

'Blue suits me. What d'you think?'

'Is that a real uniform?' Viv nodded, but Madge was still confused. 'But how can you be in the . . . ?' She made little circles in the air. '. . . and work at . . . ?'

None too articulate a lass, Viv acknowledged. 'Oh the Building Society gets me through the day. I'm a night person, Madge.' Going over to the table, she reached into a glass jar for a mint. 'Want one?' Madge declined.

Viv spoke confidentially, repressing a grin. 'We don't want to breathe vodka over Freddy.' Still inarticulate, the tilt of Madge's head continued to ask questions. 'My partner on the beat . . . usually . . . but is he on tonight? I'm never too sure.' Vodka did wonders for Viv's confidence.

'Is this how . . . ? You know . . . having a second job?'

'You mean this?' Pointing to her uniform, Viv laughed aloud. 'Special Constables don't get paid for this. I do it for love, Madge.' In an instant she realized her teasing might be misinterpreted. 'But *not* . . . for love of Freddy, if that's what you're thinking.'

The telephone interrupted Madge's denial. Viv picked up the phone before it rang again.

'Freddy?' She covered the mouthpiece and whispered to Madge. 'Speak of the devil.' Once again she talked into the phone. 'You what?'

Madge couldn't discern what was being said on the other end, but judging from Viv's reaction, she figured it must be juicy.

'Well, tell me again. I didn't hear what you said . . .'

Viv was concentrating on the conversation with the man named

255

Freddy and nodding vigorously, all the while her face gradually lighting up until it was a veritable shining beacon for lost sailors.

23

Keeping a low profile in the sitting room, Freddy was half-listening to the conversation with Viv on the telephone while half-listening to the noises of his mother washing up in the kitchen. And while listening to both, his mind somewhere else entirely, he nervously tapped a business card on the telephone table.

'. . . That's right.' Abruptly the washing-up noises ceased, and he knew what that meant. 'Look. I can't say any more . . .' He looked anxiously toward the kitchen. 'I'll tell you all about it . . . bye.'

He managed to replace the receiver just as his mother entered the room with a glare, ostensibly to remove some tea things, odds and ends, and the white cloth covering the table.

'Just checking with one of the lads . . .' He stopped tapping the business card and laid it down quietly on the telephone table. '. . . Got to be going, Ma. Busy night tonight . . .'

Hilda Calder waved away her son's words. 'I've told you a hundred times, I'm not the slightest bit interested in what you do with your drinking pals down at the police station.'

Though her statement might be true enough, it always pained him to hear. 'Ma!'

His mother simply shrugged. 'Anyway. They seem pretty useless friends if they can't find out who stole your car.'

At this point it was useless for him to stop and argue. 'I've got to go, Ma.'

Freddy gave his mother a peck on the cheek before dashing off. Sensing in some way that even so slight a kiss from him was an unusual act, she frowned, becoming more suspicious than usual.

Parked out front on the street was the wretched replacement for Freddy's memorably and hauntingly enchanting, but stolen, fancy car. He studied the substitute with open and outright disgust. First looking up and down the street, he was thankful there was no one in the immediate vicinity to watch and stare as he clumsily attempted to squeeze himself into the tiny tin can.

Gathering in the parade room at Division 'S' were the Specials, leaving behind their day jobs and getting ready for night duty. Tonight Viv was partnered with John Redwood instead of Freddy, who was nevertheless the subject of their conversation, as Wally Harris leaned over to listen in on the gossip.

'Any word about Freddy's car?' Redwood asked.

'Didn't see anything on the six o'clock news.'

Viv turned to her partner, ignoring Wally's sally. 'No. And he must be peeved. Especially tonight.'

'What's happening tonight?' Redwood inquired.

'It's Freddy's big night. More than that I'm not at liberty to say,' Viv concluded with a wink.

'Taking his Mum to the pictures is he?'

Viv silenced Wally with a nasty look. 'Put a banana up your exhaust pipe, will you?' Then she turned to her partner and confided in a quieter voice, though not quite out of Wally's range. 'He has a date, her name is Rita. Apart from that, my lips are sealed.'

Big Jess wasn't dressed in the ideal costume for her profession, although she stood out from the crowd nonetheless, despite any suggestion of modesty. Pacing in front of a brightly lit shop-front, she appeared to be waiting for someone. That notion was confirmed when she turned down a trick without a second glance. When the trick tried to get stroppy with her, Big Jess switched into her hellfire mode, her head thrust forward aiming directly for the trick's nose. Evidently the trick got the message, backed away, and melted into the night.

Observing from the parked panda car were two fresh recruits: WPC Karen Clark, in the driver's seat, and PC Ronald Eaton, who was nodding in the direction of Big Jess.

'Interesting . . . ? A prostitute turning down work. Maybe she doesn't take credit cards.'

24

Freddy's miniature automobile came to an abrupt stop just in front of the *Golden Pagoda* restaurant, a perfect fit, but then he had a hell of a job squeezing out of the so-called door: probably designed for midget clowns in the circus, he mused. But he failed to get to the other side in time to open the door for Rita, although she seemed to extricate herself with little trouble and no expectation of gallantry on his part.

'Sorry, Rita.'

'What for?'

'For . . . well . . .' He started to indicate her door, then expanded the sweep of his gesture to take in the whole car, such as it was. '. . . this sardine can.'

'What's wrong with it?' she asked. Of course, a woman with her petite figure never need worry about getting caught in a tight spot.

'It's all the firm could find . . . you know . . . because of my car being whipped.'

'Freddy, do give over. You've been apologizing all the way here. I know your car was stolen,' she reminded him. 'I was there – remember?' She pushed open the door to the restaurant and walked through.

Inside the *Golden Pagoda*, the head waiter was standing alone at a small counter. As Freddy and Rita approached him, he looked up and regarded them impassively, offering no help when Freddy removed her coat.

'I booked a table. Name is Calder.'

Remaining po-faced, the head waiter indicated that they could sit anywhere they pleased. The restaurant was empty.

'But I did book,' Freddy insisted with the utmost courtesy.

The head waiter shrugged. Rita sighed, deeply.

Picking up the 'Reserved' marker, the head waiter led them into the restaurant to a table he offered by placing the marker in the centre. However, Freddy moved on, preferring a table further into the room. So the head waiter picked up the marker once again.

Still carrying his own coat as well as Rita's, Freddy tried to pass them along to the head waiter, who pointed to a nearby coat-stand instead. When Freddy returned from hanging the coats, Rita had moved to another table and sat down, so he followed suit. So did the head waiter, who moved the 'Reserved' marker to the new table as well.

'I bet if I hadn't booked, the place would have been jam-packed,' remarked Freddy as they settled in.

Rita seemed a bit doubtful. 'Maybe it gets busy later.'

'That'll be it. Unless they're up for serving sweet and sour Kitty Food.'

Rita winced.

Noticing one of Freddy's jackets carelessly slung over the back of a chair, Hilda Calder picked it up, smoothed it out, and marched into her son's bedroom. She aimed straight for his wardrobe. Opening it, she looked for and found the matching trousers. She took them out, added the jacket to the same hanger, replaced the suit, closed the wardrobe . . . then froze. Was she seeing things? she asked herself.

Aggressively she pulled open the wardrobe again and seized one of the hangers inside. On it hung Freddy's uniform, when it was supposed to be hanging on *him*.

Whereas the head waiter handed menus to both of them, he didn't take his eyes from Rita. 'Would Madam like a drink before dinner?'

'A dry white wine, please,' she requested.

'That'll be a dry white wine for the lady,' repeated Freddy, establishing his authority. Both of them stared at him, although the head waiter made no acknowledgement of his demand. 'Right. And . . . a non-alcoholic beer for moi.'

'We have only Pils,' replied the head waiter, unconcerned.

'Then make mine an aspirin and a glass of water,' Freddy shot back, grinning at Rita.

Rather than entertained, she seemed slightly embarrassed. 'Freddy?'

'I'll just have a Seven-Up,' he told the head waiter, who turned and left without comment. Freddy leaned across the table, taking Rita into his confidence. 'It's a well-known fact that Chinese waiters have no sense of humour.'

'I thought you said you came in here a lot? He didn't seem to know you.'

'Ah . . .' He had to think quickly, not his natural talent. 'I usually come in on a Thursday. Tonight's Tuesday. It confuses them,' he explained.

She shot him a quizzical glance, then remarked, 'Look, Freddy . . . I'm going to leave the ordering up to you.'

'You are?'

'I want it to be a surprise. So you choose.'

Ah, now they were getting somewhere. He positively glowed. 'Okay.'

But before their good feelings could fall into step, the head waiter returned, breaking the spell by placing the drinks in front of their separate noses. 'Are you ready to order now, sir?'

Freddy gave Rita a huge wink, simultaneously bringing up Foxy the hand puppet just above the table, and barked his order in Foxy's falsetto voice.

'How 'bout shark-fin soup, and make it snappy!'

The head waiter was totally unimpressed. 'You want two shark-fin soup?' Even Rita seemed nonplussed.

Freddy dropped his grin, at once less facetious and more pragmatic. 'Ah, no . . . Just . . .' He turned to Rita and spoke in an undertone he knew the head waiter couldn't fathom. 'See. No sense of humour.' Then he looked again to the head waiter. 'Uh . . . give us a coupla minutes . . .'

Now hanging from the mantelpiece was Freddy's uniform, and Hilda stopped again to glare at it.

'Just like your father,' she scolded the uniform. Then she looked up toward the ceiling and past it to the heavens beyond. 'It's all your fault, Joseph Calder. Like father, like son. There'll be no flowers for you this week.'

He had been a man of no self-discipline, backbone, morals, loyalty, sensitivity, consideration, or consequence. Now more clearly than ever, it was apparent that the son was stitched from the same cloth.

Wearily and with a heavy heart, she sat down on the chair beside the telephone. On the table she happened to notice a business card. She twisted it round and read the inscription: '*The Golden Pagoda*.'

25

Scanning the menu for the umpteenth time, Freddy still couldn't make up his mind. Finally he decided to go for broke and get something with everything.

'I got a great idea. Why don't we go for the set meal?'

'Whatever you decide will be fine I'm sure,' she sweetly concurred.

He showed her the menu and placed his finger on the set meal he had rather arbitrarily selected from too many choices. 'This one . . . "Bee" . . . looks okay.'

Rita saw where he was pointing and matched the place in her own menu. Reading what dishes were included in the set meal he had chosen, her nose curled. 'I'm not too keen on sweet and sour . . .'

'All right.'

'Or chop suey . . .'

'Right,' Freddy confirmed. 'We'll get them to change these . . .'

'I'll ask them if they've got prawns in ginger . . . I like that.' She was wonderful when she talked about anything she liked. 'And maybe we could have some duck . . . but definitely not that eggy dish.' But not quite so wonderful when contemplating the unpleasant.

'It's out of here,' Freddy agreed.

She looked up at him with those dazzling, penetrating eyes underneath a tangled jungle of hair. 'It's not that I'm picky, but . . . when you're in the trade, you get a nose for bad fish.' What was she saying? 'It takes a good cook to know one, I always say.'

'I'll drink to that.' He didn't care what she was saying. 'Which reminds me . . . a toast . . .'

'Yes . . . ?' she asked expectantly.

Raising his Seven-Up, he waited for her to lift her wine glass. 'A toast . . .'

Rita began to brighten until Freddy picked up Foxy, who actually proposed the toast.

'To the girls and guys on the beat, and the villains you meet on the street.'

Rita didn't know quite what to say. 'Well . . . you certainly know how to impress a girl.'

Although she gave him her lovely smile, he wasn't entirely sure which way she meant that remark.

In the fading afterglow of twilight, the detached house was already resting in darkness. From an upper bedroom window, a man who looked to be a window-cleaner climbed out onto a small balcony carrying a large black plastic bag.

The window-cleaner retrieved a metal ladder from the floor of the balcony and extended it so that the ladder reached a wall adjoining the house. Once there, from the wall to the ground was only a matter of climbing down the ladder in its folded size.

Quickly the window-cleaner crossed to an expansive shrub, where he removed a bicycle that had been hidden beneath its covering branches. He clipped the folded ladder to the bicycle frame, then transferred the contents of the black plastic bag into two pannier bags that straddled the bicycle's back wheel.

Satisfied that everything was okay, he mounted the bicycle, started to glide, and pedalled casually down the drive and out the gate.

No doubt about it, there were simply too many dishes on the small table, which threatened to collapse under the burden into one giant mess. Freddy groaned when the final dish of Szechuan prawns was balanced on the table's edge by the waiter.

While transferring noodles to her plate, Rita glanced up and suddenly saw something that made her mouth go slack and her jaw drop open. Likewise, the noodles were sliding from the serving spoons onto the table and floor. Yet she was impossibly tongue-tied. 'Uhhh . . .'

'Something wrong?' Freddy inquired.

'I don't believe it.' She was trembling. 'It's her.'

'Who?'

Freddy looked into the mirror on the wall behind Rita just as Hilda Calder spotted him in the reflection. He was appalled.

'Oh my God . . . It's Ma!'

Rita stared at him accusingly: 'Freddy . . . you didn't . . .'

'I swear I had nothing to . . .' It was too late. He didn't know what he could possibly do or say to forestall the impending disaster.

A galleon in full sail, Hilda Calder navigated through the sea of empty tables to join them. Upon arrival, she couldn't help staring in disgust at the plates of Chinese food on the table in front of them, particularly Freddy's plate, bulging with a grotesquely colourful mixture of everything else from the other dishes.

'You having that?' she asked her son in nauseated disbelief. 'Or have you had it?'

Silence descended over the trio, as they peered at one another. While a waiter hovered nearby, Mrs Calder fried him with a microwave glare. The food remained untouched, and time stopped.

Eventually Rita gave up and got up. 'I'm going to the toilet,' she announced with a fair amount of composure.

Hilda Calder watched her go, or rather, bounce away, since the super-short hemline of her fake leopard mini-skirt was riding up and down on her barely covered bum. Keeping her thin lips tightly shut, Hilda was absorbing every detail of the picture for future reference.

'I know what you're thinking . . .' Freddy began in a halting voice.

His mother watched Rita's last undulations as she disappeared into the toilet. 'I sincerely hope you don't, Freddy Calder . . . or you'll get the back of my hand across your face.'

'Keep your voice down, Ma . . .' Freddy pleaded.

'So. You don't know her. She doesn't know you.' His mother shook her head at him with sheer contempt in her eyes. 'For a time you had me going, Freddy Calder.'

'Believe me –' Freddy interjected.

She cut him off. 'Never in this life or the next,' she pronounced the final judgement upon him.

Without warning, her chest began to heave to an alarming degree, and her breath came in spurts. And yet incredibly, she appeared to be enjoying this sudden attack of palpitations.

'Unless you want me to die in this godless place, I advise you to take me home. Now,' she insisted. 'What you do after that doesn't interest me. Because I shall be beyond all the pain and suffering you can heap upon me.'

26

Rita Loosemore opened the door and emerged from the ladies' room at the *Golden Pagoda* to discover the table where she had been sitting now empty. Freddy and his mother were waiting for her by the front door.

As Rita came closer, Freddy tried to flash hopeful messages to her, but none appeared to be getting through. In fact, the problem was that Rita's visage was set in granite at the moment, while none of Freddy's thoughts carried a chisel.

In the meantime, Lady Macbeth was lurching against the door, her son having to support her and lead her from the restaurant. Freddy looked to Rita, hoping she could at least sympathize with his predicament.

'She's not well. I've got to get her home.'

His eyes begged her to 'please understand,' but for all she cared, he could be making signs in Swahili.

For the first time, the head waiter smiled at them on their way out, probably figuring, Freddy thought, on reselling the food they left behind.

After easing his mother gently into the miniature car, Freddy turned to Rita to say something. Instead he pecked her quickly on the cheek, although a dying sigh from Hilda Calder cut short any further passion between them.

As he hastened to crouch down into the driver's seat, his mother lowered the hand from her face. She looked directly at Rita with a subtle smile of triumph.

Unsure as to whether she had just seen what she had just seen, Rita watched Freddy and the car drive out of her life. Still smouldering, hunching her shoulders, she walked in the direction of the nearest bus-stop to wait for the next 223.

Observing from their parked panda car, PC Ronald Eaton and WPC Karen Clark were watching the prostitute known as Big Jess huddled in a darkened doorway with a man whose features were obscured by the raised collar of his raincoat. But oddly enough, the money was clear as day, passing from the man in the raincoat to Big Jess. Then abruptly, the man in the raincoat slipped away and vanished.

Big Jess paused a few moments for the man in the raincoat to get away before making her exit from the darkened doorway. As she set out, her shoulder bag mimicked her jaunty swing until her mood was suddenly dispelled: her nostrils flared as she came up and leaned over to talk to PC Eaton. 'What the hell do you want?'

'Not what you're selling, lady,' Eaton replied acidly.

'Then don't let me stop you finding a nice fella,' Big Jess wisecracked as she pushed on.

PC Eaton's words stopped her in her tracks. 'Into the car.'

'What for?' demanded Big Jess aggressively.

Ron Eaton recited the same old litany of charges against her. 'Soliciting . . . receiving payment for services rendered in a public place . . . Need I say more?'

'Why don't you go clean out your police dogs' ears?' Big Jess scowled.

PC Eaton quickly opened the back door of the panda for their guest, while WPC Clark circled round the car to cut off any avenue of escape.

'You heard me . . . into the car.'

As WPC Clark approached, the piercing eyes of Big Jess bore into her, and she halted nervously, checking with Ron before taking another step. What next? her look asked him.

PC Ron Eaton stared at Big Jess and fingered his radio. 'Please yourself . . . Do I call out the van, or are you going to be sensible.'

Though heaving with anger, Big Jess moved reluctantly toward the rear of the car, and started to climb into the cramped back seat. She made a point of exaggerating her bulk in the squeeze through the door so as to make everything harder for everybody.

'You're making a big mistake, you and Wonder Woman,' she warned Eaton.

Coordinating their efforts, WPC Clark and PC Eaton applied their shoulders to the ample rear end of Big Jess to pop her through the opening and inside the vehicle.

'I know . . . you're a royal checking out the architecture,' quipped PC Eaton.

Specials Viv Smith and John Redwood were walking slowly along the posh, wide suburban street with large houses set back, when they saw a bicycle coming toward them. The front light on the bicycle was blinking on and off erratically.

'D'you want to make the pinch?' Viv asked Redwood in a mock serious tone of voice.

'After you,' he courteously offered.

Viv held up an arresting hand, and the bicycle came to a halt just in front of them.

'Officers,' the fellow on the bicycle nodded nervously.

'Your front light, sir,' Special Constable Smith pointed out to him. 'You're meant to change the battery every now and then.'

There was a look of relief in the cyclist's eyes, and he relaxed. Unhooking the light, he gave it a hard tap, which extinguished it altogether. He shrugged his shoulders and stared unhappily at the two Specials.

Slowly and methodically Viv circled the bicycle. When she came near the pannier bags, the rider stiffened, but she didn't seem to notice. Instead she gripped the folded ladder and tested the rig's strength.

'This is a bit loose, sir. Can I ask why you have it on the bicycle?'

'I'm a window-cleaner,' the man explained. 'I'm not always out this late . . . That's why I forgot about the battery, I suppose. I'm usually home before it gets dark.'

'Remember that the light is for your own protection, sir,' Redwood spoke up.

'You're right,' the window-cleaner conceded.

'Goodnight, sir,' said Redwood.

'Goodnight, officer.' With a cursory nod toward Viv, the window-cleaner propelled his bicycle forward and lifted his feet to the pedals.

'Sir?' Viv called loudly.

The window-cleaner stopped his bicycle once more, then turned back to confront Special Constable Smith.

'Walk it, sir. You've no lights. Walk it home, sir.'

The window-cleaner took a deep breath, got off the bicycle, and started walking next to it, one hand steering, without looking backward again.

27

In the interview room, Big Jess sat behind the desk glaring at WPC Karen Clark, who was, at least for the time being, pretending to be invisible. McAllister walked into the room followed by PC Eaton. Sitting down, Andy tried to assume an affable expression while glancing through the PC's report in his hands.

'Well now, Jess . . . We're in trouble again, are we?'

'No . . . *I'm* not . . . but your baby bluebottles could be.'

'What?' McAllister queried, raising his eyes in a mute question to PC Eaton, who shrugged his own indifference to what Big Jess might be talking about.

But she wasn't backing down. 'One word from me, and they're deep in the smelly stuff.'

Eaton was shaking his head. 'She keeps making these remarks –'

McAllister held up a silencing hand, continuing to focus on Big Jess. 'Go on . . .'

Big Jess rearranged herself behind the desk and straightened her shoulders, preparing to begin anew.

'I've been falsely accused.'

Andy returned his eyes to the report for a brief glance. 'Well that's not what it says down here . . . Openly soliciting . . . ?' He shook his head ever so slightly. 'Money being passed in a public place . . . ?' Pursing his lips, he looked her in the eye. 'I would've thought you'd be a bit more discreet . . . a girl wi' your experience, Jess.'

'Sod off.'

Andy merely sighed as he looked up at PC Eaton. 'Also a woman of few words . . . And that was two of them . . .' As he rose to his feet, his voice and manner hardened.

'Well, if that's all you've got to say, we'd better get the book out.'

Jess remained adamant. 'I'm saying nothing until I see my solicitor . . . and I want to see him *now*.'

'Your solicitor?'

Big Jess simply echoed his mockery. 'Aye . . . my solicitor . . . the one who works here.'

The seed of suspicion was sprouting in McAllister's mind. 'What are you talking about, Jess?'

'I'm talking about the freebie bobby,' she explained evenly. 'My lawyer.'

John Redwood, Andy surmised.

Bob Loach was shuffling the last of the paperwork in the parade room when Viv and Redwood walked in and immediately flopped down on the nearest chairs, both shivery from the cold night air.

'Bit parky out there, is it?' Loach sympathized.

Viv was still shaking. 'If you've got a cup of hot cocoa handy, just pour it in my shoes.'

Abruptly and noisily, Andy McAllister swung the door open from the outside, and, after a quick look around the room, spotted his prey.

'Mr Redwood? Can I be having you sharpish like.'

The Special/solicitor was caught off-guard. 'I was just about to sign off –'

Completely contrary to expectation, Andy smiled sweetly. 'Oh, do that, by all means.'

Redwood was plainly puzzled, as were Viv and Loach. McAllister paused at the door for another word.

'However . . . you do have your civvies with you, I hope . . .' He waited for Redwood's baffled nod before continuing. 'I'm glad . . . because it would have meant interviewing a lady in your Y-fronts.'

Back in the interview room, the door opened and bumped PC Eaton sideways. McAllister entered while ushering Redwood, now dressed in his everyday jersey and jeans, to Big Jess.

'Your solicitor, as you requested, Jess.'

Redwood blinked. 'Miss Tolliver . . . ?'

Andy answered for her. 'The one and only. Your *client* refused to make a statement.' Instantly realizing he might be committing some sort of judicial error, he hurried to correct himself. 'Not that she is being coerced into making one . . . oh dear no. It's just that she felt bashful until her lawyer was present.' Deleting the sarcasm, he switched his attention back to Big Jess.

'Well, here he is.'

An awkward silence prevailed as client and solicitor gawked at one another. Once they had made a visual connection, Jess again became aware of the other uniforms in the room, especially Andy McAllister.

'Well . . . ? Push off then. I want to speak to him . . . alone.'

Fidgeting uncomfortably, McAllister nevertheless realized that the request was not improper, and indicated to PC Eaton and WPC Clark that they should also make their exit with him. However, as the last one out, Andy was careful to leave the door just slightly ajar.

With deliberate purpose, Big Jess walked to the door, turned around, and thumped it shut with her broad backside. 'They think they've got me by the short and curlies . . .' She burst out laughing as she crossed the room to Redwood. 'Well, we'll show 'em, handsome.'

She pressed her considerable influence down on Redwood's chest, then withdrew and tottered back into a convenient chair.

28

Leaving the parade room for the night, Viv Smith and Bob Loach were walking toward the lift just as PC Ron Eaton was punching the call button.

'Fancy a drink?' Loach invited Viv.

'Sure . . . if you're buying?'

From the other direction, chirpy as an overweight sparrow, Big

Jess walked by, recognized Loach, and whacked him with her shoulder bag. Taught by past experience, Loach was immediately on the defensive.

'Hullo, Jess. What brings you down here?'

In reply, Big Jess cocked her thumb at PC Eaton. 'Well, that little piddlegerm for a start . . .'

Eaton flinched, and Big Jess reassured the poor devil. 'It's all right, darling. I shan't be needing the motor. You can take the rest of the night off and study how to be a policeman.'

She dismissed him in an instant, then turned to convey her farewells to Loach and Viv. 'Ta-ra, luvs. Must fly. I need to lie down pretty quick if I'm to pay for a month's rent.' Waving goodbye without looking back, Big Jess headed through the door into front reception on her way out.

The lift door opened, and Ron Eaton entered along with Loach and Viv.

'What was all that about?' she asked Ron.

'You'd better ask your mate Redwood the answer to that one,' said PC Eaton sourly, and with that he walked out of the lift.

Andy McAllister sat at his desk, alone in his office with John Redwood, having a quiet chat with the Special/solicitor. His mood had changed.

'I'm obliged to you, Mr Redwood. The force never likes to have egg all over its face.'

'I'm sure the two policemen only did their duty as they saw fit.' As someone with limited experience in police work himself, he sympathized with the plight of PC Eaton and WPC Clark.

'Aye . . . maybe if they'd been around the patch longer, they'd've recognized Big Jess's customer as a CID man.'

Aye, there's the rub, and Redwood didn't care to insist on putting too fine a point on it, but he did feel that something needed to be said . . . by him. 'As a solicitor, I should frown on the police making payments to informers like Big Jess –'

Andy interrupted him right there. 'Then you'd do well to remember that it's the only way we damned well keep half a step in front of the villains.'

'I said, as a *solicitor*, Sergeant. As a *Special*, I'd have to agree with you.'

McAllister looked speculatively at John Redwood. 'Let me buy you a drink, Mr Redwood.'

Although the pub on 4th was getting busier, Viv Smith and Bob Loach were sitting by themselves awhile, commiserating with each other. Viv was hugging her drink.

'I wouldn't exactly say the night was a total washout. F'instance, we did have a close encounter with the criminal classes . . . a man on a bike without lights . . .'

'Tut, tut,' Loach allowed.

'He was a window-cleaner,' Viv continued. 'That's what he said anyway. Personally, I think he's Mr Big in the drug trade.'

Some vague memory kept trying to pop into her conscious mind, but she couldn't quite grab hold of it for closer examination. 'But come to think of it, there was something . . .'

Loach waited for her to remember and continue, but for now her memories appeared to have dried up, and she let it drop. That left him with his own thoughts.

'What did that bloke mean: "Ask Redwood?" Ask him what?'

'Sorry?' responded Viv absently.

'That bit downstairs . . . about Big Jess and Redwood.' Once again he found himself reflecting on his once-bitten thumb, nearly severed in the course of action steering Big Jess into her cell. Of course, that was before he had inadvertently been responsible for Big Jess taking a beating, along with her harlot friend and informer, Jackie, who had been beaten within an inch of her life. 'I mean . . . I'm only Section Officer . . . Nobody tells me anything.'

Viv pulled a face and snorted. 'Well go ask him.'

'What?'

'Go ask him. He's up at the bar with the sarge.'

Surprised, Loach swung round and verified that it was true when he noticed Redwood. Picking up his glass, he moved toward the bar. Viv merely sighed and decided to go along with him.

As Loach joined Redwood and Andy McAllister at the bar, Viv was right on his tail.

'Buy you gents a drink?'

'I won't say no, Mr Loach,' said McAllister in his version of a gracious reply.

Redwood, however, declined, much to Loach's obvious

disappointment. 'Thanks . . . but I've got to be going. I have an early start tomorrow.'

'A nice juicy divorce, is it, John?' quipped Viv with a twinkle in her eye.

He managed to share a smile with her. 'No. Nothing as simple as that.'

'I didn't know divorce was a simple matter,' McAllister offered.

But Viv topped him. 'Sarge, believe me, it's getting married that's difficult.'

Again Redwood smiled at her – twice in one night for him was like lightning striking twice in the same spot – as he took his leave.

Sorely tempted, Loach wanted to shoot a last question at Redwood before he was gone, but the moment passed. Eventually, he tried turning his curiosity to Andy McAllister.

'Bit of a do, was there, tonight, Sarge?'

McAllister seemed deliberately mysterious. 'What do was that then?'

'Big Jess . . . ?'

Andy nodded and smiled a wee bit at the corners. 'Oh . . . Big Jess? Dinna worry about that. Her thumb-biting days are over. She gave me her word on that . . .'

Still frowning, Loach couldn't get over the feeling that he was being had once more.

'I'll have a wee half and a half, thank you, Loach.'

29

Denzil Taylor, his mother, and his stepfather, whose last name he had adopted, crowded around John Redwood at his desk in the office within his home. The solicitor was attempting to explain and develop his strategy for Denzil's defence.

'We've only got Denzil out on bail. We haven't won the battle yet . . . That's why I thought we should have this meeting, so that there's no misunderstanding later when Denzil comes before the court. Magistrates always take a close interest in the home life of a young offender – especially his parents.'

Denzil interrupted, already having problems controlling his temper.

271

'Just a sec. Whaddya mean, parents?' He thumbed at Mr Taylor. 'I didn't want *him* here today. This loser's not my father. He lives in our house 'cos he got nowhere else to go. It was my Mum who asked him to come.'

As Mrs Taylor whimpered, her husband put a protective arm about her and shouted: 'You got no cause to talk that way, not in front of Mr Redwood. You know that kind of talk upsets your mother. I came 'cos Verna needs me.'

'You came 'cos Mum's got the purse.'

Mr Taylor immediately stood up to leave. 'I don't need this aggravation.'

However, Mrs Taylor pulled his arm. 'Neville . . .'

Redwood also tried to keep him in the group. 'Please, Mr Taylor . . .'

With ill-concealed resentment, Mr Taylor resumed his seat, and Redwood turned his attention back to his client.

'Denzil . . . We're all going to have to pull together if we're to have any hope of securing your release.'

Nonetheless, Denzil couldn't contain his sense of bitterness and futility, convinced that his colour would find him guilty of something he didn't do, either now or a month from now or sometime later. 'I told you before . . . it won't make any difference. The Paki lady says it was me. I say it wasn't me. Who cares?'

'There's your mother for one. And I wouldn't touch your case if I thought you were guilty.'

Denzil shrugged.

Next Redwood addressed Denzil's mother. 'And let's begin by putting a few facts on the table. Like the fact that your son, Mrs Taylor, does have a criminal record.' Mrs Taylor lowered her eyes, but Denzil appeared quite unruffled by this revelation. 'We have to face the truth if we're going to get anywhere.'

Mrs Taylor was shaken. 'I was frightened you wouldn't see me, Mr Redwood, if you knew he'd been in trouble.' She gazed with love upon the surly young man who wouldn't meet her eye.

'I know my Denzil. He's a good boy.'

This embarrassed him. 'Mum . . .'

'That's what I intend to establish in court, Mrs Taylor. And to a great extent, it depends on the answers I get from Denzil.'

'Like what?' asked Denzil stiffly.

'Like . . . Why were you in the Mall?'

'What d'you mean why was I in the Mall? That's a dumb question.'

'Just answer the man,' his stepfather admonished him. 'He's trying to help you.'

'Please, Mr Taylor.' Redwood again faced the younger. 'Denzil, you'll be asked these questions in court by the prosecution. I'd like to hear your answers before they do. For instance: Why did you ask . . . Mrs Nazur . . . for the time, when you had a watch of your own?'

It was obvious he hated being pinned down. He couldn't concentrate longer than a few seconds on any topic that threatened him, and he tried to avert his eyes from anyone else's.

'I freaked out . . . I can't remember.'

'Why did you run away?'

'I already told you why! Hey, man, you on my side or what?'

'I am on your side. When I stand up in court, I don't want any surprises. Here . . .' He handed Denzil a sheet of paper with the list of questions about the case that he had prepared. 'Go through these . . . make up your mind in your own time how you'd respond to them.' Checking to make sure Denzil was listening, Redwood paused.

'But I warn you . . . don't be smart . . . or cool. It won't work.'

Denzil was still reading the list of questions. 'This is a joke, man. Right?'

Out in the waiting room, Stella sat at her desk working on the computer terminal and trying to ignore the raised voices from the office. She was even more concerned about their effect on the next client, Mrs O'Day, a quiet, mousey woman seated in one of the chairs and furtively glancing toward the office every few moments as the arguments became louder and angrier, each voice cutting across the other.

'One big joke, huh?' the young West Indian shouted.

'Denzil, why don't you listen to Mr Redwood,' his mother pleaded.

'He never listen to nobody,' the stepfather remarked.

Instantly Denzil yelled back: 'I've had it with you! You hear me, muso? Get your face outa my –'

As they barked at each other, Stella raised her eyes and caught the frightened Mrs O'Day's. Stella smiled apologetically; Mrs O'Day tried to bury her head in a magazine.

The mother's plaintive voice could be heard from the office. 'I'm sorry you gotta hear all this, Mr Redwood –'

273

Then the stepfather stepped back into the fray. 'You see, Verna. This is why he get in trouble all the time!'

From the passageway beyond, Simon Redwood propelled his wheelchair toward the waiting room, and he too could hear the voices shouting in his father's office.

'I gotta get outa here!' the young man's voice exploded.

'Sit down, Denzil!' the woman's voice ordered.

Simon wheeled into the waiting room toward Stella, who kept trying to maintain some semblance of calm amidst the sounds of battle.

'Yes, Simon?'

'You got my spreadsheet manual . . . ?'

The shouting in the background almost drowned them out.

'You hear your mother –?' brayed the stepfather.

'Denzil . . . ?' the mother implored.

Stella concentrated on the routine request, 'I don't think so, but let me check . . .'

The office door flew open, and Denzil hovered, ready to take off. Right behind him his mother was hanging on, trying to stop him from leaving, the stepfather in turn trying to hang on to and anchor his wife. Finally Redwood appeared to straighten out the tangled family.

'It's all right, Mrs Taylor. Let's leave it for now. Perhaps it might be better if I meet Denzil on his own next time. Okay, Denzil?'

Perhaps only to escape, the young man nodded sullenly and turned to leave through the waiting room. To do so, he had to pass in front of Simon sitting in his wheelchair.

Denzil's eyes met Simon's, betraying the faintest hint of recognition, though on the surface their faces remained impassive.

Meanwhile, Redwood acknowledged Mrs O'Day, as he ushered Mr and Mrs Taylor to the door. Preoccupied with comings and goings, none of the rest of them even noticed Simon and Denzil staring into each other's souls.

The moment of confrontation went on and on in tense silence until Mrs Taylor called back to her son.

'Come on, Denzil.'

Breaking the deadlock, Denzil squeezed past the wheelchair, leaving Simon gazing into empty space.

30

Special Constable Anjali Shah was escorted into the ostensibly empty office of Division 'S' Police Chief Superintendent Frank Ellsmore. Anjali took a seat by his desk, as the WPC went to another door and knocked softly. She opened the door, which led to a small dressing room, just slightly, so she could announce Anjali's presence in a voice only a bit louder than a whisper.

When Ellsmore appeared in the doorway to this annexe, he nodded, and the WPC took her leave. Though in uniform trousers and shirt, Ellsmore still appeared somewhat casually dressed, as he was currently engaged in tying and adjusting his uniform tie.

'Sorry about this, Anjali. I have one of those high mucky-muck meetings in . . .' He checked the clock on the wall. '. . . about twenty minutes. How's the shoulder?'

Demonstrating her progress, Anjali flexed her arm outside of the sling. 'It's nice being waited on,' she answered with a grin. 'But people are getting suspicious.'

Ellsmore laughed, releasing some of his tension and formality as well. 'Well . . . in your case . . . you deserve all the attention you can grab . . . for as long as it's going . . .'

Abruptly his expression became more serious. 'Anyway . . . my secretary said something was troubling you. Something to do with the Asian community?'

Anjali took her time to compose herself. 'There's a certain situation that might get out of hand, sir. And I am very grateful you could see me.'

He waved her polite explanation aside. 'If there's something I ought to know, I'd rather hear about it before it develops into something else.'

In essence he had authorized her to proceed, so she got right to the point. 'There have been five women hit by air-gun pellets over the last six weeks.'

'So I gather,' he nodded, taking a step back toward his dressing room. 'And the last one wasn't as harmless as the others?'

'They were all . . .' She paused as Ellsmore disappeared into his dressing room.

'It's okay . . . I'm listening,' he called out.

Getting up and moving toward the door, she raised her voice. '. . . They were all potentially dangerous, sir.'

'Section Forty-Sevens always are,' he replied. 'And we fully understand the concern the Asian community feels about these incidents.'

'That's just the trouble, Chief Superintendent. They see nothing being done . . . no arrests made . . . They don't think the Police are taking it seriously enough.'

Her words were greeted with silence, leading her to wonder if she had gone too far.

Once again Ellsmore entered the room, this time in the full uniform of a Police Chief Superintendent, an aspect that could be quite intimidating. Regarding Anjali with raised eyebrows, he beckoned her attention to the pie chart on the wall.

'Do you know what our detection-arrest rate is so far, Anjali?'

Feeling a touch of embarrassment, she shook her head.

'Eighty-three per cent. That's pretty damn good in this day and age. Especially when you remember that we're way under strength. Nevertheless . . . that still leaves seventeen per cent slipping through the net . . .'

Shifting his attention to the view from his window, Ellsmore looked into the distance, his back to Anjali. 'What I'm saying is that sometimes, it has to be a case of the majority outweighing the needs of the minority.'

'Surely the safety of one person is just as important as that of the many?'

Ellsmore remained silent for a moment, then slowly he turned to confront her questions, a mournful look on his face. 'Of course it is. And I shouldn't have to stand here making slick PR statements.'

Although she understood his position, she felt dejected, and lowered her head as she got up to leave. Just as she reached the door, he spoke to her in a more confidential tone.

'Anjali . . . I can tell you what we know so far . . .'

She turned back to him, her hopes rekindled.

'. . . but it may not help. We believe the perpetrator is taking pot shots from one of the shops around the square.'

Now it was her turn to raise an eyebrow. 'But that could mean it was one of our own people doing these things?'

Ellsmore shrugged, unwilling to commit himself officially to that conclusion. 'That's not for me to say . . . Remember, it may not be malicious . . . And much as I'd like to search some of the premises, my hands are tied. Because the ownership of an air pistol is not against the law.'

He hated to discourage her hopes, but his own position required that facts be faced honestly, whether the news was good or bad. 'It's not much help. But you should know by this time that Police work can be bloody frustrating.'

She may have known, but she was still learning.

Anjali made her way through a busy crowd in the Asian open-air market with a specific destination in mind, although she wasn't quite sure where it was. She had to ask a question here and there before being pointed in the right direction.

Finally she found the general area where all of the air-pistol shootings had taken place, as well as the stall where the most recent victim had been shot in the neck. Standing still, she began to make a detailed visual survey of what was around her, conducting her own investigation.

People milling around her looked curiously, trying to figure out what she was up to, though she took little notice, instead concentrating on where the shots could have come from. And as soon as she asked herself that question, she realized that there were perhaps only four or five adjacent shops in a row that had an unobstructed view of the stall that sold silks.

Above one of the shops on the first floor, a curtain was drawn aside slightly, offering someone an unobstructed view of Anjali Shah. She approached the shops below, then hesitated, appearing uncertain as to her next step. The curtain dropped back into place.

Moments later, Anjali was still attempting to figure out the trajectory of the air-pistol pellets when a woman's voice startled her from behind. 'Can I speak to you, please?'

Anjali turned around to discover a slender Indian woman whose anxiety was evident in every corner of her face. 'I own the shop over there,' she said in a confidential voice, pointing to a place selling fancy goods, one of the few shops that Anjali had determined to have an unobstructed path of sight to the shooting victims.

Nodding, Anjali waited patiently for the anxious woman to continue.

277

Meanwhile, the curtain on the first-floor window above the shop was again drawn back. Behind the window, a vague shape haunted the shadows.

'You are the girl who works with the police?'

'Well . . . in a way . . . but how did –'

Before Anjali could finish the thought, the Indian woman interrupted with the answer. 'Someone pointed you out to me at the temple.'

'Ah,' Anjali responded, pleased to be recognized. Still she waited for the woman to proceed.

'Can I ask you something? Something private?'

'Of course.'

The Indian woman came closer to confide in Anjali, although no one near them could possibly overhear what they were saying, or understand it if they did. 'You see . . . I have a friend . . . and I don't want her getting into trouble . . .'

Behind the curtain and the window, imperceptible from the street, was a small, wide-eyed, inquisitive face hiding in the shadows, watching the two Indian women conversing below. Ever so delicately, the curtain trembled.

The Indian woman became quieter moment by moment, more afraid of where the conversation must lead.

'My friend has a young boy . . . I know he owns an air gun . . . Just a toy, really . . .'

She stopped, unable to continue, and Anjali quickly reached out to comfort her. It was all the woman could do to hold back her tears.

'I understand,' Anjali said gently. 'And I'm sure we can settle everything quietly. But first you must promise me one thing . . .' The woman looked up at Anjali through watery eyes. '. . . that you will take the gun away . . .' Slowly, sadly, the woman began to nod.

'. . . from your son.'

The woman dropped her head, but there was denial.

Up at the window, the curtain was again at rest.

31

Madge, the young trainee at the Bromsgrove Building Society, was having trouble balancing all of the files being handed to her by the manager, Mr Maynard. Yet she was certainly making a valiant effort.

'See these go back in the filing cabinet, Miss Pyke. And you will see they are replaced in proper alphabetical order . . .'

With files practically up to her chin, she had to bob up and down in order to answer in the affirmative.

'Good . . . er . . . wait. Let me look at that last one.' Maynard removed the top file without noticing that he had almost tipped over half of the others. 'No . . . I'd better hold on to the Barker one myself,' he decided, seeming momentarily to forget she was there. Then the spell was broken, and he looked up again. 'That's all . . . Thank you, Miss Pyke.'

Half-opening the Barker file, he thought for an instant, then stopped Madge for a second time. 'Ah . . . Miss Pyke . . . a moment . . .' He quickly slipped ahead of her and shut the door to his office, shielding them from prying ears, and led her back into the room. After all, she did seem like a nice young girl, generally cheerful and sincere: perhaps a carefully aimed question or two might elicit some pertinent information.

'I've been meaning to ask you, Miss Pyke . . . have you any problems, any difficulties . . .' Her face was a blank. 'Sometimes young trainees like yourself find it hard to settle down in their first year. You know . . . jumping in the deep end after school.'

Whereas she didn't understand what he was getting at, it didn't sound right: his manner was too friendly. 'Oh, no, Mr Maynard. Everybody's been so kind.'

'Good, good . . . Wouldn't like to think any of the staff were picking on you just because of your age.'

Madge showed a charming smile. 'No. As a matter of fact, Viv . . . that is . . . Miss Smith, even invited me round to her flat for a drink.'

He couldn't help frowning. 'Not leading you off the straight and narrow, I hope?'

'Ooh no,' Madge assured him. 'I'm not too keen on vodka. But I don't think she had any lager . . .' She looked up at the manager and bit her lip. '. . . or lemonade. Just vodka and gin . . .' She bit her lip again, '. . . and stuff like that.'

'You make it sound as though Miss Smith has a well-stocked bar . . . Lives well, does she?' he asked cheerily.

Her enthusiastic reaction was worse than he had feared. 'Phew! I'll say!' Realizing her excitement might be misinterpreted, she hastened to correct any such impression. 'Oh I don't mean anything . . . She made jokes about it, that's all.'

'Jokes?'

Her brow wrinkled in the effort to find words to explain what she did mean, or at least what Viv said. 'Well . . . that she did well on the horses . . . had a second job . . . stuff like that . . . I told her she must be blooming lucky . . . on the horses, that is . . . to afford a flat like that. But she was very sympathetic when I mentioned I had to share a room with my –'

He cleared his throat, having heard more than enough. 'Yes, I'm sure she was.' Holding her by the arm (and nearly tipping the files again), he guided her back to the door without further ado. 'Thank you, Miss Pyke.' He opened the door for her. 'And remember, Miss Pyke . . . alphabetical order . . . with the files.'

Freddy Calder and Viv Smith were by themselves, apart from the other Specials gathering in the parade room. Viv was trying to get him to unburden himself, but his lips remained sealed.

'I don't want to talk about it.'

'Oh I see! Well next time you need help with your love affairs, Freddy Calder, go write to Claire Rayner, and see how far you get.'

'I didn't mean it that way.'

'Then what *did* you mean?'

Freddy still couldn't look her in the eye, or stop fidgeting. 'Just that I don't want Division "S" and the Flying Squad knowing intimate details about my love life.'

'Why should they?'

'Because if I tell you, it'll be the main story on the nine o'clock news.'

Now she *was* insulted. 'That is charming. When did I ever open my mouth and blab about your private life? Go on. Tell me.'

'What about the redhead in "T" Division I fancied? I walk into the Pub on 4th, and there's a bunch of PC's wearing ginger wigs waiting to jump me.'

Viv was not entirely successful in swallowing a gurgle of laughter.

'Oh, very funny that was,' Freddy groaned.

'All right . . .' So now she had a guilty conscience again. 'But when else?'

Before he could recollect another instance of her treachery, Section Officer Bob Loach came in and signalled for Freddy and Viv to join the rest of the Specials at the table.

'When you're ready, SC Smith, Special Constable Calder.'

From the kitchen door, Anjali said goodnight to the Indian woman, who wished to remain unseen as much as possible. When she was gone, Anjali turned around and – since she was holding a rather large wrapped parcel in her good hand – shut the door with her bottom. The door made a loud thud, as she had pushed a bit too hard.

No doubt hearing the noise, her uncle called to her from the sitting room. 'Anjali? Was it for me?'

'Yes . . .' she called back, then continued to herself, '. . . in a way.'

'What?' he called out again.

She moved through the entrance to the sitting room, where Uncle Ram had been reading his newspaper. But immediately upon seeing her carrying the ungainly package, he jumped up from the stuffed chair to take it from her.

'You should not be carrying things.'

'Uncle Ram, I'm not a complete invalid.'

He was looking at the package curiously. 'What is it?'

'Open it and see.'

Uncle Ram split open the package, revealing a well-used air-pistol. His shock was apparent, and he looked at Anjali in astonishment. 'Is this the gun . . . ?'

Anjali nodded modestly.

'Shiva, Shiva, Shiva,' Uncle Ram intoned. 'Now look here, Anjali, the culprit must be brought to justice!'

'Of course he must.'

Her ready agreement left him shocked and suspicious. 'What . . . ? Why are you agreeing with me? Suddenly I'm smelling a kettle of fish.'

'No, no, no,' Anjali insisted. 'He deserves to be punished for what he did . . .' She started to re-wrap the weapon. '. . . even though he is only ten.'

'Ten? What are you saying?'

'That it was a ten-year-old Indian boy from a good family who thought it was fun to shoot at ladies' backsides.'

'A ten-year-old boy? You are absolutely sure?'

Her haughty look was enough to confirm her answer.

He paced about the sitting room, concentrating his thoughts, until he eventually arrived at a tentative position.

'Now look here, Anjali, we must be very careful what we tell the community. And how we say it . . . Above all, it must be done with great *discretion*.'

'Sounds right up your street, Uncle Ram.'

He took this as a compliment. 'Naturally. I am not one to shirk my responsibilities.' Yet still, the sadness of it all depressed him, and he shook his head in sorrow.

'Ten years old. From a good family. Ai, ai, ai,' he wailed in futility. 'But why am I shocked . . . ? When nowadays, they have turtles coming out of the sewers . . .'

32

As Viv Smith walked the beat with Freddy Calder, she had finally just about coaxed him to tell her all about his big date with Rita, the one she had practically brain-washed him to arrange.

'It was a bloody disaster,' he admitted with a sigh.

'Oh God . . . !' Her eyes rolled. 'What did you do?'

'I did nothing . . . It was my mother –' he blurted out, immediately clapping his hands over his mouth to prevent what had already escaped, to his infinite regret.

'Your mother? You took your mother on your first date with Rita?' Viv gasped.

Freddy punched himself in the hip again and again. 'I knew it. I knew I should've kept my mouth shut.' The he turned to explain: 'No! I didn't invite my mother. She . . . she turned up.'

By now, Viv was thoroughly exasperated with the utter hopelessness of guiding her partner to romance and adventure. 'I don't think I understand your philosophy of life, Freddy. Maybe when we've a spare month, you can explain it to me.'

An unexpected bicycle bell diverted her attention momentarily. Instantly she recognized the window-cleaner she had seen before, and he seemed to recognize her. In a cocky mood when he cycled up to join them, he pointed out that his light was now in good working order, and that his ladder was firmly fixed to the bicycle frame.

Viv circled the bike, ducking in for a closer inspection. Everything appeared to check out, and she nodded her approval. He gave her and Freddy a cheery wave, then pushed down on the pedals to pull away.

'No!' Viv shouted, suddenly changing her mind. 'Hold it a second!'

Her alarm startled Freddy into action. He reached out a hand and grabbed hold of the last rung on the ladder clamped to the bike's frame. Unfortunately, although he held tight, the ladder extended as the window-cleaner kept pedalling forward.

By the time the ladder reached its fullest extension, Freddy was holding on like the anchor-man in a tug-of-war. There was a sudden jerk, and the bicycle tilted over and crashed, throwing the window-cleaner to the ground.

But when the pannier bags hit the street, they split open and spilled silver booty all over the road. Immediately the supposed window-cleaner was up and running, in the other direction.

Viv dashed after him. Cutting him off on an angle, she planted her right foot for the take-off, leapt into the air, and brought down the fugitive with a flying tackle.

Freddy would never have believed it unless he had seen it with his own eyes. Puffing forward to offer her the assistance of at least his brute strength, he was surprised to find his partner kneeling on the window-cleaner's chest, the weasel having given up the struggle long before Freddy got there.

'I knew there was something funny last night,' she announced triumphantly. 'I knew there was something Redwood and I never noticed.'

'What?' Watson asked Holmes.

'It was when feller-me-lad here, said he was a window-cleaner.'

'So?'

'He didn't have a bucket,' Holmes remarked. 'And all window-cleaners have a bucket.'

33

In a vaguely unsettled mood, and for some submerged reason, John Redwood returned home that night with a heavy heart. As he parked in front of the house, he could see a few rays of light falling from a chink in the curtains in his son's bedroom window on the ground floor. While he was watching, the curtain fell quickly, and the light extinguished.

It had happened before, but it always had a melancholy effect on him, on this occasion accentuated by the mournful melody lingering on the car radio. He switched it off, and then the engine.

In the passageway inside the house, he approached his son's closed door, knocked . . . waited a few moments . . . and went in.

His back to his father, Simon was sitting in front of his computer, as usual. Except that the screen was dead.

'You all right?'

'Yeah!' Simon shot back, though he made no effort to turn around and face his father.

There was nothing but silence between father and son now. With a forlorn shrug, the father made to leave, but held his ground for the moment instead. There was something he had to say to his paralyzed, crippled, bitter, quietly hostile son.

'We're losing one another, you know, Simon. And the time is coming when we could end up being complete strangers. It's mainly my fault, but I need you to meet me part of the way.'

Simon didn't move.

'When you're mother was . . .' he almost choked on the word '. . . *alive,* I confess I left it all up to her. I know that you were closer to her . . .' Getting a grip on himself, he felt the strain of tears. '. . . but losing her was just as . . . heartbreaking . . . for me as it was for you.'

Redwood sighed and turned toward the door.

All of a sudden Simon spoke up. 'That guy today . . . The black guy? Who is he? What was he doing here?' Though his body was still, his voice was quaking.

'Why?' asked his father, puzzled.

'He was one of them,' said Simon after a pause. 'One of the gang responsible for *this!*'

In one movement, Simon slammed his hands on the arms of the wheelchair, swinging around fiercely to face his father.

'He did this to me, Dad.'

Walking through the Pub on 4th, Police Sergeant Andy McAllister went over to a table and sat down beside Viv Smith, joining a mix of PC's, WPC's, and Specials crowding around her.

'You're looking pleased with yourself,' he remarked.

Not knowing quite how to interpret this, considering the source, she shrugged it off, looking over to the bar where Freddy was filling a tray with drinks.

Unfortunately for her, McAllister wasn't finished. 'Did I tell you that window-cleaner is thinking of swearing out a complaint about being assaulted by a policewoman?'

It was the 'Assault' that did it. 'What?'

'Well, you did sit on him, didn't you, lassie?' the sergeant persisted.

As far as Viv was concerned, however, he had stepped over the line. 'He's swearing out a complaint? Wait till he gets the bill for my tights.'

She stood up, hauled her skirt to a mounting chorus of wolf whistles and howls (though not from the stunned Sergeant Scotsman), in turn lifted each leg up to the chair for a closer view – revealing holes on both knees in her black tights and ladders from ankle to thigh.

McAllister rose from the table with a shy grin on his face and made his retreat. Before he could get away, Freddy called after him with a final word of consideration for the window-cleaner.

'Tell him he can buy Viv's size from me at a good discount.'

34

In Police Sergeant McAllister's office, Special Constable John Redwood waited patiently for Andy to finish counting his way through a wad of dockets. Finally he wrote down the total, sighed heavily, and looked up at Redwood with a dour face.

'Evening Sarge,' Redwood began with a hesitant smile.

'Aye,' McAllister sniffed.

It was a delicate subject, and he had to be careful about what he was asking the sergeant to do. 'I appreciate your help. If I'd gone through . . . more conventional channels . . . it might have taken weeks.'

McAllister's brusque manner didn't make it any easier. 'I'm not doing this because I like your face, Redwood. It's a favour.'

Redwood smiled and nodded. 'So when you get in trouble with your wife . . . ?'

'Exactly,' said McAllister, deadpan.

Leafing through one of the folders on his desk, the sergeant removed two sheets of paper, then briefly scanned each of them before continuing.

'The thug you're looking for is Laurie Kerrigan. He and your client, Denzil Taylor, were nicked for petty theft a few years back.'

'Any idea where I can find this Kerrigan?'

For once there was a perceptible grin on Andy's face. 'No problem there. He's detained at Her Majesty's pleasure, Scalebrook.' Indeed that was a place where an inmate could always be located. 'Booked for the next two years.'

Outside the parade room Freddy Calder was hurrying down the corridor after Viv Smith, who had no intention of waiting for him.

'Viv, hang on . . . ?'

'It'll have to wait, Freddy. We're going to be late.'

'This is very important, Viv,' he urged breathlessly. 'Only you can help.'

She rolled her eyes. 'How did I guess?' she asked in a rhetorical monotone. 'After parade, right?'

'No, please Viv . . . I . . .'

As she went through the door, it slammed behind her. But as Freddy tried to push it open and follow her, Viv's shout stopped him dead in his tracks.

'Don't you dare!'

He stared at the closed door as gloom descended on his face, and sighed in resignation. It was the ladies' room.

Fresh-faced Police Constable Albert Coles marched smartly down the corridor with a brisk guardsman's step. As he came up to the waiting Sergeant McAllister, he snapped to attention.

'Sarge?'

Consulting his clipboard, McAllister managed an uncharacteristic smile. 'PC Albert Coles . . . first night out on your own, I see.'

'Yes, Sarge.'

'I've got something special for you,' he offered.

The young PC's eyes gleamed in innocent anticipation. 'Yes, Sarge.'

'Your partner's in court tomorrow, and he'll be up all night doing the paperwork. So you'll be with Special Constable Freddy Calder tonight.' The ghost of a smile settled on the sergeant's face.

'A Special, Sarge?' Coles cried disdainfully.

The smile evaporated like a saucer of iced tea in the desert sun, 'Perhaps you'd allow this to penetrate your mighty intellect, laddie. Calder knows this patch like the back of his hand, been doing it for years. He knows the ropes. Not that I'm suggesting you'll need a wet-nurse.'

'Certainly not, Sarge.'

The phoney smile returned. 'Good.'

Straightening his spine even further, Coles started to take his leave.

'PC Coles . . . ?'

'Yes, Sarge?'

'Naturally, you – as the regular officer – will carry the responsibility for the tour of duty.'

The gleam came back to his eyes, and he saluted. 'Right. Thank You, Sarge.'

While the Specials were milling round the parade room waiting for their orders from Bob Loach, Freddy had managed to corner Viv. However, she was busy trying to make last-minute adjustments to her mascara with a fine brush using a small hand mirror, so she wasn't giving him her full attention.

'Please, Viv, as a favour to me?'

She stopped brushing her long lashes for two seconds and glared at him, freezing her hands and make-up tools in mid-air. 'You're as mad as a wet hen. You've finally got another date with Rita, and you want me to come with you?' she scoffed. 'Date one: Your Mum tracks you down. And date two: I'm going to pitch up. What the hell's she going to think?' Returning her eyes to the mirror, she went back to concentrating on Operation Mascara.

'You're two sandwiches short of a picnic, Freddy Calder.'

'You don't understand . . . we'll have to be subtle,' Freddy urged

287

'Make it look like we bumped into each other by accident.' He touched her arm, gently, but with urgency. 'Please, Viv, this is important.'

As soon as he touched her, Viv smudged her make-up. Glaring at him, she dabbed on some more to paint over the mistake. 'Why me, Freddy?'

'Because you're a woman . . .'

'Oh, ta very much . . .' She didn't miss a beat with her mascara brush.

'. . . and you'll know straight away whether she fancies me. You know, intuition . . .'

'Why don't you just try asking her?'

Freddy crumpled under her questioning. 'I don't want to hear the answer. I can't do it, not face-to-face. I couldn't handle it.'

In the meantime, Bob Loach had arrived at their corner checking over his clipboard. 'Come on, Freddy. Get on with it. McAllister's waiting for you downstairs.'

Freddy grabbed his hat and lumbered off, although he tarried behind just a moment, gazing back at Viv with a despairing look on his face, hoping for a last reprieve.

Viv glanced at him, then sighed. 'Where will you be?'

Instantly Freddy brightened. '*The Four Pigeons*. Twelve thirty.'

Viv nodded her assent without taking her eyes from the mirror.

'Twelve thirty sharp?' Freddy called back at her just as he collided with John Redwood coming in. They both looked at each other in surprise, then without another word went their separate ways.

Redwood, too, was deep in thought, rereading the photocopies McAllister had give him. Viv broke her concentration from the mirror and looked up, shaking her head.

'It's worse than a second job. No pay and no holidays.'

Having no idea what she was babbling on about, Redwood's expression indicated he also was baffled. With her head and eyes, Viv gestured toward the door.

'Freddy. Who else?'

35

Growing impatient, Jimmy Duncan, an excitable young Canadian in his early twenties, sat at the table in the interrogation room opposite Police Sergeant Andy McAllister, who was writing notes from their conversation. Behind him stood PC Albert Coles and SC Freddy Calder.

'Look, I've already told you, I've been to Social Services, and they told me exactly the same thing. They said it's nothing to do with them. They sent me here.'

McAllister was doing his best to be diplomatic. 'You must appreciate, sir, we can't just break into a house on uncorroborated evidence.'

Delving into his pockets, Jimmy Duncan dumped piles of bundled letters on the table. 'Here's your evidence. He's my grandad. He's written to me every month since he went back to England. And then . . . he stopped.' Not only anguish, but fear lurked in his eyes and thoughts.

Sympathetic to his feelings, McAllister nevertheless cautioned the lad about jumping to conclusions. 'It doesn't necessarily mean . . .'

But the grandson was stubbornly inconsolable at this point. '. . . What *does* it mean then? That's what I've spent all my savings to find out. Ticket from Toronto, lodgings, the works. But now I'm running out of money.'

Freddy spoke up with a question. 'Who did you say was living at his house, sir?'

'Grandad's daughter – my Aunt Margaret – and her husband.'

The sergeant frowned. 'They must have some explanation?'

Seething with anger, Jimmy Duncan still appeared reluctant to talk about his relationship with his relatives, other than his grandfather. 'They say . . . that he just up and left a year ago with a woman half his age.'

'It does happen, sir,' remarked McAllister.

Jimmy shook his head vigorously, brandishing the bundles of letters. 'No. I'd have known. He wouldn't have just stopped writing . . . not told me.' He looked desperately at the impassive McAllister for some hint of reassurance, but it wasn't there.

'Look . . . I think he's dead . . . murdered.' The young man let his accusation sink in a moment. 'And his body . . . could still be inside the house.'

PC Albert Coles shot a disbelieving glance at Freddy. But Freddy looked thoughtful rather than cynical, going over the plausible details of Duncan's story.

District Commandant Peter Whittaker and Sub-Divisional Officer Rob Barker had chosen a quiet corner of the Pub on 4th to discuss the latter's resignation. Over a cup of coffee, deep in conversation, Whittaker was lending the SDO a compassionate ear, but the issue now seemed a foregone conclusion.

'If that's your decision . . .' Whittaker asked one last time.

'No real choice, I'm afraid, sir. My wife's been ill for some time now. It's made us think . . . about the future. She really wants to go back to Scotland to be with her family. I feel . . . well, she's got to come first.'

'Of course. I do understand. Very sorry to lose you, Rob.'

Barker accepted his words with a show of gratitude, making a good job of his martyrdom. That form of response, however, still left it to Whittaker to think of something to say next.

'Naturally, we'd like to make some sort of presentation, to mark all the years you've put in.' As soon as he said it, he realized that Barker would have to share the spotlight with someone much more popular right now, although there might also be a redeeming factor in the economy of getting both done in one ceremony. 'We're having this do for Anjali Shah shortly, for her Commendation . . . So maybe . . .'

'Right. Thank you very much sir.' Privately Barker was miffed that the DC would run the two ceremonies together: Anjali's was sure to become a display of wild enthusiasm over the bravery of a woman who'd had the luck to survive the collapse of a construction site on top of her culprit. So much for his own moment of glory!

Out of the corner of his eye, Whittaker happened to spot Section Officer Loach trying to flag him from the doorway, where he was hovering uncomfortably with a file of paperwork under his arm. Whittaker signalled that he should wait.

'Have you given any thought to your successor?' He gestured toward the doorway. 'What about Loach? He's been a good section officer, fairly solid. Seems to have handled the paperwork well.'

Barker pulled a sour face. 'Bit of a rough diamond. Would have thought you could have done a bit better, sir? I mean, people who run buses aren't quite the calibre? Specials get enough flak as it is.'

He took another sip of his coffee, but it had turned cold by now. 'Maybe this would be a strategic time to get a man in from one of the other divisions?'

'Inject some new blood, you mean?'

'Exactly that, sir.' Barker nodded.

PC Albert Coles braked the panda to a clean stop in front of a bleak and austere detached house. He and SC Freddy Calder got out of the car, and Coles turned back as he headed for the door. 'Leave the talking to me, Special Constable Calder. We did a lot of this kind of thing in training. Application of psychology . . .'

Freddy beamed him a look of mock admiration as he folded his arms and slumped against the panda to view the proceedings.

PC Coles gave the door-knocker a sharp rap. After a brief wait, the door opened a crack, though restrained by a heavy link chain. Inside was a dry stick of a woman in her fifties, presumably young Jimmy's Aunty Margaret.

'What do you want?'

Showing his I.D. through the chink in the castle's armour, PC Coles tried to coax the woman's cooperation. 'Mrs Ruddle, my name's Police Constable Coles, and I'd like to ask you some questions . . .'

'Go away.'

With a foot firmly placed, PC Coles kept the door from closing. 'Madam, please . . . Mr Duncan has asked us . . .'

'I told the authorities all I know,' Mrs Ruddle snapped at him. 'And my nephew.'

'Mrs Ruddle, I must insist . . .'

'Very well,' she muttered after a moment.

The door closed, the chain was released, and the door opened again abruptly. Standing in the door was a glaring, thickset, middle-aged gorilla, presumably Mr Ruddle, with an obviously nasty temper.

'Look, we're sick of all this, right? Her Dad just took off with some tart, about a year ago. He's old enough to look after himself. He's not our problem any more. Nor's his crazy grandson. Goddit?'

Lost for words, PC Coles was mouthing air as the door slammed shut. Frustrated, he turned around and saw Freddy at the panda, a wide grin decorating his face.

*   *   *

Escorted by District Commandant Whittaker to the doorway of the Pub on 4th, SDO Rob Barker passed Bob Loach and gave him a cool nod before leaving. Whittaker stood back to observe their interaction, then stepped toward Loach to take the reports for signing.

'How did you know he was resigning?' Whittaker asked him.

'There were lots of rumours,' Loach shrugged.

'I didn't hear them,' commented Whittaker testily. Loach simply responded with a knowing smile. 'Anyway, Rob's just confirmed it.' He began to sign the reports, one by one.

Thinking that now the moment was ripe for a timely word, Loach proceeded cautiously. 'Perhaps this is an appropriate time to remind you, sir, that my hat's still in the ring for promotion. As you know, I've been practically doing the job for the last few months.'

'But not actually, Loach.' Whittaker contradicted him. 'That's the difference. And I'd suggest that, in your position, you didn't mouth off quite so readily.'

Loach was stunned by the DC's reaction. 'Sir?'

'I don't suppose you've investigated the reasons for the rumours, have you?' His voice was stern, almost contemptuous.

Embarrassed, Loach muttered, 'Well . . . no, sir . . . I . . .'

'Like the fact that Rob Barker's wife is critically ill?'

'Sorry to hear that, sir. But . . .' Loach dried up, embarrassed.

'Right. Let's just leave it at that, shall we?'

Without looking at Loach, he handed back the reports and stalked off down the corridor. Loach was left feeling like he'd just been sandbagged.

PC Coles was still in two minds as to the next step when Freddy, the wide grin still on his face, arrived at the front door. 'Another victory for applied psychology, heh?'

A rueful look on his face, PC Coles watched Freddy thump loudly on the door with his fist. The door opened immediately, framing the ferocious Mr Ruddle.

'I've told you . . .'

Freddy quickly eased a foot and a leg into the doorway. 'Mr Ruddle, why don't you just let us in, and then we can sit down and discuss this in a civilized way over a nice cup of tea.'

Ruddle continued to glare at them.

292

'It'll just save us time and effort getting a warrant,' continued Freddy casually.

'Go get your warrant,' Ruddle scowled. 'I know my rights.' Ejecting Freddy's foot, he slammed the door in his face again.

That was it for tonight. Freddy shrugged and retraced his steps to the car, followed by PC Coles already beside himself with righteous indignation.

'You've ruined everything, you idiot! This sort of situation has to be handled by the book. There are *techniques* you can employ with that sort of person.'

Freddy's eyes rolled, as he considered the fresh PC Albert Coles. 'With respect, lad, there's only one technique I know of with a closed door . . . and that's to kick it in.'

PC Coles recoiled in horror at the mere suggestion.

Leaving his office, Police Chief Superintendent Frank Ellsmore ushered District Commandant of the Specials Peter Whittaker to the lift, guiding his arm in a friendly gesture.

'I know Loach is pushy, Peter. But he seems to get on well with the lads.'

Whittaker shook his head uncertainly. 'I wish I could warm to him more,' he confessed.

'He's had a chance to prove himself recently, hasn't he?' Ellsmore prodded.

'And I'm not convinced,' Whittaker explained simply. After all, he was not professionally trained as a police administrator and leader. True, he did know how to run a business, including how to hire, fire, and promote, and those were the same skills that qualified him for this position as well. 'Look, I have to offer the job around to those best qualified. For instance, there's a damned good man down in "Z" Division. I've had my eye on him.'

A quizzical smile played on Ellsmore's lips. 'He'd mind his P's and Q's, would he?'

'Well,' said Whittaker, 'supposing he did, it's not an unimportant quality, is it, sir?'

Ellsmore's face resumed a bland expression as the lift doors opened.

36

So intent was Anjali Shah on her exercise, strenuously and methodically raising weights on a push-up machine in the Physio Department at General Hospital, that it required the shrill Aussie voice of her colleague, Kerry Packman, to bring her back to reality.

'All right . . . *ALL RIGHT*, Anji . . . Point made.' She moved closer to her fellow physiotherapist and, like a maiden aunt, waved a finger at her. 'I pronounce you dangerously fit and plenty well enough to be back at work. Skiver . . .'

Anjali surrendered and gave the machine (and herself) a rest, though Kerry's approving grin was short-lived, fading as swiftly as a cloud covers the sun. Behind Anjali she could see Simon Redwood, Kerry's patient and the son of Anjali's sometime partner in the Specials. Transfixed, she watched the crippled young man's painful efforts on the low parallel bars, his face contorted as he strained every surviving muscle in his upper body to propel one foot in front of the other.

His eyelids were shut, his eyes trying to focus on some distant image unseen. Unable to overcome the dead weight of his own body, he gasped with the physical effort, then pushed himself on with anger, oblivious to the gym or anything or anyone else around him. His only purpose in life at the moment seemed to be to keep driving his legs, on and on until he couldn't go on anymore.

'Simon!'

He didn't even hear Kerry, now close to him. Gently she put her hand out and touched him.

'Slow up, Simon.'

Startled, he looked up and stopped.

Kerry tried to calm him. 'You've got all the time in the world. Rest is as important as work. Remember?'

Reluctantly Simon nodded, resting against the bars, the sweat pouring down parts of his body he could no longer sense.

Anjali, who had observed their exchange, walked toward Simon just as Kerry was leaving. He saw her, and recognized her, yet there was no change in his expression.

'Now I know how the patients feel,' she offered lightly, adding a friendly smile.

'Oh yes?'

His hard rebuke threw her off-balance. 'Oh God, I'm not suggesting . . . you know?'

He decided not to press the issue, though his attitude still remained unchanged. 'Heard you got into a fight.'

Instinctively she raised her hand to her cheek. 'Something like that. Nothing that dramatic.'

'Not compared with me, you mean?'

He resented what he immediately assumed she meant, strictly from his own perspective. Anjali was shocked by the depth and tenacity of his bitterness.

'I didn't mean that exactly, no.' Her smile was gone now as well.

Simon's eyes seemed to calculate her hidden weaknesses and motives. 'My dad's told you all about it, has he? The son of a Special, beaten up by a gang of boot-boys, tossed off a bridge and crippled.'

He seemed to be testing how much of his misery and horror she could tolerate. What he could not possibly know was the echoes of her own experience and fear of violence that his cruel remarks triggered in her stomach. What he saw was her rather successful attempt, at least on the surface, to disguise her fear from others.

'He has talked about it, Simon. We work together sometimes.'

'Yeh, I know,' he scoffed sarcastically. 'Playing policemen.'

Anjali faced his angry look squarely, without pretence. 'Look, I know me and your dad aren't exactly going to change the world, but we're doing our bit. Who knows, we might give the police time to solve a few more crimes?'

'Like mine you mean?' he sneered. 'Maybe it's not time they need. Maybe they should just get a bit more interested? Or maybe, they're just not smart enough.'

She waited before responding. 'Getting bitter and giving up is the easy way out, isn't it?' Her eyes narrowed on his. 'Just a moment ago, I didn't get the impression that was your style at all.'

He looked away, yet wouldn't surrender his anger. 'No . . . well . . . the only thing I believe in these days is that one day I'll see them suffer the way I have.'

Anjali winced. Recovering her composure, she spoke to him in a quieter, more intimate voice. 'Simon, have you told your Dad you feel like this . . . ?'

All of a sudden Anjali was aware that a man had been standing and waiting next to her. Suppressing her immediate instinct to jump, again she turned slowly and deliberately to look at the man. Built like a gnarled tree trunk, he must be, she thought, an athlete or a fighter, or a labourer of some sort. His physical presence and power alone threatened her inside, although she tried not to show it, especially to him.

In turn, he looked her up and down, though in a sexually neutral manner. 'You . . . Miss Packman?'

'She's with another patient. I'll go and tell her you're here.'

'Thanks. It's Doug Storer, tell her.'

Without another word, Anjali nodded quickly and left the room to find Kerry.

Grinning at Simon, Doug Storer took the lad into his confidence. 'That's a relief.'

'What is?'

Still grinning, he indicated the recently departed woman of Asian extraction. 'Our brown brothers and sisters . . . you know . . .'

Registering the reaction on Simon's face, he hastened to correct the crippled lad's misinterpretation. 'Don't get me wrong, mate, I'm no racist. Christ – I fought alongside them. In Africa. That's where I got this.'

Pulling up his shirt, the ex-mercenary revealed the long scars of deep wounds on his shoulder and chest. 'Still gives me gyp.'

He let his shirt fall, as he recounted his worst adventure to Simon. 'I was caught in crossfire. My squad should have been right up there with me, but all I got was my brown brothers a hundred yards back of me.'

For his part, Simon still seemed unsympathetic to the ex-mercenary. Neither of them noticed that Anjali had reappeared at the door, nor that she could hear what Doug Storer was saying about her.

'Listen, I've got nothing against that bird . . . I'm sure she's good at her job.' He groped for the words to articulate his feelings. 'It's just that I don't want her brown hands on me, see . . .'

Though furious, Anjali waited, and did not interrupt. She was sorely offended, but intensely curious as well. And she wanted to see how Simon would react.

Simon didn't reply, but rather avoided the ex-mercenary by using his anger to start his exercises again . . . in silence.

Storer gave him a patronizing grin. 'Anyway, looks like you've got the right idea, mate.'

296

Simon stopped, unable to contain his anger. 'Oh yeh? What's that then?'

'Attitude . . .' Storer said thoughtfully. 'Don't put your life in someone else's hands. Just get the job done yourself.' He gave the lad a nod of approval.

Yet, Anjali noted, Simon was profoundly struck by what the ex-mercenary had said.

37

Ideally, Loach thought, this was where the business meetings of his company should be held. In his overalls, he was getting the lowdown from John Barraclough under a coach in the pit.

'I'm sorry, boss. Whichever way you look at it, this Redbird Express outfit's bad news. I've had a good look at their setup: rusty buckets on wheels. Don't even think about it.'

Loach rubbed his chin, in no hurry to reach the inevitable conclusion. 'Okay, so we're talking reclamation? If we gave 'em a facelift, what do you reckon?'

Barraclough shook his head, but didn't seem to be in much doubt. 'Bringing 'em up to the standard we believe in? You'd be lucky to squeeze twenty coaches out of that pile of scrap.'

Loach looked at him in disbelief, just as he also spotted Dicky Padgett's suave BMW lurch to a halt in the yard. He waited until the works foreman had completed his assessment.

'Too many years of naff maintenance and duff back-up, Bob.'

In the meantime, Loach was setting his jaw for a fight. 'You're speaking the language my partner should understand, John.'

Redwood walked his secretary, Stella, to the car while reassuring her that the trip to the prison was neither ill-conceived nor unreasonable, let alone dangerous.

'What exactly are you hoping to get from going to see Kerrigan in prison, John?'

'The truth. That would be a start.'

'And you think this man will give you that?'

He shrugged his shoulders. 'What am I supposed to do, Stella?

My son tells me Denzil was one of the gang who pushed him off the bridge and crippled him. I'm his father. I have to believe he's telling me the truth.'

'You're also Denzil Taylor's lawyer,' she reminded him firmly.

The reminder made him uncomfortable. 'Don't tell me things I already know, Stella.'

She was stung by his rebuke. 'I'm sorry. I only wanted to help.'

'Don't worry – this is all legit. When I meet Kerrigan, I'll be wearing my lawyer's hat. The records show that he and Denzil were both up before the juvenile court round the time that Simon was attacked. If they were involved in an incident together, it's just possible that Kerrigan might know something about Simon.'

Stella would have to drive. He was too preoccupied with other thoughts.

'You're turning the deal down?' screeched Dicky Padgett, his face purple with rage and incredulity. 'I don't believe what I'm hearing!'

Just as angry, but much quieter, Loach carefully summarized the evidence. 'We've given them a thorough going over. Redbird's nothing but spare parts and advanced rust. Not a new fleet for us.'

Dicky glared at the lurking Barraclough as if he were a mangy dog with diarrhoea. Then he turned away, motioned to Loach, and headed straight for the office door.

'Just shut up,' Dicky warned Loach. 'Get inside. And listen up.' He was livid. But Loach was building up a head of steam as well.

Noreen was in the office at the filing cabinet as Dicky and Loach came in. Yet they were so locked in battle that they ignored her presence and kept on shouting as if she weren't even there. At first she watched in amusement, which soon turned to irritation.

'I've got the finance on tap!' Dicky yelled. 'I've had an off-the-record chat with the liquidator working on Redbird Express, and we could lose an incredible deal with him, right now, if we're prepared to get off our arses and make a decision!'

The volume of his shouting and the intensity of his glare left Loach altogether unaffected.

'I don't care if you've had an audience with the Pope, Dicky. We're running a reputable business here, not kamikaze coach tours. If we don't maintain our high standards . . .'

Dicky was disgusted. 'Spare me the sermons. You've become holier than thou since you joined those mickey mouse coppers, Bob. They've ruined you, and now you're trying to ruin me! But no chance, buddy boy, I've taken advice . . .'

This time it was Loach who was disgusted. 'You wasted money on a lawyer?'

They stopped circling each other and moved closer. Visibly agitated, Noreen was afraid it would come to blows.

'I've got my interests to protect,' Dicky warned. 'I own half this company, don't forget!'

'And half is mine,' Loach countered evenly, standing firm and making fists at his sides.

It was a stand-off, both of them staring at one another, ready to go for the throat.

Finally announcing her presence, Noreen caused herself to make a rather assertive cough before entering the fray as referee.

'Correction.'

Both men swivelled to face her, suddenly aware someone else was with them.

'Each of you owns forty-nine percent,' she explained sweetly. 'The last two percent belongs to me. You may recall we made that arrangement in case a situation like this ever blew up.'

Listening in amazement, both of their faces revealed that, although this knowledge may have been buried awhile, they recognized that what she was saying was indeed the case.

'So when you two great pillocks have stopped beating your great empty heads together, perhaps you'd take time out to explain to me, why I should give *you*, what is, after all, the casting vote!' She smiled sweetly.

Dicky was first to recover his wits, and checked his watch before looking up at Noreen with all his charm. 'Look, I know it's only just gone twelve, but how about a nice spot of lunch, Noreen? Up at the golf club. Just the place for a cosy little tête-à-tête?'

'Now just a flipping second . . .' Loach fumed.

Noreen was quick to accept. 'Sounds good to me,' she said. And with a mocking smile for her husband, she put her arm through Dicky's.

'I can pencil you in for dinner, Loach?'

38

Redwood's car was approaching the gates of Scalebrook Prison. Stella was still worried about John's meeting a hardened criminal under false pretences.

'Why should Kerrigan tell you anything?' she continued arguing until the last possible moment, though realizing she had already asked the same question several times.

'Why indeed?' was all he could answer.

The old clock on the wall of the Bromwich Building Society showing twelve twenty-five, Viv was sitting at her position, her 'Closed' notice in place, frantically hurrying through a check of withdrawal slips, when the phone finally rang.

She grabbed the receiver. 'Freddy . . . ?' As they connected at last, she also noticed her sentinel manager, Mr Maynard, expressing his annoyance with her by clearing his throat noisily. What a bore, she thought. 'No, I haven't forgotten. I'm leaving now. *The Four Pigeons* . . . yes . . . I'll be subtle.'

That was it. She slammed the phone down, but before she could get away, Maynard darted forward to cut her off.

'Private calls, Miss Smith, most unacceptable, especially when you have a customer waiting,' he chided her.

Viv looked over to see a small, grey lady with a grey face waiting at her window. She pointed out her 'Closed' notice to the manager.

'But I'm already on my lunch break, sir.'

Maynard's warning look clearly instructed her to reopen (that is, if she wanted to return to her job after lunch), which she did with a sigh. Glancing at her watch first, she then turned her attention to the grey lady and smiled obediently.

'Can I help you, madam?'

The woman proffered a pink slip to Viv. 'I'd like to make a withdrawal, please.'

Taking the withdrawal slip, Viv speedily tapped Mrs Lawson's account number in the database of her computer. However, she frowned as she saw the numbers that appeared on the screen.

'I'm very sorry, Mrs Lawson, but your account only appears to have fifty pounds left in it.'

Viv pushed the pink slip back towards Mrs Lawson, who was gripping the counter anxiously, her knuckles growing white. 'But there must be some mistake. I deposited eight hundred pounds only a fortnight ago.'

'I'll double-check it,' Viv promised. 'Just a moment.' She went through the same procedure, reaccessing the information. As soon as it came back on the screen, she frowned as before. The numbers were the same. She swung the computer screen around so that Mrs Lawson could see it as well. Viv pointed to the balance and the deposit column with her pen.

'There you are, Mrs Lawson. No deposits at all for this month. And only fifty . . .'

The grey lady seemed totally confused. 'I don't understand, I . . .' She turned away from Viv's desk, mumbling to herself and wandering slowly toward the door.

With a shrug, Viv suddenly remembered to look at her watch and suffered instant agony. She flicked off the computer screen, flipped her 'Closed' notice, and grabbed her handbag to make a flying exit.

Rita Loosemore and Freddy Calder sat uncomfortably together at a corner table in the *Four Pigeons*. A study in distraction, Freddy craned his neck to watch the door. Much confused, Rita touched his arm.

'Freddy?'

He pretended not to notice, although it was all he could do to refrain from pulling his arm away. But he couldn't stall her forever.

'Look, I don't have much time,' she informed him. 'Can we order?'

Evidently with some reluctance, Freddy turned to her.

'Who are you looking for?' she asked him.

'Looking for . . . ?' he nearly croaked. 'Nobody . . . I was . . . er . . .' He grabbed the menu like a drowning man reaching for driftwood. '. . . looking for somebody to take our order.'

Her pained expression suggested she didn't believe a word of it. 'All I want's a drink . . . a white wine.'

With a rapid glance, he looked at his watch, trying not to attract her attention for then she might ask to see it and thereby force him to expose his phoney Rolex.

'Right.'

Biding his time by smiling winningly at Rita, he was loathe to leave his seat to check for Viv outside. A passer-by even went so far as to try to take the third chair away from their table.

'This one free, mate?'

Desperately Freddy grabbed the chair. 'No . . . no, sorry.'

'Yes,' stated Rita emphatically at the same time.

The poor passer-by appeared confused, and veered away to find an emptier chair and someone less crazy.

Awkwardly Freddy took his hand off the chair, as Rita inhaled dangerously.

In the interrogation room at Scalebrook Prison, John Redwood sat waiting, having already taken off his coat, when the noise of clanking metal nearby alerted him to the imminent arrival of the prisoner he had come to see.

A warder entered the room accompanying the man Redwood assumed was Laurie Kerrigan. He was a tall, lanky white man trying to look and walk like a dangerous black man, though on him it came out just a cocky swagger. A permanent smirk was glued to his mouth like a moustache. Insolently chewing his gum, Kerrigan sat down opposite the solicitor.

Redwood swallowed uneasily.

With considerable concern, Rita watched Freddy's rapid gallop back to their table at the *Four Pigeons*. He put the glasses down in a hurry and slumped back to his seat with a nervous smile. Deciding to take matters into her own hands, she clamped one of hers over one of his.

'Look, Freddy, I came here because you said you wanted to apologize for your mother . . .'

'Yes, well . . .' He was still hopelessly tongue-tied.

'But I also came because I want you to stop lying for her . . .'

Suddenly his attention wandered and his heart jumped when he saw Viv arriving breathlessly and hovering only a few feet away.

'Freddy . . . you're not even listening to me.'

All he could feel was a tremendous sense of relief. 'Rita, I am . . . it's just that . . .'

All of a sudden he made a dramatic wave, and his face brightened with surprise. 'Holy cow, would you believe it, there's Viv!'

Watching Viv Smith smiling and weaving her way through the crowd, Rita grew even more irritated, her eyes narrowing murderously, 'Viv? Who's Viv?'

Just then Viv arrived with a beaming face. 'Well, well, well, Freddy – This *is* a coincidence.'

Freddy beamed back at her, as if they were preparing for an ice-skating exhibition. 'Rita, I'd like you to meet Viv, my fellow crime-fighter, my partner, a Special . . .'

As he tailed off, Rita was already scrutinizing Viv with a frosty look.

'Rita? Well, well, well, Freddy's always talking about you,' cried Viv effusively.

'Oh yes, when's that, then?'

Not expecting such a direct question, Viv floundered. 'Oh . . . sometimes after a late night on the beat, he takes me home, and we chat about this and that over a . . . cuppa cocoa . . .' She trailed away as well, realizing she was headed in the wrong direction.

Rita shot a look at anxious Freddy, who immediately galvanized himself into action.

'Right. I'll get the drinks in . . .' He swept up their glasses, even though Rita's had hardly been touched. Before Viv could sit down, he leaned over and whispered in her ear.

'Hells bells, Viv, be subtle.'

As he escaped to the bar, Viv and Rita settled in to stare across the frozen abyss, Viv holding a permanent smile, Rita leaning forward to figure out what Viv was trying to do to her.

'Okay, Viv, what's going on?'

'What's going on?' Viv repeated, smiling wanly.

'You heard me,' Rita pursued. 'I wasn't born yesterday, luv. You didn't just happen to walk into this pub. You know it and I know it.'

Her smile faded, Viv glanced to Freddy, then slowly came back to Rita and sighed. She took a deep breath and faced Rita squarely.

At the bar, Freddy waited for his round, frequently looking cautiously round at Rita and Viv. They appeared to be getting along famously, leaning into each other and chattering away. With a sigh of relief, he smiled broadly. All going according to plan.

303

39

When Laurie Kerrigan asked Redwood for a 'ciggie' and the latter said he didn't indulge, Kerrigan pulled out his own and lit up. He seemed to enjoy blowing smoke.

'So whaddyuh want?'

'I was hoping you could help me,' Redwood suggested, trying to maintain a professional, impersonal tone.

'I don't remember signing up for no Samaritans.' Leaning over and gawking, he tried to get a look at the papers in Redwood's file.

'I'm handling a case for a young man called Denzil Taylor . . .'

Kerrigan blew smoke and nodded slowly. 'Yeh, I know Denzil. Haven't seen him in a while though. So he's gone and got himself in deep trouble again, yeh? Man, he's some stupid black. Good enough bloke, but stupid, like alla his kind.'

'You did a job together, you and Denzil, two years ago. Stealing radios from a school.'

He laughed with disdain. 'Radios . . . ? Please, whaddye trying to do, destroy my reputation?' He pointed to Redwood's folder. 'But hold it, mister. If it says we did that job together, forgeddit. I don't do nothing together with nobody, right. I may hire in some muscle, another pair of hands . . . but I work alone,' he boasted.

'But it was Denzil's school you broke into. So that would make it look like Denzil's idea. That's how it looks to me.'

Jumping up, Kerrigan slapped the wall with the flat of his hand. Redwood tried to remain impassive and composed, although his heart had jumped as well.

'You don't know doodly, mister. All I needed Denzil for was lay-out of the school. He was nothing. All my plans come from here.' Kerrigan squeezed his finger against the side of his head. 'All mine, right?'

'Just like the time when you did some muggings? You and Denzil?' He opened the file and looked at one of the pages briefly. 'I'm reading here about some white kid who fell from a bridge and broke his back.'

After searching his memory for a moment, Kerrigan laughed. 'Right . . . Yeh, I remember . . .' The experience seemed to grow on him. 'Yeah! That was really something.' Gesturing with his hands, Kerrigan pantomimed the scene with relish.

'He floated down like a butterfly, and hit the pavement, *spul-latt*!'

While apparently listening without emotion, Redwood's fist had bunched convulsively, shattering the pen in his hand.

Freddy returned to the table at the *Four Pigeons* with a tray of drinks, his face glowing at Rita and Viv. Getting up, Viv patted her partner on the shoulder.

'Subtle didn't work, Freddy. Sorry. It's over to you now. I suggest you try unsubtle.' And with that, she left.

Scared and shaking, Freddy slumped in his seat.

Rita was not aggressive, nor disapproving, but rather straightforward in a calm deliberate way. 'Do your own talking, Freddy. I really want you to talk to me.'

Forlorn, Freddy fumbled in his inside pocket for Foxy, his glove puppet, but Rita stayed his hand.

'No. I don't want to hear it from a puppet.'

He cast his eyes downward, but she made him look up at her. 'Whatever you've got to say, I want to hear it from you, Freddy Calder.'

Despite her patience this wasn't going to be a picnic. Freddy swallowed hard.

Back in the interrogation room at Scalebrook Prison, Laurie Kerrigan was on his feet, chewing angrily, when he wheeled round and pointed at Redwood's file.

'You finish your story, man. What other lies you got in that book of yours?'

Redwood opened the file and held it like a poker hand, close to his chest. That way, Kerrigan wouldn't see that the paper was blank. Redwood put a finger on the page, pretending to read.

'. . . That Denzil said . . .'

Kerrigan stopped him. 'No, you shut up about that black, don't even bother to spell his name. Would you really like to know what that little punk was doing?'

Redwood felt giddy, on the edge . . .

'He was in the stands, man – crapping himself,' Kerrigan sneered. 'Whatever he says, I only took him along because I felt sorry for him.'

'Sorry for him?' the solicitor inquired.

Kerrigan was building a case of his own against Denzil, getting angrier the more he thought about him. 'It was my gang, right? I was top gun. You ask them. What's this Denzil schmuck trying to do?'

Trying to absorb the information he had heard and remain cool, Redwood closed his file and took a deep breath, looking at Laurie Kerrigan for the last time, as Kerrigan kept a shifty eye on him as well, jerking his head up out of his shirt collar in order to look taller.

'Heh, I reckon I'm gonna be a lawyer,' Kerrigan proclaimed proudly. 'What's the book I godda read?'

'Read, Mr Kerrigan?' Redwood asked with some scepticism and distaste. 'You are full of surprises, aren't you?'

Simon Redwood's wheelchair was wedged near the desk in his father's empty office, as he dialled the telephone number from one of the cards in his father's card index. He waited patiently for it to ring out. At last he heard a voice.

'Is that Denzil Taylor . . . ? This is John Redwood's office – I have an urgent message for you. Mr Redwood says could you come and see him right away . . .'

He looked around again to make sure no one was there listening.

'We must see you right away . . . Yes . . . I believe something important's come up.'

When Denzil Taylor hung up on the other end, Simon put down the phone, his face set in bitterness.

40

By the time they had reached Redwood's car in the Scalebrook Prison car park, he looked haggard. Stella unlocked the door for him.

'He did it, Stella. Kerrigan – he's the one who pushed Simon off the bridge.'

'Are you sure?'

'As sure as anything in my life.'

There was no way, in her own limited experience, Stella could comprehend the full impact of his discovery. She wasn't sure even how to talk about it.

'So what about Denzil?'

'Oh, he was there,' Redwood stated without a trace of doubt. 'Didn't want to be, by all accounts. In the eyes of the law, of course, that makes him as guilty as the others.' Yet his long-buried anger was now threatening to erupt.

'. . . But Kerrigan did it. And there's not a damned thing I can do about it.'

He stared down at the palm of his hand, bloodied from the broken pen. Stella noticed it for the first time. Hurriedly she opened her bag and dug out a tissue. As he glanced up to reassure her, the look on her face asked how it had happened.

He shook his head slightly, then gave her a wry smile instead. 'Let's go home, shall we.' Touching her hand, he took the car keys from her. 'I'll drive – it might stop me thinking.'

For a time, she didn't let go of his hand. The moment registered in his sensual mind.

Denzil Taylor rang the doorbell at the front door of John Redwood's home and office. After a short time, the door swung open, manoeuvred from behind by Simon Redwood. When Denzil saw Simon, there was an uneasy ominous moment between them.

'My father's waiting for you in the garden,' Simon said in a deadpan voice.

Behind the house, Denzil walked into the garden through French windows. Outside the garden was hot and steamy, calm and peaceful, apparently empty. Denzil abruptly turned round to confront Simon, who had followed behind him.

'Where is he then?'

Simon didn't answer, but he was no longer hiding his hatred. It was seething from every pore of his lifeless body, and staring through his haunted eyes.

Denzil was suddenly alarmed. 'Hey, what's goin' on?'

All of a sudden three burly lads jumped out from the bushes and surrounded Denzil then began pulling him to the ground and pounding him. Caught by surprise, Denzil was immediately overwhelmed by the louts, and before he could shout for help, they were kicking him in the face and the chest.

Simon shouted at his friends, urging them on to make it hurt. 'Hit him harder! Make him suffer . . . the bastard!'

Denzil looked up at Simon in horror, but then his face was

smashed in by a heavy boot. He screamed as they laid into him, but he couldn't be heard any more.

Simon was taking it all in, when suddenly his mind revolted and recoiled from the violence, and he sent his wheelchair lurching back. Hitting the kerb on the patio, the chair wedged itself in tight. In his efforts to move the chair, it toppled over, and Simon was thrown to the ground.

Now he watched the beating compulsively, yet helpless to avoid it. Closing his eyes immediately brought flashbacks of his own beating.

He staggered backward until his legs pressed flat against the parapet of the bridge, a leering face forcing him further back, with no place to go. Then losing his balance, pushed over, losing his hold, his grasp, and falling . . . floating down . . . taking forever, but any moment now, ending in a solid wall of concrete . . .

'Don't hit me . . .' he whimpered to himself.

John Redwood and Stella drove up to the house when they saw that the front door was open. Suddenly alarmed, he dropped his briefcase and ran inside.

As the gang heard John Redwood shouting, they dropped their victim and ran through the garden to escape over the wall. Denzil slumped to the ground, semi-conscious.

When his father finally reached Simon, he grabbed him almost roughly and hauled him back into his wheelchair. Then he glanced back at Stella, who shuddered in fear and retreated back into the house.

Denzil dragged himself up and tried to make a run for it, but merely flopped against Redwood and into his arms. Redwood let him down easy, then turned to his son furiously.

'And what the hell was that meant to achieve?'

Simon was drained. 'I wanted to hear him say . . . "No more." Just like I did. I wanted him to admit he did this to me.'

Once again climbing to his feet, Denzil swayed in the direction of Simon and screamed at him. 'I swear to God I never did no stuff to you. I was there . . . but I never . . .'

Denzil was out of breath, leaving Simon confused. Pushing away from Redwood, Denzil left a splash of blood on his shirt. Dazed, he rocked on his feet, cursing his solicitor.

'Thanks for setting me up, man. You're just like all the rest after all. Yeh – so now you can nail me real good.'

He lurched past Redwood violently, then brushed past Stella just coming out with the First Aid box.

John Redwood was left stunned. He looked back at his son. Simon had turned his head away, silent tears falling down his cheeks.

41

The Specials poured out into the forecourt at Division 'S' headquarters.

'Just bury yourself in your work, Freddy,' was Viv's professional advice to the lovelorn.

Resolutely she walked away from him. Still as he watched her go, he nodded thoughtfully. In the meantime, Anjali Shah came up behind Freddy and put a gentle hand on his shoulder. When he saw it was Anjali making this friendly, innocent gesture, he pretended shock-horror at her sexual advances.

'Please. I've already had enough excitement for one day.'

At that moment, as PC Toby Armstrong was backing out his panda, the car backfired. This time it was Anjali who nearly jumped to the sky. Once the scare was gone, again she instinctively raised a hand to where her face had been cut, the scar still quite visible.

'Hey, you alright, Anjali?' Freddy asked her with genuine concern.

'Yes. Yeh, course I am,' Anjali responded defensively, as she straightened herself out and went to join PC Armstrong in the panda that had backfired at her.

While Freddy was watching this little drama take place, PC Albert Coles backed out another panda and very nearly creased Freddy's toes. As the car moved slowly within a moth's wing of SC Calder's slightly protruding Midlands midsection, in fact probably tarnishing the outermost button on his uniform jacket, he stood perfectly still, not moving a muscle. The car came to rest as Freddy's plumpish form was even with the side window, which PC Coles had thoughtfully rolled down to speak to him.

'Getting in, Calder? Or are you helping out the Special Branch tonight?'

Rather than twist the new PC's head completely around a few

times, Freddy gave Coles the smile of a diplomat . . . plus another gesture with the middle finger of his hand below the window that PC Coles couldn't quite see.

Back in the parade room, Loach, now dressed in his best suit, was knotting his tie. The sound of footsteps interrupted his reverie, and his back stiffened. When the footsteps stopped, District Commandant Peter Whittaker poked his head around the corner.

'I'll be down at "Z" Division if anyone needs to know, Loach.'

'Right, sir,' Loach barked, still feeling awkward and self-conscious in a civilian suit.

Taking note of the same phenomenon, Whittaker threw Loach a quizzical look.

'Plain clothes, sir,' Loach explained.

Whittaker nodded thoughtfully, then left. Loach waited until he was sure the DC had gone. Then he quickly searched through his drawer for the red rose buttonhole, smiling nervously while he attached it to his lapel. He hadn't been so anxiously adolescent since the first time he asked Cora Batten for a dance.

Travelling in the panda control car, Freddy was becoming fascinated with a new bleeper gadget, which was driving PC Albert Coles – who in turn was trying to drive through the town traffic – nuts.

'Will you stop fiddling with that damned thing?' Albert finally begged him.

Freddy nodded good-naturedly, and started to put it away.

'What the hell is it anyway?'

He picked it up to play with again. 'It's a bleeper. You know . . . it goes –' Freddy pressed the button twice, and the gadget went 'Bleep! Bleep!'

A wary eye on his partner for the evening, PC Coles let out a dangerous breath. However, Freddy couldn't resist one last extra 'Bleep! Bleep!' Albert winced as if Freddy were practising the violin.

'By the bye,' Freddy mentioned in passing, 'one of my contacts has been watching the Ruddles' house . . .'

'One of your *what*?' Coles queried.

Actually Freddy was a bit sheepish about using André Mazade as an undercover source on police operations. 'He's a cabby . . . it's on his patch.' PC Coles had a half-scornful, half-dismayed look on his face. 'Look, Coles, he thinks . . .'

'No way, Calder,' Albert shook his head. 'We have a specific duty route mapped out, and it doesn't include tip-offs from cabbies who've been watching too much TV.'

Frowning, Freddy shook his head and took a deep breath. That merely served to antagonize PC Coles, but it also slightly unnerved him. Freddy guessed correctly that Albert was the kind of person who couldn't tolerate uncertainty.

'What's the problem now?' asked Albert, finally giving in.

'Oh, nothing . . .' muttered Freddy casually. 'Just that Frank Ellsmore was holding forth about this sort of case only the other day. It's a bit of a classic really . . .'

At the name-dropping of Police Chief Superintendent Ellsmore, PC Coles suddenly became more curious, as well as less sceptical.

'You know – no smoke, just the smell of burning. Reckon it calls for a spot of fire-watching, that's all.'

Albert could hardly believe his ears, though he was tempted. 'Hang on . . . you're saying . . . that the Super wants us to look into it?'

Freddy nodded enigmatically, trusting Albert would read into the gesture a reason for pursuing the Ruddle case. Then the great Holmes covered his tracks. 'This conversation has been strictly off the record, PC Coles. So just forget you even heard it.'

In silence, Albert was left to discover the strange mysteries of being and nothingness, while Freddy went back to playing with the bleeper gadget.

42

WSC Anjali Shah stared out of the window as PC Toby Armstrong handled the driving, as usual. Yet something wasn't the same. He wondered what she might be thinking.

'What's on your mind, Anjali . . . ?'

She didn't respond immediately, and that was typical. So he responded in his own typical manner, by trying to make a joke out of it. 'You can tell me about him . . .'

The beginning of her reply was interrupted by the familiar voice of WPC Baxter on the radio. 'Sierra Control to PC Armstrong . . . ? Report position please.'

Toby handed over the radio to Anjali.

'Control . . . this is WSC Shah. We're in Danemere High Street, over.'

Toby could hear a slight quavering, a kind of fear in her voice. He looked over at her, concerned about Anjali's state of mind and health these days.

At the car park outside Division 'S' headquarters, Noreen Loach sat in her Renault 25 checking her carefully prepared hair in the mirror and adjusting the low shoulders on her sequinned Jean Muir dress. Ready for action, she looked through the windscreen, saw someone emerging from the front doors right on time, smiled to herself, and got out of the car.

Bob was running across the car park, his mac blowing open to reveal his best suit in full glory. When he arrived, breathing heavily, he actually looked quite dashing.

His assessment of her was lusty, eager, and approving: she was dressed to kill, he was ready to commit suicide.

She gave him her sexiest smile. 'Come on, big boy, let's talk . . . business.'

In Control at Division 'S' headquarters, Sergeant Andy McAllister was keeping an ear open while flicking through a report. At the radio, WPC Baxter leaned into her mike.

'Look, I hate to ask you . . . specially after . . . you know what . . .'

McAllister moved closer, tuning in to the conversation as he was ostensibly reading the report.

WSC Anjali Shah's voice replied to the message. 'Go ahead, Control, over . . .'

'. . . It's just that you're nearest to the disturbance,' Baxter explained awkwardly. Andy leaned forward on the desk.

'Disturbance?' Anjali asked, glancing at Toby.

'In a pub . . .' WPC Baxter answered.

Anjali swallowed involuntarily at the word 'pub', though trying to keep her nerves from jumping. Seeing her expression, Toby leaned over to take the radio.

'Control, this is PC Armstrong, you sending some back-up? Over.'

Although he regarded Anjali sympathetically, she avoided his eyes.

At Control, McAllister stooped over WPC Baxter's shoulder to speak directly into the mike. 'Keep your hair on, PC Armstrong. From what we hear, there's only one drunk involved, over.'

Anjali sat expressionless as the panda prowled the night, her hand moving absent-mindedly to her scarred face.

'Just the one, Sarge? And what d'you bet he's son of Rambo?'

'Look on the bright side,' McAllister's voice came through the radio. 'He may only be a mutant turtle. Out.'

Toby grinned, handing the radio back to Anjali. He noted that her smile seemed forced, as she braced herself for what might lie ahead.

A beer glass rolled along the bar counter to the edge, dropped over, and smashed to the floor. Doug Storer, ex-mercenary, was rocking unsteadily against the bar at the *Maybush*, drunk as a skunk.

'Another beer, barman.'

'Take it easy, mate. The police are on their way. Be a nice guy . . . you've had enough.'

The ex-mercenary glowered at the barman, then at his nemesis across the room a thickset Jamaican by the name of Marv something or other. 'Listen, squire. I don't like people touching my drink. And I specially don't like it when the hands belong to our brown friends. So, be a nice guy, and gimme a fresh beer.'

The barman anxiously checked his watch, as Doug Storer stood up and staggered toward Marv. 'And you . . . if you want my drink that badly . . .'

The Jamaican stood his ground, not launching the first strike, but not backing off either, and waiting to retaliate. 'Lay off, mister. I didn't touch your poxy drink . . . so just back off . . .'

But the drunken ex-mercenary kept on coming. 'If you want it that badly . . . then go lick it off the counter.'

Suddenly the old soldier flicked beer at the Jamaican, who prepared to lunge.

'Too bad you don't like brown hands, knucklehead,' Marv warned.

The bully never had a chance. The Jamaican walloped him with a first punch that knocked the ex-mercenary reeling backward over a round table and crashing heavily to the ground, hitting his head with a final thud. He didn't get up.

* * *

Out on the street in front of the *Maybush*, WSC Anjali Shah jumped out of the panda as PC Toby Armstrong switched off the siren and the blue light. Setting off down the pavement, he was suddenly aware that his partner wasn't next to him, or just behind him. Toby turned to see her standing by the car, frozen solid.

'Anjali . . . ?' he called.

'I'm sorry . . .' she faltered. He was walking toward her with all deliberate speed. 'I . . . I haven't felt anything . . . till tonight. And now I'm . . .'

She looked plain scared. Apparently cold and dispassionate, Toby took her by the arm anyway.

'C'mon, Anjali. We've got to get in there.'

The long-suffering PC Albert Coles, new kid on the block, sat in the car and watched SC Freddy Calder knocking on the door of the Ruddles' house. As far as Coles was concerned, it was a sheer waste of valuable time, as well as an amusing demonstration of the bumbling ineptitude of Hobby Bobbies like this imbecile ladies' lingerie pusher.

As before, the front door of the Ruddles' house opened a crack, and Albert could just imagine the sales talk Freddy was pitching to the cantankerous couple.

'Good evening, sir,' Albert mocked sarcastically, 'I know you've already refused us entrance . . .'

The front door opened all the way to reveal the tempestuous Mr Ruddle himself, apparently listening to Freddy's persuasive sales spiel.

Albert continued to fill in Freddy's words. 'We've still got no warrant and no evidence, but maybe a look round your house on the off chance?'

Sure enough, Freddy seemed to finish his argument, now simply waited for the door to flatten his nose. Abruptly Albert's smirk evaporated, however, as the door opened wider. Even more incredible, Ruddle stood back, ushering Freddy inside!

Freddy turned to the panda with a broad grin and waved at PC Coles in triumph.

PC Armstrong marched into the *Maybush* followed by an anxious WSC Anjali Shah. Inside it was deathly quiet, as they surveyed the immediate aftermath of the brawl: an upturned chair, a spilled table, and a body sprawled on the floor.

The other customers had opened out a space around the knocked-out brawler and the Jamaican standing over him. Rubbing his fists, the Jamaican saw the uniforms, then knelt down next to his victim to check out the damage.

Thankful the brawl appeared to be over, Toby glanced back at Anjali with a reassuring smile. He got out his notebook and turned his attention to the barman. 'Okay, what happened?'

All of a sudden the Jamaican bending over the fallen brawler interrupted in panic. 'Hey, this guy's not breathing!'

Immediately Toby and Anjali were there, turning the body over. Anjali was stunned to see someone familiar: Doug Storer, the physio patient from the hospital.

'Do you know him?' asked Toby, seeing her reaction.

She felt for the jugular pulse and listened to the man's breathing. 'No . . . not really.'

Not knowing exactly what to do, Toby was anxious, yet he could see that Anjali was back in gear.

She tried his pulse. Nothing. Quickly she tore open his collar and shirt, adjusting his head for mouth-to-mouth resuscitation. He needed the kiss of life.

'I'll handle this, call an ambulance,' she ordered calmly.

Without further delay she started mouth-to-mouth alternating with heart massage, the standard procedure. Above her, PC Armstrong pushed the onlookers back and grabbed his radio.

43

PC Albert Coles stepped through the front door of the Ruddles' house to a dingy hallway. As SC Freddy Calder shut the door and turned to his partner, he registered a wallphone, and remembered it for future reference. Then he grabbed Albert and whispered quietly while they walked.

'We'll get them talking, and then one of us has to slip out and give the place the once-over.'

Immediately PC Coles insisted that they stick strictly to the book. 'No way, Calder, we don't even have a . . .'

The funereal Mr Ruddle was waiting for them at the entrance

to the sitting room. Ignoring the caution of his partner, Freddy walked by the old crock with a bland smile.

'Thank you very much indeed, Mr Ruddle.'

Mrs Ruddle sat with her arms folded, and her husband stood behind her like a pillar of stone. Before PC Coles could begin the questioning, Freddy took the initiative.

'I'll come straight to the point. Your father's departure doesn't really add up, Mrs Ruddle.'

She bridled instantly at his impertinence.

'We've told you . . .'

'In fact,' Freddy cut her short, 'we've been led to deduce that maybe he didn't leave at all.'

'What the hell are you getting at?' put in her husband.

Freddy launched a direct assault. 'You can tell us the truth, Mrs Ruddle. Is your father dead?'

The woman stared at Calder with vengeance in her eyes, while Freddy, with his hand in his pocket, buttoned his gadget, and suddenly there was a bleeping sound coming from his trousers. Hand on the button, he pulled the gadget out of his pocket and held the bleeping whine up to his ear.

'Please excuse me,' he said as soon as he let go of the button to stop the bleeping. 'I'm afraid I'm going to have to use your phone urgently.'

PC Coles swallowed in utter disbelief, while Freddy kept on smiling.

'But please . . . continue our discussion with my colleague, PC Coles.'

Making his exit with a wink at his partner, Freddy left an extremely miffed PC Coles facing the irate Ruddles.

'Now look here, laddie,' Mr Ruddle threatened.

'All right, Mr Ruddle. Why don't we just calm down and discuss the situation further . . .'

Inside the *Maybush*, the ambulance paramedics had taken over, and now Toby and Anjali stood on the edge ready to leave. In the meantime, the paramedics were preparing to put Doug Storer on a stretcher, having fixed him up with oxygen and a portable electrocardiogram. He had not only come round, but was already conscious and thrashing about.

316

Toby gave his partner a knowing smile. 'You did okay, Anjali.'

She nodded, still shaky, and looked over at the patient, who was struggling with the ambulance men. He ripped off his oxygen mask and tore away the ECG pads.

'Get off! I'm not goin' to no hospital.'

A wry gleam in her eye, Anjali watched the ensuing struggle as she and Toby went to the door.

'A real gentleman, eh?' she quipped.

Storming down the hallway of the Ruddles' house, having been unceremoniously summoned by Special Constable Calder, Police Constable Albert Coles met him running down the stairs.

'You're a lunatic!' raved PC Coles in a loud whisper. 'We could both get –'

'I was right,' Freddy wheezed breathlessly. 'There's a locked door up there. We need to break it down.'

Flabbergasted, PC Coles lowered his voice to an undertone: 'You're crazy!' Abruptly he turned, smiling and perfectly calm, to the Ruddles waiting at the front door.

'Well, I'm sorry troubling you again . . .'

As Mrs Ruddle wished them both a lingering death and her husband grimly opened the front door for them, Freddy whispered to PC Coles, 'What about the locked door?'

Albert was barely able to keep his reply down to a whisper. 'Calder . . . if you don't get out of this door now, I'll –'

Freddy cut him off.

'Listen . . .'

Now quiet, they listened, only to hear the sound of a loo flushing upstairs.

'So?' whispered PC Coles.

Freddy looked past Albert to the unhappy couple. 'Mr and Mrs Ruddle said there was no one else in the house . . . That's what you said, wasn't it, Mrs Ruddle? *Soooo* . . . who's using the lavatory?'

'I don't give a damn!' Ruddle thundered. 'We're going to have you! For harassment . . . no warrant . . .'

'. . . Threatening behaviour . . .' the wife added.

Each accusation brought another lump to Albert's throat, but Freddy already had one foot on the stairs. He gave his partner one more chance.

'Well?'

At the moment, Albert was indecisive. 'Er . . . I think . . .'

Freddy snorted; there was no time to waste. 'Right . . . you can have a think. Me – I'm going back upstairs.'

Turning away, Freddy bounded up the stairs, leaving PC Coles behind.

'Just a second, Calder, you can't . . . Wait for me!'

Unwilling to be left alone, Albert followed after Freddy. At the bottom, the Ruddles now had no option but to follow.

44

From the upstairs landing in the Ruddles' house, Freddy mounted the small steps leading up to the attic. Nearly at the top, his path was blocked by a heavy door firmly shut. Freddy banged on the door with his fist and shouted to whomever might be in the attic.

'Is there anyone there?' He stopped a moment to listen. There was no answer. 'This is the police! We're going to give you five seconds to unlock this door, or else we'll break it down.'

The Ruddles and PC Coles crowded in behind him, all listening intently.

Through the door came a thin, frail, quavering voice. 'No, no, I'll give up. I've signed. I give in.'

A piece of paper slid under the door; PC Coles made a grab for it.

Behind the door, three bolts were drawn back, followed by some scuffling noises of moving furniture. Freddy pushed the door open.

Inside, cowering on a simple pallet bed, was a scruffy, frightened old man, obviously in fear for his life.

Freddy turned angrily to face the Ruddles. 'Who's this?'

'My father,' Mrs Ruddle admitted.

'Who left two years ago with a tart?'

Her husband spoke up in their defence. 'Don't look at us. It was his idea to lock himself up in there.'

Meanwhile, PC Coles had been looking over the paper the old man slipped under the door.

'What is it?' Freddy asked him.

'His last will and testament,' replied PC Coles.

Unable to bear more than a glance at the cowering old man, Freddy turned instead to glare at the Ruddles, shrugging their shoulders innocently, yet also averting their eyes from the feeble old creature huddling on a mattress in their attic.

Near the entrance to the Division 'S' headquarters, Sergeant McAllister looked up from his paperwork to see a muscular, powerful man who had obviously been on a drinking spree and still smelled of it.

'Hope you didn't drive here, sir?'

The man leaned heavily on the counter for support. 'No sir, walked all the way. Needed the air.'

'Fascinating,' McAllister observed. 'What can we do for you?'

'I want to thank the guy who saved me. A man remembers that kind of kinship for the rest of his life.'

'One of our officers, was it?' asked McAllister.

'The *Maybush*.' The man jerked his head back, as if the pub were just over his shoulder. 'This guy lumped me one . . .'

Ah yes, now McAllister could place the chap as the troublemaker who had been rendered unconscious in a brawl and then had to be revived. 'Oh aye, I heard . . .' Andy recalled, his eyebrow raised. Down the corridor he saw Toby Armstrong talking with Anjali Shah and Viv Smith.

'PC Armstrong. A gentleman to see you.'

Toby Armstrong broke away from the women and walked over to the sergeant, immediately recognizing Doug Storer as well, though not so difficult since he had just seen the ex-mercenary earlier that evening lying dead on the floor.

'Hey? You well enough to be out and about?'

The tough guy grinned. 'Listen, mate, I've been worse in Africa. They didn't manage to kill me there. They're not goin' to here.' He offered his hand, and shook Toby's. 'Wanted to thank you for savin' my life.'

'It wasn't me,' Toby confessed. 'It was my partner . . . gave you the kiss of life.'

Slightly shocked and more than a little embarrassed, Storer rubbed his chin and moved up a bit to wipe his lips. 'Don't remember a thing, you know. Tell you the truth, I'd had a few drinks.'

Toby nodded, half-smiling, then looked back at Anjali. 'She's over there.'

Anjali had her back turned, but a grin slowly spread on Storer's face as he contemplated recent history.

'A woman . . . You don't say.'

Turning her way, Toby called her over. 'Anjali . . . somebody wants to thank you for saving his life.'

Anjali was walking toward them; when she recognized Doug Storer she stopped. His hand was outstretched, but his face collapsed. His eyes dropped, unable to confront his own shame.

PC Coles and SC Freddy Calder were escorting Mr and Mrs Ruddle along the corridor of Division 'S' headquarters to the interview room. Coles stopped to tap on Sergeant McAllister's office door.

Waiting in a chair in the corridor, Jimmy Duncan, the young Canadian, seemed a bit disconcerted to see his aunt and her husband glaring at him. He stood up, his eyes questioning Freddy.

'My grandfather . . . ?'

'He's all right, lad,' Freddy told him gently. 'They've got him down at the hospital. Just to check him over, but he's all right.'

Aunty Margaret couldn't restrain her contempt for her nephew. 'I hope you're satisfied. None of this would have happened but for *you* . . .'

'What are you talking about, Aunt Margaret?'

His innocent question opened her floodgates. 'Me and Albert sweat our fingers to the bone looking after that old man . . . for fifteen years . . . and he tells us he's got other ideas about the house and his money. Suddenly he's got a bloody grandson! Well what about me? I'm his daughter . . . Don't I count . . . ?'

As Andy McAllister emerged from his office with PC Coles, he moved between the disputing parties and broke up the confrontation. 'Can we have this conversation somewhere more private?' he suggested quietly. He and Coles gathered the Ruddles and drew them into the interview room.

Bewildered by events and accusations, Jimmy Duncan sank back into the chair. Freddy patted him on the shoulder, and Duncan looked up at him questioningly.

'What was I supposed to do? He's my grandad. He could have been . . . dead, couldn't he?'

Freddy wanted to end his torment with a simple answer, but it couldn't be done. 'You did right, lad,' he assured him, then shook his head sadly. 'But there's nothing as queer as family.'

Leaving him to his thoughts for the moment, Freddy joined the others in the interview room, standing with PC Coles by the door. Sergeant McAllister sat at the desk opposite the Ruddles. Mrs Ruddle was near to tears.

'What was your father so frightened of?' McAllister questioned her softly.

'He got this stupid idea stuck in his head . . .'

'And what was that?'

'He thought . . . he thought . . .'

Under McAllister's dark stare, her husband apologetically stepped in to finish her sentence. '. . . we were going to put him into an old people's home.'

'And were you?' McAllister prompted him.

'Of course not,' Mrs Ruddle insisted.

'Sometimes we all say things we don't mean,' explained her husband weakly. 'Old folk can try your patience . . . it isn't easy.'

'I would never have seen Dad in one of those places,' Mrs Ruddle formally declared.

'He got this bee in his bonnet . . .' Mr Ruddle continued. 'Wouldn't listen to a word we said. He went up to his part of the house –'

'The attic, Sarge,' PC Coles interjected. 'That was where we encountered the missing male.'

'Well, he said he wouldn't come out . . .' Mr Ruddle ended lamely, flashing an accusatory look at his wife.

And so, frightened out of his wits, the old man had decided to become a recluse, locking himself up in the barely furnished attic flat for months.

McAllister still wasn't clear on certain parts of the story, or its accuracy. 'But what is all this business about a will?'

That subject sparked the anger of Margaret Ruddle. 'My father was behaving like a child. All right, I told him . . . stay there as long as you like, but you'll only get bread and cheese . . .'

From the exchange of glances around the interview room, she realized that she might have said more than she should have to strangers, but still there were no pangs of guilt or regret on her part.

'He could've come downstairs any time he liked and eaten with the rest of us. All he had to do was change his mind about the will . . .'

The faces around the room continued to haunt her with unspoken questions.

'He went and changed it, you see . . . after we'd looked after him for all those years . . . signed it away to his grandson out there.'

The silence was deafening.

'We'd waited on him hand and foot . . . you know what that means?'

The eyes were closing in on her. They didn't understand. They had never known her father . . .

45

Entering the darkened house, Bob Loach was floating, amorously drunk and sensing the perfumed scent of the only woman he had ever loved.

'You're a wonderful woman, Noreen . . .'

They kissed again for a brief moment, then climbed the stairs together. Except that Loach stumbled and sat down hard on one of the steps. He reached for one of Noreen's legs, and the smooth touch of silk gave him ideas. He pulled her down with him, and kissed her again and again, and fumbled to undo her dress.

'Come on, you gorgeous . . . desirable . . .' The clasp still wouldn't unhook. '. . . delectable . . .'

Giggling helplessly, she disentangled her silk-clad leg and pulled away. 'Don't be ridiculous, Loach. I'm wearing a five-hundred-pound Jean Muir dress, and you want me to rip it off?'

'You used to be more adventurous, Noreen,' he chided her softly.

'Oh, yeah?' she challenged him.

'Remember, remember that time when we did it in a Renault 5?' he mused. But they were still entangled on the stairs, and wound up giggling again at the thought.

'We never did . . .'

'The earth moved, the stars rattled . . .' he bragged.

'Give over . . .'

She considered for a moment. 'Hang on . . . It wasn't a Renault 5.'

'It wasn't?'

'No. It was my brother's motorbike.'

Unable to recollect such a scene, he seemed nonplussed. Noreen smiled seductively. 'Don't tell me you've forgotten that sidecar?'

Playfully Noreen broke free and struggled up the rest of the stairs to disappear, leaving Bob stranded, in search of his memory.

When John Redwood came into his son's bedroom to say goodnight, Simon was lying on his bed fully dressed, his wheelchair skewed next to him. The curtains were drawn, and the room was in darkness. His father stood in the doorway.

'Simon . . . ?' Walking into the room, he sat on the bed. 'You asleep?'

Simon was lying motionless, back to his father, eyes clenched shut. 'Asleep . . . ?' he asked in a bitter voice.

'Simon, look, I want to help . . .' He put his hand gently on his son's shoulder.

Screwing round, Simon caught sight of his father's uniform.

'Forget it. You've done your bit for tonight, haven't you?'

Again Simon turned away. His father got up and walked out. Pausing at the door, feeling miserable, he looked at the uniform he was wearing, then back at the crouched shape of his son on the bed. Pulling the door to, he felt like weeping.

Just as Loach ambled into Noreen's bedroom, he watched her vanish into her ensuite bathroom. He fell across her bed, then arose to switch the light on.

'Do you know? Do you know the last time I was in here?' His jacket fell to the ground, and he unsnapped his braces.

'When was that . . . dear . . . heart?' she trilled from the bathroom.

Struggling manfully, he was teetering in his trousers, mainly because he had not yet remembered to remove his shoes. 'Christmas.' Then he thought again. 'No, I tell a lie. It was New Year's Eve. Flippin' 'eck!'

At last he was down to socks, suspenders, and boxer shorts – quite a sight. Then Noreen appeared, framed in the doorway, shimmering in her slip. She glided toward him . . . closer . . . closer . . . then veered away at the last moment, teasing him to distraction.

Sitting down at her vanity table, she began to brush her hair, continuing her tease, knowing he went crazy running his fingers through the fine hair on the back of her neck. Meanwhile, he sat on the bed, laughing quietly to himself. She watched him in the mirror.

'And what's going through that dirty mind of yours, Bob Loach?'

He smiled to himself, rocking back and forth. 'Dicky Padgett.'

Her hairbrush froze in mid-stroke. 'What?'

He was enjoying going over it in his dirty mind after all. 'Dicky Padgett's face when we tell him tomorrow.'

With a frosty edge to her voice, she turned to face him. 'Tell him what?'

'That your two percent and my forty-nine percent equal hard bloody cheddar for Dicky boy.'

Sobriety returned with a vengeance. 'Loach? Are we making love or discussing business.'

It was only then he first detected the change in her. Even so, he didn't take it too seriously.

'Well, I wouldn't be sitting on your bed in my jockstrap if you weren't colluding with me, would I?'

She had no recourse now but to proceed, step by step. 'So . . . there are conditions, are there?'

Exasperated, he threw up his hands, beginning to feel that he had no idea whatsoever what human relationships were about, except they were never what one expected, or wanted, or hoped.

'Flippin' 'eck, Noreen, you're not telling me you're siding with that greasy article, Padgett, are you?'

Her backbone was straight as a broomstick now. 'Would it make a difference?'

''Course it bloody would! I thought we were having a good night out?'

'A prawn cocktail and a chicken Marengo doesn't buy me all, you know, Loach.'

His heart sank to the bottom all at once. They had been down this road enough times in eleven years of marriage for him to guess where it was going, and for him to realize there was no turning back . . . at least not tonight. He picked up his trousers and started to get dressed; at least he would sleep in his own bed.

'That's blindingly obvious. The way things are going, I'll be lucky to qualify for your nail clippings.' He tried to hop into the other trouserleg. 'I suppose Gobby Padgett threw in a bottle of snotty French plonk at that tight-arsed golf club of his . . .'

While he had managed to pull most of his trousers back on, he still had an arm through the wrong sleeve of his jacket. But he had what he needed, if it were time to go.

'I'm not going to beg, Noreen.'

She reached out her hand as a peace offering. 'Don't lose your rag, Loach,' she gently chided.

'I'll have you know, I'm totally in control of all my faculties.' And with that, he stormed out of her bedroom.

When he was gone, Noreen almost cried, hugging herself miserably. 'Loach . . .' But she was too stubborn to follow him. Picking up his shirt from the bed, she held it up, then threw it down, kicking one of his shoes across the room.

Waiting on the other side of the door, he held his breath, hoping, listening . . . but there was nothing to hear. Holding his head sadly, he thumped down the stairs.

PC Albert Coles was holding court, buying everybody rounds at the Pub on 4th. Among the Specials gathered around him, Viv Smith, in a show of sympathy, had linked arms with Freddy Calder. They were just saying goodbye to Toby Armstrong and Anjali Shah, who were both leaving early.

Seeing her troubled face, knowing there was something left unsaid that she wanted to say, Toby touched Anjali's arm, his own questioning look asking what was wrong. Near the doorway, she stopped, looked as though she were about to speak, then dropped her eyes.

'Look, Toby, about earlier . . . I'm sorry. I don't know what happened. I . . .'

'You got through it, Anjali. That's all that matters, isn't it?'

Gratefully, she nodded, smiled a bit, and gestured that she was ready to go. They left the pub together, Toby waving at Briggsy the barman on their way out.

Back at the table with PC Coles, the new hero was holding up Freddy's bleeping gadget for all to see, as he bleeped the tone that conquered the world. Freddy himself, however, was hardly overjoyed at Coles taking all the credit as he nursed his envy with a mug of non-alcoholic beer and a squeeze from Viv.

'Not bad for a first assignment, eh?' young Albert was boasting. 'Needed a fair old bit of detective work. The old boy had remade his will two years ago, see, and his daughter and her hubby threatened to shove him in a home.'

Although Freddy might be sour, Albert was enjoying himself immensely.

'Frightened out of his wits, he goes and locks himself in the attic. His daughter left him bread and marge and water . . . it's been going on for two years!'

The crowd was suitably entertained, and PC Albert Coles was pleased with his performance. But there was still one last piece missing, and he turned to his Special partner for the answer.

'Thing I still don't understand, Freddy, is how did you persuade them to let us in?'

At last Albert had given him an opening.

'Oh . . . didn't I mention the sledgehammer?'

'What sledgehammer?'

'The one they thought I had in my hand when I said if they didn't open the door after a count of three I'd hack it down.'

Albert stared at Freddy Calder in absolute disbelief. Freddy merely gave him a patronizing smile.

'Think you'll find that one in the appendix of that book of yours, Constable?'

The crowd roared with merriment, and even PC Coles was taken in by the hilarity. Once again the champ had won the unofficial centre of attention contest at the Pub on 4th.

Responding to the ovation and the catcalls, Freddy reached into an inside pocket for the final encore. Standing at attention on Freddy's hand, Foxy took the salute.

III

•••••

Over and Out

1

Bob Loach didn't like what he saw in the mirror. What felt like a solid granite mountain of a headache looked like a mud slide. Staring into the reflection of his own tired eyes, the relentless pressure of his hangover was a constant reminder that there was nowhere to go from the night before. To himself he couldn't help wondering if so many warning signs meant that his life was coming to a dead end.

There were his problems of the heart, for one thing: everything had started to go wrong, yet only last night matters seemed finally to be moving in the right direction. His wife Noreen, the only woman he had ever really loved, who had been teasing him to distraction lately, only to reject his advances at the last moment over some petty argument, had led him down the garden path and into the bedroom once again. At last, just as the roses were within sight, she found some reason to fight instead of surrender, withdrawing into her impenetrable thicket of reserve. At the last possible moment, just as he was about to have it all, she dashed his hopes to nothing. He slept alone. In the end, as he had long suspected, Noreen was unwilling to surrender herself, to become a true and full partner in their marriage.

In fact, partnership was the very issue which had driven the wedge between them: in this case, his 50–50 business partnership with Dicky Padgett in Cougar Coaches, up until recently a healthy and growing coachtour enterprise. Then Dicky had turned greedy and in the ensuing dispute they discovered that they were *not* 50–50 partners, but rather 49–49 partners and Noreen, holding two per cent of the stock, held the casting vote.

Now she was using that two per cent to play both ends against the middle – her own husband versus his business partner for *her* approval – and finally it was clear to him that his wife had in effect become the controlling partner of his business as well. Nor did she have any predisposition to favour her husband, or even trust him. The behaviour of Dicky Padgett was easy for him to understand, if impossible for him to condone, but for the life of him Bob Loach couldn't understand why his own wife had – for all intents and purposes – deserted him over such a clear-cut issue.

In the past, the rivalry between the partners – Loach the master mechanic, and Dicky the seemingly well-bred gent who was actually a fast-talking salesman – worked to their mutual benefit, and Dicky's aggressive approach, Bob had to admit, was a positive force in the company. Now his scheming threatened to ruin everything Loach had worked so hard to build.

Dicky was chasing some deal for bus tours to Spain, but the obvious problem was that Cougar Coaches simply did not have enough buses to meet the operational demands of such an undertaking. Dicky's brilliant plan for overcoming this minor obstacle was to loot the rolling stock of Redbird Express, a competitor gone bust. The only impediment to this keen idea seemed to be that the Redbird vehicles were only fit for scrap.

That minor detail didn't stop Dicky from going full speed ahead and trying to take Noreen along for the ride. At this point, Noreen's unwillingness to give her full vote of confidence to her husband threatened to turn Dicky's Folly into a nightmare.

But it was the disappointment in the bedroom that grieved him most; celibacy loomed as the permanent rather than temporary condition of their marriage. What was left for him? He was empty without her, he could see that in the mirror. And if the business went bankrupt, he would be left with nothing. Simply nothing.

'What's for breakfast then?' He looked down at the empty cup on the table.

Noreen didn't stick so much as her nose out from behind the newspaper. 'Whatever you want.'

Another nail in the coffin. 'Come off it, Noreen. You always cook me breakfast.'

'*Always* . . . is always a mistake,' she said carefully before dropping the newspaper curtain for just a moment to take a sip of coffee.

Wearily he went in search of his own coffee. 'You're bloody predictable, you are . . .'

Abruptly she jumped on the opportunity to needle him. 'Doesn't take long for your ardour to evaporate, does it, Loach? Or were you seriously trading a quick Indian meal and your less than impressive physique for my casting vote in the business?'

Some enchanting evening. 'You were just stringing me along, Noreen.'

She gave him a bitter smile as she got up from the table, indelicately thrusting his polished black patent-leather evening shoes in his face.

'These were left on my bed last night. They're about as seductive as their owner.'

He took the shoes from her as she turned and swept away, leaving him tied up in knots of anger and frustration. Scowling to himself, he dumped the shoes on the worktop, and they knocked the milk over. No use crying, etcetera, but it didn't make him any happier either. Finally he located the coffee jug, only to discover but a few drops left. Nothing, really.

El señor Ricardo Padgett – better known as Dicky to his amigos and las señoritas – was happy as a lark, cruising through suburban traffic in his Jay, ready to conquer the world all over again. Must be the Latin influence.

Time for his Spanish lesson. He switched tapes, ejecting the *Disco Holiday Hits From Sunny Spain* and replacing it with *Conversational Spanish Lesson* #1.

'Buenos días, Señor. ¿Cómo está?' said the standard voice on the tape.

'Bonus deays, sinyour,' Dicky mimicked, then tripped on the next part. 'Con . . . con . . . too right this's a flippin' con . . .' Exasperated with the bloody next part, he punched the stop button and popped the cassette out. 'Bloody dagos,' he muttered to no one.

Switching the tapes back the way they were, he popped in the *Disco Holiday Hits From Sunny Spain*, pressed the play button, and turned up the volume.

'Yes, of course . . . I'll ring you if I hear anything.' Solicitor John Redwood, dressed in the uniform of the law, as a Special Police

331

Constable, gave the telephone handset back to his secretary for her to replace. The phone call was bad news, and yet he felt strangely in between – an enforcer of the law, a defender of the accused – and a failure in all.

One of his clients, Denzil Taylor, had vanished. Run away from home was probably closer to the truth. And Redwood felt partly responsible for his disappearance.

Denzil had been charged with a daylight mugging at a shopping mall, although he claimed to be an innocent bystander and witness to a robbery executed by a well-rehearsed gang of young thieves he had never seen before. Yet while visiting Redwood's office, which was in his home, Denzil had been identified by Redwood's son, Simon, as part of the gang that had attacked him two years ago. That complication had just exploded in Redwood's face.

The attack on Simon had happened only about a year after his mother and Redwood's wife, Caroline, had suddenly died of a cerebral haemorrhage, as if that weren't enough tragedy for one family. Simon was only 14 at the time, when he got caught in a mugging himself. He had tried to escape the young thugs, who trapped him on a pedestrian bridge over the Aston Expressway. He had fallen over the parapet, breaking his back on the concrete below. Although he had survived, Simon would spend the rest of his life in a wheelchair.

However, when his son identified Denzil Taylor as having participated in the attack on him, Redwood made some inquiries (through Police Sergeant Andy McAllister at Division 'S' headquarters) and located a former acquaintance of Taylor's presently residing in Scalebrook Prison. In an interview at the prison, Redwood had learned that his son's principal attacker was the prisoner, Laurie Kerrigan, as vile an example of the human species as could be found anywhere. Yet Kerrigan had also revealed that Denzil Taylor was an unwilling bystander in the attack on Simon Redwood.

On his way home from the prison, Redwood arrived to find that his son had lured Denzil Taylor into a trap, and he was just in time to interrupt the tail end of a severe beating administered to Taylor by a gang of 'friends' Simon had recruited. Denzil escaped with his life, after denying responsibility for Simon's accident, and now he had disappeared from sight altogether.

Meanwhile, Stella looked at Redwood with an unspoken question on her face, and waited for him to answer in his own time. His secretary had even more patience than he did, and his was running out fast.

'That was Mrs Taylor. Denzil didn't come home last night. And when she checked his room, she found some of his clothes missing.' It must have been obvious that the news unsettled him.

Stella was shocked as well, knowing the seriousness of the young man's flight. 'He's skipped bail?'

'No big surprise, is it?' he answered bitterly, 'not after the beating my son organized for him here . . .'

Simon, meanwhile, was out of sight, listening behind the door; he had fallen out of the wheelchair during the ambush of Denzil Taylor, and the bruise on his forehead was growing red under the pressure; he clenched his grazed, raw knuckles into tight fists.

In the office, Redwood slumped into his chair, his head in his hands.

'I feel so bloody responsible.'

'That's crazy, and you know it.'

Poor Stella: a good heart, but limited vision. He just looked up at her without a word, and sighed.

'What are you going to do, John?'

He shrugged. 'I honestly don't know. If he's done a bunk, then he's digging himself a hole he'll never get out of.' He shook his head. 'Damn it, what a mess we make of our lives . . .'

Redwood couldn't see his son abruptly turn his wheelchair from the door and propel himself slowly away toward the kitchen.

2

Gearing down, Loach cornered his white Jag into the yard of Cougar Coaches only to find his partner's parked in his wife's spot and his wife's Renault 25 just parked in his spot. He screeched to a stop, as Noreen emerged from her car and slammed the door. Crossing in front of his Jag, she glared at him defiantly as she headed for the office.

Redwood found his son sitting at the kitchen table, mindlessly spinning a knife on its point and watching it fall, then doing the same again, and again. Simon was aware of his presence, and probably of his growing irritation, but gave him no sign of recognition, just concentrated on the knife.

'What are you doing with yourself today?'

Simon didn't even bother to turn around and face his father. 'Why don't you just say what you mean?'

Redwood didn't know where to begin, but he knew that he had to make a beginning somewhere, sometime. 'We have to talk about this, Simon.' Cautiously he took a step closer to his son.

'Bit late for talking, isn't it? You think I'm as bad as them now . . . and that's what you can't stomach, isn't it?'

Reaching out in anger, Redwood grabbed Simon's chair and abruptly turned him around. 'Damn right! You can't just go taking the law into your own hands, son.'

'No?' he asked in bitter sarcasm. 'And what would you do, Dad?' With a quick snap, he wrenched the chair away from his father's grasp. Inspecting him up and down, Simon sneered at the uniform, and what it represented that had failed him. 'I know what you do . . . and it's pathetic.'

As they glared at one another in silence, Stella came to the door. He was grateful for the excuse to disengage and followed her immediately.

'Give him a break . . .' she said gently.

'What?' he shot back, still absorbed in his anger.

'That's not going to solve a thing.'

Perhaps she wanted to help somehow, but she didn't know how.

'He won't talk to me, Stella. We haven't talked properly since his accident.'

'He will. Don't give up on him now.'

He just shook his head. 'It's a two-way street, Stella. It's about time he comes to terms with his handicap and gets a grip on his life.'

'That's your time-scale you're talking about, John. Not his.'

From the woman who worked as his secretary, this was not the kind of sentiment he wanted to hear. He was sure his frown would be misinterpreted by her as concern about Simon's future.

Dicky Padgett leaned against the filing cabinet on one side, while on the other side, Loach discreetly closed the door behind them.

Then both of the men focused their gaze on the woman between them.

'Okay,' Dicky shrugged, breaking the silence. 'It's the sixty-four-thousand-dollar question, Noreen. Who's going to get your two per cent?'

She turned to Dicky with a knowing smile, yet said nothing. Loach nervously licked his dry lips.

'But before you even think of answering,' Dicky went on, 'let's just remember what we're discussing here, shall we? We're talking serious expansion, Noreen. The difference between Big Business coaches and small-time buses.'

That was too much for Loach and he butted in. 'She knows the options alright: Expand into big-time bankruptcy with Dicky Padgett, or move forward with caution.'

Noreen held up her hands in mock surrender. 'How am I meant to make a decision when you two keep going on at me?' The two men turned and glared at each other to keep quiet. 'Anyway, I've already decided what I'm going to do . . .'

At that, they turned on her, riveted to her words.

'. . . I'm going to think about it . . . over the weekend. And I don't need any more speeches from either of you. I'll make up my own mind.'

Loach shrugged his shoulders as if shaking off dead bugs, though secretly he was relieved. 'Fair enough.'

Nonetheless, it wasn't good enough for Dicky. 'But that gives me one big problem, Noreen. You see, in a few hours, Señor Gomez will be getting off a plane with one red-hot contract burning in his hand.' Gomez was the Spanish businessman who had dangled the carrot in front of Dicky, proposing that Cougar Coaches handle all of his tour buses from the Midlands to Spanish holiday resorts. 'So when Bob and I meet him, I think we'd better be telling him the same story.'

Dicky's pressure tactics made Loach angrier than ever at his nonchalant recklessness. 'You're a maniac, Dicky. You've got this geezer jetting in to talk tours from Brum to Barcelona, and we're sat here with just about enough coaches for Blackpool and back. We . . . haven't . . . got . . . enough . . . coaches. *Comprenez*?'

Dicky merely responded with a bland smile. 'Calm yourself, Loach. I've got a plan.'

'Oh, no. No thank you, Dicky. I'm not available for free-fall parachuting today.' He moved toward the small bathroom off the back of the office to change into his Specials uniform. 'You've just cooked your own goose, Dicky. And it's got crackling on.' He pulled the door to, but strategically neglected to shut it.

Out in the office, Dicky shared a confidential smile with Noreen, though she felt uncomfortable as the target of his persuasions.

3

The smart, crisp, clean Specials uniform made Freddy Calder look trimmer, taller, almost dashing, even if he did think so himself. Admiring his reflection, he sleeked his hair into place and smiled, as if Rita had just noticed him. Then his mood changed and he put on a scowl, enough to frighten the criminals who would have to face him. He put his hat on with the authority of Field Marshal Montgomery and stood at attention to take the salute.

Suddenly at the corner of the mirror he saw the witch spying on him: his mother observed his primping with a critical eye. Freddy removed his hat sheepishly.

'So . . . ? Now you're starting to do it during the day,' she let fly.

'It's a police parade, Mum, not an open air orgy.'

Hilda raised an eyebrow and gave him a withering look. 'I suppose that hussy of yours is going?'

He tried evasive action, checking his tie and tight collar in the mirror. 'It's Anjali Shah's commendation ceremony, Mother. Strictly business.' Surely she couldn't expect him to skip an official occasion honouring the courage of one of his colleagues.

This parry merely deflected her attack on to another target, *the* other woman in Freddy's life.

'That Rita's a tart. Only a woman of loose morals would wear the clothes she wears. Skintight – you can see everything. And who in their right mind would want to?'

She eyed him coldly, daring him to answer back, but he chose not to argue.

'And she's working-class,' the wicked witch droned on. 'We may be many things, Freddy Calder, but we're not working-class.'

'Rita's a lovely girl, Ma.' Freddy swallowed audibly, as he rallied to his true-love's defence. 'And . . . you've got no right to talk about her like that . . .' He tried to squeeze his ears shut in anticipation of the dire outburst to follow.

Sure enough, she reacted as though she were utterly scandalized. 'Don't you raise your voice to me, Freddy!' she shouted. 'She's done this to you, hasn't she? Turning you away from your old mother.'

Still incapable of intentionally wounding the mother Freddy nearly gave up the struggle, even though he knew her diatribes were only a mask for her fear. Yet this time her attack wasn't just against Freddy and his many failings: it was against someone he respected. Freddy straightened his uniform and stared back boldly at his mother.

'What Rita has done for me, Ma, is to give me a bit of self-respect. She likes me for what I am, not what she wants to make me.' He could see that this argument was getting him nowhere, but he pushed onward stubbornly in Rita's defence. 'And . . . she's fun to be with. Is that such a crime?' he concluded with a meek smile.

His mother was almost too enraged to speak, though she finally managed. 'Yes! I'm your mother – not a doormat to be trampled all over!' Her lips trembling, she glared at him, unable to find words for the fever of her condemnation. 'It's taken me thirty years to make a man out of you, Freddy Arthur Calder.'

Freddy winced.

'. . . and in five minutes, that . . . *trollop* . . . makes a monkey out of you!'

Inwardly, Freddy groaned. Outwardly, he just stood there like a man in a monkey suit with an empty tin cup to show for all of the acrobatics he had just performed.

Dicky Padgett drew his chair up opposite Noreen Loach, leaning over for a serious word in her ear, yet cheated on the angle to the side just a bit, projecting his voice toward the crack in the door to the back room.

'Stage management, Noreen. *Marketing*!' Dicky pronounced the term as if it were a great and powerful voodoo magic. 'He need never actually see our operation here. The last thing businessmen want is sump oil on their Gucci shoes, believe me, I know.' He raised his voice slightly, throwing it off to the side.

'He's not coming here for a busman's holiday . . .'

Grinning at his own pun, Dicky toned down again somewhat, though he only seemed to be making a point of confidentiality, when in fact John Barraclough, the works manager, could probably hear him just as well from out in the yard.

'No,' Dicky continued, 'what he'll want is some excitement: a touch of the old glitterati. Bit of baccarat at the casino, some disco dancing, and a couple of sexy . . .' Although he was leering, he could plainly see her frown, so he made a mid-course correction. '. . . companions.'

Unfortunately, his attempt at verbal compromise did not erase her frown. 'No offence, Noreen, but this is how deals are done.'

Before she could reply, or even blush, the back room door opened abruptly. When Loach emerged in full dress-uniform, Dicky blinked, then his sleazy smile faded rapidly.

'Do me a favour, Bob. I said we're going to meet Gomez at the airport and show him a good time, not give him a coronary.'

'You're the one meeting him,' Loach reminded his partner. 'It's your arrangement. I've got a prior engagement.' He tugged at the cuffs on each sleeve of his jacket, fully aware of the effect of a uniform on various types of people.

His relaxed attitude clearly unnerved Dicky. 'But there are things I can't explain – drivers' rotas, petrol consumption, maintenance details . . .' There was still anger in his eyes, but now they were imploring as well.

'Come on, Loach, we're running a bus company here! Not playing cops and robbers!'

But Loach wasn't budging. He wasn't even bothered. 'Save your breath, Dicky, I've got no choice. We're honouring a very brave woman this morning . . . And before you go to see Gomez, maybe you should take a gander at this.' Acknowledging his silent wife with a nod, Loach reached into his desk drawer to retrieve the newspaper. 'If we stick ourselves with buses which are sub-standard, look at what will happen.'

Folding the newspaper into a cricket bat, he smacked it against Dicky's chest as he walked out of the office. Dicky watched with dismay, then threw the paper back on Loach's desk.

Although the men often acted as if she weren't even there, Noreen had been carefully observing every blunder in their clumsy ballet.

All that nonsense aside, she was still curious as to Ricbard Padgett's intentions, and wondered whether he truly believed hecould realize them through clever salesmanship.

'Was all that stuff you were saying for real, Dicky? Do you really think you could swing the deal without having Gomez come near the place?'

'Just watch me,' said he with a sly grin.

She was still sceptical. Was he claiming to be a magician? 'You could kid him into believing we're something we're not?'

'Noreen . . . I'm a salesman. I can sell anyone *anything*.'

'Yes . . . I know,' she said thoughtfully. 'That's what worries me.'

His grin widened as he stalked out his objective. 'With or without Loach. I'm going out there to sell Gomez something I know he wants.'

In the meantime, Noreen had picked up the newspaper Loach had left behind. At first, as they talked, the front page was a blur, but then as she stopped listening to him, the lead story came into focus. Plastered with photographs of a disaster in Greece. Mangled bodies and twisted junk by the side of a road somewhere. A coach had lost its brakes and crashed into the solid rock wall of a mountain at high speed. The driver was among the many dead.

4

'Closed' read the nameplate on Viv Smith's window at the Bromwich Building Society, as she was nowhere to be seen. At the next window, attending her own position, Madge, the young trainee, was counting the stack of bank notes for the third time and tried to maintain her concentration while Mr Maynard, the manager, walked up quietly behind her. Madge thought a great deal of Mr Maynard and worried about making a positive impression on him every day, though today she could only pretend to keep count and hope that she had been accurate on the previous try.

Frowning, Mr Maynard looked at his watch, and scowled, 'Where's Miss Smith this morning, Miss Pyke?'

Madge was happy to know the answer to one of Mr Maynard's many inquiries, and gratified to be able to provide him with the information he had requested. 'She's gone to some service, she said. Maybe it's a funeral, Mr Maynard? Anyway, she did say she wouldn't be in till midday.'

Her superior appeared far from satisfied. 'Certain employees treat this place like a holiday camp. Sometimes I think I'm the only one who's doing anything.'

Madge was stung by his oversight, and her face must have crumpled because he at once corrected himself: 'I don't mean you, Miss Pyke,' he said with a benign smile. 'You've greatly impressed me with your commitment.'

She felt herself blushing: whenever praise did happen her way, she immediately became totally flustered. 'I can't tell you . . .' she mumbled, shielding her eyes from his by staring down at the bank notes in each hand, '. . . how much I appreciate . . .'

Just as abruptly Maynard's imperious manner returned. 'But I mean what I say, Miss Pyke. The very instant Miss Smith returns, tell her that I want to see her urgently.'

'Yes, of course, Mr –'

'And you may emphasize the "urgently".'

Maynard turned on his heel and marched away smartly, filling Madge with admiration for his decisive authority. 'Yes, Mr Maynard.' Her eyes couldn't help following him all the way into his office, where a woman was sitting at his desk waiting to see him. The visitor was an older woman Madge had seen before: a Mrs Lawson, if memory served her accurately this time. Mr Maynard was proud of Madge when she remembered names.

Already late for for the ceremony and still stuck in her flat, Viv Smith hurried to squeeze into her shoes while checking herself in the mirror and absently brushing non-existent specks from the jacket of her Specials uniform. She glanced at her watch while making a frantic last-minute search for her hat, and found it on the shelf reserved for the Belgian twin sisters in her international doll collection. After all that mad scramble, Viv was finally ready to leave when the telephone rang.

Hesitating for a moment, she turned back and irritably lifted the receiver.

'Yeah?'

It was Madge, who immediately launched into a stream of gabble, to which Viv listened until she could no longer contain herself.

'Madge, you can tell him to put a banana up his exhaust pipe for all I care . . .'

She listened for a little while longer, but it was no use. 'Okay, okay, don't tell him. I'll tell him myself when I get in. Is there anything else? Because I've got to be –'

Before she could even say 'going,' Madge had embarked on another harangue until Viv had no choice but to hang up on her.

That's all she needed, she thought as she carefully replaced the receiver – to worry about her job and Maynard the Prig on top of being late for something more important. She looked at her watch again: time was not standing still for her.

Amidst the landscape of the parade ground at Tally-Ho, the Police Training Centre where Police and Specials alike were prepared for duty, the colour scheme contrasted two groups of people in attendance at the ceremony. The knife-creased blue uniforms aglimmer with gold braid and the formal elegance of white gloves provided a background to the bright bursts of the summer print dresses worn by the wives and girlfriends, the mothers and aunts.

Sitting with her proud family, between her mother and Uncle Ram, Special Constable Anjali Shah appeared to be listening attentively to the speech in her honour being delivered from the platform by Police Chief Superintendent Frank Ellsmore. Actually her mind was a blank, and it required all of her powers of concentration to remember to sit up straight and try to look intelligent without seeming either too pompous or too meek.

In the row behind the Shahs were her colleagues: her Section Officer, Bob Loach; Special Constables Freddy Calder and John Redwood; Sandra Gibson, Administrative Secretary and the acknowledged 'Mother of all Midland Specials' as well; and Anjali's partner on the night of the incident in which both were injured, Special Constable Toby Armstrong.

There was also an empty seat beside Freddy Calder on the aisle.

Viv Smith knew at a glance that the empty seat was hers, and before the Police Chief Superintendent could conclude his oration, she made her late entry quietly and, she hoped, inconspicuously, and settled in beside Freddy.

'Special Constable Anjali Shah,' Ellsmore intoned, 'without a

341

thought for her own safety, went to the rescue of a fellow officer facing a violent criminal.'

Anjali tried to keep the video replay of the incident out of her mind for just a while longer, just a few moments more, and then it would be over. But the image of her partner began to surface against her will, the bloody face of Toby Armstrong lying in an alley as a thug stood over him about to finish him off with an iron bar. She remembered tackling the thug, and getting smacked out of the way as he escaped.

'We ask a lot of all our officers, but we could never insist on bravery in the face of extreme danger. Today we honour a young woman who gave us that, and more. In recognition of her exceptional courage, we present this commendation . . . to Special Constable Anjali Shah.'

Suddenly Police Chief Superintendent Ellsmore stopped speaking, and looked straight at her. Realizing it was time for her to come forward, she stood up and moved past Uncle Ram to the aisle.

As she passed in front of Freddy, he leaned forward to whisper his personal congratulations. 'Good on you, Anji.'

Unfortunately, he had forgotten that a beam had broken her fall off the wall and patted her on the shoulder. She winced, her arm retracting instinctively in a sharp reminder of the dull pain still lingering there.

'Thanks, Freddy,' she murmured in a low voice as she reached the aisle.

Viv turned back to Freddy and punched *him* in the shoulder, outraged at someone even more stupid than she was. 'You wally,' she admonished him, though also in a low voice.

'I'm sorry . . . I didn't think . . .' Freddy whimpered.

'You should try it once in a while,' she scoffed.

5

It was not until the moment she was about to receive the commendation from Police Chief Superintendent Frank Ellsmore that Anjali Shah allowed herself a moment of personal pride. She realized that she was more lucky than brave, and that she had not

342

permanently conquered her fear. She felt uncomfortable as a symbol of courage among fellow Specials far more fearless and heroic than she could ever be. Yet she was proud to be standing up for what she truly believed: that society must join together in common cause to free society from a constant threat of fear. If she could do it, so could anyone. They were all Specials. This time, she as a Hindu might serve to reflect the Christian philosophy that even the least would have the chance to be first, and that notion of herself she could accept.

So as Ellsmore clipped the insignia to her jacket sleeve and shook her hand, the burden was lifted from her shoulders. She was standing here for all of her friends, all of the Specials, because wherever they had come from, each one of them had stepped forward.

Finally, Anjali was in a position to show everyone that she stood on the side of life, not death, and that she refused to accept the violence that had once threatened her own life, as she rejected – by the way she had chosen to live, and by what she had chosen to do – the inevitability of violence altogether. If that was heroism in the modern world, she would wear the insignia with pride.

For one moment, as she looked out over all the people watching her, the artificial formality of the ceremony no longer made her nervous and self-conscious. And for once, she allowed herself to smile and enjoy being the centre of attention. It was her humanitarian *values* that were being honoured today.

Uncle Ram, however, was bursting with family pride and simply couldn't sit still. Resisting the clutches of his sister – Anjali's own mother – he dashed forward to the podium with his trusty instamatic camera. As the bulbs flashed, tears streamed from his eyes, and he only hoped that he was aiming in the right direction to capture the memory of his niece being awarded a medal as an outstanding subject of the United Kingdom.

The police brass band struck up a rousing march, and the hearts in every breast swelled with a bit of pride in themselves as well – sentimental perhaps, somewhat contrived by the trappings of tradition most probably – yet inspiring feelings of hope for this old world.

Having made the quick change into civilian clothes, Viv Smith was ready to face Mr Maynard with the same brave front Anjali Shah

343

had shown at her commendation ceremony. Bracing herself, she knocked on his door and entered without waiting for an invitation.

She was surprised to find someone else in the office besides Mr Maynard, who rose to greet Viv with a stern unforgiving look on his face.

Viv recognized Mrs Lawson, who was eyeing her with an apprehension verging on dread, and her lanky son, Warren, who appeared to have a perpetual scowl tattooed on his eyebrows. Although she had not seen Warren often in the past, this was the first time she could remember seeing him in a suit.

'Miss Smith, come in and sit down,' Maynard ordered.

Uneasily, she managed to do so, meanwhile noting that Mrs Lawson averted her eyes.

'I presume you remember Mrs Lawson, Miss Smith?'

'Yes, of course . . .' she said uncertainly.

'Mrs Lawson has brought a serious complaint to my attention,' Maynard charged. 'I want you to listen very carefully.' Then he turned to the older woman, and nodded for her to speak. 'Mrs Lawson . . . ?'

Still unable to confront Viv directly, Mrs Lawson spoke to Maynard instead, shifting uncomfortably in her seat. 'Last week I came into the Building Society and deposited £800. When I came to make a withdrawal, I was told I only had £50 in my account.' Faltering with emotion, she paused to regain composure before continuing. 'I just can't believe it . . .' Again she lost control of her voice.

Viv was remembering the occasion, which stuck in her mind because Mrs Lawson had come in just as Viv was about to go out for lunch to meet Freddy Calder at a rendezvous with the object of his hopeful affections of late, one Miss Rita Loosemore. Mrs Lawson had asked to make the large withdrawal, but Viv didn't recall any deposit the week before, nor had any such deposit shown up in Mrs Lawson's account as revealed on the screen of Viv's computer terminal.

'Hang on . . . Mrs Lawson, I remember . . . yes, you were trying to make the withdrawal, and I –'

Right away she was interrupted by Mrs Lawson's son, Warren. 'No you don't,' he scolded. 'Let my mother have her say before you start, right?' He appealed to Maynard, who turned to Viv and glared at her, nodding.

Feeling the pressure from all of them, Mrs Lawson hesitated before going on. They waited.

'Now I've realized what must have happened. When I brought the £800 last week, the girl –' She indicated that she was referring to Viv. '– the girl . . . gave me a pink slip to fill out, not a white one . . .'

What Mrs Lawson was saying took Viv's breath away. 'Now wait a minute –'

Again Warren interrupted. 'That's right! I came in with my mother last week, because she had so much cash on her.'

Viv was confused. 'I didn't see you . . .'

Yet there seemed no doubt in Warren's mind. 'I was sitting waiting the whole time.' Again he turned to address Maynard. 'It's pretty obvious what's going on. Miss Smith must have confused my mother into signing a pink slip for withdrawal, not a white one for deposit.'

'No!' Viv objected. 'Mr Maynard, this is outrageous . . .'

Acting as unofficial prosecutor, the son summarized his mother's case. 'It's not for me to say what has happened to this money, since it has failed to be deposited in my mother's account . . . but the implication seems clear.'

Viv could hardly speak, she was so outraged. 'How dare you! Mr Maynard, I must speak to you in private.'

But Maynard shook his head in stubborn resistance. 'Whatever you have to say in explanation, Miss Smith, should be said here and now in front of the Lawsons.'

'I can only tell you the truth,' Viv stated for the record, measuring her words. 'Mrs Lawson did not deposit any money last week.' Of that much, Viv was certain. 'And she definitely filled out a pink withdrawal slip. She was trying to take out eight hundred pounds which she didn't have.'

Then, as an afterthought, she added: 'I remember she was surprised.' Unable to understand why Mrs Lawson did not seem to have the same recollections, Viv turned to her once more. 'Don't you remember? I double-checked it for you?'

Instead of questioning Mrs Lawson, Maynard continued the interrogation of Viv. 'Are you absolutely sure about this?'

Viv couldn't believe what she was hearing, and stared at Mr Maynard. 'Are you accusing me of lying, or what?'

Challenging him directly, she expected him to recognize, however half-heartedly, her basic honesty. On the contrary, he made no answer. Viv turned to Warren Lawson, but all he had to say was: 'It's your word against ours, lady.'

He turned to his mother for confirmation, but instead found her in an extreme state of distress. Reaching out for her, Warren put an arm around his mother and guided her up from the chair and toward the door.

'I'm not willing to subject my mother to this any further. We'll obviously have to inform the police.'

Incredulous, Viv checked again with Maynard, and again was shocked to find him nodding gravely in agreement. Not knowing where to turn, she went after the Lawsons. Outside Maynard's office, she caught up with them and grabbed hold of Mrs Lawson's arm.

'Mrs Lawson, please! You've got this all muddled up.' Her son tried to interfere, but Viv dodged his efforts. 'Please, you must remember that day . . . ?'

But Viv's own efforts were futile, as Mrs Lawson began to cry, appearing to be near collapse. As Viv couldn't maintain her grip on so fragile a creature, Warren finally succeeded in pushing her away.

'Leave her alone!' he commanded Viv in a thunderous voice. 'Haven't you done enough?'

Cursing with an ugly stare, Warren dragged his mother away and stormed out of the Building Society. As feelings of helplessness drained her energy, Viv watched them go. Warren Lawson never looked back.

In despair, Viv turned back to Mr Maynard's office, knowing she had to return to his judgement. She felt abandoned and adrift in a universe of lies.

6

Returning to the seat of his authority, Mr Maynard went back into his office and sat down behind his desk, waiting for Viv to join him. Eventually she followed, though by now she was so distraught that she wasn't sure what to say, or what not to say. Maynard was cool and controlled, and did nothing to reassure Viv or ease her discomfort.

'So . . . I'm guilty until proved innocent. Is that what you're saying?'

He didn't respond directly. 'I simply wish to know if you've told me everything. The critical difference between your story and Mrs Lawson's is whether £800 passed over your counter or not.'

She was incensed at his complete lack of faith in her. 'I've told you! It flaming well didn't! And if you're willing to take the word of some half-senile old bat and her scheming son –'

Maynard interrupted her, while barely keeping a lid on his own anger. 'If you'd try and calm down, Miss Smith, I might be more disposed to believe you.'

Why wasn't he already disposed to believe her? Why wasn't he on her side? Viv's temper exploded.

'Why bother? You've obviously made up your mind that I'm guilty already.'

'Miss Smith, when £800 goes missing, and I know that the employee accused already has a large mortgage with this company, a lavish apartment . . . and that she is something of a gambler . . .'

What did he mean, 'something of a gambler?' Vaguely she began to remember joking with Madge Pyke about making up the monthly mortgage payments for her tiny flat with added proceeds from gambling and petty thievery on the side. Obviously her little flight of fancy had been taken quite seriously by the young trainee, and she in turn had found a receptive ear in Mr Maynard.

'. . . then I think I am more than entitled to be suspicious,' Maynard concluded.

'Who's been gossiping about me?' she asked straight out.

Maynard looked at her a moment without responding, probably wondering how she knew the source of his 'evidence' against her. Avoiding her question, he said: 'Until this affair is sorted out, Miss Smith, I insist that you relinquish your position and confine yourself to clerical work.' He started rearranging the papers on his desk.

'In case I run off with some more money, is that it?'

'Shut the door when you go, Miss Smith.'

'Shut the door, my arse!' she snapped. 'It's good to know that when customers stick fingers in your face, there are creeps like you waiting to stab us in the back.'

Maynard's jaw went slack in disbelief at her defiance. Before he could reply she added: 'You can take your job, Mr Maynard, and shove it!'

* * *

Her anger seeking an outlet, Viv burst into the staff lavatory and made a quick survey. The tiled room was quiet, except for a solitary drip from one of the taps every few seconds, and apparently empty. The stall doors were all open save one, which was closed and engaged. Furtively Viv stole a glance under the door, yet found no sign of feet. She frowned.

Obviously Madge Pyke was hiding inside the cubicle perched on the loo. This entire episode was becoming pathetic, Viv concluded, as she hammered on the door.

'Come on out, Madge. I know you're in there.'

After a moment, Madge's squeaky voice piped up from behind the closed door. 'I didn't tell him anything, Viv, honest.'

'Which is why you're sitting in there like a constipated hen, I presume?' Viv inquired indelicately. 'Come on out here . . . or I'll drag you out.'

Another moment passed, then the door was unbolted from the inside and pushed open slowly. Fearful of Viv's wrath, Madge peered out at her, while temporarily holding her ground, as it were, perhaps leaving open the possibility of escape by diving into the toilet.

'It's not my fault, Viv,' she pleaded. 'Mr Maynard kept on and on at me. I might have said a few things, but I didn't tell lies.'

Viv shook her head, though at present she could find no room in her heart for fools. 'Yeah . . . ? I'm sure they don't come much purer than you. When the blessèd Bromwich Building Society are looking for a virgin to sacrifice, I'll be sure and give them your name, Madge . . .'

Madge responded with a puzzled smile.

'. . . although I have a feeling you'll fail the qualifier.'

Abruptly turning her back on Madge, Viv stormed out, leaving the trainee in her ill-chosen hideaway.

Rob Barker began to have second thoughts about meeting his paramour at the *A La Swallow* Hotel, especially after his experience with Viv Smith a few weeks ago when he had to deny having been the person she had seen lunching at *The Game Bird* with someone she knew, someone other than his wife. The hotel offered a discreet atmosphere, and the bar section overlooking the restaurant area provided elegant camouflage in the form of a jungle of decorous palms and creepers, blending in cool greens and pearly-grey whites.

But he was nervous nonetheless: this was no place for a public scene, which he must avoid at all costs.

Still the background ambience of New Age music soothed the distant surf of Piña coladas as the cocktail hour floated along. Yet Rob's whisky was sour, and he didn't have a lot of time on his hands at the moment. He glanced at his watch, then up to the clock, holding at sixteen minutes past the hour while digital seconds flipped by inexorably.

From the corner of his eye, he saw her hurrying over to him, and quickly readjusted the concerned look on his face, pretending not to have noticed her as yet. Just as she arrived, he turned and acknowledged her, although he was careful not to offer a kiss.

Someone might recognize Sandra Gibson, an administrative secretary renowned in certain circles as 'the Mother of all Specials'. And then perhaps, certain of them might recall her quasi-official connection to him, since Rob had recently resigned as a Sub-Divisional Officer of the Special Constabulary. In fact, he was about to be honoured for his service as he left the Specials, and it simply wouldn't do for the two of them to continue running the risk of being linked romantically.

From the smile on her face, it was apparent that she hadn't yet reached the same inevitable conclusion. Sandra slumped onto the bar stool next to him and tried to explain why she was late, as always, though she was evidently happy to see him. 'Sorry, sorry . . . There's always someone else needing a shoulder to cry on.'

'Yeah . . . I know,' he nodded, pushing the waiting gin and tonic toward her.

Before picking it up, she gestured to the restaurant below. 'Do you want to go straight in?'

He shook his head. From her reaction, it was clear that he had not successfully disguised his worries. Concerned and compassionate (also as usual), she placed her hand gently over his. 'I know . . . We've got some talking to do, right?'

He couldn't help frowning, slipping deeper into anxiety, yet his darkening mood only seemed to brighten hers. Smiling with reassurance, she stroked his hand as if with a feather, trying to keep a light tone. 'Don't worry. It's going to be okay, Rob. I'm an expert, remember?'

When he looked at her hopelessly in reply, he could see that this sign finally unnerved her.

7

In the afternoon, the empty parade room at Division 'S' headquarters, where the Specials would first gather in the evening, now seemed eerily quiet, like school during the holidays. Alone, Viv Smith, in civilian clothes and unemployed at the moment, walked back and forth across the room, lost in her thoughts.

Suddenly the doors burst open and Viv jumped out of her skin, twisting around to see Police Sergeant Andy McAllister barrelling along with a rare grin on his face.

'Viv . . . ? I thought we'd got burglars.' Moving toward her again, his assumed pleasantry appeared to be a clumsy attempt to put her at ease. 'Bit early for your shift, aren't you?'

While she attempted a smile, it didn't match her answer. 'Sorry, Sarge. I'm not in the mood.'

Immediately McAllister's jovial front dissolved.

'What's wrong, Viv?'

'Nothing . . . nothing I can . . .' Flustered, she couldn't think how to cope with his sympathy. 'Just leave it, okay?'

That only sharpened his curiosity. 'Is there anything –'

Abruptly she cut him off. 'No . . . I've told you . . . no.'

Realizing she was far more upset and ready to explode than she had thought, Viv made a determined effort to regain her composure.

'Thanks all the same, Sarge. I'm just waiting to see someone . . . okay?'

Judging from his raised right eyebrow, he observed her distress, but he didn't pry any further; he nodded to her, if a bit stiffly, then turned and walked away.

His footsteps echoed crisply on the polished floor, and as she watched him disappear through the swing doors she grew more forlorn by the minute.

Handling delicate subjects was not among Sandra Gibson's social skills, and her supposed lover, Rob Barker, wasn't making the process any easier, except for having chosen the right spot for a quiet talk in the bar area at the *A La Swallow* Hotel. Still, after observing him carefully, she knew it was up to her to dig out whatever he was going to tell her. She had to know.

Nonetheless, she approached him softly, having learned from long experience. 'Whittaker's told me . . . that you're leaving the Specials . . .'

He looked miserable, and didn't try to hide it. She began to fear the worst.

'It's all right, Rob. We can still make it work, can't we?' It was an effort to keep the desperation out of her voice.

His face – his mouth, his eyes and cheeks – appeared numb, lifeless. 'Leaving the Specials will be a whole lot easier than leaving you.'

The shock was instantaneous, though she had been anticipating it for months now. Still she couldn't believe that he had spoken the words.

'You don't mean that?'

He had no expression. 'Yes . . . I do.'

Seeing her reaction of pain and disbelief, he softened a little, reaching out to touch her hand, to reassure her in some way. 'I don't want to do this, believe me. You're the best thing that's ever happened to me, Sandra . . .'

For a second, she thought she heard a faint possibility of hope.

'. . . but things have become impossible.'

'They were always impossible, Rob,' she muttered wanly.

His fragmented attempts at explanation plunged the dagger home again and again, though by now she felt quite numb. 'Look, if I left my wife now . . .' he whined. 'She's ill, Sandra! How do you think I'd feel if she . . . How would *we* feel . . . ?' Unable to face the conclusion of his own question, he put his head in his hands, covering his eyes. 'It would be ugly, horrible.'

But the murderous shock had left her cold. 'Rather like this, then? Or don't you see us in the same category?'

'That's the problem, isn't it?' he shook his head. 'It's not the same. She's my wife, and we're just . . .'

He didn't find the phrase he was looing for, but glanced instead at his watch.

'We're just nothing?' she suggested with a hint of sarcasm.

'You know, I used to think, one day he'll stop looking at his watch . . . the way you're doing right now . . . one day he won't say "I've got to get home." One day I won't sit in an empty flat waiting for the sound of your car, and asking myself why I let this happen.'

'I can understand how you must feel . . .'

'No. You never did,' Sandra burst out. 'Not really. And I didn't make you. I damn well loved you too much to make you make a choice for us.' Her eyes implored him, but Rob was still in full retreat. 'And now you sit there as if you don't give a monkey's whether I'm hurt or not . . .'

As the tears leaked from the corners of her eyes she tried to remain focused on him through the blur. So far as she could discern, the uncomfortable, defensive look on his face implied that he saw *himself* as the victim.

'My god, how do you think I felt . . . ? Having to walk away from you . . . ? Every night . . .'

Her tears stopped flowing, and her vision began to clear. Her voice became harder. 'I never worked that out.'

Unable to confront her bitterness, he turned aside. She couldn't feel any sympathy for him in his present embarrassment.

'What is it that you want from me, Rob?'

'Your forgiveness, Sandra.'

She was speechless. This was the kiss-off, and he must have been planning it for some time.

'Please . . .' he begged her quietly. During the hush that followed, his eyes glanced furtively to each side, and he became aware that people around them had begun to stare. When they had started, he couldn't guess, but he worried about what might have been overheard, and by whom.

Yet that got him moving. He took a £10 note out of his pocket and left it on the table, then checked his watch with a guilty frown.

'I'm sorry, I've got this appointment.'

One look at Sandra told him she knew he was lying. Yet there was no way to make a graceful exit. As he repeated to himself many times, he would just have to plod through until the end. 'I'm sorry, lunch is out . . . but stay and have another drink.' He had to ride over her frozen stare. 'I'm sorry . . .'

He stood up, though his knees felt a bit unsteady, and as best he could, assumed dignified posture.

'I suppose you're coming to the party tonight?' he asked, hoping she would now discreetly decline.

'It would look rather strange if I didn't, wouldn't it?'

'Yes, of course,' he sighed. Obviously there was no point in trying to win an argument right now. 'I mean . . . Listen, Sandra, my wife'll be there . . .'

So *that* was the problem.

'There was not way round it,' Rob explained. 'So . . . no scenes . . . right?'

'You bloody flatter yourself, don't you . . .'

Uncertain of whether she had understood or not, he affected a formal smile for the witnesses, taking his leave of Sandra with a slight bow as he slowly backed away. 'Yes . . . right . . . thank you . . .' And he was gone.

Fingering the heavy gin glass in her hand, weighing the possibility of heaving it at Rob's departing skull, she decided not to waste the effort after all. Instead, she set the glass down carefully on the glass-top table. Sandra was the one who was shattered.

Police Chief Superintendent Frank Ellsmore had been listening dispassionately to Viv Smith's tale of woe concerning accusations of her acquiring funds by dishonest means through her position at the Bromwich Building Society, and of her swindling a Mrs Lawson out of some £800. Tilted back in his executive chair, his fingers steepled, he fixed his gaze on the view through his office window, letting her finish her story.

'. . . So it feels like an impossible situation, sir.'

Not breaking his gaze for the moment, he let the dust settle in silence, then slowly swung round to face her.

'Viv, why have you told me all this?' he asked, trying not to sound too stern with her. 'Why did you come and see me?'

Caught off-guard by his tone, Viv felt flustered by the direct question as well. 'Because . . . you're the Chief Superintendent. I thought you . . .'

He cut her short, not mincing any words. 'You're a special, a part-time Policewoman, Viv. You're job's the Building Society . . . Are you looking for a shoulder to cry on? What do you hope to achieve?'

'I don't know, sir. Maybe I'm stupid. It's just that I thought I might at least get a fair go here. It's like I've already been tried and convicted at the Building Society.'

'Viv, all I can do is give you advice . . . off the record.'

Her eyes fell, and she nodded bleakly in anticipation of the door shutting on her.

What she needed now, he thought, was someone to tell her the plain truth. 'Firstly, you were damned stupid coming to see me. Secondly, you were even more stupid to leave your job. And thirdly, you better get yourself a good lawyer.'

Viv was stunned. 'Is that it?'

'What did you expect me to say? "Don't worry, Viv, you can have the whole police force to prove your innocence? We'll put CID and forensic right onto it?" You're not that naive, surely?'

She crumpled. 'No, sir . . . but as a Special, I had hoped . . .'

'The police haven't been called in yet. And even if we were, you'd only get the same consideration as any member of the public. We don't take sides and fight private battles.' He spelled it out for her.

'There's nothing I can do.'

8

Jumping the gun, the party goers exploded into the room, bombarding the Pub on 4th with a burst of noise and showering Briggsy the barman with streamers, incidentally scaring him half out of his wits as well.

A volunteer crew of off-duty PC's and Specials, dressed casually in their civvies, busied themselves decorating the place for Anjali Shah's party that evening. Briggsy had been putting the finishing touches to his own contribution, having looped some fairy lights across the bar, but they wouldn't switch on, so now he had been reduced to screwing and unscrewing every lightbulb.

Around the room, the festive preparations were finally taking shape. The glitterball above the dance floor was being tested and adjusted, a platform had been set up in the corner for the disc jockey and disco paraphernalia, and the microphone and sound system were being connected. Having just hung a rope of old Christmas spangles across the room, as well as some shimmering metal-foil strips to bring a flash of fire to the darker corners, Bob Loach stood back to admire the crew's handiwork.

All around them – in a low, husky, sexy baritone – the voice of Freddy Calder pervaded the entire domain, adding his distinctive imagination to the simplest task of testing the MC's microphone.

'One . . . two . . . three,' he purred, then thumped the mic with his finger, amplified throughout the Pub on 4th to sound like the heartbeat of his passion.

Briggsy frowned and covered his ears.

'If I hear there's been any dirty phone calls, you're top of my list, Calder,' Loach warned. He glanced at his watch. 'Freddy, there's something I've gotta do. Everything's okay, isn't it?'

His thumb and forefinger making a circle, Freddy answered in the affirmative. Catching Loach just in time for a sneak preview, Freddy held him back momentarily while removing the pack of cards from his pocket.

'Magic . . . just watch . . .'

Beaming his best showman's smile, Freddy squeezed the pack of cards from both ends in one hand, flipped them through the air, and casually caught them with his other hand, in one motion. He could tell that Loach, in spite of his stubborn scepticism, was impressed.

He should have quit while he was ahead of the game. Instead, Freddy nonchalantly flipped the cards through the air once again, only this time he bungled the job, and the pack spilled to the floor.

Only then, as Freddy fumbled to pick up the pack did it become obvious to Loach that the cards were simply joined together, like an accordion, and he couldn't stifle a laugh.

'That good, eh? I'll have to take a chance that you don't demolish the place before I get back.'

A smirk curling his lip, Loach made his exit, leaving Freddy, slightly crestfallen, to reconsider his vaunted talents as an illusionist.

Her shaking the vodka bottle was of no use, as Viv could see it was already dry as a vacuum tube. Dejected, she plonked the bottle down on the drinks cabinet in her sitting room. Just then the doorbell rang, and she went distractedly to the door.

'Who is it?'

'Viv . . . it's . . . er . . . Peter Whittaker,' said the voice, from the other side, belonging to the District Commandant of the Specials.

Immediately she opened the door. 'Good of you to come round, sir.'

As Whittaker moved hesitantly past her, Viv remembered something stupid she had forgotten. Closing the door, she nimbly skipped around DC Whittaker to the drinks cabinet, where she surreptitiously hid the empty vodka bottle, even though, despite her self-conscious feelings of guilt by association, she had touched nary a drop. After recovering her composure, Viv gestured to the small sofa, and Whittaker sat down. She noticed, with a measure of satisfaction, that he was a mite uncomfortable, being careful not to muss her Specials hat lying on the cushion next to him.

'Would you like some tea?'

'Uh . . . no thanks . . . not for me.' Apparently he hadn't come just for a social chat. 'Look, Viv, I'll come straight to the point. I had a phone call from Superintendent Ellsmore . . .'

Oh-oh, here it comes, she thought. 'I was going to talk to you this evening . . .'

Whittaker nodded, still uncomfortable. 'We've discussed the best thing you could do, Viv . . .'

She looked into his eyes, searching for a glimmer of hope, some sharing of her concerns.

'. . . both for yourself and the force, is to take leave of absence, and just let things run their course.'

Viv was stung. 'You mean . . . I'm an embarrassment . . .'

That made Whittaker *very* uncomfortable. 'I didn't say that.'

'You've probably forgotten another time you gave me some advice, sir,' Viv reminisced, her anger rising. 'I was making a scene over a certain ginger-haired bloke.' In fact a PC by the name of Ginger, who had stolen Viv's affections, apparently along with several other paramours at the same time, let alone his wife, although Viv decided that DC Whittaker probably didn't need to be reminded of all the particulars.

'What you said then was: "We're not running a lonely hearts club, Viv. We're here to support one another."'

'I remember,' he nodded.

'So what's happened to this wonderful support you talked about? We get back-up on the street. So what about now? When I need it?'

But he didn't budge. 'You're asking for something we can't give. Be reasonable Viv.'

'Your idea of "reasonable" is to close ranks. You can't have your Specials contaminated with the likes of Viv Smith, can you?'

'All I said was: It would be difficult for you to carry on your work as a Special while all this is going on. Innocent or guilty, people would say we were taking sides.'

'People?' she challenged him. Whom did he think he was talking about? 'That's great,' she murmured, no longer disguising her sarcasm.

In a flash she realized why he must have come here. 'You want my warrant card,' she blurted out. 'Is that it?'

'I didn't say that,' he muttered in his embarrassment.

'Well, you can have it . . .' Determined to make a show of he gesture, she immediately crossed the room to retrieve her handbag. After rummaging through it roughly, she located her warrant card and tossed it onto the coffee table.

'It's about as much use to me as my library card right now,' she informed the District Commandant.

Dressed in his best suit, Loach had felt awkward while putting up party decorations at the Pub on 4th, but here in the stately foyer of the Hotel Excelsior, with his tie now neatly in place, his choice of attire appeared perfectly appropriate. Nonetheless, feeling confident in being properly groomed did not prepare him for the surprise of being recognized by the receptionist at the front desk.

'Mr Loach? Can I be of any help?'

Puzzled by her familiarity, he hesitated.

'Didn't recognize you at first,' she smiled. 'Without the uniform.' From his blank expression, she obviously realized that he was still lost. 'My car, I lost the keys,' she reminded him. 'You broke in for me.'

'Yeah, that's my line of business,' he nodded, still not recognizing her.

She gave him a polite smile.

'Look, is there a Mr . . . Señor Gomez staying here?' he asked, trying to sound casual.

Her smile disappeared, and she quickly checked the register. 'Yes . . .' She squinted at the key pigeonholes. 'And the gentleman's been in his room all afternoon . . . Number 625.'

She gave him a secret wink, most probably under the impression that Special Constable and Section Officer Robert Loach, crimefighter, was about to lead an undercover raid on Señor Gonzalez.

'Thanks . . .' Deciding he was, perhaps, taking himself a bit too seriously, Loach smiled back at her. 'Thanks a lot.'

As he hurried off to the lift, she remained behind, watching after him, utterly fascinated by his undercover exploits.

The lift doors opened on the sixth floor and Bob Loach emerged into the corridor. Catching sight of his reflection in the mirror, he stopped briefly to make last-minute adjustments, and to rehearse his speech.

'So . . . Mr Gomez . . . as Senior Director, I've regrettably decided that . . .' He cleared his throat. '. . . we should call it a day. I'm afraid the deal's off.'

Still muttering to himself, he marched down the corridor, straightening his collar just a tad so it wouldn't slip, until he stopped in front of the door marked 625. Nervous, he waited for a moment, swallowed hard, stood up straight, and knocked on the door.

After only a few seconds, the door opened. Standing there, inside, was Noreen. His wife. Loach's mouth fell open.

'Noreen? What the hell're *you* doing here?'

Her only answer was an enigmatic smile.

9

The formal ceremonies honouring Anjali Shah having concluded that afternoon, this evening's informal ceremonies at the Pub on 4th were in full swing as the Master of Ceremonies himself, Freddy Calder, kept his eager audience alternately in wonder and in hysterics with silly magic tricks and even sillier remarks in his own inimitable style. Yet just as their laughter and enthusiasm seemed to be riding the crest of the wave, the MC defied their expectations once more. Instead of trying to top his own best jokes, he reversed direction completely, suddenly becoming serious and shifted the spotlight back to Anjali Shah. He raised his glass to her.

The transition seemed perfectly smooth and fitting. Every man in the house arose, everyone raised their glasses in tribute.

'. . . So it's your night, Anjali, and a big thank you from us all . . .'

Simple enough, in the end, but enough to loose the floodgates. After sipping the toast, the crowd broke into whoops and cheers. No one's grin was wider, or prouder, than Freddy's.

And when the roar began to subside, Freddy stirred them up

again. '. . . and it's a helluva big round to buy! So, cheers, Anjali . . .' He gave her a broad wink from the podium, and the ceiling nearly collapsed from the resulting explosion of laughter.

'. . . No, seriously, she's a brave lass . . . and so are her physiotherapy patients, by all accounts.'

The whoops erupted again, this time with Freddy getting the bird.

Meanwhile, Anjali was thoroughly enjoying the occasion when she happened to glance aside and catch her mother's eye, which betrayed an anxiety behind Mrs Shah's otherwise pleased expression. 'Where's Uncle Ram got to?' she asked her daughter in a stage whisper. 'Maybe we should be worried? He could have been run over . . .'

Anjali privately entertained this notion for a moment, then dismissed the suggestion as mere wishful thinking. 'No such luck,' she assured her mother, gently squeezing her hand on the table. 'Stop worrying.'

Nonetheless they both kept worrying, yet allowed themselves to be distracted and entertained by Freddy Calder, who had now recruited his partner, Foxy the hand puppet. His appearance was inevitably punctuated by catcalls.

'Moving on swiftly now, MacFoxy tells me that we've got raffle tickets going spare. And if they remain unsold, the price of beer will go up.'

Foxy nodded in agreement, but many members of the audience were not so easily manipulated, and greeted this announcement with hearty booing, which only appeared to make Freddy even happier as ringmaster. 'And on that sobering thought . . . some smooth music for all you smoothies out there . . .'

Freddy pointed to the disc jockey, the cue for him to roll out the music, which suddenly hit the sound system with a boom of heavy metal rock. Instantly Freddy tried to cover his ears as old MacFoxy dived under his armpit. Yet several couples seemed to gyrate naturally to the noise as they took to the dance floor.

Bob Loach, uneasily seated in an overstuffed armchair in the Excelsior Hotel suite of Señor Gomez, felt trapped into observing the pageant being played out before him. The unexpected third party at their impromptu conference turned out to be his mystifying wife,

359

Noreen, who was at present mixing his drink. Sitting opposite Loach was Señor Gomez, a handsome man with an athletic build, dressed in tasteful suit, perhaps in his early forties, though he looked older in some ways.

Neither of them was making it any easier for Loach to enter the conversation, and he wasn't sure where to start, but evidently the ball was in his court. 'You speak good English, Señor Gomez,' he began tentatively.

'My mother was English,' Gomez explained, his pronunciation and diplomacy both semi-polished. 'I undertook my prep school days near Windsor.'

'Yeah?' Loach twigged, not knowing what else to say. Inept at casual social conversation, as well as nervous in Noreen's presence, he decided it would be better for him just to lay his cards straight on the table.

'Well, Mr Gomez, I wanted to clarify some details concerning our proposed business venture . . .'

'Yes,' Gomez put in. 'I undertake it is problematic?'

Loach turned sharply to Noreen, who was handing out the drinks. Her bland smile was enigmatic.

'Unrealistic?' Señor Gomez pressed on. Still trying to figure him out, Loach nodded cagily. '. . . if nothing to say unsafe?'

Glaring at Noreen, Loach wondered what she had said to Gomez. 'Not at all . . . Not yet.'

'Precisely,' Gomez responded, as he acknowledged Noreen for delivering his drink, then continued to smile at her. 'Your very gracious wife has already underplayed some very intricate background.' Loach must have looked perplexed when Señor Gomez turned to him once again. 'But perhaps now we could concentrate?'

Loach felt lost. 'Sorry?'

'Summarize?' Noreen suggested, offering her husband a clarification on the term 'concentrate' as employed by Señor Gomez, who nodded and smiled at her.

Loach turned to the side and spoke to Noreen in a low voice only she could make out – 'How come your Spanish got so good?' – then returned to face Gomez.

'Very well, Mr Gomez. To be absolutely honest, the deal as it stands would overstretch us. Our present capacity of coaches –

leaving us some slack for unforseen delays, etcetera – would only meet half your requirements.'

Gomez appeared neither shocked nor even surprised. 'And what is the about-turn of your maintenance?'

Finally Loach was on more familiar ground, and he gained confidence, even though he couldn't remain unaffected by Noreen sitting to the side staring at him.

'Every vehicle receives a three-thousand-mile service, without fail, and we can turn that round in about three hours.'

Apparently satisfied with that, Gomez proceeded, though his pace slowed, indicating the mounting importance of his questioning. 'And how are your feelings about road safety?'

Honesty, Loach reassured himself, was the best policy: not just most of the time . . . but always . . . even if it might be painful. He took a deep breath.

'There's not enough done, basically. Coaches should have the same structural safety factors as railways rolling stock.'

Señor Gomez raised an eyebrow. 'These are the new rollover cages you are referring to?'

Nodding, Loach began to ponder whether he had underestimated Señor Gomez.

'All my companies have them fitted,' Gomez affirmed.

Loach sighed: pleasantly surprised at the sensible attitude shown by Señor Gomez, unpleasantly disappointed that his own company could not yet meet that standard. 'Perhaps you still might like to come and see us?' he suggested, hoping to salvage some measure of goodwill from this half-English gentleman who had impressed him with his understanding of the business they both had in common (if, alas, not as partners).

Señor Gomez, however, was still full of surprises. 'Indeed, I have, in advance, made this arrangement with your wife.'

'You don't say . . .' Loach remarked, just as the telephone rang. Cagily he sipped his drink, ignoring Noreen, as Gomez answered the phone next to his chair.

'¿Sí? Ah . . . Buenos tardes . . . But of course. You know my room number? Bien, I wait for you with anticipation.' Señor Gomez replaced the phone before returning to his guests. 'Your Mr Padgett has just arrived. He tells me he has an exciting evening planned.'

By now Loach should have become used to surprises, yet he

turned to Noreen anyway for more answers on this one. 'Oh aye?'

Before she could answer, Señor Gomez had more questions. 'Your Mr Padgett. It is my hope that he is a lover of opera. Classical music?' he suggested. Loach detected a pleading undertone to these inquiries.

Loach couldn't offer Gomez any comfort on this point. He cleared his throat. 'I believe Dicky had different ideas in mind.'

'Ah . . .' replied Gomez, obviously disappointed.

'More like a trip to the casino and a lively night at the disco with some bunny girls.'

This preview didn't seem to suit Señor Gomez, and he got up from his chair rather stiffly with the aid of a walking stick, which had previously remained hidden by the chair. When standing, he looked down again at his lame leg with a rueful smile, and Loach and Noreen exchanged glances.

'What a shame,' Gomez sighed, shaking his head. 'I know someone who loves such evenings. He is of an age to appreciate such entertainment.'

Loach nodded compassionately. 'Young chap, is he?'

Señor Gomez reflected for a moment, then smiled and shrugged. 'In some ways . . .' he agreed. 'The chap I speak of is my father.'

Noreen cracked up in laughter and delight, and even Loach felt a slow grin widening across his face as he watched her.

10

Partners for the evening, Special Constable John Redwood and young Police Constable Albert Coles emerged together from Division 'S' headquarters and walked slowly toward their assigned panda car.

'Draw the short straw, did you, Redwood?' PC Coles asked sardonically.

'No, not really,' said Redwood. 'I need to make up the hours if I'm going to meet the commitment.'

Coles scoffed anyway. 'Yeah, your commitment is some poor copper's overtime.'

As Redwood was thinking of a rejoinder, Viv Smith appeared at the car-park entrance and spotted him, though her wave seemed half-hearted. 'Give me a moment,' he asked PC Coles abruptly, and broke away to go meet Viv without waiting for his answer.

She started explaining herself as soon as he was within range of her voice. 'Hi! I ducked back here because I suddenly changed my mind . . . about the party. I can't face it . . . Guess you've heard?'

He didn't tender her the kind of sympathy she seemed to be asking for, but instead offered her his business card. 'Look, Viv, come and see me tomorrow in my office . . . say . . . about ten?'

Awkwardly grateful, she wasn't able to raise her eyes. 'Thanks, John. I didn't like to ask.'

'We'll talk it all through then,' he promised, then waited for her to meet his eye. 'Now go to the party.'

She shook her head.

'You haven't got anything to hide, have you?'

'No.'

As best he could, he tried to instill a little courage in her heart. 'Get in there and show them. Try not to worry. Enjoy yourself.'

Unable to spare any more time, what with PC Coles waiting for him at the panda, Redwood had to get going. In the meantime, Viv was left behind, still uncertain. She looked at the solicitor's card in her hand wondering whether she should risk getting into more trouble by going up to the Pub on 4th for a drink in tribute to a brave woman.

Just as Dicky Padgett – dressed to the nines in a shiny suit to attract the female of the species while club-hopping later that evening – stepped out of the lift into the sixth floor corridor of the Excelsior Hotel, he ran smack into Bob and Noreen Loach and nearly knocked heads with them.

Loach smiled nonchalantly as if nothing had happened and it was no surprise for them all to bump into each other like this. 'Gomez'll explain everything, Dicky,' he reassured his partner, 'but I should cancel your disco companions . . .'

As he simply stared at Loach, Dicky was ambushed by Noreen from the blind side. '. . . and any plans you were making to float our buses on the stock exchange,' she added, patting Padgett's little pink cheek.

As she and her husband entered the lift, Noreen turned back

with an afterthought. 'And close your mouth, Dicky, love. It doesn't do you justice.'

As the disco beat was being pounded into the dance floor at the Pub on 4th, Sandra Gibson was anchored to a table staring at Rob Barker dancing uncomfortably with his laughing wife, Brenda. Sitting with Sandra, however, Freddy Calder was oblivious to her private suffering, as he concentrated on the card tricks he was trying to show her. He had to strain in order to speak to her above the disco noise.

'Is this music too loud, or what?'

'What?'

'I said, who's that with Barker.'

'His wife, I hope,' Sandra replied before bitterly tossing down the rest of her gin and tonic. 'Why . . . ?'

Freddy glanced over at the dancing couple, then returned his attention to the pack of accordion cards. 'I expected someone . . . with one foot in the grave, that's all. I mean, that's why he's leaving, isn't it . . . ?'

Fuming inside, Sandra turned on him. Seeing her reaction, yet not sure just what he had said wrong, Freddy flipped the cards and withdrew from her glare.

Viv Smith hesitated a moment longer, hovering in the doorway of the Pub on 4th while watching the heaving bodies of some of the better dancers. Again she scanned the room looking for a friendly face, but this time she finally spotted Freddy Calder at the same time he was looking over at her, and they made a connection. He appeared relieved to have discovered her at last, and waved for her to come over.

Instead, Viv faltered, then turned back to make a run for it. Unexpectedly, however, she found the way blocked by two Indian gentlemen; one she recognized as Anjali Shah's Uncle Ram, dressed in the formal, colourful finery suitable for a special occasion in their homeland. They, too, were hovering in the doorway, uncertainly.

Both gentlemen beamed at Viv. Uncle Ram executed a small bow and gracious gesture to usher her into the club before them.

No longer having a choice, she took a deep breath and walked in. Eyes followed her, and tongues were wagging, but she made up her mind to get through this situation somehow. Setting her jaw, Viv headed for Freddy's table.

From behind, Uncle Ram and his friend, Nuresh Prakash, watched Viv merge into the crowd. Taking his guest's arm, Uncle Ram urged him to proceed likewise, leading him forward.

'Courage, my friend.'

Moving through the club, Ram located his niece sitting patiently with her mother. Finally they both noticed him coming. As he passed through the crowd with Nuresh Prakash, many good-natured comments and compliments regarding their costume were directed to them. Ram truly enjoyed every moment of his own parade, beaming regally as if he were a member of the royal family.

Parked outside a fast-food store with the engine idling, John Redwood sat in the passenger seat of the panda rifling through his notebook as fast as he could. Meanwhile he tried to keep an eye on the gangly youth who, after stowing some stuff in the luggage ports, was climbing aboard a flashy motorbike parked closed by.

As PC Coles returned and got back into the car carrying his double cheeseburger and a packet of french fries, Redwood pointed at the motorcyclist. 'Follow him, quick!'

Without asking why, Albert thrust the food into Redwood's lap while simultaneously putting the car in gear and stepping on the accelerator. As the panda lurched into traffic after the motorbike, the french fries slipped out of Redwood's hands and landed on his shoes. Albert glanced at the mess, irritated beyond his limits.

'That's my supper you're wiping your size tens on,' noted Albert, then turned his attention back to the pursuit. 'What is it, Redwood? He's not even speeding.'

'No,' Redwood conceded, 'but he's on a stolen bike.'

PC Coles picked up the pace, closing the gap with the motorbike. 'Yeah . . . ? Are you sure?'

No sooner were the words out of his mouth than the biker spotted them in his mirror, and suddenly the motorbike shot forward, weaving rapidly through the dense traffic.

'I am now,' Redwood answered. He barely saved the cheeseburger packet from joining the french fries as they hurtled round a corner.

Freddy was standing and gesturing to the disc jockey in an effort to persuade him to lower the volume when Viv Smith came up behind him and tugged his arm. He jumped in surprise, then held up a finger to ask that she wait a moment until he could get the disc jockey's attention.

'Come on, sit down, Freddy. I want a word.'

'Won't be a minute, Viv. I've just got to sort this little problem out.'

'Freddy, please,' she insisted, tugging a bit harder. 'This is important.'

Squinting into the hubbub, trying to find the DJ, Freddy hardly wasted a glance in her direction. 'Viv, I am meant to be the MC,' he explained with a certain authority. 'Not everyone likes it this loud. Did you see the look Barker –'

Viv interrupted him without concealing her bitterness. 'I thought you were meant to be . . . my *friend.*'

Startled by her tone, he turned to see what was wrong. For her part, Viv was furious that self-absorbed Freddy couldn't see past the nose on his own face.

'Don't tell me you're the only person who hasn't heard.'

Flushed with embarrassment, he tried to apologize. 'Yeah, of course, Viv . . . Look, I'm sorry, it's just that –'

'Yeah . . . Whenever you've got some piffling girlfriend problems, you can call on me anytime. But when I'm faced with no job, criminal proceedings, and being drummed out of the Specials, you're too busy!'

'No, Viv, no . . .' Freddy protested.

But Viv had already stormed off and escaped into the festive crowd.

11

The motorbike skidded around another corner and howled down a street of derelict, bricked-up houses, PC Coles and SC Redwood in their panda following in hot pursuit. Beyond the street they could see a huge, gaping wasteland fast approaching. Just as the motorbike reached the edge of the wasteland, the biker roared back and jumped the machine over the remains of the old road and took off across the rough terrain.

When Redwood and Coles hit the wasteland, however, the panda came to a jolting halt. They sat and watched the lights of the bike bouncing away over pitted ground. Relaxing, Redwood attempted to slow his heavy breathing. 'That's it then.'

'Not bloody likely,' Albert responded. He threw the car in gear, and the panda lurched into the wasteland. 'Hang on, Redwood! This is what you hobby bobbies sign up for, isn't it?'

The thought occurred to John Redwood that these might be the last words he would ever hear.

After deferentially delivering a tray of drinks to their table at the Pub on 4th, Uncle Ram turned to address Anjali in a more serious manner.

'I'm sorry to be late and cause this misunderstanding, Anjali. But you will understand when I introduce you to my good friend, Mr Nuresh Prakash.' With an intense smile and a grand flourish, he presented his guest. 'He has just returned from Bombay.'

Balanced rather precariously in a somewhat diffident stance, Nuresh had to make an effort, though clumsy with reserve, to hold out his hand to her. 'Honoured to meet you at last, Anjali.'

Shaking hands, Anjali acknowledged him and smiled, amused at his sense of decorum. 'Please, you are welcome to the party.' As she gestured for them to sit down to their drinks, she kept smiling until they were seated, then moved away from the table, heading purposefully for the dance floor.

While her sudden departure left Nuresh bewildered, Ram leaned over to confer confidentially with him. 'You see, my friend, she likes you.'

'But she doesn't seem to know who I am,' Nuresh worried.

His face beaming once again, Ram put his hand on his friend's shoulder. 'Of course she does. But she is a shy girl. That I also told you,' Ram reminded him.

Nuresh nodded, although he seemed unconvinced. Having observed his behaviour since he arrived at their table, Anjali's mother now turned away, anxiety beginning to eat at her nerves.

The panda nearly became airborne as it careered into a small hill, bounced up, and sailed over the other side, skidding around a bit, then accelerating through a huge puddle and into the wet mud. Queasy in the stomach and rattled to the bone, Redwood hung onto the dashboard for dear life, blinking at what he could see ahead of them through the windscreen. Albert was frowning.

The motorbike seemed to be heading toward a huge bonfire burning a pile of large salvaged timbers and other refuse. As they looked intently at the dazzling glare, the motorbike appeared to drive straight through the flames.

Albert slammed on the brake, and the car screeched to a stop. Catching their breath, they peered through the windscreen, trying to trace the path of the motorbike. Looming beyond the bonfire was a massive warehouse, and they just managed to catch a glimpse of the light on the motorbike disappearing near, and most probably into, the warehouse.

'Gotcha!' Albert exclaimed.

Redwood was not so sure. 'I damn well hope so . . .'

Viv was attempting to leave Anjali's party discreetly, picking her way through the dancers, when abruptly she came face-to-face with Police Sergeant Andy McAllister, who had just come off duty. 'Where are you off to, Viv?'

'Home,' she answered, trying not to appear too upset.

'No you're not,' he announced 'I want to talk to you.'

'You're the only one, then,' said Viv with a rueful smile.

'Don't be silly. Come on.'

He led her toward the bar. 'Thanks. I was beginning to think I didn't have a friend brave enough to talk to me.'

'Why didn't you tell me what this was all about earlier?'

Viv lowered her gaze. 'Nothing personal, Sarge. I didn't know what to do.'

'But you shouldn't have gone over everyone's head to the chief,' he admonished her. 'You know better than that.'

'You're right,' admitted Viv sadly. 'Fat lot of good it did me.'

Andy shook his head, and she gave him a quizzical look.

'Now us poor infantry can't do a damned thing to help you,' he explained. 'Don't you see?'

PC Albert Coles and SC John Redwood had left their police vehicle in order to get a closer view of the warehouse on foot. Turning back to check the panda, Albert groaned, and Redwood looked to see what was the matter. They had a flat tyre.

'Radio for back-up?' offered Redwood hesitantly.

The suggestion only served to irritate Albert. 'I know that.' He buttoned his radio, and the static crackled.

Sergeant McAllister and Viv Smith were walking away from the dance floor when they came upon Anjali Shah and her family and guests. Awkwardly cornered at the table, Anjali was grateful to see her friends, and waved for them to come over.

'Sarge . . . come and meet my mum.'

Andy began to shake hands all around, as Anjali grinned happily at Viv.

'And this is Viv, another Special.'

Smiling through her discomfort, Viv shook Mrs Shah's hand. Meanwhile, Anjali continued relentlessly.

'. . . and this is my Uncle Ram . . . and . . . his friend . . .'

Amongst the polite smiles, Uncle Ram stepped forward and put his arm around the shoulder of his friend, Nuresh Prakash. 'No, no, Anjali. Let's do this properly.' Swelling his chest and putting on his proudest face for Viv and McAllister, Uncle Ram extended his hand in a grand gesture to Anjali.

'Sir! This is Nuresh Prakash – Anjali's betrothed.'

Andy and Viv observed an early frost descending on the gathering. Apart from Nuresh, who appeared to be terribly pleased with himself, everyone else felt terribly for Anjali, while wishing they were somewhere else. Anywhere else.

Recovering from her shock, Anjali shot a steely glance at her newly betrothed before returning her attention to Uncle Ram. She slipped her arm through his, and forcibly directed him away from the table, calling back over her shoulder to the others.

'Will you excuse us for a moment?' she asked, but didn't wait for their answer.

12

Although the windows were blackened, one end of the warehouse was brightly lit. PC Coles and SC Redwood had crept inside and made their way to a vantage point where they could observe the operations. They counted four young men wearing a strange assortment of overalls, parkas, and modern Gothic armour, working on a car, one using an acetylene torch. Actually, the car now looked more like a burst fruit. The roof was the sliced-off top of a pineapple, the bonnet a peeled banana, the doors jagged apple wedges, the bodywork was being elaborately sprayed in hi-glo paisley.

Next to the parked motorbike, another 'unzipped' car sat on a trailer, and a few others were still awaiting treatment. They were all Sierras. Incredulous, Redwood watched as one of the men started to spray another car. Suddenly he blinked, and stared at the number plate on the back of the blue Sierra being sprayed.

'My God . . .'

Albert turned to quiet him, as Redwood winced when the first spurt of paint hit the side of the car. Both of them were so intently engrossed in the scene that they were startled by a noise behind them.

Two of the men had surreptitiously worked their way around the flanks of Redwood and Coles and were now at their backs. A heavy chain dangled from the hand of the motorbike rider. His companion had a blowtorch: he flicked his cigarette lighter, and the yellow-blue flame shot out from the nozzle.

A melancholy Viv Smith sat at the table in the Pub on 4th watching the melancholy Sandra Gibson at her side, who in turn was staring over the rim of her glass at Mrs Rob Barker, who in turn didn't appear to be melancholy in the least.

'She looks pretty healthy to me, Sandra,' Viv remarked with the Mother of all Specials.

Sandra had requisitioned her own personal bottle of gin and so far had swallowed the contents about a third of the way down. 'You know what, Viv?' she asked, nursing her bitterness. 'I've got a good mind to go right up to her table and say: "Mrs Barker? You don't know me, but my name is Sandra Gibson. And I'm the bird your husband's been bonking for the last two years."'

Instead of being hilarious, her words made Sandra even more miserable. Viv put a restraining hand on her shoulder.

'That would be a dumb move, Sandra.'

'Look who's telling me about dumb moves . . .'

Viv withdrew her hand recalling an incident that took place only a few metres from where they were now standing, that involved a certain PC by the name of Ginger Stokes. 'Yeah, you're right,' Viv conceded. 'What do I know?' She threw up her hands. 'Go on, then. Go and tell her.'

Immediately Sandra rose to her feet like a soldier springing to attention, though a rather unsteady soldier perhaps. Just as abruptly, she sat back down. Then she reached for the gin bottle and poured out two large ones.

'. . . After I've had one more drink.'

SC Redwood and PC Coles were outflanked by a gang of car butchers who appeared none too happy at being caught in the midst of their late night slaughter.

'What do you mean stolen?' said their leader, the one with the blowtorch. 'We've just borrowed them; we're no thieves. We're artists . . . By the time we give them back, these cars'll say all we wanna say about materialism.' Taking another step forward, he smiled and shrugged: 'All we're doing is making a statement.'

Redwood was somewhat disconcerted when young Albert, without a trace of either fear or common sense, challenged the gang leader with only his fists to back him up against the blowtorch and chains. 'The only statement you'll be making, Charlie boy, is down at the station.'

Redwood seemed to remember being in a similar situation not so long ago, although he was able to escape suspicion then by faking a love scene with his partner, Viv Smith. With Albert, that was not such a pleasant prospect.

Nevertheless, despite Albert's idiotic bravado, once again it would seem as though Redwood were about to be rescued just in the nick of time. From the outside came the sirens of approaching police cars, thanks to Albert's call on the radio . . . and the flat tyre on their panda.

At the Pub on 4th, Brenda Barker was aware of the woman's presence before she spoke. Careful to maintain her poise, she turned ever so slowly, with a cool gaze, to face the woman.

'Mrs Barker, you don't know me, but my name –'

'– is Sandra Gibson,' she interrupted, finishing the woman's introduction for her. 'Yes, I know. You're one of Robert's little Specials, I believe . . .'

Sandra blinked, caught completely offguard.

In the meantime she was given a thorough inspection from top to bottom, yet she didn't know what to do about it.

'What a pretty dress,' remarked Mrs Barker, the polite smile still painted on her lips. 'And so cheap . . .'

13

A nervous Rob Barker sat drinking at the bar in the Pub on 4th with an unusually garrulous Peter Whittaker, though both were under the watchful surveillance of Briggsy the barman. While Whittaker had been spouting forth, Rob's main concern was simply to get through this awkwardly uncomfortable social occasion as quickly as possible, pick up his goodbye gift or whatever it was, and vanish into the night without further ado.

'I'll have to make a decision about your replacement soon, Rob.'

'Yes . . .' automatically responded the otherwise preoccupied Barker, soon to depart as Sub-Divisional Officer of the Specials.

'Integrity – that's the key,' his superior observed.

Barker felt a twinge of conscious he tried not to reveal. 'Yes . . . right . . .'

Sneaking a look over his shoulder to his table, Rob almost choked on his beer when he saw his former mistress sitting and talking with his wife.

Sandra Gibson stared blankly at Mrs Barker, unable to believe what she was hearing.

'In case you have any wild illusions of stealing my husband, I think I should acquaint you with a few facts . . . it may surprise you, Sandra, but I have no intention of leaving Robert. And neither will he leave me,' his wife emphasized. 'You see, he works for J. G. MacIntyre Ltd., who pay him a remarkably generous salary. Indeed, they will continue to do so when we return to Edinburgh, where they have their head office.' She seemed to be enjoying herself. 'The fact that Robert is merely an average draughtsman in neither here nor there. You see, J. G. MacIntyre is my father.'

At last Sandra twigged to their marital arrangement, and she nodded in defeat. She hadn't noticed Rob coming over to the table. Rather unsteadily she stood up to look him in the eye.

'I was just about to tell your wife . . . that the last thing I want to do is stand in the way of true love . . .'

Rocked on his heels, Rob looked to his wife, who turned away in disgust, as Sandra left them to each other.

Freddy was distracted by the sight of PC Steve Northcott waving his arms at the doorway entrance to the club. When Freddy realized Northcott was waving at *him*, motioning for him to come over, he jumped to his feet and moved quickly through the crowd.

Sitting at the table with her family, Anjali Shah could feel the eyes of Nuresh Prakash boring into her back. When she wheeled round suddenly, sure enough, she caught him staring. At first he looked startled, then slightly confused, but gradually his face became serene.

'You are very beautiful,' he said, almost with a sense of devotion.

She was prepared for anything but that. Yet now she was speechless. What could she say?

When Bob and Noreen Loach strolled into the Pub on 4th, arm-in-arm and clearly in good humour (under the terms of a newly arranged truce), Specials Wally Harris and Phil Warren were among the first to spot the surprisingly happy couple.

'Who's the skirt with Loachey, then?' Warren asked.

'That's not a skirt, mate. That's Noreen.' Phil played dumb. 'Loach's wife.'

'Didn't even know he was married!'

'From what I hear,' Wally grinned, 'neither does he most of the time . . .'

By then the strange couple had become lost in the sea of humanity rocking to the disco music.

Fumbling to open his formerly missing salesman's sample case, Freddy was also obediently following and trying to keep up with Sergeant Andy McAllister marching down the corridor of Division 'S' headquarters to the rear entry cell area. Telling himself not to get his hopes up too high didn't seem to help him coordinate walking and pushing two briefcase buttons at the same time.

When he finally managed to flip the lid of the sample case open, his heart sank. It was as empty as a graveyard except for Freddy's name sewn into the lining, like the evidence left behind of a ghost from his own past. With a shiver, he closed the case forever and caught up with McAllister.

'No sign of my car, then?' Freddy couldn't help adding.

'As it happens, yes.'

Unsure he had heard what he had heard, Freddy's brow began to lighten, although he didn't fail to notice that McAllister maintained his usual dour expression.

'It's outside in the yard.'

Freddy was hardly able to contain his emotions until he got out of the station and hurried over to the trailer, only to stare in utter horror at the 'unzipped' remains of a sierra. Truly stricken with grief, he put his head against the stone wall and closed his eyes.

'Why are you showing me this?' he inquired of McAllister, not opening his eyes. The Sergeant seemed incensed. 'You ungrateful barmpot! How about thanking us for bringing it in?'

Suddenly Andy snapped his fingers, and the trailer was rolled away. Freddy's eyes were barely open to see what was behind it, but immediately they popped. There was his *car*! His bonny beautiful Sierra! His very own lovely blue machine! He couldn't believe this miracle, nor could he disguise the joy he felt as he turned to thank McAllister.

The sergeant almost smiled.

14

District Commandant Peter Whittaker cautiously tapped the microphone at the podium. Reluctantly the party at the Pub on 4th quieted to a hushed silence.

'Thank you, ladies and gentlemen. We now come to another important part of this evening, when we must sadly say farewell to an esteemed colleague.'

There was precious little indication of any regret on the faces of some of the Specials in the audience – including Bob Loach, Viv Smith, and several of the others who actually knew Rob Barker –

but they were keeping a low profile until the final curtain had fallen, although they privately hoped it would be sooner than later.

'However, to remind you of your years of service, Rob Barker, and in recognition of your unswerving devotion to duty, we would like to present you with a small memento of our appreciation – something we're sure you'll cherish . . .'

Whittaker picked up said memento, a polished wooden replica of a mounted truncheon, and motioned for Rob Barker to join him at the podium.

'We're going to miss you, Rob . . . and we won't fill your place easily.'

The audience, with some notable exceptions, began to applaud. Sandra Gibson had to make a deliberate effort to hold herself together, let alone clap for Rob Barker. Viv and Loach simply kept their heads down.

Barker's wife was leading the applause. In the meantime, having just returned to the club positively elated, Freddy Calder joined in the applause enthusiastically. When he happened to notice that none of his friends were sharing his enthusiasm, he suppressed his clapping immediately, and the general applause soon subsided as well.

Barker stood at the podium clasping the Truncheon of Honour for all to see, though his expression seemed strangely ambivalent. 'I'll try to be brief.'

A storm of whistling and cheers greeted his unintended humour, and he waited stoically for them to die down.

When all was quiet, Barker continued his acceptance speech. 'I owe a debt of gratitude to my colleagues and friends . . . and above all – my dear wife.'

Brenda Barker held her head high and smiled strongly. Her husband raised the truncheon like a soccer trophy.

'This . . . *treasure* . . . will have pride of place on my mantlepiece . . .'

The applause thinned considerably this time, as Viv leaned over to offer a sympathetic word in Sandra's ear.

'Shall we tell him where else he can put it, Sandra?'

Sandra would only shake her head. Somewhere in her heart, the embers were still too warm . . .

As Rob Barker was already in the process of making his farewell waves and leaving the stage, Viv decided to place the responsibility squarely on her own drunken shoulders, and although they were thus weighed down, she stood up for her friend, Sandra.

'Hypocrites! The lot of them! If you won't tell them, Sandra, I bloody will.'

Before anyone could stop her, Viv was making her way toward the stage. Being congratulated and shaking hands, Barker was unaware of her approach. Viv had no trouble acquiring the microphone when she reached the podium, and instantly she felt its power.

'I'm sure we would all want to wish Rob Barker very well,' she began. Again there was a hush, as Viv looked around at the silent, expectant faces waiting for her words of appreciation.

'. . . which all goes to show, doesn't it? . . . how popular you can be, even when you're a greasy, two-timing bastard willing to kiss a porcupine's bum.'

Before anyone else could do anything about it, however, Freddy Calder had already made his move, leaping onto the podium. Glancing at Viv with a stricken smile, Freddy easily wrested the microphone from her.

'Thank you, Viv.'

Immediately flicking the microphone off with his finger, Freddy bundled Viv off the stage.

'Why are you doing this to me?' Viv objected, making a half-hearted show of resisting his efforts.

Connecting with the disc jockey, Freddy made a 'finish it' gesture to him, without letting go of Viv's arm. The strains of the last waltz – in this case, the rock smooch version – wafted through the club, and some of the couples made their way to the dance floor, while others started to leave or to prepare to do so.

Off to the side and hiding from her friends, sobbing on Freddy's shoulder, Viv felt hopeless and abandoned.

'Why are you all doing this to me?'

15

There were only a few diehard couples remaining on the dance floor, and everyone else had left. Dancing cheek to cheek, Bob and Noreen Loach didn't even notice the others.

'I'll give you one thing, Loach,' she conceded.

'Yeah?'

'You were always a smoothie dancer.' She nestled against his shoulder.

'Well, that's why they gave me the cup in Hartlepool,' he boasted.

'They never did. It was Butlins.'

'Was it?' He must be getting senile.

'And you won it in the "Best Pair of Legs" competition. Don't you remember? I wanted to shave your legs.'

Now he did. Grinning in spite of himself, he held her tighter. 'Now that I do remember . . .'

All at once the music stopped, quickly followed by a loud thud as the amplifier was switched off. Rather surprised, the Loaches looked round to find they were the last couple left standing on the dance floor.

Freddy walked Viv up to his car in the yard, attempting to comfort and encourage her with his own recently rediscovered happiness.

'She's come home, Viv.'

Preoccupied with larger concerns, Viv couldn't concentrate on the Sierra. 'Yeah?'

Nonetheless, Freddy went through his usual spit and polish routine on his beloved chariot, while disconsolate Viv wandered around the car making a cursory inspection. But when she got to the other side, her eyes suddenly widened in amazement.

'Oh-oh!'

'Don't tell me, it needs washing.'

His grin disappeared as she shook her head and motioned him to come round to her side of the car. As soon as he saw, he froze in his tracks, and his eyes rolled as if he were about to faint dead away. Instead he made a pathetic, strangled cry as he beheld the side of his formerly blue Sierra painted and smeared with hi-glo squiggles and spills.

'It's only paint . . .' Viv offered lamely.

'It's only paint? . . .' echoed Freddy, holding back the tears.

'You're lucky that's all you've got to worry about, Freddy . . .'

'Yeah . . . you're right, Viv. It's only paint.' And suddenly, it did make sense. 'Yeah . . . I'll sand her down, get a decent paint respray. No problem.'

'I wish my life was as simple as a paint job,' she confessed, a growing hangover of regrets expanding her headache. 'Freddy, my life's become a pile of junk.'

Now it was Freddy's turn to be preoccupied, staring at his own pile of junk. 'You're right. But let's build on that.'

In spite of all her troubles, Viv took one look at his earnest face worried about his bloody car, and burst out laughing in the dark.

Now there were only two cars left in the car park outside Division 'S' headquarters: Noreen's Renault 25 and Loach's white Jaguar. The respective owners were walking amorously, arm-in-arm. When they found their cars parked side by side, he pulled her to him seductively.

'Damn, Noreen. We've brought two motors.'

'I didn't want to drive home with your hand on my knee anyway,' she teased.

That brought a grin to his lips. 'Sorry about that.' He gestured toward the Jag. 'I'm coming back to collect mine tomorrow. Come on, princess.'

As he escorted his wife to her car, she handed him the keys. 'Steady on, Valentino.'

Gallantly he unlocked the driver's door and graciously offered her the honours. Instead of getting in, her face fell.

'No, you drive, Loach.'

'It's your car . . .' he insisted.

'But you don't like my driving. You've told me often enough . . .'

'Nonsense,' he smiled. 'It's only when you take corners on two wheels.' After all, he was a partner in a transportation firm.

Noreen was not amused. Nor was he.

'Noreen, drive, please.' He thrust the keys at her. 'I can't risk my license – a man in my position . . . on the brink of promotion . . .'

She sighed and took the keys, her romance evaporating as he meandered round to the passenger side. When she was in the driver's seat with the door closed and the seatbelt fastened, she reached for a cigarette, and so did he. Rather than start the motor, she lit her cigarette from his lighter and sat for a moment, letting off some steam.

For a while, they sat smoking in silence. Eventually, he spoke first.

'He's a good-looking guy I suppose . . .'

'Who?'

'Gomez.'

'Yeah, I suppose . . .' She couldn't quite figure out what he was getting at.

'No, really, he is. In a sort of Spanish way.'

'Uh-huh.'

The hush fell upon them once more, and they smoked. Again he broke the silence.

'What I meant to ask you was . . . how long were you up there? In his room? Alone . . . ?'

Instantly deflated, she was reminded that her husband certainly knew how to puncture her balloons. She answered him with a distant weariness.

'Loach . . . I was up there all afternoon. I'd just put my clothes on when you knocked on the door.'

After a moment of silence, the engine started, then roared as the throttle was depressed. The headlights flooded on. The passenger door swung open, and Loach swung out. Slamming the door, he stamped over to the white Jaguar.

They left separately.

16

In a hurry, Anjali Shah hopped down the steep stairs in her home while buttoning up her uniform jacket. She made a quick stop at the hall mirror, adjusted her neckerchief, straightened a stray curl, and hastily brushed her hat. Frantically she searched for her bag, but couldn't find it in any of the usual places. So she scurried off to the living room, though reluctantly, knowing whom she would find there.

To be sure, upon entering the room she immediately confronted an awesome array of disapproving faces. Her mother dropped her eyes, too embarrassed to reveal her anxieties to Anjali. Showing his discomfort in a different way, Uncle Ram simply stood and stared at her. Nuresh Prakash, already camped out in her living room soon after their supposed betrothal had been announced, nervously stood when she entered, affecting a rather feeble smile.

Anjali was greeted with silence, as they all watched until she found her bag. As soon as she saw it by the sofa, she grabbed it, managed a watery smile, and made for the door.

'See you later . . .'

But it wasn't going to be so easy, as Uncle Ram, sternly stepped forward and blocked her path.

'Not so fast, Anjali. Close the door, if you please.'

She shrugged, wearily went to close the door, and impassively braced herself to listen to Uncle Ram's lecture.

'You really must start behaving like a mature woman. You are always speaking about being given your rightful place in family matters which involve you . . .'

'Yes . . . ?'

'Well, here we all are.' He spread his arms to encompass the gathering of the multitudes all four of them, 'and *you* are the matter under discussion. But what are you doing at this moment, Anjali? You are rushing off in your uniform. We must settle this situation now.'

But she drew the line at negotiating her entire future while waiting to rush to Division 'S' headquarters for duty. 'I'm not aware that any *situation* exists, Uncle,' she said pointedly. She leaned over to kiss her mother's cheek, then did the same to a more hostile Uncle Ram, but only smiled as she passed Nuresh Prakash on her way to the door. 'Good to see you again, Mr Prakash.'

Three unhappy people watched her leave. When she was gone, Nuresh turned an accusing look at Ram, still fuming at his niece and trying to avoid the gaze of his friend.

At Division 'S' headquarters, parade for the Specials was being taken by District Commandant Peter Whittaker as a temporary replacement for the departed Sub-Divisional Officer, Rob Barker. Though frequently consulting his clipboard, Whittaker was trying to disguise his nervousness with a show of brisk efficiency.

In the meantime, his audience of Specials was taking a sceptical attitude before making a final judgement, although there was little enthusiasm expressed for the rather stiff formality of the DC taking parade. On the other end this time, Bob Loach shifted from one foot to the other, thoroughly out of sorts.

'Good evening to you all. As you know, Rob Barker has, sadly, resigned. Until a new sub-divisional officer is chosen, I shall be taking parade.' He surveyed his troops, however thin, as a gesture more than an assessment. 'So, if we're all here, I'll begin.' Then the DC began by reading off the clipboard. 'Special Constable Freddy Calder, off-duty. And Viv Smith . . .' – he paused, looking up –' . . . is on leave.'

Bob Loach and John Redwood exchanged glances. Again Whittaker peered over the assembled Specials, although this time he looked more closely, and found fault even in their general disposition.

'Before I assign the roster can we have notebooks and pencils at the ready, so I don't have to repeat anything.'

Eyebrows were raised, but the notebooks were produced, in some cases emphatically. Without thinking, Steve Northcott finished the last swig of his Coke, instantly arousing Whittaker's ire.

'And I'd appreciate it if some of you would remember that it is a parade, not a queue in the canteen.'

Mid-swig, Northcott froze, then whisked the can out of sight.

Observing all of this, yet holding his tongue, Loach rolled his eyes in silent wonder.

Mrs Shah closed the front door as Ram finished pouring Nuresh Prakash a whisky. Ram walked over and held the glass out to Nuresh, who courteously waved it away . . . so Ram drank it himself, in one gulp.

Now that Anjali was gone, Nuresh leaned to his side, retrieved a slim attaché case, and lifted it to his knees. He flipped open the case, and inside were revealed neat, tidy bundles of £10 notes.

'I'm willing to honour my part of the bargain, Ram,' he offered, although his tentative tone seemed to belie his words. 'But I do so reluctantly. Your niece shows no inclination to like my company. Always, she is excusing herself . . .'

Ram tried to dismiss his concern with a wave of the hand. 'She needs time to accustom herself . . .'

Nuresh didn't let Ram finish. 'I thought from our last conversation, when I agreed to pay you this sum in advance, that you had talked to your niece about *everything* – about me, Ram, *and* working for the police.'

'All these things *will* be talked about, Nuresh . . .'

'I told you that this was one of my conditions before marrying

Anjali. It wouldn't be suitable for my wife to be seen walking the streets with another man.'

'All of these things take time, my friend,' said Ram.

Yet Nuresh was shaking his head. 'I am not a young man, Ram. I would like to have a family before I am too old to enjoy children.' As if to underline his meaning, he tipped the lid of the attaché case closed.

'Perhaps the money will help you to concentrate on making Anjali my life partner . . . ?'

Ram breathed a great sigh of relief when he realized Nuresh was not after all taking the attaché case away. He poured himself another whisky, then turned to present a new idea to his niece's suitor.

'Nuresh, you and I, *we* should go and see Anjali's superior at the police. We shall tell him the problem together.'

The suitor's immediate reaction was unenthusiastic. 'I don't like being involved with the police.'

Disregarding his apprehension, Ram sat down beside Nuresh as both friend and counsellor. 'I kept telling you that Anjali is not a policewoman. She only helps them – that is what Specials do. It is quite a different thing, believe me.'

Nuresh remained unconvinced. 'Then you go see them. It's your problem, she's your niece . . . your dowry payment.'

Although he liked the last part of that statement, Ram was still uncomfortable about shouldering the burden of his niece alone, since he had just discovered the ideal resolution. With an understanding frown on his brow, Ram put his arm round Nuresh's shoulder.

'They will comprehend better if they see you there. You are a respectable businessman, and it will help them to understand that this is not a matter to be taken lightly.'

Nuresh remained doubtful.

Just as DC Whittaker put his clipboard down, finishing up his remarks at parade, Anjali managed to slip in behind the standing ranks. She caught Redwood's eye, and smiled.

'You probably think I've been a touch severe with you this evening . . .' Whittaker concluded 'But it's important we behave like a team, and not as a group of individuals relying on the other man to take down what I'm saying.' His eyes narrowed, as he looked into their faces, one by one. 'Maybe we could all do with tightening up our acts . . .'

When Whittaker's gaze reached Loach, the latter made no effort to conceal his resentment.

'Locker room camaraderie is one thing, but outside, on the streets, you're not a one-man band. You're the uniform of the whole police force.' He paused, and sighed. 'Okay, dismiss, and have a good and productive evening.'

As the Specials relaxed and started to move about, Whittaker's enquiring look at Anjali indicated that she hadn't really gotten away with her little deception. Apologetically she approached the District Commandant to explain why she was late.

Lost in thought, Redwood waited for his partner, Anjali Shah, near the entrance to Division 'S' headquarters. Suddenly he was distracted by a shadow moving from the edge of the building, then surprised to recognize the shadow as Viv Smith.

'Viv. You startled me.'

He assumed a polite smile, which she didn't return. 'I've got to speak to you, John. Won't keep you so long . . . please?'

Redwood nodded in agreement, and walked away with her. Anjali saw them just as she was rushing through the door, and instinctively she stopped, keeping her distance.

Standing to the side, Anjali observed Viv speaking earnestly with Redwood. The strain on Viv's face was clearly evident.

17

DC Whittaker was inspecting the locker room, realizing that he should have stepped in earlier to take a close look at the slackness creeping into the system during Barker's extended absence. With a critical eye that had long become a habit, he noticed a pair of shoes left on the floor, a rather offensive postcard from one of the Specials on holiday, that sort of thing.

Appearing in the doorway, hovering for a moment, Bob Loach then walked purposefully toward Whittaker, who turned to him without bothering to hide his impatience.

'Loach?'

'Can I have a word, sir?'

'I can only spare a minute . . .' Whittaker warned him. 'It's about the SDO vacancy, sir. I think you know my feelings . . .'

'Yes, I do,' the DC responded testily.

Section Officer Loach seemed undeterred. 'I'd just like to know where I stand, sir . . . Am I to understand that you are considering candidates from other divisions?'

Whittaker cut him off with a curt reply. 'Loach, the way you speak, you'd think the decision was up to you. I've already told you that there are many factors to be considered. Your name has been logged. You'll be called before a special board, which will make the decision. You'll be informed of that decision as soon as it has been made. I promise you . . .' Now, if there's nothing else . . .'

Again Redwood tried to reason with Viv, who was distraught, angry, and frightened all at once.

'Viv, as I told you in my office the other day, you don't have to sell *me* your innocence. It's the *law* you've got to persuade.'

'But the law isn't *fair*!' she protested.

'Did I say it was? My advice remains the same: get yourself a good private investigator. I can help with that, put you in touch with one. The only way to refute the charges against you is to find tangible evidence that this woman and her son are lying. At present, it's simply your word against theirs. Your only chance is to let an investigator find some proof of your innocence.'

'John, you might as well tell me a fairy tale,' she said in a despairing voice. 'I've got a mortgage, and no job as of two days ago. I couldn't afford to give an investigator a ham sandwich, let alone pay his fee.'

Feeling particularly awkward at this moment, he didn't know what to tell her. As a defender of the downtrodden Redwood had many clients who were hard-pressed, but lately he had been unable to maintain a proper professional and emotional distance with people he knew personally and cared about.

Viv lowered her gaze. 'I suppose it's down to me. Is that what you're saying?'

'No, it isn't. That would be the worst thing you could do – getting personally involved. Doing it that way would really put the lid on the box.'

She considered his advice. 'You mean I shouldn't get personally involved . . . like you did?'

Instantly recognizing her reference to his getting involved in the case of his client, Denzil Taylor, who had also been mixed up (though perhaps as an unwilling bystander) in the gang attack that left his son paralyzed two years ago, Redwood knew that his own admonitions wouldn't satisfy her in this case. He didn't know what to tell her.

Seeing his indecision, Viv glanced round to find Anjali Shah, who had been waiting at a distance. 'Night, Anjali. Night, John. Watch the bugs don't bite.'

Redwood smiled at her, though not without a touch of sadness, and went to join Anjali. Enviously Viv watched them walk off together, not looking back. She swallowed hard.

Drumming his fingers on the steering wheel, PC Albert Coles stopped at the junction looking straight ahead, while his partner for the evening, SC Bob Loach, idly surveyed the detached homes in the nouveau riche neighbourhood from the side window of their panda. Loach was the first to notice the big Cadillac approaching, but Albert only began to pay attention when the Cadillac roared past them. Nevertheless, once alerted, Albert pulled out sharply to follow.

'That's a bit tasty,' he smacked his lips.

'Just a bit,' Loach concurred. 'Thirty-five grands' worth . . . and that's not counting his flashy number plate.'

'I meant the speed,' Albert growled, continuing to exhibit no sense of humour whatsoever. Peering ahead, he frowned, the Caddy already having disappeared in the traffic.

'Well, constable, it's long gone now,' Loach pointed out.

'People like that get up my nose,' Albert ruminated rather less than gracefully. 'Cars the price of houses – they think they own the street!' He shook his head in disgust. 'I'd throw the book at 'em.'

Loach merely shrugged, unwilling to waste the energy. 'Live and let live, sometimes.' Maybe he was just getting older.

Shifting his gaze from driving just for a second, Albert gave him the eye, then went back to watching the road. 'Of course. You're the Special with the white Jag?'

Chuckling, Loach realized that he'd left himself open to a sneaky attack.

'Listen, Loach, I wouldn't care if it was the Chief Constable himself driving the Queen home in a Roller. If he's over the limit, I'd have him.'

Chalmers slowed the Cadillac to a crawl, gradually coming to a stop in front of a particular house, identified by an ornate suspended number board emblazoned with an elegant polished brass 19, and by an American-style letter-box at the end of the drive proclaiming the name Egerton. Moving forward once again, he turned sharply, swung across the driveway, and pulled in front of the entrance, parking right there and blocking the way completely. Damian, his 12-year-old son, grinned up at him, though with an edge of anxiety at the corners of his mouth.

After switching off, Chalmers picked up the car-phone and dialed directory enquiries with his gold-ringed finger. '. . . Egerton. It's a Mosley number . . .' His eyes glanced at the road, then the letter-box. '19 Hillcrest Avenue . . . Yeah, that's right . . .'

Patiently he sat waiting for the number.

18

Egerton himself – who sported a small and somewhat pedantic moustache, and today was dressed comfortably in his golfing outfit, his colour-coordinated casuals – was actually watching his video recording of today's golf match on the huge-screen TV in the excessively tasteful living room of his sumptuous home when the telephone rang. He absently picked up the cordless phone, but the next moment he grabbed the remote control and zapped the sound of the TV; he listened to the voice on the telephone with ever-growing alarm while the golfers flashed silently on the telly.

'Does a kid with a red anorak and a baseball hat with NY on it live here?' the voice asked.

Egerton was stunned as his son Billy, who matched the description perfectly, was at that moment strolling through the overly tasteful living room.

'Yes . . . ? But who is this . . . ?'

'My name's Chalmers,' said the voice. 'I'm the father of a lad who's just had his bike stolen by the kid I've just described. We spotted him down at the supermarket, and followed him to this address. Now who am I speaking to?' demanded the voice of Chalmers.

'My boy stole a bicycle?' Egerton blinked. 'Now listen, I don't know whether this is some kind of a joke . . .'

'This is no joke. Get yourself through that front door of yours. I want the bike returned now.'

'Where the hell are you speaking from?' asked Egerton, quite unnerved.

'Look out of your window, and you'll see.'

The cordless phone still pressed to his ear, Egerton walked over to the window. Outside there was a dinosaur Cadillac sprawled across the entrance to his drive.

His mouth dropped open.

As Egerton's voice rose in anger, Chalmers sat in the Cadillac outside, squared his jaw, gripped the car-phone, and listened to what the weasel had to say for himself and his thieving son.

'Now look here, Chalmers, or whatever your name is – *get off my property or I'll call the police!*'

'Suit yourself, mate,' Chalmers replied calmly. 'It'll save me the call.' He looked over at Damian, watching his father yet hearing only one side of the conversation. 'And in the meantime, I'm warning you: If that bike – if that five-hundred-quid bike – isn't out here in the next five minutes, I'm coming in there to get it myself!'

A few stallholders were still packing up as Anjali and Redwood walked their beat along the shopping street. All of a sudden Anjali stopped. Not knowing what had crossed her mind, Redwood gave her a questioning look.

'Mind if we cross over?' she asked.

Following where her eyes turned he understood. Across the way was a shop by the name of Prakash Video. Trying to communicate his confidence to her by sounding firm and appearing resolute, Redwood touched her arm: 'Come on, Anjali . . .'

She swallowed, and allowed Redwood to guide her forward.

Two of his young employees helping him, Nuresh Prakash was putting up the shutters on his video store, covering his name across the window. Looking up as the uniformed Anjali Shah and John

Redwood drew level, Nuresh was startled to see her, then couldn't keep from staring at Anjali.

'Mr Prakash . . .' she nodded stiffly, walking by.

He nodded vaguely, and turned to busy himself with the task at hand. His two young employees, however, glanced knowingly from Anjali back to their boss and then to each other, while not entirely successful in stifling bubbles of embarrassed laughter.

Pretending not to notice, Anjali and Redwood walked on in silence. When they were safely out of range, he looked over at her, attempting to convey reassurance.

'It's his problem, Anjali . . .'

Her expression suggested her own view that the issue was considerably more complicated.

PC Albert Coles answered the radio as he was driving the panda: no problem. Except that he had to jiggle the wheel to avoid tapping into an oncoming truck.

'19 Hillcrest Avenue? It's just round the corner. We're on our way.'

He lowered his foot on the accelerator pedal with a sigh, glancing wearily over at Loach. 'Just a neighbourhood ruckus. Big deal, eh?'

19

Chalmers got out of his Caddy shouting at Egerton, who hovered uncertainly under the protective shell of his porch. Partly hidden, Egerton anxiously lowered his hand, reached sideways, and grasped a number nine iron.

'Clear off, you . . . lager lout!' All he needed to do, Egerton told himself, was hold off this maniac until the police came. Yes, that was it: 'I'm warning you, the –'

Paying no attention to his warning, Chalmers began taking deliberate strides toward the porch. 'Come over and say that to my face, wanker.'

Before Chalmers could get to the porch and tear Egerton limb from limb, his rush to vengeance was abruptly thwarted by the arrival of the panda, which pulled up next to the Cadillac. As PC

Coles and SC Loach jumped out of their car, Albert grinned from ear to ear as he recognized the Caddy blocking the driveway, and observed the threatening bulk of its owner.

Albert shared a private wink with his partner. 'I'd say this motor was less than adjacent to the kerb . . . How 'bout you, Loach?'

Ready to go, and eager as well, Freddy was having trouble containing his impatience. His precious love – his gorgeous, Sapphire Sierra – was once more ready as well: newly resprayed, rebuilt, and fully restored to mint colour and condition. The motor purred, yet Freddy remained ill at ease, scanning his surroundings as if expecting an ambush at any moment. He was in one of those moods, half-expecting to find a mother hiding behind every bush.

Finally Rita appeared at her front door, and scurried from the house into the car, although the look on her face betrayed her irritation.

Freddy didn't notice. Hardly had she shut the door before he hit the accelerator, and away they went.

PC Albert Coles found himself in a rather ineffectual position, standing in the middle of the front lawn with Chalmers and Egerton on either side – one a thickset, ebullient bully dressed casually in an expensive, high-fashion leather jacket and clean jeans; the other a wealthy twit with a voice that could cut glass – both boiling mad.

Meanwhile, Loach leaned against the panda, watching carefully from a distance. At the moment he was keeping an eye on Chalmers, who was pointing an accusing finger at Albert.

'I phoned the police two days ago, and of course, what happened? Sweet FA. "We'll keep a look-out," they said. Some look-out. It took me less than an hour to see this idiot's kid riding it down at the supermarket.'

Attempting to referee the dispute while recording the details in his notebook at the same time, PC Coles had his hands full simply keeping the warring factions apart. 'That is no reason, sir, to take the law into –'

The slight yet feisty Egerton intruded into the dispute, though using Albert to screen him from the heftier Chalmers. 'I've told this man till I'm blue in the face, officer, that I know nothing about a stolen bicycle.' He gestured to his stately property. 'Look around you. Does this look like the kind of place you'd find stolen goods? It's laughable!'

Chalmers wasn't laughing. 'You're the joke, mate! You're just the sort . . . bloody *yuppie*!'

Ignoring him, Egerton appealed furiously to poor Albert. 'My boy has no need to steal anything, officer. He has an expensive bike of his own. He can only ride one bike at a time . . .'

'Cut the one-liners, tache-face,' Chalmers menaced.

Albert tried to intervene, but Loach could see it was a temporary holding action at the moment, and he turned his attention to the Cadillac blocking the drive. For the first time he noticed a boy sitting in the Caddy, staring back at him, his face revealing a stream of tears running down each cheek.

Curious, Loach headed for the Cadillac. As soon as the boy saw him coming, however, he slid down in the seat and out of sight.

Parked proudly on the lip of a hill, the glistening blue Sierra overlooked the civilization below, where lights began to blink on as the dusk was advancing. Outside, looking through the windscreen at lovely Rita, Freddy breathed on the glass, then caressed the surface with his handkerchief, careful to avoid the new security sticker announcing that his beloved baby was now wired and protected with an alarm.

'They'll never do this to me again,' he murmured to himself. 'I've made sure of that.'

Yet he failed to notice that Rita didn't look best pleased, as she stuck her head out the window.

'Freddy, I can now see for miles through that windscreen.'

Nonetheless, Freddy spotted a fleck of dust he'd missed, then buffed it lovingly away, as he gazed alternately at the spotless glass and at Rita's clear blue eyes, her head still stuck out the window and now extremely close to his. She spoke to him quietly, but firmly.

'So, do you want to kiss me, or would you rather grope the car?'

Freddy stopped polishing in an instant.

Bending over and looking through the window of the Cadillac parked across the driveway at 19 Hillcrest Avenue, Loach found Damian, the young son of the hothead Chalmers. His nose running, Damian was sniffing in an effort to stanch the flow of tears. When he saw Loach watching him, for a moment he seemed terrified, perhaps because of the uniform. Loach smiled to show he was not threatening, then signalled the boy to lower the window. Cautiously Damian reached for a button on the door, and the window glided down.

'Nothing for you to worry about, lad. Let the grownups slog it out, eh?'

Loach grinned and winked at him, and Damian appeared to relax somewhat. Putting his hand gently on the door – no sudden moves – he opened it.

'Come on, I'll show you what crime detection's really about.'

The boy hesitated at the open door. Not waiting, Loach ambled off, apparently talking into his radio in a muffled voice. Turning back to the Caddy, he motioned with a reassuring wave for Damian to follow him.

Loach couldn't fail to note in passing that the argument between Chalmers and Egerton was still burning hot, with Albert in the middle trying to cool them off. As Damian joined him, they strolled casually toward Egerton's garage.

Suddenly another lad – about the same age, wearing a baseball cap with NY on it and a red anorak – slipped out the side door by the garage, and froze.

'Stop right there,' stated Loach, pointing at the lad.

When the lad saw Damian, he was immediately frightened, and made a run for it. Loach and Damian set off in pursuit.

The other lad, however, had a strong headstart, while Loach and Damian were forced to pick their way through unfamiliar obstacles in the semi-darkness. Yet by the time they sprinted round a corner in the back garden, the other lad had come to a dead end, trapped and cowering on the raked roof of the garden out-building.

'Come on, lad,' Loach advised him in an even, calm voice. 'Let's be having you.'

But the lad was having none of it, turning away and scrabbling toward the ridge of the roof. 'No way . . .'

He didn't make it. Losing his grasp, the lad slipped and slid down the roof, clawing at the tiles as he went. Loach charged ahead and arrived at the outbuilding just as the lad fell heavily into his arms.

When the lad realized what had happened, he was back on the ground in the firm grip of Special Constable Robert Loach.

'Okay, let's talk . . . shall we?'

20

Trapped in the perfect car with the perfect woman, Freddy was still uncomfortable. He glanced sideways at Rita, who was clearly waiting for him to make the first move. The erotic intensity at the moment registered zero on the Richter scale. Needing some suggestive atmosphere to help trigger an earthquake, Freddy flicked the buttons on the tape deck, and instantly soothing mood music emerged to soften the edges of anxiety.

Feeling a bit more hopeful and emboldened, Freddy made a tentative move, putting his arm around her, though somewhat stiff and clumsy in his execution of the manoeuvre. Impatiently Rita pulled him toward her and jammed her mouth hard against his. This triggered a search for romance in each other, fuelled by the surging desire of hungry mouths and tongues.

Then the car-phone bleeped. Freddy couldn't believe his misfortune, as he pulled apart from Rita. He couldn't simply ignore the bleeping, so he grabbed the phone with an apologetic nod to Rita. He was still breathing heavily as the dreamy look on his face drained away.

'Ma . . . ? What did you say?'

At the word 'ma,' a storm cloud descended on Rita's brow. Impulsively she reached to the tape deck to turn up the music, requiring Freddy to strain in order to hear his mother's voice over the car-phone.

'Where did you say you were? *Casualty*?' Panicstricken, he covered the mouthpiece, his eyes bulging. 'Judas Priest, Rita – she's in casualty!'

Rita seemed unmoved, but Freddy became immediately decisive and determined.

'I'm on my way, Ma! Take it easy . . . No, we'll talk about it when I get there. I'm on my way.'

He replaced the car-phone and moved to start the car before

sneaking a glance at Rita. Now, of all times, the earthquake was rumbling inside her, although she certainly couldn't be accused of hiding her sentiments.

'And you're absolutely sure it was your son's bike you saw, Mr Chalmers?'

Still standing between the two hostile antagonists and holding them at bay, PC Albert Coles was also writing furiously in his notebook as he made a sincere attempt to record their stories on paper. Nevertheless, neither was being very cooperative.

'How could he possibly tell?' Egerton answered for Chalmers.

'I'll bloody prove it . . .' Chalmers offered, charging forward to pound Egerton to a pulp.

PC Coles stopped him cold with an authoritative shout. 'Quieten down, both of you! Or we'll have this conversation back at the station.'

In the meantime, none of them had noticed SC Loach and the two boys emerging from the dim light of the garage until they were all standing behind PC Coles. Startled, Albert turned to find his partner holding two expensive mountain bikes in custody.

'That's my kid's . . .' Chalmers blurted out, starting toward one of the bikes.

Loach held up his hand, halting Chalmers, then turned to each of the boys. 'No. They're my bikes now. Aren't they, lads?'

Dolefully, each of them nodded. The elder Egerton looked astonished; Chalmers was outraged.

'What the blazes is going on here?' Chalmers demanded.

Loach addressed him tersely. 'Something you should have found out for yourself, sir.' Still engaging Chalmers in his explanation, he reached into his pocket. 'I won these bikes from both your sons the same way your lad lost his . . .'

From his pocket he produced a pack of playing cards, which he then handed to Egerton.

'. . . in a game of pontoon.' The next question Loach directed to Egerton. 'These are yours, I think sir?'

Accepting the playing cards in a shaking hand, Egerton confronted his son. 'Is this true, Billy?'

Shame-faced, Billy nodded. Young Damian stared defiantly at the elder Egerton, Billy's father.

'Your lad's as guilty. Not to mention the small protection racket they've got going at school to fund other gambling debts.'

'Protection racket?' Chalmers sneered.

'Bullying is the word I'd use,' Loach replied.

Chalmers tossed a glance at PC Coles, then an almost indiscernible wink at Egerton. To him, the incident had now been defused.

To the lads, on the other hand, Loach stressed the gravity of their transgressions. 'This is a very serious matter, but what I'm prepared to do is give your bikes back . . .' The faces of the lads began to relax. '. . . on loan.' Now they were just as puzzled once again.

'That way, if you ever gamble with more than matches again, we'll be down on you so hard you won't believe it. We'll have you for theft next time, understand?'

Nodding his head, his eyes downcast, Billy Egerton needed no further persuasion, Loach reasoned. He turned to include Damian in his official warning. 'So clean up your act! Threatening behaviour doesn't go down too well in juvenile court, believe me.'

Both Damian and Billy indicated their agreement, sheepishly accepting the bikes Loach then returned to each of them.

The elder Egerton appeared to be more shaken than the boys. 'I blame myself,' he admitted. 'I'm sorry. If we'd kept them on a tighter rein . . .'

'More money than sense, sir,' Albert interjected.

Egerton nodded, though his confusion suggested he hadn't really taken in the remark. He turned to his son Billy and directed the youngest into the house.

Exchanging glances, Loach and Albert were about to return to their panda when Chalmers launched attack at his son.

'You little pillock, Damian! Why the hell did you tell me it had been stolen?'

The silent fear that came over Damian answered the question. But his abject fear wasn't enough. His father punched him sharply on the cheek, and it hurt.

'You think I've got time to play your stupid games? Get back in the car!'

Chalmers was suddenly aware that PC Coles and SC Loach had been watching him critically. 'Kids. You'd think they'd be happy with what they've got. I didn't have half the stuff that boy of mine has. If I'd pulled a stunt like that, my dad would have belted me one.'

Loach remained unsympathetic. 'Yes, sir.'

In an effort to buy back their good wishes, Chalmers pulled out a wad of notes. 'Still, no real harm done, eh?' he said. 'Maybe you could . . . er . . . donate this to the Police Benevolent whatssit, yeah? For all the trouble you've been put through?'

Chalmers put on his most ingratiating smile, but Loach took the money and rammed it back into the breast pocket of the high-fashioned leather jacket Chalmers was wearing, giving it one last extra-hard shove for good measure. 'I don't think you've been listening to a word I've said. Sir.'

For the first time that night, Chalmers wisely kept his mouth shut.

21

The blue Sierra raced up the drive leading to the hospital complex and braked to a sudden stop in front of the main entrance. Jumping out in a panic, Freddy left the car door open without a thought. The waiting automatic doors at the entrance opened just as Freddy bolted through on his way to save his dying mother.

Arriving at the main reception area for casualty cases, he looked over to the desk, and spotted someone with a blanket round her, obviously an elderly woman, being helped by a nurse. Out of breath, Freddy lurched toward his mother.

'Ma . . . ? Ma . . . ?'

It wasn't his mother. The woman under the blanket turned to Freddy with a puzzled expression, and the nurse gave him a funny look as well. Smiling in embarrassment, Freddy backed away from them.

'Sorry . . . er . . . sorry . . .'

Viv Smith waited patiently at the open door to her neighbour's flat. When Mrs Walker returned, she held a crying baby in one arm and dragged along a toddler at her knee, but she was also carrying a small tape recorder. Awkwardly she tried to untangle the strap with her 'free' hand, while the toddler tried to drive a pushcart of bricks over her foot. Not to be outdone, the baby grabbed the tangled strap and started to chew on it.

Meanwhile Mrs Walker was turning over the Walkman with a look of doubt. 'It's Barry's. You know how to work it?'

Viv had never tried, but she assumed she could figure it out somehow, and she certainly did not want Mrs Walker to try and explain it to her in detail while the baby was crying in her ear.

'Yeah. Doesn't everybody?' Without waiting for a reply, Viv gave Mrs Walker a tight smile and took the tape recorder from her.

Feeling extremely irritated, Rita Loosemore waited in the car, flipping through the same magazine for the third time, when at last she saw Freddy leading his mum by the arm. Looking consciously deadpan, Rita lowered the window.

Hilda Calder stared down at Rita with undisguised contempt. 'I usually sit in the front, Rita.'

She simply stared at Freddy's mother, and then at Freddy, who looked like a cat on hot bricks. Freddy gave Rita a hopeful glance, but that was all he had to offer.

Grumpier by the moment, Rita got out of the car. 'Far be it from me to interfere with the pattern of history.'

The triumphant queen was assisted onto her throne by Freddy, while Rita plopped down resentfully in the back. Round One to Hilda Calder.

Señor Gomez walked along slowly and deliberately, inspecting the rolling stock and maintenance benches and talking shop with the works manager at Cougar Coaches, John Barraclough, who was also explaining the work he had been doing on the engine hanging from a hoist at the far end. Occasionally Gomez asked a question, and seemed to be nodding appreciatively.

Following behind, Bob and Noreen Loach and Dicky Padgett tried to figure out what the Spaniard was saying and thinking, as they conferred amongst themselves in low voices.

'What'd'ya think?' Dicky whispered, referring to their previous talks with Gomez.

Loach shrugged, though he desperately wanted to believe. 'Maybe we're in with a chance after all?'

The pair in front of them stopped abruptly, and Señor Gomez

turned back to them with a broad grin, apparently satisfied with whatever Barraclough had been able to explain to him. Without a direct word, Señor Gomez beckoned to Dicky Padgett, and they went off toward the office, Loach and Noreen bringing up the rear.

Loach lagged behind to get a quick impression from Barraclough. 'What do you reckon?'

Barraclough remained noncommittal. 'A quick prayer's not a bad idea.'

From the backseat driver's point of view, Freddy was proceeding with excessive caution, wary of his mother's stony presence like the Rock of Gibraltar next to him.

'Com'on, ma, are you okay?' No answer. 'What happened?' No answer. 'What did they say?'

'Stop fussing, I want to get home. I'm perfectly alright.'

'Did they do any tests?'

'Certainly not.'

'But they should have done something . . .' Freddy protested. 'Shouldn't they, Rita?'

'Like freezing her in liquid nitrogen,' said Rita under her breath while seething in the back seat.

Not hearing her response, Freddy glanced over his shoulder at her, taking his eyes off the road. 'Should have done some tests, surely?'

'Not if the patient is already dead,' Rita replied, again to herself.

The irascible Hilda couldn't hear either one of them. 'Give over burbling, Freddy, just get me home.'

But the burr was in his tail, and Freddy couldn't get it out of his mind. 'You don't go to Casualty without someone telling you what's wrong . . . ?'

The question hung in the air forever, until at last Hilda Calder deigned to speak. By then her voice bad soured to vinegar.

'It was my nextdoor neighbour. She felt queer, so I went in with her on the bus.'

'So there's . . . nothing wrong with *you*?'

Pursing her lips, she shook her head slightly in a show of bad temper. She pulled down the eye-shade vanity mirror to check her hair and spy on Rita.

Although his mother had mentally gone on to other matters,

Freddy was still stunned by her revelation, as the Sierra shuddered to a stop at the traffic lights. Seizing the opportunity, Rita grabbed her bag, pushed the door open, and climbed halfway out of the car.

'That does it, Freddy. I'll find my own way home, ta very much.' She got out, then leaned back in. 'You've obviously got your hands full with Madonna, here. If I get really stuck, I'll call an ambulance.'

With that, she slammed the door so hard that the car alarm set up a piercing wail. Putting his head in his hands on the steering wheel, Freddy failed to notice when the traffic lights changed. Other cars began to honk, but because of the car alarm screaming in his ears, he failed to notice them as well.

22

Viv Smith walked down the suburban street made up of dwelling houses some of whose lower floors had been transformed into shops. When she came to a small grocer's, she stopped, reached into her handbag, and removed a notebook. She was checking the name on the shopfront just as a customer went in, so she held back awhile, waiting for an opportunity to enter the grocer's when it was otherwise empty of customers.

Once they had Señor Gomez captive in their office, the Cougar Coaches management team went into action. Dicky ushered Gomez into the best seat – behind Noreen's desk – while Noreen plied their guest with a cup of coffee. Loach gathered extra chairs for their conference, but none of them could sit down; they perched in anticipation.

Not a man to be hustled into anything, Gomez sipped his coffee, then sat back and sighed, while his audience held their breath.

'I'm not going to burden your time . . .'

Dicky felt a sudden leak in his balloon, glancing uncertainly at Loach.

'I had, in fact, already made a decision before I came here.'

At the last moment, Noreen looked at her husband sympathetically, realizing she still felt concern for him, even in the worst of times.

'There is another company at Manchester . . . not unlike your own . . .'

The balloon burst. Gone, vanished in the blink of an eye. Even Dicky didn't have any hot air left.

'So this is the intention which I wish to do. I'm giving the company in Manchester a contract for a year – to handle all my business in the south of Spain.' He paused, thinking before speaking again.

'The operation in the north . . . I wish you to handle. Same contract . . . for one year.'

Loach looked at Noreen, who looked at Padgett. Their faces brightened all of a sudden. 'That's great, Mr Gomez!' Dicky said enthusiastically.

Señor Gomez held up his hand. 'Wait for the whole deal, Mr Padgett. When the year is ended, I shall decide which of you two companies will undertake the whole territory.' In no hurry, he looked at each of them in turn. 'Does that meet with your approval?'

Both of the Loaches were too choked with relief to move, let alone speak. To the rescue, redoubtable Dicky, glancing at them and grinning, took charge. He moved forward with his hand outstretched.

'I speak for us all, Mr Gomez. You've just got yourself a deal.'

Señor Gomez, with the aid of his cane, stood formally to receive the handshake. For his part, Dicky gave it the extra moment, the added squeeze, the final touch of personal sincerity. Then he put his arm around the shoulder of his new partner in bus tours through northern Spain.

'Now, if my colleagues don't object . . .' Dicky tried to throw a quick warning glance in Loach's general direction. '. . . we should discuss the kind of PR and I think a deal like this will need . . .'

Finally noting that Loach and Noreen were encouraging him rather than opposing him, Dicky beamed at them. Noreen got the message, and led Loach with her to the door, nodding at Dicky in passing. He flashed a smile of appreciation for their timely exit before turning his full attention to Señor Gomez once again.

As she closed the door behind them, the last works Noreen heard from Dicky were: 'And then we'll adjourn to the golf club . . .'

She caught up with her husband as he walked to the yard, hopping up to give him a peck on the cheek. Stubbornly unresponsive, he marched off to the coach he had been working on, got down underneath, and disappeared from view.

Noreen followed him with a purpose, bending to peer under the coach. 'Well . . . ?'

He pulled himself out a fraction, although he was already oily. 'What?'

In a celebrating mood, this time she decided to set her trap with honey. 'In a Mills and Boon romance, you'd be sweeping me off to some exotic location for a candlelit dinner. But since we're Cougar Coaches, I at least expect a portion of chicken nuggets and a can of shandy.'

Loach considered her suggestion and on second thought emerged from underneath the bus, and stood up again. 'You're a hard woman, Noreen. But you're on.'

All at once he remembered, though.

'No, you're not. Flippin' 'eck, I've just remembered, I'm on duty.'

The arctic chill turned Noreen into an ice statue. 'Oh, well then . . .'

'Noreen, let me explain. It's downright crucial that I'm there tonight. It's Whittaker, you see: he plays everything by the book. And if I'm not there, he'll count it against me.'

'Not seriously?' she scoffed.

'Straight up.' Ignoring her tone, he forged blindly ahead. 'I wouldn't be surprised if he's not considering someone from another division for the promotion . . . someone better educated . . .'

Looking at her sheepishly, he realized that Noreen couldn't care less if someone else were promoted to Sub-Divisional Officer.

'So, how about another coffee?'

She just shook her head and walked away talking to herself as she went. 'Well, Noreen, love . . . if you didn't know it before, you certainly do now. On the scale of things, you're somewhere below a Wimpy and just above a plastic cup of freeze-dried decaf . . .'

23

'But I had no idea that Anjali was getting married,' said Police Chief Superintendent Frank Ellsmore to his visiting guests, Anjali's Uncle Ram and her fiancé, Mr Prakash. He was pleasantly surprised.

Ram nodded in a dignified manner while closing his eyes slowly, which Ellsmore took to mean that the betrothal was a sacred commitment.

'Then let me be the first on the force to congratulate you, Mr Prakash. Anjali is much respected here. We only wish there were more like her.'

Although Ellsmore may have assumed his comments were appropriate to the occasion, apparently he had erred, as the two Indian gentlemen exchanged wounded looks.

'Yes, yes . . . and I'd like to discuss her involvement with the police,' Ram began diplomatically. 'Naturally, we are very proud of her, and what she has achieved. But in our culture, Superintendent, a married woman cannot be seen walking the streets with another man who is not her husband. Or even driving in a police car . . .'

Ellsmore started to comprehend the gist of what Ram was saying. 'You mean . . . ?'

'The husband would lose face, you see. He would be the laughing stock of the community. My good friend, Nuresh Prakash here, is a highly respected member of the Indian business community.'

'Mr. Shar– . . .' Ellsmore stumbled, once again demonstrating why, despite the best of intentions, he would never be appointed ambassador to anywhere.

'He owns three video stores,' Ram continued. 'It would damage his reputation, and his customers would vanish.'

Finally Ellsmore grasped what he thought to be their mission, and he smiled with relief. 'I think I understand the problem. Anjali believes that there might be some disgrace attached to her leaving the Specials, is that it?'

But again he had missed the point, as Ram and Prakash appeared to be alarmed by Ellesmore's words.

'Not quite,' Ram countered gently. 'You see, superintendent, in our country a marriage is arranged between families of the two parties.' Knowing this was a delicate subject with the English, Ram proceeded in an especially polite tone. 'In Anjali's case, it is not what *she* decides, it is what is decided *for* her.'

Ellsmore took a deep breath before trying to clarify the facts. 'And you and Mr . . . Prakash . . . have decided between you that Anjali should no longer be a Special? Does Anjali know about this?'

Ram's shrug was noncommittal. 'Yes and no, Superintendent. But that is of no consequence.'

401

'Oh, but it is, sir,' Ellsmore hastened to contradict him, courteously but firmly. 'Anjali's commitment to the Specials is voluntary. The police don't employ her. She doesn't get paid.' He looked at each of them. 'It's up to her to tell us that she no longer wishes to be a Special.'

For the first time, Nuresh Prakash spoke up. 'Sir, we wish you to use your influence in her best interests.'

Ellsmore shook his head. 'I can only discipline her and force her to resign if she does something foolish, or is under suspicion of any kind.'

From the looks on their faces, Ellsmore knew this was not what they had hoped he would say.

Except for Mrs Lawson behind the counter, the small grocer's shop was empty when Viv Smith came in. Without delay, she picked up two cans of beans from the shelf, walked slowly over to Mrs Lawson, making herself plainly identifiable, and slammed the beans emphatically on the counter. Mrs Lawson jumped, a hint of panic in her eyes.

'Why are you doing this to me, Mrs Lawson? I don't understand.'

Nervously pretending to ignore Viv, Mrs Lawson mechanically put the cans in the bag. 'If there's nothing else you want . . . ?'

'The truth would be a start,' Viv declared. 'Do I look like the kind of person who would get involved with theft? Or even perjury? Because that's what you're saying, Mrs Lawson.'

Again the panic flickered in her eyes, and only the entry of another customer saved her from cracking up. Yet the customer spent but brief time and less money purchasing a package of pretzel snacks, then left without having said a word. The door was opened, letting in the street noises from outside – the dying roar of a motorbike engine cutting out – and the door was closed, leaving Viv and Mrs Lawson alone together once more.

Distracted by the sound of the motorbike in the outside world, Mrs Lawson was still looking anxiously at the door. After taking a deep breath, Viv brought Mrs Lawson's attention back to the matter at hand by taking a thick packet of money from her bag and tossing it on the counter between them.

'This is for the shopping, Mrs Lawson. there's five hundred there. It's all I've got.' She hadn't planned to get to the imploring stage quite so soon, nor to have tears welling up that couldn't be held back for long. 'I'm begging you, if you don't tell me the truth, my life's ruined. I don't have a job. Not even references. I'll have a record . . .'

While Mrs Lawson obviously did not want to hear all this, she couldn't avoid listening, and Viv's pleading was having a visible effect. She looked thoroughly ill at ease.

'All you need to say is that you and your son made a mistake. That the money turned up elsewhere. The Building Society will be only too pleased to have it sorted. There'll be no comeback, I promise you.'

At long last, Mrs Lawson crumbled. 'Oh God. I'm so ashamed . . . I've never done anything wicked in my life.' Now it was her turn to appeal to Viv's compassion. 'You must believe me!'

Viv moved closer and spoke in an even voice. 'Tell me . . . What did you do?'

In contrast, Mrs Lawson spoke in halting voice. 'I gave my son the £800 to put in my account. Only he never did. He said he'd fix it . . . told me that there was no way the Building Society would want trouble once I'd convinced them that there'd been a mix-up with slips.'

Although Viv was not really surprised at her revelation, she couldn't quite imagine this woman as a master-thief either. 'You thought all that out?'

She broke down, crying and shaking her head in denial. 'Warren told me what to do. I never thought you'd lose your job . . . My son said –'

'My son said . . .' echoed a sneering male voice.

Viv and Mrs Lawson immediately turned to see her son, Warren, who had just entered from the back room, still clad in his tough leathers. Too late Viv realized that the motorbike noises she had heard outside were probably from Warren's machine, and had probably contributed to Mrs Lawson's fear.

For it was his mother at whom Warren was now glaring in disgust. 'Yakety-yak . . . You stupid old cow. I told you to keep your mouth shut . . .'

As he moved forward, his mother and Viv were both terrified.

24

'I'm ashamed, Warren,' admitted his mother.

'Who gives a toss, Mother?' Instead of threatening her, Warren spotted the wad of cash and immediately scooped it up, ripping the money out of the packet and flicking through the bills. He whistled in appreciation.

Viv made a grab for her money. 'Give that here!'

As if he were swatting a fly, Warren brushed Viv aside roughly and pushed past her. 'Out the way . . .' He moved quickly to lock the front door and pull down the blind. Strolling back toward his mother, he glared at her, brandishing the wad of money in her face.

'Maybe you were just going to keep this for yourself, eh Mum? Not tell little Warren?' *he taunted her*.

'Don't be stupid . . .' Viv intervened.

Instantly Warren turned to her. 'Keep – it – *shut*!' His eyes narrowed. 'A nice little bribe to get us to tell lies, is that it? Well, I'm sure the police would be more than interested to hear this one.'

Pulling herself together, Mrs Lawson made her way toward him, putting a gently restraining hand on his shoulder. 'Give her money back, Warren, for God's sake. It's finished.' Again she began to waver. 'I haven't slept since we did this . . .'

Disgusted with her, he moved away. 'I'm warning you, Mum! I've warned you before, and I bloody mean it! You say one word, and you'll be putting me away. I'll walk through the door, and you'll never see me again. Think about it! You'll never see little Warren again.'

Viv could see that, in spite of Mrs Lawson's desire to do the right thing, Warren had managed to get through to her. The older woman, noticing Viv watching her, had a helpless look on her face.

'Just a minute, Warren,' Viv interrupted him. 'There's something you ought to know . . .'

She pulled the little 'something' out of her bag – the Walkman tape recorder – and placed it on the counter. Warren and his mother stared at the device, and seemed somewhat startled by the discovery.

That was the opening she had been hoping for. Seizing her chance, Viv broke away from them and made a dash for the back room.

She was well beyond Warren's reach by the time he noticed she was trying to escape.

To her surprise, however, the back room was a dead end, as she didn't find the exit in time. Frantically she looked for some way out, as Warren burst in and quickly cornered her. He dug into a pocket in his leathers, and pulled out a flick knife. Holding it up to eye level, so she could see the menace clearly, he sprang the lethal blade. Then he slowly extended his hand, the knife outstretched toward her face, and advanced step by step as Viv flattened herself against the wall.

'You smart-arsed little bitch! You taped what she said? Give it to me . . .'

He held out the other hand for the Walkman, grotesquely curling his fingers and inviting the object into his grasp, as he moved closer. Behind him, Mrs Lawson appeared at the door, blinded by her weeping until she saw the knife in her son's outstretched hand.

Immediately she screamed and ran toward her son. '*Warren*!' She threw herself between the two of them, but the knife got in the way and sliced into her arm. In sudden shock, her body jerked away and fell backwards. While sliding down to the floor, she looked stupidly at the blood streaming through her sleeve.

Warren simply stared at her while his attitude appeared to go through a bewildering metamorphosis, the sneer and the swagger dissolving into jelly. He didn't even bother to look at his captive, but rather let the knife slip from his hand to the floor, then knelt beside his mother, the tears streaking his face.

'Mum . . . mum . . . mum . . .' he moaned over and over.

Viv saw her chance for escape, coiling her muscles to spring past him, but then she looked down to check the obstacle she would have to jump over: Mrs Lawson. She was bleeding profusely; her eyes were vacant, not only in shock, but obviously in danger as well. Viv realized that she couldn't leave the woman who had saved her lying on the floor with her blood draining from her body.

Kneeling beside the woman and unconsciously pushing Warren aside, Viv grabbed Mrs Lawson's apron and tore it off roughly. Stricken by the sudden rending of the fabric, Warren stared at Viv as she steadily ripped the apron into wide strips.

'Call an ambulance, Warren. Now.'

Snapping out of his trance, Warren got up and rushed out. Viv was trying to make a tourniquet to squeeze off the flow of blood from what appeared to be a bad wound. Worried she might be too late, Viv anxiously took the woman's jugular pulse. It was faint. Her eyelids closed and she was fading away.

25

Back from Division 'S' headquarters, the silver Lexus pulled up outside Prakash Video, and Nuresh switched off the engine. Maintaining his silence, he got out of the car, and Ram followed him.

'Nuresh . . . ?' Ram hoped his friend was not hopelessly discouraged.

'The Superintendent has made things perfectly clear, hasn't he?' Nuresh asked in a way that concluded there was nothing left to be said.

'I don't think you were listening. Did he talk to me in Bengali and you in Urdu? I thought he was most sympathetic to our position.'

Nuresh let his anger show for the first time. 'Ram, you're fooling yourself. I wanted to fool myself, too, for a time.' He shook his head sadly. 'But only Anjali can change her way of life.' Pausing, Nuresh looked Ram in the eye. 'I don't believe you are capable of arranging this marriage.'

'You must give me time to –'

Nuresh waved away Ram's protest. 'I am not a young man. And I let myself be charmed by the idea that I could have Anjali for my wife.' With no bitterness, he looked at Ram, nodding slowly. 'But it's time we woke up from the dream, Ram.'

'Nuresh, listen to me . . .'

'No. I'm tired of listening. Anjali does not listen to you. Far better we end our arrangement now.'

Alas, Ram's hopes began to fall.

'Naturally I expect the money I gave you to be returned.'

Hiding his panic, Ram took the offensive. 'So, you are giving up? The great businessman Nuresh Prakash! Is this how you built your fortune? You surprise me,' Ram teased him. 'You fall at the first fence.'

'Leave it, Ram,' advised Nuresh.

'Tell me you love Anjali. It seems your idea of love is as lasting as the summer snow. I can see you are not worthy of her.'

Inflamed, Nuresh faced Ram. 'I love her. I will always love her. But I cannot be married to someone who will make me look foolish.'

'Nuresh, I agree,' Ram assured him in a softer voice. 'Why do we argue? We want the same thing, my friend. Just give me some more time, that is all I ask.'

After due consideration, Nuresh nodded his assent.

'Forty-eight hours, Ram. Middle-aged men cannot afford to be patient.'

As Nuresh turned and walked to his store, one of the employees, who had clearly been watching, scuttled inside. Meanwhile Ram was left alone with a forty-eight-hour ultimatum.

The paramedics had carefully placed Mrs Lawson on a stretched trolly, the drip up and her arm strapped to the post, allowing new blood to flow into her limp body. Her face ashen, she appeared very weak, but alive. Warren stayed close to her, holding and pressing her hand as the paramedics wheeled her from the grocer's shop to the ambulance outside.

On their way past Viv, one of the paramedics turned to her with a comforting smile, touching her arm. 'You did well, love. She owes you one.'

Viv nodded, still rather dazed. She looked over to find Warren staring back at her, the shame haunting his face.

Freddy Calder and John Redwood were among the Specials arriving early for evening duty at the back entrance of Division 'S' headquarters. Worried about Viv Smith, Freddy was down in the dumps over the insensitive remarks he had made to her the last time he had seen her at the Pub on 4th.

'Have you seen Viv . . . ?'

'Not since the other night,' Redwood acknowledged.

His misery confirmed, Freddy nodded. He was about to speculate further when they were interrupted by the appearance of Police Sergeant Andy McAllister at the door.

'Redwood, spare me a minute?'

'Right, Sarge,' Redwood agreed.

'There's something you ought to see,' McAllister said mysteriously.

407

Redwood frowned at Freddy, as they exchanged puzzled looks, then left him to follow the sergeant.

In the office of Cougar Coaches, Bob Loach, in full Specials uniform, brushed himself down, making sure to remove every stray hair, piece of lint, and speck of dust. Finally he put his hat on and adjusted it carefully, then picked up the small mirror to check the results. For just one self-indulgent moment, he savoured the thought of promotion, trying the rank on for size.

'SDO Loach . . .' he murmured. '. . . Sub-Divisional Officer Loach . . . Yeah.'

He smiled upon his noble reflection, then saluted the mirror smartly . . .

It was then that he noticed Noreen standing in the doorway watching him. As he blushed and put the mirror away, Noreen shut the door behind her, then turned back and folded her arms. Loach's anxiety grew as he waited for the storm to break.

Sergeant McAllister nodded to Redwood, indicating the viewing grill, and Redwood took a look inside. In the interrogation room were the four young people – three white, one black – who had steamed an Asian woman at a shopping mall, a crime for which Redwood's client, Denzil Taylor, had been apprehended. The black member of the gang removed a woolly hat, and Redwood gasped in astonishment upon discovering the person to be both female and bald: a teenage girl, no more than sixteen years old, who had shaved her head. He quickly checked with McAllister.

'But . . . she's a girl!'

The sergeant sniffed and shrugged. 'Not that easy to tell, if they shave their heads.' How times had changed since he was a lad, Andy mused. At least no one had any trouble telling the difference, *visually*, between the sexes back then.

Redwood had to ask the obvious question, although he had known the answer for some time. 'So the case against Denzil was completely inaccurate?'

'Looks that way,' Andy replied.

District Commandant Peter Whittaker walked Viv Smith along the corridor of the hospital away from the casualty department. Viv still seemed a bit shaken, and Whittaker braced her arm for support.

'She's going to be okay,' Viv concluded, offering the DC a weak smile. 'Thanks for coming, sir.'

Whittaker had some news of his own he thought she might like to hear. 'I had a very apologetic Mr Maynard from the Building Society on the phone for over half an hour. He wants you back, Viv . . . He said you put the phone down on him. Is that right?'

'I was frightened of what I was going to say to him,' she confessed. She remembered her anger at the way Maynard had fumbled his apology while trying to save himself further embarrassment. Thinking it over, perhaps now was not the best time to express her resentment to Maynard anyway. 'It's better this way,' she concluded.

But Whittaker had yet another surprise in store for her this evening. 'In that case, maybe you'd like to consider working for me?'

'You're joking?'

'I pride myself on being a good judge of people. And I need someone with a good head for figures.'

'Look, sir . . . I . . .'

'Before you say anything, Viv, let me explain. I wouldn't blame you at all for disliking me intensely for what I did when you came to see me. When you asked for my support, I said I could do nothing. But after you left, I kept remembering what I said on that night you reminded me about . . .'

'We're here to support one another?' she suggested in a wry tone.

He acknowledged her memory with a rueful nod. 'But when it came to it, there wasn't a thing I could do. I know I appear a little stuffy to some of the Specials. I'm old-fashioned, don't take a lot of risks.' He stopped short, lifted his head and looked her in the eye. 'But I hope you'll believe one thing. If I could have offered you a job that day, I would have.'

Indeed she was touched, even if his show of concern had been somewhat delayed. 'That's very kind, Mr Whittaker.' Then she added an afterthought: 'And *forgiving* . . . after my outburst at the party.'

'What outburst was that?' he asked innocently.

Gratefully she returned his smile, although she still wanted to keep her options open for a while. 'I'd like to think about the job . . .'

Whittaker nodded while reaching into his shirt pocket. He took

409

out Viv's warrant card, her identification card as a Special, and handed it to her. 'This is yours, I believe?'

She was as amazed to see her warrant card as she would have been to see a magician produce a bouquet of flowers for her out of thin air. 'You didn't turn it in then?'

'I'm a pretty good judge of people, remember?' He winked at her just as they reached his BMW, then stopped to add another thought. 'I hope you'll be available for duty tonight?'

'You bet! Think of all the people who'll have to buy me a drink.'

Whittaker shared a smile, opening the car door for her.

Leaning against the wall of the corridor outside the interrogation room, John Redwood was still trying to cope with the bombshell that new evidence – the gang of young thieves inside the room – would vindicate his client, Denzil Taylor, when he saw the victim of the crime, the Asian woman, walking toward him accompanied by a CID man. The woman also recognized Redwood, and immediately shied away from him.

'You're the solicitor . . . for the . . . ?'

Redwood nodded slowly. Extremely upset, the woman could barely face him.

'I didn't know she was a girl. I thought it was your person. I honestly didn't know.'

'I can see how you made the mistake.' At the least, she had the courage to admit making a mistake in identifying Denzil Taylor as one of the thieves.

Anxiously she looked up into Redwood's face. 'Nothing will happen now . . . with your person?'

'All charges have been dropped against my client,' Redwood assured her.

The woman sighed with relief as the CID man escorted her past the interrogation room. Only when he knew she was gone did Redwood add, to himself: '. . . if I can ever find him to make it official . . .'

26

The Specials were in high spirits, and although DC Whittaker tried to maintain his usual sense of propriety during parade, tonight his audience was irrepressibly rowdy and good-humoured. Modestly convivial himself, Whittaker tried to get into the swing of things as he brought his remarks to a close.

'So, finally, it is with great pleasure that we have Special Constable Viv Smith back in our ranks.'

The reaction was a mix of catcalls, whistles, stamping, howling and cheers. Freddy was transformed with happiness, while Foxy danced on his hand around Viv's shoulder.

'Who loves ya, baby?'

Viv grinned at Foxy and stuck her tongue out at everyone else. Then she turned to Freddy and gave him a hug. 'Thought you'd got rid of me, did you? You miserable old sod!'

As the Specials dispersed, John Redwood positioned himself near the door to hand out photos of Denzil Taylor, one of them to Freddy Calder. 'Keep an eye out for this lad, will you, Freddy? Client of mine . . .'

Freddy looked at the photo again, nodding as he walked out with Viv Smith. They almost bumped into Maggie, the receptionist, who was just entering the parade room to bring a note to DC Whittaker.

When Whittaker received the note, he brought it closer in order to read it, then closer, then closer, unable to decipher the scrawl. 'Is this coded, or are my eyes going?'

Maggie diplomatically took the note back. 'It's from Loach, sir. He apologizes he can't make it tonight, but he has an important business meeting. He's at the Britannia Hotel, if you need to reach him.'

Flustered, Whittaker waved the note away from his sight. 'That won't be necessary, thank you, Maggie.'

The cell area at Division 'S' headquarters was congested with a mob of youths brought in for causing a disturbance by setting off fireworks. One of the wiseguys still had a rocket tucked into his boot, which he was obediently removing under the watchful gaze of Sergeant McAllister.

411

'Okay, so it's not November the Fifth,' the wiseguy argued. 'Does that make it a crime?'

'No,' McAllister reasoned with him. 'But building a bonfire in the grounds of an old folks' home does, laddie.'

As the mob was being moved away, John Redwood walked in with WPC Morrow. She waited near the door while Redwood came to the desk.

'Do me a small favour, Sarge?'

Andy raised one eyebrow. 'What, another one?'

Redwood handed him a wad of photocopies he had made of Denzil Taylor's photo. 'Get your lads to keep a look-out?'

Andy nodded wearily, then noticed WPC Morrow near the door. 'You're with WPC Morrow for your sins tonight, Redwood,' he grunted.

WPC Morrow grinned at the gruff sergeant, and he grinned back. 'Look after him, Mo.'

Waiting outside for WPC Morrow to bring the panda over to pick him up, Redwood decided it would do no harm to check on whether McAllister had taken his request seriously. He leaned over and glanced through the door. Sure enough, Andy was handing out the photocopies to everyone going out on patrol. Smiling to himself, Redwood was reminded that Andy's bark was considerably worse than his bite . . . at least so long as you were on his side of the law.

Dennis, a scruffy kid of 14, waited in the phone box for his call to connect. The phone box was one of the few structures in decent working order in a neighbourhood resembling a bombed-out war zone.

'That the police? . . . Listen, man, it's about the Houldsworth Buildings. Know it? . . . Right . . . I've heard a lot of smashing noises coming from there, glass and that . . . No, can't give ya my name . . . I'm just trying to help, right . . .'

He replaced the phone without finishing the conversation, then turned to receive the delighted whoops and war chants of the gang, all of them young teenagers.

Matt, the leader and oldest (at 17), was outfitted, from top to bottom, in a small braided skull cap, flat-top haircut, a mechanic's overall plastered with badges and emblems of various sorts, a thick leather belt, and baseball boots. He grinned from ear to ear.

'Come on, posse. Let's get ready to give them a warm welcome . . .'

Matt's sniggering passed through each of the soldiers in his gang . . . rather, in his army of trained urban guerrillas.

Redwood was driving when they first received the call on the radio; WPC Morrow had answered it.

'Houldsworth Buildings, possible vandalism? No other details?' she was complaining.

'Nothing, sorry,' responded WPC Sheila Baxter on the radio from the control room at Division 'S' headquarters. 'Anonymous call.'

'Yeah, right, Sheila,' WPC Morrow sighed. 'We're on our way.'

Mo replaced the radio, bracing herself as Redwood made a sharp turn. While scanning the pavements, they were driving down a street getting darker by the moment.

Trying to exorcise her demons of the night by pretending there was nothing unusual out there, Mo picked up the strands of their previous conversation prior to the radio call. 'There's a lot of Denzils out there, John. You can't expect to find a needle in a haystack.'

By then, Redwood was listening without paying any attention to her. He glanced at Mo and nodded, but carried on with the task of searching the dark for signs, either of life or of danger.

At first glance, the warehouse building on a cleared site in an area known as the Houldsworth Buildings appeared normal enough. On closer inspection, however, the ramshackle structure seemed derelict: windows broken or boarded up with rusting corrugated metal; masonry pitted with holes and crumbling into rubble; weeds proliferating everywhere, reclaiming occupancy.

Near the top of the warehouse, there was a very faint light glowing behind one of the broken windows, which was covered by a ragged plastic flap. A shadow moved between the light and the window in silhouette.

The shadow belonged to Denzil Taylor, living alone in a small, shabby, empty room barely lit by a solitary candle. Ragged and tired, he had been sleeping rough for days. Now he was too hungry to sleep, and he had to eat something, anything to take the edge off, even if he didn't have much of anything left.

Hearing a noise outside, he went to the window and pulled the plastic back. He looked down to see the lights of a police car as it laboured over the uneven ground moving toward the warehouse. Frowning at the unnecessary inconvenience, Denzil ducked back behind the plastic curtain.

The panda car jolted to a halt outside the Houldsworth Buildings, and SC Redwood and WPC Morrow got out quickly. But then there was nothing to see or hear, no sights or sounds of vandalism. Rather, it was all eerily quiet.

In the fading daylight of the murky area, WPC Morrow could see that the building was constructed around an open courtyard with a main entrance archway cut in the middle of one side. Straining to see the details of the warehouse, she was suddenly startled by a rustling noise behind her. She turned just in time to see a stray dog running in her direction, then jogging to the side and trotting across open ground. With great relief, Mo caught her breath.

Inside the warehouse on the ground floor, the posse worked in silence under Matt's direction. A large slab of concrete was being pulled into place to an upstairs window, hanging poised and ready to fall into the courtyard.

In an upper room of the building, Denzil could sense something going on below. Huddled under a blanket eating cold baked beans out of a can, he was frozen in place, keeping still, listening. Through the old lift shaft he could hear activity down there, most probably the posse. Yet if the activity did come from the posse, it should have been louder. Then he remembered the police car snooping around outside, and he shivered. Why couldn't everybody just leave him alone?

Redwood didn't like the looks of the situation. Craning his neck and looking up, he had scrutinized every single window and corner he could view from this vantage point. He didn't see a thing, and that was what worried him. Nothing. After an anonymous complaint about excessive noise and destruction, the only sound or motion they found was caused by a stray dog. Something wasn't right, he told himself, and the light was fading all too rapidly.

*   *   *

414

Through the crack in the wall, Matt spotted the uniformed constable outside, hesitating before walking into the trap. But he wasn't running away, so it was only a matter of time. Matt spat at the image.

'Nothing personal, copper. It's just the uniform I hate.'

Looking back into the room, where members of the posse were waiting at their battle stations, Matt surveyed his preparations. He was particularly proud of the old tyres soaked in paraffin, the product of many hours of their labour. Pleased with his plan in the moments just prior to his execution, he shared his grin with the posse, giving them the sign that the hot fun was about to begin.

27

It was a moment of decision: to go forward, or stay back. WPC Morrow looked at the Houldsworth Building and couldn't help feeling a sense of foreboding.

'Don't mind telling you, John. I'd rather face a football crowd who's just lost at home on an own goal. How the hell do we know what we're going into?'

The decision wasn't his alone, and Redwood had to take his partner's doubts into consideration. 'We could sit tight and wait for back-up?' he offered.

Apparently that strategy was hardly a tempting option to WPC Morrow's ego. 'And have a donkey like Coles taking the Mickey? Do me a favour . . .' Mo suggested.

Just then they heard an odd noise from the direction of the building. Though partially covered by Mo's talking, the noise echoed for a moment, sounding as if it might have been human – a yell. They waited, holding their breath, but no other sound broke the silence.

'What'd you think?' Mo asked quietly.

Staring ahead at the warehouse, Redwood didn't answer but shrugged and began to move forward. Swallowing her trepidation, WPC Morrow followed after him while opening the channel on her radio. They walked slowly, picking their way over the rough ground toward the main entrance archway.

'This is Charlie 3, over.'

After a moment's pause, the familiar and welcome voice of WPC Sheila Baxter at control came out of the radio to greet them. 'Come in, Mo.'

'Houldsworth Buildings . . . We're going in.'

'Roger . . .'

Keeping a reasonable space between them, Redwood and Morrow proceeded cautiously to the archway, then stopped. Redwood scanned the empty rubble around them, but beyond it was too dark to see without their torches, which threw only a narrow beam of light. He cupped his hands and shouted into the courtyard.

'Anyone there?'

Their torches crossed the building walls, searching for anything out of the ordinary.

'We're police officers,' Mo yelled. 'Show yourselves!'

There was no response, as her voice reverberated in the empty space bounded by a ghostly fortress.

'This isn't a game,' Redwood warned in a loud voice, though no longer shouting, 'This is a very dangerous building. Someone could get hurt.'

Suddenly a voice echoed back to them from the darkness. 'You're dead right, mister policeman!'

Denzil Taylor had heard the approaching voices of the police outside, and he had recognized one of the voices. Momentarily stunned, he had immediately jumped to the conclusion that they were after *him*. But after hearing the general commotion on the ground floor, he realized that this had nothing to do with him, but rather with the covert activities of the posse over the last few days. Obviously something big was about to happen, and Denzil didn't like the smell of it.

Taking along his guttering candle, Denzil had worked his way down through the gloomy passageways and crumbling stairways to the floor above the ground to get a better view of the courtyard outside and the situation below. As he got closer, he took a last look at a beam across an open space where the floor had collapsed beneath it, and snuffed out the candle. When his eyes had readjusted to the dark, he got to his knees and felt for the beam. Remembering the picture in his mind's eye of where the beam was, he crawled across – balancing ever so carefully – to the other side. He breathed a sigh of relief as he reached safety at the top of a staircase.

From that perch, he could clearly see the room below. There wasn't much movement or noise, but they were there. One of them was holding a rock the size of a soccer ball, with a pile of similar blunt weapons at his feet. Another was hanging onto a rope leading to a primitive pulley system and then to a concrete slab the size of a refrigerator, partly balanced on a ledge by the window. And in the middle of the room was a pile of old tyres all covered with some sort of solidified goo. Denzil could guess what it was.

Stepping over and through and onto the uneven rubble, Redwood and Morrow had reached the bottom of a rise up to the wall where they had thought the voice came from, but the torches showed no sign of disturbance anywhere near.

Maybe the vandals were playing hide and seek, simply trying to annoy them and wear down their nerves in a futile chase through a dark and abandoned building. Redwood rather hoped the scenario was something like that, something harmless, even though unnerving.

The sound of a nearby click startled them. It had come from inside, and to WPC Morrow it reminded her of the cigarette lighter her old boyfriend had used. As she was about to check with Redwood, the ghost of a shadow flew across the wall, and they both looked up in alarm, swinging their torches to see what was going on just above their heads.

Matt, leader of the posse, stood silhouetted on the stairs holding one of the tyres that was starting to burn wildly. Now was his moment of glory. The fire going strong, out of control, he gave the tyre a shove down the ancient stairs, aiming at the uniformed intruders beneath him. He fondly watched the blazing tyre bounce and roll down the stairs, the flames spreading with a whoosh spewing black smoke in all directions.

WPC Morrow screamed as the ball of fire rolled by, narrowly missing them, but her partner simply stared, paralyzed by the sight of another flaming tyre hurtling toward them. Somehow realizing it was up to her, Mo shook herself out of panic and cleared her head just as the second tyre flew by on the other side. She grabbed Redwood's sleeve.

'Come on, John, move it!'

He didn't. And now they were being showered with heavy rocks also landing dangerously nearby. So this time she rattled his bones and shouted in his ear. 'Let's get the hell out! Redwood?' She tugged at him while punching the button on her radio. 'Sheila! Come in, for Christ's sake!'

From above, Matt gazed out at the inferno raging below, and held out his hands for more refreshments to add to the party atmosphere. One of his minions supplied him with a fresh tyre beginning to blaze, and young Dennis was preparing another. The rocks were flying everywhere, as the posse let them have it. Best of all, Matt reasoned, there were only two fuzz out there, both of them were under attack and pinned down, so all of the escape routes remained clear.

Except for one. Perching on the staircase above, Denzil could see everything, fitfully between the spirals of dense black smoke. There was no time to lose. Springing into action, he ran down the staircase to catch the posse by surprise.

At the same time, Redwood and Morrow were making a rush for the building from outside, their way back cut off by choking black smoke and flames and burning tyres spreading more of the toxic fumes. Redwood scampered up the hill as fast as his feet could move, then stumbled into the rubble. Painfully he dragged himself to his feet, concentrating on getting to the stairway directly above him. He couldn't see Mo anywhere ahead of him, but he couldn't look back now.

Smiling down on Redwood, the leader of the posse was taking final aim on his skull, an easy shot from where he stood, as soon as the fire was hot enough so the incendiary bomb couldn't fail to ignite its intended target. But just as Matt was above to rock 'n' roll, he heard a noise above him. He swivelled in time to see the crazy guy from upstairs descending on him with a wild cry.

The force of Denzil's tackle sent Matt flying smack into the concrete wall. The flaming tyre Matt had been holding now simply obeyed the law of gravity and followed his declining path to the wall, bumping into his fallen body and engulfing his torso in the horrible flames.

Matt's screaming pierced the night air, as Denzil tore off his bomber jacket and jumped on the burning body, trying to smother the flames and pull the suffering victim away from the source of the fire.

When Redwood reached the ground-floor room, he recognized Denzil Taylor immediately, and was quick to jump to the conclusion that he was there to help. He took off his own jacket and rushed to join Denzil in extinguishing the fires.

WPC Morrow arrived a moment later and went to assist the injured gang leader. The other members of the posse seemed too frightened to move, let alone escape.

Dennis, the one who had telephoned the police to set the trap, was sobbing and watching in horror. Sirens blared in the distance, getting louder by the second.

But at least the fires had been extinguished. Relaxing just for a moment, Denzil looked over at John Redwood, wary of his reaction to all this, but too tired to run anymore.

Redwood smiled and held out his hand to show he was shaking like a leaf.

28

Surrounded by an impromptu band of rowdy admirers round the bar at the Pub on 4th, Viv Smith was distracted by the gentle tugging on her sleeve. Again Freddy was at her side to plead for a few moments of sympathy in regard to his continuing romance with Rita Loosemore.

'Hey, Viv, let's go somewhere a bit quieter . . . need to talk to you about something . . .'

But this was her night, and this time his problems would have to be postponed. 'No way, not tonight, darling.'

Meanwhile, Police Chief Superintendent Frank Ellsmore and District Commandant of the Specials Peter Whittaker were standing in the doorway watching the festivities. Briggsy the barman spotted the brass and nudged Viv.

'You've some heavy compensation owing tonight, Viv,' Briggsy advised, 'so make the most of it.'

'Don't worry. I intend to.'

Behind her, Freddy popped the cork from a bottle of champagne, setting loose an eruption of foam and of cheering in Viv's honour.

The area approaching the Houldsworth Buildings had become a veritable car park: a blue police light was still pulsing next to the ambulance next to the panda car that had been the first to arrive (with SC Redwood and WPC Morrow) next to several other police cars, most with their headlights still blazing. The police were mostly busy rounding up the subdued members of the posse and bundling them into a van.

As Redwood and Morrow watched the gang leader, Matt, being loaded into the ambulance, he put an appreciative arm around his partner. 'You were great . . .'

Mo smiled and hugged him in return. While in their embrace, Redwood noticed Denzil Taylor nearby and caught his eye. They grinned at each other. Denzil turned around, showing the word POLICE emblazoned on the back of the jacket he was wearing. After checking to make sure it was okay with Mo, Redwood moved toward Taylor.

Still facing in the opposite direction, Denzil turned edgily when Redwood touched his arm, unsure of their relationship now.

'It's all over, Denzil. And thanks . . .' he shook his head. 'You were an idiot to be here in the first place . . . but thank God you were.'

Denzil started to smile when a paramedic behind him swung round and pointed at him. 'Hey! You! Yes, you!' he shouted.

Denzil stiffened. Redwood put a steadying hand on his shoulder, to demonstrate that cooperation was the easier option. But the paramedic chose to grab Denzil's arm. 'Come on, lad. Let's give you the once-over.' He made a cursory examination of Denzil's face and eyes, then sniffed, and winced. 'Not that you deserve it,' he commented with more than a trace of bitterness.

Taking the paramedic's arm much more delicately than the paramedic had grabbed Denzil's, Redwood pulled him to one side, though still within earshot of Denzil Taylor.

'Not him, mate. He saved our lives. This lad's a bloody hero.'

The paramedic backed off with an apology. But Denzil looked at Redwood with a new sense of shared understanding and slowly he smiled in thanks.

*   *   *

Superintendent Frank Ellsmore and DC Peter Whittaker sat talking by themselves at the bar, surrounded though they were by Specials in riotous celebration.

'Had any more ideas about the SDO?' Ellsmore asked. 'I don't think we should leave it too long . . .'

'I agree,' confirmed Whittaker, sipping his whisky.

Speaking of candidates for SDO, Ellsmore looked around the bar for the section officer, remembering he hadn't yet seen Bob Loach that evening. 'I don't see Loach?'

Whittaker couldn't hide his smile. 'My sources tell me he's under house arrest. Thank the Lord, I didn't have to duck him tonight.'

'He's a hard man to shake off . . .' Ellsmore chuckled. Then he looked Whittaker in the eye, '. . . the kind the service needs.'

Whittaker grunted in a begrudging manner, but Ellsmore had already moved over to Viv Smith. As soon as she saw him, she escaped from her conversation and turned to him with a grin that matched his. The others quietened down, as Ellsmore initiated his unofficial inquiry.

'What's all this Cagney and Lacey stuff I've been hearing?' he asked.

Her eyes twinkled, she reached into her bag, and produced the tape recorder, which she placed on the bar for all to see. 'I got it all on this little beauty,' she boasted. 'But in the end, I didn't need it. The threat was enough. Mrs Lawson's signed a sworn statement now.'

Her listeners around the bar applauded, though a bit less raucously than before: more a sign of genuine respect for her guts and ingenuity than of simply having a good time in her name.

'Good work, Viv,' said Ellsmore.

'I still feel a bit shaky when I think about it all,' she confessed with a laugh.

'She obviously needs another vodka and orange, Super,' suggested Briggsy.

Ellsmore smiled and nodded. But before Briggsy left to attend to the order, he suddenly became curious about the tape recorder, he picked it up and raised it to his eye for closer examination.

'Here's a funny thing, sir,' Briggsy remarked.

The Super didn't exactly share Briggsy's curiosity. 'A tape recorder's a tape recorder, Briggsy.'

'No,' Briggsy disagreed, 'not this one.' Everyone gathered round, as he pressed each of the buttons on the tape recorder in turn. Freddy craned his neck over a taller shoulder to see what was happening.

Nothing was happening. Viv couldn't take her eyes off the Walkman. 'What?' she asked no one in particular, thoroughly confused by the tape recorder's malfunction.

Briggsy turned the Walkman around and flicked open the lid to the battery compartment. It was empty.

'It's got no batteries,' Briggsy announced, displaying it to the assembly.

Viv was speechless.

But not Freddy. 'Better make that a double vodka, sir.'

29

Viv Smith got off the bus on High Street and immediately walked over to a shop window where she could catch a glimpse of her reflection to check out the new, summery, black-and-white number she was wearing. Only when her face fell in dismay did it match her feelings about the outfit she had already paid too much for.

'Well,' she concluded, 'you're stuck with it now.'

That decided, there was nothing else she could do abut it, so she dragged herself away from the window mirror and looked around to get her bearings. Because it was a cul-de-sac, High Street looked more like a mews, with a mix of terraced houses, small shops, and lock-ups. The businesses included a body-repair shop, a DIY store, and finally, Whittaker's Printing Works. Arriving at the door, she stopped for a moment, smoothed her dress, took a deep breath, and walked in.

She entered a small, cramped, rather inelegant reception room, used primarily as a collection point for stuff going in or out. A side door led past a glassed-in office, through which Viv could also see a shop floor. On the walls were various samples of the firm's work: letterheads, wedding invitations, business cards, sales brochures, and other ephemera.

A woman Viv took to be a secretary was stacking boxes on the counter. A sharp dresser, thirty-something, and seemingly ice cool, the secretary looked just the kind of woman Viv most envied.

'Can I help?' the secretary asked Viv, expressing just the proper note of disdain.

'Is Mr Whittaker about?'

'Do you have an appointment?'

'Well . . . no,' Viv admitted, caught off-balance. 'But he was expecting me to pop in.'

The secretary looked sceptical, but merely remarked: 'He's at the bank.'

Viv actually felt relieved, though she wasn't sure why. 'Oh. Well. In that case . . .'

'You can wait,' offered the secretary, while hardly extending the warmest welcome. 'He shouldn't be long now.'

Viv nodded, but the secretary kept looking at her, as though waiting for her to go on. Viv tried to figure out what she wanted to know.

'I don't know . . . It's difficult to know if people are serious.'

'Serious?'

'He offered me a job.'

A glimmer of surprise showed on the secretary's stony face.

'He knew I was on the point of resigning, you see,' Viv explained.

'Sorry?'

'He knew I wanted to resign from the Building Society,' Viv went on, but she could see that the secretary was absorbing none of it. 'Look, I'll speak to him tonight down at the station.'

'Ah . . . I think I understand. You must be one of his . . . Specials.'

'That's right,' said Viv with a smile.

'But you look so ordinary,' the woman said, unthinkingly.

Viv was stung.

'I'm sorry. I didn't mean it like that. What I meant was . . . that I wouldn't have you down as a part-time police woman.'

'The regulars look even more ordinary than us.'

The secretary, obviously more experienced than Viv in this sort of bitchy give-and-take, remarked superciliously: 'I wouldn't know. I haven't met any of them. Mr Whittaker's Specials, I mean. He talks about you all, of course. Makes you sound like waifs and strays.'

A few of them did fit the description, Viv admitted. Freddy came immediately to mind. 'Well, some of them do look like something the cat brought in . . .'

Viv stopped short, wondering why she was making herself endure this unpleasant situation, and abruptly she decided to give up the illusion that she was getting anywhere here. 'Look . . . could you tell Mr Whittaker I've had a good think about his offer, and –'

She stopped again and changed her mind again as well, all because of the man who had just entered the reception. He was a hunk: he embodied that indolent, sleepy-eyed sexuality she loved in men. She devoured him with her eyes, in spite of herself.

'You got the new artwork for the Bentley Development, Carol?' asked the hunk, glancing at Viv out of the corner of his eye. 'Oh, I'm sorry. Am I –?'

'No, no,' Viv gave him her shy smile. 'Go ahead.'

Carol, began to answer his query. 'They're in . . .

In a split second, the hunk and Viv exchanged looks: his a quick flirtatious grin, hers an amused smile. The instantaneous rapport between Viv and the hunk did not escape Carol, who was put off her stroke. '. . . in the drawing office,' she finally managed to say.

'You wouldn't be a love and pop up there and get them for me?' he asked Carol with a heart-melting smile.

'Well . . .' Even an ice queen had to consider that kind of persuasion, although she was searching for some reason to say no.

'Only I've got to phone Andrews about the wedding invites,' the hunk added. 'He'll be out if I leave it much longer.' Before Carol could think of an argument, the hunk had turned to Viv. 'This Andrews is a bit of a comedian. He's ordered two hundred wedding invites with a black border round them.'

He threw her a grin, and she smiled back, even though she had no idea what he was talking about. The secretary was not in a mood to budge, though and the hunk gave her a healthy push. 'Don't worry, Carol, I'll stand guard. And I've got this young lady here for back-up.'

'Being a Special, of course, she's used to that,' remarked Carol tartly.

'I get by.'

Unable to find any justification to stay, Carol departed reluctantly.

No sooner had she turned her back than the hunk extended his hand to Viv. 'Dave Hucheson. I'm the Works Manager.'

'Viv Smith,' she introduced herself, shaking his hand.

At this moment, Peter Whittaker walked in from the street. 'Viv! Hello,' he greeted her with a broad grin.

Viv was a bit uncertain as to their understanding. 'Mr Whittaker . . . you suggested I drop by when –'

'Yes, yes,' he interrupted, 'I remember. I'm glad you did. I couldn't be absolutely sure you would,' he suggested, perhaps trying to explain why Carol had never heard of her. 'You never know if people are serious.' Then he took Viv gently by the arm, guiding her toward the side door. 'Come on through.'

As Whittaker escorted Viv to his glassed-in office, Carol returned to reception with the artwork Dave had requested. She observed him undressing Viv through the intervening glass.

'How's Anne and the two kids?' Carol asked Dave sharply.

Dave simply returned a knowing smile. 'Wife's fine. Kids are fine. Thanks for asking. Thanks for asking last week, too . . . when that bird in the hotpants ordered the letterheads.' He turned again to watching Viv, who was concluding a spirited conversation with Whittaker.

'You're so damn sure of yourself, aren't you?'

'You know the answer to that one better than anyone, Carol.'

She slapped down the artwork on the desk in front of him. 'Well, I wouldn't get too hungry for this one. She's not going to take the job.'

As Whittaker ushered Viv back into reception, he turned to his secretary. 'Viv'll be starting next Monday. She'll be looking after accounts.'

Carol's expression was frosty. Dave tossed her a lopsided grin before turning his full attention back to Viv.

Their eyes met, and from that brief moment each knew that this was only the beginning.

30

Freddy looked round surreptitiously to make sure his mother's prying eyes and ears were nowhere near, then crept from the sitting room into the hallway. After a hasty glance upstairs, he went to the telephone and punched out a number.

The phone rang at Rita Loosemore's new flat, which still seemed empty somehow, since there was really not enough furniture from her old flat to fill all the corners here. The phone rang again, and Rita ran out of the bathroom in her wet hair and a dressing gown to snatch the receiver. Peeved at having to go to all this trouble, she told herself that the party on the line had better be worth this aggravation.

'Hello,' she answered.

'It's me,' announced Freddy's voice on the other end.

Rita plopped down on a stuffed chair.

'What do you want, Freddy?'

Keeping his voice low and keeping an eye on the upstairs landing, he set to work straightening out their tangled feelings.

'Why'd you get off like that, Rita?'

'Maybe I'm getting tired of your mother turning up on our dates.'

'How was I to know Ma hadn't been taken to casualty?'

Rita sighed. 'You just can't see it, can you?'

'You were there,' he reminded her. 'I just got this message Ma was in casualty. I wasn't to know . . .' He stopped himself, realizing he was raising his voice, then looked anxiously upstairs again before continuing in lowered tones. '. . . it was the neighbour who'd been taken poorly.'

'You let her take over . . . let her order me into the back of the car like I was so much rubbish! And you were happy for me to get the bus home . . . Again.'

'I couldn't just leave her there, Rita.'

'That's just the point,' she argued. 'You were happy for me to get the bus, but not her.'

'I didn't want you to get the bus. 'I wanted . . .'

'The truth of the matter, Freddy, is that you're married to your mother.' And with that, she slammed the phone down and went back to the bathroom to dry her hair.

Disheartened, Freddy also put the phone down, then picked it up and punched out Rita's number once again. Looking up the stairs, he saw his mother out of the corner of his eye. Hilda Calder stood framed in the kitchen doorway watching him with a stern glare.

'Thought you were upstairs,' Freddy stumbled, embarrassed at being a 38-year-old man caught by his mother calling his girlfriend on the sneak.

'She'll only hang up on you again,' his mother commented acidly.

'It's private, Ma.'

426

'Maybe I don't like being discussed behind my back. Certainly not by the likes of her.'

Although neither of the Calders could see her at the moment, the woman in question was still in her dressing gown and wet hair, still listening as the phone rang next to her while she attempted to lounge on the sofa. Angrily Rita jabbed a cigarette into her mouth and lit it, considering whether to answer the phone and give Freddy another lecture. If it rang another five times, she was going to pick it up and scream into the mouthpiece.

Meanwhile Freddy slammed the phone down with a vehemence that startled even his cold-blooded mother.

'Will you stop this, Ma?' he implored her.

'Stop what?'

'My private life's my own affair,' he insisted. 'For God's sake, I'm nearly 40!'

'I just want what's best for you. I won't be around forever. I want you to take up with a decent girl who'll make you happy.'

Freddy had to laugh. 'Face it. None of them are decent as far as you're concerned. You find fault with all of them.' But it wasn't laughable at all, not to him. 'For crying out loud, Ma, I'm not even past first base with Rita yet. And already you're trying to wreck it.'

'You forget,' she took pains to remind him, 'I've met her. And I know a schemer when I see one.' She shifted in disgust. 'One look. That's all it takes. Men never see these things. Women do, though. Women know women.'

It was no use talking to her, and no use listening to her any more. Freddy threw up his hands in despair as he walked away to mount the staircase. His mother followed right behind, her sermon as yet unfinished.

'You're just like your father. He was led by the nose by his fancy women, too.'

He stopped, then turned to stare in disbelief.

'Oh yes,' she cackled, 'he was carrying on, too. Just like you. The sins of the fathers . . .'

'You're making it up.'

'Why do you think that? Because I haven't mentioned it before? I didn't tell you because I didn't want you to lose your respect for your father.' That was a cruel joke, Freddy was thinking. '. . . and because . . . well, I find it difficult to talk about these things. I tried

427

talking to him about it once. He didn't even have the backbone to own up to it,' she added, her bitterness as fresh as if he were alive.

Freddy just shook his head sadly. 'Sometimes, Ma . . .'

'I don't intend to go through all that again . . . all the hurt your father put me through . . .' After pouring more salt into his wound, she warned him not to open it again. 'You'd better come to terms with that now!'

Lowering his eyes, Freddy just stood there for a moment, then eventually nodded and sighed, and started the long climb. 'Okay, Ma, I'll see to it you won't get hurt.'

'You'll tell her you won't see her again?' she demanded, pursuing her inquiry up the stairs.

'No, Ma, that's not what I meant.' He kept climbing.

'Then . . . ?' What was he trying to get away with this time? She decided she would have to follow him and force a final conclusion to this lunacy.

'I'm leaving,' he said in a quiet voice, not even turning to face her as he reached the top of the stairs.

Though her jaw dropped just slightly, she knew enough not to believe his idle threats. Still . . .

Freddy went into his bedroom, closed the door behind him, locked it, and leaned against the ramparts waiting for his mother's assault, though with a calm determination he had never felt before.

Hilda tried the door handle, surprised and irritated to find it locked. 'Don't be childish, Freddy.'

There was only silence from the other side. She was locked out.

'You were just like this when you were little. With your sulks and tantrums. You'd sulk for hours on end in your room.'

No answer, only more silence.

Her own resentment began to grow, as she recalled the resentments of the past. 'Your father'd always give in to you, of course. He spoilt you. Completely spoilt you.'

Still there was no reaction from Freddy.

'You get more like him the older you get. He was determined to get his way, too . . .'

All at once the lock clicked, the handle turned, and the door opened. Freddy emerged carrying a small travelling case in his hand.

'Where do you think you're going with that?' his mother demanded tartly.

'I'll be back for the rest,' he told her, walking wearily down the stairs of his family home.

She called down after him. 'I hope you don't think I'm going to get down on my knees and beg forgiveness.'

Descending the last stairs, he kept on going, his mother now in hot pursuit.

'This isn't the first time you've threatened this.'

'That's the difference,' Freddy informed her. 'All the other times I just threatened it.' Finally he turned to face her.

'It's for the best, Ma. What the eye doesn't see, the heart doesn't grieve over.'

'You won't find anywhere to stay at this time of day. It'll be dark soon,' she warned, hanging on till the very last second.

'I'll find somewhere,' he shrugged, turning away.

Suddenly she was struck by an inspiration. 'Of course! You're going to *her*. You're going to stay with her.'

Freddy opened the front door and walked out. Only when he was out of the house at last did he turn back for a final glimpse of his mother by the bottom of the stairs, still ranting and raving at him.

'She won't want you! That one's only interested in a good time. She won't want you hanging around the place all hours.'

That was enough. He was gone.

At last reaching the safety of his home away from home – his familiar blue Sierra – he unlocked the front door and opened it. Still no sound of his mother. Freddy threw the travelling case on the front passenger seat, then climbed into the driver's seat.

After closing the door and fastening his seat belt, Freddy allowed himself a last look. 'Bye, Ma,' he whispered. Then he started the car, and pulled away.

Standing in the hallway, Hilda Calder, suffused with anguish now, listened to her son driving away. 'Freddy!' she called to no one. In a trance, she walked slowly to the living room.

As she wandered aimlessly, she spied one of his suit jackets draped over a chair. Carefully she picked up the jacket, smoothing and cradling it, then collapsed into a soft chair in tears. 'Freddy . . .' she gently cried his name.

31

At Division 'S' headquarters in the office of Administrative Secretary Sandra Gibson, 'Mother of all Specials', Bob Loach was at her feet practising his presentation for the interview on his candidacy for Sub-Divisional Officer before the Promotion Board. Step by step, Loach was explaining a complicated flow chart and diagrams relating to his bus company that Sandra found absolutely incomprehensible.

'It's quite simple. We have to have our vehicles up and ready. If a front line bus goes down, we have to have a coach ready,' he repeated.

While it all sounded quite sensible, Sandra was rather bemused by the intricacies, much more impressed by his immaculate uniform. 'So?' she asked again, not sure what she was supposed to make of this.

'So it's just the same with the Specials. We're back-up to the regulars. We have to be ready in case they go down.'

'Is all this meant to be evident from the chart?'

Loach was none too happy with her question. 'The chart's just a learning aid,' he informed her in a somewhat patronizing tone.

Sandra considered whether to encourage him, or to tell him the truth. Which was her duty? 'It's a promotion board, Bob. You're not marketing learning aids.'

Loach decided she simply didn't understand, but he couldn't see why: his diagrams were so clear, so dramatic. 'Look,' he started again, showing her the first chart. 'The flow lines are the stages between one management process and another. Take this box here . . .' He pointed to the box marked PR, then looked up at her with a smile of patient understanding.

'PR doesn't only stand for proportional representation, you know, Sandra,' he quipped. 'It also stands for public relations.'

'Right,' Sandra replied, still none the wiser.

'So why do you think we've got this bottleneck at PR, then?' Loach pressed on.

'Can't wait to find out.'

Loach didn't notice the sarcasm. 'Because too many people keep going down a one-way street. What's needed is some traffic dispersal measures.'

'Traffic dispersal measures? I thought we were talking about –'

Before she got her thought out, he jumped in to complete his own. 'The Specials are seen as a PR problem, when they should be seen as a resource!' he concluded.

Sandra remained blank.

'. . . applying the principles of sound commercial management, that is,' Loach amended, doggedly trying to get through to her.

'Sorry,' she apologized. 'You've lost me.'

'Once you start looking at the Specials from the point of view of whether they're value for money . . . well, they cease being a problem. I mean, you can't get better value than a bunch of lads who cost you nothing.'

'So where's the value for money flow-line, then?' she asked, referring to his flow chart.

'There isn't one,' he answered, now confused himself. 'The point is –'

Sandra stopped him in his tracks. 'Can I give you a piece of advice, Bob?'

He was taken aback, but nonetheless was still willing to listen. 'Sure.'

'Leave the chart here when you go in for the interview.'

Loach looked at her as though he couldn't believe his ears. 'I'm only trying to show them I've got ideas,' he insisted, though no longer so sure of himself.

'I'm sure you are. But Bob . . . these promotion boards are very conservative. Of course they're looking for blokes with initiative, but not a whiz-bang Special with a plan to change the whole police system!'

As he listened to her, she could see that he was considering her message. 'When you go up there,' she explained, pointing a finger upstairs, 'they're judging you against some charlie from what's-his-face's division. They want to know if you're the right stuff for promotion.' She reached over for his charts, and ever so gently began to tug them away from him.

'In other words, Bob, keep your mouth shut until they ask the questions. Then make your answers prompt . . . and short.'

He gazed uncertainly at his stack of charts, now in her hands: hesitating to part with his ammunition and face the interview unarmed, yet knowing in his heart she was right. 'Okay. No chart then.'

Empty-handed, he looked down at his uniform, spotting a non-existent particle of dust and flicking it away. 'It's that damn garage,' he muttered nervously. 'Dust everywhere.'

Sandra beamed at him. 'You look great.'

At that moment of enlightenment, the telephone rang, and Sandra lifted the receiver. 'Sandra Gibson . . . He is, yes. Right. I'll tell him.' She hung up. 'They're ready for you.'

All of a sudden he felt terribly vulnerable, unsure of anything. He swallowed, unable to look her in the eye, fearing her judgment. 'D'you think I'll get it?'

'What do you think?'

He straightened up, and this time he did look her in the eye.

'I'm the best of the bunch, and you know it.'

Sandra merely lifted an eyebrow. 'That's my Bob Loach.'

Although Freddy's precious Sierra had been stolen, partially vandalized, then recovered, and finally restored to sapphire splendour, somehow it remained the one constant in his life of continuous ups and downs. Yet a glance at the travelling case on the passenger seat reminded him that he could not actually live here.

Suddenly coming to an executive decision while pulling into the passing lane, he picked up his car-phone and punched out Rita's number. By now he could almost do it without looking, though he made another executive decision not to test his hypothesis at the moment. The phone rang once . . . twice . . .

Making still another executive decision, he threw down the telephone altogether.

Roz Mitchell was also someone whose identity was revealed by her car, a maroon Volvo Estate littered with baby seats, toys and more kids' junk than she could cope with, yet overflowing with the unmistakable signs of a full and active, though impossibly disorganized life. Nonetheless, the rear window was surprisingly uncluttered, save for two discreet stickers near the bottom that would not obstruct her vision nor impair the safety of her children: GREENPEACE and NO THANKS TO NUCLEAR POWER. The stickers might just as well have read: YUPPIE and THIRTY-SOMETHING.

She pulled the car into a rectangular area next to a parade of

432

shops and parked it there. When she got out of the car, she looked around for some indication that she was in the right place.

Keogh was watching her from an old Ford transit van parked facing her car, at the same time reading the *Star* and munching on a small pie.

Eventually she saw him, then hurried over to speak with him. What she saw was a tall, lean, greasy-haired young man perhaps ten or more years her junior, his youthful attitude characterized by a long, lanky leg carelessly slung out of the van's open door.

'Excuse me,' Roz chirped, interrupting both his reading and his dinner.

Either preoccupied or definitely thick-headed, Keogh seemed only barely capable of lifting his head to acknowledge her presence.

'Do you know if it's okay to park here? Only there are no yellow lines . . .'

Keogh managed to shrug.

So did Roz. 'I thought you might be from round here, that's all.'

'No,' was all Keogh said before going back to his more intellectual pursuits, reading the *Star* and feeding his face.

'I suppose it'll have to be alright,' Roz half-grumbled to herself, seething at the rudeness of some people. 'Thanks for your help,' she added under her breath. Taking care to lock her Volvo, she hurried off to the shopping parade.

Keogh scrunched up the pie bag and tossed it out, then shook the crumbs from his newspaper and folded it neatly. Getting out of the van, he walked to the back and opened the rear doors, then lifted out one of the yellow wheel clamps.

In no particular hurry, he carried the wheel clamp over to the Volvo, and within a few seconds he had quickly fitted the clamp to the inside of the rear wheel. Then he got up and strolled to the front of the car, where he sellotaped a notice to the windscreen.

Returning to his van, Keogh shut the rear doors, got back in, and slammed his door. He whistled tunelessly through his teeth, looking casually in the direction of the shops, and turned the ignition.

32

Just in time Freddy spotted an old Ford transit van pulling out of the parking area outside the shopping parade and heading straight for a collision with his Sierra. He swerved to the side while jamming his hand hard on the horn.

Half out of the parking area and into traffic, the imbecile driving the van – one Keogh by name, though Freddy never would have known – finally decided to brake. Freddy's quick detour allowed him just enough room to miss the van by a whisker.

Once past, Freddy turned round and screamed bloody murder at the imbecile, though it was surely a waste of precious breath. What to do, he brooded, about all those imbeciles who failed to respect the conventions of human society. He couldn't keep his mind on such issues forever, though, as thinking about social conventions led him back to thinking about his mother, and that led him back to Rita, which was exactly where he was going anyway, no matter how he might try to avoid dwelling on the immediate problem.

When he finally got there, the Sierra pulled up outside a three-story block of flats that, to Freddy's eye, looked quite new and attractive. He switched off the engine, while he remained seated behind the wheel, looking off moodily at the flats.

Truth be told, he didn't know what to do next.

When Roz Mitchell returned from the shops with all of her bundles, she first had to find some way to set each of them down without dropping and breaking anything: a challenging task in itself. Then she had to search through her bag to find the car keys, and that seemed to take forever as well. At last she found them, but as she fumbled to find the right one, she happened to notice something behind one of the rear tyres.

Moving closer, she saw what it was, although she had never seen a wheel clamp until that moment. Cupping her hand over her mouth to keep from screaming, she was horrified to find her Volvo, and herself, made prisoner.

Rita was depressed, as might easily be discerned from her choosing to wear her floral kimono. Listlessly she turned over the toast under the grill, then proceeded to break a couple of eggs into the small frying pan. Wandering to the sink, she stared aimlessly out the window for a while, switching on the radio, trying another channel, and switching it off again.

She was on her way across the room to check if the curling tongs had heated up when the doorbell rang. With a sigh, she went back to the oven and took the eggs off the heat. Then she went to see who was at the door.

When she opened the door and saw Freddy standing there with an apprehensive smile on his face, she might have been surprised a bit, but hardly shocked.

'Freddy,' she announced. She was not thrilled to see him.

'Is now a good time?' he asked.

'Well . . . not really. I was going out soon.' The state of her costume suggested that she had no more concern for truth in conversation than he did.

'I tried ringing . . .'

'What do you want, Freddy?' Although Rita wasn't usually so blunt, at the moment her patience was severely limited by a headache.

He tried to find the key to her forgiveness. 'I know you're annoyed about this hospital business . . .'

'Annoyed? I'm bloody furious! That's the second time I've had to get a bus home.'

The smallest argument defeated his spirit, and he became downcast. 'Look . . . I'll go. I can see you're upset.'

'That's it,' Rita sarcastically agreed. 'Walk away. If someone turns the heat up, you just do a disappearing act.'

'But if you're going out . . .' Freddy reminded her.

She sighed. 'I just said that,' she confessed. But then, abruptly, she sensed something amiss, sniffing the air.

'The toast!'

Charging off to the kitchen, she called back to him over her shoulder. 'Well, don't just stand there looking pathetic!'

The door was open. Freddy reached for his travelling case, hidden out of sight until now – or, rather, not previously exposed to view – and entered Rita's flat, closing the door behind him.

In the meantime, Rita consigned two pieces of charred toast to her pedal bin and switched off the grill. When she returned to find Freddy in her half-empty living room, however, her heart softened.

435

'Sorry about the smell. I forgot to turn the grill off.'

Freddy glanced around the sparcely furnished room, his smile beginning to wear a bit thin. 'Still got a few holes to fill, I see.'

'And a hundred and one things to do,' she said in her own defence. 'It's just a question of getting round to everything.' And having money, which she conveniently thought not to mention.

Trying to become more accustomed to a strange environment in a short time, he wandered about, making conversation. 'They say moving's one of the most traumatic things you can do . . .' He picked up a dead plant from the window ledge. 'I see this didn't survive the move.' He wondered if *he* would.

Rita came up behind him. 'Probably not used to being blasted by the sun all day. It's a south-facing . . .'

Halting mid-sentence, her jaw dropped, and she stared at an object standing flat up against the sofa that vaguely resembled luggage.

'Going somewhere?' she asked pointedly.

Freddy thought a moment. 'No . . .'

'That's what I thought,' she concluded.

He could feel the door closing, shutting him out. 'Listen, you keep saying I'm a weakling and gutless . . . but I'm not!' he protested.

'Look, Freddy . . .'

'I had it out with her, see. With Ma, I mean. Told her straight she was screwing everything up.' He thought that he noticed her perk up a little after that revelation. 'You'd have been proud of me. I know you wanted me to stand up to her more.'

'But that doesn't mean –'

'I had to get out, Rita,' he interrupted, desperately needing to complete his confession. I'd've burst if I hadn't.' He looked sadly and longingly into her eyes. 'It was as bad as that.'

She tried to hold back what she knew was coming, hoping she could contain him somehow. 'Hang on, Freddy. Before you say what I think you're going to say . . .'

He swallowed, but didn't take his eyes away from hers. 'I know it's not fair to drop you in it like this . . .'

'I'm not looking for a lodger, Freddy,' Rita informed him. 'Do you hear what I'm saying?'

He heard, but tried to deny, appealing to her as a friend, and as a woman. 'I need time,' he said softly, repeating a phrase he had often heard women say. 'Time to sort everything out. I can't think straight at the moment.'

He could say that again. 'You want me to make it easy for you,' said Rita resentfully. 'You want to leave one ready-made home and just plonk yourself down in another!'

Freddy backed away from the onslaught. 'I just thought . . .'

It was no use. 'For God's sake, I don't even know what sort of relationship we've got here! Or even if we've got one at all!' she said. 'One kiss in the car . . .'

He looked up, hoping it was starting to get better now.

'. . . Well, it's hardly a basis for living together.'

'Just until I get myself sorted out. Please, Rita. I promise I won't get in the way.'

Incredulous, at both Freddy and herself, she shrugged in surrender and flopped down on the sofa, wondering at her own sanity. Yet she was moved by his plea, knowing what it was like to worry about having a roof overhead.

So she relented, and decided to make the best of it just for the time being. Welcome home. 'I was about to sit down to some scrambled eggs on toast when you arrived,' she admitted.

'And I've ruined them,' Freddy guessed.

'Too bloody right,' she confirmed. 'So . . .' A glimmer of a smile began to appear on her lips. '. . . you're going to have to take me out to dinner.'

All at once, after all that careful build-up, his face fell and he went back to being sheepish again. 'Ah . . .'

'What?'

'I'm on duty tonight,' Freddy finally told her. His uniform was stuffed into the travelling case.

Too boiling mad to screech, Rita looked down at the case, then looked up to Freddy, then looked and pointed to the door.

33

Keeping her Volvo in sight – although it certainly wasn't going anywhere with a wheel clamp locked on – Roz Mitchell stood in an open phone kiosk holding the notice that had been plastered to her windscreen and shouting till she was blue in the face.

'I want it unclamped! . . . No – *now!* You get someone down here *now!* . . . That's blackmail! . . . You've got no right . . . Okay, we'll see what the police have to say!'

She slammed the phone down and tried hard not to cry. The sun was beginning to set.

While DC Whittaker presided over parade, several of the familiar faces – Bob Loach, Viv Smith, Freddy Calder, Anjali Shah, John Redwood – seemed disturbed, with more than the usual shuffling, coughing, and fidgeting on the line. Clearly it was not the most electrifying parade and Whittaker's rambling remarks weren't helping to galvanize them.

'Just as well the Inspector has nothing planned for us tonight . . . in view of our depleted numbers. Still, I'm sure something'll turn up. It always does. Criminals don't go away, do they?'

He paused, but 'no comment' seemed to be the answer.

'Now . . . what else? Oh yes.' Whittaker surveyed the troops. 'I'm hoping you'll have a new SDO before long. The board met today, and the quality of candidates for the post was extremely high.'

His gaze happened to stop at an embarrassed Bob Loach, who stared down at his feet. Looking back at his clipboard, Whittaker resumed: 'Well, let's run quickly through the roster . . .'

Something was wrong. He took a closer look, then smiled. 'Glad I spotted that. I was just about to read out last night's roster.'

Loach traded glances with Freddy, who rolled his eyes.

Having forgotten her coat, Roz Mitchell huddled in the driver's seat of her imprisoned Volvo, Radio 3 playing above the noise of the engine running and the car heater blowing out warm air. Suddenly she saw two bright headlights growing larger in the driving mirror.

Keogh stopped the old Ford Transit van behind the Volvo, turned off the ignition, and took his time disembarking from the vehicle, in no particular hurry to listen to another tirade.

As soon as Keogh got out of the van, Roz marched up to him and recognized him right away – the person who had *not* warned her to avoid parking in the spot where her Volvo was now held immobile.

'You can get that thing off my car right now!'

'You know the charge for declamping,' he droned. 'It's on the notice.'

'I'm not paying you a penny,' Roz refused. 'You're not the police.'

'I don't want a penny. I want seventy-five quid.'

'If you think I'm going to hand over that kind of money, you've another think coming.'

'Suit yourself,' Keogh shrugged, starting back for the van.

She shouted after him. 'You let me park here without telling me who you were!'

He turned again to face her, a menacing look in his eyes. 'Look, lady . . .'

'I asked you earlier if it was okay to park here.'

Keogh played deaf. 'You going to pay the fine or not? If not, you're just wasting my time.'

'I want to know by what right you can come along and clamp people's cars!' she demanded.

He winced, her voice hurting his tender ears. 'Don't shout at me, lady. You won't get your car declamped by shouting at me.'

'I can get a lot louder that this!'

Yet before she could make good on her threat, someone distracted her attention. Weaving through the small group of onlookers who had gathered around the altercation were two Specials, Viv Smith and John Redwood.

'All right, what seems to be the trouble?' Redwood asked, as he and Viv broke through into the circle.

'This . . . this man clamped my car,' shouted Roz Mitchell, barely able to spit out the words.

Keogh immediately dismissed her complaint. 'I don't need no police permit to carry out clamping.'

'You expect me to believe that?' Roz shouted at him.

Redwood tried to calm her down, and, as a solicitor, he did know what he was talking about. 'That's correct in law, I'm afraid. He doesn't actually need a permit.'

'What!' Roz was incredulous at the injustice of it all.

'All I need is the permission of the owner of the space,' said Keogh with a sneer.

'And who might that be?' Viv asked.

Keogh pointed to the parade of shops. 'The Chinese takeaway over there.'

'Are you saying I've got to pay the fine?' Roz howled.

Again Redwood tried to explain the law. 'It may not be entirely fair . . .'

'You're telling *me* it isn't fair!'

Viv put herself in front of the angry woman. 'Calm down. This isn't helping anyone.' Neither of them noticed that Redwood was then blocked from their view, soon slipping away unobtrusively through the surrounding onlookers.

Meanwhile, Roz Mitchell was becoming incensed at Viv. 'Calm down?' she laughed cynically. 'I've been here an hour and a half. The kids are still with a neighbour. And we've got people coming to dinner at eight.' She stared at Viv, as if she expected more understanding and sympathy from a woman.

Getting no satisfaction, Roz marched to her Volvo, Viv and some of the crowd slowly following. 'Well . . . if you're not going to do anything . . .' Opening the hatchback, Roz rummaged through the kids' junk until she found the toolbox, then lugged it out and set it down. She unfastened and opened the lid, taking out some sort of iron implement resembling a jemmy.

Viv spoke to her in a low voice as Roz kneeled down with her weapon. 'Look, love, I'd think about what you're doing if I were you.'

Roz paid her no mind and immediately set about trying to wedge and wrench the clamp off the wheel. Keogh hadn't been watching closely until he saw Roz Mitchell duck down below the shoulders of the onlookers out of his view. When he finally made his way through the onlookers and saw what she was doing, he turned to Viv.

'Are you just going to let her vandalize my gear, then?'

Viv considered interfering, but too late. With a mighty jerk of the iron jemmy, Roz snapped the clamp. Victorious and contemptuous at the same time, she pulled the clamp clear of the wheel, then stood up to Keogh.

'Right. What are you going to do about it?'

While previously languid, Keogh was now worked up to the point of strangling Roz Mitchell, but as he moved to threaten her, Viv Smith once again interposed herself between them.

'Can we all please calm down?' Viv demanded, a threat in her voice as well. Quickly she checked the vicinity for signs of Redwood, but now that she really needed him, he was nowhere to be found.

'That's criminal damage, that is,' charged Keogh, now fighting mad. 'And all you do is stand there and do sod all!'

There was no denying that Viv was getting rattled, even frightened, for Keogh was getting angrier by the moment. She tried to hold him off for as long as she could.

'Do you want to swear out a complaint against this woman, sir?'

'Too right I do. I want her nicked! Now!'

Just as Keogh leaned down into Viv's face, she heard John Redwood's voice close by. 'Hold on a second, Viv.'

Keogh pulled back and Viv straightened up. Standing next to Roz Mitchell and Redwood were two rather small though solemn Chinese gentlemen.

'This is Mr Lee,' Redwood introduced the older gentleman. 'He's the owner of the takeaway. And this is his son,' Redwood gestured, indicating the junior.

Keogh nodded his head aggressively at the elder Chinese gentleman. 'I've met Mr Lee.'

Redwood turned to question Keogh. 'That would be when you spoke to him about his parking space?'

Keogh shrugged. 'Stands to reason we'd've had a natter at some point.'

'The question is – what about?' Redwood asked him. 'As you know, sir, Mr Lee doesn't speak English too well. And it seems he misunderstood what you said. His son tells me that Mr Lee thought you were a cleaner.'

The junior Lee spoke up to confirm Redwood's interpretation. 'Cleaner – yes. From the council.'

'A cleaner?' Keogh scoffed, quickly attempting to discredit Junior. 'Are you serious?'

'Well, he seems to know nothing about giving you the right to clamp vehicles.'

Keogh objected vehemently. 'Oh, I get it. I'm being made to look the bad guy around here.'

The younger Mr Lee shook his head at the bad guy. 'My father does not want trouble with authorities.'

Attacked from all sides, Keogh turned on Lee the younger. 'I made it perfectly clear to your old man what this was all about. He seemed very happy with his percentage.' Keogh had pulled a folded scrap of paper from his pocket, and he waved the paper in front of the younger Chinese gentleman's nose. 'Is that – or is that not – his signature?'

Redwood continued his objection. 'But if Mr Lee believed he was signing a paper signifying that the areas had been cleaned . . .'

'Too bad,' Keogh shook his head angrily. 'This gives me the right to protect his parking space.'

Redwood paused for effect. 'I'm afraid not.'

'What?' Keogh bawled.

'Mr Lee's son tells me one of the conditions laid down by the council was that this area be made freely available to shoppers.'

'Does this mean I don't have to pay the fine?' Roz asked gleefully.

'Exactly that,' Redwood assured her.

Roz turned to the helpless Keogh, beaming her pleasure. Finally she laughed and turned her back on him, glancing at her watch. 'Well, I've got just over an hour to prepare a three-course meal for six people.' She replaced the toolbox, closed the hatchback, and walked round to her door.

As Roz started the engine, Viv Smith leaned down and offered her a word of advice. 'I suppose I ought to warn you about breaking open clamps. You may not be in the right next time.'

'Don't worry,' Roz laughed. 'I don't make a habit of it.' And with that, she rolled up the window and drove away.

As they walked over to the van, Viv confided with Redwood in a low voice: 'God! I've always wanted to do something like that. It must've felt great.' Not one to wear his heart on his sleeve, Redwood seemed content with a slight smile.

Meanwhile the small crowd of onlookers had begun jeering and applauding as Keogh took his shattered clamp and dumped it in the back of his van. Just as he closed the rear doors and was about to make his escape, Viv stopped to have a final word with him.

'One other thing, sir. Does it have an up-to-date motor insurance?'

Thoroughly frustrated, Keogh sloughed off her inquiry with a shrug. 'There's nothing wrong with this van . . .'

Viv stood in his path and cocked her head. She wanted an answer. Finally he surrendered. 'I don't carry it around with me.'

Viv just grinned, happily writing out an HRT pad. 'That's okay, sir . . . as long as you produce it at a police station within five days.'

Before leaving, she wrote down the number of the van in her

notebook, then looked up at Keogh. 'Just to be on the safe side. We don't want your vehicle being impounded, do we, sir?'

34

Bob Loach and Anjali Shah were walking their beat on a suburban street, Loach complaining about his tribulations with DC Whittaker and his interview for promotion to SDO, Anjali keeping a watchful eye on the neighbourhood while only half-listening to her partner.

'You heard Whittaker,' Loach grumbled. '"The Inspector has nothing planned for us tonight." Those were his words.' Briefly interrupting his diatribe, he checked to make sure that the door to the paper shop was secured. 'It's bad management. A failure to make proper use of resources.'

Meanwhile Anjali was observing a battered Datsun cruising slowly by on the other side of the street in a rather suspicious manner. There appeared to be three youths in the car, and the driver seemed to pick up a bit of speed as he passed the uniformed Specials, perhaps concerned about attracting any attention. The young people seemed to be crouching and hiding from view, as well as searching each of the shops along their route.

'Still, it won't take long now,' Loach continued, referring to the promotion process.

Anjali pointed across the street. 'We've still got the other side to do yet.'

Loach wasn't listening. 'I meant before the promotion board makes its decision.'

The Datsun Anjali had been watching turned down a side street, Gifford Road, and disappeared, although Anjali couldn't take her mind off the image of the young men cruising around and looking for trouble.

'Well, as long as you felt it went okay,' she mumbled.

'The important thing to remember is keep your answers short and to the point.'

Again Anjali was only half-listening, more interested in an elderly, turbanned Sikh on the other side of the street. He was a short but stocky man with a small, military-style moustache and an erect,

443

dignified bearing. Just discernible at this distance were three military medals of some kind on his chest.

'Of course, it's how you handle these people,' Loach continued. 'It's not just a question of agreeing with everything they say, you see.'

Walking on just ahead of her partner, Anjali checked the door of a fishmonger's shop. When she looked back almost across the street, the elderly Sikh gentleman had moved on, almost certainly down Gifford Road, the side street where the Datsun had disappeared only moments earlier.

'I mean . . . what you don't do is barge in there and tell them how to run the police force . . .'

Anjali stopped suddenly, and Loach nearly collided with her. 'I don't like it,' she said, her eyes gazing off to Gifford Road.

The elderly Sikh, Shambji, was coming down the alley when he saw three youths blocking his way. As he approached them warily, gradually he slowed, then came to a stop.

'Evening, Granddad,' mocked one of the youths, apparently their leader. He turned to the side to share a joke with his buddies. 'He should be tucked up in bed with his Horlick's.'

Shambji, sensing the danger, yet unafraid, pulled himself up to his full height. He had been a soldier for many years, and was not easily pushed around.

'Will you move out of the way?' he asked politely, 'I wish to pass.'

'We just want to know the time,' the leader said, his attitude suggesting otherwise.

Gingerly taking out his fob watch, Shambji clicked it open, and the music box played *The British Grenadiers*. Smiling, he looked into the face of the watch. 'This time is now . . .'

'Hey! Real funky, Granddad,' enthused the leader, snatching the watch. 'What else you got – a guitar in there?'

'I would ask you to return my watch,' Shambji requested firmly, bracing himself for more trouble.

The leader merely laughed. 'You've got bottle, Granddad. I'll give you that.'

'Your families have not taught you respect,' the elderly Sikh admonished them.

His observation was greeted with hoots of laughter and derision from the three youths. 'So why don't you teach us?' inquired the smallest of them.

The leader moved in closer to Shambji, clearly threatening him with harm. 'I asked you what else you got . . .'

Instinctively the old gentleman made a quick, involuntary move to his inside pocket, then realized he had given away his secret.

'Turn out your pockets,' ordered the leader, as the others moved in, surrounding Shambji.

'So . . . cowards, too,' he nodded, with no further recourse than to put up his fists in self-defence.

WPC Sheila Baxter clicked off her microphone in the control room at Division 'S' headquarters and turned to Police Sergeant Andy McAllister, busy checking through a pile of dockets.

'I knew it was only a matter of time,' she said, Andy squinting up at her with a puzzled expression as to what she might be talking about. 'A complaint from Alfredo's,' she explained.

Of course, McAllister knew of the place, had even seen it from the outside, but he had never accumulated the fortune required to set foot inside. And if, by some miracle, he had indeed acquired sufficient wealth, he'd never dream of spending a penny of it at Alfredo's.

'Customer find a rat bone in his nouvelle cuisine?' he quipped.

Baxter shook her head. 'Sounds like someone doesn't like the size of his bill.'

'Lot of bawbees, that place,' Andy observed. 'Cheapest bottle of plonk is thirty quid. God knows what they charge for mince and tatties.'

'There but the for grace of God, eh, Sarge?' Sheila grinned.

McAllister frowned. 'I hope that wasn't a veiled crack about Scotsmen blowing the moths out of their wallets,' he warned.

'Never,' Sheila replied. 'Thought you ate there every night.' She ran her finger down the roster, looking for a likely candidate. Her finger stopped at Mo. 'WPC Morrow's on panda duty there. I'll get her to check it out.'

McAllister across the table in an attempt to see the roster. 'Who's on with her?'

'Uh . . . Special Freddy Calder.'

445

The trace of a rare smile appeared at the corner of Andy's mouth. 'If there's any evidence, he'll probably eat it before he gets back . . .'

'We can't even be sure he came down here,' Loach protested as he walked along Gifford Road with Anjali.

'I'm sure,' she insisted.

Loach just shrugged, willing to go along with her judgement for a while. 'Well . . . there's no sign of the car . . .'

'Something wasn't right,' Anjali repeated for the umpteenth time, her eyes darting here and there in search of something out of place. 'They were looking for trouble.'

They stopped at the mouth of an alley. Loach tried to calm her nerves. 'It's an easy trap to fall in, Anjali. Three kids in an old banger, and the warning bells ring. Likely as not, they're just out for a good time.'

Anjali saw something down the alley, a pile of clothes perhaps, half in and half out of the light from the alley's only streetlamp. Loach turned and saw the something as well. Then they recognized the something as a body.

'It's just a drunk,' Loach surmised from the look of the situation.

Anjali blinked, starting to move. 'No. That's the man I told you about.'

As they got closer, Loach noted that there was no covering on the head of the body. 'But Sikhs would rather die than be seen without their turbans,' he called after her.

'That's what worries me,' Anjali answered, breaking into a run.

When she reached the body, immediately she knelt down, shocked at what she saw. 'Oh no . . .' There was blood streaming from the man's face, his eyes fluttering weakly; he appeared to be near death. She snuggled the old man in her arms, as Loach came up behind her and buttoned his radio.

'Section Officer Loach to Sierra Control. Over.'

Semi-conscious, the old man brought his hand up to his bare head.

'His turban,' Anjali guessed. 'He wants his turban.'

Loach quickly looked around for the turban, as WPC Sheila Baxter's voice came to them from the radio.

'Go ahead. Over.'

'Request ambulance immediately for Gifford Road,' Loach reported into the radio. 'Adult male with head injuries. We don't know how severe yet. Over.'

'Understood. Out.'

Loach spotted the turban over by the wall and quickly went to retrieve it. 'Looks like they've used it for a football.'

'While he was wearing it, judging by the state of him,' Anjali observed, cradling the old man in her arms. Loach handed her the turban, and she gently eased the turban back on the old man's head.

The old Sikh's eyes opened, though his vision was remote, looking somewhere far away. 'I am so ashamed . . . I could not defend myself . . .'

Anjali laid him down carefully, trying to comfort him with her soothing voice. 'Rest. An ambulance is on the way.'

Standing up beside Loach, she immediately tugged out her notebook and offered it to him. Quizzically he stared back at her.

'The number of the car,' she suggested.

Loach took the notebook from her and looked at the first page. There was the number. 'Thinking on your feet,' he said, truly impressed. 'I never even . . .'

'You had other things on your mind,' she recalled with a nudge.

He nodded sheepishly, flicking back the cover of the notebook and buttoning the radio again to sound.

35

The ultra-chic Alfredo's was tucked down the end of the mews, announcing its presence only with a striped awning and a discreet sign in flowing neon script. WPC Morrow and SC Freddy Calder got out of their parked panda, the latter most eager to witness and perhaps to sample the culinary delights within.

'I wonder if they do takeaways . . .'

As they entered the foyer on their way to the dining room, Freddy sniffed the air, and his appetite soared. 'Maybe I'll save up and bring Rita here. It beats scrambled eggs on toast.'

Mo smiled, while Freddy stepped up his pace. At the entrance to the dining room, he gazed into paradise: the angels dressed divinely, eternally serene and endlessly amused, their only purpose to relish tasting an infinite variety of the most exquisitely delicious foods in heaven, and enjoy them forever.

'No! Not there,' called out the voice of the manager, as he hurried to head off the slightly overweight Special.

Freddy was distracted by the manager, whose name, he had been informed by WPC Baxter over the radio, was Sergio. The diminutive Sergio had anxiety written all over his face, and Freddy's longing gaze into the dining room was not helping the manager's mood.

'This way, please. My office.' Sergio requested, though it may have sounded more like an order. The manager also signalled to WPC Morrow with an imploring look in his eye, perhaps hoping that Mo might do something to stifle Freddy.

The office of this grand palace of the palate, as it turned out, was rather small and drab. Sitting in the corner was a middle-aged gentleman who, by his clothing, appeared to be the typical Scotsman.

'This is Mr Menzies,' Sergio gestured toward the Scot as WPC Morrow and SC Calder came in. 'He does not pay his bill.'

Hamish Menzies, florid of face and expansive of temperament, as well as waistline, leaped from his chair to greet the officers. '*Mingis*, officers. Spelt Menzies, but pronounced Mingis.'

Sergio was unimpressed. 'Mingis, Menzies . . . he still does not pay.'

'Correction, my good man,' Menzies boisterously interrupted. 'I have never failed to honour a debt or discharge an obligation in a long, interesting, and only occasionally disheartening life.'

WPC Morrow stepped in to clarify the situation. 'Let's get this clear,' she addressed Sergio. 'You're saying this man here refused to pay his bill?'

'I already say this two times,' Sergio fretted. 'He must pay.'

An affable smile on his ruddy face, Menzies appealed to Morrow for sympathy. '"Refuses" is an emotive word, officer. "Temporarily unable to commit the necessary funds" would be closer to the mark.'

Sergio could barely contain his fury. 'You will pay, or I have the police arrest you!'

Menzies ignored him, continuing his commentary to Freddy Calder and WPC Morrow. 'Let me explain. I arrived in your much underrated city late this afternoon . . . checked into my hotel . . . took my usual constitutional. I needed sustenance after my long and arduous journey, and came upon and rejected many an eaterie before selecting this estimable establishment. Imagine my distress when –'

Mo cut him short in an attempt to edit his rambling remarks. 'So what you're saying –'

But Menzies hardly paused for breath. 'Imagine my distress when I found that I had omitted to transfer funds or articles of identification from my travelling clothes to my gadabout clothes! It is this oversight that has brought me to this wretched and humiliating state.'

Throughout the discourse, Sergio kept shaking his head. 'They will try anything not to pay. Even be sick in the toilet. So they can take us to the public health!'

Menzies turned to the manager with exaggerated courtesy. 'I had no quarrel with the bill, sir. The bill was equitable enough. As was the service. I would have given more than an adequate tip – a tip reflecting my sense of well-being – if my funds were not languishing at this minute in my travelling clothes at my hotel.' Then he added an afterthought. 'And *if*, of course, service wasn't included.'

Sergio dismissed his assurance with a wave of disgust. 'Enough of this. He wastes my time.'

Instantly Menzies jumped at the manager's remark. 'Ah! An interesting choice of words, under the circumstances. You see, our friend here neglects to mention my offer to leave my watch as a pledge.'

'Your watch?' Freddy asked, suddenly curious.

'Let it go on record that I made the offer,' Menzies insisted to Freddy. 'You can take it down in writing, and use it against me at a later date. I offered a timepiece of great market and sentimental value to offset against the bill.' Taking out his watch, his thrust the timepiece of great market and sentimental value under Freddy's nose.

Freddy's eyes stared out of their sockets. 'Is that a Rolex Oyster you have there, sir?'

'What?' asked Menzies absent-mindedly. 'Oh – the watch. Yes, I think so. I didn't actually buy it,' he admitted. 'I was given it by my dear wife, for our twenty-fifth.' Looking fondly upon his treasured watch, Menzies for the first time lapsed into an uncharacteristic silence.

WPC Morrow couldn't quite swallow the Scotsman's supposed

naiveté. 'And you'd give something of sentimental value to a total stranger?'

Menzies, however, was quick to contradict her. 'No, no. That's just it. I'd return as fast as it took a horseless carriage to whisk me to my hotel and back. I'd probably even urge its driver to contravene the bylaws of your parish in hurrying me back here.' He gestured to include Sergio in his plan. 'I would also insist that our friend here store it in his safe.'

Freddy smiled and shook his head, taking a more trusting view than his partner. 'I doubt if that'd be necessary, sir. I'm sure the manager could be trusted to –'

Again Menzies interrupted to disagree. 'I'd have to insist on that. You see, it's not just the fact of our twenty-fifth.' His eyes began to water with tears. 'My wife died the day before our anniversary.'

'Oh . . . I'm sorry,' said Freddy in embarrassment.

Audacious and ebullient just a moment before, Menzies at once became glum. 'Fate showed us the winning line, and then at the last moment revealed it to be a mirage. Just one day,' he lamented. 'Surely one day wasn't too much to ask for?' He looked at each of them, then turned away, overcome with grief. The listeners averted their eyes as well.

Finally Freddy spoke up. 'So which hotel are you, uh, booked into, sir?'

'The Marchmont.'

'You legged it all the way from the Marchmont?' Freddy asked, wondering at the Scotsman's intelligence after all.

'Sturdy highland stock, officer. Used to walk ten miles as a young sprout to the kirk every Sunday. And even further in my courting days.'

Despite the storyteller's colourful conversation, Freddy was distracted by his own thoughts. 'Would you, uh, excuse me for a moment, gents?'

'What?' asked a confused WPC Morrow, as Freddy ushered her out of the small office. When they reached the foyer, she halted and confronted him. 'What was that all about?'

'Listen,' whispered Freddy, 'that guy doesn't just talk, he recites monologues. You want to write up this report? It'll take all night. No. I'll tell you what I'm going to do . . . I'm going to pay Menzies's bill.'

'Oh yeah?' she questioned, not quite believing him.

'Seriously,' he affirmed, strangely humourless and out of character. 'I pick up the tab. And Mr Menzies gives me the Rolex as security.'

'You're *not* serious,' she argued, still looking for a twinkle in his eye.

'How can I lose?' he asked. He was serious.

'And if this Mingy-thingy doesn't show?'

Freddy scoffed at her ignorance. 'Have you any idea what a watch like that costs?'

'Two hundred?'

'Five would be closer.'

His mind made up, Freddy started back to the office, with a sceptical WPC Morrow in tow. 'In fact, part of me hopes he doesn't show.'

Mo shook her head with a sigh. 'Once a salesman . . .'

Entering the office again, Freddy took the lead. 'I think, gents, we've got a way out of this impasse.'

Already Sergio was objecting to what he assumed Freddy was about to propose. 'No washing up. I don't put him to work on the washing up. He pays the bill.'

'I was going to suggest I act as banker. I pay the bill. And look after the, uh, collateral.' He smiled at each of them. 'How does that sound?'

Try as he might, Sergio could discover no immediate objection. 'I don't care who pays. As long as Sergio is paid.'

Menzies was overjoyed at Freddy coming to his rescue, and beamed his pleasure at the brilliant peacemaker. 'You have the wisdom of Solomon, officer. Why aren't you Lord Chief Justice?'

In the meantime Sergio had gone to his desk and picked up the bill, which he then handed to Freddy. 'Service not included.'

One look at the bill, and Freddy blanched. Taking out his wallet, he started counting out tenners till he came to the end, then turned to his partner. 'I'm a fiver short.'

With an audible groan, Mo hunted around in her shoulder bag for a fiver. She handed it to Freddy. 'I'll be wanting that back.'

In turn, Freddy handed the money to Sergio, then moved to the beaming Menzies. 'Now then, sir. The watch,' he requested.

'What? Oh – the watch. Of course.' Menzies carefully gave the watch to Freddy. 'You look after that. Don't go getting involved in fights with young sprouts anxious to flex their manly credentials in front of the lassies.'

Freddy proudly strapped the watch to his wrist, then held up his wrist to admire how handsome it had suddenly become.

Yet it appeared that Mr Menzies was not quite finished. 'Could I . . . trouble you for a receipt?'

Mo tugged out her notebook, scribbled a receipt, tore out the page, and handed it to Menzies, who beamed brighter than ever.

36

By the corner, in one of the eight beds of the small ward at the hospital, rested an elderly Sikh gentleman, Shambji, staring up at the ceiling and suffering in silence. Although his head was bandaged, he was still wearing his battered turban.

Also still in uniform, Special Constable Bob Loach and Anjali Shah were talking quietly with the young nurse at the door. 'We won't tire him,' Loach promised. 'We just need him to fill in a few missing details, that's all.'

'Well, try not to excite him,' cautioned the nurse.

'Wants to go home already, does he?' Loach chuckled at the feisty old goat.

'It's not that,' the nurse reported. 'He wouldn't take his turban off for the x-ray.'

The three of them shared a moment of quiet understanding, then the nurse left them alone, and Loach and Anjali walked across the room to the foot of Shambji's bed. While he seemed to be awake, he was very still, breathing very shallowly.

'Mr Shambji . . .' Anjali called to him gently.

As she came closer, the old man weakly tried to turn his head away, tears welling up in his eyes. His fragile voice was like a wounded bird trembling in the nest.

'There is nothing to talk about. I am a foolish old man. I have let everyone down.'

Anjali crouched by the side of the bed. 'Don't blame yourself, Mr Shambji. There was nothing you could do.'

'There was much I could have done,' he disagreed quietly. 'They

452

were not yet men. I am shamed by boys.' The well of tears began to cascade over his cheeks.

Loach didn't want to press the old man, but he did want very much to capture the lads who could have done this to an elderly gentleman who wished no one any harm. He also felt the need to get their questioning over as quickly as possible so the old man could rest.

Loach cleared his throat to get the old man's attention. 'We need to know how many of them there were, Mr Shambji. Their ages . . . what they were wearing . . .'

Shambji, however, was preoccupied with his own disgrace. 'My comrades trusted me with their money,' he mourned. 'Money they could not afford . . . but it was a good cause. They gave because it was a good cause.'

'How much did they take?' Anjali asked patiently, speaking closer to his ear in softer tones.

'Fifty pounds,' he answered, his voice in the distance. 'We collected fifty pounds . . .'

'And it wasn't your money?'

There was silence as Shambji took a moment to gather his thoughts. 'Every year we give money to the temple for the benefit of the poor children.'

Loach had leaned over behind Anjali. 'When you say "we" . . . ?'

The tears stopped for a moment, as the memory stiffened his features with pride. 'The Undivided India Ex-Serviceman's Association. There are so few of us now . . .' Starting to fade into nostalgia, Shambji halted his recitation, then picked up the threads of his story.

'My comrades say: "Shambji, this year you will take the money to the Gnani." It is an honour to do this. I am proud to be chosen. But . . .' He choked on the words, '. . . but because of my senility and foolishness, I allow the money to be taken from me like a weak child. And by no more than children themselves. The children we collect for could have done better. I shame my comrades. I shame myself.'

'So this money belonged to members of your old regiment?' Loach reiterated.

'Battalion,' Shambji corrected him. The One Fourteenth Punjabis. We bore our colours in two world wars. The battalion was given two posthumous Victoria Crosses by King George himself. And ten

Military Crosses,' he recited with pride, which then dissolved into shame. 'And I – RSM Shambji – now bring disgrace to them because I cannot defend myself against children.'

Again he tried to turn away, the tears flowing freely down the furrows of his worn face. 'Please,' he pleaded with them. 'I do not want you to see me like this. Go away, please,' he implored them. 'Go away . . .'

The fob watch was open, playing *The British Grenadiers*, lying on the table in the interview room at Division 'S' headquarters. To the eyes of Andy McAllister, Anjali Shah, and Bob Loach, even the Crown Jewels would have suffered by comparison at that moment.

'But no money?' Anjali repeated.

'I'm afraid not, lass,' McAllister confirmed. 'That went on booze. Most of which they sicked up in the yard.' In the end, the drunken louts were hardly worth capturing, except for Shambji's fob watch, which was now winding down as *The British Grenadiers* faded into memory. 'At least we've got them,' he concluded. 'That's what matters.'

Anjali kept looking at the watch. 'It was a collection for underprivileged children . . .'

'What was?'

'The money,' she answered absently.

Loach was also fascinated with the timepiece, and what it was worth in emotional terms. 'I hope we can make this stick, that's all.'

'Don't see why not,' Andy assured him. 'They've got to explain how they come to be in possession of the watch. That's a tricky one to get round.' He picked it up for their closer inspection, and all were focused on its fine filigree. 'It's even got this Shambji's name on it . . . an inscription or something. His regiment probably gave it to him when he retired.'

'Battalion,' Anjali corrected him.

'What?'

'It's a battalion.'

Without another word, Anjali abruptly turned and left the room.

Frowning, McAllister wondered what he might have said. 'What's the matter with her?' he asked Loach, hoping he hadn't insulted the Asian community somehow.

37

By the time Loach and Anjali arrived at the Pub on 4th, their simmering argument had heated up considerably.

'You've got to stand back. There's a hard luck story on every streetcorner, if you look for it. You'd have to be the Bank of England to bail out everyone down on their luck.'

'You're deliberately misinterpreting what I'm saying,' she said, while following him along to the bar.

Loach went over to Briggsy the barman, who busied himself cleaning glasses. 'Pint, please, Briggsy.' He checked with Anjali to see what she wanted.

'Tonic water,' she requested.

After a moment, looking at her fingers on the bar, she started in again, obsessed with her compassion for a poor, innocent, yet noble gentleman. 'He's got hardly enough money for himself, and yet he collects for a charity,' she reflected sadly. 'It's a pity someone can't do the same for him.'

'I'm not arguing about that. I'm just trying to be sensible about this, that's all.'

It was his sensibility that irritated her. 'Well, you're lucky. I don't feel sensible. I feel bloody *angry*!'

'And I don't?' he inquired, staring back at her. 'What makes you think you've got the monopoly on compassion?' He shook his head in frustration. 'Women!'

Anjali realized it wasn't Bob Loach she resented, for all that he wanted to be was the first millionaire Special.

'It's never people in fur coats who put their hands in their pockets,' she observed. 'It's always people who can't afford to who give. People like Shambji.'

'Right!' Loach finally concurred. And, taking out his wallet, he extracted a fiver and slapped it down on the bar. 'Match it!' he challenged her.

Reappearing with this drinks, Briggsy was startled to find himself in the middle of a wild argument between two close friends. As he set the drinks on the bar, Anjali stood up and rummaged through her bag.

'I'll do better than that,' she retaliated, counting out five pound coins of her own into a large, clean ashtray, adding Loach's fiver to the pile. 'I'll double it. Treble it, even. You've given me an idea, Loach.'

Instead of slapping his cheek, she gave him a quick peck, then headed off into the crowd with her makeshift collecting bowl. Briggsy was startled more than Loach, who merely watched Anjali wending her way through the club.

'That's a lousy way to win an argument.'

Briggsy leaned over to recapture Loach's attention. 'Now how about paying for these?' he grinned.

Near the far corner of the bar, Anjali approached Freddy Calder, drinking non-alcoholic brew, as usual, and his partner of the evening, WPC Morrow. Freddy couldn't help but eyeball the cash lying in the ashtray.

'You read my mind, Anjali. I was just about to suggest a collection on my behalf.'

Anjali was not amused. 'This is for a brave old man who had fifty quid stolen.'

'There you are, Freddy,' Mo elbowed him in the ribs, 'It *is* for you,' she teased, alluding to a certain bill from Alfredo's.

'Fifty quid?' Freddy sneered, 'What's fifty quid these days? Some people spend more than that on a meal these days.'

'Put your hand in your pocket, Freddy,' Anjali asked in a no-nonsense tone. 'Every little bit helps.'

'I'm absolutely skint,' he protested. 'Honest. Ask Morrow here.'

Mo vouched for his temporary poverty. 'It's true. I watched him part with the entire contents of his wallet a couple of hours ago. I even had to buy him a drink.'

Switching tactics, Anjali moved the ashtray under Mo's nose instead of Freddy's.

'It's turning out to be an expensive night,' Mo commented, digging deep in her shoulder bag and ultimately adding a pound coin to Anjali's growing collection. Anjali reproved Freddy with a sharp look, shared a smile with Mo, and moved along to the next opportunity.

Freddy was still preoccupied with his outstanding loan. If earlier he had been hoping that Menzies would default and he could keep the Rolex, he had come round to the view that he'd sooner have cash in hand after all. Mo shook her head, amazed that he still expected Menzies to appear any second at the Pub on 4th.

'You realize,' she said, thinking that he must. 'He's not going to show. It's getting on for eleven.'

'No it isn't,' Freddy disagreed. 'It's only . . .' He called across to Briggsy, who was standing at the till. 'Give me a time check, Briggsy!'

Looking at his own watch, Briggsy called back: 'Ten to eleven. I'm about to call last orders.'

Suddenly alarmed, Freddy put his wrist to his ear and shook the watch, then listened intently for the ticking.

'What's the matter?' Briggsy inquired in a loud voice. 'Watch bust?'

'Don't even think it,' Freddy said, more to himself, the very words sending a chill through his spine. Mo merely gave him a look that said 'I told you so.'

Worry now spreading over his face, Freddy laid his wrist on the counter, the Rolex in plain view. Remaining calm, for the moment, he carefully tapped the watch case. Nothing happened. He tapped it again, this time a little harder. The casing and the dial and some of the springs and screws inside all fell to pieces on the counter.

'There's your problem, Freddy,' Briggsy observed. 'No wonder it wouldn't work.'

'I want my fiver back, Freddy,' Mo reminded him.

His hopes in ruins, Freddy stared at the junk he had purchased for an exorbitant sum, cursing his miserable fortune, and wondering if he now qualified for Anjali's charity.

Meanwhile, Anjali was gazing at Andy McAllister – who sat by himself, eyes closed, reclining with his feet propped up on the corner of the table. She went ahead and approached him gingerly with her ashtray.

'Sergeant.'

Andy opened his eyes, saw her, then saw the ashtray. 'What's this?' he asked warily.

'I suppose you're going to lecture me, too. Tell me I shouldn't take pity on every hard-luck story who comes along.'

'So who's leaving?' McAllister inquired drily, praying someone else had decided to resign so he could enjoy another party. For that, he would contribute a penny or two.

'It's for Mr Shambji.'

McAllister frowned. 'How much have you so far?'

'About thirty quid.'

'How much did he lose?'

'Fifty. Look, I'll understand if you don't –'

She stopped and stared as he removed two £10 notes from his wallet and drop them in the ashtray as if he were tipping a flower lady.

'Pity Baxter's not around to see this,' he chortled, knowing Sheila would die of a heart attack on the spot.

Anjali was stunned by his gesture. 'I can't take this,' she told him, deeply touched.

'Don't be daft. It's from all of us downstairs . . .'

As she absorbed his simple explanation, Andy drank up, rose from the table, and pulled his tunic down smartly, giving her a twinkly smile on behalf of all the brothers and sisters in the family.

'. . . villains and police alike.'

38

Only when the milk van was driving away up the street did Hilda Calder emerge from the front door of her home to get the milk in. Puffy-eyed, and half clothed in her old dressing gown, she'd had a bad night, so she didn't care to show herself to anyone this morning.

Closing the front door and walking back toward the kitchen, she glanced up the stairs and noticed Freddy's door closed. She put down the milk bottle and decided to investigate, mounting the stairs without wasting any time.

She hesitated at his bedroom door, then decided that if it weren't what she thought it was, it would make no difference anyway. So she slowly turned the handle and opened the door.

Lying in the bed covered with blankets was a lumpy form, which Hilda recognized as her sleeping son. Softly, so as not to awaken him, she closed the door, a smile of smug satisfaction on her face.

John Redwood sat leaning on the desk in his office, his hands cupped together, listening to his client, Denzil Taylor, who sat slumped in the chair opposite, hands in the pockets of his bomber jacket. While Redwood's secretary, Stella, took notes, Denzil was attempting to clarify some of the details involved in the attack by Kerrigan and his gang that culminated in Redwood's son Simon being thrown from a pedestrian bridge.

'You don't admit to being scared,' Denzil was telling them. His confessions had been painfully honest, and he continued to force himself to tell all, despite the pain and embarrassment. 'You pretend you aren't,' he admitted, though remembering how terrified he was at the moment Kerrigan was toying with young Simon's life. 'But Kerrigan knew. He could sense it.' The fear of him was in Denzil's eyes as well. 'He picks up things like that. And uses it.' Remembering, the fear began to become unbearable. 'So when things started getting heavy . . .'

Suddenly he broke off and jumped up from his chair, unable to cope with his fears. He tried to make himself sit down again, but couldn't, and needed a moment to catch his breath.

Redwood was sympathetic. After all, he had been watching this young man come clean. 'We don't need to go over this,' he told Denzil. 'I've got most of this stuff from Kerrigan . . . the extent of your involvement, I mean.'

Denzil seemed unwilling to give up his struggle at the moment. 'I gotta put myself in the picture,' he insisted. 'We can't talk about this like I wasn't there. I *was* there, man. The day Simon . . .'

'I think we've established that,' Redwood interrupted, cutting off the replay for his own sake more than Denzil's.

'I gotta say it,' Denzil declared. 'So it's on the record. She's gotta write it down,' he went on, pointing to Stella, 'so it's official.'

Mentally exhausted, Redwood sat back in his scat. 'I think we've done enough for one day.'

'We only just got going!' Denzil objected.

'I've got someone else coming at eleven-thirty,' explained Redwood.

'Maybe you've got problems with this part of it, too,' Taylor challenged him.

'Problems? I don't think so.'

'Least I know I have to get my head round it somehow,' Denzil tried to explain. 'Maybe that gives me a start over you.'

Although Redwood seemed at a loss, Stella knew exactly what Taylor meant. She looked up from her notebook, wanting to intervene, yet knowing her boss would resent it; so she held her tongue, as always.

'You realize,' Redwood advised, 'giving evidence against Kerrigan might expose you to danger.'

'I know it,' Denzil confirmed. 'He's major league. He don't take prisoners.'

'So are you sure you want to go ahead with this?'

Denzil walked to the window and looked outside. In a small, walled garden below, Simon was sitting in his wheelchair. Denzil couldn't tell what Simon was doing; he was just there.

'I'm sure,' Denzil repeated.

Redwood wasn't finished. 'I also have to ask you if you want someone else to represent you. I'm more than a little . . . uh . . . involved.'

'It's gotta be you, or I don't do the business.' He turned to face the solicitor. 'Okay?'

'Okay,' Redwood agreed, then exhaled a long sigh. He got up to walk Denzil to the door. 'Come tomorrow. At about half two.'

'I'll be here,' Denzil promised. Redwood opened the door for him, and Denzil stopped before walking out. 'You just make sure *you* are,' he said enigmatically.

When Redwood shut the door and turned round, Stella was waiting, having swivelled in her chair to confront him.

'What was that supposed to mean?' Redwood asked.

'Maybe one day you won't be. Here, I mean. You very nearly weren't this time. Denzil won't be around to save your bacon next time.'

Upset with him, Stella flipped her notebook shut, stood up, and walked to the door. 'And what would happen to Simon then? Have you thought about that?'

His eyes closed, wired to a CD Walkman, listening to the blissful chaos of heavy metal, Simon sat motionless in his wheelchair, meditating, breathing in the scents wafting from the garden. When a shadow fell across his face, he opened his eyes. Denzil Taylor stood blocking the sun.

'I want you to know something,' Denzil told him without asking. 'I know it don't mean much, but I'm gonna say it anyway.'

Simon pulled off the Walkman to listen to Denzil, but looking at him directly required shielding his eyes from the sun's halo around the young West Indian.

460

'I'm blowing the stuff on the guys who did all this to you. Not 'cos of you. I ain't doing this just for you. I'm doing it for me. It's me I gotta live with. And it ain't gonna be a life if I don't.'

Staring at Denzil, Simon's expression gave nothing away, as if his face and feelings were paralyzed as well.

Denzil hesitated, then shrugged. 'Well . . . I guess that's it.'

He started to walk away when Simon's voice stopped him. 'It may not be much of a life if you do,' he said. 'Dad says Kerrigan . . .'

'Kerrigan don't scare me. He's the cat we gotta skin.' Nodding a casual farewell, Denzil walked towards the shurbs cloaking the back gate. 'Take it easy, man.'

'Good luck . . .' Simon called to him, just as Denzil disappeared from view, then added, under his breath, a name, '. . . Denzil.'

39

The old coach bearing the Redbird Express insignia was speeding along the skid-pan in the bus test area at about 70 miles per hour when it suddenly braked and swerved, water spraying up from behind, and almost toppled over before righting itself and roaring away.

Loach had seen such demonstrations so many times that they no longer seemed so exciting as they once did. What got his heart beating faster today was talking gossip over his cellular telephone with Sandra Gibson, Administrative Secretary of the Specials, speaking from Division 'S' headquarters.

'So what do you think?' he asked her eagerly, trying to get the latest odds on his chances for promotion to Sub-Divisional Officer.

'Positive,' Sandra assured him, though she didn't elaborate.

'Not even unofficially?' he quizzed her.

Loach was absolutely incorrigible, Sandra decided. 'We've got juicier things to gossip about than who's going to be the new SDO at "S" Division.'

'You would tell me?' he asked again, just to make sure.

'I promise you, Bob. You'll be the first to know.' She glanced down at Loach's flow chart still leaning against one of the desks and grinned. 'Now get off the phone. I've got work to do.'

461

While clearing the line on the cellular phone, Loach walked over to where the old Redbird coach had just pulled up. His partner, Dicky Padgett, and Works Manager John Barraclough were disembarking with wobbly legs from their ordeal.

'So what do you think?' Dicky demanded.

'I don't know,' Loach shook his head. 'It's a lot of money.'

Apparently Dicky was in no mood for conversation. 'Come on Bob! This is the day the dithering has to stop. Management decision.'

Loach checked with Barraclough for a more reliable opinion.

'They're not without their faults,' Barraclough conceded. 'But I reckon they're worth what we're paying.'

'We've got to have 'em, Bob,' Dicky insisted, 'The Spanish deal – remember?' Maybe Dicky was right; maybe he was just being too cautious. Maybe it was time to give in gracefully.

'Okay. Get the contracts drawn up.'

Dicky reached into his inside pocket and just happened to find a contract there waiting for him. 'As they say on Food and Drink – Here's one I prepared earlier.'

In the small ward at the hospital, Shambji was checking the locker to make sure he hadn't left anything behind. His belongings were wrapped in a brown paper parcel on the neatly made-up bed, where Anjali Shah stood waiting for him.

'Mr Shambji . . .' she said quietly.

He turned back to face her. 'Is my tie straight? There is no mirror.'

She came over to him and centred the knot of his tie.

'Appearance is very important,' he told her. 'My commanding officer would say: "Shambji, appearance is your calling card on the world."'

Anjali smiled. 'How are you feeling today?' she inquired of her patient.

He didn't know quite what to say, or how he felt, but he did know he was still alive. 'I cannot lie down and die like a dog. It is not in my nature.'

She, for one, was happy he had survived. And now that he was ready, there was something else to tell him. 'Good news. We've caught them.'

Though interested in what she was saying, he didn't appear overjoyed at news of the capture of his attackers.

'And that's not all.' Delicately, proudly, she placed his watch on the bed next to the parcel of his belongings.

He couldn't believe his eyes. Picking it up in one old, withered hand, he gently stroked it with the other, and finally he could no longer hold back the tears from streaming down his face.

'Forgive me . . . I have always been an emotional man . . .'

Close to tears as well, Anjali took his hand. 'Goodbye, Mr Shambji. And good luck.'

She smiled through her tears and rushed out of the room, nearly bumping into the nurse on her way in. Looking after Anjali, her curiosity now aroused, the nurse went over to Mr Shambji. She laid a hand on his shoulder.

'Are you all right, Mr Shambji?'

The elderly gentleman had to wait a moment – to stem his tears, to catch his breath – before he could speak.

'The girl from the police is a very good person. She was not to know the stolen money was all in five-pound notes . . .'

On the bed, a pile of money had been left beside his parcel of belongings . . . in coins, silver, and notes.

'You see,' Shambji said to the nurse 'it is a *miracle*!'

40

Although the suburban shopping area was well lit, there were still many shop entrances hidden in shadows, fortunately for Ram. Striding purposefully past the shops, he suddenly saw his niece, Anjali Shah, approaching from a distance, and needed a place to hide. Anjali was in uniform, walking the streets with her 'partner', who was almost surely a man. Ram did not want to be seen by his niece here, least of all now.

Choosing a dark doorway, Ram hunched his head down into his shoulders, pretending to be absorbed in the shop window. Anjali took a long time getting there, but finally he could hear her voice as they approached. When they reached his doorway, he cast quick sidelong glances to check whether she had spotted him, but they went by without any change in their normal behaviour.

He decided that he was safe after all. Yet just at that moment, an elderly Indian lady stopped at the doorway and stared at him with disapproval. Only then did he realize that the shop window he had chosen was filled with mannequins barely dressed in the flimsiest female undergarments.

With as much dignity as he could muster, Ram marched stiffly past the reproachful gaze of the woman, and in a while was hovering uncertainly outside the Prakush Video store.

The houses on Grovelands were mainly detached homes of the well-to-do, if perhaps not the super-rich and famous. Yet each of the properties included plenty of bedrooms and bathrooms and an ample back garden, and no one here was starving. Someone might be prowling, however, and in answer to WPC Sheila Baxter's radioed summons, Redwood and Anjali Shah were there to investigate.

As the panda pulled in to the front drive of number 16, Redwood was already whispering into the radio. 'It looks quiet enough . . . but I'll get back to you. Over.' Without the noise of their engine, the neighbourhood grew even quieter.

When they arrived at the front door, Anjali rang the bell, and immediately the door opened. Greeting them was Liz Bellamy – a lean woman, perhaps in her forties, with an angular face revealing a hint of hardness – who seemed extremely relieved to see their uniforms.

'Thank God! I was worried you wouldn't get here in time.' With a quick gesture, she invited them into the house.

Just as the front door closed behind them, a Rover turned into the front drive and parked. Out jumped the woman's husband Richard – in his late forties, though dressed much younger, somewhere in the up-market 'next' category. Having seen the police enter his house, he was anxious to get out of the Rover, which then began to beep because he had left the lights on. Cursing to himself, he reached back into the car and fumbled to turn off the lights.

In the meantime, Liz Bellamy was leading Anjali and Redwood through a spotless hallway to the back garden. 'This isn't the first time, you know,' she told them.

'You've complained before to the police?' Anjali inquired.

'Not exactly, last few times I thought I was jumping at shadows. But tonight's different. I definitely saw someone in the garden . . .'

As she directed them to the back door, they suddenly heard a

464

scuffling at the front door when Richard Bellamy burst in, then charged down the passageway toward them.

'Chrissakes, Liz! What's going on?' he demanded. 'I saw the police . . .' All of a sudden he had a terrible thought. 'Where's Susie? Nothing's happened –'

'Susie's fine,' his wife assured him. 'She's up in her room . . .' Then she turned to explain to the Specials. '. . . our daughter . . . GCSE's coming up . . .'

'Then what the hell's going on?' Richard wanted to know.

'Your wife called us in,' Redwood informed him. 'She saw a prowler in the garden, Mr Bellamy.'

He shook his head wearily. 'Oh God, Liz. Last time it was the neighbour's dog.'

His wife sniffed. 'Well, you weren't here this time, Richard. I know what I saw . . . and it was too big to be a cat.'

Redwood nodded and the Specials turned toward the door to the back garden. 'We'll take a look, sir. Set your wife's mind at rest.'

But Bellamy violently objected. 'No!'

Anjali and Redwood stopped, and his wife was even more startled.

Bellamy hastened to reassure them. 'Look, officers, I can handle this myself. So there's no need for you to do anything further.'

Redwood raised an eyebrow, becoming a mite suspicious. 'I'm afraid we'll still have to check it out, sir, seeing your wife called us in.'

Bellamy turned on his wife. 'Dammit, Liz, look what you've started!'

Unlocking the back door, Redwood traded baffled expressions with Anjali as they ventured into the garden, leaving the arguing couple to follow. 'What the hell is your problem?' they heard the wife ask her husband.

In the garden, the beams of their torches scissored the dark. The garden was quite large and surrounded by ornamental fencing. Toward the rear was a greenhouse, and beside it a diminutive toolshed. Mrs Bellamy joined them, observing that Anjali was looking back toward the light spilling from an upstairs window.

'That's Susie's bedrom,' Mrs Bellamy pointed out. Craning her neck upwards, she shouted in a loud whisper. 'Susie! Susie!' Soon she gave up, turning back to Anjali. 'They hear nothing with those earphones on. How she can study is beyond me.'

465

'She'd bloody well better be studying,' Mr Bellamy chimed in. 'It costs a bloody bomb, that school of hers.'

'My husband wants Susie to go to Oxford,' Mrs Bellamy confided in Anjali.

'Because nobody gave me the bloody chance,' he added, moving over to join Redwood. 'There's no one here now . . . if there ever was anyone,' he whispered.

'I'll still check it out.'

Bellamy's tension seemed to be getting worse by the minute.

41

Ram was stuck with Nuresh in a tiny office at the back of Prakash Video: Nuresh was unloading cassettes from a small carton onto a desk already stacked high with videos, while Ram was busy avoiding a direct answer on the question of changing his niece's mind about betrothal. Spying a poster on the wall promoting Eddie Murphy and Nick Nolte in *48 Hours*, Ram took it as an omen.

'I know you only gave me forty-eight hours, but I need more time, Nuresh. You know as well as I do that I cannot give Anjali an ultimatum.'

Putting down the cassettes he was holding, Nuresh leaned heavily on the desk. 'That is precisely what you must do,' he asserted, turning to face Ram. 'And precisely what you won't do. Why deceive yourself, Ram? The truth is, you cannot force yourself to take such a step.'

In despair, Ram flopped down on a stool and confessed 'I idolize the girl, Nuresh. I couldn't bear it if she were ever to hate me.'

This Nuresh could understand, yet Ram's personal feelings for his niece were clearly in conflict with his promises to Nuresh concerning the betrothal.

'Then let me make it easy for you,' Nuresh proposed. 'I too love Anjali as you do.' Nuresh swallowed his regrets, though it was difficult due to the lump in his throat. 'Let us cancel our arrangement.'

Ram jumped from the stool, 'No, no, no,' he pleaded. '*Time*, Nuresh. Be a little more patient . . .'

'Ram . . .' Nuresh began, '. . . we cannot keep going round the trees. It's time you and I faced facts. Anjali will go her way regardless of what you or I say.' A headstrong woman, Nuresh reflected, was stronger than the heads of two men. 'Let us end our arrangement now.'

An invoice in the empty canon provided Nuresh with a timely reminder to be tacked on to his previous words. 'Naturally, I will expect the money I gave you to be returned.'

After an awkward pause, Ram realized he had to say something. 'But of course,' he fumbled. 'No problem, dear fellow. I shall get it for you . . . first thing tomorrow morning . . . if that is your wish?'

Nuresh nodded, and Ram likewise yet hoping his friend might still change his mind. But before he could press him further, they were interrupted by a shopgirl tapping on the door, an urgent look on her young face.

'If you'll excuse me then, Ram,' Nuresh bowed. 'I shall expect you tomorrow?'

'Of course,' Ram agreed, bowing in return. Making every effort to maintain his smile, he withdrew from the office.

Having completed their search of the back garden at 16 Grovelands, Special Constables John Redwood and Anjali Shah returned to an unwelcome reception from Richard Bellamy.

'See? Nothing. No prowler.'

'I'm not surprised,' his wife snapped back. 'The din you made, he'd've had to be stone deaf not to hear you. Christ, Richard,' she berated him, 'I was scared! Why d'you think I called the police?'

But Bellamy was paying little attention to her; instead he was watching the Specials as they ambled off toward the greenhouse and toolshed. 'Now where the hell are they going?' His tension once again on the rise, he set off across the back garden in hot pursuit, his wife hurrying to keep up with him.

By gesture Anjali conveyed the message that she would check the toolshed while Redwood probed the greenhouse. Yet as Redwood turned to carry out his assignment, his path was suddenly blocked by Richard Bellamy.

'Oh, come on, officer. It's obvius my wife's made a mistake . . .'

This fact, however, was not quite so obvious to his wife, who glared at her husband. Next to her, Anjali was opening the door of the toolshed.

'. . . of if there was someone, he's long gone by now . . .' Bellamy persisted.

Anjali and Liz Bellamy peered inside the toolshed. Cowering inside among the garden tools were two adolescents, one male and the other female. The female Anjali presumed to be Susie Bellamy, whose clothes created the impression of having been thrown on in some haste. The buttons on her blouse, for instance, were out of sync with their proper buttonholes, which left little doubt as to what Susie had just been up to.

Liz Bellamy's eyes widened, her lips mouthed one word – 'Susie?' Meanwhile Susie was making frantic gestures to her mother and Anjali to keep her misdemeanours hidden from the eyes of her father, who was in conversation with Special Constable John Redwood.

'It'll only take a second to check out, sir . . .'

Liz and Anjali looked at each other, then Liz shut the toolshed door with her back and leaned against it. Her eyes implored Anjali to join the conspiracy.

Her husband's constant complaining finally broke their concentration. 'Maybe . . . But I've got some tender plants in here, dammit!'

'I'll be careful,' Redwood assured him, although he was rapidly losing patience. 'Now, if you'll just let me pass, sir . . .'

Stepping aside just sufficiently for Redwood to get by, Bellamy followed on his heels into the greenhouse, his nerves stretched.

His flashlight picking out a light-cord, Redwood gave it a tug, and a dim light hovered in the air. The greenhouse was fairly large, and the sheer number of plants made it difficult to inspect every corner. One glorious aisle was entirely given over to numerous varieties of chrysanthemums. Yet strangely enough, considerable space here and there had been devoted to a species of rather dull green weed, though none seemed to be thriving, and Redwood had no idea what it could be, or what might have happened to keep the weeds from flowering.

Still, he could see fairly quickly that, in spite of the dark corners, nobody could hide in here and remain unseen. What had happened to the weeds was now more of a curiosity than what had become of the supposed prowler.

'Don't think I know this one?' he inquired, indicating the weeds.

Bellamy's face looked pale in the dim light, and even his voice sounded as though he were feeling a bit sickly. 'It's . . . uh . . . an experiment . . . that failed. Got attacked by some spider mite, I think. I've been meaning to hoik it out . . . Never seems to be enough time in the day.'

'I know what you mean,' said Redwood. 'But it's a pity you can't save it.' With a final look at Bellamy's weed disaster, he edged out of the greenhouse. 'Well, I won't take up any more of your time, sir . . .' While talking to Bellamy, he looked also at Mrs Bellamy. '. . . But don't hesitate to call us again should the need arise. We've probably frightened your prowler away, but he might try some other time.'

A glance of thanks passed from Liz Bellamy to Anjali Shah as Anjali rejoined her partner.

'Good night, sir . . . Mrs Bellamy,' Redwood concluded. 'We'll let ourselves out.'

'Good night,' Mrs Bellamy replied.

Immediately her husband started back toward the toolshed and greenhouse before she could cut him off. 'Richard? Where are you –?' She caught hold of his arm, and he dragged her along with him.

'I've got something to do in the greenhouse.'

She tried to hold him back. 'It can wait. Come on inside . . . I think we both need a stiff drink.'

He wouldn't budge, and she noticed a look of secret determination in his eyes. 'Richard? You've been acting like a madman all evening. What's going on?'

He spoke not a word, but instead took her by the hand and led her into the greenhouse. Groping in the dark, he found the light cord, and the eerie illumination returned. Then he pulled her closer to some of the weeds.

Bewildered, she had no idea what he was trying to tell her. 'Well . . . what is it?'

Richard pulled one of the green leaves from the withered weeds. 'See this? Look at it!' he exclaimed. 'You and your damned prowler . . . inviting the police in . . . Be my guest! Great God Almighty!'

'You're not making any sense, Richard. Why are you so frightened?'

'I could go to jail, you silly cow! This damned stuff is *marijuana* . . .'

469

42

As Redwood and Anjali reached the panda, he paused and looked back upon the house and grounds at 16 Grovelands, still trying to figure out what was bugging Richard Bellamy.

'Damn funny bloke. Couldn't get rid of us fast enough. Wonder if he'd be so unconcerned if the prowler had been after his silver?'

'The prowler was after more than silver,' Anjali quipped.

'What?'

'I suppose you might call it an inside job,' she teased him. 'A case of love in the toolshed . . .'

Although he waited, no further information was forthcoming from her. 'I take it you are going to explain all of that to me?'

Naturally Anjali nodded, opening the door of the car and climbing into their private confessional, eager to fill him in on everything he had missed . . .

. . . and he had missed everything.

The door to the toolshed creaked open. Plucking up his courage, the lad made his move to get out while the coast was clear, but he hadn't considered the power of Susie's desire. As he made his move, she pressed him back against the wall by the force of her lips, planting a passionate kiss where he couldn't speak up to object. While his wide-open eyes may have suggested she was out of her tree, he was certainly enjoying the tasty fruit. So he decided to stay awhile.

Having returned home from her tour of duty that evening, Anjali, still in uniform, went into the kitchen to find a snack before going to sleep, but discovered her mother peeping through a crack in the door to the sitting room.

'What's going . . .' Her mother shushed her, and she finished in a whisper. '. . . on?'

When her mother turned to face her, Anjali could see she had been crying.

'See!' her mother urged in low tones, pointing to the peephole.

Anjali went to the crack in the door and looked through. In the sitting room, Uncle Ram was slumped in a chair, a whisky glass clutched in his hand and tears running down his cheeks.

'He has been sitting there like that all evening,' her mother said. 'You are responsible for this, Anjali.'

'Don't be ridiculous. What have I done?'

Although Mrs Shah had remained quiet for many years, now it was necessary for her to speak out, both on behalf of her brother and her daughter. 'Your uncle is a good man. He worried for your future. But you have forgotten how to behave like a good daughter.'

'Ma, don't start on this again. It's been a long day . . . let me go to bed without my future being mentioned.'

Clearly her mother was angry with her about something. 'Anyone would think Nuresh had horns growing out of his head,' she wailed. So that was it: marriage again.

'I'm sure he would make a good husband for someone . . .'

'Well then . . . ?'

'But not for me, I don't love him, Ma.'

'English nonsense,' she scoffed. 'I didn't love your father when he and I were married. But we understood that what our families had arranged was a good thing. Love would come later.'

'If that is true, Ma, what about the nights Father came home drunk? How did you feel all those times he struck you . . . ?'

Suddenly blinded with anger, Mrs Shah slapped her daughter's face.

In the heavy silence that followed each of them realized the enormity of what had just happened. Breaking away, Mrs Shah bustled over to the sink where she could hide her face and keep her hands busy with dirty dishes.

Coming up behind her, Anjali tried to catch hold of her mother, not to display her anger, but rather to plead for forgiveness.

'I didn't mean it. I'm sorry, Ma. Please, I was angry.'

Mrs Shah did not turn to face her daughter, but spoke with her back to Anjali. 'You father is dead. He cannot speak for himself.'

Pulling herself free of Anjali's grasp, again she moved off by herself, padding over to the kitchen table to find something she could tidy away.

Later, Uncle Ram was reclining in the sitting room, staring into space, when Anjali came over and sat down on the arm of his chair. At first he didn't react to her presence, but then she tucked his head into her arm, and he couldn't hold himself aloof.

471

'I am a foolish old man, Anjali.'

'What has happened?' she asked him in a quiet way.

He couldn't bring himself to answer.

'Uncle Ram?' she gently prodded him. 'Tell me.'

Still he was silent, unable to look at her.

'He is going to prison because he cannot repay Nuresh Prakash the money,' her mother abruptly declared, having appeared by the door to the kitchen.

'Prison? Money? What money? What are you talking about?'

Her mother opened her mouth to speak, but Uncle Ram stopped her with a raised hand.

'No! I shall tell her. It is my own folly which has caused all this.' Finally, he looked into his niece's questioning eyes. 'I received a considerable amount of money from Nuresh Prakash – a kind of dowry – for your hand in marriage, Anjali.

I invested the money, to ensure it would grow while in my safekeeping . . . Unfortunately, I was misled by certain factors in the marketplace . . .'

'The money's gone,' said Mrs Shah simply, finishing her brother's thought.

Ram glared at her, then continued. '. . . and now Nuresh asks for its return, which is only right and fair.' When he reached the end, he hung his head in shame.

'How much, Uncle? How much do you need?'

'More than you have in your account,' he said bluntly, without a trace of sentiment.

Anjali blinked in astonishment; she wondered if there were anything in this house sacred to her, except for family ties. 'We must ask for time to repay it, Uncle Ram.'

'I cannot,' he confessed. 'I have promised to return it tomorrow.'

She saw the road before her coming to a dead end. 'Is there nothing we can do?'

In vain he had searched for some other way out, but he had always reached the same conclusion in the end. 'I shall pay for my stupidity. I shall go to prison.' Anguished, he raised clenched hands to his face, hiding his shame behind them.

Mrs Shah intervened. 'Or, you could end this nonsense by marrying the man. Oh, I know you don't love him, whatever that has to do with it. But he is not too displeasing to you, is he? He is a wealthy man. You will not be tied to a stove, if that's what worries you.'

From behind his hands, Ram watched Anjali to see which way she would jump.

Of course, Anjali had heard this entire speech many times before. This was nothing new. The only new element in the mix was the overwhelming burden of debt her uncle had assumed, though it had her signature in blood on the I.O.U.

Eventually she gave in, breathing a weary sigh of resignation. 'All right. I shall marry him,' Anjali announced. 'There, I've said it. I shall marry him.'

Shaking with joy and relief, Ram stood from his chair and reached his arms out to embrace her. 'Anjali, you are the most wonderful girl . . .'

She stopped him with the palms of her hands before he could embrace her, fixing him with a hard look. Indeed she had surrendered, but she felt no compelling need to help them celebrate her defeat. Ram subsided in his chair, and she walked slowly to the door, unbuttoning her uniform.

'Er . . . there is just one small thing, Anjali,' Uncle Ram added as an afterthought.

'Yes?'

'Nuresh does have one condition . . .'

'Yes?'

'It's just that . . . well, you cannot expect a man of his standing in the community to have his life partner walking the streets at night in the company of another man,' Uncle Ram explained delicately.

Removing her uniform jacket listlessly, Anjali dumped it on a chair. Perhaps tonight was the last time.

'I have to give up the Specials, is that what you're saying?'

43

Bob Loach had died and gone to heaven. Standing in the yard of Cougar Coaches was a vision of utter perfection, truly a chariot of the gods – a glistening, gleaming, brand new *supercoach* – a sleek extravaganza that made his other buses look like tin boxes on wheels. Even Loach's white Jag appeared cheap and flimsy by comparison.

As soon as he got out of his car, Loach ran over to the supercoach, and there he found John Barraclough, who had been 'feeling' the quality of the machine.

'What the hell's this, John?' he marvelled.

But Barraclough had the face of a reluctant messenger. 'I believe Dicky was talking to Eric Parmenter . . . on the golf course?' . . . meaning Eric Parmenter, the salesman.

Loach slapped a hand to his forehead and groaned.

Barraclough hastened to disclaim any responsibility for having any dealings with a salesman. 'I tried to explain how things were at present, but you know Eric.'

'You told him, and he still left it?' Loach queried.

'Said he'd rather leave it here than park it on a meter.' There wasn't a meter big enough for this jumbo cruiser even in Texas. 'Said it's name was Delilah . . . hoped it might tempt you.'

That it did, and that made him mad. 'I could strangle bloody Dicky Padgett. He knows we're overextended at the bank as it is, buying those damned Redbird coaches! What the hell's he playing at?'

Walking nervously around the yard, he noticed that not only was a supercoach there that shouldn't be there, but also that coaches were not there that should have been there. 'And incidentally, where are the Redbird coaches? Weren't they supposed to be here this morning?'

'They were,' Barraclough agreed. 'But it's early yet.'

Loach looked up at the sky to check the time of day – it was a glorious morning – and then he looked down at the supercoach. The sheer beauty of the beast softened his mood and made him sentimental.

'Just look at it, John,' he murmured. 'It fair makes you weep . . .'

'In fairness to Dicky . . .' Barraclough said tentatively '. . . It was a conversation he and Eric Parmenter had a while back. Seems three of them are going abegging. Some company defaulted on its downpayment, and Eric wants them off his hands fast. He mentioned an attractive discount . . .'

Loach just shook his head. 'We couldn't afford to fill its tank,

John. Let alone buy three of them.' But of course, he couldn't help musing what might have happened if he had procrastinated just a little longer before signing a contract. '. . . If we hadn't been so damned quick purchasing those other buses . . .' He could kick himself now for giving in to Dicky so easily.

'What's the old saying?' Barraclough reminded him. 'A bird in the hand?'

Loch laughed drily. 'Oh, aye . . . in this case, two old decrepit Redbirds in the hand . . .' A hundred Redbirds would never be a match for one golden eagle supercoach, but at least that was closer to a balanced equation.

Sailing along in his saucy blue Sierra Freddy was having a private counselling session with his psychotherapist, Dr MacFoxy, who happened to be sitting on Freddy's free hand while the other was taking care of the steering.

'All right. So I go see Rita. But what do I do, MacFoxy?' It was a rhetorical question, and Dr MacFoxy was not required to answer that one. ''S all right for Rita to tell me I have to make a clean break . . . up and leave Ma . . .'

Dr MacFoxy asked Freddy how he felt about that.

'Sure I wanna get away, but . . . Ma would never forgive me,' Freddy confessed, pinpointing the real problem. 'She'd hate me for the rest of her life, she really would . . . for the rest of her life.'

Freddy had a quick glance down at Dr MacFoxy, responding in the psychotherapist's high, puppet-like voice. 'Well Freddy . . . no one lives forever.'

Freddy looked around furtively, hoping no one had been there to hear Dr MacFoxy making such an odious, distasteful remark. 'What kind of advice is that, you dummy?' he chastised Foxy.

Suddenly the car swerved hard to the left, and it was all Freddy could do to fight the wild rocking of the vehicle, gripping the wheel with both hands. He couldn't use the brake, for fear it would throw the steering off even more, so he just rode it out, hanging on for dear life, with horns honking everywhere. Eventually the Sierra rolled to a stop.

He took a deep breath, then got out of the car and circled round to the rear. As he had suspected, the left tyre was a blow-out. He kicked the damn tyre and shouted at his damn car.

'I take you back, and this is how you repay me!'
The moment he said it, he was sorry.

44

The new supercoach sparkled like a jewel in the morning sun, to adorn the yard at Cougar Coaches for only a few more moments. Standing by till the last, Bob Loach was admiring it with the salesman, Eric Parmenter, a quiet Aussie. It was hard telling which of them was gloomier about Cougar Coaches not snapping up the supercoach when the market was depressed.

'I know it's going back a few weeks,' Eric admitted, 'but Dicky was real shook on the idea. Mind you, he'd just licked the tar outa me, three and two at a tenner a hole.'

Loach could barely resist the offer. 'I would if I could, Eric. I mean . . . this is a real cracker.'

'Don't forget the discount,' the salesman said with a grin. 'It sorta lets you in on the ground floor.'

'And follow *their* company into liquidation, Eric? No! It's tempting, but I'll have to pass . . . And you don't know how hard it is for me to say that. But . . .' he hinted '. . . it may be a different story next year.'

Eric shook his head. 'Vehicles like this . . . at the price I've quoted you . . . don't come on the market every day, Bob. I wanted you to have first go.'

'I appreciate that, but we can't underwrite any more rolling stock until next summer. We're just about to take delivery of coaches from Redbird. They're going under, you know.'

''Course I know. It was bloody Redbird who ordered three coaches like this and defaulted on the payment.' Still chuckling, he signalled the driver. 'Right, Bruce . . . when you're ready, we'll take this beaut back home.'

Loach stayed his arm. 'A favour, Eric.'

'Surely,'

'Can I . . . can I have a last look inside?'

Again Eric laughed. 'No sweat.' He called up to the driver in the cab. 'When Mr Loach is through, Bruce, I'll see you back at base.'

Gesturing for Loach to climb aboard, Eric then offered the same hand for a shake. 'See you around, Bob.'

After shaking hands, Loach mounted the steps of the supercoach, and Eric Parmenter walked across the yard to his car, stopping for a moment to talk with John Barraclough.

'If only we'd known about this a coupla days ago, Mr Parmenter . . . because I know what Bob Loach is going through right now . . .'

Meanwhile, what Bob Loach was going through was an experience similar to the scenes of Richard Dreyfuss inside the big mother spaceship at the end of *Close Encounters of the Third Kind*. He was awestruck by a preview of the future. Scenic coach travel was not a relic of the past, but an affordable luxury with modern conveniences: personal viewing screens, double lavatories, and all the other amenities. What a dream. With a fond farewell as he strolled down the aisle, caressing the upholstery on the back of each seat as though it were silk.

When he emerged from the supercoach, he took one last longing gaze, then turned to find Anjali Shah waiting for him.

'It's beautiful,' she said.

Her words brought him out of his daydream, though he was surprised to see her here. 'Anjali? Hi!'

'Business must be good. I didn't know you had buses like this.'

Not any more. Slowly the supercoach pulled away and drove out of the yard, leaving Cougar Coaches behind in the mundane present.

'I don't,' Loach finally answered her. 'But don't I wish?' he sighed. The supercoach was gone. 'There's always something in this world you can't have . . .'

'Don't I know it,' Anjali said to herself.

Loach heard what she said. Anjali seemed nervous. Something was on her mind.

Ram was about to pay for his purchase of Tums when the shopkeeper, a woman of Indian background like himself, appeared to recognize him, though he couldn't remember ever having seen her.

'You are the uncle of Anjali Shah?'

He nodded with a smile, yet he was not altogether pleased to be recognized by way of his niece.

'She would know all about the police, wouldn't she?' asked the shopkeeper in a loud voice.

Ram winced, but another woman, a customer – and not of Indian background – overheard the remark and leaned into the conversation in front of him.

''Course she would,' the woman declared. 'She works for them, you know.'

Why didn't they ask *him* about her? After all, he was the one with the answers. The trouble was that complete strangers were frequently of the opinion that they knew someone better than that someone's own family.

He opened his mouth to tell them so, but the shopkeeper spoke up first. 'Reason I ask is, I have a son who wants to join the police force,'

'She'd be able to help, wouldn't you think?' the customer suggested.

Ram tried to shush the customer, but the shopkeeper jumped in again, finally addressing him.

'Would you ask your niece if she would come by one day and advise us perhaps? If it isn't asking too much?'

He was about to answer the shopkeeper when the customer interrupted him. 'They had a special ceremony where the police gave her a medal.' She turned to Ram. 'Did you know that?' 'Of course I know. I was there. I met all the top people from the police. They hold Anjali in the highest esteem, because she is good at her job . . .'

His voice trailed away, as he listened to what he was saying. And thinking about that, he became aware of the avid faces in the shop waiting for him to continue telling them about his wonderful niece, the one who was a Special . . .

Instead he picked up his Tums. 'I shall speak to my niece,' he told them.

45

In the office of Cougar Coaches, Anjali and Loach were having a private counselling session, although he was a better talker than listener. He was certainly adamant: he didn't want Anjali to resign, period. She was what the Specials were all about.

He wasn't very subtle about it, nor perhaps very sensitive. On the other hand, she wasn't going to be confused about where he stood on the issue.

'Don't go near Whittaker,' he warned her, shaking his head forcefully. 'Promise me you won't resign, Anjali.'

'I don't have any option.'

'Of course you have,' he insisted. 'Listen . . . you can take a leave of absence. It's a free country, remember?'

'For *some*.'

Parked near Rita's diner at a lay-by, Freddy locked his car, this time checking it twice to make absolutely sure that everything was secure. He also assessed the rear, noting that the spare tyre looked very much out of place. Nonetheless, he gritted his teeth, stood up straight, and walked into the diner wagon.

Rita saw him as soon as he walked through the door, but she pretended that he was no different from any of her other customers. They were the usual group – a couple of truckers, two young female vegetarians with backpacks, and a motorbike messenger in leathers. She kept herself busy with all of them, but eventually she could no longer avoid standing in front of him, so he had the chance to speak to her.

'Sorry,' he apologized, 'I got held up.'

She seemed apathetic. 'Uh-huh?'

'Yeah, the back tyre.' He made an explosion noise like a blow-out, using his hands as visual aids exactly as he had done since the age of four.

'Oh,' said Rita, none the wiser.

Freddy leaned forward confidentially. 'We need to talk about *us*.'

'Freddy, this isn't the best time or place in the world for intimate conversations,' she told him without lowering her voice.

One of the truckers asked for a sausage roll, and Rita popped one into the oven.

When Freddy spoke again, it was in a voice that only she could hear. 'Well . . . maybe if you'd let me stay the other night, I coulda –'

She cut him off. 'I told you, Freddy. I don't take lodgers. That's not the way you're going to get your trousers on the back of my chair.'

Everybody in the diner snickered. One of the vegetarians clapped.

And one of the truckers began to look at Freddy in a new light.

For his part, Freddy was mortified, and he spoke to her in an even lower voice. 'It's not easy, you know, with a mother like –'

'Any trouble you're having with your mother is your look-out, not mine.'

'Excuse me,' interrupted the backpacker who had applauded. 'A Fanta. To go.'

Rita got the Fanta from the chest freezer, and the backpacker gave her exact change, as well as some sort of feminist salute.

'I swear, Rita. From now on, I'm a changed man,' Freddy asserted. Rita checked the oven and the trucker's sausage roll, getting an plate ready. 'But if I just stood aside and let Ma go find a Fisherman's Friend, you'd think me a funny bloke. Now wouldn't you?' he whispered at the top of his lungs.

'A funny bloke?' she mocked in disbelief. 'Sometimes, Freddy, you're the biggest nutbucket I've ever met!'

The two truckers exchanged amused looks, then grinned at Rita as she delivered the hot sausage roll.

'Well, apart from that,' Freddy continued, 'I thought we had something good going. Something to work on.' Now that their laundry was being aired in public, he saw no need to whisper.

'Freddy . . . love might be some kind of building site to you. But I've got news for you . . .' The trucker with the hot sausage roll pushed his cup forward. '. . . You can't patch it up with wet sand . . .' She filled the cup with more tea while making an aside to the trucker. 'Sugar 'n' milk's over there, luv.' Then she walked over to Freddy. 'You want my honest opinion?'

He glumly awaited her judgement.

She stood and looked him in the eye. 'I don't think it's going to happen with us. That's the honest truth.'

Crushed, he leaned his head against the counter. 'They say bad things come in threes . . .'

'What?'

'Nothing . . .' Freddy replied. 'But this bloody well makes it number two . . .'

Bob Loach's white Jaguar stopped outside Anjali's home, and she got out. Over the purr of the engine, Loach called to her. 'I have your promise, Anjali. Yes?'

Anjali nodded good-naturedly and made herself smile, as Loach waved and drove off.

From an upper window, Ram observed Anjali arriving home. He heard her come in, climb the stairs, and go into her room. Troubled by his thoughts, he crossed the room and then the passageway to reach her bedroom door, which was ajar. Quietly he pushed the door open further, and apparently she didn't hear him.

Lost in thoughts of her own, Anjali had placed the jacket of her Specials uniform on her bed. Taking great care, she removed the commendation she had received, then put it in a brightly painted box. The box she carried over to her dresser, and buried it deep toward the back of the bottom drawer.

What Ram saw made him more miserable than all his previous worries about spending a lifetime locked away in prison.

What had he done?

46

At the behest of Nuresh Prakash, Ram had consented to sit with him and watch a video on a small TV in the cramped office at the back of one of his Prakash Video shops. It was an Indian video, very colourful, very nice singing and dancing: a fantasy something about a prince who loved a princess, yet whose love, it would seem, was unrequited. But Ram's thoughts were elsewhere, and he couldn't allow himself to be distracted by some pleasant fairy tale. There were serious matters to discuss.

When the story was finished and the credits were onscreen, Ram pressed the remote control to reduce the volume to zero, somewhat surprising his host. With a heavy heart, yet knowing the time had come, Ram turned to face his friend Nuresh.

'Anjali agreed to the marriage,' Ram solemnly announced. 'Accepted your conditions.'

Nuresh was stunned, hardly daring to hope it were true. 'She agreed?'

'Yes,' Ram affirmed. But then he had to deliver the bad news as well. 'But wait, Nuresh . . .' As he began, he remembered to make no excuses for himself. '. . . I would never sleep again knowing that

481

I had forced her against her will in order to save this weak skin of mine.'

Nuresh questioned him with a glance.

'I am telling you this because I want there to be no misunderstanding between us.'

'I also want there to be no misunderstanding, Ram,' Nuresh agreed. 'But you are not making yourself very clear.'

There was silence, and for a moment, Ram wondered whether he had the courage to go forward. Finally, he did.

'It saddens me to tell you this, Nuresh . . . but . . . I have decided there will be no marriage. I will not allow Anjali to make sacrifices for me.'

All at once Nuresh looked as though the life spirit had been squeezed out of him. He was devastated, and tried to speak, but Ram held him back, and continued his confession.

'I have also to tell you . . . that I cannot return your money. It is all gone.' Now it was most difficult to keep himself together. 'Do not ask me how. It is a thing of shame . . .' Yet he knew he must not surrender to his fears, especially at this time, so once again he faced the disappointment and disapproval of his friend Nuresh.

'. . . But it is better for your friendship that I bare my heart to you like this.'

The kaleidoscope of bright colours from the video that was still playing were strangely reflected in the dead, grey eyes of Nuresh Prakash. Suddenly he was a single man with no prospects once again, all alone.

'I see. So you no longer have my money?'

'I shall repay you, Nuresh, even if it takes all my worthless life to do so.'

Nuresh gave a hollow laugh. 'And if I insist that the money is paid immediately?' he asked.

Ram took a deep breath, realizing that all of his worst fears could soon be coming to pass.

The spurned suitor was relentless. 'What honour will your family have if you go to prison, Ram?' He looked up to the heavens and raised his hands in supplication. 'Listen to him, Krishna!' he mocked. 'Listen to this crazy man!'

* * *

482

Hearing a noise outside the office, Noreen Loach looked up from her accounts just as Dicky Padgett burst through the door, and she jumped half out of her chair. Obviously he was stressed out.

'Loach? Where's Loach?' Dicky demanded.

'He took someone home,' she answered 'He'll be back any second. What's the matter? You look awful.'

Padgett was seething and about to explode. 'That swine Timson . . . at Redbird . . . *He used me!*'

This time she did jump out of her chair, heading for the cupboard to pour Dicky a stiff brandy. 'Slow down, Dicky, for God's sake.'

A moment later Loach entered the office 'What's up?' he asked when he saw their faces.

'I'll tell you what's up, Bobby boy,' Dicky started in on Loach. 'You took too long to make your mind up, that's what. If we'd done the deal with Redbird when I first came to you, this wouldn't have happened.'

'What the hell *has* happened?' Loach asked.

'That little swine Timson shafted us,' Dicky explained. 'Seems he got a nice back-hander from a company in Rochdale to dump our deal. While you blew hot and cold, he was looking elsewhere. Know what I'm saying? If you hadn't hemmed and hawed, we wouldn't be deep in the dirt like we are now!'

'But we signed a contract, Dicky,' Noreen pointed out.

'Yes . . . *We* signed the bloody contract. Redbird conveniently forgot to ratify it.'

'Can they do that?' Loach asked.

'You want to sue a company that's already down the tubes? What do you think?'

Quickly Loach picked up the telephone and dialled the number.

Feeling a bit dense trying to understand what was going on, Noreen turned to Dicky for some clarification. 'So we don't have the Redbird coaches?'

'At last,' he said sarcastically. 'The penny dropped.' He turned to watch Loach, who was on the phone waiting for a connection. 'And maybe Bob will enlighten us how he hopes to service the Spanish contract. That I'd really like to hear.'

Loach covered the mouthpiece on the phone so he could tell them quickly: 'I'm trying to get in touch with Eric Parmenter.' Then he turned his attention back to the phone, speaking into the mouthpiece in a lower voice. 'Yes . . . I'll hold . . .'

'Eric Parmenter?' Noreen asked vaguely.

Dicky's face lit up. 'My God! I'd forgotten all about the supercoaches!'

Now their interest in Loach's phone call went nuclear, and they focused intently on his every gesture. Soon, however, it became clear that the news wasn't going to be wonderful. Loach began to deflate like a balloon with a fast leak.

'No, I understand, Eric . . . I didn't think you'd move that fast . . . Well, that's true. You always were a fast worker.'

After they hung up, Loach put the phone down, shaking his head that there was no deal on the supercoaches. Dicky hid his head in his hands.

'I can't bear it!' Dicky hollered. 'You haven't lost us that deal as well?'

'Dicky!' said Loach very quietly. 'Get out of my face.'

Dicky drained the brandy Noreen had poured for him, then let the glass roll back and forth on the desk.

'Maybe there's something else you've forgotten about, Bobby boy. A certain penalty clause in the Spanish contract? You remember . . . ? If we're unable to meet our commitments, we pay an indemnity of a hundred thousand pounds.'

Loach and Noreen looked at each other in shock. Dicky was perversely cheered by the sight of their fear. 'You'd better be sure of one thing. I don't intend paying one cent of that. I hold you, as the managing director, responsible.'

Dicky Padgett turned his back on the managing director, and started to walk out. 'In other words, Bobby boy . . . I wouldn't count on making it as the first millionaire Special this year.'

Dicky was gone before Loach could draw a breath or Noreen could throw a shoe after him.

'That guy . . .' Loach seethed. 'Anybody would think I'd done all this on purpose.'

Noreen held him by the shoulders . . . it had been a long time . . . and he could feel the anger run out of him.

'So what do we do?' Noreen asked.

'Go out there and face the world! What else?'

'Oh, aye . . . and what's that?'

Her lip trembled, and it wasn't easy for her to say, but it was true.

'Me . . . holding your hand.'

He didn't reject her. He grinned at her, as he used to, just before he pulled her into an embrace.

47

By the way her uncle and her mother failed to meet her eye or make conversation during supper, Anjali's suspicions had grown stronger. Anxious to know what was happening in their heads, and to get it out of the way before she had to face duty that night, she decided that she must press the issue.

'There's something going on . . . and I would like to be in on the secret. Ma? Uncle Ram?'

'I don't know what you mean,' said Ram.

Tired of his excuses, Anjali was about to have it out with him when the front doorbell rang. Mrs Shah rose from her place, motioning to Anjali for her to stay where she was.

Immediately Anjali sensed that this was the moment she had been reading: the last link in the chain, the final farewell to her independence. She closed her eyes, and waited.

Nuresh Prakash had come to call on Anjali in his best suit: yet being a somewhat burly gentleman, his clothes gave the impression of being a size too small for him. Rather diffidently, he placed the bouquet of flowers he had been holding onto the table, retaining a small wrapped box in the other hand.

When Anjali opened her eyes, the stage was set. Her mother, her uncle (actually her surrogate father) and her fiancé all gathered round her – the claws of a steel trap clamping down on her.

'Now that Nuresh is here,' Uncle Ram began in an uncharacteristically subdued tone, 'I may as well tell you, Anjali . . .'

Abruptly, yet politely, Nuresh interrupted him. 'May I, Ram? Let me explain?'

Nuresh stepped forward, and addressed Anjali quietly, as if she were the only other person in the room.

'Back in the old country, things are done the way they have been done for centuries. They are good ways, but they are old country ways. We are in a new country. It has different ways. They may not be as good as the ways were back in the old country –'

'I think we understand about the ways, Nuresh . . .' remarked Ram to bring him to the point. But in case his words be misinterpreted as criticism, he hastened to add to Anjali: '. . . although there is much truth in what he says.'

Slightly annoyed at Ram's interference, Nuresh continued.

'Anjali I've come here to release you from any promise you may have made to marry me . . .'

Anjali was totally unprepared for this. She looked into Nuresh's eyes and began to see him truly for the first time. He was a stranger.

'. . . for whatever reason . . .' Nuresh paused, then proceeded: 'And I also want to say that Ram's misfortune in the money market is also my misfortune. It is something we will share *equally*.' His steely glare eventually persuaded Ram to lower his head gracefully, relieved of his own overwhelming burden.

'I have only one thing more to say,' Nuresh concluded, looking directly at Anjali, 'I would like Anjali's permission – and, of course, the rest of the family's – to call on her whenever she is willing.'

Uncle Ram and Mrs Shah now turned their gaze to Anjali. She coloured and lowered her eyes, one of the few times in her life she had felt shy.

'I . . . suppose so . . .' she said, flustered. Then she regained some of her usual spirit, and added: '. . . but no conditions, Nuresh?'

'No conditions,' he agreed, and handed her the small wrapped gift he had been holding.

To Anjali it looked suspiciously like a video cassette, and when Nuresh eagerly helped her pull off the giftwrap, her presumption proved to be correct.

'Why . . . thank you, Nuresh.' She lifted an eyebrow, as Sergeant McAllister would. 'A video. That is kind.'

'It is about a prince who loves a princess,' he explained. 'Their marriage has been arranged. However, the prince is a very wise person who gives the princess time to make her love him.'

'Uncle Ram? Let's at least have some surprises left when we see the film,' said Anjali with a smile.

Then she looked up at Nuresh, standing awkwardly by the table. 'Have you eaten, Nuresh?'

She didn't wait for an answer, but got up and fetched another chair to the table. 'Then sit down. Share some food with us.'

After so many months of worry and anxiety, Mrs Shah and Uncle Ram regarded one another with new hope. 'But be warned, Nuresh,' Anjali added. 'Tonight I intend to be with the Specials. As usual.'

Anjali just managed to beat District Commandant Whittaker into the parade room by a whisker. Everybody else was already there, including Bob Loach, Viv Smith, Freddy Calder, and John Redwood – the usual gang. As soon as the DC walked in, the clumps dissolved and formed into line.

Whittaker cleared his throat, and the room fell silent. 'Barring flood and fire, I sincerely hope that your next parade will be dealt with by your new SDO – whoever that may be . . .'

A few groans were heard and some of the Specials looked over at Bob Loach, whose face was a mask.

'All right, to business,' continued Whittaker. 'First up is . . . Oh, yes, before I forget . . . We've been getting some flak from the people who live on the canal. Section Officer Loach?'

Preoccupied, Loach didn't respond.

'Section Officer Loach?'

Freddy tugged on Loach's uniform.

'Sir?' he woke up.

'I'd like you and Special Constable Calder to show the flag down there. You're our senior men . . . and I'm sure you'll be able to shoulder any harsh words they may throw at you.'

48

'This'll only take a second,' Redwood assured Viv as they waited in front of the door to 16 Grovelands.

Viv shrugged, though obviously she was more than a little bored.

'But I phoned his wife earlier that I'd pop in.'

Before Viv could offer a clever retort, the door opened, revealing Susie Bellamy.

'Oh . . .' stammered Redwood, taken aback, '. . . Good evening, miss. I'm Special Constable Redwood . . . This is Special Constable

Smith. I spoke to Mrs Bellamy earlier . . . Actually, I was here last night – checking a prowler.'

The teenager was tongue-tied and Redwood suddenly realized the identity of the girl standing at the door. 'You must be Susie . . . Right? The hard-working student?'

She glared at him then averted her gaze, tapping the door with her foot to express her irritation.

'Actually, it's your father I've come to see,' Redwood explained, which relaxed Susie's tension considerably. 'May we . . . ?' He invited himself in, and she opened the door to admit them.

'He's outside . . . in the greenhouse,' Susie told them.

In the soft moonlight, the canal became a straight ribbon of shimmering silver. A row of colourfully converted barges and houseboats were strung along one side of the canal, all having wide gangplanks leading down to the bank. Tinkly piano ragtime music emanated from a pub at one end of the canal, the lights from the pub spilling out to splash on Bob Loach and Freddy Calder as they passed through its beams.

'Bob, I have a question. If, like you keep saying, you're getting this promotion to SDO . . . how come Whittaker is giving you this schlepp to do?'

'Maybe he's hoping I'll fall in and drown,' Loach suggested. In fact, Loach was beginning to doubt whether someone like Whittaker would ever understand enough about the position of SDO to do the sensible thing and award the promotion to him.

Discouraged, he kicked a stone into the canal and watched the rings eddy outward. 'No! That's a bit unfair. He wouldn't have given me you as a partner. He'd know you'd be daft enough to jump in and save me.'

'Why should I?' said Freddy.

'Why shouldn't you?'

'I can't swim,' Freddy informed him. 'That's bloody why.'

Crossing over the first gangplank, Loach tapped politely on the roof of the converted barge. The door opened into a box of light, framing the head of the barge-owner – a broad, strapping fellow of about 40 who looked as though he could bend iron bars with his teeth, though his midsection had spread out to the suburbs.

'Yes?' inquired the barge-owner suspiciously.

'Police, sir . . . Just checking everything's okay.'

'Did you hear that, honey?' shouted the barge-owner over his shoulder into the cabin behind him.

'Hear what?' A woman's voice shouted back at him from the cabin, rising above the noise from the TV.

'It's the police,' shouted the barge-owner.

'The what?'

'The bloody police, Shirl.' He pointed to his ear, trying to get her to turn down the volume on the TV. Shirl apparently didn't get the message.

'What do they want?'

'Checking everything's hunky-dory down here.'

There was a pause, as perhaps Shirl stopped for a moment to consider the merits of the idea. 'About high bloody time,'

She eventually shouted back.

The barge-owner lowered his voice to confide in Loach and Freddy. 'It's all right. I can tell she's really pleased.'

'Well, if everything's okay, we'll say goodnight,' Loach suggested.

'Goodnight, officers.' With a mocking grin on his face, he disappeared inside the barge and closed the hatch.

Warily Freddy and Loach retraced their steps over the gangplank, straining to adjust their eyes to the darkness. Freddy tripped on something in the shadows and stubbed his toe. 'Bugger it!' he cursed into the night.

Susie Bellamy led Viv Smith and John Redwood into the dimly lit greenhouse toward her father, who appeared to be preoccupied with some task and thus did not notice their approach. As they got closer, they could see that he was incinerating the leftover green weeds in a small stove.

'It's the police, Daddy,' Susie announced bravely behind his back.

Startled, Bellamy staggered back from the stove. Susie departed.

'Evening, Mr Bellamy,' Redwood began, noting that Bellamy wasn't looking too well. 'Sorry to disturb you . . .' He examined Bellamy more closely. 'You all right, sir?'

Richard Bellamy was looking anything but all right. Redwood smelled the air, trying to identify the cause of Bellamy's malaise.

'It's a bit stuffy in here . . .'

Viv, too, sniffed the air with a puzzled look.

'Here, let me give you a hand with that,' offered Redwood, taking the fork from Bellamy and scraping the weeds off its tongs into the small furnace. 'I spoke to your wife earlier . . .' Redwood glanced around the greenhouse only to find that most of the weed crop was gone, with only a few wispy plants remaining. 'Oh dear . . .' Disappointed he removed a small bottle from his tunic and shoved it to Bellamy, recalling the conversation with Bellamy's wife.

'I mentioned to her I have a client who runs a garden centre. When i told him about your problem, he suggested you give this stuff a go . . . but it's a bit late, by the look of things.'

Viv was picking some of the remaining weeds, gazing at them casually.

In the meantime, Richard Bellamy was sweating profusely and leaned heavily against a platform laden with dazzling flowers.

Redwood was concerned. 'You sure you're all right? It's damned stuffy in here . . .'

Bellamy's eyes rolled back in his head, and he began to fall. Redwood steadied him. 'Viv, give me a hand.'

She joined him, and each took a shoulder, supporting Bellamy out of the greenhouse and into the fresh air of the garden.

49

Loach and Freddy were back on the canal walkway.

'Show the flag . . . Isn't that what Whittaker said?' Freddy remarked. Then he considered the lovely barge-owner and his wife Shirl whom they had just met. 'It wouldn't worry them if we had the skull and crossbones sticking out of our heads.' They passed under a weak street lamp with a Neighbourhood Watch badge bolted to it, and Freddy chuckled. 'I reckon they'll need frog suits to do the job proper like.' He could see the day when Specials would swim their beat in the canal.

The Specials crossed over the gangplank to the second mooring, a flat-bottomed houseboat soaked in darkness as deep as ink. Loach knocked, and they waited, but there was no answer. Then Freddy tried knocking a bit louder, but that got no response either. He rattled the doors, but the houseboat was securely locked.

'Maybe we should leave them a note?' Freddy suggested.

Loach turned to go ashore, while Freddy pulled out his Foxy hand-puppet, who cried out in the night in his loud Foxy voice. 'Never fear – the Specials were here!'

'Put that damned thing away, Freddy,' Loach said wearily.

Freddy shrugged, jammed the puppet back inside his tunic, and rejoined Loach on terra firma. He sniffed the night air. 'Can you tell me why folk live on water? It's not natural. It's damp . . . and smell that!' Again he sniffed.

'Smell what?' Loach asked him.

'Canal Number Five,' Freddy quipped, chuckling at his own wit, as they reached the gangplank and crossed to a darkened barge.

'Old, Freddy,' Loach admonished him. 'Very old and hairy, that one.' He knocked on the barge roof.

From inside the barge there came a rasping sound that turned the stomach. Freddy tried to locate the source of the sound, looking over a particular hatch, when suddenly the hatch broke open with a crash.

The two Specials were staring down the twin muzzles of a double-barrelled shotgun.

Walking away from the Bellamy home with John Redwood, Viv wore a pensive expression, as if trying to decide whether to say something aloud. She kept looking at some of Bellamy's weeds, which she had stuffed in her pocket.

All of a sudden the realization flashed across her face.

'It bloody well is!'

Redwood was startled, and when she stopped where she was, he went back to her to find out what happened. Then she started laughing.

'Well I'll be jiggered!' Again she burst out laughing. 'D'you know what this is?'

Still puzzled, he remained silent.

'I went on a course . . . a couple of years ago . . . The dope squad showed us some of this stuff.'

'The dope squad?'

Viv reached into her pocket and pulled out a few flakes of Bellamy's weeds. 'This, John! Godalmighty, it's pot! Marijuana! Your friend Bellamy's been growing his own private supply of cannabis!'

Redwood still couldn't grasp it.

'No wonder he looked funny,' Viv went on, 'if he'd been burning the stuff and sniffing it in!' Her eyes grew even wider, staring at Redwood. 'And d'you know what you've done? Do you know what you have done, Special Constable Redwood?'

Whatever it was, Redwood began to suspect he had really stepped in it this time.

'You've just helped Bellamy get rid of the evidence!' Laughing, she slapped the small amount of marijuana out of her hand.

Redwood was not only appalled by what he had just done, but by what she had just done as well. 'What are you doing!'

Viv shrugged. 'Oh, don't worry. There wasn't enough to make a joint . . .'

50

A soft silence cloaked the canal, and there was nothing in the moonlight or the air to suggest that anything out of the ordinary had happened. There would be no alarm, no report, no witnesses.

Deep inside the main cabin of the barge, Special Constables Bob Loach and Freddy Calder held their hands in the air. Covering them with the double-barrelled shotgun was an unusually attractive woman in her thirties – tall and loose-limbed, bright eyes and high cheek-bones. She was seated on the steps leading up to the hatch, the only way in or out of the barge, and lying on her lap were two pistols.

The two Specials were standing in the middle of a long space between two identical seating areas with bolted tables flanked by bunk seats. Behind them, the main cabin ended in an area comprising a small galley opposite a slatted door to a lavatory, separated by a double-louvred door leading into a bedroom. That was their universe, and the master of that universe was a woman with a powerful weapon that could blow anyone's head off.

'Sit down,' she ordered them. When they didn't move, her voice became very hard. 'I said *sit down*!'

The two men sat down on the bunk seats, one on either side of the central space. They surveyed their world, exploring the decorations on the walls and around the cabin. There was a glass cabinet full of various types of guns, pistols and rifles, all securely clamped with iron rods. On shelves around the wooden walls there were shooting trophies, cups, plaques – the paraphernalia of competition. There were photographs everywhere: several of the woman; several of a man, usually in an officer's military uniform; several of the woman and the man together; some showing them with guns, some at sporting events; some just casual. But it was obvious from all the pictures that the two were in love.

Even though the evidence would suggest that the woman in front of them had expert knowledge of fire-arms, Loach decided that the best policy would be to take nothing for granted.

'Miss . . . we are police officers. Can I ask you to check if the safety catch is on?'

The woman flicked the shotgun a notch lower to aim at his midriff.

Loach reacted immediately to the threat. 'Okay, okay!' He waited for her to be sure he wasn't making a move. 'Look, miss, is there something wrong here?'

'That's rich,' she cackled. '*You're* what's wrong here!'

Baffled, Freddy and Loach looked at each other, wondering what to do.

'I want no talking until my husband gets back,' she warned them.

'Where is your husband, miss?' Freddy asked delicately.

Her reaction was swift – a sharp intake of breath, a vicious, hostile staring at Freddy – but without a word of explanation.

'We really are from the police,' Loach assured her. 'You've got a problem here –'

Her fury blazed. 'You think I'm stupid! I'm a trained observer – whoever *you* are – and policemen you're not.'

With the shotgun as a pointer, the woman traced the distance between the two men in tiny movements of her hands. 'Oh, you're wearing something that looks like a police uniform. Very clever. But since when did police stop wearing helmets, and wear those kind of flashes on their shoulders?' She had simply never seen an emblem of the Specials, though her face was flushed with the triumph of her logic.

'You made a mistake coming here tonight. I suppose you thought the place was empty.'

493

Freddy pursed his mouth, looking round-eyed at Loach, who was busy trying to remain as calm as possible.

'We're Specials, miss. The badge on my shoulder shows that I'm a section officer. Section Officer Loach. And this is Special Constable Calder.'

She looked at each of them in turn, apparently undecided as to what to do herself.

Very carefully, Loach unclipped his radio. 'We can get this all sorted out if I radio to base . . .'

'*Stop it*!' she screamed, pointing the shotgun at his belly. 'Lay it on the table! Do it! I warn you, I can put a hole in your chest the size of your fist with this. *Do it now*!'

Loach signified his compliance with her order by laying the radio down on the table in front of him.

'Push it towards me.'

Loach gave the radio a slide across the table. 'I understand you being alarmed. It's a bit lonely down this way, and –'

'I would rid your minds of any idea that I'm some kind of frightened woman. And be warned – I'm a first-class shot!' The swing of her head encompassed all the trophies and plaques and cups around the cabin. 'And I wouldn't have the slightest compunction in shooting . . . prowlers.' The identification, the association, had already been cemented in her mind. 'I may be here alone . . . but my husband will be back soon.'

Again the two Specials looked at each other, Freddy surreptitiously tapping his temple with a finger to demonstrate the concept of totally bonkers, a gesture he quickly adapted into a scratch when he felt the woman's eyes on him.

'When will your husband be back?' Loach inquired, wondering what kind of little errand the man of the barge might be running this evening.

'Shortly. He'll be back shortly.'

Loach noticed the expensive overnight bag resting by the woman's feet, and also noticed that she was dressed for travelling – somewhat casual, comfortable, but neat, carefully chosen, well planned and coordinated. Where were she and her husband going? And why?

'I don't know how to make you believe that, miss,' Loach continued, trying to keep her talking. 'We're *not* prowlers.'

'We really are part of the local police force,' Freddy chimed in.

'I can clear this up right away,' Loach offered. 'Let me show you my warrant card . . .'

As he moved his hand toward his inside pocket, the sound of the shotgun being cocked stopped his hand in midair.

'Don't,' she threatened. 'Don't make a move.' A grotesque smile began to twitch at the corners of her mouth. 'You're like all your kind! You don't listen. You think: "She's a woman. Who cares about a woman? She's of no account!" Well, don't make that mistake!'

Her breath was coming fast now, 'They didn't tell us about this at night school, Loach,' Freddy wisecracked in a low voice.

After a long silence, Loach spoke up. 'I need the toilet'

The woman was disconcerted by his request and bit her bottom lip.

'I really do,' Loach urged

Finally, the woman gestured with the barrel of the shotgun to a door at the back of the boat. 'Back there . . . on the right.'

As Loach made his slow walk to the rear, Freddy's face took on a glow of hope. From the back of the cabin, Loach pointed to a door opposite a tiny galley kitchen, and the woman nodded.

Loach went into the minuscule lavatory and closed the door, quickly taking inventory: a small toilet; a simple washbasin; a tiny shelf below a face-high mirror; a round window through which only a dove could escape.

The woman's voice called to him from the main cabin. 'You've had enough time. Get back in here!'

Loach hit the flush mechanism before leaving the loo, then came back into the main cabin. Freddy looked up too him with a list of hopeful questions on his face, but Loach shook his head 'No' in a tight motion. However, Loach tried to disguise a veiled interest in the double-louvred door behind him.

'I know what you're thinking . . . but the only way off this boat is right behind me.' She indicated the hatchway over her shoulder.

With a small, sharp, deft move of his foot, Loach edged the double-louvred door slightly ajar.

'What are you doing! Get back in here!' The woman set the shotgun in the crook of one arm and picked up a pistol from her lap.

Meanwhile, the bedroom door slowly creaked open. On the

inside of the door was a full-length mirror that began to show a reflection of the bedroom inside as the door opened.

'I'm coming . . . Take it easy . . .' He tired to stall her just a few moments longer to see what might be available to help them in the bedroom.

The full-length mirror began to spread the bedroom out for his view. Most of the space was filled by the large bed. On the bed were two bodies. One of them was a young woman sprawled on her side, her head hanging over the edge of the bed and her radiant hair flowing on the floor. The other body was a man, a bullet hole through his forehead, flattened against the headboard.

The dead man on the bed was the same man in all the photographs on the walls of the main cabin. The woman's husband would not be back shortly.

Gagging at the gruesome sight, Loach tried to keep himself from dropping to his knees and puking his guts out.

51

Some of the Specials were now drifting back in, gathering informally in the parade room, the task of writing reports still ahead of them. Among those who dreaded the writing of reports this evening was Viv Smith, as she searched her bag to find a light for the fag already dangling from her lips.

'God! Who do I have to sleep with to get off writing my report?'

Mike Sullivan happened to see Andy McAllister at the door, but he could also see that Viv couldn't see him. 'You could always try Sergeant McAllister,' he suggested to Viv.

'McAllister? That'd be like kissing a hedgehog!' she declared, taking another drag on her cigarette. Something made her turn to look behind her, and there was the Sarge. One look at him, and she choked on the smoke.

As for McAllister, one eyebrow went up, the other didn't waver, and the moustache twitched . . . but the eyes twinkled.

'For the last time, I'm warning you . . . Get back in here where I can see you!'

Loach was still hanging back in the no man's land between the lavatory and the small galley in front of the bedroom containing the corpses. There was nowhere to go, but it seemed unlikely that she would come after him at this point either.

'But supposing your husband isn't coming back, miss?' Loach tried to reason with her.

She became even more agitated at his question. 'Why shouldn't he be coming back? What are you trying to say?'

'Well . . . we could have a long wait.'

Freddy was frowning at him, trying to read the hidden messages in Loach's words.

'Why don't I make a cup of tea?' Loach suggested. Hiding his actions by the angle of his body in relation to her, Loach mimed for Freddy to chat the woman up. Freddy caught on right away.

'Nothing like a cup of tea, miss, to see things as they really are. And when your hubbie gets back –'

'Maybe not, Freddy,' Loach remarked.

'No?' Freddy asked him, confused.

'No!'

Freddy couldn't figure this one at all. Yet their conversation had washed over the woman, and she had been borne along with the current. But now she was beginning to show an edginess that threatened to crack her wide open.

'Both of you! Shut up! I don't want tea. You're trying to confuse me. Just like everyone has tried to confuse me. First the lying . . . then the promises . . . more lying . . .'

The shotgun wobbled dangerously, her finger tight on the trigger as she swayed to her feet. Freddy pressed himself hard against the bunk support fearing the gun was going to go off.

'I'm through with listening. The time for listening is past.' Suddenly the pistol in her hand barked, and one of the photographs of her husband on the wall disintegrated.

'Oh Jesus . . . !' gasped Freddy, sweating hard.

But the pistol going off was the slip that allowed Loach to duck back inside the bedroom.

In the main cabin, the woman was twisting in anguish as if an alien creature inside were striving to break out.

Loach rested his back against the louvred doors. He didn't have a plan, but he hoped a search would give him some idea.

The woman was trying to focus on where Loach had been, and she could see he was no longer there. Freddy tried desperately to distract her, talking in his MacFoxy puppet voice.

'Ah, miss . . . can we talk about this?'

Although she wanted to concentrate on Loach's disappearance, she couldn't completely take her attention away from Freddy – or rather MacFoxy – who had come out to dance for her a table level.

'Listen, lady. I want you to know I'm not with these guys. I'm a plainclothes puppet. Plainclothes 'cos this guy's so mean, he wouldn't pay a penny to see Lady Godiva with her hair cut short riding a white horse into Coventry . . .'

In the bedroom, Loach worked hard at keeping his eyes averted from the murdered bodies on the bed. He opened a hanging wardrobe, and inside the first thing he saw was the husband's army uniform.

'Stop it!' the woman screamed at MacFoxy, then looked again at the last place she had seen Loach. 'Where is he?' She screamed at the bedroom door. 'If you don't get back in here now, I'm going to kill your friend!'

She pointed the shotgun at Freddy's face, and MacFoxy fell from his hand onto the table.

'For God's sake, Loach . . .' he pleaded in a low voice.

The door to the bedroom opened, and the woman looked over to see. Loach came out, but he was now wearing the dead man's army uniform jacket and cap.

The lighting in the cabin was soft and shadowed. The woman was unable to focus on the figure, the image having a strange, dreamlike quality. And suddenly, she softened.

'Jeffrey? Is that you, Jeffrey?'

Freddy tried to speak to Loach, but the latter warned him off with a small wave of his hand. Then slowly, Loach began walking toward the woman.

She struggled to maintain any sense of reality, swaying to and fro, though the shotgun remained relatively steady in her grasp, pointed now at the approaching figure.

But as Loach came closer and closer, she could clearly see it was not Jeffrey, and the anger and hatred began to return to her eyes and mouth. What she actually saw now was a travesty of her husband, an imposter who would have to be destroyed.

In the meantime Freddy had carefully edged along the bunk to a position where he could take a chance at launching an attack on the woman. But he would have to do it soon, as she seemed about to pull the trigger on Loach.

Wide open, Loach knew he might have only seconds to live. Yet he kept walking closer to her, closer, confusing her, giving Freddy time to get next to her, get behind her, just another few moments . . .

The woman's finger curled on the trigger. 'No!'

Freddy threw himself at the shotgun, his hand sweeping the barrel upwards, his face almost right on top of the muzzle.

The gun exploded and blew through the ceiling at the same time the lights went dark.

52

Freddy was lying quietly in the hospital bed, a net-like bandage around his head, severe powder burns on his cheeks and face where the shotgun discharged, painkiller in his bloodstream, no hearing in one ear . . . but a smile still on his sad face. Standing at the foot of the bed, Bob Loach regarded his old friend in wonder.

'Would you believe it, Freddy? Looks like we're both heroes.' Loach made the comment as much for the benefit of the nurse tucking Freddy in as for Freddy himself.

'You didn't know I was Dick Tracy, did you?' Freddy asked her coyly.

The young nurse simply snorted at him disdainfully. But Freddy didn't give up, despite the sedative. 'Where have you been all my life?' he said to the nurse in his sexiest James Bond voice.

'For most of it, Mr Calder, I wasn't born,' she replied.

Loach howled with laughter. 'I don't think we need worry about you!' He didn't notice that Hilda Carter had joined them until he felt her push past him. Recovering quickly, he pulled up a chair for her.

Freddy stiffened as well. 'Oh, hi, Ma. Bob, this is my Ma. This is Bob Loach, my superior officer.'

Mrs Calder was annoyed, and barely acknowledged Loach. 'Seems to be a lot of hilarity for a place like this. And I'll have you know, Freddy Calder, I came here expecting the worst. I've never felt so ill in my life when I got the telephone call. And look at you! With that thing on your head, you look like a half-cooked pease pudding.'

'It looked worse, I can tell you, before they cleaned me up,' Freddy told her in a quiet voice. For a moment, he was back to being a boy again, sick in bed and staying home. 'I'm sorry they made you worry.'

Deciding the time was ripe, Loach left the battlefield on tiptoe, giving Freddy a final valedictory wave from the door.

Hilda Calder didn't even miss a beat. 'Worry? You don't have any idea, Freddy Calder, what worry is until you become a mother, and because there's no chance of that happening to you, you'll always be ignorant.'

Out by the doorway to the ward, Loach noticed Rita Loosemore hanging around, though she seemed unwilling to go in and see Freddy. Loach walked over to her for a word of advice.

Back by Freddy's bed, his mother was now droning on about his quitting the Specials. 'Maybe this will put some sense in your head . . . and make you pack up all this police nonsense before you get killed!'

As she went on and on, Freddy caught sight of Bob Loach at the entrance to the ward trying to signal a few graphic messages that there was someone there to see him who wouldn't come in until his mother was gone. His heart beating faster, Freddy guessed who it was.

'. . . But why waste my breath. Look at you . . . You're not even listening to me.'

'Ma?'

'Maybe for once in your life you'll stop being so damned selfish, and think of other people . . .'

'*Ma!*' he yelled as forcefully as he could, given that he was smothered in medications, but that got Hilda's Calder's complete attention.

'Ma, Rita's here.'

She expressed her contempt for the tramp. 'I won't sit with that woman!'

'I'm not asking you to,' Freddy told her as gently as possible. 'I'm asking you to leave.'

'Leave! I will do no such thing. I just got here. The very idea!'

'Ma? For once in my life, do it. Because if you don't, I'll bleed all over this bed.'

'Freddy Calder, you can be so crude.'

'You want crude? Just try me.'

Realizing that this time she was, alas, not going to get her way, Hilda Calder began to feel sorry for herself, though her natural bitterness made even that difficult. 'Children! You bring them into this world just so they can kick you out of it.'

She picked herself up and trudged away from her son, pausing only momentarily to fix Rita with a mean glare as they passed at the door. Rita actually smiled at her.

'Always a pleasure to see you, Mrs Calder . . .' she greeted the old bag, then added to herself as the old bag walked away '. . . going the other way.'

As soon as Noreen saw her husband at the entrance to the hospital, she broke into a full run and didn't stop until she was in his arms. She hugged him fiercely, overcoming his diffidence.

'When I heard about that madwoman . . .' she said breathlessly, then couldn't continue for fear she would break down weeping, so instead pressed herself even harder into his chest.

'Give over, lass,' he chided her, looking about him sheepishly.

'You could've been killed, Loach! Dammit, you matter to me!' Passionately she kissed him and wouldn't let him go. Eventually, it didn't matter to him if there were passers-by watching them.

53

With one notable exception, everybody who was anybody was at the Pub on 4th that night, including the core of Specials and their police counterparts who had become such a closeknit family – Anjali Shah, DC Whittaker, Sandra Gibson, Andy McAllister, Viv Smith, John Redwood, Super Frank Ellsmore, Toby Armstrong, WPC Morrow, PC Albert Coles, Sheila Baxter – and all the rest. Tonight they were celebrating just being alive . . . among friends.

And when Bob Loach and his wife arrived from the hospital, the party turned into a mob scene, beginning with a beery rendition of 'For He's a Jolly Good Fellow.' Loach's face was flushed, and he would have preferred a hole to open up in the floor.

After the cheering had abated somewhat, Chief Superintendent Ellsmore stood next to Loach and raised his hands for silence.

'I've something to say,' said the Chief, 'and . . . I'll make it mercifully short. It's very simple. Ladies and gentlemen of the Specials, I give you your new Sub-Divisional Officer . . . Bob Loach.'

That did it! the crowd went wild. It was perfect timing, in the opinion of everyone but Wally Harris, who yelled 'Fix!' Nonetheless, he immediately decided he didn't mean it when Viv walloped him in the stomach with her bag.

Bob Loach shook the hand of Chief Superintendent Ellsmore, who smiled proudly at the new SDO. 'I'm happy for you, Loach, but don't thank me.' The Super prodded DC Whittaker to come forward. 'It was his idea,' Ellsmore said. 'He's the one you should blame.'

Of all the surprises Loach had come upon that evening, Whittaker was one of the least expected. Maybe there was more to the DC than first met the eye . . . and perhaps that was the way Whittaker wanted it.

'Just remember, Sub-Divisional Officer, Loach,' Whittaker said drily while shaking Loach's hand, 'I'll be watching you all the way . . .'

After another boozy cheer, glasses were raised and requests made for Loach to buy the house a round.

'How about buying us a drink, Suby?' shouted Julie Deane.

'Yeah, champagne all round,' offered Tommy Rose.

Loach waved at Briggsy, setting the wheels in motion, and was greeted by more cheers and taunts alike. Reaching into his pocket, however, he happened to find a hand puppet – Freddy's MacFoxy.

'I must've picked it up in the barge,' Loach explained to no one's satisfaction.

He moved out into an open space, and once again the crowd quietened. 'Don't worry . . . I don't make speeches.'

'Oh yeah?' Phil Warren disagreed.

'You had us fooled,' quipped Steve Northcott.

Loach waited for the rabble-rousing to die down. Then, as all waited expectantly, he raised MacFoxy high above his head.

'To absent friends!' Loach toasted in full voice.

Despite all the laughter that MacFoxy had brought to that room, not a single giggle was heard now. But they did begin to think about the character who inhabited MacFoxy on a regular basis, and something changed in their perceptions of him at that moment.

Loach used the spotlight to look deeply into the eyes of those who were staring up at MacFoxy – he nodded misty-eyed at Anjali . . . then Redwood . . . then Viv . . .

Viv tried sniffing, but she couldn't stop the tears from flowing. She looked up at Andy McAllister standing beside her, and suddenly she stretched up on tiptoe and gave him a wet kiss on the cheek.

At any other moment on any other night he might have boxed her ears, but this time it was inappropriate. He swallowed hard, looked sideways at Viv, and placed a fatherly hand around her shoulder. 'Ach awa' wi' ya,' he said both gruffly and gently.

Standing tall over all their heads on Loach's outstretched arm was MacFoxy – his arms not working properly, his tricky little moves not working at all, his voice mute. Yet throughout the Pub on 4th, among all the Specials gazing at that silly piece of nothing, every single one of them could see MacFoxy telling jokes, making wisecracks, flirting with the girls, doing magic tricks, dancing the lambada . . . In their inner ears, each of them could hear the voice of MacFoxy as clear as a bell, offering his toast to the Specials they had all heard a million times before. With Freddy lying in the hospital, and the room perfectly quiet, everyone heard the same old voice of MacFoxy they had always known . . . and had just met:

'To the girls and guys on the beat,
And the villains you meet on the street!'